LOOSE
AMONG
THE
LAMBS

Books by Jay Brandon

Deadbolt
Tripwire
Predator's Waltz
Fade the Heat
Rules of Evidence

Published by POCKET BOOKS

LOOSE
AMONG
THE
LAMBS

JAY BRANDON

POCKET BOOKS

New York   London   Toronto   Sydney   Tokyo   Singapore

POCKET BOOKS, a division of Simon & Schuster Inc.
1230 Avenue of the Americas, New York, NY 10020

Copyright © 1993 by Jay Brandon

All rights reserved, including the right to reproduce
this book or portions thereof in any form whatsoever.
For information address Pocket Books, 1230 Avenue
of the Americas, New York, NY 10020

Brandon, Jay.
     Loose among the lambs / by Jay Brandon.
        p.   cm.
     ISBN: 0-671-76032-7
     1. Public prosecutors—Texas—Bexar County—Fiction. 2. Trials—
Texas—Bexar County—Fiction. 3. Bexar County (Tex.)—Fiction.
I. Title.
PS3552.R315L66   1993   93-17618
813'.54—dc20   CIP

First Pocket Books hardcover printing December 1993

10 9 8 7 6 5 4 3 2 1

Pocket and colophon are registered trademarks of
Simon & Schuster Inc.

Printed in the U.S.A.

for Dan Thornberry and Mark Stevens,
who are the best
on their respective sides of the street

Acknowledgments

I would like to thank all those who shared their expertise with me for this and the other books in my Bexar County legal series: Beth Taylor, formerly (I'm sorry to say) of the Bexar County District Attorney's office; Lyndee Bordini, assistant district attorney; Cruz Morua, San Antonio Police Department Identification section; Dr. Robert Bux, deputy Medical Examiner of Bexar County; Dr. Nancy Kellogg, Medical Director of Child and Adolescent Sexual Abuse Intervention Services; and counselor Dorothy Le Pere.

I also thank Bill Grose, Virginia Barber, and Mary Evans for their thoughtful, thought-provoking appraisals of the manuscript; and Dudley Frasier for his professional and kindly treatment of the book and its author.

Acknowledgments

PART ONE

The price one pays for pursuing any profession,
or calling, is an intimate knowledge
of its ugly side.

James Baldwin

1

WHEN WORD CAME THAT ELIOT QUINN WAS IN THE building, he was still on the first floor. Some enterprising clerk had called upstairs with the news, and Patty stuck her head in my office door to pass it on.

Eliot Quinn. *The boss is coming,* was my first thought. I found myself on my feet, as if I'd been caught sitting in his chair. "I guess I should go escort him up," I said. "Or would that be presumptuous? Maybe he's not even coming to see me."

"Of course he is," Patty said.

"Well—I'll give him a few minutes. For God's sake, tell Joan to buzz him right in if he does come up." If Eliot made it as high as the fifth floor he *would* be coming to see me, because the fifth floor is nothing *but* the district attorney's offices.

"I'll tell her," Patty said on her way back out, "but I'm not sure Joan even knows what Eliot Quinn looks like. She's only been here five years."

I gave him a while. Eliot would have lots of people to see on the way up. He'd picked his day shrewdly, a Thursday, when the week's trials would be winding down but the judges had not yet skipped town en masse. I walked to the end of my office, surveying it. This had never been Eliot's office. We had been in the new building almost a year. My office was a little smaller than the one in the old courthouse, but this one looked bigger because of the windows. The old office had been a burrow, hollowed out of the heart of the building. This one was

3

an aerie, perched on the top corner of the Justice Center. I often found myself at the view, which wasn't much but at least reminded me there was an outside world. It was the middle of August, the buildings looked as if they were painted on a rippling scrim; the whole landscape was liquified by heat. We'd already thought the heat unbearable back in June. By now it seemed to have been with us half our lifetimes.

After a while I worked my way down through the building to find Eliot. The fourth and fifth floors were all DA's office, warrens of offices. From the third floor down the building was all courts. All criminal courts. The new Justice Center wasn't big enough to hold all of Bexar County's courts, so the county commissioners had decreed a segregation. The civil courts had remained in the old courthouse, stretching out and breathing a sigh, undoubtedly, when the riffraff were booted across the street into the Justice Center.

I picked up my own small crowd of gladhanders at the third floor. Two or three defense lawyers lingering in the hallway said, "Mark!" and shook my hand warmly, as if we were old friends well-met in a surprising place. Pete Fortune, who had tried to block my promotion years ago and later had stolen a client or two from me, glanced up, cried "Blackie!" happily, and waved me over. I was happy to return his wave and keep moving. The really bogus insiders use that old nickname on me. Friends know I detest it.

I was not above my own gladhanding. "Hello, Judge," I said to a sixtyish man who looked uncomfortable in his suit and in the hall. He was not a judge, hadn't been for two years, but would carry the title for life. I'd never liked him, had contributed to the campaign of the woman who'd unbenched him, but it nonetheless saddened me to see him in the building carrying a briefcase and a load of worry, having to hustle for a living again. The uncharitable would have said there was an element of the personal in the sympathy I felt. I shook his hand warmly, asked after his family, and wished I had some business to send him.

One of the youngest of my assistants was so startled to see me when I peeked into his courtroom on the second floor that he called me "sir." I could tell from his face he regretted it immediately. We were all supposed to be colleagues here. But he tried through the remainder of our brief conversation to call me by my first name and couldn't make his tongue do it.

"Hi, Bill. I was looking for Eliot Quinn; have you seen him?"

"Who, mmm—uh. Who?"

"Eliot Quinn. You don't know him?"

"Quinn, Ma—? Well, it sounds familiar. Is he a lawyer?"

Paula Elizondo, the court coordinator, who had seen a thousand young lawyers like Bill during her years in the courthouse, and found each new one more ignorant than his predecessors, leaned around Bill to give me a little smile and a destination. "Judge Hernandez's office. He's been stuck there for the last twenty minutes."

"Thanks, Paula." On my way out I heard twenty-six-year-old Bill ask her who Eliot Quinn was. Paula's only response was, "You *were* born yesterday, weren't you?" I decided to reward Bill's sudden historical curiosity.

"Eliot Quinn was district attorney here about five times as long as I've been," I said.

"Oh, *that* Eliot Quinn," Bill said, and anyone could see he wanted again to slap himself in the face for sounding such a fraud. Paula laughed out loud. It was good to see one of the people who actually ran the joint laughing at a lawyer.

After making my way through another small crowd of well-wishers I did find Eliot in Judge Hernandez's outer office. I could see that Eliot had worked his way back out that far from the inner sanctum but hadn't quite been able to make that last bolt out the door. When I said his name Eliot leaned in to me as if greeting me intimately. What he murmured was, "Get me away from this old fool."

"Hello, Judge. Hope you don't mind if I steal Mr. Quinn away for a few minutes. I only have a minute before I have to be across the street in Commissioners Court."

"Certainly, certainly," Judge Hernandez said, as hearty as I. He was still wearing his robe, though I would have guessed his day's work was done. "The two of you must have much to discuss. The old gives way to the new, eh, Eliot? Eh, Blackie? Stop back and see me on your way out, Eliot."

"Of course, Judge, of course. So good to see you again." The door barely closed behind us—I had his arm, as if literally dragging him away—when Eliot said, "That man destroys your respect for institutions. I should have fired him while he was still in Misdemeanor.

"Hello, Mark," he said more warmly. "You're the one I came

5

to see. I should have just taken the elevator straight to the third floor. But you know these elevators."

"It's the fifth floor in this building, Eliot. And these elevators are pretty fast."

"A man could get lost in this building," Eliot said quietly. "I don't want to sound like one of those old dodderers lost in the past, but this is an awful building, Mark. This ministry of justice. We could be anywhere in the world in here. There's a building like this in every city in America. The old courthouse is unique, and so is every courtroom in it. You could be taken into one blindfolded and know exactly which court you were in. This, this is a cold, joyless place. All the courtrooms exactly alike, and all the furnishings gray and bolted into place." He shook his head. "The courthouse has style. Stupid style, but style. It looks like a man out on the town on Christmas Eve, wearing a red vest and a green hat, stepping with great dignity because he knows he looks ridiculous."

"But everything works here," I said. "Everything isn't falling apart." My defense of the new building was halfhearted. I missed the stupid old courthouse myself. The shiny new Justice Center is too uncomplicated, too clean. The old courthouse is a living entity, so infected with humanity that it breathes.

"But this is your building," Eliot said as if finishing my thought, but he was only interrupting his own speech. "I shouldn't criticize. I'm sure you've invested it with your own fond memories."

I gave him the brief tour, Eliot nodding and peering as if interested. He didn't stop to admire anything until the fifth floor, where he gazed up at the foot-tall letters of my name: MARK BLACKWELL. DISTRICT ATTORNEY. I ushered him under them and briefly through the maze of hallways, concluding in my office. "And this could have been yours," I said, "if you hadn't decided to bail out so early."

"Ha ha," Eliot said. His laugh was that precise; I could hear the syllables. He dropped his hat on a chair. I saw he still had a full head of white hair. "Try for two lifetimes in office instead of only one? No, no, I retired right on schedule. Of course, I never intended for that *civilian* to usurp my position." As if he couldn't bring himself to say my predecessor's name. "I wish you'd run four years earlier than you did, Mark. But at least you took the office back. I'm glad it's in good hands again."

It was so strange to see Eliot Quinn in my office. I saw him regularly, every few months, but never before here in the office. His presence seemed to drag us into the past; the room darkened and expanded in imagination, became the old office, and I felt myself turning into a midlevel assistant to the man before me. That time was not so long-gone. Eliot wasn't old. Sixty-two, sixty-three. But he embodied a past era. He had been district attorney of Bexar County for almost twenty years. He'd been the only boss I'd had during my eight years as an assistant DA, from the late sixties to the midseventies. I was forty-eight now—older, I suddenly realized, than Eliot had been when he'd hired me. But he'd been so steeped in authority he'd seemed Olympian to me.

He had hardly changed in the seven years since he'd declined to run for reelection again. It appeared to me he'd coalesced. He was smaller than I'd remembered, and thinner. His gray pinstriped suit was lint-free, his white shirt casually glistened, and his tie was held out by a collar pin. Eliot's jaw, which in final arguments he would clench into a vise of determination, as if he had a grip on the defendant and would never let go, was still firm. He hadn't taken to glasses. When he glanced at me his blue eyes still pierced, from across the room.

We still heard about him from time to time, though he avoided the criminal courts, his old venue. Occasionally he was still hired as trial counsel in a federal or civil case. Representing personal-injury plaintiffs allowed Eliot to prosecute again, in a sense. Recently he had mounted a rather spectacular prosecution—it could be called nothing else—of the managers of an office building who had sought to discourage an old homeless woman who frequented the building's lobby. What should have been a routine slip-and-fall case, with considerable jury sympathy for a business that only wanted its customers to go unmolested, had turned in Eliot's hands into an account of vicious persecution of a helpless victim that bordered on Nazism. The jury's punitive damage award would keep the old woman off the streets for several lifetimes.

"How's Mamie?" I asked.

"Fine as ever. But still not used to having me underfoot during the day. She kicks me out when I spend too many days in a row at home. And how are you doing, Mark? Will you be keeping the job?"

7

"That's not up to me, is it?" It was election year. I'd won the barely contested primary back in the spring. The party had done its job, seen that I, its best candidate, had no serious challengers. The general election coming up in November promised to be more harrowing.

"Yes, it probably is," Eliot said seriously. He continued studying me, quite frankly. "Half the battle of keeping the job is really wanting it. Do you want it, Mark? Are you enjoying it?"

"Enjoy? Enjoy." I tasted the word again, but couldn't make it work in my mouth. I knew what he meant. When I'd been an assistant DA there'd been a touch of nasty joy in getting a really ugly case, one in which the testimony would make the jurors wince in disgust and start thinking in punishment terms of decades rather than years. A great case, a prosecutor would call it. But now I was *the* District Attorney, I saw all the great cases, and there was no joy in them, just a weariness at the idea that new batches of ugly facts would appear on my desk every morning, day in and out forever, no matter how well I did my job. "It's not a job you can enjoy, is it?"

"You can't?" Eliot asked. His gaze at me had changed from friendly interest to concern. He looked like my doctor, studying me for symptoms of a disease he'd just diagnosed.

I gave him an ironic smile to show I was okay, but said, "Tell me how to enjoy this one." I sat down behind one of the files I'd been studying that morning. "This is one of the tough ones. We've got a man here, a male prostitute. He's tested positive for the AIDS virus. But he hasn't changed what we like to call his lifestyle. He won't quit. It's his living and his life. After his last arrest he told the cops he *wants* to take as many with him as he can. So he's out there killing people, and all I can charge him with, the one time out of a hundred when he's caught, is prostitution. A class B misdemeanor. He does ten days in jail, then he's screwing somebody new the next day. He's going to turn out to be the biggest mass murderer in San Antonio history, and I can't stop him. Tell me, Eliot, did you have problems like this? Somehow the job seemed simpler when you did it."

I had hoped to perturb him just a little, but I hadn't. I could see that his only concern was for what he considered my overreaction.

"Maybe it was simpler," he said. "Or maybe I'm just a simpler man than you are, Mark. But I know one thing. You're taking this job too seriously. You're not the guardian of San Antonio. It's not your job to protect everyone."

"If I'm not then who is?"

"No one is," Eliot said. "No one can be. People have to look out for themselves. As for you, being district attorney is the easiest job in the world. Other people have to make all the tough decisions. Judges, juries. Some poor hapless defendant has to decide whether to take the plea bargain offer or try his luck. Defense lawyers have to decide whether to have their defendant sit silent and be thought a criminal, or take the stand and remove all doubt. But you—you just go full steam ahead. All you have to do is hold a press conference once in a while after some particularly heinous fiend is arrested and say"—he leaned forward, forearm resting on one knee, head thrust aggressively forward—" 'We're going to throw the book at this guy. We're going to make him wish he'd never been born.' " Eliot leaned back and laughed. "Then take a nice vacation. Go to a conference somewhere. You're not getting the fun out of this you should, Mark. My God, we used to enjoy power. Your generation just seems to see it as a burden. Take it easier, Mark, or you won't last."

"I know. I fret too much," I said.

"Maybe that's the only difference between us," Eliot said. "We do the job the same way, but I basked in it and you brood over it." He was looking at me happily. "Mark, I'm proud of you. I'll bet you don't hear that very often. But I am. I keep up with things in my own small way. I hear things you wouldn't hear yourself. I know what kind of district attorney you've been for four years. You are the best. Even defense lawyers don't have anything bad to say about you. You had a rocky first year." He waved away that understatement as if it were smoke in the air between us. "Most people didn't expect you to get out from under it. But you did. You do the job just the way it should be done, without partiality. I don't hear anything about you except that you're strictly fair. That you treat everybody exactly the same."

"I try," I said.

"No. You *do*. If the public understood how well you do your job this election would be a walk. But I'm not sure they do. Lawyers do, but the public—well, most people go through life without being exposed to the criminal justice system, and of those who are, few emerge happy.

"I try to tell people," Eliot continued. "It's silly of me to take this pride in you, as if I made you what you are, when in reality I had nothing to do with it."

"You taught me everything I—" I began, but he waved me silent.

"I guess I take pride in it because I feel you've finished the work I began," he said, looking out the window reminiscently. "You know the way this office used to be run?" He laughed. "You would have thought it a horror, Mark. I remember when I was interviewed for a job here, in the fifties, fresh out of law school and damp all over. If I'd been a puppy my eyes wouldn't have been open yet. They weren't, in fact. I sat right there— Well, no, this was in the old office, in the first assistant's office. The first assistant himself interviewed me for the job. Dan Blake, did you ever know him?" I shook my head. "Fat old blusterer," Eliot continued. "He talked to me for a while, and asked me the same silly questions people always ask at interviews, then all of a sudden he excused himself and left the office. It confused me a bit. He'd left so suddenly he'd forgotten to close his desk drawer. It just sat there beside me, gaping open. I thought he was testing my trustworthiness, seeing if I'd snoop while he was gone, so I sat there rigid as an altar boy, staring straight ahead, until the interviewer came back. When he sat down he glanced in the drawer and got a sour look, like there was something rancid in there he'd forgotten about. And all of a sudden the interview was over."

Eliot nodded at my chuckle. "You're laughing, you're not as naïve as I was. I didn't realize it even after I got the letter saying they couldn't use me. I had no idea what had happened.

"But I had an uncle, he wasn't a lawyer but he knew how things worked. He asked me why I hadn't been hired and I told him I didn't know, I thought the interview went okay. When I mentioned the desk drawer business to him he scowled just like the first assistant had done and he said, 'Idiot. You were supposed to put money in it.'

" 'No,' I said. I thought he must be wrong. But my uncle made one phone call and came back and told me the proper amount. And I called the first assistant to ask for a second interview. He seemed disinclined, but when I said, 'I think you'll be surprised how much I've learned in such a short time,' he agreed. And we went through a briefer version of the same charade again, and again Mr. Blake was called away so suddenly that he left his desk drawer open. This time I deposited my bills in it. When he came back he looked in, he smiled, he closed the drawer, he shook my hand, and he said, 'Welcome to the district attorney's office.' "

My smile had died long before the end of the story. I'd heard of the practice before, and it had seemed like a funny anecdote, but as Eliot quietly sketched it I pictured it happening, such an interview being conducted here in this office.

Eliot was sober, too. "I never got to fire that man," he said. "He died long before I got the chance."

"But, Eliot," I said, "there was a vestige of that system even when you were DA. Even when I interviewed for the office, you needed some kind of connection to get in. I'd worked for Harold Adams when I was in law school, and if Mr. Adams hadn't put in a good word for me—"

"Yes, but you didn't have to pay," Eliot said, so sanctimoniously he could hear it himself, and we both laughed. "And if you hadn't worked out you would have been bounced."

He gave me a belated surprised look. "You say 'connection' as if it were a dirty word. Connections are just a way of sorting people. I get a hundred applicants a year fresh out of law school, what do I know about them? That they won the mock trial competition? You know what that's worth once you shove them into a real courtroom. But being a prosecutor is a people job. If you don't work well with police officers, you don't work well in this job. If you can't establish a rapport with the judge, you're no good to me in that court."

Unconsciously, Eliot had started talking as if he were still district attorney. I listened as if being instructed.

"Anyone with those kinds of people skills can make contacts," he continued. "You don't have to be born to them. I wasn't. You weren't, yet you met Mr. Adams, and did good enough work for him that he'd recommend you. You see? You made a contact, so there was someone I knew who I could ask about you. Can he cut it, can he do the job? That's all a connection is worth. It won't get you in if you're no good, if you're just somebody's nephew."

He gave me a grin. "And now that you've become a politician, you need all the connections you can get."

"Yes indeed," I said, and we sat in companionable silence, thinking about the distasteful aspects of the job of district attorney, until Eliot suddenly stirred himself.

"Drat me for an old fool, Mark," he said. "Don't let me talk your day away. I came for a reason." He leaned toward me. "I came to help you with your problem."

"What problem is that?"

"That one." He pointed at the newspaper lying discarded on the floor beside my desk. I picked it up, ignoring the blaring front-page headline, and handed the paper toward Eliot to leaf through and tell me what he was talking about. But he didn't take it out of my hands.

"That problem right there," he repeated, pointing at the headline, the one that screamed, WHERE WAS LOUISE? It was the newspaper's way of keeping alive a story that had kept the city buzzing the previous week. A four-year-old girl had wandered or been taken from her parents' apartment complex and been gone overnight. By late the second day volunteer search teams were combing the neighborhood, the nearby woods, culverts, the dark, crawly spaces under front porches. Hope of finding a living girl after two days in the August sun died quickly. People began searching with their noses as much as with their eyes.

And after sundown that day Louise came toddling home. She was happy, unexposed to the heat, but she couldn't say where she'd been, only that a "nice man" had taken her to a nice house. A new search commenced immediately as the old one reached its only partly joyous conclusion.

"That's not my problem," I said, "that's a police problem." Indeed, the chief of police was feeling the heat. Reporters, digging into the story, found Louise's was not an isolated case. A boy had been missing overnight the month before, another boy earlier in the summer. The newspapers and TV news hatched the phrase *serial child molester* and found ways to insert it into every day's otherwise barren news summaries. I thought it was overblown, myself. There were always such cases, and the police weren't even sure these could be blamed on the same man; children's descriptions are notoriously sketchy. But the chief of police, finding it increasingly difficult to fade the heat of that hungry media attention, had accepted the public theory, and had just assigned more detectives to the cases.

"I'd be just delighted to prosecute anybody they can arrest, but they don't seem to be having much luck at that. Until they do—"

Eliot said, "If you think this is just a police problem, you don't understand the public relations aspect of your job. The public doesn't make distinctions between law enforcement agencies. The only thing the news-watching citizens know is that a wolf is loose among our lambs. Rest assured, they will blame all the shepherds. And you're up for reelection. You're the one they can exercise their fear and outrage on."

Eliot Quinn was a much shrewder politician than I. His two decades in office had proven that. I could see he was right.

"Well, thank you," I said quietly, already trying to think of solutions. I should meet with the chief of police—

"I didn't come just to offer advice you don't need," Eliot interrupted my thoughts. "As I said, I'm here to help you."

He had my attention. He didn't immediately use it. Eliot seemed not quite to agree with the course on which he was about to launch. When he spoke it was slowly, the way a man steps on half-submerged rocks to cross a creek.

"I have a friend," he said. "An old friend. He has a client. The client wants to turn himself in."

"The client is the man who abducted the children?"

"Yes. It's only a case of indecency, Mark, not aggravated rape. Only some touching. He's a sick, ashamed man—"

"Well, it's also kidnapping," I interrupted. "Maybe aggravated. If—"

"Now we're plea bargaining," Eliot said, "and that's not why I came. I don't represent the man. Thank goodness," he added fastidiously.

"No," I agreed. "But what does he want? I can't agree to anything before he's even arrested. He has to turn himself in—"

"That's it," Eliot said. "That's exactly what he wants to do. He's overborne by guilt. But he's also afraid. The frenzy this city seems to be in, he's afraid for his life. He has a deathly fear of police. Unreasonably, but we can understand. How many people in this city would say the best solution would be just to shoot him on sight?"

"Yes. But then?"

Eliot cocked his head at me, as if I were something to regard. "He'll turn himself in to *you*, Mark. You personally. You see, you do have a reputation in some quarters. He trusts you to do the right thing."

"He does?"

Eliot acknowledged my look. "Well, *I* do. And my friend does, his attorney. This seems best for all concerned. For you too, Mark," Eliot added. "It will not be at all bad publicity for you, at a time when you can use it. You'll have the arrest yourself, you'll be the one who ended the crime spree."

That had already occurred to me. I searched briefly for any trap into which my self-interest could be leading me, and saw none. Eliot must already have made the same search himself. "But we have no deal," I emphasized. "No agreement, except that he'll turn himself in."

"That's the only agreement," Eliot confirmed. "You and Austin can work out the details later. Austin Paley, that's his attorney. You know Austin, of course. You and he can strike some sort of agreement later on as to sentencing."

"All right." Eliot and I shook hands, as if he *were* representing clients, as if he had acted for them. And of course he had, but just as an intermediary, an old friend in the middle. He bestowed his fond smile on me again.

"I hope this will do it for you, Mark, give your campaign the momentum it needs. I want to see you reelected. With you in office, Mark, I can feel my tradition is continuing."

He stood up to lean closer to me. "And I tell you frankly, you can use the help. I mentioned your reputation for treating everyone equally. The voters may not be as aware of that as they should, but it's well known in the circles that matter. And you know, not everyone likes it. A reputation for doing no favors is actually harmful to you in some cases. Because some people expect favors. This town runs on favors. Why do you think Leo Mendoza is running against you? Leo's not the smartest lawyer in town, but he's pretty shrewd politically. He's got money behind him, and more than money. Men who'd like to have a district attorney who's beholden to them. You remember that, Mark. Don't treat him lightly."

"I didn't think I had been. But thanks."

Eliot shrugged. "Advice is cheap. I've ignored more of it than you'll ever hear."

He retrieved his hat. " 'Twere best done quickly," he said, more loudly, returning to our earlier topic. "As soon as Austin gets his client in hand we'll be in touch. Done?"

"Done."

Eliot nodded once, briskly, and strode out, as confidently as if he were leaving his own office, as if this new building weren't an unfamiliar maze to him. I remained at my desk, regarding again the bold, tall type of the newspaper headline. Next week it would be my name in print that striking.

And as Eliot had said, that couldn't hurt, could it?

I wish I had the gift of invisibility, to turn on and off at will. I enjoy being recognized, I enjoy the notoriety of being district attorney, but to do the job properly I need to be able to slip unobtrusively into courtrooms, and that's a gift usually denied me. I'd like to drift into the room completely unobserved, to watch my assistants when they're chatting with the judge, or plea bargaining with a defense lawyer. I don't mind them looking a touch bored at docket call, as long as they remain professional; boredom is a part of any job. But as soon as I walk into a courtroom, backs straighten. Mouths set in grim determination. Everything turns life and death.

To diminish this air of importance, I've made it a practice to be constantly at large in the building. At least once a day I drift down and cruise the courts. People don't get that startled look when they see me any more.

That Thursday afternoon after Eliot left I made my usual run downstairs. In August the weeks seem to run short, the building clears out faster than usual. By Thursday afternoon it was already deadened, as if I were intruding on a weekend. I had to glance into three courtrooms before I found anything going on. In Judge Ramon Hernandez's court a jury trial was in progress. I took my seat among the scattering of spectators and identified the trial participants. The defense lawyer was a twenty-year veteran of the courts who had probably stopped learning anything new his first year out of law school. The first chair prosecutor was Becky Schirhart, who had been a prosecutor only slightly longer than I'd been district attorney. She was about thirty, the newest first chair felony prosecutor in the office. I'd followed her career with more than usual interest since a couple of years earlier, when Becky, still fairly new to the felony courts, had jumped at the chance to prosecute a police detective for murder.

Becky had the kind of appearance that made her the topic of occasional speculation; I'd overheard some of it. She looks both innocent and intense in the office and the courtroom, leading some men to wonder what she's like after work, whether she devotes that intensity to anything else.

I didn't recognize her second chair, which disturbed me. Even from the back, I should know everyone who works for me. This was a woman, Mexican-American, small and a little slumped. When she turned her head toward Becky I could see not only that she was very young but that she was no one I had ever seen before. What was she doing sitting at the State's counsel table?

The jury was watching a young Mexican-American man testify. He was wearing a white shirt for the occasion, but no coat or tie; he looked as if he wouldn't own either. His knees were cocked outward, leaving his feet lying on their outsides, a boyish pose that looked unstudied.

The chair beside the defense lawyer was empty. The witness was the defendant. His lawyer was questioning him, in the time-honored words of a lawyer not quite in possession of the facts himself: "And then what happened?"

"I decided I better go," the young man said. "I didn't want no trouble. So I went outside and around to the back where I was parked, but I heard somebody running after me, so I turned around quick, but it wasn't the guy, it was her."

"By her you mean Miss Flores?"

"Yeah, her." The defendant nodded toward the woman at the prosecution table. His eyes didn't quite snag on her.

So it was a witness Becky had sitting beside her. Now I was genuinely perplexed.

"What did she do?" asked the defense lawyer.

"She came up and she grabbed my arm and she said she wanted to go with me. I told her no, you better go back, but she wouldn't. I think she'd been drinking some. I don't mean she was swaying or anything, but maybe she was loosened up more than usual. I don't know, I'd just met her."

"What did you do?"

"I kept walking toward my car. And she kept following me

and when I got in she got in. So I thought, okay, and I drove us down the street to a house I knew."

"Was it your house?"

"It wasn't nobody's house. It was empty."

"Did Miss Flores say anything while you drove?"

"No, she just scooted over beside me and put her hand on my leg."

"And did that have some effect on you?"

"Well, yeah."

The defense lawyer didn't ask him to specify the effect. The defendant reached for his shirt pocket, but the cigarette pack that obviously belonged there had been removed for the solemn occasion. He went back to twisting his hands together in his lap while his lawyer led him through a tale of sudden youthful passion followed by feminine remorse and shame. As the defendant talked, my attention was drawn to the victim—that was obviously who she was, as this was obviously a sexual assault trial—the young woman sitting up front at the State's table. Early in the defendant's recital she turned animatedly toward Becky, clutched her arm, and whispered something. Becky calmed her. The victim sat quietly for the rest of the testimony. I couldn't see her face, but something in her expression kept drawing the attention of the jurors, and repelling the defendant's gaze. He would glance toward her but couldn't look at her. I wasn't alone in noticing his inability.

When he was passed to Becky for cross-examination, Becky stood and took two steps to the side, so she was standing directly behind the victim. The defendant found something interesting on the other side of the room.

"So when you left the restaurant," Becky began, but interrupted herself. "Mr. Arreola, could you look at me, please?"

"Objection," the defense lawyer said hastily. "The witness doesn't have to take direction from the prosecutor."

Oh good, Joe, I thought. *Go ahead and tell everyone your guy can't bring himself to look in the direction of his victim.* Judge Hernandez said mildly, "That's true, he doesn't."

"So this young woman forced her attentions on you, Mr. Arreola? You couldn't shake her off?"

"No, I couldn't get away."

"How much would you say she weighs, Mr. Arreola?"

"I don't know." Nor could he estimate very well, because he glanced at the victim but his glance wouldn't take hold.

"She didn't overpower you physically, did she?"

It was a silly question, but no one laughed. Becky's tone wouldn't permit it. The jurors looked very solemn as they stared at the expression I couldn't see on the victim's face.

"In fact it wasn't immediately after you left the cafe that Ms. Flores came out, was it? And it wasn't only the parking lot that was outside, the restrooms were too, weren't they? You had to skulk around the ladies' room for some twenty or thirty minutes waiting for Ms. Flores to come out, didn't you, Mr. Arreola?" Becky's questions grew more and more harsh, but her hands were on the victim's shoulders, asking *her* to bear up.

Even after both sides rested and the judge gave the jury a recess, Becky Schirhart didn't seem to see me. She spoke quietly to the victim for a minute or two, until the woman left, giving the defendant a wide berth, to join a small family group in the audience. It was as Becky followed Ms. Flores with her eyes that Becky saw me. I stood, and she came to talk. But I spoke first.

"I've seen it done coldly," I said, "as if the facts were so plain only idiots could fail to see them. And I've seen it done passionately, as if the victim were the prosecutor's sister; that usually sounds forced. But this is the first time I've ever seen it done angrily and compassionately at the same time."

Becky shrugged. She looked worried. "It was a risk, of course. Having her in the room while he testified meant I couldn't call her in rebuttal. But she'd already told her whole story, I didn't think I'd need to call her back. The defense objected, but the judge let me try it."

"Something this novel—" I began. Becky was already nodding.

"I know, I should check with someone first. But I didn't plan it. It was a spur-of-the-moment thing. You should have seen that little bastard while *she* was testifying. He squirmed, he rolled his eyes, he groaned out loud. He turns to his lawyer and says, loud enough for everyone to hear, 'I can't believe she's saying all this shit.' "

Becky turned to look at the defendant. "For once I wanted to give one of them a taste of his own medicine. They always get to sit there and put on a show while the poor victim's struggling

18

to tell her story. I wanted to see him try it. And I wanted the jury to see if he could look her in the face while he tried to spout that load of crap and he *couldn't!* They saw it. That lying little creep."

I've seen prosecutors animated by cases, but I've rarely seen one so personally involved. It is, after all, just a job. After this case was over there'd be a thousand more in line behind it. I didn't remind Becky of that.

"It was very effective," I said. "But let's not try this experiment again until we see what happens to this one on appeal."

"No," she agreed. "But if this guy gets reversed I'll try him again."

"Assuming he's convicted this time," I said gently.

"He will be. Can you picture that jury coming back in here and facing her and saying not guilty?"

I left her to her waiting. I felt restored by having watched someone so unjaded in her work. I wondered how I could spread Becky's enthusiasm through the rest of the staff, rather than allow the more common reverse effect.

Becky's performance and Eliot's visit had given me a greater sense of well-being than I'd enjoyed in some time. Events were flowing my way. I was the head of a professional, well-trained staff, and by the following week I'd be a public hero as well.

The hallway outside the courtroom was empty. There was no one lying in wait for me, which had been a problem for a while. Three years ago, shortly after my election as district attorney, my son David was arrested for rape. He'd protested his innocence and I had supported him, of course, supported him so publicly that ever since some people saw me as peculiarly vulnerable to emotional appeals. Mothers, sisters, uncles of defendants caught me in the hallways of the Justice Center to tell me that what had happened to my boy had happened to theirs, too. But I never intervened. I was not a judge; I did not usurp the jury's function. It had been three years, and the emotional pleas had slowed.

I checked the other courtrooms, but they were empty. It was time to go home. The only alternative was to watch Becky's final argument and wait for her verdict. I have seen a thousand final arguments. I've given hundreds. On the other hand, I know my empty townhouse very well, too.

I headed back to the courtroom.

2

ONCE I HAD A PARTNER. I'D HAD A FAMILY, AS well. Now I had the office of district attorney. I didn't think I'd given up the rest of my life for the office, but I could see how a neutral observer might disagree.

Fresh out of law school, I'd been an assistant DA for eight years. I loved the work, but no one with any ambition remains a prosecutor forever. Tired of being a bureaucrat of justice, and of my layers of bosses, I left the office after eight years. When I did, I wanted to learn about the only aspect of criminal law I didn't know: representing clients. I didn't want just instruction, though, I wanted a partner. Someone I could talk to about my cases; someone I could rely on to back me up.

Linda Alaniz was the partner I found. I'd opposed her in several cases, enough to be singed by her skills. But Linda was not just a capable defense lawyer. She was as true a believer as there ever was. I wanted to learn from her the secret of her faith, how she committed herself so passionately to the defense of the guilty.

Linda believed in our clients. If she didn't believe their stories, she still believed in them. She saw them as victims themselves, lost children whose causes no one else had ever taken up.

I learned from her, but she did not convert me. I couldn't treat our clients the way Linda did, like family members who'd gotten a bad break. We were good partners, maybe *because* I was the skeptic and she had the passion. If we'd been more similar, Linda and I would have gone our separate ways after I'd spent a year or two learning from her. Instead, our differences kept us together for ten years.

Ten years can pass like a long weekend, but always perform a decade's worth of change. We look around and find we are not the people we thought, we are not living the lives we'd assumed. Early in my partnership with Linda I was a happily married man, with a teenaged son and an infant daughter. A few years later I discovered that leaving the office at night and going home to my wife Lois seemed backwards. I went on feeling this dislocation for more than a year, until a moment came when Linda and I felt the same way at the same time, and we became partners completely, privately as well as professionally.

When we did, it was as if Lois knew, as if she'd expected it before I had. My wife and I didn't separate. We remained friendly partners in raising our daughter Dinah; pleasant roommates. Linda didn't want a husband and I didn't want to leave my home while my daughter was still in it, so we all drifted along for a few years.

It was the district attorney's office that finally separated us all. When I was offered the chance to run for DA I found I wanted it, I wanted it badly. Linda must have been dismayed to see me seeking so arduously the world I'd left behind to become her partner, but she understood. She helped me campaign. When I won she even came into the DA's office with me, as my first assistant.

As for Lois and me, I think we could have continued to live as we had, maybe into old age, but the terrible events of my first year in office—David's arrest and its aftermath—broke us apart. We had been divorced for two years now.

Being chief prosecutor pried me loose from Linda a little more slowly, but just as certainly. Linda was no prosecutor. She didn't last as first assistant for a year before returning to private practice. Even then we thought we could maintain our private relationship while remaining occasional public adversaries, but we were naïve. The absolute difference in our work emphasized our private differences as well. What we did was what we were. For months we did nothing but argue, until the arguments became so wearisome we began seeing less of each other to avoid them. And when we'd put a certain distance between us we found there was not much reason to bridge that distance.

But I hadn't found anyone to take Linda's place, and I don't think she'd replaced me, either. She had her clients. I had my duties and my reelection campaign. And after all, there's nothing more satisfying than work, is there?

The arrest went off without a hitch. That's what it is when a suspect is taken into custody, an arrest, even though in this case police weren't involved. *I* was the arresting officer, a first for me, one I didn't enjoy. I had tried to make sure this silly business wouldn't damage my relationship with the police department. As soon as the plans were set I'd informed the chief of police, Herman Glower, who, it was said, had "cleaned up" the department during his six years as its chief. As far as I could see he'd just made the PD colorless, like himself. Chief Glower had unsmilingly instructed me in the basics of arrest.

"There's nothing to it," he'd said. "Just remember to take a firm grip on his arm. That settles them down. You'd be surprised how many want to bolt at the last minute, even when they're turning themselves in voluntarily."

And that had been the end of my prearrest dealings with the police department. I assumed they'd closed their files on the cases once I'd informed them of the imminent arrest.

The spectacle was to take place in the well-lighted hall outside the fifth-floor entrance to the district attorney's offices. I would make the arrest out there in the hall. It had to be a public event. My campaign could use the publicity of my putting a stop to a series of horrifying crimes, and the suspect presumably wanted a very public view of his going quietly into custody, not like a monster brought to bay.

The whole hallway was secured, with our investigators, two uniformed cops, three sheriff's deputies, and the sheriff himself to take over the transport to the jail, and a sprinkling of assistant DAs who wanted to watch. With the media arriving and angling for camera positions, the small hall must have been jammed already. I was in my office, regally awaiting the appointed minute. I wished I had Eliot there to joke with. But Eliot had refused my invitation to be part of the arrest, modestly claiming he'd had nothing to do with it.

My intercom buzzed. "Ready," Patty said, and I was already at the office door, to ask her in person in the outer office if the satellite coverage was in place.

"Everybody but Oprah," she said.

I went down the long interior hall toward our front door, picking up acolytes along the way, including the chiefs of the felony and sex crimes units. They stayed discreetly in my train, waiting to do the dirty work once I'd intercepted the glory.

As soon as I emerged into the public hallway the lights hit me, making it impossible to distinguish faces. I was sure I knew everyone there, the reporters, the prosecutors, my colorful friend the sheriff, but the lights isolated me. I could picture my assistants smirking at the edges of the crowd. That would have been my reaction to this silly waste of time.

But it hadn't been, I recalled. When I was an assistant DA there'd been occasions like this two or three times a year, press performances in the hallway starring Eliot Quinn. And Eliot, a man of sharp, solemnity-deflating humor, took them very seriously, so seriously that his assistants learned not to smile at them either. "This is as much a part of the job as pointing your finger at the defendant in court in front of a jury," I'd heard him say once. "You can't just do a good job, you have to let them know you're doing a good job. Otherwise some other bumblewit will be doing this job four years from now."

I'd nodded soberly then, and the memory of it kept my face straight as I stepped into my own public performance.

"Where are they?" I asked softly into the blazing void, and a voice answered, "That sound is their elevator arriving."

A few moments later my eyes had adjusted well enough that I could see the blond man in the suit with no tie pressing through the crowd toward me. Austin Paley was right behind him, so I knew this was the suspect. The arrestee. He looked scared to death, as if the crowd were calling for his blood.

What they were calling were questions. The lights abandoned me, to center on the child molester and his attorney. Austin Paley stopped, touching his client's arm, to allow him to answer a question or two if he chose. The man to be arrested kept his head down and spoke shortly if at all. I had a moment to study him. This was my first view of Chris Davis, the man who'd chosen me to arrest him. He was about forty, I'd been told, but looked far more youthful. I fancied I could understand his fascination with children. He looked like a boy himself. His open collar made the suit look a little too big for him. He kept his eyes shyly downcast.

It was a horrible occasion for him, the worst of his life. I wondered what had made him do it. He must have believed the police were very close to arresting him anyway. But why not just quit and disappear, move to another city, rather than subject himself to this—arrest and prison and pain? Maybe it was guilt that had forced him here; a childhood churchgoing upbringing he couldn't shake, or a recent conversion, or a deep-seated revulsion at what he was.

But if conscience had been Davis's goad, it seemed to have deserted him. Now he just looked scared. I saw him hear the elevator doors closing, saw him look across the hall to the head of the stairs. "Take a firm grip on his arm," Chief Glower had said, and I realized he'd been right.

Austin Paley had taken over the press coverage. "Yes, I made this arrangement," he was saying. "Mr. Davis came to me to say he wanted to turn himself in and put all this behind him, but he was afraid. One or two experiences with San Antonio police officers in his youthful past had left him fearful of the reception he'd receive at the hands of outraged police. When I told him that I knew from personal experience that District Attorney Mark Blackwell was eminently trustworthy, and has an impeccable reputation for fairness, Mr. Davis came up with this scheme. Everyone concurred, so here we are."

Austin glanced at me. He didn't wink—he couldn't have, it would have shown up on the news footage—but that was the impression he gave me. Austin was a man who could rise to any occasion but in the midst of solemnity or passion slip one a look that said, "Only you and I know how full of shit I am." I smiled back at him, though Austin hadn't smiled. I quickly erased mine.

Austin was only five years younger than I, but like his client he bore his years very lightly. He could, in fact, have been Chris Davis's slightly older brother, a more successful, infinitely smoother guardian used to pulling his sibling out of scrapes.

They came toward me and I laid hands on the suspect. "Mr. Davis, you're under arrest," I said, managing to avoid adding, *in the name of the law.* I held him long enough for a good photo opportunity, justifying the time in the spotlight by explaining to him in careful detail just what would happen next. Davis nodded along as if I were his friend. I kept my face stern.

Finally I passed him off to the contingent of sheriff's deputies who took him into actual custody, hustling him into the offices out of sight. Chris Davis looked like a wave-borne glint of sunlight in that tide of dark men.

I stayed to answer a few more questions, confident that one of them would give me the opening to make my tough speech. When it did I said, "No, we have no deal between Mr. Davis and my office. Our only arrangement was that he could turn himself in to me rather than to police. Now the case will take its normal course. Whether I prosecute it personally or not, there will be no favors. As in all cases. I'm flattered by the faith Mr. Davis and his attorney place in my fairness, but I'm sure they realize that my job is to prosecute people like this suspect. These are particularly heinous crimes that have thrown this city into an understandable panic. It's my responsibility to prevent their happening again. I won't be taking it easy on Mr. Davis."

That was as good as it was going to get. I ignored the rest of the questions and retreated into my offices, Austin Paley at my elbow. He patted my back in greeting, I touched his arm, and we proceeded down the interior hall to my private office, loosening up further with every step, until we were laughing.

"Gosh, Mark, but you told me we had a deal, right? Two years' probation and no fine, wasn't that it?" he extemporized.

"I'm sorry, Austin," I responded in kind. "That was just a lie to get you in here. You don't mind, do you?"

We didn't do any real plea bargaining in my office; in fact, we hardly mentioned the case at all. We made cocktail-party chat about how long it had been since we'd seen each other, what we were busy with, how our friend Eliot seemed to be doing in retirement. After a few minutes Austin stirred himself and, with a small frown, as if it were indelicate to refer to his reason for being there, said, "Well, I'd better go find my client. Where are your men keeping him?"

"In the torture chamber, beating a confession out of him."

"It will cleanse his soul, no doubt," Austin said, and shook my hand again, taking me into his confidence as he said, "We'll talk soon."

After all the waiting, the event seemed to have passed quickly, leaving me alone again, though the clock told me it was almost lunchtime and I'd done nothing else all morning. It had been campaign work, not prosecution. In atonement I worked late into the afternoon, finding myself still in the office when it was time for the six o'clock news. I turned on the TV in my office and watched my act again. My God, I looked formidable in my few seconds on the screen. There was no hint of the foolishness I'd felt. *This will do me some good*, I thought. All over the city, burglars in appliance stores must be dropping their tools and repenting their trades at the sight of my stern countenance. Tearful private citizens would be murmuring, "Thank God we have this man watching over us."

It wasn't until I saw myself on screen, hours after the event, holding Chris Davis's arm, that I remembered the vileness of the man I was touching, remembered the ordeals of little Billy and Louise and Kevin. It was impossible for me to picture the frightened Davis as the villain of our collective imaginings. He looked like a victim himself.

3

THE BUILDING HUMS ON MONDAYS. I CAN FEEL IT, even in my remote perch. I remember Monday mornings perfectly well, from both sides of the docket, prosecutors getting files together, arguing with defense lawyers, the defense lawyers gliding from court to court, trying not to look in a hurry, all of them wondering if they'll be in trial that afternoon.

My morning is more predictable. My time is scheduled. I meet with the county commissioners to ask for money. I meet with my staff to ferret out recurring problems. Community leaders come to ask me to do more, or less. I seem never to hear from happy people.

Austin Paley was a welcome diversion that afternoon. Part of his appeal was that he wasn't scheduled. He was one of the rare people who could expect to drop in on the district attorney, not because of some special access, but just because of his impenetrable insouciance. I postponed a scheduled meeting to see him.

He looked fastidiously out of place. Austin was rarely seen in the criminal courts any more, though at one time he had been one of the familiar crowd. Sometime in the last eight or ten years he had moved beyond us, though, into the corporate realm where lawyers were as unfamiliar with the courthouse as was an average law-abiding citizen. But Austin hadn't lost touch. He made the social rounds, contributed to judges' campaigns, occasionally even personally steered an important client through the hazards of a DWI charge.

"How did you get into this one, Austin?" I asked after our cheerful, clubbish greetings were done.

He rolled his eyes. "Friend of a friend," he said lazily. "Chris thought— Well, you can imagine. He felt like a hounded man. Hearing footsteps. He just wants to get shut of the whole thing."

"I imagine," I said mildly, not taking up the implied invitation to make an offer.

"One reason I allowed his arrest to be so public," Austin continued, as if he had arranged it all, like a reception for a visiting dignitary, "was so that people could see how harmless he is. You saw him, Mark, so befuddled. He's really a child himself." His mouth turned wry. "That's his problem, I suppose. Children are peers to him."

I opened my desk drawer, to let him know immediately where we stood. "I've gotten letters, Austin." I dropped a representative sampling on the desk. "Saying they're breathing easier now that the child rapist's behind bars. Asking me please to put him away well into the next millennium."

That was the shorthand rendition, but someone with Austin's political savvy wouldn't need more. His gaze fell on the letters momentarily with a flicker of distaste. "Well, you will get reactions like that, won't you? But they can't dictate what you do. First of all, of course, you couldn't get a lot of years."

"For aggravated sexual assault of children? I couldn't?"

Austin's eyes had been roaming idly around my office. For a moment they returned to me, searchingly. He smiled again, as if I'd made a joke.

"I think you'll find it's only indecency. You can't prove penetration. But you know that. You've talked to the children, of course."

"Yes. Well, I've read their statements."

"And of course the defendant gave a statement too."

I had read that one, too. Davis's confession was a little more precise, and much more articulate, than the average defendant's, but still damning.

"Yes. One that would revolt a jury."

"Oh, juries," Austin said dismissively, and we both laughed.

"What he needs is treatment," Austin continued. "Ten years

of probation would be a much more effective deterrent in this case than any term of imprisonment. It would make the streets safer." Acknowledging my letters.

I shook my head. "I can't do it, Austin. Not probation."

He understood. And he was thoughtful enough not to make me spell out the political realities we were talking about. Austin waved his hand as if we'd passed beyond his attention span. We were only talking about a defendant, after all.

"All right, if it has to be years, how many?"

Years means prison. It's the word we use. A term of probation may last years, too, but they're different sorts of years.

"Thirty," I said.

"I'm telling you, Mark, you can't get thirty. If you went for aggravated you couldn't get it. There's no physical evidence, the girl's too young even to make a witness, and if the boys do remember accurately they'll just prove indecency."

Indecency with a child, basically fondling, carries a maximum sentence of twenty years, as opposed to the maximum of life for aggravated sexual assault of a child.

I shrugged. "We'll see what a grand jury says," I said, and immediately felt like a bully.

Austin sounded mildly exasperated. "You're not going to make me try this, are you? Do you know how long it's been since I tried a case? Come on, Mark, I brought this to you. I promised him you'd be fair. *Be* fair.

"Look," he went on, in the confidential tone that came naturally to him, "this is easy. You can come out of it golden. Someone leaks a copy of the statement to the media. People read that it was just some mild fondling, rather pathetic at that. The children remain anonymous, of course, but they're safe, and too young to remember much. And you, you'd like to put this man away forever, but the damned legislature has tied your hands, they put a maximum of twenty years on this crime. And in view of the relative mildness of the offense— that's not the word, we'll think of a better word—and the fact the defendant is so torn by remorse he turned himself in, you think a sentence of say, eight years, is more than adequate to protect . . ."

Austin was leaning forward, talking animatedly. I thought I was seeing him now as he must be at his best, in private meetings throughout the city, in the highest rooms of many an office tower. His client was forgotten, I was sure. Strategy itself was the enticement. We were collaborators.

That made me wonder anew how Austin had come into the case. Friends of friends, he'd said. Was Chris Davis politically connected? I'd never heard of him, but that didn't mean much. There were power brokers in San Antonio I hardly knew. I certainly couldn't keep track of their extended families, and friends and lovers, and friends of lovers.

Davis could even have been a relative of Austin's. I remembered their resemblance. It would have been rude to inquire too closely.

"Let's say twenty," I interrupted his flow. "You know he won't do much time, in that range." Due to early paroles because of prison overcrowding and intervention by a nobly humanitarian federal judge, prison sentences in Texas have become largely symbolic. A twenty-year sentence could mean as little as two years actually served.

"Whatever," Austin said. "We're in the ballpark." He exhaled, suddenly bored with the subject. "How's the campaign going?" he asked, switching to something more in his line.

We talked politics for another ten minutes. Austin was too discreet to offer me a campaign contribution on the spot, instead talking about people I should meet, the kind of people who don't normally get involved in something as low-level as a DA's race.

"We can get this settled quickly, can't we?" Austin said in leaving. "I'd like to drop back out of the limelight. I've tried to deflect it all back on you."

"I appreciate that," I said, remembering his nice speech at the time of the arrest. Austin waved away my thanks. It had been a favor too small for him even to keep track of. We shook hands at the door and Austin hurried off down the hall, with many calls on his time, I imagined, but he'd drop in on old friends on his way out of the building. *Like Eliot*, I thought. *Like Eliot's private shadow.* Austin Paley was almost unknown to the general public, but in his quiet way he wielded more influence than most public figures. I realized I felt flattered by his small courtesies.

Later that week, at a political fund-raiser, I thought I felt Austin's ghostly fingers slip into my pocket, leaving not cash but something much more valuable.

"I got a call from the firefighters' union," my campaign manager told me in a quiet corner, momentarily aside from the smiling, swirling crowd. "They want you to speak to their next meeting. You manage not to set fire to anything, I think we'll get their endorsement."

"Good, Tim. Why firemen should care who the DA is I don't know, but anybody's welcome on this bandwagon."

Tim Scheuless, my campaign manager, and I weren't friends. We'd hardly even known each other a year earlier. He'd come recommended from more-veteran campaigners. Tim owned a local ad agency, one he'd staffed so ably that he had too much time on his hands, and had gotten interested in politics. Tim understood politics better than I, but he wasn't a lawyer, and he didn't have a very good grasp of the nature of my job, as he often demonstrated in conversation.

"That's the trouble with the district attorney's race, there aren't any issues," he said, shaking his head. Tim should have been a candidate himself. He had broad shoulders and a large head that photographed well, and his teeth when he flashed them were truly impressive. "Tough on crime," he went on. "That's it. But who's gonna run for the office and say he'll be weak on crime? Where's an issue?"

"There's character," said a voice at my elbow. I knew the voice, but I was amazed to turn and see Linda Alaniz at a political function. She hated politics almost as much as she'd hated being a prosecutor.

Linda was wearing a dress held up by straps that showed off her shoulders, and the brownness of her skin. Her eyes glittered. She looked tired, but as if she'd abruptly thrown off weariness at the prospect of a good fight.

"You know some dirt on Leo?" Tim asked her. That was what "character" meant to him.

"I mean fitness for the job," Linda said acidly. "Fairness. Setting a standard to which the entire office must adhere. That's what Mark has done during his term."

"Oh," Tim said. "Yeah, sure. I mean of course, obviously. But tough on crime—that's what sells." He turned back to me. "That's where you've got the real advantage, and I don't see you using it enough. Mendoza can talk about being tough on crime, but you can do it. You need to try something, soon. Some big case, with gruesome details. A laydown, of course;

God forbid you lose it. Something long, too, so you could be in the paper every day looking tough, and there's no chance of losing. Surely you've got some case like that around the office? I read about 'em all the time."

Sure, they all look easy when they happen, when the TV reporter says police have arrested a suspect. People want to see that suspect on trial the next day. They ignore or never hear about the details that make trial an adventure—the contradictory statements from victims, the alibis false or true, the witnesses who are less than pristine themselves.

"I could do that, couldn't I?" I said to Linda.

"I could help," she said. She was looking at me, ignoring Tim. "I'll pick one of my most disgusting clients, and instead of trying to get him a good plea bargain I'll let you try him."

"Good. And if the case isn't going too well during trial—for me, I mean—"

"I'll advise him to testify, so you can tear him to pieces," Linda finished.

All this sounded like a good idea to Tim, but he knew when he was being kidded. "All right, all right," he said. He raised a finger. "But look, why do you have a campaign manager? So do what he says once in a while, okay? You listen to me, and we'll win this thing going away."

"I'll work on it, Tim, I promise."

He saluted me with an eyebrow, patted Linda's shoulder, and slipped away to work the crowd. "It's good to see you," I said to Linda. "It's *amazing* to see you here."

Linda gave me an ironic smile. "You deserve to be reelected, Mark. I support you."

Well, political support. But I was delighted to have Linda beside me again, for whatever reason. I wished it could be permanent.

I looked around at the crowd. Linda was eyeing them too, as if she might have to talk to some of them. "Aren't you glad you don't have to do this kind of crap to keep your job?" I said.

"I make no judgments," Linda said, causing me to laugh so boisterously that several people turned to smile at me.

Austin was right about the child-molesting cases. He had done his homework more thoroughly than I had. I started catching up a few days later, beginning with rereading the children's statements. The statements might have relieved a parent, but they were poor material from a prosecution point of view. The crucial part of one boy's statement read, "I was just about asleep when I felt him touching my leg. His face looked funny. He put his hand inside my shorts. I laid very still. Then I went to sleep."

As Austin had said, it proved indecency with a child, not sexual assault. Only fondling, no penetration or contact between intimate body parts.

"What about the girl? There's no statement from her."

The advocate shook her head. "It's a good thing this is going to plead. You don't want to depend on little Louise."

The advocate works for me, supposedly. We have three of them in the sex crimes section. They're counselors who help prepare children for trial, take statements from them, sit with them and play with anatomically complete dolls for the video camera. Sometimes they accompany the child to court. They're supposed to be neutral, just assigned to protect the child, but as defense lawyers always point out, the advocates work for the prosecution.

This advocate, Karen Rivera, was a pale, bony woman who smoked, even in my ashtray-free office. She didn't seem the kind children would respond to, but they did. I've seen her. Her face changes when a child comes into the room. Even her body grows more maternal somehow. With children she is wonderfully protective and reassuring. She uses up all her patience on them.

"Why?" I asked.

"Because she'd kill you," the advocate snapped. "Ask her the same question three times and get three different answers. I know, I've done it."

"What about medical? What could I prove there?"

She shook her head. "Like he knew it would come to trial. Nothing. No redness, no damage. She doesn't remember much, and I don't want to push her. Maybe she's better off not remembering."

"How is she?" I asked.

The advocate shot her half-smoked cigarette into my metal trash can from five feet away. "She's fine," she said, but her tone said something different. "If everybody'll stop asking her about it she might forget it. She might fall to pieces ten years from now on her first date, or twenty years from now when she's married and has kids herself, but right now she's okay. She doesn't know what happened. Everything's new to her, she doesn't know this was something awful. If I can save her from her damned parents she'll be fine."

"What do you mean?"

She gave me a hard look, like I was after her babies, too. She said, "They get victimized three times. First by the molester. Next by the parents. That's the most important one. The child can forget what happened, maybe, but they're much slower to forget what Mommy and Daddy did when they found out."

"Like what?"

"Like not believing. That's the worst. The kid gets up her nerve, she's scared, she suspects something's wrong, so she goes to the only people she can rely on. And if they tell her she's lying—and a lot of them do, I'll tell you; they don't want to believe it so they say the child's making it up—if Mom and Dad don't believe her, if they don't take her in their arms and promise her they'll never let it happen to her again, then she's all alone in the universe. And she knows it could happen again, because nobody's on her side."

"Who's the third one who mistreats her?" I asked.

"Us. The system. Once the parents are convinced, or half-convinced, so they call for help, then the cops come. When the cops come to a child's house because of something the child said, then she knows she's done something terrible. She thinks she's going to be arrested. Then she gets taken to a doctor who takes her clothes off and sticks a flashlight up her behind, and god damn, this is worse than what happened with the nice man in the field or the motel room. Then the prosecutors get hold of her, and some sweet friendly bitch like me who's going to be her friend just as long as we need her and not a day longer. Sometimes I think we're the worst. You and me, the whole justice system."

She'd lit another cigarette, on automatic pilot, and inhaled half of it. "You need some time off, Karen?" I asked quietly, the tone used to avoid scaring someone off a ledge.

She laughed, causing a cloud of smoke to obscure her face. "I need Green Lantern's ring. I need to scour the whole world clean. When is everybody going to wise up and put me in charge of everything?"

I could already see how difficult the cases would be to prosecute. Austin knew that. Luckily, his guy wanted to plead guilty.

"I need to meet with all the parents," I said. "We don't want them to read in the papers that it's going to be plea bargained. They'll be expecting trials."

Karen rolled her eyes. "Be gentle with them," she said. "The kids're all right, at least for now. It's the parents that're falling apart."

But they came into my office very bravely, faces set. I met with each set of parents individually, telling them what we were proposing. I talked about avoiding the trauma of trial. Kevin's parents took up my theme almost before I'd announced it.

"Yes," Mr. Pollard said. His head bobbed. "We understand. Don't worry about us."

He was Kevin's father, a big man with a heavy dark mustache and work-hardened hands. Six-year-old Kevin sat silently beside him, his mother on the other side. She reached for Kevin's hand when she remembered. Other times she worked a tissue in her hands.

There was something about Mr. Pollard I didn't like. His quick acquiescence to a plea-bargain agreement was a relief, but it surprised me and put me off. I turned my attention to Kevin, a slight boy with pale eyes anomalous beneath his shock of black hair. Kevin must be tired of being looked at by adults the way I was looking at him; appraisingly, but with mouth retaining a smile at all costs. He looked down, away from me.

"Kevin?" He wouldn't look up. "Do you understand what I'm saying? The man would go to prison, far away from you, and you wouldn't have to tell anyone else what happened. Does that sound good to you?"

"He understands," his father said. "We've talked to him about it. He'd be glad to get it behind him. Don't worry about Kevin," he said heartily.

That was what bothered me. Mr. Pollard's concern with not causing us bother. I'd seen that reaction in victims before, but I was more accustomed to those who demanded justice, who demanded more than I could provide. The suspicion crossed my mind that Mr. Pollard planned to obtain justice in his own way. He could have taken Chris Davis apart in the time it took a bailiff to cross the room.

"Does that sound all right?" I repeated to Kevin, my insistence aimed less at him than at his father. By staring intently at the boy I imposed silence on everyone else until Kevin looked up at me. His eyes were watery.

But he kept his voice from wavering by speaking softly. "Yes," he said. His eyes held me. He wanted something more. I wanted to speak to him privately. For a moment he looked as if he were still a kidnapping victim, and it was the people on either side of him holding him captive.

"Yes," he said more clearly. "That's what I want to do. Not testify in court. As long as he'll stay away."

"He will," I said. Kevin looked down again. "Karen, why don't you take Kevin down the hall and get him something to drink. And maybe something to play with."

Karen seemed glad to get the boy away, and Kevin went with her without hesitation. Karen turned at my door, took in both parents with her flat gaze, and looked at me. I nodded, and she left with Kevin.

Mr. and Mrs. Pollard were looking at me. Neither moved over to take the vacant chair between them.

"We're lucky," I said, "that this was not a violent or—extended—case of molesting." There was no good way to put this. I didn't want to minimize the harm to their son, but legally he hadn't been as much of a victim as he might have been. "I know it's frightening, but it could have been much worse. Kevin should outgrow it without much trouble. If he doesn't seem to be recovering, you should get in touch with this office and we'll recommend a counselor. We know some good ones." I assumed.

"The bad part is, *because* it wasn't worse than it was, I can't obtain a very high sentence for this man. Even if we put Kevin through a trial and did the very best we could do, it would only be twenty years."

Steve Pollard was nodding along with me. Once again I felt irritated at having him on my team.

"I can get almost that much in a plea bargain," I went on flatly. "Probably fifteen or so. I'm sure that doesn't sound like enough, but—"

"Yes, it does," Pollard said. "We won't make trouble about it."

"It's your decision," I said, giving up. "Whatever you tell me to do I'll do. Mrs. Pollard?"

"Yes?" She looked startled, as if she'd forgotten what we were discussing. Then she stiffened. Nothing had happened, husband and wife hadn't exchanged a glance. Pollard was suddenly stiff, the muscles standing out in his neck as if he had his jaws clamped. And his wife sat up alertly as if he'd grabbed her arm.

"Have you understood everything I've said?"

"Yes," she said hastily. "Yes, this is best. For Kevin. We don't want him—to have to relive it."

We had our agreement, that's what I'd wanted from them, but I found myself both anxious to get them out of my office and reluctant to let them go. We hadn't connected. I hoped Karen was doing better with Kevin.

"Is he going to be okay?" I asked her a few minutes later, after the family Pollard had taken their joyful leave of us.

"Kevin?" she said, and shrugged. "How good was he going to be anyway?"

It had been interesting to see Karen in the room with all of us. She'd been in her kinder, gentler persona because the boy was with us, but she'd been sitting behind him, behind his parents, and her eyes had told me she was still there, inside her motherly disguise, the bitter woman for whom the world was arranged all wrong.

"I hope you didn't let that Norman Rockwell family-togetherness scene fool you," she said now that we were alone. "That was the most time they've been in the same room for a year. The parents are separated."

Ah. Click, click. Nothing was ajar any more. I found myself feeling slightly relieved. "I'm stunned," I said. "They seemed such a happy family."

"That boy's going to need help," Karen said. "They haven't even bothered to get divorced, so the father doesn't have to pay support or have regular visitation. He just drops by whenever he feels like it, and he hasn't felt like it much since Kevin spent the night with a strange man. You saw him—his biggest concern is that his kid's going to turn out to be a fag instead of a fullback. He's doing his duty now, but after this is done he'll drop Kevin like a hot rock. And Kevin knows it. He's smarter than both of them, he knows his dad wants nothing to do with him. You stay in office long enough, you'll see Kevin back in this place.

Nine, ten years from now. You watch. I only hope what he's charged with is killing his old man. I'll testify for him."

I sighed. This had been the last of the interviews, the hardest and the easiest. I had all the parents' agreements. All of us, the defense included, just wanted the cases to go away quietly.

"Let's do it," I said abruptly. "Let's get these things indicted and get it over with.

"What?" I added harshly, after silence had forced me to look at the advocate again. "What do you want me to do? All I can do is prosecute somebody who's already done something. Everybody else has to get on with their own lives. I'm no more in charge of the world than you are, Karen."

When everybody wants something to happen it can get done quickly. I took the cases to a grand jury the same week, and had three indictments for indecency with a child an hour later. The cases landed in Judge Hernandez's court, and when Austin and I appeared together to ask for an early disposition setting, the judge was happy to oblige. We had a date set the week before Labor Day.

The only surprise was the call I received from Mrs. Pollard. She spoke very quickly, as if afraid she was wasting my time or as if somebody might step in and pull the phone out of her hands.

"I know you said we didn't have to be there for the guilty plea, and it won't be like a regular trial, but I wondered if it would be all right if we do come. Kevin and I. Not to talk or anything, just to watch. I think it would help for Kevin to see it happen, to see the man taken away in handcuffs. He still doesn't— Some nights I have to sleep with Kevin. He—"

It was none of my business. "Of course," I said. "It's a public event. You're free to be there. But do you really think—"

"He won't get near Kevin, will he? I've never been in a court-room." She sounded apologetic, as if telling me she'd dropped out of school.

"No, ma'am. You and Kevin will be in the audience, with a railing between you and the front of the court, and the defendant will be brought in through a side door. They won't be close."

"Good. Then we'll be there."

I wanted to ask if Kevin's father would be there too, but didn't want my tone to alert her that I'd noticed anything wrong in her family. Let them think they could fool anyone.

The day of the plea, we gathered by ones and twos as if for a secret meeting. Judge Hernandez had graciously given us a day in the middle of the week when nothing else was set in his court. The Justice Center was almost empty on the hot summer afternoon. My footsteps echoed in the stairwell.

But there was a flock of media outside the third-floor courtroom. We hadn't kept the occasion secret; to the contrary, publicity was part of the plan. It was a campaign appearance for me, and I allowed myself to be sidetracked into one of those dashing courthouse interviews—"Yes, Jim, I can take a moment to reassure your viewers, while on my way to do justice and serve the people"—so beloved in the spot news biz in which we were all engaged.

Two print journalists and a couple of their TV counterparts were inside the courtroom, scattered through the pews. There were no spectators. It wasn't an entertaining occasion. There was no potential for drama as there would have been if it had been a trial. I thought.

Halfway up the left aisle I saw a black-haired head that barely reached over the seat back. Beside him, Mrs. Pollard turned to look at me. She had no expression. Karen was with them, protectively placed on the aisle. No man.

I nodded to them gravely as I passed, but didn't think I'd do them any favor by calling further attention to them. As I passed them, another figure, inside the rail, arrested my attention. I walked faster as he turned toward me.

"Eliot!" I pumped his hand. "I didn't know you'd be here."

"Just watching out for you," he said quietly.

I chatted with him, aware that we were standing before the bench of a criminal courtroom in which he had never tried a case and never would. I wondered how Eliot felt as a spectator at the scene to which he'd once been so central.

Becky Schirhart arrived. As the regular first chair prosecutor in the court she was there to do the actual work of taking the guilty plea. She looked quite at ease. It wasn't her case, it was just a guilty plea, she had nothing to worry about. But I remembered her new to the office, when I'd still been a defense lawyer, and later when she was made insecure by having me as a new boss, when an occasion like this would have sent her spinning with worries of everything that could go wrong. She was an old pro now, relaxed in the courtroom. Becky was summer-casual, wearing a long-waisted dress instead of a suit. Her brown hair, loose to her shoulders, showed traces of exposure to sun. Her eyes, I noticed for the first time, were hazel, some subtle shade that seemed to shift as she did, as the light moved across her face.

I introduced her to Eliot. Becky wasn't as callow as many of my young assistants; she had enough sense of history to know whom she was meeting and treat him accordingly, not as if Eliot were a civilian lost inside the bar. Becky was as tall as Eliot, making him look older, though he was tanned and steady and made us both laugh with a casual story about an occasion when the judge of this court had worked for him.

I was looking past Becky's shoulder down the aisle. Kevin Pollard's reaction told me something had happened. He was suddenly sunk even deeper in his seat. Karen was leaning over him.

Austin Paley was coming up the aisle, glancing to either side, pleased, I was sure, by the sparse population of the courtroom. This appearance was slumming for him; he wouldn't want it widely observed. He stopped as he came abreast of the two women and Kevin, glanced at them disapprovingly, then hurried toward us. But he wasn't looking at either Eliot or me. Finally I turned and saw that Chris Davis had entered through the quietly sliding door behind the bailiff's desk.

He was wearing his Bexar County Jail uniform, a white coverall. His hands were handcuffed in front of him. The cuffs seemed to drag down his arms, showing their white undersides, the thin muscles apparently incapable of lifting the heavy metal cuffs.

He hadn't even shaved for his appearance. He looked fifteen years older than the last time I'd seen him. His eyes were sunken in reddened sockets, his nose had grown so thin it looked incapable of drawing breath, and his hair looked lank and thinner. He shuffled toward me in his jail thongs, his bare feet pathetically bony.

I looked back at Kevin. This was why he was here. I didn't see how anyone could be frightened of this apparition before me, but Kevin visibly was. Both Karen and his mother had their arms around him, but Kevin looked all alone, lost in a foreign landscape. He'd raised his left arm so that only his eyes showed, and I suspected beneath the cover of the arm he was sucking his thumb.

"You should have warned me we'd have an audience," Austin said, rather snippily.

"The boy's mother thought it would be good for him to see it," I said formally.

"Let's hope it's good for all of us," Austin said. "Hello, Eliot."

"Austin. How odd to see you in this place."

"And you," Austin said, recovering his good humor. "Let me just make sure my client is as happy as possible."

He went to confer with the defendant in the jury box, Eliot resumed his seat, and Becky and I went over the paperwork for the plea. Judge Hernandez kept us all waiting. I looked from Chris Davis to Kevin. The defendant never looked at the boy. He did nothing threatening that I could see, but Kevin never grew calmer. He stared at the jury box where Davis sat with his lawyer. The sight of the defendant should have reassured him. Davis looked helpless and beaten himself. It was impossible to picture Kevin letting this crazed-looking man near him.

Finally Judge Hernandez, a man of middle age and more than middling girth, entered, and we few scattered souls rose to acknowledge his sovereignty. "The State of Texas versus Christopher Davis," the judge announced.

"The State is ready," I said. Becky rose and approached the bench to represent us.

"So is the defendant, Your Honor," Austin said, always only as formal as the occasion required. He brought the defendant forward to stand between Austin and Becky, in the direct glare of the judge's majesty.

"Do we have an agreement?" Judge Hernandez asked.

As Becky read the terms and Austin agreed she had it right, I moved to the side so I could see Davis's face. It also gave me a chance to look back at Kevin. The details of the guilty plea droned on, a ritual I'd performed or watched thousands of times, until it had lost not only meaning but reality. But Kevin Pollard's frightened face opened the proceedings to the outside world, made this quasi-public ceremony hopelessly inadequate. It would be over in ten minutes. Kevin needed more.

As did the defendant. I noticed Chris Davis shuffling to the side, almost edging Austin out of his path. Austin had to put a

41

hand on his arm. Davis saw his fate coming. Until this moment
he'd probably still hoped to get away free, even after agreeing
to accept a fifteen-year prison sentence. I've seen defendants,
I've listened to them. Many of them harbor foolish hope up to
the last moment that when the time comes they'll be able to say
something, or a sign will appear on their faces, turning aside
the wrath of the State and persuading the judge to exercise
compassion.

For a defendant, the guilty plea, though he'd accepted that it
represented his only chance to receive a lighter sentence than
he had coming, also meant giving up his one chance to tell his
story. It meant that the judging authority heard only the guilty
details, not the compelling reasons. The defendant lost his
chance to evoke sympathy, to make people see that nothing had
happened as he'd intended, that he had been as much a victim
of events as anyone else. Sometimes I could see their faces
twitch with the desire to explain themselves.

Chris Davis had that look. I thought the bailiff was going to
have to restrain him. Maybe it was Davis's nervousness that
was making Kevin so fearful. Davis did look like a man about
to bolt. I walked through the low gate in the railing and back
down the aisle to stand next to Kevin. I leaned over and put
my hand on Kevin's shoulder, only for a moment, then just
stood there looking as determinedly protective as I could. Damn
his father.

It should have been over in minutes. It's hard to derail a
guilty plea. Chris Davis found a way to do it, though.

"You understand," the judge was telling him, "that by entering
a plea of guilty you are waiving your right to a trial by jury?"

Davis murmured something that must have been acceptable
to the record. "Very well," Judge Hernandez said. "How do
you plead?"

I didn't hear what he said. But the proceeding halted. Austin
looked at his client. Becky looked back at me.

"What?" the judge said.

"No," Chris Davis said distinctly, obviously repeating himself.
He shook his head. He said it again—"No"—not noisily but
adamantly.

Judge Hernandez looked displeased, as if suspecting he was
the victim of a prank. "Do you mean 'not guilty'?" he asked in
deep magisterial tones.

"No," was all Davis would say. "No, no, I won't." He began shaking his head and wouldn't stop.

"A moment, please, Your Honor." Austin pulled the defendant aside and began speaking to him with obvious growing harshness. Davis wouldn't stop shaking his head. Austin's hand came up as if he wanted to slap his client. Chris Davis's head was down, he couldn't look at Austin. He might still have been repeating his litany of "no, no, no, no."

"Cold feet," Becky said, beside me. "Send him back to jail, bring him back in another month, he'll come around."

"Well, hell," said a low, fierce voice behind my other shoulder. Becky and I turned in surprise to see Eliot Quinn standing there, as if he had joined our discussion, but his troubled gaze was directed across the room at the recalcitrant defendant.

When Eliot realized we'd heard him, he turned toward us. "I'm sorry, Mark," he said. "I got you into this. I'll get you out again. Perhaps this young lady is right." He gave Becky a more than perfunctory glance; she became self-conscious. "Let him stew for a while, he'll come around."

"It's no problem, Eliot. This gives me a chance to try him. Even better exposure for me." Neither Eliot nor Becky would have understood that I was joking, because they hadn't heard my campaign manager's suggestion that I do just that. They took me seriously. Eliot looked concerned, started to speak again, then changed his thought to goodbye. "I'll get it straightened out," he told me just before he left.

"Will I be like that?" Becky asked, watching him go. "Still wanting to prosecute people long after I'm gone?"

"I don't know. How strong is the urge now? Do you want to prosecute this one?"

She turned to look at the defendant. To me he hardly looked worth prosecuting. He looked as if he'd expire on his own in another day or two. But there was no sympathy in Becky's stare. She looked as if she were seeing the crime enacted. It is a rare quality in a prosecutor, or anyone else, to be able to resurrect from bare written details the immediate horror of crime. The cases pass before your eyes so fast you just have time to translate details into sentencing guidelines—abuse, gun, pain, fear: thirty years—not to bring them to life. This one had slowed suddenly so that Becky seemed to see it. Her gaze only softened when she looked up the aisle to the boy huddling next to his mother.

"Sure," Becky said. "I'll try it."

"Have you ever done a child sexual assault before?"

"I've sat second on two or three," Becky said.

"Then you know you have to win that boy's trust completely. Think you can do that?"

She said, absolutely unconvincingly, "Children love me."

I touched her arm, lightly, and walked up the aisle. "Okay?" I asked, and Karen said, "Yes," but her deep look at me belied it.

"What's happening?" Mrs. Pollard asked. I was looking at Kevin rather than her, so I was startled when she reached across and grabbed my hand.

"The defendant can't bring himself to say guilty," I said, as if it were no big problem.

"They won't let him go?" She tugged at me, saw she was being inappropriate, and released me.

"Oh no," I said forcefully, answering her question, but it was Kevin I was looking at and speaking to. He had sunk to the size of a child half his age, and he was trembling. *My God*, I thought, *what did Chris Davis do to him?*

"This is bad for him," I went on. "He'll go straight back to jail, and after he thinks about it for a while he'll probably beg to come back here and plead guilty. And if he doesn't I'll just prosecute him, and we'll do each case separately so the sentences will be stacked on top of each other and he'll be in prison a lot longer than he would have if he'd taken this offer. Kevin."

Maybe it was a mistake. I'm certainly no child psychologist. But I wanted to involve him, not conduct the whole discussion over the boy's head as if he were inanimate. I knelt to put my face on a level with his. "Do you think you could sit up there on that witness stand and tell what happened to you? Not today," I reassured him, "but someday, if we needed you to do that? We'd practice with you, you'd know what to say. Could you do that, Kevin?"

The challenge, as I'd hoped, made him sit up straighter instead of cowering further. "Yes," he said softly.

"Good." To his mother I said, "It might not come to that, but I want to know. Kevin would be our best witness."

When I stood up it had all fallen apart. Austin Paley threw

up his hands and stalked away from his client. The judge had already left the bench. Austin said a word to Becky, then looked at me and stopped. He looked as if he didn't want to approach me. But then he steeled himself, as if forcing himself to do the right thing by someone against whom he'd committed some social faux pas, and came through the gate in the railing. He only glanced at the little group in the seats beside me. When he reached me he took my arm and drew me further up the aisle toward the courtroom doors.

"I'm sorry, Mark. I had no idea I was involving you in a fiasco like this."

You and Eliot have been too long out of the daily grind, I thought. A busted plea bargain is no big deal, it happens all the time. "I'll just set it for trial," I said.

Austin looked disconcerted, but he didn't protest. "Maybe that's what it will take. But we'll work something out. I'll give you a call."

He glanced behind me as if the whole setting gave him a pain, and hurried away. The room was clearing. The bailiff had swept up the remains of the defendant and whisked him back through the door into the clandestine passages that led to the jail wagon. Mrs. Pollard and Kevin were coming toward me. I tried to reassure her again, telling her I'd keep her informed, when two small hands gripped mine and tugged me down to Kevin's level. He was dressed up, in black slacks, a white short-sleeved shirt, and a green tie, making him look even more betrayed. He'd gotten dressed for a special occasion and been left waiting.

My face was only a few inches from his. For the first time I was close enough to see some strength in his little face. He had a good grip on my hand, too.

"Don't let him come to my house," he said.

"He won't get near you, Kevin. I promise."

He held my hands and my eyes a few moments longer, until my sincerity convinced him. He exchanged my hands for his mother's, and they walked slowly out.

A newspaper reporter named Jenny Lord was in front of me when I turned around. Without preliminaries she asked, "If these cases have to be tried now, will you prosecute them yourself?"

I motioned to Becky. "If my schedule permits," I said routinely.

"Come on, Mark, you can give me better than that."

I looked at Jenny, remembering the times we'd joked in halls and courts about the silly doings in the courthouse. "Hey, come on, it's not fair to pretend you know me. You wouldn't take advantage of our friendship, would you?"

"If we had one, no," she said, raising her pad, pencil, and eyebrows.

"All right," I said, accepting the challenge like a schoolboy. "Here. Since becoming district attorney I have personally obtained two death penalties, two more life sentences, and other convictions amounting to hundreds of years in prison. I'm not afraid to try a case. However"—I looked at Becky—"I have also assembled a professional, excellent staff. If this defendant is foolish enough to ask for a trial, he'll find a formidable prosecutorial team opposing him, and sending him to prison."

The reporter finished writing and looked up at me, bored. "That it?"

"All right, how about this?" I deepened my voice. "We're gonna throw the book at this guy. We'll make him wish he'd never been born."

"Oh, that's good," Jenny said, writing furiously.

Becky was looking at me, trying to keep her face expressionless. She wasn't very good at it. When I looked at her I remembered what she had said when I'd rebuked her ever so mildly for not clearing with a superior her plan to have the victim sit with her in the rape trial I'd watched her prosecute. "I know," Becky had said. She'd known she should, but she hadn't. Becky was the most deferential of my assistants, but in trial she was perfectly sure of herself.

I took her out with me. "I want to look at these cases a little more thoroughly," I said. "Would you like to join me?"

"Does that mean I'm the formidable staff member who gets to hammer this guy?"

"If you ask me nicely," I said.

4

THE STORY ABOUT THE RUPTURED PLEA BARGAIN
ran on that night's news. The TV anchor reminded viewers of
the panic before the defendant was arrested and pointed out
that the saga wasn't over yet. They also reran the video footage
of Chris Davis's arrest in the hallway. We were all preserved in
the melee—Austin shaking my hand, the defendant hangdog
beside him, I the stern guardian of the community peace.

Unknown to me at the time, a ten-year-old boy I hadn't yet
met was in his living room when the tape of the scene ran on
the five o'clock news. The boy stopped what he was doing to
watch, then watched for the story again at six. This time his
parents were in the room, but they didn't notice his concentration. They thought nothing of it until the boy climbed out of
his bed that night, sat unnoticed behind them until the footage
appeared yet again, on the ten o'clock news, and said quietly,
"He molested me, too."

His parents didn't believe him. They accused each other of
overexposing the boy to the wrong kind of TV. But the next
day the boy told his fifth-grade teacher, as well. The teacher,
flustered but concerned, took the boy to the school nurse. After
pondering her official options of giving the boy aspirin or sending him home, the nurse instead called a doctor she knew. The
doctor made an appointment for the boy and called his parents.

And so Tommy's story began to make its way to me.

*   *   *

In the meantime, though, the cases I already had against Chris Davis were giving me fits. This was not going to be the laydown my campaign manager had asked me to find to prosecute. Becky and I began preparing the cases for trial, which involved much more careful study than merely talking to the parents. Since the defendant was no longer going to cooperate to convict himself, we had to see what we could prove against him, and that began to look slimmer and slimmer. Louise, the four-year-old girl, as Karen had warned me, proved useless. She identified Chris Davis from a spread of six photographs, yes. But the second time she identified another of the six. When we changed the lineup, with only Davis the same, she took another stab and missed.

"Adults are all the same to her," Karen said. "She doesn't even look at our faces. Put *your* picture in there and see what she does. You might look familiar to her by now."

I declined the experiment.

The third boy identified Chris Davis's photograph, but his story of what had happened between them had weakened to the point that the behavior he described may have been inappropriate, but it was no longer a crime. "He's successfully repressing it," Karen said. "Maybe that's best for him."

"It's not best for me," I growled.

I knew I could rely on Kevin Pollard. I'd heard him identify Davis in court. My only worry was that he'd be too scared to testify. Becky and I went to his home, hoping he'd be more comfortable there. It was seven o'clock at night, but Dad wasn't there, having abandoned the pretense of normal family life. I was glad not to see him.

As a way of easing into the idea of identifying the defendant in court, I showed Kevin my little spread of six photos. "In court," I told him, "you'll say that I showed you these pictures, and I'll ask if you picked one out. Now take your time, Kevin. Just show me the one of the man who picked you up in the car and took you home with him and touched you the way you didn't like."

The pictures were similar, young blond men, but not that similar. I expected the one of his molester to leap out at the boy. But he went through them slowly, pushing them apart with his finger. His mother leaned over his shoulder to look at them too. Somehow the mug shots, more than the court proceeding, seemed to make the experience her son had endured more real to her. Kevin lingered over the photo of Davis, but then kept going. Becky returned my look.

"He's not here," Kevin finally said.

"Could you look again, please?" I cajoled, trying to keep the exasperation out of my voice.

The little boy obliged. I watched Kevin. He no longer looked frightened. Was he successfully repressing the experience too? Were all my victims going to heal on me before I could put together a case?

"Not one of these," Kevin finally said in his thin voice. "Can I go play now?" he asked his mother.

"But you told me . . ." I started over, trying to take the whine out of my voice. "Remember the day in court, when you told me he was the one who'd touched you?"

"Not him," Kevin repeated. His mother looked up at me, as innocently as her six-year-old son.

Out on the sidewalk, as we walked toward the car, I said to my assistant, "These have now become your cases, Becky."

"Oh, thanks."

"Being a first chair prosecutor, I'm sure you know the principle by now. When the case looks perfect, the first chair plans to try it. If a glitch pops up, it's no longer worthy of the first chair's attention; it's become a second chair case. If it gets bad enough it can become a third chair trial, and that's just one step above dismissal. And that's where these cases are headed."

"Well," she said as we settled into my car and I took off too fast, eager to leave this slightly shabby middle-class suburb behind, "I couldn't really picture myself trying a case with the district attorney." A beat. She was looking out the window. "But I was looking forward to it."

"I would have liked working with you too, Becky. You know, I wouldn't have let just anyone prosecute Mike Stennett." A rogue cop accused of murder. Becky had tried him with the chief of the special crimes section. "Tyler thinks he handpicked you for that case, but I wouldn't have approved other choices he might have made. And I followed your trial work very closely."

"Really? I never saw you." Becky was still looking forward, not at me, but now she seemed deliberately to be forbidding herself from looking at me. Some strain showed in the profile of her neck and cheek.

49

"You were rather caught up in the trial," I said dryly. "I dropped in to the courtroom now and again. And of course I got daily reports from Tyler."

"I wondered."

We drove in silence for a few minutes. The atmosphere in the car was warmer but still a bit strained. Often I could forget my official position—there were a few people in the world who treated me the same as they always had—but from Becky I felt a steady awareness that I was her boss. I felt her watching me, waiting for her cue.

My thoughts returned to the case. I couldn't understand Kevin. He'd told me in court we had the right man. I would have known from his reaction anyway. Why was he denying it now?

Becky was also thinking of the boy. When the Justice Center loomed in sight, and the parking garage where we'd left her car, she cleared her throat and said, "Are these really my cases? And do you really think they're on their way to being dismissed?"

"At the moment. Have you thought of a brilliant way to resurrect them?"

She turned sideways in the seat to face me as I pulled to a stop. "No, it's probably something stupid. But if we're about to lose them anyway, maybe you wouldn't mind trying something a little unorthodox."

"Try me," I said.

In the incidental crevices of time between work and campaigning, I tried to have a personal life, too. Luckily, I didn't have much of one to squeeze in.

When I picked up Dinah on Friday afternoon Lois invited me inside. I went just a few steps into the house, into the dining room beside the entry hall. "Hello, precious," I said to Dinah, holding her against me. Lois smiled at me over our daughter's head. "Have a good week?" I asked Lois.

The question became more than perfunctory when the phone rang, Dinah yelled, "I'll get it," and streaked out of the room.

"Not bad," Lois said. "You?"

I laughed. "Hard to say."

She nodded as if she were still following my career.

"Is everything okay around here?" I asked. "The house seems

to be holding up. You look great." I stopped and looked at her, at her raised eyebrows. "I didn't mean that to sound as if you're part of the house."

She laughed again. "I seem to have more time now, Mark. Dinah helps me out. I can even leave her alone for an hour or two. I get chances to go to a workout again once in a while. It's nice."

Our togetherness had been extended longer than we'd expected by the length of Dinah's phone call. Lois led me farther into the dining room. "Sometimes David comes over to stay with Dinah, or take her somewhere while I do something else," she said. "Have you talked to David lately?"

"Of course."

She looked at me as if she knew I was lying. It had been almost two weeks since I'd spoken to our son, twice that long since I'd seen him.

"He doesn't seem very happy," Lois said.

"I guess not. I don't understand why he's still married." David's marriage had always been rather mystifying to me, and had grown more so in the last three years.

"Well, you know." Lois didn't want to criticize. But, "I wish you'd talk to him," she continued. "I don't know what's wrong. Maybe he'd tell you what he won't tell me."

I just looked at her. She acknowledged the family history with a shrug. "But maybe it's the kind of thing he wouldn't want to tell his mother."

"My God, Lois, I think I've put off telling him about sex too long."

She didn't smile. "Well, when the chance comes up, I just thought—"

"Sure. I'll try, don't worry." Talking of David reminded me, and I'm sure Lois as well, of our marriage, and how it had ended. We cleared our throats and our sentences trailed away to nothing, until Dinah rejoined us. "Let's go!" I said heartily.

"Don't forget," Lois said softly as I went out the door.

There were two slight problems with my cases against Chris Davis. Technical difficulties, we would call them: He wouldn't plead guilty, and I couldn't prove he was. I had a sudden brilliant insight. Davis now said he hadn't done it. So did the victims. Could it be—? I hoped a chat with the defendant might allay this silly fear.

Austin Paley had to be there. I couldn't talk to a defendant without his lawyer being present. So Austin Paley met me at the jail the following Monday morning. Sheriff Marrs was kind enough to let us use an office rather than one of the booths where inmates normally met with their lawyers. While we waited for Davis to be brought in, Austin and I exchanged greetings more formally than usual.

"What a mess," Austin said, shaking his head. "I'm sorry, Mark. What are we going to do now?"

I found Austin's calm assumption that we were working to solve the mystery together, on the same team, annoying, but I answered anyway. "I thought I'd see if your client's changed his mind about pleading."

"Maybe you can better the offer just a touch?" Austin suggested helpfully.

"Would that help?"

Austin shrugged. A short, jumpy-looking deputy brought Chris Davis into the room. I didn't think the handcuffs were necessary, but some deputies use them at every opportunity.

"I'll be right outside," the deputy said vigilantly.

Davis sat down, manacled hands in his lap. Austin and I remained standing across the room, as if we both were his interrogators.

"I want to ask you a few questions," I said. "It's up to you whether you want to answer, but it might help if you did."

Davis looked at Austin, who said offhandedly, "I'm sure Chris doesn't need me to tell him that he doesn't have to say anything. But if he feels he should—"

Austin extended a hand, offering his client to me, and I sat in front of the defendant. He glanced up, then back down.

"I just have one question," I said. "Why did you change your mind about pleading guilty?"

Davis wouldn't look at me. "Because I didn't do them," he muttered.

"But you confessed, Chris."

His gaze shifted still farther away, to the side. After a minute of silence I said, "Then I have to assume you *did* do them."

He looked at me sharply. Chris Davis's blue eyes were already watery. He looked scared, as I wanted him. But not scared enough to talk.

"And you knew the right details," I went on. "Facts that weren't in the newspapers. Things you couldn't have known to confess to if you weren't the one."

"No, but I—" he said quickly, then stopped again.

I could see he was tormented. I had a good idea that Davis was no innocent, as Eliot Quinn had told me, but I also had that growing suspicion. He had been on the verge of confirming it for me, I was sure, when he'd stopped himself.

I leaned my head in close to his, and spoke confidentially. "You didn't have to be here, Chris. You turned yourself in. You confessed."

"I felt guilty," he muttered.

"But you didn't do these, did you?"

He looked past me, at his lawyer. I couldn't see Austin. I kept my attention riveted on Chris Davis.

"No," he said.

I leaned back. Now I had a terrible problem: I believed him.

"Why on earth would you confess, then?"

I think if we'd been alone he would have told me. But it was a secret so awful he couldn't say it in front of Austin. I put the question a different way. "What could they threaten you with that would be worse than this?"

I didn't mean the police officers who had taken his confession, and he knew it. I meant whoever had sent him into the glare of publicity to absorb the heat of the public's fear and indignation.

"Who put you up to it?" I asked. But whatever the hold on him was, it held still. Davis clamped his jaw and shook his head.

Behind my back, Austin chimed in as if we were working together. "You can tell him, Chris. Who sent you to me?"

The defendant just shook his head again. He was growing older every time I saw him. His white jail coverall seemed to be leeching color from his skin. He was so pale I could see his veins running blue under his skin. The only dark spots on his body were around his eyes. His frightened eyes were retreating into the caves of darkness under his brow.

We hammered at him for twenty or thirty minutes. Once in a while I'd throw up my hands and say something like, "Well, I've got him, and I need somebody. I'll just convict him anyway.

I can do it with my witnesses and his confession." And Austin would say, faithfully trying to good-cop his client, "You hear that, Chris? You're the only one who can save yourself." But we were wasting our dramatic talents. Chris Davis kept shaking his head at first, even spoke a few times, evasively, but after a while he began to withdraw from us. His thin arms, with the hands lying limply in his lap, began to draw closer across his chest. His head lowered. By the end of the session he looked like an overgrown autistic child, his response to the outside world reduced to one shaking foot.

I looked at Austin, who looked back alertly, ready to follow my lead. But I was done. Not bothering to lower my voice, I said to Austin, "I'm going to dismiss one of the cases, where the child says positively Davis wasn't the one."

Austin nodded. "That was honest of him."

"But the other two I'm keeping pending. As soon as he wants out of jail he can have it, in exchange for a name. I assume he understands that."

"Let me talk to him for just a minute."

I went out into the hall. The deputy who'd promised to remain on guard had deserted his post. I looked back to see Austin leaning earnestly over his client, a hand on Davis's shoulder. Austin had managed to animate him sufficiently that the defendant was nodding again. It was only a minute or two before Austin straightened and walked out to where I was standing.

"Let's walk out together, Mark. Um—" He saw that we were locked in too. "I'll get a guard."

He walked farther down the hall. I returned to the doorway of the office, feeling a vague obligation to keep watch over the prisoner. He looked too pitiful to guard, though. At the sound of my footsteps he looked up. He must have been expecting Austin again, but he kept watching me so intently that I reopened the conversation.

"Who could have made you do this?" I said, shaking my head. It was a rhetorical question, I thought.

But Davis swallowed and looked past me and said, "Ask him. Ask my lawyer."

5

BUT I'D REALIZED THAT ALREADY. AUSTIN PALEY hadn't been tricked into this scheme, he was part of it. Austin was connected. If a powerful manipulator wanted to arrange this substitution scheme, he'd go to Austin. And Austin had arranged it beautifully, even conning someone I'd trust blindly, Eliot, into fronting for him. But who was Austin's real client in this business? It must have been a complete insider, someone who knew where the bodies were buried. Maybe he'd black-mailed Austin, too, into helping arrange the scheme. I wouldn't have thought Austin would willingly do something so unethical. But I also knew I'd never find out the name of his shadowy client from Austin or, apparently, from Chris Davis. Davis prob-ably didn't even know. So I had to try the back door.

If someone had devised this scheme to get a substitute, Davis, to take the heat for these crimes, it must have been because the real molester felt the heat himself. The police investigation must have been getting uncomfortably close.

I went to see the detectives who'd worked the cases. From the one who'd taken Chris Davis's confession I got only disap-pointment that he was back at work on the cases. "Shit, you close a case—three cases, this time—you take some satisfaction from putting some jerk away, you go on to the hundred other cases you got, then *boom!* it all falls through. What happens to these things over in that damned courthouse?"

His partner was cagier. Lou Padilla, his name was. He was

older, probably old enough for retirement, and in anticipation he'd started letting himself get fat. But his face was still hard when he wanted it to be. He didn't stand up from his desk and shake my hand, just grunted as if he wasn't surprised to see me.

My entering his office had reduced the floor space almost to nil. I sat in the metal visitor's chair, my knees hitting the front of his desk.

"I guess you've heard these child-molesting cases are open again?" I said after the preliminaries. Padilla nodded toward three files open in front of him. I had a sudden conviction that the files had never left his desk. "You have any other good suspects?" I asked.

"Got several." The two words must have hurt his throat terribly, because he didn't try any more.

"Such as?"

He waved a hand. "Just suspects, you know? The usual. I don't wanta blacken anybody's reputation by droppin' their name before I'm sure."

I didn't say anything else for a minute or so, because there wasn't any point. Suddenly the whole conversation was between our eyes. He was looking at me languidly, but steadily. There was something he didn't like about my being there. I looked back at him hard, trying to pry it out. He managed to bear up under my stare.

"Any of your suspects what might be called highly placed?"

"Highly placed?" he repeated, as if I were speaking over his head.

"Rich, or politically connected, or the son of somebody who's got some influence somewhere, that sort of thing?"

"I don't concern myself with that kind of crap," Lou Padilla said.

The hell he didn't. "What is it?" I asked. "Somebody you're afraid to go after? Who are you protecting?"

"Just being careful, sir." He had a way of saying "sir" that made you think it was his dog's name.

"Somebody forced Chris Davis to fade the heat for them. That means somebody with money or power or both."

"Good theory," the detective said. He hadn't moved from his slumped position in his desk chair. He didn't break into a sweat, either, under the weight of my suspicions.

"How about if I glance through your files myself?" I asked, reaching for them.

"Be my guest," he said, so I knew it would be useless. He wouldn't have written the name down.

I had expected that at least the investigating officers were doing their jobs. I hadn't thought the cover-up would extend this far. This seriously disrupted my theory that the child molester had thrown Chris Davis up as a screen because the police were getting close to the real offender. Maybe he'd done both, devised the substitution scheme *and* bought off the cops. He was a careful man, in some matters.

Suddenly I was furious. I'd been duped, but here was a man deliberately neglecting his job. I stood up. "So who're you going to come up with as a suspect this time?" I said on my way out.

"Look," his voice called me back, with an edge of anxiety, but when I turned back he looked imperturbably the same. "I'm a nobody," Lou Padilla said. "I put in my ten hours a day in this pit, I go home and eat supper, I sit in front of the TV with a beer. I don't own a tux. I don't run for office. I'm not looking for an in with anybody."

If he felt he had to justify himself, then it must have been bothering him. "Tell me what you know," I said, closing his office door.

"Just leave me out of it," he said, glaring, but not at me, at an empty corner.

"You're not," I said. "You're right in the thick of it."

He shook his head as if he'd just shake me off. When I didn't leave we stayed encased in silence for a long minute. I decided I wouldn't ever leave. Detective Padilla acted as if he'd read the thought in my mind. For a moment his voice sounded uneasy again, just a shade.

"Why don't you ask somebody who *would* know?" he said. "Some insider. Somebody who collects those things."

"Like?"

He looked at me. He studied me. Then his face grew hard again. This would be the last word I'd get from him.

"Ask Eliot Quinn," he said.

At first I thought, *Yes, it makes sense now. Eliot has known from the beginning.* Then I thought, *No, Eliot would never set me up that way. Especially not to protect a criminal.* Then I thought, *But maybe once I tell him it was all a hoax, he'll have a good idea who might have been behind it.* There was nobody who knew more about the dirt in San Antonio, for the last thirty years, than Eliot Quinn. And then I thought, *No, Padilla was just being sly, throwing me off the track.* Then I thought—

This array of thoughts kept me from going to see Eliot. In my state of mind, it wouldn't have been helpful, because I couldn't have trusted whatever he chose to tell me anyway. I kept putting it off, while trying to develop my own investigation.

"This is the crazy thing you wanted to try?" I asked.

"I don't think 'crazy' is the word I used," Becky Schirhart replied.

"You realize you could hopelessly taint the witness? If this came out at trial—"

"What good is he to us now anyway?" Becky answered.

She was right. The risk was minimal.

"Besides," she said, again reasonably. "Kevin was already in the courtroom. How much more could this taint him?"

So we found ourselves once again at Kevin Pollard's house two evenings later. It was nice to have something to do at night. After seeing Linda at the campaign rally, I'd almost reached the point of calling her again. Work postponed the decision for me.

We settled cozily in the living room. Becky sat beside Kevin on the couch, but I took a seat to the side, so I could see the boy as well as the TV screen. Mrs. Pollard stayed on her feet. We'd politely refused her offers of coffee and dessert, but she wanted to be ready in case we changed our minds.

Becky had called ahead to make sure they had a VCR. She had to eject a tape of turtles or dinosaurs in order to insert ours. Kevin stared at the screen like a born addict. As Becky straightened and resumed her seat she explained.

"I obtained this videotape from the TV station. It's very short. Kevin." She had to say his name again to tear his gaze from the screen. "Remember we showed you pictures before, and you identified the man who touched you? But then later you said it wasn't him." Kevin nodded. He was very quiet, waiting for us to tell him what he'd done wrong, and what his punishment would be. Becky smiled at him reassuringly, but she spoke like an adult who had no children of her own, overelaborately, making too much of everything.

"But sometimes pictures don't really look like the people,"

she continued. She looked up at Mrs. Pollard and me and laughed. "I'd hate to think I look like my driver's license photo." Kevin's mother smiled back politely.

"So we thought we'd show you this instead. A videotape where people move and turn different ways and look more like themselves." As she started the tape she said, "Now don't get nervous, Kevin. Just tell us if you see the man who molested you. Who touched you. And if he's not here, tell us that too."

The screen came to life. It was the tape of my heroic arrest of the infamous serial child molester, in the crowded courthouse hallway. There was no sound. The speed seemed slightly off, so that the figures moved like some weird breed between humans and cartoon animations. This was not such a crazy idea of Becky's, at that. The videotape was as good a lineup as a defendant could ask for. Chris Davis edged into the scene, but he wasn't handcuffed, nothing shouted that he was the suspect. And there were many other men in the picture, some of roughly similar appearance to Davis. We weren't influencing Kevin with a hopelessly suggestive showing.

Kevin looked much calmer than he had in court, but he still grew stiff as the figures filled the screen. When Chris Davis entered the picture with his lawyer, Kevin's eyes grew big. A minute later the scene was over.

"Did you see him?" Becky asked. Kevin said nothing.

"Run it again," I said.

This time as the scene started Kevin stood up. His back was to his mother and Becky, I was the only one who could see his face. His mouth was pinched into a tiny circle. His eyes were watery again, but he didn't just look as if he were on the verge of tears. He showed a mixture of emotions. I couldn't believe, looking at him again, that he hadn't seen his molester in court. Tonight's was a much diminished version of his reaction then, and it was still disturbing.

"Him," he said, touching the screen.

I looked at Becky and rolled my eyes.

She couldn't see the screen, Kevin was blocking her view. She moved around him, but by that time the figures had moved so that Kevin's immobile finger rested on nothing. Becky ran it back and asked him to try again. "Him," Kevin said again. This time Becky froze the picture.

"Which one?" she asked, and Kevin made sure we all could

see. Becky and I looked at each other, she ruefully, as if the
label I'd applied to this experiment had proven correct.

But Kevin was convinced of his choice, however wayward.
He was trembling again. I wanted to reach out and hold him,
but I was afraid to touch him. To my relief, Becky put her arms
around him, murmuring reassurance, but Kevin remained stiffly
standing, staring at the screen.

"Something happened to that boy all right," Becky said later
in the car. "But by now he's so confused I don't think he knows
what."

"No," I said. "But somebody knows." I was beginning to
think I should take Detective Padilla's advice. Ask Eliot Quinn.

The sun hit me as soon as I stepped out of the Justice Center.
It was barely noon, but already one of those days. The sky was
cloudless but not blue. It had been bleached of color, white as
the sun that burned in its center. It made people scurry for
cover the way heavy rain would. I had to walk across rubble to
cross one street. Workers had excavated a ten-foot hole to get
at something and had the tar bubbling ready to replace the pavement. Its fumes blended with the heat to make it seem we were
under noxious attack. The downtown streets were always torn
up, in a pattern seemingly designed for no reason but to frus-
trate motorists. Something was always broken. Five thousand
years from now archaeologists will uncover this city and conclude that it was built by a race of titans who mysteriously died
out and their city was taken over by a lesser race who couldn't
maintain it and eventually smothered in their own garbage.

Even the short walk left me feeling a little light-headed. The
office building was pleasantly cool and the elevator brisk, but I
still arrived at the entrance to the dining club feeling clammily
inappropriate for the dim, elegant surroundings. The maître d'
looked as if he agreed with my thought. "This way," he said.

On the way we collected Eliot, who was in the bar talking
and laughing with a man who appeared to me underdressed
until Eliot introduced us and I realized the man could dress any
way he damn pleased, because he owned the building.

"Drink?" Eliot asked when we were seated, but I declined,
both because I was still a bit sun-dazzled and because I didn't
want what I had to say to sound merely like the product of a
loosened tongue. When Eliot finished the amber drink the

maître d' had carried for him from the bar the waiter brought another, with no signal from Eliot.

Our chairs were very comfortable, and our table bore a white cloth. There was only a scattering of other lunchers, all of us far enough apart to be private. All through lunch I tried to bring up what I wanted to say, but the elegant surroundings seemed to impose a murmuring inconsequence on the conversation. Eliot kept up an amusing flow of stories about other rich, important men he spotted around the room, but he punctuated it with questions for me about running the office. Once in a while he'd smile at my answers as if to say there was nothing new beneath the broiling sun.

The next time the waiter replaced Eliot's glass I said, "Me too." It turned out to be a bourbon old-fashioned, not one of my favorites. The taste made me suck in my breath, and it emerged dragging the train of words I'd been rehearsing.

"Something's happened that points away from Chris Davis, Eliot. I'm beginning to suspect Austin Paley set me up, trying to protect someone. How he forced Davis to confess I don't know, and it doesn't matter. What I want to know is who he was trying to protect."

Eliot didn't answer. With one finger he swept the table, clearing the space between us. I barely even saw the waiter's hands. Eliot dropped his boulevardier's air but didn't look perturbed. He just gave me his full attention.

"The cases are crumbling," I began, before I remembered I wasn't sure whether what I said would find its way into the enemy camp. I stopped so suddenly Eliot must have sensed my reason, but he didn't say anything. The silence grew as we watched each other.

I realized, looking at him, that I would never be Eliot. I'd never match his record of longevity; my current term as district attorney might be my last. Even if I did remain in office I'd never develop Eliot's contacts. At his age I'd feel as out of place in this quiet, rich club as I did now. I lacked that combination of toughness and gregariousness that gave Eliot such ease anywhere he found himself. It seemed to me as I sat there that an old ambition of mine was falling away. The feeling made me change the subject.

"When I was one of your assistants," I began, "I never had delusions about my place in the hierarchy. I didn't picture myself as felony chief. I knew I was just one of the troops. But it did seem to me I had a peculiar string of luck in one way. Once in a while I'd have a problem with a case. Like knowing the case would be tough to prove, maybe impossible, but not wanting to let it go. The defense lawyer's pressing me for a dismissal or a low offer and I know he has it coming, in the normal course of things, but the *crime* was worth more. Yes—" I grinned. "Once in a great while I stepped outside the system and thought about the crime itself instead of how good or bad a case it was, and I'd get angry. But I knew it wouldn't do any good to try a case I couldn't make. It certainly wouldn't make my stock in the office rise any higher."

Eliot cleared his throat. "And often on one of those occasions," I hurried on, "not every time but often enough that it seemed more than coincidence, you would appear. You'd come into my court to talk to the judge or my first chair, or you'd be passing in the hall and step into my office to ask how it was going. You must have done that a lot, but the times I remember were the ones when I was having a problem. As if you'd come because you knew about it, like some sort of"—I didn't say what I was thinking, which was "fairy godmother"—"guardian. Not just like the boss. And you always said something that helped. You'd tell me to go ahead and try it and let the chips fall where they would, or that you'd assign another investigator who might dig something up. One time just the fact that you appeared in court and seemed to confer with me about the case made the defense lawyer think there was more weight behind the case than he'd been thinking, and he agreed to plead to what I'd offered."

Eliot and I both smiled, at having put one over so long ago. There was something I wanted to say, but even now I was too embarrassed. Instead I said, "You must have been all over that building all the time, dropping in on courts and offices, to leave all your assistants with that feeling. It's something I'd like to learn."

"Mark." Eliot shook his head slightly, still smiling. "I *did* take a special interest in your career," he said. He'd heard the thing I couldn't bring myself to say. "I watched you, I watched your cases. Eventually I made you a first chair prosecutor, and you know there were people who stayed in the office years longer than you who never made that. I'm sure you know why, now that *you're* the office guardian. You have assistants you watch more fondly than the others."

"But you didn't know me well enough—"

"I did," Eliot said. "Oh I know, I didn't have drinks after work with you, or bring you to my club. But it doesn't take socializing. You know who you can count on, don't you? It doesn't take many times of watching in court or strolling through the halls after five o'clock. You can tell the real prosecutors, the ones who believe in what we do, from the ones who are just in the office to get trial experience or a paycheck. Can't you?"

Yes, I made those distinctions, usually unconsciously. It was no random chance I was working with Becky Schirhart on these important cases.

"I think you've proven I was right about you," Eliot said.

Then why did you help Austin Paley screw me? That was my question I didn't ask. Intuitive as Eliot was, I was sure he heard it, especially when I returned to the topic.

"I'm sure Austin lured you in just as he did me, Eliot. But now that you know it was all a fraud, you should have a good idea who he's trying to protect. You know his associations. You must have heard rumors." Eliot didn't look like a man searching his memory. He began to look like a cagey opponent. Damn. "There's something old about this case, Eliot. Austin himself, for one thing. How long has it been since he was in a criminal court? And the investigation seems to be leading back in time." That was a wild shot, based on Detective Padilla's age and attitude. "Something that goes back to your administration, maybe. Tell me."

Eliot said, "I'm glad you don't think I took any knowing part in duping you. If that's what it was. I'm still not convinced—"

"Because I couldn't imagine you doing that without being forced. And no one could have forced you. Who could threaten you, Eliot? You know where all the bodies are buried."

He smiled gently into his fading drink. "No, I dug them all up. I prosecuted all the crimes I knew about."

"Bullshit. I know better than that, Eliot. You can't have been district attorney of this town for twenty years, somebody as sharp as you, without learning things you couldn't prove in court. Hell, I know a few myself, and I haven't even been in office four years. Some underling is stealing from the customers and you know damned well he couldn't have done it without kicking back some to his boss, but he won't admit it, so the employee goes to jail or gets probation and you keep running into his boss at public functions and saying, 'Hi, how you doin',' but you know he's a fucking thief and he knows you know it. Somebody else knocks his wife around every time he gets drunk, but she drops the charges every time he sobers up. You can't make a case out of everything you know. But you know." I emphasized the pronoun. "Tell me who to suspect, Eliot."

He was no longer smiling. He sighed deeply. That made me hopeful. It sounded like a man who knew his disguises had been penetrated. But it also sounded like a man stalling for time. Eliot drained the last of his drink and made a gesture of negation that may have been aimed at the waiter rather than me. And his answer seemed off the subject.

"In the old days," he began, "even before my time, this was what was called a wide open town. Meaning it was completely closed up. If you knew the right people—and I mean maybe five men—you could get things done without anyone ever knowing. I don't mean get away with murder. The people one knew didn't commit murder. Murderers have very little influence on society. I mean you could get a historical building torn down without any fuss, if you needed the lot for a good reason. In crime it was DWIs, that sort of thing. That was something people could understand. Everyone ran the risk of being DWI once in a while. Nobody would mind if the case went away. Even reporters would keep it quiet. Once in a while something bigger, too. A rape case, maybe, if the girl wasn't from a good family and the boy was. She got compensated. Nobody got hurt.

"It filters down, you know? It wasn't just the big boys working things out. It's a way of life. No one wants to be unreasonable.

"But one thing leads to another. Once you start trading favors, even *receiv*ing favors becomes capital. 'You did me one before, I'd hate somebody to find out about that, how about another one now?' It wasn't that bald, but you know what I mean."

I knew. But I'd grown up in a different, less genteel system, thanks to this man across the table from me. "But you changed all that, Eliot."

He smiled. As usual, being with Eliot made me feel young and naïve. "Nothing ever changes, Mark."

"Austin Paley's a part of that old system, isn't he? He's too young, but somehow he's connected to everyone. I've always known Austin moved behind the scenes, but—"

"Austin's not very forward," Eliot agreed. "He likes his position in the deep background. Men like him usually have a longer life than people who get right out in front and have to stand for reelection."

"But he's not rich," I said. "Is he? It's not just about money, the kind of influence he wields. Politicians can always find other money cows. Tell me about him, Eliot."

There was no reason why he should, except the pleasure Eliot took in sharing a story. And perhaps the amber drinks were having some effect on him. "I can tell you exactly how to become Austin Paley," he said. "Austin did have some family money. Father was a lawyer, you know."

No, I hadn't known that. I couldn't think who Austin's father might have been.

"He didn't leave Austin a fortune," Eliot continued, "not enough to live on. I remember when Austin first started out he was scrambling like every other young lawyer fresh out of law school. You'd see him in county courts looking for appointments to DWIs, that sort of thing. Just trying to make a living.

"But Austin had plans, even back then. He got interested in politics early on. He used that money his father had set aside for him, and he made contributions. He did it smart, too. He didn't try to go over his head. The governor would never have heard of him. Even a state senator would have been out of Austin's league in those days. But you know, Mark, in local races, especially back then, the budgets were tiny. They didn't get big contributions. That's where Austin made his mark. A county court judge running for reelection would have been enormously grateful for a hundred dollars. Five hundred would get a city councilman's attention."

Or a district attorney's, I thought. But Eliot didn't have a confessional attitude. He was a man of the world offering some of his stored knowledge.

"Still, there must have been more than campaign contributions," I said. "How deep do Austin's connections go?"

Eliot sounded almost cheerful again, as he got to continue his explanation. "It only *started* with campaign contributions," he said. "You can't buy your way in to the inner circle, not with the little amount of money Austin had. But it can get you noticed. You can buy your way a little closer to the candidate. Austin didn't just contribute to campaigns, he worked on them. He did favors. He was at the right spot. For a couple of people he was indispensable. He came through for them right when they needed it.

"That's what you have to do, you see. Work your way far enough inside to find out the way things are done. Who did what to whom, and why. You don't do favors just to win favors in exchange, you do them to show you can be trusted. Do something a little bit unethical so insiders will know you're not judgmental, they can let you help with even worse things they have in mind. Or they'll tell you things other candidates did. People love to talk. You know that, don't you, Mark? They'll spill secrets they've held for twenty years if you happen to be there when they're in the right mood, and they think they know you enough to trust you. It doesn't take long to learn where the bodies were buried."

And next they'll trust you to bury one or two yourself. At some point, past favors admit the bearer to real corruption. On one level it was fascinating to hear a real insider tell me how things worked on the real inside. But it was Eliot. It scared me to hear Eliot reveal knowledge like this. A few minutes earlier he'd denied knowing about any crimes he hadn't prosecuted. Now he sounded as if there were a rampant underground of crime, or at least sleaze. And as if he were a full member. He couldn't have been talking about the dim past, either, before his time as district attorney, because we were discussing Austin Paley, who'd been a teenager when Eliot first became DA.

Eliot must have sensed what I was thinking, because he stopped talking. His lips were pursed, his eyes downcast.

"Give me an example," I said.

Eliot answered my unasked question instead. "He never did anything for me. I never had a need for anything like that." He looked up at me. Eliot's eyes were limpid and sincere. He could have sold me the courthouse. "You know yourself, Mark, I ran unopposed for my last two terms. I didn't need favors from anybody."

Not necessarily. That could have meant the favors were done

far backstage, that any potential opposition had been dissuaded very early on. I believed I would have heard rumors of that kind of activity, though. After all, any lawyer thinking of running for DA would mouth off about it to other lawyers long before taking any official steps. All I remembered hearing during Eliot's years in office was that Eliot was too popular and too highly regarded for anyone to want to challenge him.

"I don't understand the kind of favors Austin could have done that would win him this kind of support," I said.

Eliot grew reminiscent again.

"A few years ago," he said, "we had a little political scandal here in town. A developer wanted to build an office complex, but there was a community center in the way. The county government issued the permits, but the city couldn't let the land go while the community center stood on it."

Little political scandal was typical of Eliot's downplaying. It had been the biggest scandal in recent memory. "I remember," I said.

Eliot looked at me indulgently, as if I were a child who had just told him I knew all about World War II. "Somebody torched the community center," I said, to demonstrate my familiarity with the details.

"Yes. Somebody. And after that it turned out a couple of the officeholders who'd helped the project along had an interest in it."

"Financial interest," I said.

"Yes." Eliot smiled quietly again.

"Heads rolled," I prompted him.

"One or two," he acknowledged. "But when something like that breaks, what the public hears is the least of it. Somebody resigned, somebody else got defeated at the next election. But the ones who took the fall, Mark, might not have been the dirtiest. They were the ones who failed to protect themselves. Who didn't have enough markers to call in. When a story like that starts breaking, there's frantic damage control going on subsurface—bodies being thrown overboard to lighten the load; promises made. 'I'll take care of you down the road, trust me.' The people who were really in deep, you never heard about them."

"And Austin was one of them."

Eliot chose his words carefully. "Austin—helped out. He

wasn't in on the deal from the beginning. But after the first torpe-
does struck he happened to sail by in his yacht, and he took a few
survivors on board. Am I being too metaphorical for you?"

"No." I thought about what I wanted to ask. What first occurred to me was, "Did Austin keep *your* name out of it? Is that
one of the favors he did you?"

Eliot shook his head again. "I was never in it. I'm not rich
and I was out of office by then. Nobody asked me into the
deal."

I still had the illusion that Eliot wouldn't lie to me. I *knew* it
was illusion, but I felt it nonetheless. I believed him.

"But Austin helped cover up for other people," Eliot continued. "Men who are still in office. That's the main source of
Austin's power now. People owe him."

I thought we had neared the end of what Eliot would tell me
by implication and example and speculation. It was time to confront him. "And what has Austin Paley done with this power
of his?" I asked.

Eliot's answer was oblique. He wasn't looking at me. "I
should never have let you inherit this problem. I should have
settled it once and for all. I thought I had."

I stood up. "Eliot, I'm developing a terrible suspicion. You
know what it is. Tell me I'm wrong."

"Sit down, Mark. Don't run off half-cocked. I'll take care of
this."

He was looking at me sternly, and he spoke with his old
authority.

But it wasn't his any more.

To get the answer I had to find someone with nothing to lose,
someone who might even take pleasure in telling me. I knew
where to start. Ben Dowling had been the courthouse reporter
for one of the papers when I was a young prosecutor and for
twenty years before that. He was a press-pass-in-the-hat kind
of guy, not literally, but he harked back to that era. He continued to wear a suit every day even after his younger colleagues
were prowling the courthouse halls in jeans and Nikes. Ben was
retired now. He'd talked about finding a small-town weekly that
needed a senior editor, but he couldn't bring himself to leave
San Antonio. After my lunch with Eliot I found Ben that night
at home, a freshly painted three-bedroom house on the near

south side, with small rooms that were much neater than I'd expected. There were two walls of crowded bookshelves, but very few things on the walls otherwise. It didn't look like an old man's house. Ben saw me glancing around as he led me into the living room.

"You should've seen this place before my wife died," he said. I sank into the comfortable chair he gestured me into. "She not only couldn't throw anything away, she'd put it up on the walls. We didn't have an inch of wall space. And I mean just crap. Framed seashells and menus from places we'd eaten in once on trips. After she was gone I got rid of it all. Looked at everything one more time and remembered where we'd gotten it and cried like a baby, but I don't want to be looking at that junk every day for the rest of my life. Besides, I knew the kids would dump it all later on, so I saved them the trouble. Now once in a while I think— Ah, but the hell with it. Drink?"

"No, thanks."

Ben frowned at me. He was still on his feet. "You worry me, Mark, don't you know how to do this? You come to pry information out of some old codger, first you ply him with drink. I got more stories that way than with my good looks, and you don't have that advantage."

He laughed and I joined him. "All right. Whatever you're having," I said. He disappeared into the kitchen for less than a minute. He must have had it already prepared. He returned with two small but brimming liqueur glasses.

"Sherry," he said. "Now you know my terrible secret, but there's nobody left down there you could tell it to who'd give a damn. Salud."

He drained his glass, so did I, and he carried them away and returned quickly. He was enjoying himself and making me start to enjoy it too, though I'd come on a bitter errand.

Ben was tall and thin and his curly hair was still thick. He moved like a dancer. He must have been over seventy, but age hadn't slowed him.

We chatted about times old and new. He showed more interest in the latter. It was five minutes before I realized he had painlessly dug out of me not only facts about pending cases but a statement or two about my personal philosophy of running the office I wouldn't have revealed to the current crop of reporters. "This is all off the record," I finally said.

69

He laughed and spread his hands. "What record?"

We worked around to my reason for coming. Ben had heard about Chris Davis's uncompleted guilty plea.

"I'm looking for background," I said. I gave him a quick sketch of developments in the case, not everything, but enough details that hadn't been in news reports to make him think he was hearing the real skinny. Ben sat forward restlessly on the edge of the couch, eager to interrupt with questions. He wasn't used to being the interviewed. I fended off his questions until I could conclude. "So it seems obvious the real molester is somebody with influence. And I have a strong feeling this has happened before. I was hoping maybe you could tell me anything you might have heard about other dropped cases."

I've never heard a reporter talk about a story who didn't know more than had seen print, and they are most passionate about the stories that never got written. Ben settled back with a happy look in his eyes that didn't reflect the emotions of the story, only of his pleasure in sharing inside information.

"Eliot Quinn is right about the old days. We had a sort of gentlemen's agreement to let certain stories pass. And in return they gave us others. They made us feel we were all in the same club, and you didn't betray fellow club members. I remember there was one state senator, a real family-man type, who practically had a police escort on his way home from his girl friend's every Thursday night, to make sure he didn't bang into cars and pedestrians on the way home. Everybody knew. But it didn't seem like a story, it seemed like a family secret, and we were all family. If there'd ever been a rumor that he was stealing votes or state funds, all bets would have been off. We would have been all over him. But the other indiscretions, they seemed like his own business. We didn't want to embarrass his wife and children.

"And like I say, we were fed stories in return. The press was almost like another arm of government in those days." He gave an apologetic sort of shrug. "This was when I was just starting out. I chafed under it a little, I'll tell you, but I couldn't have bucked it. There were no mavericks then, because it went all the way to the top. And I mean the *top*. You think no reporters knew about Jack Kennedy back then? Or even Eisenhower and his jeep driver? But it would have been bad manners to report it. If I'd tried to print one of those stories my editor would have killed it and I would have found myself writing obituaries for the next six months.

"Nowadays reporters have got no manners, and I say that's a good thing."

Ben sounded nothing at all like a crabby old fart complaining about the kids today. He sounded still in the thick of things. But he had a long perspective.

"So what are you telling me," I asked, "that none of you would have reported on some rich guy who couldn't keep his hands off children?"

Ben thought about it, uninsulted. "I don't think the gentlemen's agreement would have covered that. But it doesn't matter. I'm talking forty years ago. I don't think you need to worry about somebody who was active back then. You want something of more recent vintage. And by then things were different. I don't need to tell you. You were in the DA's office twenty years ago. Would you have ignored a case like that, just because of who the defendant was?"

"No."

"No. Or even a DWI. And I wouldn't have either, by then. The gentlemen's club disbanded around the early seventies. And you know one of the people who killed it."

"Eliot," I said.

Ben nodded. "When Eliot Quinn became DA, all agreements terminated. One of the first things he did was prosecute a city councilman's son for assault. Personally. He pissed off a lot of people in the early days, Mark, but by the end of his first term he was so popular he didn't even draw an opponent. The old boys even took him under their wings. He's one of the reasons things are different now."

This didn't do me a damned bit of good, but I was glad to hear it. I didn't want to believe Eliot had taken orders from fat-assed criminals. I didn't want my memories twisted; to think I'd naïvely accepted his preachments that we treated everyone the same, unaware there was one stratum of offender laughing at us all.

Ben sat quietly on the couch, lost in thought. His face showed no trace of the pride that must have suffused mine. He wasn't here to praise Caesar. He was just reporting the facts.

I made a small joke, as prelude to departure. "So, Ben, forty years as a reporter in this town and you don't know any dirt that could help me?"

He ignored my tone and spoke from a deep well of thought, still staring off into the past. "I was just trying to think," he murmured. Then he revived, and looked at me. "There's nothing I can specify. But there were rumors.

"Your old boss, Eliot Quinn, was as tough a prosecutor as this town's ever had. Once a case was indicted he'd take it as far as it could be taken. But once in a while over the years there was just a whiff, nothing anyone could confirm, about a case that would get derailed, somewhere between the police investigation and the courthouse. It would never get as far as a courtroom. It just went away."

Ben reached for his sherry glass, found it empty, kept holding it as if he'd get up in a moment. "I can't tell you it was true," he said. "I tried to dig into it a couple of times, but it was the kind of thing if you tried to track it to its source it dried up into nothing. Some people claimed Eliot knew about the lost cases. That was the kind of rumor that would follow any public figure, in these mean-spirited times of ours. No one believes in saintliness, you know?" He laughed. "Neither do I."

My unease returned, like the chill from the breeze he stirred as he walked past me back into the kitchen, because I don't believe in saintliness either.

"But you can't give me a name?" I called.

Ben reappeared, with two full glasses. "Wish I could. If I'd ever found it, it wouldn't be a secret."

"You said maybe Eliot knew about the cases. But some of them might have gotten lost before they reached the courthouse. Like where?"

Ben said, "I'll tell you how I think it would work. It would have to be someone with a lot of influence, at several levels. When he starts feeling the heat, a city councilman or a councilman's aide goes to see the chief of police. Now, the chief serves at the pleasure of the city council, so he needs every council vote he can get, all the time, because if he ever loses a majority he's out. So he listens."

"When the councilman tells him to halt an investigation?"

Ben shook his head. "It wouldn't be that ugly, Mark. The councilman would just say that he's heard his good friend is being investigated, and that he happens to know that this man is a very solid citizen, so he'd better not be being harassed by police without good cause. And the chief passes the word on to his detective that before he makes an arrest he'd better be damned sure of his facts." Ben shrugged. "A case like that, one involving a child witness, it could never be that good a case."

No, not that could stand up to that kind of scrutiny from above.

"It would be very discreet and gentlemanly," Ben said.

"But of course there'd have to be something ugly back of it, to provide the mystery man with his clout in the first place."

"True, true."

Ben Dowling snapped his fingers, then pointed one at me. "I'll tell you who you should talk to. McCloskey. Did you know Pat McCloskey?"

"Sure. Detective McCloskey. Is he still alive?" That was out before I realized it might offend my septuagenarian host, but Ben took no offense.

"Oh yes. Pat's younger than I am. But you know cops, they take early retirement, put in twenty years at something else, too. I don't know any old cops who aren't drawing two pensions. But then, I don't know too many old cops, come to think of it."

There was nothing good to say to that.

"But Pat," the old reporter continued. "He only retired seven or eight years ago. He might still have all his faculties. I talked to him once, I don't know how many years ago, when I was following up one of these rumors. He stonewalled me from 'Hello' on, but I thought— You know, I should have followed that up when he first retired. I thought, maybe once he's had his last promotion and nobody's over his head any more, he might tell me something. But I forgot." He shrugged, forgiving himself. "It would have been an old story by then anyway."

"Maybe not," I said. It might have been a story of renewable interest. Ben knew what I meant.

"You track McCloskey down, then. There was something, he didn't like it but he had to take it. He might have just been mad at his boss that day, who knows? You let me know, will you, Mark? I'd be very curious."

"I will," I lied. Well, it might not turn out to be a lie; it depended. I thanked Ben most politely, and made my last glass of sherry last another hour, to let the old man talk. He was quite entertaining, too. Told me a good deal of local history I'd never heard.

Pat McCloskey, former vice detective, twenty-year veteran of the San Antonio Police Department, retired, had a new job that wasn't law enforcement–related. He was the manager of a cafeteria. "They've got great benefits," he said.

He and I were having a cup of coffee, sitting in the middle of a sea of empty tables at three o'clock in the afternoon. The place was closed between the lunch and dinner shifts, but Pat was on duty, supervising the cleanup.

Pat was barely over fifty, but he'd been retired for ten years. He looked like a man with ready access to food, but as if he still put in time in the gym, too. His arms stretched the short sleeves of his shirt almost to the breaking point, and his chest and stomach did the same to the shirt's buttons. Similarly, his head was thrusting through the top of his hair. His wide nose rested atop a bushy brown mustache.

"That guy," he laughed, shaking his head. He was referring to Ben Dowling. "Still tryin' to get to me. 'S been a long time since anybody asked me anything newsworthy."

"This isn't for the news." I didn't know McCloskey well, I didn't know if that would reassure him or if he missed being in the thick of things. So I got right to the point. "Was Ben right? Did you know something?"

McCloskey sipped his coffee, stirred it, tried to fish a speck out with his spoon. He was stalling, trying to decide whether to bullshit me. After a minute he realized he'd paused too long to say no, he'd never known anything. He twisted his mouth to acknowledge that he'd given himself away, but he still didn't speak. If he'd been bought off, I thought, it had been years ago. Had he given his money's worth of silence yet? But if it was something else that had kept him from talking, as Ben had implied, the pressure should be off now. No one going to demote him now.

"It's happening again," I prompted him. "Maybe it's been happening all along. Now we have the extra added attraction, of course, that this guy may not just be fucking children, he may be fatally infecting them, too."

"I read about these new ones," McCloskey said quietly, "and

I wondered. But there's so many perverts around now, there's no reason to think these are my guy."

"I have reason to think so," I reminded him.

He nodded. "I'm not even sure I knew anything," he said, beginning to tell his story.

"I was working on a case. This was ten, eleven years ago. Kid in an apartment complex. Eight-year-old boy. He started acting funny, doing things with his toy soldiers his mother thought was damned peculiar. Took the boy to a doctor and the doctor thought yes, he might have been abused. Mother reported to us. And she also kept an eye on a guy in her apartment complex who'd been friendly with the boy. Babysat for her sometimes, even. She'd been glad to have his help. She was single, she was trying to work and go to school too, she didn't have any money." McCloskey shrugged, not making a judgment. "She told me the guy's name, but it didn't mean anything. I couldn't even prove he existed. And apparently he'd sniffed the wind, 'cause he was gone. She never saw him again.

"She knew where he lived in the complex, of course, she'd taken her son to his apartment before." The former detective gave that thought a moment of silence before continuing. "But when I got a warrant the apartment was empty. Furnished but empty. The manager told me it'd been vacant for months.

"It didn't make any sense. I asked him who else would have a key and he said nobody. I checked out the manager, I checked his friends, nobody fit the description. Then I did something just silly, I thought. I tried to find out who owned the apartments. You ever try something like that? Go through a management company into a holding company into a parent organization. I must've been real bored."

I had my doubts about that. I wondered what had become of the eight-year-old boy in the last ten or eleven years. I wondered if McCloskey had children of his own.

"Pretty soon I was in thick among more blue suits than you could sort out in a year. I tried to find out who was enough into the actual hands-on business of managing the apartments to get a key to one. That narrowed it a little, but at that level nobody'd have a key to any individual apartments. If for some reason they wanted to see one they'd just have the manager let them in. I asked if anybody'd done that a few months earlier, about the time the boy's mother remembered this friendly neighbor appearing. People with important things on their minds don't remember little things like that, but I knew who to ask. A secretary remembered getting a key one time. She couldn't say when. It wasn't for her boss, it was for some consultant the company'd hired, who had some expert coming in for a couple of weeks who didn't want to stay in a hotel. That's what the boss had told her, anyway.

"I checked out the boss and the consultant—some hotshot lawyer the company'd hired to do something I didn't really follow: bribe somebody, probably—and the expert, who was from Dallas. This was really far afield by this time, you know. I felt sure I was wasting my time. But I managed to get pictures of all three of these guys, without them knowing. They didn't have mug shots, needless to say. These were pictures from business journals, the company's annual report, that kind of thing."

He was talking faster, assuming I'd know what followed. I could guess. "I mixed the pictures in with some fillers and showed them to the boy," he said. "And he picked the lawyer right out. So did his mother."

The hair on the back of my neck had stirred at the word *lawyer*. But there are a lot of lawyers, representing a lot of people. "What did you do?" I asked.

McCloskey looked at me and laughed. "I finished out my career in Internal Affairs."

"What?"

McCloskey had the same free and easy tone as he finished his tale, but I could hear behind his voice what this had once cost him. "I took what I had to my boss," he said. "I knew for what I wanted to do I needed more clout than I had. I wanted to do a live lineup, and for that I needed to make an arrest. I went to the captain and told him what I had, who my suspect was, and what I wanted to do. He listened and said he'd get back to me, and the next week I was reassigned. To Internal Affairs."

He looked at me to see if I understood the import of that, then he spelled it out. "Internal Affairs is where you finish out your career. At least I did. You don't make a lot of friends. Not too many people outside the division want to work with you after that. I just held on long enough to get my twenty and quit."

"And the case with the little boy?" I asked.

McCloskey watched me. "Left it behind, of course. Oh, somebody else took over my cases, but nothing ever came of that one. I checked."

We sat quietly for a minute. I was starting to grow stiff from the plastic chair I'd been sitting in for half an hour. The cafeteria served good food at good prices, but it wasn't designed to encourage leisurely dining. McCloskey looked around his kingdom of chairs and tables, wondering, I imagined, if he was safe now, if they could get to him here. His right fist was clenched, making me think his shirt sleeve really was going to pop.

"That just leaves one thing," I said. "The name."

He looked at me hard, trying to judge my interest. I realized it was the same look I'd gotten from Detective Padilla. A sort of standard-issue department stare.

"Would I know him?" I asked, trying to ease it out of him.

"I'm pretty sure you've run into him," McCloskey said.

Padilla was so delighted to see me that his emotions must have embarrassed him. As soon as I walked into his office he stood up and turned his back on me.

"I have more now," I said.

I'd expected some sarcastic reply, but he didn't say anything. He pulled his jacket out of a locker as if he were going somewhere; somewhere preferable to here, because I wouldn't be there.

"I owe you an apology for what I was thinking about you," I said. "And you owe me one, too."

He glanced at me over his shoulder just long enough to let me know he didn't find me amusing.

"You might as well sit down and listen," I said, "because if you leave I'm going with you. I don't think you can outrun me." I continued as if I didn't care what he did.

"I owe you an apology because I thought you were on the take. I thought you were covering up for this molester. But that wasn't it, was it, Padilla? You wouldn't tell me who your suspect was because you've seen what happens to cops who suspect this guy."

He hadn't turned around, but he'd stopped pretending to be leaving. All I could see was his motionless back.

"You thought I was here just to see if you were on to him. That's why *you* owe *me* an apology. You thought I wasn't really trying to find out the name, you thought I knew it. You thought I was part of the cover-up when your chief told you I'd said the cases were closed, and it turned out I was taking a guilty plea from a guy you knew wasn't the molester."

Detective Padilla turned around. His wide shoulders were sloping, his arms dangled at his sides. He looked wary. I hadn't disarmed him with my honesty. "I don't know that," he said quietly.

"Well, I do. That was all a setup and I fell for it. It would've been nice if somebody who knew had told me I was making a mistake, but then I should have checked harder myself. But I wasn't helping set it up, Detective. Not willingly. I'm a prosecutor. That means you and I are on the same side."

He snorted. "You're a lawyer," he said. "Lawyers protect their own. I've seen it before."

Padilla hadn't been able to resist saying that. He *should* have resisted, if he'd wanted to go on convincingly pretending there was no cover-up. He'd just implicitly admitted he knew of one.

"It's not just lawyers protecting this one, is it? You don't have to worry about lawyers."

He didn't say anything. I felt anger creeping up me, up my back, over the tops of my shoulders. "Let's cut the crap, okay? I don't care why you wouldn't tell me, because of me or you or whoever you suspect. Just tell me the name now."

"I'm still working on it," he said. He was asking me for time, maybe for time to check me out himself. But too much time had already been wasted.

"You've run into a wall, haven't you?" I asked. "You've run into this wall before and you think you're about to hit it again."

"No, sir. This time I'm not."

His face was stony, but he kept giving himself away. He couldn't help it.

"Every day you stall me is another day he's still out there," I said. Padilla's face told me he knew that. He might even have been thinking of doing something about it, but not what I wanted him to do. "Just breathe the name to me," I almost begged. "I'll work up the cases from there. I'll fade the heat from whoever's trying to ruin this case. No one will know I got the name from you. I just want to see if I'm on the right track."

I saw him waver and I saw him fall back. He had no reason to trust me and I had no way to convince him he should.

"All right," I said. "Then I'll tell you the name." He shrugged. He didn't care. I moved around in front of him. "Austin Paley," I said distinctly.

Detective Padilla's face changed as if a spell had been broken. But he still didn't look happy.

"If you already knew, why're you bugging me?" he growled.

"Because we've got work to do," I said. "And I need your help."

"You said all you wanted from me was the name," he said.

"I lied."

McCloskey and Padilla had their suspicions, and they coincided with my own, but they didn't know. They had some pretty good evidence, but they couldn't be positive. There were at least a couple of people, though, who did know for sure. It was time to return to the source.

"Do you really think this is going to help?" Becky asked. "Billy's already positively identified Chris Davis. And now he's not even saying Davis fondled him. He's just talking about a sort of lingering tucking-in. I'm not even sure it's a kidnapping case. He seems to have—"

"Billy's five years old," I said. "Some grown-up asks him, 'Is this the man?' he says yes. He says what he thinks adults want him to say. The first time somebody showed him a photo spread they thought Chris Davis was the one, and maybe they somehow subtly tipped off Billy which picture was the right answer. I don't mean to shock you, but it happens sometimes."

Becky in the passenger seat beside me was wearing a thin blouse over a casual blue skirt. It was a Thursday afternoon, her court work was done for the week, and she hadn't worn a suit to the office. She hadn't expected to be making this surprise trip with the boss. She looked a little uncomfortable. And of course she didn't want to challenge what I was saying. I was pressing her, trying to make her think I thought her naïve and inexperienced, so she'd come back at me harder. I wanted someone to tell me if I was acting crazy, and there was no one else I trusted at the moment. I hadn't had a good sounding board since Linda left the office. I thought Becky could fill that role, if she'd get over her deference toward me. I'd been thinking about her since Eliot had told me it was easy to know the real prosecutors in one's employ. That was true. I knew Becky was one of the good ones.

But I tried to put myself in her position. Fifteen or twenty years ago if Eliot had plucked me out of the felony section to sit second on a big case with him, and he'd spun wild theories about cover-ups and years-old conspiracies, would I have had the nerve to tell him he sounded like he was full of shit? Sure. I couldn't tell him even now.

"That's why you're coming along," I said. "You can show him the pictures, so we know it'll be a fair test." Because I hadn't told Becky who my real suspect was. "I threw a couple of surprises into the lineup," I went on. "Why don't you look at them now, so you don't look startled when you're showing them to Billy?"

I passed her my six photos. Five of them were police mug shots with the identifying marks excised, so they'd more closely match the sixth, the one of Austin I'd gotten from the bar association directory. The six pictures were pretty close matches in appearance—maybe *too* close, I was afraid Billy wouldn't be able to pick one out, but I wanted the test to be fair—but I'd had trouble finding five ringers of about the right age. Most mug shots are of young men. They get arrested early. Only a very rare criminal gets away with his crimes as long as this man had.

"Why, who did—" Becky said as she started sorting through the pictures, then came to a dead halt. She looked up at me, eyes wide, her expression asking what sort of vengeful quest I was embarked on.

"Remember, that's who Kevin identified on the videotape."

"But that—"

"No, we didn't take him seriously. But I've done some more checking. Other people have suspected Austin in the past."

"Other people?" Becky said. "Police? Then why have we never heard about it? Have we?"

"Maybe there's nothing to it. We'll see what Billy has to say," I said, as if speaking of going to have a chat with an adult witness.

We didn't go to Billy's house, we found him at the daycare center where he spent afternoons after kindergarten. His father had given us permission over the phone to see him, but neither of the parents left work early to meet us there. "Just see Mrs.

Kelly," the father had said. I pictured my third-grade teacher, a sweet-faced grandmotherly old Irishwoman who'd come over from the old sod about the time of the potato famine. But this Mrs. Kelly turned out to be maybe twenty-two, wearing shorts against the lingering heat of early September. She seemed to have more energy than the five-year-olds in her charge, which probably made her good at her job but was a little frightening to see.

When I offered her identification she said, "Oh, that's okay. Mr. Reynolds called. You'll want a private room, won't you?" Maybe Becky made me look respectable. She was close at my side, like a military attaché. Becky stood very straight and held her purse at her side, and had the alert, cold look of a secret service agent checking out where the President was going to be spending the night. She gave Mrs. Kelly a tight little smile doled out by the millimeter.

We were in a big carpeted room with windows on three sides, filling the room with light even through the half-closed blinds. There were four or five little tables, several bookshelves, and plastic laundry baskets full of toys: stuffed animals and puzzles and things on wheels. Most of the kids were staring at us. One boy asked, "Is that your daddy?" and the three-year-old beside him glanced up at me, said, "Yes," and looked back down at the important coloring that occupied him.

Mrs. Kelly deftly cut Billy out of the herd and delivered him to me. "There's nobody in the office," she volunteered, and plunged back into the melee, clapping her hands to stir her charges from their group lethargy. "Who wants to play kickball?" she shouted.

Billy Reynolds looked up at me timidly but prepared to do whatever he was supposed to do.

"Hi, Billy. Remember me?"

He nodded unconvincingly. Becky took his hand. In the hall she explained to him that we just wanted him to look at some pictures. He nodded. He was an old hand at the routine.

The office had an unoccupied desk, a couch, and a couple of chairs, which we took. Becky pulled a small end table close to the couch in front of Billy. I tried to distance myself from the proceeding. I let her do the talking.

"Billy, I'm going to show you six pictures. They're pictures of men. Some of these pictures are just here because they look like

like the man you described. The real man might not even be here in these pictures. You don't have to tell me one is the right one. Just look at them very closely and tell me if one of them does look like the man who kidnapped you. Can you do that?"

He nodded, already studying the top picture curiously. He had a canny little expression, as if he were playing a game that involved secrets. He didn't give anything away as he looked closely at the first two photos in the small stack Becky had handed him. By the third one I thought he was growing bored. His study of it was more desultory.

But when he saw the fourth picture he dropped the one he'd been lifting out of the way. It fluttered to the floor. Billy was staring at the fourth photo. After a long moment he pushed back from the table and pulled his hands back against his chest.

"Turn it away," he said.

We didn't. "Why?" Becky said. "Is there something about that one you don't like?"

"It's him."

Billy's voice was tiny. He shrank back farther against the back of the couch. I'd seen him identify Chris Davis's picture before, but I hadn't seen a reaction like this.

"Don't be scared, Billy." Becky put her arm around him. He huddled against her. I tried to be invisible. I didn't want to be there, I didn't want to be a man in the room with him. "No one's going to hurt you," Becky said. "But you said he *didn't* hurt you," she went on. "You said you didn't remember anything except the man leaning over you right before you went to sleep. Remember, Billy? Is that all that happened?"

Billy started crying. We didn't ask any more questions. Becky turned the pictures over.

At the last ID session, Billy had been as composed as an expert who'd testified a hundred times. After picking out Chris Davis's picture he'd told us his revised story, that he didn't remember anything bad happening. He was successfully repressing it, Karen had said. I was glad the child advocate wasn't in the room with us now. I think she would have slapped both Becky and me.

Becky was rocking back and forth with Billy. He was still crying, but more softly. He was telling her something in mutters. "It's all right," Becky kept saying. Her voice was calming, but there was tragedy in her eyes. She was looking up at me.

We had thought Kevin had gone completely unreliable when he'd identified what we thought was the wrong man on the videotape. But it explained Kevin's behavior that day in court. He'd been terrified not by Chris Davis, in custody, but by the real molester in the courtroom with him, unconfined, unsuspected, free to walk out into the same world to which Kevin had to return after court. When both Detectives McCloskey and Padilla named the same man as their suspect, and then Billy identified him as well as Kevin, I was convinced. The identity of the molester made everything else make sense—the way the cases had come to me to begin with, and the skewed course of the investigations, reaching years into the past.

I went to the grand jury the next day and described the identifications I'd seen. Indictments can be based on hearsay, on descriptions from people who never witnessed the crime. Usually grand juries just hear a bored assistant DA read from police reports and victim statements. I was a livelier witness than they were accustomed to; perhaps in appreciation, they gave me the indictments I wanted. I used the indictments to obtain an arrest warrant.

This all happened very quickly. It can, if you walk it through. The only hitch was finding police to serve the warrants. Padilla refused, and I didn't blame him. Finally two patrolmen were assigned. No one of higher rank cared to participate in the arrest.

I led the patrolmen into the office building. The uniformed officers hung back, confused about their status, maybe. They weren't used to being led by a civilian. We rode the elevator in silence.

The receptionist seemed unfazed by the cops, but she admitted me deeper into the offices without squawking. Down two hallways I found the private secretary, who was already standing. "Is he in?" I asked.

"It will be a few minutes," she said. "He's occupied at the moment."

A light on the telephone on her desk went off. Both of us glanced down at it, then I looked back at her. "If you'd care to have a seat—" she began.

"I wouldn't." I walked past her and opened the door at her back. It was a big office inside, it took me ten steps to reach the desk. Austin Paley looked up from the other side of it.

"Mark, you should have called," he said easily. "I would have had something prepared."

He'd practiced enough criminal law to recognize the arrest warrant I held in my hands. "Don't tell me another of my clients has done something naughty," he said.

"No, Austin. This is for you. You're the one who needs a lawyer. You're under arrest for kidnapping and aggravated sexual assault, in three separate cases."

6

By the time I arrested Austin, Tommy Algren was on his way to me. After identifying Austin Paley on the television news he'd made his way through the layers of his parents, teacher, school nurse, doctor, and cops by his quiet, stubborn refusal to back down from his story that the lawyer on TV had molested him—two years ago. The news of Austin's arrest breaking publicly eased Tommy's way.

Tommy was ten years old. He looked like a little adult to me; by now I was used to dealing with younger children. He sat straight in his chair as he told his story. His voice didn't get away from him. But as he talked he seemed to slip back through the years to the young boy he'd been when his involvement with Austin had started. His carefully combed light brown hair dried and loosened and fell onto his forehead. He started swinging his legs more freely. His feet didn't quite reach the floor.

"At first we just talked. For a long time. We'd go for walks. He'd pick me up from soccer practice and take me to get ice cream and we'd walk around. There were a few other boys at first, but later on it was just me."

"We knew nothing about this," Tommy's mother interjected. She was a too-heavy woman who could have been in her thirties or forties. She looked like the former but spoke and dressed like the latter. For her formal appearance in the district attorney's office she wore a dark but patterned dress and a choker of pearls she kept fingering, especially when she spoke of her absent husband. "Mr. Algren and I thought Tommy was getting a ride home with another boy's parents. That's what he told us."

Tommy kept looking at me, as if his mother were inconsequential. I nodded at him and he continued.

"Then we'd—" He swallowed. I could see him rearranging the story. "In the summer I was supposed to be in daycare all day."

"His father and I both work," Mrs. Algren said, moving a hand like a shrug.

"Of course," I said consolingly.

"It was so boring," Tommy continued. "What were we supposed to do, push the little kids on the swings? Sometimes Waldo would come and get me—"

"Waldo?" I said. I was hiding half my face behind my hand, showing no reaction. I can do that for days on end.

"That's what he told me his name was," Tommy said. He smiled slyly. "But I knew it wasn't."

"How did you know that?"

"Sometimes he left me alone in the car. I looked in that box between the front seats. I found envelopes and things with his name on them."

"What was his name?"

"Austin Paley." He waited for reaction. I just nodded.

"Anyway, summers, that was better, because we had all day. Sometimes we'd go swimming. At first in pools, but Waldo knew other places we could go swimming when he'd forgotten to bring swimsuits for us. He said that was okay 'cause there were no girls around.

"We did that lots of times—I mean and other things too, going for walks or riding horses in Brackenridge Park. And just talking, you know. Waldo wouldn't ever say we shouldn't talk about something, or, you know, try to act like I was too little."

Mrs. Algren stared away toward a corner of the ceiling, looking stoical.

"The first time something happened—is this what you want to hear about?"

"Whatever you want to tell me, Tommy. Whatever happened."

He nodded and went on, unembarrassed.

"We'd gone swimming in the river he knew. No one else was around. It was way out in the country. After we got tired we laid down on an old quilt Waldo had brought. It was in the shade but it wasn't cool. It was August, I think. Waldo said we'd just let the air dry us. We laid there and talked a little, but not for long. Waldo closed his eyes and was breathing louder. I started getting sleepy too."

It was easy to picture. I could feel it: the deadened air of summer, bugs droning, the scratchiness of the quilt, long stems of grass tickling, water droplets evaporating off the skin. The imagined warmth made me drowsy in the cool of my air-conditioned office. I could put Tommy in the picture because he was right in front of me, but the man was just an anonymous length of shaded flesh, until I remembered with a shock that it was Austin Paley I was hearing described. The man in my imagination became harder to picture when I remembered who it was. "What happened?" I asked.

"Waldo turned over and his arm landed on me. It was hot, but I didn't move it because I was sleepy too. His arm just laid on my stomach for a long time like he was asleep, but then it moved down to my, my crotch."

"You know they never said one thing to us?" his mother suddenly said loudly. "Mr. Algren and I are thinking about suing that daycare center. Of course we didn't give any permission for these day trips. We didn't know anything about them. This man told them he was Tommy's uncle and Tommy didn't tell them any different."

Tommy was watching me. I tried to let him see that I knew there are some things you don't tell parents. "I understand," I said. "You couldn't be blamed." I looked at his mother, but I was speaking to Tommy. "Go on, Tommy."

"Well, he was touching me, my legs and stomach and—everything. I didn't stop him, but it woke me up. Then he opened his eyes too. He talked to me real seriously, the way he had before about other things. He said there was nothing wrong with it, it was just something some people did, and he thought I was ready and he asked if I thought so too. I didn't say anything."

"Were you scared?" I asked.

"Sure. But it wasn't awful or anything. After a minute he took my hand and put it on him, too. On his leg, up at the top. Did I say we still didn't have any clothes on?"

Color had crept up his mother's neck into her face. Even the pearls weren't cool enough to stop it. "Must we go into all this now?" she said suddenly. "Tommy's given a statement to the police. A very detailed statement, I might add." She didn't look at me as she asked.

I had the written statement. "No," I said. "We needn't continue today. I just needed to know enough to know what kind of charges to file, what the exact offense was." I'd also wanted to get a glimpse of the kind of witness Tommy would make. Telling his tale in a courtroom wouldn't be as cozy as in my office, but the way he'd held his composure in front of me, a stranger, as well as Becky, Karen Rivera the child advocate, and his own mother made me hopeful.

"Of course," I continued, "when we start preparing the case for trial Tommy and I will have to go over this again and again. Or Tommy and another prosecutor."

"Trial?" his mother said. "Do you think there will be a trial?"

"We have to prepare as if there will be. And I'd say at this point the chances are there will be a trial. Several trials. There are other children, you know." I thought it might comfort her to be part of a crowd, but that wasn't the crowd she wanted to belong to.

"I just thought—" She was fingering the pearls like mad, as if they could teleport her out of this sordid place. "Mr. Algren and I assumed the man would plead guilty once he was confronted with the evidence. Don't they usually?"

Yes, they do. But Austin wasn't a usual defendant. I couldn't picture him pleading guilty.

"Often they do, Mrs. Algren, but often they don't. And in order to induce someone to plead guilty, we have to offer them a lower sentence than we could get from a jury. I wouldn't want to do that in a case like this. We went to take this man out of circulation, don't we?"

She sat for a moment as if she hadn't realized the question was directed at her. Then she came awake with a little start. "Of course," she said. "He certainly won't get near Tommy again, I'll assure you of that. Tommy's father has threatened to shoot the man."

Out of the corner of my eye I thought I saw a quiet smile cross Tommy's face, but when I looked at him directly he wore the same calm, serious expression with which he'd recited his story. He looked heartbreakingly old, as if he could endure anything.

"You see why I prefer children?" Karen Rivera said after she'd shut the door on Tommy and his mother.

"Think he'd make a good witness?" I asked Becky.

For once she didn't wait to hear my opinion first. Becky was standing with her arms folded, staring after the departed child. "He's *too* good," she said. I nodded.

The cases against Austin continued to pile into the office. Some of them came to us, after his picture appeared in the newspapers. Some we sought out. After I obtained the first indictments, Lou Padilla went back to some of the children he'd interviewed over the last few years, showed them new photo spreads. For some of them it had been too long, they couldn't remember the face. In at least a couple of cases the parents, or parent, wouldn't let the detective in the door. But one child, then two, three, looked at Austin Paley's photograph and picked it out. They, too, appeared in my office. It began to be a horrible, normal facet of life, this parade of broken children. Some of them hadn't seen their molester for two years, but they still wore the haunted expressions they'd carry into old age. They bore secret knowledge that had turned them from average children into something else. One boy wouldn't let his father near him, hadn't for two years. One five-year-old girl was horribly flirtatious, standing so close I could feel the warmth of her skin, and smiling at me with an expression that would only have been appropriate on the face of an old whore.

One boy was an aberration. When he waddled into my office the first thing I wondered was why Austin had suffered such a lapse in taste. The other children had been cute as a litter of puppies. Their skins glowed, their eyes showed quickness, their little faces could have sold Kodak film. This boy, though, was on the revolting side. He must have been sixty pounds overweight, which is a lot of fat for a four-and-a-half-foot-tall nine-year-old to carry. His skin was mottled. A candy bar stayed in his stubby fingers. He looked dirty. I kept catching whiffs of him. To hear this creature give his saga of intimate contact while looking at him and smelling him was enough to put one off the idea of any form of sex. I didn't believe him. Austin Paley was nothing if not fastidious. He wouldn't have stayed in the same room with this child.

After he left I just cleared my throat, and Dr. McLaren knew exactly what I was thinking. She opened her file and put it on the desk in front of me. "Here's a picture of Peter taken two years ago."

"You're kidding. This is his little brother, this isn't him."

"Cute as a button, wasn't he? He was *too* cute. That's what Peter thinks. He's spent two years turning himself into something no one would want to touch. He's destroyed the thing that made him vulnerable. This is what we call effective response. He's protected himself very well."

So well I wouldn't think of putting him in front of a jury, I thought.

Janet McLaren was a psychiatrist who specialized in the treatment of children, particularly children who had been sexually abused. The chief of my sex crimes unit had suggested I talk to her, and after one meeting the doctor had attached herself to the cases as an unpaid consultant. I think she saw in me someone desperately in need of education.

"I haven't seen them all, of course," I said. "But Detective Padilla tells me some of the children seem to have recovered without any damage at all. Why are some okay and some are so—" I didn't want to say "twisted," but I didn't need to finish the sentence.

Dr. McLaren nodded. "I'm not sure I'd put much reliance on the detective's professional psychological opinion after one meeting with an abused child—"

That remark sounded gentler than one would think. Dr. Janet McLaren was about my age, late forties. At that age there is a wide variety in feminine appearance. Some women still look like Joan Collins. Others have already turned into everyone's memory of Grandmother. Dr. McLaren was somewhere in the midrange; she could probably go either way to suit the occasion. She was a bit too heavy and looked as if she didn't fight it too hard. The extra weight softened her face, and the flowered dress she was wearing didn't try to hide it. She had blue eyes and a full-lipped mouth that broke easily into smiles. Her hair was mostly gray, blending easily into the original blond; it was twisted atop her head into a neat but indifferent mass. Her voice was melodiously kind even when criticizing, or explaining psychological concepts. The kindness didn't disguise her apparent feeling that she was sometimes speaking over my head.

"—but it's true, many of the children seem to display no bad effects. Some have adjusted so well that, if they were my patients, I wouldn't let you put them through this pain of recalling it."

"You wouldn't want them to suppress it, would you?"

She smiled at me, at my attempt at psychoanalysis. "Suppression isn't necessarily a bad thing. They can remember what happened to them without dwelling on it every day. If we think they've managed to resolve the conflict, that it's not just festering inside them waiting to explode later, such as at puberty or after they're married, then that's fine. What's wrong with forgetting something terrible that happened but that doesn't affect your life any more?"

I was more interested in the children as witnesses. "You've seen all the children I've seen, Dr. McLaren. Are they all telling the truth?"

"I'm not a lie detector, Mark. There are indications. Peter, whom you just saw, of course demonstrates the symptoms. Peter was molested, I'm quite sure. Whether it was your suspect who did it, that's another question."

Her voice deepened, indicating a shift from the particular to the general, to a renewal of my education in child psychology. "Children want desperately to please us, Mark. Nothing is as important to them as adult approval. That's what we try to teach them, isn't it? We love them and reward them when they do what we want, ignore them or punish them when they don't. Do the same thing to a dog and you'll get the same result. When you start questioning these children, particularly *these* children, who've been hurt, who may feel rejected by their parents, when you bring them in here to this very adult, formal place, and look at them seriously and try to be their friend and then ask them important questions, they don't start searching their memories to try to find the true answers. They try to figure out what you want to hear. And if they can give it to you they will. The same is true when a police officer brings them photographs to look at.

"I'm not saying they lie. Certainly they do try to tell the truth, because that's what the grown-up says he wants. But if that grown-up drops any clues as to what *he* thinks the truth is—" She shrugged. "There's no better detective than an abused child."

I sat and digested that. She wasn't helping. The inevitable next question occured to me: "Then *are* they all abused? If they think someone wants to hear that they were—"

The psychiatrist nodded at me approvingly. I felt some pleasure myself at having pleased her. *Stop that.* I frowned, seriously. This was a conversation between adults, not a session between teacher and pupil.

"You'd like medical evidence, wouldn't you?" she asked.

"Well, of course. I assume we have some." I hadn't delved into that aspect yet.

She gave me that smile, that knowing, pitying smile, only a flicker of it this time, because we were talking seriously about something important to both of us, and she did want to help. "Sometimes," she said softly, "a child is brought to me right away after reporting the assault, within a day or two. When I get that opportunity I do a physical exam. I'm looking for evidence of sexual assault, of course, but it's also a way of gaining the child's confidence. And of reassuring the child. Sometimes I do it even if the reported assault isn't recent. Then I can reassure the child there's been no permanent damage. They're often worried there's something wrong with them, with their bodies. I can assure them there's not.

"And usually it's even better than that. Or worse, from your point of view. In most cases I find no physical evidence of assault at all."

"None?" I asked, startled, wondering for a moment about the competence of this my supposed expert.

"None," she repeated, and perhaps she'd caught my thought. "Check with your doctor who does the initial exams and you'll find the same thing. I find definitive evidence of assault in maybe fifteen percent of the exams I perform. In approximately another thirty percent there's something I can spot that indicates abuse to me, but it's subjective, it's not definite. And these are only in the recent cases. If a child is brought to me well after the fact there's almost never any physical evidence."

I sat digesting this blow to my court cases.

"I have my own opinions, of course. Look at Peter. That boy was abused. There's no question about it, even though he doesn't have any scar tissue. His whole life is a scar. And Katrina, the flirtatious little girl." The five-year-old who'd stood so close and looked at me so knowingly. "Katrina didn't get that way from watching cable TV."

"Is that just a phase?" I asked.

Dr. McLaren sighed. She was sitting in one of the visitor

chairs in front of my desk, which I knew from experience weren't comfortable for long sitting. She leaned back and stretched her legs in front of her. Long legs, I noticed. "No," she said sadly. "It may get better, if someone handles Katrina just right—which her parents aren't. They're afraid of her and Katrina knows it." She frowned at herself. "I shouldn't have said that, forget it, please. But these kids—they're sexual beings from now on. They're not going to forget what they know. They've been exposed to this world of adult knowledge long before they can handle it. Which of us can? But these children certainly aren't ready. Look at Katrina. She gets no pleasure out of the way she behaves. She's not really trying to seduce you when she acts that way. She'd be terrified if you touched her intimately. But it's a way of behaving she knows, it's a way she found approval once. She can't forget it."

She shifted to the general again. "None of them can. It sets them apart from other children. It's very hard for them to fit in at school after that, or find friends their own age. They have this dirty secret they think everyone can see in their faces."

She made it sound like a horrible, isolated world of never-ending pain. She spoke with a certain urgency, because we both knew I wasn't a real student of that world. I was just here to reach into it and pluck out one or two of the inmates for my own purposes. For those purposes a child like Peter or Katrina was of no use to me. Dr. McLaren knew how badly wounded they were; she'd made me see it a little. But you can't count on juries for imagination. I wasn't going to put some grubby fat boy or leering little monster in front of them. No, I needed a child obviously and conventionally damaged. One in pain and embarrassed and needing the protection of the adult community. Sorting through them, I felt like a pitchman for a charity. *Find me a pitiful one. Don't you have any with scars?*

"What kind of man," I asked, "can look at a four-year-old girl and think of her as a sexual object?"

"It's not about sex, Mark, it's about control. Just like a rapist of adult women is trying to assert control, not achieve sexual gratification. A raper of children is looking for *absolute* control. Who could you control more completely than a child?" She held up a hand, open fingers upward, enclosing a small soul. "These children's whole lives can be his, Mark. Everything they think, the way they react to everything they see, it can all be a reflection of him. You probably know this: Many of these children go on to become abusers themselves. After they're grown they molest children. They're still emulating him, a generation later."

"Let's talk about him," I asked. "This man, what would he be like?"

"He's not my area of specialization," Dr. McLaren said. "But I can tell you some things." She paused to get her thoughts in order, looking up over my head. She seemed to be sorting through a lineup in her mind, wondering which one to have step forward as an example.

"We divide these men—some of them are women, but usually it's men—into two types. The rapist and the molester. The rapist wants to hurt kids." She dismissed him. "The molester—your man is a molester—he likes children. He seduces them. Each one may take a long time. Because he wants so much more, you see. He doesn't just want the child's body, he wants to be loved."

"And power," I said, being the bright pupil.

"Love *is* power," she confided.

"But he—" I was frowning. "Most of the cases we have are against live-ins. Father or stepfather or boyfriend. I understand that. There's access. But this man, he's found victims all over. How does he get close to them?"

"With their help," Dr. McLaren replied without hesitation. "You'll find, if you haven't noticed already, that these children come from poorly organized families." Nice phrase, I thought. So much more descriptive than the currently fashionable "dys-functional." "Single parents," she want on, "divorced parents, or just ones where the parents don't have much time for the child. The molester"—she spoke of him almost admiringly— "fills a need in the child's life. He gives them the nurturing they need and haven't found. The child loves him. The child needs him."

I remembered Tommy Algren's abetting of his own abduction from the daycare center, repeatedly. And again of the damage to my own cases.

"I hope you're not saying the child then is willing to cooper-ate—I mean willingly—"

"Has sex with him?" She shook her head adamantly. "These are young children. When a strange man starts treating them kindly and getting close to them and acting affectionate, they don't know he's after sex. They don't know sex exists until he exposes them to it. And they hate that part of it. It scares them; it ruins them."

Janet moved her head slightly, as if easing a neck growing stiff. She was still watching me. There was strength in her gaze, holding me, making me think for a moment that she was exercising some psychological technique on me.

I thought about Austin Paley. We weren't talking about an anonymous case study, we were talking about a man I'd known most of my adult life, with no suspicion of his real life.

"We haven't found nearly all his victims, have we?"

She shook her head. "A man his age, who probably started in his teens: Hundreds. Hundreds of attempts, anyway, and as careful as he seems to have been, most of them were probably successful. Even if it was only half—"

Started in his teens, I thought. That meant there was already an adult generation of Austin's victims—his spores, many of them already embarked on child-molesting careers of their own. Austin had already left his mark on generations.

I suddenly thought of Chris Davis. Maybe it wasn't blackmail that had made him step forward to own up falsely to Austin's crimes. Maybe it was love.

We sat in silence. I felt oddly close to Dr. McLaren after only a few minutes, maybe because we were collaborating on a common cause. Her manner contributed too. She acted as if she knew me, or had in a past life. I hadn't enough experience to know if all psychiatrists treated everyone like that. I had a childish urge to disrupt her assumptions about me, to prove myself better or worse than she thought.

"Will I need to repeat all this to the prosecutor who'll be trying the case?" she asked. "Of course, I've worked with most of the sex crimes prosecutors enough to—"

"I think I can pass it on to anyone trying the case with me," I said confidently.

She gave me that look. I returned a reassuring one. Thorough professional, master of a thousand arcane details.

"I didn't see you making any notes," she said.

"I didn't know there was going to be a test."

She arched her back to sit up straighter in the chair, and gathered her feet under her. But before she rose she said, "Trying the case with you? You're going to be trying one of these cases yourself?"

My campaign advisers wouldn't like it, but if I convicted Austin myself, putting an end to the menace to San Antonio's children, nothing would be better for my reelection chances. And I had my own reasons for wanting to prosecute Austin Paley personally.

"I think so. You'll help me, won't you?"

"Oh yes," she answered, as if to say I'd need it.

While I was making my preparations for trial, Austin wasn't sitting idly by. His war opened on two fronts. Publicly his implacable nonchalance remained untouched. He was free on bond, of course. He didn't go cowering into seclusion as most defendants would. On the contrary, he seemed more publicly active than ever. He gave interviews, and made them count. He appeared not to be bitter about his indictments. Instead he affected sympathy for me.

"The district attorney found himself in a tight spot. There was a growing public fear he had to play to, for the sake of his hopes of reelection. He had a suspect in hand, he saw himself getting the kind of favorable publicity he so desperately needs, then it all fell apart. He had to find another scapegoat, quickly. I was available."

"Do you think there was any personal animosity involved?" the television reporter asked, falling into Austin's scenario.

Austin reluctantly concluded that the reporter might be on to something. "Well, I *was* the attorney who brought forward the suspect who then refused to plead guilty, throwing a wrench into the district attorney's plans. And of course the district attorney and I have opposed each other on cases in the past," he went on. "But I doubt any of that affected his decision, consciously. I was just the most readily available suspect. I think this will all blow over after it's no longer a political necessity. Don't look for this case to be tried before the election. He wouldn't risk that."

To a newspaper columnist who followed up on this last line, Austin expanded: "There's no case against me. Mark Blackwell just wants the public to think he's put a stop to the threat against the city's children by arresting me. By arresting anyone—anyone would have served. But he doesn't have the evidence to actually try me, because he knows that would end in acquittal, because I'm innocent. I expect the cases will be quietly dismissed after the election. It's really rather a cynical manipulation of the system."

The columnist, who wasn't as gullible as his television counterpart and had done more research, asked, "What about reports that at least two of the abused children have identified you?"

I could picture Austin looking deeply troubled. That's how the columnist described him. "I wouldn't be at all surprised," was Austin's answer. "As anyone knows who has tried this kind of case, a child can be made to say anything, if someone works at him hard enough. I feel sorry for those children."

I didn't know what the public thought. Surely the small percentage of citizens who would vote in the district attorney's race was following the story. I couldn't help wondering how I was perceived. Austin, it seemed to me, was beginning to appear rather victimized himself, and I was his persecutor.

But Austin was no victim. He held a lot of strings, and he was pulling them behind the scenes.

"Blackie! Hey, hoss, if you're gonna go crazy, why don't you give your friends some warning, so we could steer you the right way?"

"Well, Harry, that's how craziness is, you know, it sort of sneaks up on you."

"Yeah, I've seen that happen." Harry's eyes shrewdly took me in. Those penetrating blue eyes looked out of place in the hearty bonhomie of his expression as he leaned toward me, one hand over my shoulder, the other pumping my hand.

There is an underground tunnel that connects the new Justice Center with the old courthouse. It was there Harry accosted me. I was on my way to his bailiwick, he had just entered mine. Lawyers have business in both court buildings; there is always a wealth of foot traffic through the tunnel. People hurrying by slowed to look at us curiously, the two elected officials having a very public conversation. Because Harry didn't lower his voice a decibel. Harry was of the old school of public figure, who thought a hearty manner and vaguely rural expressions made him seem a man of the people, though he'd never forked a load of hay in his life.

"Well, you sure could've picked on somebody more guilty

than ol' Austin Paley, son. I think that case can stand some more investigation, you know what I mean? I mean, I can't believe it, myself. I *don't* believe it. And if Austin calls me as a witness, I'll have to get up and tell a jury that."

Harry was a much better politician than he was a lawyer, but he knew enough law to know that his personal opinion of a defendant's guilt or innocence would never be admitted in court. There in the public hallway, though, his opinion was perfectly admissible to everyone within earshot, which at Harry's volume took in two or three city blocks.

"You're certainly entitled to your opinion, Harry," I said calmly, "but you haven't talked to those children the way I have. You haven't seen them point out Austin Paley as the man who molested them."

"Well, I know most of us look pretty much the same to little kids. Hell, if somebody else went home wearing my suit tonight, my kids wouldn't even notice, long as he doled out the allowances like he was supposed to."

I happened to know that Harry's youngest child was a sophomore at SMU. We were deep in the realm of metaphor, which is no place to prosecute a case. Neither is a public hallway. I didn't respond.

"Well, look for my name appearing on Austin's witness list as a character witness," Harry boomed anyway. "That man's done more for this county than"—*Than any one-term district attorney*, I heard—"than any ten other people," Harry concluded. But his little ice-chip eyes confirmed what I'd heard. I stared back to let him know I understood what this was all about.

"Whyn't you come see me?" he said in his lowest tone, the one a secretary sitting on his lap wouldn't overhear if he didn't want her to. For public consumption he repeated loudly, "Better find some better investigators, Blackie!" He clapped me on the back and went on down the hallway, shaking every hand, whether offered or not.

I hate that nickname. And the people who use it on me. But I could ignore Harry only at my peril. He was a county commissioner, one of five who run the county government: awarding contracts, setting salaries. Among other duties, they oversee my budget.

*   *   *

The next week I wanted to investigate my speculative insight into Chris Davis's motivation. This time I had no qualms about interrogating him without his lawyer present, since he and the lawyer had conflicting interests, but I discovered Austin had taken Davis out of my reach. He'd made his bonds. Chris Davis was no longer in custody.

That made sense. Once Austin's first scheme had failed because his substitute's nerve had, it was dangerous for Austin for Davis to remain in custody, where he might decide to talk at any time. In fact, it occurred to me, Chris Davis was a continuing danger to Austin, because of what he knew. I assigned an investigator to find Davis, but he had no luck. Chris Davis never returned to the apartment he'd given his bail bondsman as his address.

Well, I hadn't expected Davis to help me much even if I did talk to him. Even things that should have been important to me, that *were* important, began to seem nuisances, such as the calls from my campaign manager, Tim Scheuless.

"I had a booking fall through," Tim said in a puzzled tone. He called my speeches bookings, as if I were a rock band playing the Ramada Inn. "You know, that south side what was it?"

"Yeah," I said, holding up a hand to tell Becky to stay in the room. She went back to her reading. "The Concerned whatevers for something-or-other."

"Yeah, them. They said they're canceling their Meet the Candidates series. They already had Leo Mendoza speak to them, though. I think they're going to endorse him."

"Well, that's not a surprise."

"Yeah, but still. I thought— Well, anyway." He must have remembered he wasn't supposed to discourage the candidate. "Say, aren't you going to try something soon? Remember what I told you? I still think that's our best chance for good coverage. Don't you have somebody really horrible who's got a lousy lawyer and no chance of—"

"As a matter of fact I'm preparing a case for trial now." I winked at Becky, who was pretending not to listen.

"It's not Austin Paley, is it?" Tim asked quietly.

"Why do you ask that?"

"Jesus, Mark, you need to stay away from that one. That's the hottest potato in town right now. I've gotten a couple of calls—"

"You too?"

He went on as if I hadn't interrupted. "I think it'll be okay if you treat it like it's just another case, you know, let it fall wherever it falls, have some assistant handle it, that'd be okay. But if people start thinking it's some personal vendetta of your own, there's going to be some fallout. The man's got friends. I mean—"

"He's a criminal, Tim."

"Well, nobody's convinced of that. Until they are, people are going to stand up for him. I've already had somebody tell me he's not going to send in the contribution he'd promised because of your false accusation of his old buddy Austin."

"I'm sorry to hear that, Tim, I really am, but what do you want me to do?"

His hesitation told me he knew perfectly well how much weight whatever he said would carry with me. "At least tell me you're not going to try it yourself," he begged.

"Don't you think voters will be happy for me to send a serial child molester to prison, Tim, no matter how many fat cats are offended by it?"

"Well, yeah. But it's not even that good a case, is it? I said a laydown, Mark, not something risky. Hand it off, all right?"

"I'll think about it," I said, and hung up.

He was right. I knew he was right. There was no reason to put my career at risk over this one case. I had a staff of competent prosecutors, some of them better than that. My sex crimes chief had already volunteered, and she had an impressive record in cases like this. I should take Eliot's advice: Talk tough, then let my staff do the work. I'd be shirking what I felt to be a personal responsibility—I'd brought the case into the office, I was the one who'd been duped by Austin's initial scheme—but no one expected the DA to try every case personally. No one would look askance if I let an assistant try the case.

What about Becky? I certainly trusted her. But when I looked at her and thought of handing these cases—*my* cases—over to her, I couldn't bring myself to do it. Why not? Because I saw a torturous path through a tangle of hazards to reach a conviction in this case. Isn't that terrible? I trusted only myself to negotiate it.

There must have been another reason for my reluctance to hand over the cases to someone else, someone as able a prosecutor as I. I sensed that reason lurking in the back of my mind, but I hadn't poked at it enough to goad it into revealing itself.

"So what do you think?" I said. "Pick your victim."

"I like little girls," Becky said. Once upon a time I would have made a joke from that line, but by this time I was so immersed in the world of child sexual assault that I barely saw the opening as it passed me by. "Little girls look more vulnerable and precious. You can drive fathers of daughters absolutely over the edge with the idea it could have been *their* babies instead. Juries want to protect girls. Boys, though—"

"They're supposed to look out for themselves," I said.

"Exactly."

"The trouble is," I pointed out, "our cases with the little girls are lousy. They're the youngest, I don't know if they can even identify him. Plus, he didn't—"

"Yes," Becky said, already ahead of me. "So if it has to be a boy it has to be Kevin, obviously. He's a good age, he looks good." She looked up at me. "When he tells his story *I* want to run up and hold him, and I'm not a pushover for kids."

No. And that's good right now. But for trial you'll need a rapport with them. Have you spent much time with children, Becky? Are you interested in them?"

"Of course," she said, but that was just a defensive response.

"It's no disgrace if you're not. Not everyone has to be interested in children. Do you want— Never mind. It's none of my business."

She answered me anyway. "No, I do. But you can't just decide to have children. You need some help, I understand." She cleared her throat. She was actually blushing a little.

"Come on, Becky, I don't believe that. A woman like you, with your—advantages. You must be hounded by men."

"Hah," she said. The blush was fading. "Besides, you're not going to pick just anybody and say, 'Hey, you wanta have a kid?' It's— Well, you're a parent. You know."

"Yes. When you first have a child you think this is the most important thing you've ever done, this is the one part of you that will live on. Then time goes by and you get caught up in your work again and the child grows up just a little. Just a tiny bit and already he's so changed you wouldn't recognize him if you went away for a week. You start to wonder if you're really a part of him at all." I lapsed into thought, and I would have

101

stopped talking then, but Becky was watching me expectantly. "Then years go by and you think maybe that was the most important thing in your life after all and you realized it too late."

"Why is it too late?"

I just let the question float by. "So you think Kevin? I think you're right, the others—"

"I have this—friend," Becky said. It was odd the way her face changed, from one word to the next. Sometimes I thought she looked like a child herself, but then, without her even moving, a shadow dropped down her forehead and she seemed to be speaking from a perspective of long years; lost years. "Donny. I knew him from law school, and that goes back a long way now. Sometimes I think if things had been just slightly different, if one weekend had turned out different, or one job interview, we'd be married now, with kids or talking about it. But it didn't. And now we're both so caught up in work it doesn't seem to matter. But I think some day, maybe in years, he'll realize what you said, that something important passed him by."

"You still see him?"

She smiled. "Yes, definitely Kevin," she said. "Maybe we can get some parents of boys on the jury. If we do it right it might be even more heartbreaking than having a little girl up there on the stand."

I pushed aside the other files, opened the one, and Becky came and leaned over my shoulder as we went through it again.

7

"WHY KEVIN? WHY DOES IT HAVE TO BE HIM?"

I'm not the one who singled him out, I wanted to say. I'm not the one who made him a victim.

"Because Kevin's is the best case," I said. "Kevin can identify the man positively, and I'm convinced Kevin would make the best witness."

I didn't tell them all the reasons. Tommy Algren was the most articulate of the child victims, but he was too old and too controlled. Becky and I had decided that Kevin Pollard would look more pitiful.

Technically I didn't need his parents' agreement. I could just subpoena Kevin and he would have to testify. But I needed a cooperative witness. I needed to rehearse with him before trial, needed his trust when he looked at me from the witness stand. I needed his damned parents.

I'd done too good a job of informing the Pollards what the odds were in this kind of case. They read the papers, too; they reminded me that a man had been acquitted of a similar charge in federal court the month before. Jurors are reluctant to accept a child's story if an adult vehemently denies it. After all, we can imagine ourselves being unjustly accused by a child too young to understand the consequences.

Mr. Pollard said, "If Kevin testifies, he'll be marked. All the other kids will make fun of him."

And the guys at the bowling alley will look at you funny, I thought.

"No," I said. "The media won't identify him. They don't report the names of child victims."

He and his wife looked at me hopefully. "Really?" he asked. "Is that the law?"

"No, it's just a journalistic tradition. But it's very strictly followed."

They kept looking at me. "Uh-huh," Mr. Pollard finally said.

I wondered if it would help to have Kevin in the room with us. He was playing in the back yard so we could discuss his future freely. Kevin would be willing, I thought. I stopped pleading and just stared at them, as if I knew they were good folks who would do the right thing.

Mrs. Pollard grew embarrassed by their slowness. "It'll be okay, honey," she said to her husband. "When the jury hears all those other children say he's done the same thing to them . . ."

I cleared my throat. I thought about not correcting her. Becky saved me the trouble of deciding.

"We won't be able to do that," she said. "Unless the defense slips up, the jury won't be allowed to hear about the other cases. We can only try them one at a time."

And the defense won't slip up, I thought. Whoever Austin hired would be too good for that.

"No one will ever be safe," I said abruptly.

"What?"

"If I can't send this man to prison, no child in this city will ever be safe again. Including Kevin. Do you think he's safe just because we've caught the man who molested him? That doesn't count for anything unless we can convict him. And we can't do that by ourselves. People complain about crime, but they have to help put a stop to it. Victims have to fight back. They can't back down."

I thought this was language that would appeal to Mr. Pollard. But all he said was, "Mind if we talk about it alone for a few minutes?"

"Okay," I said shortly, and strode past them, across their brown shag carpet and through the sliding glass patio door into their back yard.

"I have seen more public-spirited citizens," Becky said outside. "What do you think they'll say?"

"I don't care what they say. To hell with him. If he says no I'll come back after he's gone. Two can play at intimidating that wispy wife of his. Absentee fathers don't get to dictate what's best for their sons. I'll get her to give us the go-ahead. Or you can."

"Gee, thanks," Becky said.

"Kevin," I called.

He was alone on a swing set, on one end of one of those gliders made for two children. I wished I were small enough to take the other seat.

It was dusk, magic hour, when the day arrays all its previously hidden possibilities just before opening into night. It was early September, Kevin would be back in school. I remembered schoolday afternoons as precious, and twilight most precious of all, the air growing so still and clear it could carry a mother's voice calling you home for blocks and blocks. Dusk made every activity the most wonderful of the day, the one we could least abide giving up. But Kevin looked like a boy who didn't mind school, who probably had already done his homework.

"How are you?" I asked.

"Fine," he said placidly, not bored, a boy used to being alone. *What are you worried about?* I wanted to ask his father. *This boy's got no friends to lose anyway.*

"We arrested him, Kevin. The man you told me touched you. I didn't understand that day in the courtroom, did I? We had the wrong man. But when you told me the right one I had police officers go and take him to jail."

"I know," Kevin said. I tried to detect some reaction in his voice, eased fear, or even pride that he'd made such a big thing happen in the adult world, but I couldn't hear anything from Kevin. He might have been waiting to learn from me how he should react.

"But I can't keep him there," I said, "unless you help me. You have to tell your story to other people. Not just me, not just in my office. You need to tell it in front of a lot of people in a big room. Do you think you can do that?"

"We'll be there with you," Becky added helpfully. She knelt to his level, awkwardly in her skirt and heels.

"Will you help me?" Kevin asked. Promise of mere presence wasn't enough for him.

"Oh, yes," Becky said, reaching out and hugging him in what appeared a perfectly spontaneous response. "I'll help you,

Kevin," she said. "All you'll have to do is watch me and answer the questions I ask. All right?"

He nodded. Very docile boy. He'd show more animation in court, though, after we'd rehearsed. And Austin would be there then. If Kevin had anything like the reaction to his presence he'd had that other day in the courtroom, the jury could have no doubt of his sincerity.

"Mr. Blackwell?"

It was that twilight voice, calling me home. A thrill ran along my arms, and I realized I'd been expecting the call, waiting for it. Time to go in. Becky and I trudged up the gentle slope of the yard to the back door, Kevin with us. Mrs. Pollard looked down at my hand on his shoulder.

"We've decided," she said.

"Yeah," Pollard said gruffly. "Can't let the bastard get away with this, can we? Sorry, hon," he apologized for the obscenity, then dropped into a squat in front of Kevin, his black pants stretching tight enough to create an embarrassing moment if the material was as thin as it looked. "How about it, Kevin, is it all right with you? Do you want to testify about what happened to you?"

"I already said I would," Kevin said.

Pollard gave me a funny look. "We've discussed it," I said. Pollard kept his stare on me for a long moment. I returned it blandly.

The next day I was making my usual rove through the courts, looking for Becky but in no hurry to find her. The sights of confrontations and deals being made raised my energy level, as usual, but also made me feel left out. It was with this soft jangle of emotions that I reached Judge Hernandez's courtroom and found Becky deep in conference with Linda Alaniz.

I went up the aisle faster. I was smiling. Linda was not, as she turned away from Becky. I knew the intensity of her expression. Someone's life was in her hands.

"Linda! I'm glad to see you. You know, I've tried to call you a couple of times lately, but you're never at home."

Linda smiled at me, too, but hesitantly, as if afraid a smile would convey too much. "Hello, Mark. You need to warn your prosecutor against being too harsh. She might make me try the case."

I certainly wasn't going to intervene. I barely glanced at Becky. But I wasn't done with Linda. "Are you through here? Do you have time for lunch?"

"There you are," someone interrupted, in a hearty lawyer's tone, so I thought it was aimed at me, but the thirtysome-thingish man with the sculpted nose and wide forehead and dark-rimmed glasses came up to Linda instead. "Listen, I'm having a little trouble in the 175th. You think you could come— Oh, I'm sorry."

Linda's face was blank, an unusual expression for her, one she had to work to achieve. "Mark, do you know Roger Guerra? Roger and I are officing together now."

"Oh," I said. "No, I didn't know. Yes, Roger and I've met."

Roger smiled enough for all of us. "Yes, Linda's retraining me, telling me everything I learned wrong. She's the best." He laid his hand on her forearm. His look spoke of devotion. Linda was watching me, still blankly, still working hard. She patted his hand, and he removed it. "But I don't need to tell you that, do I?" Roger said to me.

I said that he didn't. To Linda I added, "I just wanted to thank you again for what you said about me to my campaign manager."

Her eyes warmed a little. No, they'd been warm all along, but carefully restrained. "It was all true."

"Gee, Linda, I thought you were just buttering me up, hoping for favors."

She finally smiled, because we both knew her tongue would stick to the roof of her mouth before she could make it say something insincere. Then her new partner hustled her away to deal with his problem in another court. Linda never looked back, maybe because she knew I was watching her, all the way out.

"You know, she wasn't a very good first assistant." Becky was standing with me. I barely heard her. "But then, she's a great defense lawyer." Brief silence. "On the other hand," Becky concluded, "my opinion of her probably isn't all that important to you."

It was a big chunk of my past that had just walked out of the courtroom, one that I'd thought might just possibly be in my future, as well, but I'd been wrong.

"What?" I said.

*　　*　　*

107

Later that afternoon I left the office early and went home. Becky was coming in my office door as I went out it, and she seemed confused by my early departure. "Where are you going?" she asked. "It's just personal," I said. That made her confusion turn to concern. "Really?" she said.

"Family personal." I wondered why I felt compelled to explain, and Becky must have realized it was strange, too.

"Oh, sorry," she said. "Well . . ."

It seemed eerie to be home before dark, as if I might surprise the daytime owner. I sorted through my clothes, trying to decide what to wear to my own house. I was going by invitation, but I wasn't supposed to appear a guest.

"Listen," Lois had said, on the phone. "I have a favor to ask."

"Sure," I'd said automatically.

"I'd like you to come to the house next Friday night, for dinner. And stay after dinner," Lois hurried on. "I just want you to be here." She stopped and laughed at herself. When she started again she sounded more relaxed. "Here's what it is, Mark—Dinah has a date."

"A date?"

"Yes, her first date. I would have spared you the anxiety of knowing about it, but I'd like you to be here. The boy's coming to pick her up and I thought it would be nice if her father were here to meet him."

"Want me to put the fear of God into him, eh? All right, I'll get Muggsy and the boys together and we'll all be lined up at the door when the little terrorist shows up." Lois endured this stoically. "Okay, Lois. I'm sure we can pull this off. After all, the kid's only, what, thirteen? Want me to bring some of my dirty clothes and scatter them around? It'll be all right as long as Dinah doesn't trip over me and say, 'Dad! What are you doing here?' "

Lois ignored my attempts at humor. "Come for dinner early," she said. "I want the remains of dinner on the table when the boy arrives."

So it was that I found myself dressing for dinner at my old house, trying to strike the proper casually-at-home-but-formally-receiving-a-visitor tone. The silliness of it improved my mood, but the occasion disturbed me. My baby's first date. Date. She was much too young. Only a little jerk with too much self-confidence would ask a thirteen-year-old girl out on a date, especially so early in the school year. What did the little thug think he was after, anyway?

"You're not going to make me regret inviting you, are you?" Lois asked patiently, as I explained these concerns later in her kitchen. "Just meet the boy and don't say anything."

The doorbell rang. "Awfully early, isn't he?" I asked. Lois was just taking a roast out of the oven. "No, that's probably—" she began, but I was already heading for the front door. It opened before I reached it.

"Oh," I said. "David. We *are* going to present a united front, aren't we?"

I started to hug my son, thought that was a bit much, and ended up sort of grasping his shoulders like some dopey variety of French Foreign Legion officer. "How are you?"

"Fine," David said. "Fine. I invited myself. Couldn't miss this."

I pulled the front door farther open and peeked around it. "Where's Vicky?"

"She didn't come. Hi, Mom."

David crossed the dining room to hug Lois. He looked like a boy doing it, though he towered over her. David is twenty-six, my height or taller, but very slender. He looks too tall for his size, in constant danger of breaking, or tripping.

"Well," he said, stepping back, "where's the dream date?" and went down the hall to find her. I heard Dinah's door open, heard her greet her brother happily. I was surprised to hear that they sounded like such good friends. They had grown up separately, David already a high school boy by the time Dinah was aware of him, a married man with a home of his own before she was old enough to be of any interest to him. I was glad to think they'd found the time to become real brother and sister after David was already grown and gone. Lois and I looked at each other. She knew I was wondering if this had been a secret part of her arrangement, inviting David without telling me.

When Dinah emerged from her room she came shyly to greet me. She didn't overtly ask for my approval, but the request was in her approach. She wore a cream-colored dress with a sort of cowl covering her shoulders. It was fairly casual, by no means a prom dress. Wearing it, Dinah looked like a pretty little girl, not a miniature adult.

"You look beautiful, darling," I told her. She smiled, and in the next moment busied herself helping Lois carry dishes to the table. I filled the drink requests, iced tea and water and Coke. For a few minutes we were all busy between the kitchen and dining room; there was a pleasant bustle that sounded like conversation.

But when we found ourselves sitting at the table together, I turned to David and fell silent. Whenever I saw David now I remembered talking to him with bars between us. It had been three years, but I could never forget my son in jail, his bewilderment, the helplessness I'd felt. I still felt it when I saw him, that guilty certainty that there was something I'd neglected that had kept him imprisoned. I don't know if David felt that way too, but I felt it *from* him, and it still made me uncomfortable to be near him.

He looked all right, though. He had none of the haunted look one might have expected. Here with his family he seemed perfectly at ease. He looked older, of course, than he had before his jailing. There were moments when he frowned, or leaned solicitously toward Dinah, or paused before answering a question, when he could have been the man of the house. Lois leaned toward David just as Dinah did, waiting for his answers.

"So who is this boy?" I asked. They all turned toward me. I understood at once that I was the only one uninformed. David gave Dinah a sly sidelong look she acknowledged by slapping his hand without looking at him.

"His name's Steve," she said. "He's very nice."

"Steve? What happened to Jeff and—what was the other one's name?"

"Mutt." David laughed. Dinah regally ignored him.

"What about them?" she asked me, as if I were Barbara Walters getting a little too personal.

"I thought Jeff was the one you liked, but Danny'd been calling. Does this mean you like Steve better, or is he—"

"I'm not going to *marry* him," Dinah said, overly exasperated.

David leaned toward me confidentially. "Jeff's just a little slow."

"You mean," I said in the same tone, gesturing toward my head, "not the brightest boy in class?"

"Not slow like that," Dinah said. "Slow to *phone.*"

Dinah was even prettier when being teased. "I hope we're not going to be talking abut Jeff when Steve arrives," Lois said.

"Maybe these two shouldn't even *be* here when Steve comes," Dinah said. David and I grinned at each other.

Banter made us a family again. We fell easily into our roles. It was easy after that to talk about other things, Dinah's school, David's job. I tried to follow what he said about computer software. He'd had a good job before his arrest, with a small company through which he seemed to be rising rapidly. They'd taken him back after he was free again, but neither of them was the same any more. The company had expanded into other areas than the software for small businesses, in which David was expert. His degree was in accounting, he'd written a couple of the computer programs himself. But he was no longer as important to the company as he'd been before the interruption in his career. He told us this only by implication. What I really wanted to ask was, if after the tragedy of his arrest for rape he'd grown dissatisfied with his old job and old friends, then what about his marriage? How did he continue with Vicky, to whom he'd never seemed very attached even before the crisis? That was the question I might never ask.

I felt myself settling in now, comfortable, as if we were still what we appeared to be, an unbroken family. But it hadn't been like this when Lois and I were married, not in the last years of our marriage. I wouldn't have sat there extending dinner for the sake of its society. I would have been up and pacing, reading cases or on the phone, rehashing the day at the office or preparing for the next one. I don't mean I would have devoted the whole evening to work; just a few precious minutes snatched from family obligations. I hadn't thought of myself as a workaholic. But work was where my *interest* lay. I could see now that while work hadn't filled all my time at home, I'd devoted just enough important minutes to it that my family could see that's where my heart was. I was killing time with them until I could get back to the office or the courthouse.

Starting the affair with Linda had been secondary. I had already betrayed my home long before that. Now sitting among them, one of them but only as a visitor, the family life I'd neglected seemed terribly sweet to me. If I had kept just a fraction more of my life among them I could have saved my home, saved us all. We'd be here now just as we seemed, without the aura of temporariness.

"Yipes," Dinah said, having turned David's wrist so she could see his watch.

"You're already gorgeous!" I called after her as she bolted from the table. "I'll help," I added, as Lois stood and picked up plates.

"Sit, sit," she said.

"I thought you wanted the boy to see the family dinner still on the table when he got here," I reminded her.

"We don't want him to think we're pigs, do we?" she answered, disappearing into the kitchen.

David and I were left alone, rather artfully, if one chose to look at it that way. "Want to go in the front room and peer out the curtains?" he asked. I followed him. We remained standing in the living room. The early American furniture in that room was designed for appearance.

"What's Vicky doing tonight?" I asked casually.

David answered casually as well, but I thought I felt a tension that hadn't been there before. "Went to a movie. I wasn't interested in seeing it, and she thinks I'm silly for wanting to be here for this."

I didn't remember ever having been to a movie without Lois while we were married. I saw quite a few movies I wasn't interested in seeing. So did she. And I wondered if being married to a woman who thought family milestones like first dates "silly" made David question their future together. I wondered if David went meekly along to Vicky's family occasions and only she balked at attending ours, or was it mutual? Lois and I would never have thought of having such separate lives. It wouldn't have seemed an option.

All this speculation left me silent long enough, probably, to let David in on my thoughts. That's how we'd always communicated, by reading each other's minds. I remembered Lois's telling me that David seemed troubled, and that she hoped he'd confide his worries to me.

I said, "It sounds as if you do most of your work alone."

He answered as if he'd never thought of that before. "I guess I do."

"Did you plan that? Do people at the job make you uncomfortable?"

He laughed, humorlessly. David looked older now than the lighthearted boy who'd entertained us at dinner. "More like the other way around," he said.

"Well . . . But you can't just withdraw from everybody, David. Nothing that happened was your fault. I know it will take even longer than this to feel your life back to normal, but you have to—"

"No." He was shaking his head, cutting me off, and he gave that dry chuckle again. "That's not it. I wasn't embarrassed. When I said I made them uncomfortable, I don't mean just people studying me when they thought I wasn't looking. Everything was fine, I slipped right back into my job. But—"

He dropped onto a wooden love seat that looked as spindly as he. "I mean I *deliberately* make them uncomfortable. Sometimes I'll give them this look." He stared at me, head slightly lowered, eyes very deep and direct, sizing me up as if deciding to slash my tires on his way out or do it to me instead. I'd seen that expression before, always on the face of someone charged with a terrible crime.

David laughed and looked boyish again. "I *use* it, Dad. I *want* to be this scary thing in their midst. I didn't want everything just to revert to normal. And if they were going to look at me I was going to give them something to look at.

"I still do it. I think." Now he did look embarrassed. He was looking away from me, out the curtains, down at the floor. "When I meet somebody new I wonder if they know my story. And you know what? I'd be disappointed if they *didn't*. And once in a while I've been negotiating with someone, and it's been pretty tough, real give-and-take, you know, and all of a sudden they give in. And I have to wonder, Did I just do it without knowing it? Or did they suddenly remember about me? Either way—" He laughed again. "I can't tell this so you'd understand."

"Maybe you couldn't if I didn't understand already," I said. His eyes stopped wandering around the room. "I know just what it's like, David. I think I do. You know, there are a lot of people who think they know the whole story of what happened in your case, but they don't all know the same thing. And a lot still wonder. They wonder what *I* did. Who I got to, or threatened, and how. And I've never yet claimed innocence. I just let them look at me. And sometimes I look back."

David was studying me, wondering if we really had this secret in common or if I was just trying to convince him we did. "Be a shame to have something awful happen to you and not be able to use it afterwards," I said.

Slowly, not the quick, false reactions he'd made during his speech, David smiled at me. I realized again how much he looked like both me and Lois. He probably didn't realize it. I think you have to look backward to see those things. But I'm sure he felt kinship in that moment.

The doorbell rang.

"Yipes," I half-shouted, "the kid sneaked up on us."

We were on our feet, milling toward the door as if we were a crowd. I put a hand on David's arm.

"Now don't terrify him, David." He looked at me as if I were making fun of him, as if it had been a mistake to tell me. "Unless it seems called for," I finished. He grinned.

"Hello," I said, before I even had the door fully open. I had to lower my gaze a little. Young master Robbins stood on our doorstep. He was less formally dressed than I'd expected, no tie, no jacket, but he wore conservative navy trousers and a plaid long-sleeved shirt.

"You must be Steve."

"Yes sir."

I brought him inside. David nodded to him and said, "I'll see how Dinah's doing."

I settled into a chair. Young Steve remained standing. He looked more composed than I would have been. I suppose he was a handsome boy. Hard to tell about a thirteen-year-old. He had a few freckles across his nose, no acne, straight white teeth. His dark hair was rather short on the sides but longer in the back.

"They always keep you waiting," I confided to him, by which I meant to ask whether this was his first date.

"I guess so," he answered.

David returned, with Lois, who made small talk with Steve about school, even calling a couple of teachers by name. I just stood by, trying to look like someone only a fool would cross.

Dinah entered, with a shy, measured step. Her home had become a theater. Steve turned and saw her. Dinah was obviously aware that she and Steve were the observed of all observers. It made her very stiff. Not so her date. He smiled unselfconsciously.

"Hello, Dinah," he said. "You look lovely." It sounded like a line he'd heard on TV, but he said it well.

Dinah and Steve didn't sit down with us. After only a minute or two they were walking toward the door. I stopped Dinah to give her a hug. "Have a good time," I said to her.

"Be careful," I told Steve, by which I meant to say, If you ever do anything to hurt her, I'll pinch your head off and beat you to death with it. I hoped he was as perceptive as he seemed, but if he had been he would have drawn back from me in fright instead of giving me the manly little handshake he did.

When they were gone I asked, "Someone did tell him I'm the district attorney, didn't they? I didn't want to say it myself, but he knows, right?"

David and Lois both laughed. "Come on in, Dad," Lois said. "Is your past coming back to haunt you?"

"I never did anything to be ashamed of on a date. Certainly not in the eighth grade."

We passed through the formal living room and went on into the den. "I remember some dates of ours that would have scared the wits out of *my* father if he'd known," Lois said.

"Hush, you'll shock the boy."

The phone rang, and Lois slipped out of the room to answer it. Realtors, I remembered, get calls at all hours, like lawyers.

"How are things at home?" I asked David, knowing I couldn't keep my tone casual enough to prevent his resenting the inquiry.

"Fine," he said. That was all. I had a flood of follow-up questions: Any chance of divorce? Am I ever going to have grandchildren? Is Vicky always as cold as she seems? Are you happy?

"Really?" I pressed.

David seemed ready to pounce on anything I said. "I know you never liked Vicky," he said suddenly.

"I don't dislike Vicky." I was genuinely shocked. "I hardly even know her. She seems very nice. It's just I wonder—"

"She thinks you don't," David said.

"Is that why she's not here? I don't know how she could think that. I don't disapprove of people."

He laughed, harshly.

"I just want to know if you're happy with her, David. That's my only interest in Vicky." That sounded much too mean. I moderated it. "I like her just fine, but that doesn't matter if she doesn't make you happy."

"It's not her job to make me happy."

"That's not how I meant it. I mean if you're happy together."

"We are," he snapped. "I said we are, didn't I?"

Had he? "Well, good," I said mildly.

David cooled. He had heard the uncalled-for anger in his voice. "How's the campaign going?" he asked. And that was the end of the personal conversation. I was left where I usually was left with David, hoping I could fix things the next time.

8

. . . BECAUSE OUR CAMPAIGN HAS CONVINCED THE people of this county that it is time for a change in the office of the district attorney. That is why the incumbent has concocted this case against an upstanding, and I might also say *out*standing, public citizen. Trust me, there is no evidence behind these accusations. There is only the desperation of a public official who knows . . ."

"He's bought the whole Paley party line," Tim Scheuless said.

"Leo doesn't buy. He sells," I answered.

"TV just slurps this drool up, don't they? Are they ever going to ask him anything?" Tim asked angrily.

"Wait." I turned up the sound on the tiny TV on my desk.

"But there haven't been any more children molested since Austin Paley was arrested for the crimes," the television interviewer said.

Leo Mendoza dismissed that fact. "The real molester isn't an idiot," he sniffed. "He's just lying low, happy that someone else is being made to suffer for his crimes. Once I am the district attorney, believe me, I will uncover the true offender."

Leo had chosen to conduct the interview on a street outside the courthouse. He was an imposing but oddly shaped figure. His stomach was oversized, but his legs and chest were very thin. This gave him a wedge-shaped appearance, the point of the wedge thrusting toward anyone standing in front of him.

He seemed to be leaning backward, his head withdrawing as he talked. He wore a white hat that further obscured his face.

Leo was a longtime defense lawyer who had paid his dues to the party without ever asking anything in return, until now, so he had the solid backing of his party in his race for district attorney. Years ago, half my lifetime ago, he had been an assistant district attorney for a while, so he claimed the background for the job. Since then he had prospered in a small way, handling low-profile misdemeanors and minor felonies, almost never drawing the public's attention. He had no record to attack. He could say what he liked about mine, with impunity. He knew how to run a campaign, paying proper subservience to the power groups, giving fierce interviews without saying much, courting the organizations that would encourage their members to vote.

"The cases will not be tried in court," he assured his interviewer. "The incumbent district attorney will never risk allowing his victim to prove his innocence. The arrest was just a campaign ploy."

"Aren't they giving Leo a lot of time?" I asked. "What is this, an endorsement?"

"They always have long features on the noon news," Tim said. "Wait, here's the big wrap-up."

"Crime is more rampant in this city than it's ever been," Leo was saying soberly, talking directly to the camera.

"No shit," I said.

". . . while my opponent spends all his time sitting in his office spinning plots against innocents. Once I hold the office, all that will stop. Then we will see nothing but the impartial administration of justice."

Tim snapped off the television. "You see," he said at once. "He's gonna kill you with this. He's finally—"

"You don't think anybody's going to buy this crap, do you?"

"I *know* they are," Tim said emphatically. "Let me tell you what happened yesterday. I got a call from the North Side Civic Betterment Council. They're endorsing Leo."

"What?" I said, coming out of my chair.

Tim nodded. The North Side Civic Betterment Council was one of the groups that had first encouraged me to run for district attorney. Their support for my reelection was supposed to be a given. "Why on earth?" I asked. "They must know I'm the better candidate."

"It's Austin Paley," Tim said, indignant but calm. He'd had time to absorb his outrage. "I don't mean he's behind it, but it's about him. John Lyman called me himself to say that he was the one who'd insisted his group support Mendoza, and he wanted me to know it. He said, 'I told 'em flat out, anybody who trumps up charges against an innocent man doesn't care who he hurts. Any of us could be next.' And he was sincere as a nun, too. He absolutely believes—"

"Austin got to him," I said quietly, but not believing it. What Tim said next was true.

"No sir," he said emphatically. "How do you get to John Lyman? He doesn't give a damn what anybody thinks. But he believes Austin." Tim leaned toward me. "Everybody doesn't just dance to Austin's tune, you know, Mark. The man has genuine friends. He's given a lot of money to charities over the years, he's worked for the right causes, he goes to church, he's—" Tim spread his hands, delivering the blackest condemnation of all. "He's *charming*, for God's sake. *I* like him. My *mother* likes him. Think of people who've known him for years, think how they—"

"I'm one of them, Tim."

"Well, there you go. Look. I'm not asking you to ditch the case—"

"Cases," I said. Tim gave me a stern look: Don't get technical.

"Just let it cool off. It'll fade to background after a while if you don't do anything on it."

"No. I have to disprove what Austin and now Leo are saying. I have to show that I personally believe in Austin's guilt, that it's not just a politically expedient charge I've trumped up. Besides, didn't you say I need the exposure? Or are you going to buy TV spots for me out of your own pocket? You have any more speaking engagements lined up for me?"

"One or two," Tim mumbled. But they were dying, and my campaign treasury had sunk below empty into red.

I could still get news coverage, though. If I prosecuted Austin personally, I'd get myself on TV and in print, for good or ill.

"It's not personal," I said. I was lying. "It's something I have to do."

"Well . . ." Tim said. "At least for God's sake . . ." Suddenly

119

wondering why I was seeking his approval anyway, I tuned out his admonitions.

"Why don't you take his advice?" Becky Schirhart asked later. "I'll prosecute Austin Paley, and I won't let it get postponed. You can have it both ways."

I didn't answer, and not because I didn't think Becky deserved an answer. While I remained aware of the difference in our ages, I no longer thought of her as a kid, or as an underling. When we talked it was to plan our trial strategy, and that partnership demanded an equal footing, if she was to be of use to me at all. I didn't answer because my answer sounded sappy, even to me.

"It's the smart thing to do," Becky added.

"I know that."

I was looking out a window of my office. Becky was on the couch behind me. From the corner of my eye I saw her come toward me, hesitate, then take another seat from which she could see me better. I turned toward her.

"Why *is* it personal, Mark?" she asked. "It's obvious it is."

I decided to be sappy. I owed her that, because I'd drawn Becky into the case, too.

"I feel like he's stolen my past." I didn't have to identify "he." "This has been going on so long. Some of it must have happened while I was an assistant DA, fifteen years ago. Austin molesting children and having people quash the cases for him. While I—"

I leaned closer to her. Becky hadn't changed expression. There was no way she could understand this. "I believed in what I was doing," I told her. "I believed in Eliot. I listened to those speeches Eliot gave us about how every case was the same, you didn't hold back because you liked the defense lawyer, and how all the defendants were the same, it didn't matter if it was somebody's son or a nobody, and I believed it. I listened to other people making jokes under their breath—I even made some myself—but I believed in what we did in that office. I believed we were the law's last guardians, and that we could make a difference, and all that crap."

Even as I ended on a note of ridicule I remembered the feeling, one Becky couldn't share. I had believed that I'd chosen a life's work that made a difference in the world; that I served an

ideal higher than money or power. Years of watching the out-
comes of cases skewed by corruption or just laziness or stupidity
had taught me better, but it hadn't touched the pride of those
first years as a prosecutor. My cynicism about the system was
deeply engrained and hard-earned, but the only true cynics are
burned believers. I could admit it now: I believed in justice. I
believed I personally could wrest it from an unfair world. I had
once believed that.

And even as I'd changed, grown a coarser layer of protection,
I still believed far in the back of my mind that I'd once been
part of something noble. Austin had stepped on that bit of cher-
ished pride. While I'd been relishing my role as a player on a
team with an almost sacred mission, Eliot Quinn had quietly
been killing cases against his political ally. It made me feel dirty
to think of it now. It had rewritten my whole past. I hated to
think of Austin oozing through the courthouse, being charming,
expecting a certain deference and being accorded it. Confident
of his power and his standing; perhaps thinking that more people were willing parts of his protection than actually had been.
How many knowing looks had he given me in the past that
I'd missed, that I'd just interpreted as expressions of general
camaraderie?

"He's tainted everything," I said. "I'd thought I was part of
something important, something uncorrupted."

"I know what you mean," Becky said, the kind of remark you
make offhandedly to keep someone talking.

"Remember what I told you Ben Dowling, the old reporter,
told me about the gentlemen's agreements they used to have,
how they—"

"—would cover up for everybody from the President on down
just because it was unseemly not to?" Becky said.

I nodded. "That had an effect, you know. I grew up thinking
there really were noble institutions in this country, people who
were genuinely heroes. I looked for them when I went to find
a life's work. Your generation, you never heard anything from
the time you were children but scandal and corruption and lies,
and *that* became your norm. You can't be disappointed because
you don't expect anything better of anyone."

"Don't assume too much," Becky said. "You can't explain
everybody's personalities just by the times they grew up in.

I understand what you mean about feeling part of something important."

I gave her some attention. She looked serious. But she was giving me the kind of scrutiny I'd never given Eliot years ago, and I knew she couldn't possibly share the illusions I'd had.

"Really?" I said. "You mean you're not just here for the money?"

She smiled back at me.

I supposed it was still possible, even in this latter age, for someone to idealize prosecution work. In a way, I did myself. Why else had I returned to the district attorney's office? I had made more money in private practice. But in my ten years as a defense lawyer I'd never defended anyone with half the fervor with which I'd prosecuted some of my cases in the DA's office.

"Just because there was one thing going on you didn't know about doesn't mean you were wrong about everything," Becky said.

I made a disgusted sound. "I was an idiot."

"And now you're going to do something about it," she said, once again drawing me out of my contemplation of the changeable past. Of the two of us, Becky looked like the hard-edged one now.

Suddenly I had a strong desire to win reelection. I wanted to regain my sense of purpose. In these cases against Austin Paley, I had.

"Let's go to work," Becky said. "Unless you wanted to go on whining about your childhood a while longer?"

I made a sound as if testing an empty tank. "No, I think I bottomed out, thanks."

She laid her hand briefly on mine, in sympathy.

"Let me ask it this way, Kevin. Was it your idea to go camping, or was it Austin's? Did you suggest it? Did you say, 'I know what, let's camp out'?"

Kevin studied Becky's face, searching for the answer. When she remained impassive, only smiled gently at him, he glanced away, seemed to search his memory.

"It must've been his idea," he said quietly. "I'd never been camping out."

Becky and I glanced at each other, and she turned back to the boy on the makeshift witness stand in his room. We'd brought a big chair in from the living room and ensconced Kevin in it, where he looked like a young prince suddenly elevated unwillingly to the kingship. I was letting Becky take a turn questioning him. She was getting better at it. Kevin watched her as she moved about the room, thinking of her next question.

"Did you ask your parents if you could go?" Becky asked.

"Yes."

Becky nodded. She smiled at Kevin. He didn't smile back. He sat waiting tensely for the next question. He had a stuffed elephant he was holding against his side, his arm so tight around the elephant's neck he would have choked it if it required breath. Nice touch. It might be overplaying if we let him bring it to court, but it was something to think about.

"Did you tell them who you were going with?" Becky asked. She'd stopped looking to me after every question. She was following her own train of thought. Becky was wearing a loose white blouse that left most of her arms bare. Occasionally, at a certain angle, she looked to me closer to Kevin's age than to mine. She could have been the older sister pretending to be a grown-up questioner. But there was an essential adult sternness about her, as well. Once in a while, turning away from Kevin, she clenched her fist.

"I told them I was going with some other boys," Kevin said. Again Becky nodded for his benefit.

"Let's look at the dolls again," Becky said.

Kevin immediately got down on the floor and picked up the two dolls, which were anatomically complete. Not impressive, but complete. Both male, one larger than the other. Becky took Kevin through the whole story, joining him on the floor. If one watched them only peripherally they looked like children playing with dolls. One had to look closely, and listen, to be aghast at the explicitness of the tale. The dolls started out side by side, sleeping. They wore no clothes. "It was hot," Kevin explained.

"And what was happening when you woke up?" Becky asked. A nice neutral question. But it wasn't the first time Kevin had been asked.

Kevin brought the man doll close to the smaller one. The man doll's penis touched the boy doll's shoulder, then his neck.

"Did you touch it?" Becky asked softly. "Why? Was it your idea, or did he ask you to?"

With every telling Kevin had brought the larger doll's penis closer to the smaller one's mouth. In two or three more sessions, I was sure, he would insert it. But I didn't know if I would believe him when that happened. I didn't know if Kevin was edging closer to the truth, because he was beginning to trust us and overcome his embarrassment, or if he was trying harder and harder to please. He knew what we wanted, I was sure. Kevin was six years old, but he was older than his peers. He was adept at pleasing adults.

When I'd ferreted my way through the years of stalled investigations, rumor, and reined-in suspicions, I'd become convinced of Austin Paley's guilt. It fit so well. I'd heard the children identify Austin with complete credulity. But as I began preparing one specific case, doubt crept in. Children *aren't* very reliable. They say what they think is expected of them. I know how investigations work, too. Once a man is accused, it's easier to bring other charges against him as well. Clearing cases, the cops call it. They can empty a file drawer of unsolved cases at a suspect's feet and turn it into a bonfire. Once the accusations begin to pile up, it's almost impossible to keep a clear view of the real man behind them.

I shouldn't harbor these doubts. That wasn't my part of the system. Eliot could have stilled my doubts, when I was working for him.

"Mark?" Becky asked.

"Well, that's enough for today," I said. "It's not a very fun way to spend a day, is it?"

Kevin answered my smile.

I put my hand on his shoulder. "You know we just want you to tell the truth, don't you, Kevin? Whatever you say happened, we believe you."

He nodded soberly, then asked, "Can I play now?"

"Sure."

"With the dolls?"

Becky and I looked at each other. The kid kept throwing us loops. She shrugged at me. We weren't damned psychiatrists. Should we let Kevin keep the dolls, with their vacant eyes, slightly slack-jawed mouths, and their anatomical completeness hanging out? Maybe it would be good for him to familiarize himself with them. Maybe they'd scare him if he woke in the middle of the night to find them in his bed. And maybe when his mother found them on the floor she'd wonder what kind of perverts she'd let into her house.

"Why don't you play with them while we talk to your mom, if you want?" I stalled.

As we passed through the doorway I leaned close to Becky to ask, "Shouldn't we take them with us?"

"Not for me," she whispered back. "I've got my own at home."

I gave her the startled look she wanted. Becky looked slightly aghast herself—not, I thought, at the joke itself, but at the fact she'd told me a joke, as if I wouldn't think her sufficiently serious for the solemn occasion.

The dolls were back in my briefcase when we hit the sidewalk. We were in the middle of a northern suburb, far, far from the courthouse, it seemed. The day seemed both late and timeless.

"Do we have to—" Becky began.

"Go back?" I looked around. "Let's get a drink," I said. "But for God's sake don't say anything to make them search my briefcase."

All the courtrooms look alike in the new Justice Center. Small, functional, industrial beige. Some judges have found ways to customize their courtrooms with posters or other decoration, but it's futile. The walls seem to absorb adornments. But there are other distinctions. Courthouse regulars know they're in Judge Hernandez's court by the look of the staff. The judge seems to hire the same type of person, man or woman, armed bailiff, or clerk armed only with a lip. They lounge around the court, talking idly to one another or otherwise loafing. If anyone approaches one of them, the court staffer turns the same knowing, disdainful look on the intruder. "Don't just tell me what you want," you can almost hear them say. "Tell me why I should do it for the likes of you." Their attitudes don't change when the judge enters the room. If anything, they intensify.

I've spent years looking for the good side of Bonita, Judge Hernandez's court coordinator, and decided it doesn't exist. Instead I've adopted an attitude of my own toward her, of distant professionalism as frosty as her own. Sometimes it works.

My elevation to eminence and power doesn't seem to have impressed her. "Mr. Blackwell," she said as I approached her desk. But she's always called me that. Anything less might imply something personal.

"Ms. Vargas," I returned. "Thank you for the special setting."

"We wouldn't want this mob messing up our regular docket," she replied. I shouldn't get the idea she'd done me a favor.

By "this mob" she meant the four reporters in the courtroom and the three cameramen in the hall, drawn to this quiet court on a Thursday afternoon for nothing more than to see us wrangle over a trial date. I had already talked to them. My stern line was that the cases must be tried right away, to remove the danger to the children of San Antonio. "You mean the voters of San Antonio?" Jenny Lord, the newspaper reporter, asked slyly.

"Children don't vote," I said, snappishly, because she'd made a joke I might once have made myself, in carefree days gone by.

Since he was a free man on bond, Austin had to come through the public hallway, running the gauntlet of reporters like everyone else. Austin, of course, would not duck the opportunity. He came across well on television. He appeared mild and unthreatening but with an underlying confidence and a glint of humor. He should have had his own talk show.

Austin kept us waiting while he indulged in an impromptu press conference in the hall. Becky and I just sat, having nothing to discuss today. Our only strategy at this setting was obvious.

Austin was the soul of friendliness when he arrived. I had turned my back on the courtroom doors by then, but I couldn't miss his coming. He spoke to everyone in the room. Austin stood over me with a smile. I didn't rise or offer my hand. He didn't appear offended. He called me by name and said, "How are things going?" as if he genuinely cared for my welfare. Even I couldn't tell we'd ever had a trace of acrimony between us.

"Fine, Austin. And for you?" He had a way of forcing you to play the game his way, because he'd react the same affable way no matter how inappropriate his partner's response.

He wiggled one hand at waist level and said, *"Así así."* "Soso" in Spanish. He continued smiling as he said it.

"Haven't you hired an attorney?" Becky asked him.

Austin's only answer was a smile. Missing the cue by just a minute or two, the door behind the bench opened and Judge Hernandez entered, chuckling appreciatively. Buster Harmony leaned closer to add a secondary punch line, and they both laughed. The judge stood behind his chair and Buster, in as much of a scurry as a large man in his fifties could manage, came around the bench and stood beside his client. He leaned across to shake my hand and say, in as *sotto* a *voce* as he ever employed, "Hello, Blackie."

I felt a wave of satisfaction because Austin was being so true to form, but not for that reason alone. If I had had to guess the kind of lawyer Austin would hire, fat old blustery Buster would have headed my list. He'd been around as long as any criminal lawyer in town, had made a lot of money over the years and lavished much of it on campaign contributions, was best friends with every judge, knew their children's names, had known every public official for years and years, since they were children together. As a lawyer he didn't do much any more and didn't have to do much, having won a few big civil judgments in the previous high-spending decade. He had a reputation as a fierce trial lawyer, but he hadn't been tested in a long time. Even in his prime, when I was an assistant DA, he'd had three shots at me and never won. He would be easy to anticipate, I thought.

After greeting me, Buster riveted his attention on the bench. Judge Hernandez slipped him a wink as he took his seat. The judge was in his late fifties, had been on the bench more than a decade—long enough, in his case, to forget any previous life. He was heavy but not extravagantly so, not enough to make the robe bulge. His dark complexion looked healthy, his eyes were sharp behind his dark, heavy glasses. His hair was thick, iron gray on top and white at the temples. He looked every inch a judge. He was the only person in the room who believed his own facade.

"Well, Buster, Blackie. Young lady. What a formidable assemblage of legal talent. You quite intimidate me."

While Buster chuckled extravagantly, I rose to say, "Good morning, Your Honor. We're here to obtain a trial setting for the State of Texas versus Austin Paley."

"Of course," the judge said grumpily, as if I'd interrupted him. "Well—are both sides ready?"

"The State is ready," I answered crisply.

"Well, Your Honor, if we can slow down just long enough for me to catch up," Buster drawled. "Which case are we announcing on? There's more than one with that style."

Judge Hernandez hated being told something wasn't simple. "Of course," he said by rote, and shot a look at his coordinator, Bonita. Bonita leaned over to push the folders on his bench toward him. The judge nodded sharply and pushed her hand away. Bonita sat down, visibly rolling her eyes. Judge Hernandez did not, of course, hire exclusively surly, disrespectful staff members. He created them.

"Yes, there are three cases," he said. "No, four." He read off the numbers at tedious length. "What is your announcement on each case?"

"The State is ready on number 4221," I said, and sat down. Fortuitously, the first indicted case had been the one in which Kevin Pollard was the victim, the one Becky and I had chosen to try first.

"We're not ready on that one," Buster Harmony said, shaking his ponderous head. "The defense is ready to try number 4222 or 4223. On the others we need more time for investigation."

The numbers he named were the cases involving the girls who couldn't quite identify their attacker. I'd kept them alive only for bargaining chips. The fourth case was the one in which ten-year-old Tommy Algren was the victim. There were other cases waiting in the wings, but I hadn't obtained indictments in them yet. I was going to try my best case first. Buster, of course, had other ideas. If he forced me to try one of my weak cases first, and Austin was found not guilty, it would make any later prosecution less credible—and less likely.

"State?" the judge asked.

"Not ready on 4222 or 4223," I replied blandly.

"Not ready?" The judge scowled at me.

"No, Your Honor, those cases are still being investigated," I said. "We are ready on the first case on the court's docket, and the State requests the earliest possible trial setting. This defendant remains free on bond, and the number of cases against him demonstrates clearly the danger to the community in allowing that situation to continue through many trial settings. The State requests an immediate trial." There are reporters in the room, I was as good as saying. It won't be me who has to fade the heat from the public for letting a serial child molester pass freely among them, Judge: it will be you. I had no doubt Judge Hernandez understood that. His scowl deepened.

"How can I force him to try a case he isn't prepared to try?"

he asked me, waving his hand at Buster, who nodded politely in acknowledgment of the judge's courtesy. "Why aren't *you* ready on the others?" Judge Hernandez continued.

"The State is prepared to try number 4221, the first case," I said doggedly. "To answer Your Honor's first question, the way to force the defense to try the case is to set a trial date."

No one could force me to try a case I wasn't ready for. I could if I chose dismiss every case except the one I wanted to try. Such a dismissal on the State's motion would allow me to refile the cases later. Nor could the defense escape trial indefinitely simply by announcing they weren't ready. At some point, when the judge insisted, the case would be tried no matter what the defense announced.

We all knew these things. Buster and I weren't arguing legal issues. We were sparring for control of the judge's will. Judge Hernandez was a ditherer. As with most judges, he would do what he thought was right and what he thought was expedient, hoping like hell the two coincided. Judge Hernandez was known to go back and forth, often responding not to the force of the law but to the lawyer who could best wheedle him into something.

The judge didn't like to be confronted with this kind of stalemate. He preferred, by being blustery and unreadable, to bully the parties themselves into reaching a compromise. Situations that called for decision rather than compromise upset him.

And in a stalemate, I expected the judge to side with his old friend—who along with his client brokered more political weight than any other two people in the county.

"If all the state wants is speedy prosecution," Buster said helpfully, "we'd be willing to try the two middle cases together. That would dispose of half the cases at once."

"Thank you for the suggestion, Mr. Harmony," I said, turning to him. Buster smiled at me, just trying to help. "But I'm sure Judge Hernandez is quite capable of managing his own docket without—"

"It is not at all a bad idea," the judge said slowly.

There was a slight tug at my sleeve. I had forgotten Becky was there. When I looked down, annoyed at her interruption in this crucial moment, she handed me two sheets of paper: dismissal motions, already filled out with the names of the cases and the case numbers of the two indictments involving the little girls.

I glanced at Buster. For a moment I felt I was being maneuvered. But Becky was right. Drop the distractions.

"Your Honor, the State tenders motions to dismiss in cause numbers 4222 and 4223. In hopes of wasting no more of the court's time."

"Mr. Harmony," the judge asked.

Buster spread his hands as if graciously accepting defeat. "I can't hardly object to the dismissal of half the cases against my client, Your Honor."

"Good, then," Judge Hernandez said decisively. "Then I shall set the other case for trial in, um, thirty days. October fourth. Can you be ready then?"

"I'll make my announcement that day," Buster hedged.

The judge stood up, and his naturally grumpy tone returned. "You had better be ready. Both sides. Or I will hold you in contempt." But before he turned away the judge pointed at Buster, making a gun of his finger and thumb. Buster pointed back. He shook his head, still the jolly old friend even after Judge Hernandez left the courtroom.

Early October was a fine trial setting for my purposes. Still a month before the election, and the trial should last not much longer than a week, if that. But I couldn't afford a reset past that setting.

"Smooth move, Blackie," Buster Harmony was saying. "Slid my cases right out from under me. Maybe I'm getting too old for this business." His smile shifted focus. "Or maybe I need a pretty young assistant, too."

Becky smiled back as if he were tolerable. "If I were flattered enough to take that for a job offer, Mr. Harmony, I'd have to say that I'm very happy where I am."

"Well, who wouldn't be? Prosecutor's always in the catbird seat, right, Blackie? Isn't that why you went back? Come on, Austin, let's get away while they let us."

Austin shrugged apologetically, as if he'd been caught cheating, as he followed his lawyer up the aisle. "Look forward to the trial," Buster's voice came floating back.

"Is he for real?" Becky asked. She was standing close at my shoulder.

"Before your time, he was considered a real terror in trial."

Becky's smile returned, this time for real. "Oh, good," she said.

In two weeks Becky and I had Kevin primed. He would tell his story to either of us, in detail. Sometimes it wasn't until Becky and I were talking about it after practicing with him that we'd realize *what* detail. While we listened to him we were clinically detached, no matter how much we smiled at him and patted his back and praised his sincerity; mentally we were consulting checklists as he talked. Now we have this element of the crime. Now that one. Good, he just raised the punishment range to life. It wouldn't be until later, in the Kevinless quiet of the car or a restaurant, that Becky and I would realize what he'd just told us, what a real memory it was for him. Only then would we picture the scene, picturing Kevin as he relived it for us.

"I think I can get him to cry again," I said. "Just by pausing a little between questions. Letting him dwell on it."

Becky nodded. We fell silent.

I stopped the rehearsals, afraid of Kevin's losing his naturalness for trial. Becky went back to her regular court docket. I was left with an occasional campaign appearance, with making humiliating calls asking for contributions, and with sizing up Buster Harmony. He wasn't the fool he projected. No matter what he might have owed Austin or what Austin might have paid him, Buster wouldn't have taken on the defense unless he saw a prospect of victory. I wondered what strategy he had in mind. I wondered how I would have run the defense myself.

As it turned out, I should have devoted more thought to Austin than to Buster. Buster wasn't the only one working on the defense case.

It was late in September when Becky and I went to Kevin's house to pick him up for our last rehearsal. This one was going to be in a courtroom. Mrs. Pollard opened the door, but not very wide. "Kevin's not going to come with you," she said.

"What?" I pushed the door open, gently; it didn't require much force to overcome Mrs. Pollard's resistance. "Is he sick?"

"No," she said quietly. I didn't ask her any more, because I'd seen Kevin. He was standing in the open doorway that led to the living room. He looked very young today. He was clutching a plastic soldier.

"Are you all right, pal?" I knelt in front of him.

"I made it all up," he blurted. "It didn't happen, Austin didn't do anything to me."

"Kevin," I began. Becky was kneeling beside me. She touched my side and shook her head slightly. I let her lead him back to his room. He'd tell Becky what was wrong.

But I already knew. Austin would do anything. He wouldn't confine his efforts to preparing for trial; he'd much rather ensure that there'd *be* no trial.

How do you bribe a six-year-old boy? Easily, as I recall: with candy, balsa wood airplanes, the promise of a trip to the zoo. But how do you make sure he'll stay bribed?

"We just don't want to put Kevin through this," I heard an offensively familiar voice say. When I looked up, *Mr.* Pollard was there, standing behind his wife, his hands on her shoulders as if he were thrusting her toward me. She looked embarrassed.

"Through what?" I asked quietly. I was going to make them earn their money.

"The trial," Pollard said. "And everything that goes with it, the teasing, the name-calling at school . . ."

"I told you we'd keep his name out of the papers."

"Well, kids have a way of finding out," Pollard said defiantly. "Somebody hears a teacher talking to another one . . . The kids figure it out. We'd have to leave town."

I had come up close to them. Mrs. Pollard reached up and touched her husband's hand. They were united. One hears about crises pulling families together.

"I don't need your permission," I told them. "I can call Kevin as a witness whether you like it or not. I'll have him subpoenaed."

"Try it," Pollard said pugnaciously, looking like the schoolyard bully I'll bet he once was. Thrusting his chin forward looked oddly comic, since he was still standing behind his wife. "You'll have to find him first."

Mrs. Pollard patted his hand. She gave me a pleading look. "What good would that do, Mr. Blackwell?" she asked. "You heard what Kevin said. Nothing really happened between them. It was all just make-believe."

In answer to that I just stared at her. She kept her eyes resolutely on mine, but her eyelids fluttered. "He changed his story once," I said. "He'll change it back when I question him during trial."

But I couldn't be sure of that. I might get only one shot at Austin. I couldn't take it with a witness I was unsure of.

But they didn't know that. And Pollard was an angry man. A man's man, the kind who couldn't bear what had happened to his son. My best bet was to stir that anger.

"You're going to let him get away with this? The man who kidnapped your son and took his clothes off and touched him and put his penis in Kevin's mouth?" I made it as brutal as I could. I saw Pollard swallow hard. "You're going to take Austin Paley's money and let him get away with what he did to your boy?"

"Nobody took any money," Mrs. Pollard said, but that time she couldn't look at me.

I kept my eyes on her husband. "Don't you want to see him punished for what he did to Kevin?"

Pollard's pride was hurt. I had managed to humiliate him. But this humiliation wasn't a public one. He swallowed again, and when he answered me he was no longer blustering. He sounded like a reasonable man. He was asking me to be reasonable too. "We're more concerned with the rest of his life," he said.

That was probably what they'd convinced themselves of. It would require comfort like that to allow them to do something so despicable. I strongly doubted they'd dealt with Austin himself. He would have sent an emissary. The emissary would have spoken softly and reasonably, pointing out the uncertainties of trial, but the certainty of its outcome: the public humiliation for Kevin and for them. He would have weighed that against what money could provide: therapy for Kevin now, a college education later on. The benefit was tangible. And after all, what good would a conviction do Kevin?

"Becky," I called, and heard her voice answer me from the back of the house. I heard her footsteps. The Pollards looked relieved. In a minute the officials would be out of their house and they'd have their lives to themselves again.

"Whatever you do," I said, "don't you dare spend the money on yourselves. It's Kevin's. He earned it."

I took some satisfaction in the redness of their faces, in the silence of the house, as I took Becky's arm and escorted her out, but that satisfaction dissipated quickly once we were outside. The neighborhood, which we'd grown to know so well, looked completely alien. So did my car. Nothing looked familiar, because we were nowhere. We had a trial date in five days, but we had no case.

9

It's ALL RIGHT, JUDGE," I SAID TO THE SPUTTERING Judge Hernandez. It was October 4, our special trial setting, and I had just handed him another motion to dismiss. I was tubing the case involving Kevin. I turned from the bench to look at the defense table.

"This comes as no surprise to the defendant," I continued. "In fact, it's at the instigation of the defense that I'm dismissing the case that was set for trial today."

The judge went from blustery to confused and back to blustery by the time he spoke. "The court should have been informed—" he began.

"We haven't been negotiating with the State," Buster said. "I don't know what the DA's talking about."

"No. Nonetheless, the defendant knew I would come into court today without a case, because I have no witness."

Buster sounded baffled. "If the State is having some problem, we'd consider—"

"My witness has been bribed," I told him. "How are you going to fix that?"

Buster went immediately to full court bluster. "That's an outrageous allegation! Unless you're—"

"That's why I said it quietly."

"Address the court," Judge Hernandez said peremptorily.

I wheeled to him. "Yes, Your Honor. The state offers its motion to dismiss in cause number 4221 and announces ready in the last remaining case styled State of Texas versus Austin Paley. The State is prepared to try that case today, Your Honor."

That was a lie. I counted on Buster to help me out. He came in as if I'd written his lines.

"Well, the defense is *not* ready," he said. "That case wasn't even set for trial today."

"I believe both cases are on today's docket, aren't they, Your Honor?" As a matter of course they were, in case we reached a settlement on both before trial.

"Indeed," Judge Hernandez said portentously, staring at the docket sheet in his hand.

"That may be," Buster said loudly, "but we all agreed that the first case was to be tried today. The defense was prepared to go to trial today in the case the district attorney has just dismissed, not in the other."

Judge Hernandez pointed a finger at both of us. "The two of you are interfering with my docket. First one of you isn't ready, then the other. Do you think you are privileged characters, that you don't have to answer to the court? This time," he continued sternly, "I give you only three weeks. And I warn you—I warn you both—the case *will* be tried that day."

Buster and I stood for his departure, so it was easy to turn toward each other immediately afterward. "Mark, you're wrong. I have never been accused—"

"You still haven't," I said shortly, and stepped around him to where Austin still sat, with an air of baffled curiosity as if he were some rube to whom everything that happened in a court-room was too complex to follow.

"I'm not forgetting Kevin Pollard," I told him. "I'll revive his case, too, maybe by the next setting. People who'll take a bribe will cave in to a threat, too. Once I find out how you got to them—"

I had been putting on an act, but the act overtook me as I stood over Austin. The muscles in the arm I was leaning on locked up. His bland face begged to be punched. A memory picture replaced the scene before my eyes, the picture of Kevin Pollard alone on his swing set, the hostage of the adult world, of not only his abuser but of the parents who wouldn't protect him, and wouldn't let me.

The memory had the effect of calming me. I couldn't give in

to anger. I had to be crafty, not explosive, because my adversary was the craftiest man I'd ever known.

But Austin Paley had seen murder in the way I stood over him. He had the good sense to speak quietly to me.

"Mark, I didn't do it. I don't know what those people told you, but if they decided the case shouldn't go forward it was because of their own doubts, not because of something I did. They know their son better than you. They know better than to believe his lie."

I wouldn't be drawn into discussion. Buster must have given some sign to his client, because Austin stood suddenly. Buster said he'd get back to me, then took Austin's arm and walked out.

Becky was standing slightly behind me, patting my back so gently, so discreetly I had no idea how long it had been going on. "I've never had a handler before," I said to her.

"Who knows how long you've needed one." Her gaze was troubled, and it was on me. "It's just a case," she added, echoing me.

My anger had receded, but it hadn't been replaced. I felt no sense of triumph. I'd only staved off disaster for a few weeks. Now reporters were coming toward me up the aisle, and I had to explain to them that I had indeed dismissed three-fourths of the cases against Austin Paley, just as he'd predicted I'd be forced to do, but that he was still guilty as sin and I'd prove it soon.

"Hell of an ugly way to practice law," I said.

I was in disguise by the time I reached the elementary school, dressed like a real person rather than a lawyer. The first time I'd come in a suit, of course, looking official as hell, but they knew me now, even in my khakis and open-necked shirt. One of the supervisors waved to me as I opened the gate to the playground. The children looked up, not in fright, in anticipation—any novelty a distraction.

Tommy Algren was standing apart, under a tree, watching two younger boys rolling cars down the slide, trying to aim them to crash into plastic soldiers standing unsuspectingly in the sand at the bottom. I stood beside Tommy and we both watched. His only acknowledgment of me was to nod toward the boys and say, "Psychopaths."

"Definitely prison material," I agreed.

Tommy smiled. We began walking away. This time the two high school students in charge, a boy and a girl, didn't notice me. They were sitting on a concrete bench very close, comparing the notes on their clipboards, leaning into each other, pointing out items of interest on the papers.

Tommy's parents no longer sent him after school to the daycare center from which Austin Paley had so often and casually abducted him, but they couldn't possibly have thought he was more secure now, if they'd spent ten minutes checking out the program. Tommy's elementary school allowed children of working parents to stay after school, on the playground or in the cafeteria, "supervised" by the two teenagers. The kids were left pretty much to create their own amusement. There were fewer of them than I would have supposed, maybe thirty. Other children of working parents were picked up after school by daycare centers or maids or, if they were older—ten or eleven—walked home and spent an hour or two alone until Mom and Dad got home.

"Anything you need to do today?" I asked Tommy as we left the playground.

He shrugged. "Not really."

"Done your homework?" I asked as we got into the car, and we both laughed. It was one of our jokes.

After Kevin fell through I'd felt paralyzed. I'd tried to think how to force him to testify for me anyway. Becky felt confident of opening him up on the stand if we got him there, but I didn't discount his father's threat to take Kevin out of our reach. I quickly discarded him and decided to move on to the one case I had left, the one involving Tommy Algren.

Tommy'd been slick as vinyl in my office, recounting his relationship with Austin. That was the main reason Becky and I hadn't liked him as a witness. He'd healed too thoroughly, he sounded unruffled about the abuse he'd suffered. And of course, he was older than I would have wanted. At ten years old he was on the cusp of adolescence. His experiences with Austin dated back two and three and four years, but Tommy was no longer the little boy to whom those things had happened.

But Tommy was all I had left. I'd begun cultivating him the day after the Pollards told me Kevin wouldn't testify. I wasn't going to make the same mistake with Tommy I'd made with Kevin: I wasn't going to let the parents stand between us. I would make Tommy my own, I'd decided, so that he'd do what I asked no matter what his parents said.

Of course, Austin would try to get to him too, but he'd have to do it surreptitiously and cautiously, while I could do it openly.

Austin didn't have to win. He just had to delay. I needed to prosecute him before the election—now little more than a month away. If I failed, and if Leo Mendoza was elected in my place, Austin would never be tried. Leo'd already announced as much. Austin just had to stall me until I was off the stage. He'd done it successfully with Kevin. I was determined he wouldn't with Tommy.

"Want to hit a few?" I asked.

I parked the car at Batter-Up. Tommy followed me to the counter, hanging back a little. I'd already decided that little Tommy was no athlete, but I didn't want to make a major league slugger of him, I just wanted to find things to do with him, put in the time.

Tommy put his hands in his pockets while I judiciously ran my fingers over the bats, selected one, and took a couple of practice swings. Tommy was of about average height for his age, but thin. His arms were thinner than the bat I was holding. He looked good in his clothes, like a little model. He always seemed to have had more grooming than other kids, and he had an air of cool sophistication, but it evaporated when he tried to do something physical, when his limbs and body seemed barely connected. I know about playing cool.

"I was always one of the tallest kids in my class," I said as I selected a smaller bat for Tommy and handed it to him. He leaned on it like a cane. "But for years I was also the clumsiest," I went on. "My arms and legs were just too long for me, you know, they were so far out there I didn't even know where they were half the time."

I demonstrated, stretching my arms, rotating my hands on their wrists. Tommy laughed. He looked cool as Reggie Jackson leaning on his bat.

"So after a while I just said the hell with sports, you know? It's no fun having everybody think you should be the best at something and instead you trip going after a ball and throw like a girl. So I retired. I acted like I was just too good for everything, like it wouldn't even be fair if I played. You know? And that was okay, except I really did want to play. Sometimes my dad and I would shoot baskets and that wasn't so bad because he never made fun of me. He even gave me a few tips."

"Like what?" Tommy asked. He swung his bat a couple of times in a swing that started behind his head above the level of his shoulders and ended up down around his ankles.

"Simple stuff," I said. I traded dollars for tokens and we headed for an empty batting cage. There was one gang of kids, probably a team, but they were down at the fast-pitch end and I chose the slow-pitch machines for Tommy and me. We were out of earshot of everyone else when we stepped into a cage. "Like paying attention. You know, I'd be trying to throw the ball toward the hoop and start running to get my own rebound at the same time. My dad just told me to concentrate on the one thing I was doing. Something you could figure out for yourself but never do, you know?"

"Yeah," Tommy said. He had stepped up to the plate. I casually adjusted his bat. "Straight across," I said offhandedly, as if reminding him of something we'd already talked about. He took a more level practice swing and I fed a token into the machine. Fifty feet in front of us the metal arm attached to the metal box of softballs stirred, revolved, lifted a ball, and hurled it toward the plate, toward Tommy, who swung and missed.

"You think it's coming fast but it's not," I said. "Watch it. You can see right where it's coming. Keep your eye on the ball, don't worry about the bat, it'll go where you're looking."

Another ball came in, fat and slow, so slow it bounced on the plate as it crossed in front of Tommy. He just watched it. "Good eye," I said.

"Then in junior high the basketball coach spotted me," I went on. "I mean, you couldn't miss me, I was already almost six feet tall. I didn't grow much more after I got to high school, but in junior high I was a real freak. You could see me coming from one end of the hall to the other."

The next pitch from the machine was perfect, just at shoulder level for Tommy. His bat met the ball, not a very good cut, he was under it, so the ball leaped up in what would have been an easy pop-up, but in the fielderless confines of Batter-Up its arc looked spectacular. "Good shot," I said. Tommy hunkered down and raised the bat again. I pulled it back a little farther. The metal pitching arm quivered and started around again.

"So the coach saw you," Tommy said.

"Concentrate," I said. The pitch came in, about waist high, but Tommy was crouched low enough to get it. He hit a line drive that would surely have been foul outside the first-base line. "A little slow," I said. "See, I pulled the bat back so you'd have more power, but that means you've got to bring it around faster. Watch for the pitch." He nodded.

"Yeah, so this big dumb basketball coach saw me in the hall and he made me go out for the basketball team. I mean I didn't even have any choice, he called my parents, he'd be waiting in the hall after my last class to take me to practice. I didn't get to decide at all. It was nice."

Tommy nodded, understanding how attractive it would be to be forced to do something one secretly wanted to do but didn't have the nerve to try. Another pitch came toward him and he swung ferociously. The ball slammed untouched into the netting behind us.

"That time you closed your eyes," I said. "That's the first thing, to watch the ball. That's all you have to remember."

"And to keep my swing level and to bring the bat around faster and to lean back instead of forward," Tommy said grumpily.

"Yeah, it's tough. This is the hardest thing in sports. Want to go shoot baskets somewhere instead?"

"Let me try a couple more times first."

I fed another token into the coin box.

The next pitch came toward his head. I was already darting toward it, trying to deflect the ball just enough that it would miss him, but long before I got there Tommy had jerked his head back out of harm's way.

"Dropped my bat," I said casually, picking it up again. "That was good watching, Tommy."

He might not have heard me. He was gritting his teeth, glaring as if the machine were a human rival who had just tried to take his head off. "Keep your eyes open," I muttered.

The next pitch was a good one and Tommy met it dead square. It leaped straight off his bat along the same line it had come in on, and smashed into the metal box of balls, making the whole thing quiver.

"That'll teach him," I said.

When the machine had given me my token's worth again, Tommy turned to me and said, "And by the end of the season you were the MVP, right?"

"It's not that kind of story, Tom. We didn't get into the play-offs and I wasn't the star of the team. But I got to play, and I liked it. Got to travel with the team, you know, made a few friends. By high school I even was pretty good. And it was fun. Beat the hell out of acting like I was too good to play. You know? You ready to go?"

"Let me take another couple of cuts," he said.

During the second batch of pitches Tommy hit one that arced high over the machine, almost brushing the top of the netting, hitting the high fence thirty yards away. It might have been a long fly out in a real ballpark, but it might have been a home run, too, and I acted as if it were. "Man," I kept saying. "Man, what a hit. You weren't aiming for that spot, were you? You didn't even know you'd hit it, did you? You just closed your eyes and swung."

"I was watching," Tommy insisted. "I watched it all the way in."

"Man," I said, and whistled through my teeth.

It was five o'clock, late, but Tommy's parents wouldn't be home yet. I drove slowly. "How did you meet Austin?" I asked, without emphasis, discussing a mutual friend.

"He had a house in my neighborhood," Tommy said. "I thought he lived there, but I guess it was a rent house, because when I went inside, later on, it was empty. But he showed up there one day, working outside like he'd just moved in and was fixing up the place, and we started talking. Just, you know, about the neighborhood, who lived where and where there was to go to the store and like that. There were other kids around too."

"And he was there again the next day."

"Yeah, or the day after, or some time. He was always outside. After a while he asked if I could do some work for him. I was only seven, you know, I couldn't mow the yard or anything, but I picked up trash and raked leaves and stuff like that, and he paid me two dollars. He said I really helped him out."

"Were there still other kids around then?"

"Some. We kept hanging around him. It's not a real exciting

neighborhood, you know? One day he had to go to the store, and a couple of us rode with him, and the next day he asked us if we wanted to go on a picnic.''

Tommy told the story with an admirable completeness of detail and not much prompting. He knew by now the significant aspects. He looked out the car windshield as he talked, his eye catching on points of landscape. His voice was calm. He seemed to remain emotionally level. This wasn't the first time we'd talked about Austin. Tommy knew I wasn't spending time with him just because I liked him. He knew we'd get to Austin eventually. He didn't seem to mind. He had told me more intimate details than these, but always in the same bright, reminiscent tone. It was just a story, one he knew interested his audience.

"Any more problems at school?" I asked him abruptly.

Tommy looked at me, put off his stride. We were stopped at a stop sign on a trafficless side street, so I could look back. After a moment's perusal of my face he shrugged. "No," he said, but he'd lost that cool, self-sufficient air.

"No? Has anybody found out you're going to testify?"

"I don't think so," he said, uncertainly, like a child. "I sure haven't told anybody," he added. I was certain of that. This was my fourth meeting with Tommy. I'd usually picked him up at school, but I hadn't seen or heard him mention a friend. I hadn't tried to explain that it was his friend Austin who'd set him apart from the other kids. Tommy was a smart boy, I'd rather he realize that for himself. But I could raise the subject.

"What about Brian?"

"That moron," Tommy said.

"Is he still picking on you? More than he was?"

Tommy shrugged again. He was leaning against the passenger door, not looking at me any more.

"There's always guys like that, Tommy, believe me. You can handle him."

He stirred. "Did you ever have to?" he asked.

"Me? No. No, I usually *was* the bully."

He laughed. "I'll bet."

It was my turn to shrug. "Not something I'm proud of, but it did give me a certain insight, you know?"

"I guess. So what d'I do with him?"

"Threaten him with a bigger bully, for one thing. If things

143

get too tough, tell him your friend the district attorney is going to come see him and his parents."

From the look on his face I knew Tommy would never resort to that. It would single him out as a freak even more. "First I'd have to explain to him what an attorney is," he said morosely.

I laughed. At first it was a surprised response, but I kept laughing, more than the joke was worth, until Tommy joined me. We were still laughing when we pulled up to his house, a nice brick home in an upper-middle-class neighborhood, the yard mowed, the hedges trimmed. I could tell by looking at it that it was empty.

"It's okay," Tommy said. "They'll be home in a little while."

"I'll come in and wait, if that's all right with you. Maybe I could use your phone."

"Sure."

As we walked up the driveway my hand dropped casually toward his shoulder, but I stopped it. Tommy took his key from his pocket and let us into the big empty house.

"You can touch him, it's okay," Janet McLaren said. "He's got to learn somehow that people do touch each other just out of fondness, it's not necessarily sexual."

"I think I'll let somebody else try that experiment," I said. "I don't want to spook him. I'm not trying to rehabilitate him, Doctor, I just need to be sure of his testimony."

"Is there some reason why you couldn't help with his therapy at the same time?"

"Yeah, there's some reason. I don't know what the hell I'm doing. I don't want to go blundering around in his psyche like some half-assed amateur psychologist and risk giving him a breakdown two weeks before trial."

"You've seen too much TV. You're not going to send Tommy into a coma by putting your hand on his arm. As a fully assed professional psychiatrist, I assure you of that."

Dr. McLaren was wearing beige slacks and a short matching jacket over a striped blouse that showed a little more cleavage than she would normally have displayed in a professional appointment, I thought. When we'd shaken hands I'd noticed her quietly shining fingernails and that her blue, almost purple eyes were somehow more prominent than at our first meeting. I flattered myself that she'd taken extra care preparing for our appointment today. I know I'd looked forward to seeing her again. But almost as soon as we started talking about Tommy we were at odds.

I fetched her can of Diet Coke from the table and poured the remainder into Janet's glass, smiling as I did, hoping to restore socialness to the occasion. She nodded thanks.

"I've tried to get into the story almost without mentioning Austin to him," I said quietly. Janet's expression grew alert to match the concern in my voice. "I have to hear the details but I'm afraid to remind him. I'm also—unsure. No, I'm afraid, that's what it is, afraid of how he feels about Austin."

She nodded. "Yes. You're wise to be concerned about that. Children hate what happened to them but still love the molester. If you think he's going to be vindictive toward Austin Paley, you're dangerously oversimplifying Tommy's reaction."

"I know. But—love? Isn't that putting it a little too strongly?"

"No." Dr. McLaren had this knack of focusing all her attention on me. Her voice lowered, as if we were discussing secrets, which made me lean toward her. Her eyes held me the way a good teacher's voice holds students. "Who else does Tommy love?" she asked. "He has no friends, you're right about that. He used to have, but no more. No siblings. Until he found his abuser he was all alone in the world."

She paused, still watching me. I said, "You want me to say, 'But, Doctor, what about his parents?' "

She smiled sadly. We were comrades again, the only ones who understood the world.

"If Tommy were really sure of his parents' love, he would never have fallen into this man's trap," she said. "Has he told you how they met? Well, you see. There were other children in the initial group, but Tommy was the one who kept returning, day after day. Austin Paley knew Tommy was the one he wanted, the one looking for someone.

"The Algrens don't think they're bad parents," she went on. "They're *not* bad parents. They've put Tommy in a good school, given him a nice home, bought him everything he needs. They take him to the zoo or the museum, when they can manage. They buy him a book or a computer game at least once a week. They conscientiously remind themselves to do that for him."

"Like another appointment in their Filofax."

"It's not their fault they don't have time for him. Maybe they could get by on one salary, maybe they could both work shorter hours. But even if they did, it would be out of obligation, not desire. They're committed to work, that's the most important thing in their lives, and Tommy knows it."

"Then he met Austin Paley, who always had time for him."

Janet nodded. She put a hand on my knee, which was intriguing, but I couldn't escape the feeling that she was giving me a demonstration of the appropriateness of touching. "There was a void there not just of affection," she said. "There was a training gap. Tommy doesn't see his father enough to know what he's like. Tommy's getting old for a child, he needs to see how to act like a man."

"Austin was a role model for him."

She nodded.

"That's scary," I said.

I could see the truth of her observation. That's what had put me off about Tommy, not just that he was too cool to display his hurts to a jury, but that he was like Austin himself—charming, imperturbable. A dapper little socialite in a child's body and a child's confusing world.

I sat thinking about Tommy's future. But after a moment I shook off that concern. He wasn't my child, he was my witness. "There's something else that worries me. We're sitting here talking as if we're sure at least we've got the facts straight, but I'm not so sure. Tommy scares me. He didn't report he was molested and then we found a suspect and Tommy picked him out of a lineup. He saw Austin on TV and that was the first time he'd ever reported what happened to him. He told his parents."

Janet understood. "It sounds like a grab for attention."

"Even his parents didn't believe him at first. Why should I?"

"I don't always believe the children who come to see me," she said. "I tend to believe boys more, because—and this would explain too why Tommy didn't tell anyone he was being molested—boys are afraid to tell, more than girls. They're afraid of being called fags."

"Ten-year-old boys? Nine-year-olds?"

She was almost amused with me again. "Is that too dim a memory for you? Trying to be a manly little ten-year-old, playing catch with the boys instead of house with the girls?"

"Well, yes, but I don't think I even knew what homosexuality was then. We weren't so sophisticated back—"

"You'd have known there was something queer about touching a man's penis. Would you have been friends with a boy
you'd heard stories like that about?"

She was sitting on the small couch in my office, I was sitting
in the armchair just in front of her, facing her. I tried to be very
adult as we discussed this, but being a psychiatrist she could
probably read my body language. "I see your point," I said.
"But do you see mine? I've got a trial. I've got to make people
believe Tommy, over the vehement denial of an adult. There's
no physical evidence, not this long after the fact. If I gave him
a lie detector test, I couldn't get the result before a jury. Is there
anything, some kind of objective evidence, that what Tommy
says happened happened? Not that it was Austin, just that it
happened at all. Something Tommy—"

"I have my own little test," Janet said. "I ask them to describe
semen. Kids can pick up the outlines of seduction from TV or
other places, but in the normal course of childhood they haven't
come across semen. Without telling them what I'm looking for
I ask them what happened, and if they finally say something
came out of the man's penis I ask them what it looked like, what
it smelled like. What it tasted like, if that seems appropriate."

I was sitting very still. Janet was talking quietly, watching me.
She'd grown more clinical. "Did Tommy describe it?" I asked.

"Yes."

I nodded slightly, as if it weren't much. I didn't want her to
see how happy the news made me. It was tragic for Tommy
but good for me. Janet kept watching me. She knew just what
I was thinking. She was the savior of children; I was only using
them.

She wouldn't let me get away with anything, even within the
supposed privacy of my mind. Janet put her hand on my arm
and looked into my eyes.

"You know what you're doing with Tommy is dangerous,"
she said. "You could hurt him as badly as Paley has."

"I do understand that," I said. But I didn't make any
promises.

She was still looking at me. "I think I need to work on you
some more."

"Professionally?"

She nodded. "But so subtly you won't even know what's

147

happening. It's best to start in a relaxing setting, like lunch. Or is it dinnertime yet?"

"Of the day, or in our relationship?" I asked.

The corners of her eyes crinkled, but whether in a small smile or in continued study it was hard to say. "You see?" she said. "I've already done wonders for your self-esteem."

"Austin's a licensed realtor, did you know that?"

I nodded, not to say I'd known it, just that it made sense.

"He's very elaborate, Mark," Becky continued. "He doesn't seem to have ever done anything on impulse. He has these systems. His neighbors are shocked that he's been arrested. The people at his church are outraged. He taught children's Sunday school, Mark. And he's never been anything but perfectly proper with the kids he comes into contact with."

"The ones that people know he's been in contact with." Not to my surprise, Austin lived by the code that says, Don't shit where you eat.

"That's right," Becky said. We were in her office, and she seemed more in charge in that setting. She leaned toward me across her desk as if I were a recalcitrant witness she had to bring into line. "But meanwhile he has this secret life. We'll never track down all his lairs. There's only a couple of rent houses he owns himself, I think, but being a realtor gives him access to empty houses all over town. He can just appear, start acting like he's moved in, and there he is, the new neighbor. But nobody knows his name or where he really lives. He must've had several of these going at once, in different stages of cultivating children."

Becky had a plant atop her filing cabinet, a sad lost cause beneath the slit window of her office. It was an ivy of some kind that had crept across the top of the metal cabinet and started down the side, searching. The plant had only a few leaves, it was mostly just thin vine, but it was green, it gave Becky's office slightly more homelike an atmosphere than most, which was rather sad in itself.

"It's kind of creepy, isn't it?" she said. "We can show some of this elaborate preparation he put into the seduction. The stalking."

I stood up. "You're doing good work, Becky. I'm sorry you're getting stuck with all the crud work, but that's how it falls out on this one. Meanwhile, I have to go cultivate the victim some more."

Becky stood up and already had her purse strap over her shoulder. "Okay," she said.

I shook my head at her. "I'll go by myself again this time."

Becky looked concerned. "Mark, don't you think I need to get to know him too? Even if you're going to do the examination at trial, two of us talking to him might draw more out of him. Maybe he's different with men."

"I do want that," I said. "But first I want him very dependent on me. That's not strong enough to dilute, yet. Next time, I promise."

As I turned in her doorway to wave goodbye Becky was still standing, looking at me worriedly. No one trusted me any more.

As I drove to Tommy's house that evening I thought about something else Janet McLaren had told me about him that might or might not be true. "If he's so afraid of how the story will make him look," I'd asked, "then why *did* he tell?"

"Maybe it *was* to get attention," she'd answered. "I don't discount that idea. But it was probably jealousy." She could see she'd surprised me. "I'm sure Austin Paley didn't brag about his other conquests to Tommy," she'd sensibly explained. "Tommy thought it was something new for both of them. He thought he was special to Austin. Then he saw him on TV, part of a case involving several children, and he knew immediately Austin was behind it. He felt betrayed. That's probably what undercut his loyalty to Austin enough to tell his parents what had happened."

It was, to use Becky's phrase, a little creepy. It wouldn't be the first time I'd used a jealous lover to testify against a defendant. But I wanted Tommy to have a more reliable reason for testifying, too.

This time his parents were home. Mrs. Algren answered the door, dressed like a sitcom mom on old TV, wearing a dress and necklace and stockings even at home after work. When she took me into the living room I expected her husband still to be wearing his tie and suit, but he was in sweat pants and T-shirt.

"Sorry," he said about the sweat as he shook my hand. "I've been riding the exercycle."

The living room was very big, high-vaulted. Through an archway the room blended into the dining room, making it appear even bigger. The carpet was white, and unstained. The fireplace was made of white brick. Beside it glass shelves held a variety of fragile knickknacks and one family portrait in a silver frame.

"I need to talk to you," I said. Mr. and Mrs. Algren looked uneasy, until I started talking, when they visibly relaxed. He ducked his head a little, keeping his eyes on me, and nodded in rhythm to what I was saying. His receding hairline gave him a serious air. He was very trim but not particularly muscular, as if too much exercise wasn't worth his time. Mr. Algren was a young man, by my standards, no later than midthirties, but he already looked like someone who'd come far in the business world, and had done it by shucking nonessentials like humor.

Mrs. Algren was the one who could have profited by time on the exercycle. That's why she looked older than her husband. She lacked his intensity, too. She had the look of a woman who wants to help you out but always hears something more urgent going on in another room.

What I said to them was, "You know I wasn't planning on Tommy's case going to trial this soon. I was forced to move it up because I lost my witness in the other case. I believe the defendant managed to bribe his parents."

"Bribe?" Mr. Algren said. I nodded sadly. The Algrens shook their heads in sympathy, appalled at the idea of parents who would take money for ignoring the best interests of their child.

"You see what will happen next," I said.

"He'll come to us."

"I don't want that man near this house," Mrs. Algren said. She drew closer to her husband.

"It won't be him, honey." He looked at me and I shook my head. "It will be some lowlife creep he's hired to approach us. Some lawyer, probably."

No one seemed to think I might be offended by this analysis, which I suppose was complimentary. There were lowlife creep lawyers and then there were ones like me.

"You don't have to be worried about us, Mr. Blackwell," Algren said. "I'll show that son of a bitch the door so fast he'll think he got hit by a train. I may put him *through* the door. Unless—"

He really was very quick. "Now you understand," I said.

"Understand what?" his wife said. She was looking past my shoulder.

"You want us to play along when we're contacted," Mr. Algren said.

"Exactly."

He nodded. I nodded. If Joe Friday had been there, he would have nodded. "And maybe we can lay another indictment on Mr. Paley's doorstep," Algren said.

"But won't he know you've warned us?" Mrs. Algren asked.

"It doesn't matter. He *has* to try to get to you. He's so afraid of trial he's desperate."

"Then mightn't he try to do something to Tommy?"

"That's something for me to worry about," I said. "I don't think Paley's the type to try something violent, but we've got the possibility covered. I'm seeing Tommy almost every day after school anyway, preparing for his testimony. The days I don't, I'll have an investigator with him. That only leaves school and home."

"And we'll take care of him here," Mr. Algren said.

"Excellent," I said.

What had passed unspoken in our conversation was any suspicion that the Algrens might actually accept a bribe—not the kind that came in cold sordid cash, but the promise of job opportunities, contacts, and, best of all, keeping Tommy—and themselves—out of the public spotlight. I didn't think they'd be susceptible even to that, but I had another way of protecting myself against that possibility.

"Let's just keep this to ourselves," I warned them. "I'm going to go talk to Tommy for a few minutes so he won't know why I came."

They nodded, ready to conspire in the deception of their son.

"What were you talking to Mom and Dad about?" Tommy asked when I found him in what the Algrens called the study, which contained a high techish metal-and-blond-wood desk, a computer at its own desk, and one tall bookshelf holding mostly bound manuals. Tommy was at the computer. He pressed a button and the words on the screen disappeared.

"Just telling them you're going to be all right. They're worried about you." He looked pleased to hear that. I continued. "Listen, Tom, I came by to talk to you because I got an idea."

This "Tom" business was a deliberate ploy of mine. I figured

I was the first person in his life to call him by his name without diminution. I wanted him to appreciate me for seeing his maturity. Tommy'd been in therapy for weeks now, and he understood the implication of therapy, understood that everyone thought he was damaged. Tommy was going to drag this extra shadow at his heels for the rest of his life. When he was sixty he would still be the abused boy. But he could have something else, too: an early understanding that everyone was as fragile as he, that adults are only scared children too. He need never be afraid of anyone again. I could show him that.

"I've been thinking about this Brian business," I said, frowning. Tommy's own face opened. He'd looked resigned to going over details of the case again. But no, I was here because I'd been thinking about his problem at school.

"I was all wet when I told you to threaten him with me. That was stupid."

"Yeah," Tommy agreed.

"I know, I know. You'd just make it a bigger challenge for him. He'd eat that up." Tommy looked relieved at my enlightenment. He'd thought I'd lost touch with reality. "But you know the worst thing you can do to a guy like that? Give him something to think about. Because he can't do it; it hurts him to try. It'll burn out his circuitry. Whenever he sees you from then on he gets this pain between his ears. He starts avoiding you. It hurts to look at you."

Tommy had a little of that look himself. "You think so?" he asked doubtfully.

"Look, Tom, you think Brian's the only Brian in the world? I prosecute stupid jerks for a living, remember? I see Brian every day, sitting there in handcuffs and jail slippers, on his way to prison. These guys are morons." I touched the tips of both index fingers to my temples, like electrodes. "You can't outrun him, you can't beat him up. But up here, you're about eight feet taller than he is."

"So what do I do, tell him math problems every time he comes close to me?"

He was perking up and he was talking like a kid. I liked it. I said, "First off, tell him you've always admired him."

Tommy's face twisted. "That greasewad?"

"I said tell him, I didn't say mean it. Hey, *are* you smarter than this guy, or am I wasting my time? Put it to him like this.

Tell him you saw him doing something nice once, taking up for somebody else, and it made you realize he's a better person than anybody else realizes."

Tommy had to set me straight. "This guy never took up for anybody in his life. If ten guys were kicking a girl who was down, he'd come and take *their* side."

"I know that. *You* know that. But you think this idiot remembers every day of his life? Tell him it happened, make it sound good enough, and he'll be saying, 'What? No. Well . . . Oh yeah, I remember that.' Believe me, you tell somebody they did something noble, they'll believe you."

"Maybe," Tommy said. He still sounded doubtful, but he was thinking.

"If this works, you're golden. When he sees you he's going to remember what a hero he is, and he isn't going to sully his reputation by being a jerk to you. Maybe to everybody else, but not to you, the one guy in America who looks up to him."

"I don't know," Tommy said. "Do I have to keep this up just 'til I puke, or for the rest of my life?"

"After a while it's automatic. Look, Tom, you're acting like this is a chore. It's fun. You take a guy who hates you and you turn him to your side, and he's sweet to you from then on while you're laughing up your sleeve about what an idiot he is; believe me, that's why God created the planet. There's nothing more fun in this world."

I hadn't meant to deliver a paean to the joys of manipulation, that was a little too close to giving myself away, but you get caught up in these things.

"Is it worth trying?" I asked. "Or are you having a better time eating dirt every time he catches you on the playground?"

"It's not bad," Tommy said slowly. He didn't want to come around too fast. "What's your other idea?" he asked.

"What makes you think I have another idea?"

He smiled at me.

"Okay, if this first brilliant idea doesn't work, if he comes around and starts picking on you again, its because he's managed to get over having to think about how much you admire him. But it's still in the back of his mind. He wants to reduce it to something simple, like you're a fag, but you don't let it be simple. Give him something else to think about."

I'd passed quickly over the "fag" aspect, as if only an idiot like Brian would entertain that thought.

"Like?" Tommy said.

I spread my hands. "You know the situation better than I do, Tom. Use something at school. Use what he says to you. If he says he hears you've been seeing a shrink, tell him, Yeah, and now you understand *his* problem. The shrink explained why Brian has to keep hanging around you. Don't tell him why, just tell him you understand, and it's okay."

Tommy was nodding. I went on offhandedly. "I'm going to have an investigator from my office picking you up from school the days I don't see you. If Brian gets wind of that and says something to you about it, just look real alarmed and say, 'You haven't said anything to anyone, have you?' Let *him* worry what he's done wrong. Or if you think it would work better, confide in him. Confide a lie, of course."

"Sure," Tommy said. He was as quick as his father.

"Just remember, the thing a guy like Brian hates worst is thinking. Keep it complicated, keep him off balance. He'll either wind up being your pal or he'll start staying away."

"And either one's fine with me," Tommy said. He sounded very adult, he had the mannerisms, too. He swept his hand in front of him in a worldly gesture I'd seen before. But it was a child's hand making the gesture, a small hand with fingers thin almost to the point of translucence.

"That's the best I can do," I said, wondering, *Did Austin Paley ever give you swell advice like this? Did he concern himself with your problems?* "If all else fails, tell me and I'll have my investigator pound him into oatmeal."

"You'd get sued," Tommy said.

He followed me out into the living room, which had the effect of making everyone furtive. We closed as if it had been a business call. I let myself out. When I looked back from the doorway the Algrens were standing as if for another family portrait, Mrs. Algren beside her husband, Algren's arm draped across Tommy's shoulder. Father and son both wanted to wink at me. I returned their waves with a significant nod and look at each of them in turn. I had them all well in hand, I thought.

"Well, it's happened," Tim Scheuless said on the phone. "I guess you've already seen it, haven't you?"

The latest poll, he meant. Leo Mendoza had just passed me in supposed voter popularity. "It looks like I lost more to 'undecided' than I did to Leo," I said.

"Yeah, that's the good part," Tim said, but his tone of voice needed work. It sounded as gloomy as November. "What we've lost," he said, "is the advantage of incumbency. But we could get it back. Don't you have anything ready for trial?"

"I'll see," I said shortly. "Meanwhile, let's plunge into debt. Put up some billboards. Let's run those radio spots again. Is there time to make some new ones?"

"Maybe. I don't know if I can buy the time. Or the signs. Things are pretty well booked up already. But I'll see what I can do."

As usual when I hung up from talking to my campaign manager, I was depressed. I put on a brave front for the benefit of the troops.

"See if anybody's got a really ugly, easy case going to trial this week," I said, "so I can take it over from them."

"I'll pass the word," Becky said. She was responding in kind to what I'd said, but I couldn't tell if she thought I was serious or joking.

"And, Jack," I said to my chief investigator, "see if you can find any evidence Austin Paley got to the Pollards. Sudden deposit in their bank account, you know the kind of thing."

"Sure."

"Oh, and assign somebody to pick up Tommy Algren after school. Some days—"

"Already done," Jack said, and left my office with the busy air that was perpetual with him.

Becky Schirhart was studying me quite frankly. I remembered the air of uneasiness that pervaded the district attorney's office during close election times when the chief's job was on the line, which meant everyone else's was too. Maybe a new broom would sweep the place clean. People would be busy brightening their resumés and having lunch with lawyers they knew in the outside world. I'm sure I wasn't the only one in the office who'd seen the new poll. I attributed Becky's concern to that.

But she said. "The trouble with Tommy is—?" prompting me to complete the sentence that had been interrupted by the ringing of the telephone.

"The trouble with Tommy is he's modeled himself on Austin," I said tiredly, my enthusiasm for rehashing the case at a low ebb. "The most worldly man on the planet. Everything's an amusement for him. I need to break through that to the pain if I have any hope of convincing a jury that this boy's been hurt."

"Maybe—this would be tougher, but maybe what you could show them is how deadened Tommy's been made by this, how all his reactions now are inappropriate. I'm sure you could get psychiatric testimony to that effect. What always strikes me about that little boy is how empty the whole rest of his life is going to be. That's just as frightening as him crying all the time, isn't it?"

"Maybe," I said.

"Let me talk to him this afternoon." Becky was leaning toward me. If I were an energy vampire, if I could absorb her enthusiasm, I could lift myself out of this paralysis. But I intended only to deflate her.

"Becky," I said, "I think I can take it from here by myself."

She looked at me as if she couldn't think what I meant by "it." "This really isn't a two-person prosecution," I elaborated. "I appreciate all your work on it, but I won't need a second chair at trial."

I expected her to think I wanted only to grab for myself whatever glory was to be had. I was prepared for her to think that. But if she had thought that, she wouldn't have argued. She would have just left, offended.

"You'll need me," she said.

"It's best if I do it alone."

She sat there. I hadn't the heart to dismiss her, but that was the effect of my silence. We'd grown closer while working on the case, but I was still the boss. In a moment, when I had the energy, I'd stand up, and the interview would be over. Becky understood. Her shoulders hunched inward, as if she were lowering her center of gravity, anchoring herself in the chair, defying me to pull her out of it.

"I know why," she said.

"There's no why, it's just—"

"You think it would be bad for my career to be associated with you so publicly if this turns out to be your last case. You think I need to pull back in case Leo Mendoza wins the election."

"As it looks like he's going to," I said.

"You don't think I'd stay here anyway if he wins, do you?"

I smiled slightly in gratitude. "That's nice to say, Becky, but it's tough out there in the real world. There's a recession going on. Some of the big firms are laying off lawyers, not hiring new ones."

"It doesn't matter, I wouldn't work here," she said. "I've heard what this place would be like without you. Having to worry about who you're dealing with, whether he's connected, having to make better offers to lawyers who helped out Leo in the campaign."

"That's just talk," I said. "There's always talk like that. This place is a machine, it runs itself, no matter who's at the top."

"No," Becky said, with some ferocity. She still had her head lowered slightly. Her determined air made her look even younger than she was, but that didn't make the determination ring false. On the contrary, she looked young enough never to have been disappointed, to believe that what she thought must happen would happen. "I was here before you came," she said. "I saw who got promoted, and why. You had to hang out with the section chiefs after work and go to meetings for causes the boss believed in. What you did in the courtroom didn't matter so much."

Becky was probably right that the character of the office would change if Leo was elected. Leo wasn't a bad man, I didn't suspect him of harboring one evil intention. But he believed in the system of favors and personal loyalty. If he did win the election it would be because he'd been faithful to that system. He wouldn't forget the favors. That wouldn't make much difference in the day-to-day running of the office, though. As Eliot had said, murderers don't wield much influence. Any district attorney has to go after criminals as hard as he can.

"I'd never have made first chair under the old system," Becky continued. "And I won't go back to it after I've seen how the office should be run."

Her loyalty was flattering. But I felt the lure of private life. It would be so easy to let go, just give up the office gracefully. Give up the hard decisions and the badgering by citizens, the phone calls from angry cops, the endless stupid meetings with other public officials. I'd been curious about what it was like to run the district attorney's office, I'd found out, and it stunk. It would be a relief to let go.

Before Becky's comments I couldn't remember the last time I'd been praised for my job performance. Criticism was the only constant. No one was ever satisfied with the results that emerged from the criminal courts. I didn't blame them, I wasn't satisfied either. True justice was a possibility so faint that it wasn't even a day-to-day goal. Every day was a compromise. I was tired of compromise, deathly tired of the burdens of the office.

"All right," I said to Becky. "It's your head. But you know, there's a good possibility we could lose the trial *and* the election. Then your prospects would really be dim."

"We can't lose the trial," Becky protested. Quickly she realized I might question her priorities, and added, *"Or* the election."

"Trials like this—" I began instructively.

I was discussing reality, but Becky—she *was* as naïve as I'd suspected—was telling me what *had* to happen. She interrupted me. "He can't get away with what he's done to these children. We can't let him go on doing it."

I hadn't realized she was so caught up in the facts. I hadn't see Becky evince that much sympathy for the children, and when we'd talked about the case we'd talked about the practical aspects of it. I'd forgotten what had impressed me about Becky to begin with: her passion for the victim.

She was no longer sunken into herself. She was leaning slightly forward, eyes shining. I'm sure that would have disturbed her; I'd seen Becky make efforts to look as blasé as the rest of us. But she couldn't pull that off. She could have been one of the child victims herself.

I gestured toward my office door. Becky took it for dismissal and stood up. But, "Do you think," I asked her, "if we barricaded that door and locked the windows I could stay here even after January?"

Because I *wasn't* ready to let it go. To hell with private life. I *liked* making the decisions. No one could run that office better than I could. The compromises hurt me, the injustices gnawed at me. I didn't want to see the place taken over by someone who could take them in stride.

"We'll try it if we have to." Becky smiled.

At least I sent her on her way more cheerily. I was left looking around my office with a premature case of nostalgia.

10

I APPRECIATE THAT, SIR. I HOPE YOU CAN APPRECIATE *my* position as well. I can't—"

I felt like a shnook for having called him "sir," but it certainly wasn't a discussion between friends.

"You may be right," I inserted into a lull in his speech, waited for him to interrupt me with the inevitable assertion that he *was* right, and continued, "But that's not for me to say. That's going to be up to a jury."

"Don't give me that," my phone caller said. "You know more than any jury will know. *You* decide who to prosecute."

I let him go on haranguing me. I was polite. I was deferential. But finally I felt compelled to ask, "May I ask, sir, what your interest in the case is?"

After a moment I put my hand over the mouthpiece of the phone and whispered, "He's just interested in justice." Becky smiled.

"I'll give that a lot of thought," I finally said, sounding painfully sincere, I thought. It wasn't my tone that convinced him, though, it was my caller's assurance of his own importance. He couldn't be ignored.

"That was the mayor," I said after I hung up. Becky raised her eyebrows. "He'd appreciate it if I could postpone Austin Paley's trial long enough for more investigation."

It had been my first conversation of any substance with the mayor of San Antonio. Theoretically he had no influence over my decisions. He was city, I was county; he oversaw city departments, I prosecuted criminals: our functions didn't overlap. But the mayor's real authority derived from being the acknowledged local leader of my political party. That gave him control over campaign funds, endorsements, any number of tidbits he could throw to local officeholders.

I stared at the phone. "I swear, the last few days politicians have been swarming over me like I'd stepped in an antbed. I've never known a man with so many friends."

"You were his friend, too," Becky said.

I didn't deny it. "But I wouldn't do this kind of thing for him. What are they all so worried about?"

She shrugged. If I couldn't answer that question, Becky certainly couldn't. "Are you thinking about agreeing to a continuance?" she asked quietly.

"Of course not. If you and I don't try it next week, nobody ever will. Don't they think I know that?"

"This is a lot of—pressure," Becky said carefully.

I shrugged. "What are they going to do to me?"

Becky wasn't that naïve, even as uninterested in politics as she seemed to be. It wasn't a question of what local leaders could do *to* me; it was what they could refuse to do *for* me, in the closing days of a campaign I was beginning to lose. They were starting to make me feel pigheaded. Maybe there was something to Austin's claim of innocence, when it was supported by so many people. Maybe I should accede to their demands, or at least appear to do so: delay the trial, win back my campaign support, have a chance of retaining my office. Then I'd have four more years in which to decide whether to prosecute Austin.

But being pigheaded was not entirely a bad feeling. Having a host of politicians arrayed against me tended to make me think I was right.

"Well, I've got to get out of here anyway," I said. "Ugly duty calls."

"I'd like to go with you,' Becky said.

I frowned at her. "You're kidding."

"You must have had something better to do than this," I said to her half an hour later.

"No," she said quickly, then realized the answer was something of an embarrassment to her. "Insider politics," she added, "it should be fascinating."

I made a noise. She felt comfortable enough with me to be sarcastic, and by now I knew her well enough to recognize it. Becky and I had grown quite accidentally close in the last month or so. As my life outside the case fell away in large chunks I found myself talking to her more. Our intense trial preparation meant there were days when we saw almost no one but each other, when we ate all our meals together. Though she was still making appearances in her regular court, Becky had turned over most of her responsibilities to the other two prosecutors there. I knew, from things she didn't say, from seeing her in the halls when she didn't know I was watching, that our isolation was telling on her, too. She felt set apart, even from other people in the office. We'd imposed such tight secrecy on our case that we could talk to no one but each other. Inevitably, during little breaks, over sandwiches, we'd talked about things other than the case, as well. She'd seen Linda definitively walk out of my life, and I hadn't seen anyone else *in* Becky's life.

"Why don't you call up that guy"—I'd almost said boy—"Donny and do something with him? Surely—"

"You don't intrude on Donny," Becky said, "you wait for him to come to you." Her tone was so neutral, almost amused, she seemed to be reciting a poem she'd learned through hours of repetition. "And please," she added in a more lively voice, "if you ever meet him, don't call him Donny. That's our little secret. He goes by Don now."

"Did you consciously deepen your voice when you said that, or—?"

"That's how you say the name," Becky said, lowering her chin toward her neck to say it deeply again: "Don."

"That's how the announcer will say it when introducing our next governor," I suggested.

"Oh, Donny'd never have anything to do with politics," Becky said quickly. "He—"

And stopped abruptly. She'd embarrassed herself again. Actually I was flattered that she'd forgotten she was in the company of a politician. To cover her discomfiture I said, "You're not afraid to call him because you don't want to appear forward or something stupid like that, is it? Because let me tell you, guys love that. Smart ones, anyway. Every girl who ever pursued me, I fell in love with."

Becky grinned at "every." These lawyers, you can't slip one word by them. "The whole crowd, huh?" she said mockingly.

I grew lost in thought. Literally lost: it took me minutes to find my way out. When I did I realized Becky had fallen silent for that long too. I was embarrassed at brooding in front of her.

"This will be humiliating," I said, pulling into the brewery parking lot. The lot should have been filled. It wasn't half so. This was my big fund-raiser, the last gasp of my campaign. There'd be at least a small crowd here no matter what. Lawyers hedging their bets in case I did stage a come-from-behind win; other candidates using my event to make appearances of their own; small contributors not enough in the know to have heard what a political pariah I'd become. From the looks of the parking lot there were few of those.

Becky was staring at the low blocky building, looking far away in the gloom of twilight. "You should let people know," she said quietly, "about what they're doing to you on this case. About the calls you're getting and the pressure you've had to resist. If people knew what you're fighting on this case—"

"It probably wouldn't matter."

We stepped out of the car. The interior lights illuminated our bodies briefly but our heads were shadowed. Becky must have liked it that way. "Can I tell you something?" she asked.

"Sure." I closed the car door and started walking. She caught up and stopped me. She didn't want to say it on the fly.

"You know, you give the impression of playing no politics and no favorites, and that's how the office seemed to run," she said hurriedly, "but I was never close enough to know if it was true. I figured you had to do the crummy little things that politicians do to keep their jobs. We all figured that. But now I have gotten close enough. And I know it hasn't been just an act. You know I'm not political at all, I try hard to avoid all that stuff, but I've been telling everyone I know to vote for you. I'll bet everyone who really knows you is doing the same thing. Maybe if—"

"Becky," I said, feeling rather pained and flattered at the same time, "thank you. But let me tell *you* something. Don't have heroes. Heroes are bad for you."

"I didn't say you were my hero," she said snippily.

162

"Good. Because there aren't any heroes."

The impetus for my speech had been the sight of someone going in the doorway we were approaching. He'd reminded me of someone. Someone who wouldn't be here.

But he was. "Eliot!" I said happily. It *had* been him. And in spite of what I'd said to Becky, I was delighted to see him. He clasped my arms warmly. "It's great of you to come. Hello, Mamie." Eliot's wife of about forty years was standing back just a step or two from our reunion, wearing the hat she'd worn to every political function I'd ever seen them at. I'd have recognized the hat if it had come on its own. Mamie beamed at me. She looked so much like my grandmother that I felt myself shrinking to the size of an eight-year-old boy.

There was a crowd of fifty or sixty people, enough to stave off absolute political embarrassment. There were quite a few other candidates, desperately looking for civilians to gladhand. In this crowd of insiders Eliot drew more favorable attention than I did. I would have had to wait my turn if he hadn't drawn me aside. I wasn't going to take this public occasion to ask him what I was curious about, I just wanted to tell him I was glad he'd come. Eliot Quinn's appearance at my rally carried some weight. Not enough, unfortunately, but that made his coming even nicer.

He cut off my expressions of gratitude. "How bad has it gotten?" he asked.

"Worse than I expected," I said jokingly. The way I towered over my old boss embarrassed me, like a gawdy bid for attention. I lowered my head toward him.

"Are they being subtle about it, or have they come right out and threatened what they'll do to you if you prosecute Austin?" Eliot asked. He sounded as if he were joking, too, and anyone seeing us from across the room would have thought he was, from his smile, but his eyes were dead serious.

"Increasingly less subtle," I said. These men were Eliot's old friends. He knew them, even if he wasn't in active conspiracy with them. So I asked, "Haven't these people bothered to learn anything about me? Don't they know the best way to ensure I'll prosecute Austin Paley is to tell me I can't?"

Eliot smiled slightly, rather wistfully. He must have been thinking of the years when he'd shared power with these old pols, when he'd had to deal with them, help them out or seek their help.

"These men don't think that subtly," he said. "They're used to telling people what to do and having it done."

"What are they afraid of, Eliot? Because this is starting to sound like fear, not like favors for a friend. What does Austin have on everyone?"

"I wish I could tell you, Mark. If I find out, I will."

We stood quietly. I wanted to believe that Eliot didn't know. Eliot had a lifetime's experience of reading people. He knew I *didn't* believe, not quite.

I made my speech, the audience applauded politely and immediately headed for the doors. Becky was waiting for me when I'd shaken the last hand. We drove back to the Justice Center in silence that seemed to be imposed by the night. It was after eight, our end of downtown was cleared out. Anyone on the street had nowhere at all to go.

"Mark?"

"I'm okay." The failed rally had made me mournful, but I didn't feel like sharing the reasons with anyone.

I found Becky's car and saw her safely into it, then drove away as if I had somewhere to go, but instead found a parking space of my own.

The Justice Center loomed bulky and ugly, almost as wide as it was tall, a plaid block. The soft light that made the old courthouse next door look romantic didn't soften the hard edges of the new building. I didn't stop to gaze on it fondly, I just went in. The corridor was dark. A few of my ambitious assistants would have worked late, but not this late. The elevator seemed to lift off with a groan, protesting that it was off duty.

The DA's offices were empty, I was thankful to find. There were enough lights to find my way to my office; I didn't light more. Once the door closed behind me I began breathing more deeply, the way a man does who is happy to be home after a weary day.

No thoughts. The site did away with thinking about my life. That's why I'd come. The papers were already laid out on my desk. I didn't have to look for a thing. I sat down and put hands on them and my personal life went away. I wanted only to immerse myself in the abstract problems of the case. I checked the indictment for the thousandth time, making sure Austin's victimization of Tommy was set out with sufficient exactness. I let the picture of the act described in the document form in my mind, filling in details, hoping the scene would be as vivid for the jury.

My thoughts returned to Tommy instead. He scared me. I wasn't sure what the jury would think of him: a boy mature beyond his age, calm as he told his tale, with that little twist to his mouth. A miniature Austin Paley, in fact.

David flashed across my mind. Tommy'd reacted to his father's distance by seeking love elsewhere. David had reacted by giving up on it, settling for a loveless marriage. I didn't want to feel responsible for him—he was a grown man—but I was. I always would be, no matter how old he grew.

Night had stolen over the city, cool and dark, and over these offices as well, because I hadn't turned on any lights. I wanted dimness, quiet. I wanted sleep, but I knew sleep wouldn't come tonight.

I could no longer keep my mind on the case. In the lonely dark the shambles of my personal life seemed to surround me. Linda and I would never recover. She had started to put together a life free of our differences. I wondered if it would take as long to see her without pain as the years we'd been together.

My family had dissolved in my wake, as well. David and I might develop an uneasy truce, but anything warmer seemed unlikely. Lois had quite rightly made a new life for herself. Dinah had given up her endearing efforts to keep me close. The most recent weekend I'd kept her what she'd talked about was school, which obliquely meant boys. Now a veteran of three dates with two different boys, Dinah was eagerly examining the future, not brooding over the past where I lay. I would never figure very prominently in her thoughts again.

Even old friends like Eliot had grown distant. There was no one I trusted any more.

Which left nothing. No human heart held me first. There was no one to whom I'd be the first person to run, with good news or tragedy. I didn't know where *I* would go, for a celebration or commiseration.

I found myself outside on the tiny fifth-floor balcony, where I was arrested by the rising of the moon. It rode a hand's breadth above the horizon, low and huge and orange, its color diffused beyond its outline, as if colored by a young child. It rose in flame like a phoenix. I stood and watched. The moon was not quite full, which made it look lopsided, tilted like the head of a questioning person. I forgot it for a few minutes and when I looked again there was a different moon, smaller and tightly contained and dead white. I remembered nights in my youth when the full moon called me outside, called me away, told me other people, women, were staring up at that same moon that warmed the night, dreaming of a man like me. The world was full of romance and I could be part of any one I could find. I had limitless possibilities. The moon of my youth was close enough for me to mount and ride.

But this wasn't that moon. This was a cold stone that blocked the stars.

I was quite self-consciously aware of my mood. After a while it grew almost laughable. But I wasn't ready to be amused. What I did achieve was a certain coldness of my own. I could be hard as stone, too. If all I had left was my work, I would throw myself into it. I would be the finest prosecutor this world had seen. If I had only one case left to prosecute, I'd prosecute it in a way people would talk about for years.

I returned to my office and stood at the desk, trying to decide whether to gather up the case file or go home completely alone, when I heard steps in the outer office.

My first thought was that I was all alone, and Austin Paley was a desperate man. But I had nowhere to retreat. The steps began slowing before they reached my door, as if the walker had faltered in his resolution.

But the door flew open, banging back against the wall, startling me even though I'd been expecting it. The visitor stopped in the doorway, where dim light rendered her a charcoal sketch. "I knew it," she said.

It took me a long moment to recognize her. I was expecting someone more ominous, and at first she did look ominous, with her face shadowed. She looked tall and slender and the slow way she moved spoke of purpose. She came toward me, adding, "I didn't even have to follow you, I knew this was where you'd come."

"Becky," I said. "This is a surprise."

"Not yet," she said. She walked straight up to me. In her heels she was tall enough to put her palms on my cheeks and pull my face down only slightly, to reach hers. But her lips didn't quite hit mine, she had to slide them an inch or so across my face before our mouths met. Mine was already open from surprise. Becky's was open too, with a purposefulness I'd only seen in her when pursuing a prosecution. I bent to her willingly, put my arms around her automatically. Her hands stayed on my face, then slipped to my neck, my shoulders.

Becky drew back from me as if to make certain I knew who she was. The night's light through my windows illumined the side of her face. By moonlight she looked untouched, skin as smooth as a child's. I wanted to put my palm on her cheek, just to feel something so warm and soft. Becky no longer looked sinister. In the gentle light she looked completely guileless.

We kissed again. Her lips were softer than the first time. But there was determination behind them. Her teeth lightly clenched on my lower lip. I could feel her individual fingers on my shoulders.

After a long time she drew back. "This has crossed your mind, hasn't it?"

She talked tough, but she was too close to me for disguise. I could feel her trembling. She'd really had to work her nerve up to come here.

"My God," I said, "are you real? You're like something I conjured out of the moon, because I needed you so bad."

Her face lit up as if she were indeed moon-wrought. She stepped into me and we encircled each other with our arms. The hug was better than the kiss, because it wasn't startling and it covered more ground. It warmed me. I hadn't realized how chilled I'd grown in the lonely dark.

We held each other until it began to feel awkward to stand so still. Her fingers moved softly, making me suddenly sad, because they forced thinking on me, driving away the lovely thoughtless reveling in sensations we'd had for a minute or two.

I desired her the way anyone desires sweet young flesh, firm and yielding, that can be molded into any shape desire asks. I felt her mind, too, the way we'd come to know each other without meaning to, so that she'd known where I'd gone and what I was feeling. She'd felt the same, I knew, consumed with one passion that seemed like another, because it had to fill all the empty spaces in her life.

But there was a gulf between us of years and of experience, and of authority. I knew that if I followed the flow of this lonely, inviting night, by the next day I'd feel I had taken advantage of her, because I hadn't thought of her this way until I needed someone and she was the closest person.

I was still holding her. "Damn," she said against my neck, quietly and emphatically, telling me in one word that she knew me as well as I knew her, that she knew exactly what I was thinking, and how I regarded her.

"It's not that way," she said, looking up. "I was thinking about it long before tonight. Look." She pointed at what she'd set down on the table beside my couch. "I brought a bottle of wine. It's been in my desk for a week. I thought some night after we'd worked late . . ."

She had broken our contact with the gesture, and I kept it broken by stepping back, subtly, I hoped.

"Becky, I'm very flattered, and I'm enormously attracted to you, but I can't take the chance, because I need your help more than I need—the comfort you want to give me."

She laughed softly, derisively, at my word choice. She looked flushed, but in laughing she was recovering herself. When she spoke she sounded very sure of herself, but she had folded her arms across her chest self-possessively, acknowledging that our contact was over. "Why can't we have both?"

I spoke flatly, looking at her, not being evasive. "I put you on this case because I could trust you, because you were a nobody. Everybody I trusted had failed me. If I sleep with you now you'll be connected to me, you'll have an in. I won't be able to trust you any more."

Her expression grew concerned. "Is that how things work in your world?" she asked.

"It is lately."

But this wasn't true. This wasn't my reason. The main reason, probably, was that I was an idiot. I had no doubt I'd regret rejecting what Becky offered. But I'd have regrets either way. I'd feel deceitful if I let her close to me, because as lonely as I'd been, Becky hadn't crossed my mind. I'd be using her. And some day when we inevitably broke apart, she'd find that I had wasted part of her precious youth. Worse, she might end up the way I was now, with only work to sustain her. And if she didn't hate me for that, I'd hate myself.

There'd been a few moments of silence. Becky was looking up toward the ceiling, hugging herself. "Can I just creep back

out under cover of darkness and we pretend I was never here?"
she asked. The jaunty tone she sought sounded more like her
voice was on the edge of breaking.

I took her hand. "I'm glad you came," I said. "I do need you.
This case is giving me fits. You're the only one I can talk to
about it. Be my partner."

I said the last sentence quietly, and as quietly she answered,
"Okay." I walked across the office and turned on a light. Becky
still looked beautiful. She was wearing a dress, not a fancy one,
but not one of the suits I was used to, either. She probably felt
uncomfortable. And I was probably selfish to keep her there,
but I did want her. I did want to talk. And as soon as we began,
as soon as I drew her attention to the papers on my desk and
took up the conversation we'd broken off that afternoon, Becky
lost her self-consciousness and immersed herself in argument.
She even, as she reached for a notepad, brushed my arm with
hers without seeming to notice. We were such lawyers, it was
embarrassing when I thought about it later. Romance is a nice
little diversion, but a case is a case.

"Just ask the question," Becky was saying animatedly. "We
can't lose. If the defense objects, they've told the jury the answer. If they let us get into it, explore his romantic history. The
jury will be interested, I guarantee. A forty-three-year-old man
with no serious involvement with an adult woman, ever?"

"Maybe he'll show up at trial with a girl friend," I suggested.

"If he does we'll call *her* as a witness," Becky said eagerly.

I laughed, touched her hand without thinking, then turned
quickly away before she could react. We'd made a pot of coffee.
The cup I poured was the last of it. Becky's unopened bottle of
wine still stood on the end table, a reproach to our seriousness.

The truth was, I was more attracted to her during our brain-
storming session than I'd been when holding her. It reminded
me of old times with Linda. I wanted to touch Becky more
intimately, to ask if her offer was revivable. Only my strict self-
discipline stopped me. That and that I would have looked like
an idiot.

"We have to talk," Austin Paley said on the phone.

"Fine. Your lawyer's office? Or mine?"

"No. This has to be very private." He spoke quietly, even
furtively, utterly without his usual offhand air.

169

Then he surprised me by giving me directions to an address I'd never been, in a south side neighborhood I might have trouble finding. "What's this place?" I asked.

"It's just a house, that no one else knows."

"Austin. Tell me why I should come."

The line was silent for several seconds. Austin seemed to be fading from me. "Mark, do you really think I'll have a gunman waiting for you? Or a naked whore? Tell your assistant where you've gone, or anyone else you trust. But don't let it go any further. And come alone."

"You haven't told me why I should."

"Because you want to know the truth," he said.

As always, leaving the courthouse during daylight hours was a guilty pleasure. The courthouse is my home, more than any other building of my life, but my responsibilities there are constant. I drove away with the thrill of a boy skipping school. That Wednesday the weather had finally turned, south Texas's version of autumn at last appearing. The air hadn't lost its morning chill, but the sun was warm. By afternoon it would feel like summer in a normal climate. The kind of weather in which kids wore sweaters to school, then left them lying in tangles on the playground.

I got turned around trying to find the house, in a tangle of streets such as seems peculiarly indigenous to San Antonio, where a street would change names at the end of a block, or run parallel to another street for blocks only to meet it perpendicularly. Dead ends abounded. One of those dead ends turned out to be my destination, a narrow street so short it held only eight houses, four on each side. My address was one near the closed end of the street, a tiny woodframe house with a sagging porch the size of a welcome mat. The house was no better kept than the ones around it. It needed paint; the windows were so dirty they were obscured without being curtained.

I assumed this was one of Austin's many hideaways, the lairs he'd scattered around town as child traps. I couldn't picture him in it.

But he was. Before I could knock the door was pulled open, jerkily, because it dragged on the floor. There was Austin, looking as I'd never seen him: underdressed. He wore slacks, an open-necked yellow shirt, and brown loafers without socks. Yellow wasn't a good color for Austin. His skin seemed to absorb it, making him look sickly. Even his smile wasn't as hearty as I'd always known it. His manner was a diminished version of itself.

"Mark. Come in. Please excuse the dreadful surroundings. Don't touch anything, you'd catch a disease."

He didn't offer to shake hands, but otherwise he was hostly, ushering me into a dim living room made smaller by a clutter of old-fashioned furniture, scratchy love seat, wooden-armed chairs with doilies. We had left daylight behind. Inside the little parlor it could have been midnight. Austin turned on a floor lamp, which accented his paleness.

It didn't cross my mind that Austin might actually be sick or scared. I had grown used to thinking of his life as a facade. This was only a new facade for a new situation. I was impressed, though, at being given a peek behind his veil, even if all I glimpsed was another veil.

Austin was more solemn than I had ever seen him. "Let's speak quickly," he said. "I know you don't want to be here any longer than you have to be. But Mark. Promise me you'll keep an open mind. I tell you this not just because I need your help, but because I'm tired of carrying it alone. So listen, please. Even if you decide not to give me the time I need, promise you'll look into what I'm about to tell you. Something has to be done."

I nodded skeptically. Austin leaned forward and began talking in a rapid voice. He rubbed his hands together as he spoke, rubbing each finger in turn as if desperately trying to get warm, or clean. His story quickly became familiar.

"About four years ago a man named George Pendrake had plans to build an office tower. With shops on the ground floor, a bank, fountain. Beautiful little white model of the place he had. He schlepped that thing all over town, trying to interest backers. He found the land—close to here, as a matter of fact. Poor neighborhood, but close to downtown. George's center could have revived the whole area. That's what he said. He raised the money fairly quickly."

"From you among others?" I asked.

"No." Austin shook his head ruefully. "He didn't need as small an investor as me. The project went ahead very quickly. Pendrake got the permits he needed with amazingly little trouble. The lot he wanted was vacant, the county condemned it and sold it to him for virtually nothing. Construction began.

"Then everything went bust," Austin said—sadly, as if he *had* been afflicted personally by the loss. "The recession finally reached San Antonio, money dried up, construction costs began to overrun as they always do. Some people claim George Pendrake had underfinanced the place from the beginning, by siphoning off too much of the money he'd raised, but it doesn't matter, he went broke too. His creditors forced him toward bankruptcy. Which isn't a disgrace at all these days, it's a normal business move you pick up and go on from, but in this case George and his friends fought like hell to keep that from happening."

"Because?" I asked. Austin looked at me hopefully, glad of my attention.

"Because if Pendrake Plaza had been forced into bankruptcy, a receiver would have been appointed to untangle the debts and the assets and which of the partners owed what. And Pendrake had secret investors who didn't want their names coming to light."

"I know this story," I told Austin. "Pete Jonas resigned his county commissioner post. Alice Sylvester was defeated in the next city council elections."

"You know some of it," Austin said. "The fact is, Pete and Alice weren't even in as deeply as several others. I felt sorry for Alice especially. She was barely involved, but she went down. She had a future, too."

"So you did know about the project," I said.

"Not yet, I didn't. I'm sorry, I'm getting ahead of my story. At this point I was going my own merry way. But nobody knew anything yet, except the people on the inside."

"Politicians who'd helped smooth the way for Pendrake because he'd cut them in for shares of the profits on the tower," I said. "And they didn't want it leaking out in bankruptcy proceedings because it made them look sleazy."

I was surprised that Austin didn't protest such a judgmental word, because I had a feeling the secret investors we were discussing were going to turn out to be Austin's friends, the people who'd been pressuring me to forego prosecuting him.

"But then hope gleamed," he continued. "Pendrake found another speculator, someone from Houston, who'd buy the unfinished project. Nobody'd make any money, but they could all get out from under. You could almost hear the sighs of relief.

"But the buyer had a condition. He'd only buy the tower if he could also buy the property adjacent to it, which would give him access to the expressway. He said the project was a loser without that adjacent property included.

"But no problem." Austin smiled. "The city owned the adjacent property. The same people who'd cut through the red tape to obtain building permits for George could help the new buyer buy the adjoining land too. Because the city owned it and they *were* the city. But they ran into a hitch."

"Because there was a community center on the adjacent property," I said.

Austin grimaced. "A lousy community center. Ever see it? One little wooden building, one story and a basement, a couple of meeting rooms not much bigger than this living room, no use to anybody. Basketball court with the hoops perpetually in ruins. Nobody used the place. It would have been no loss to the neighborhood."

"But."

"But there was a technical problem. The land had been willed to the city, with a clause requiring the city to build and maintain a community center on the property. If the community center were ever removed, or if the city tried to sell the property to a private owner, the property would revert to the grantor's alternate heirs."

Austin paused, kindly, but, also kindly, didn't ask. "I'm keeping up," I volunteered. "I remember these terms from law school. It comes back to you."

Austin smiled. "Yes," he said. And returned to his story. "But again, no problem. The heirs would have been glad to sell. They'd love to inherit this land out of the blue and have a buyer all ready to take it off their hands. But there were too many threads, you see. The city couldn't sell while the community center stood on the property, and the heirs couldn't sell either. The buyer was on the verge of saying it was too complicated and walking away. Too many inquiries had been made, word was starting to leak out that this little tract was important to somebody important. The community activists got into the act and started trying to force a referendum to vote on a bond issue to improve the community center. The investors were getting frantic."

"That's when they turned to you," I said.

Austin shook his head. "They didn't need a lawyer. They already knew the legal problems. They needed an *extra*legal solution. So one night—"

"One night the community center burned to the ground," I said.

"Everybody knows that part, don't they?" Austin said.

Yes, that was the event that had nudged the scandal into the light. The fire had obviously been arson, though no one ever determined who had given the order. Pendrake Plaza's corrupt foundation couldn't bear its weight any more. The project collapsed under public scrutiny. A couple of the secret investors were uncovered; but not, as I'd now been told by both Eliot Quinn and Austin, all of them.

"Why did a couple of the conspirators allow themselves to be exposed without exposing all the rest, too?" I asked. "It seems overly noble."

Austin had gradually stripped himself of mannerisms. He'd grown calm, lost in recollection of the story. "Because there was another aspect of the story that *never* came to light," he said. "I told you, the community center had a basement. The night of the fire, it was occupied."

I blinked. I sat there picturing a family, or a crowd of children, scrambling through the dark, frantically searching for a way out through the smoke until the burning roof collapsed on them. "That's horrible," I said.

Austin nodded. "The body was discovered during the cleanup. A fire department investigator found it, and by that time the scandal had started breaking enough that he realized the news might be worth something to someone. Instead of including it in his report the way he should have, he thought he'd try to supplement his income."

"Who was he?" I asked.

Austin shook his head. That was one of the secrets he was holding. But I could find out. The inspector's identity would be a matter of public record.

"*This* was when you were brought into it," I said.

It wasn't a question. Austin nodded. "I helped smooth things away," he said. "Then we all sat tensely for weeks, waiting for someone to report that their brother or husband or father was missing. But no one ever did. Apparently it was a homeless vagrant who broke into the center to spend a warm night. Or looking for something to steal."

Which didn't diminish the crime, which was murder. Knowingly or not, the arsonist had murdered the man in the basement. Under the law of parties, so had whoever ordered the arson. It hadn't been just a financial scandal or the loss of an election that had been at stake. It had been criminal charges and the prospect of life in prison.

"Who knew?" I asked.

"The secret investors," Austin said.

I couldn't be sure who they were. Maybe some of the people who'd been calling me the last few weeks to ask for clemency for their old friend Austin Paley. But maybe the callers were just unwitting pawns of the real conspirators, doing favors for friends. There was a wide web of friends.

"The arson inspector," Austin continued, "who's now retired and living in—another state. And me."

My mind spun with the plot. I'd be able to find the fire inspector; I might be able to coerce him to talk. Doubtful: the story implicated him as well. But if I could make him think I already knew . . .

It could have been a minute that passed while I was beginning to put together a case. It may have been only seconds. I remembered who was telling me the story, and I realized how far afield we were from the case that had brought us together.

"I'm not going to bargain away the cases against you to get these people," I said. "If that's what you were hoping, I might as well leave."

He shook his head slowly. "No, Mark, you don't understand. I am innocent of the charges you've brought."

We seemed to have changed subjects. Austin's face was drawn. He was beginning to look like the portrait in Dorian Gray's attic; still handsome, but with his paint peeling off in spots.

"I've been set up," he said. "I was planning to come forward with the story I've just told you. I couldn't keep it to myself any more. That body in its anonymous grave, it was starting to haunt me, Mark. Two or three nights I even dreamed of him, standing at my door, shuffling up to my bed."

Austin shuddered. He did look like a haunted man. If he was lying he was a hell of an actor.

"You may think my conscience isn't what it should be," he said soberly, "and I'll admit I've kept some ugly secrets. That's why they trusted me to help hide this one. But not murder. I balk at that. I couldn't live with it."

So? I was thinking, still trying to hold on to the thread of the child sexual-abuse cases we had pending. Austin saw my doubt.

"I decided to break my silence," he said. "And I made the mistake of telling people. I tried to get someone to come forward with me. I didn't have enough evidence of what had happened by myself. I hoped someone else was as troubled by it as I. But they have more to lose. No one would agree to corroborate my story. One of them seemed susceptible to persuasion, though. He kept me talking until suddenly I found out I was the subject of a police investigation. That I was the prime suspect in these child abductions." He stretched a hand toward me. I remained immobile. "You see what happened, Mark. They struck first. They stalled me to keep me quiet and then they saw to it that no one would believe me when I did come forward. They've tarred me with the worst crime a man can be accused of. If I accuse *them* now, it will just look like I'm blowing smoke, trying to cover up my own guilt."

"Yes," I said.

Austin stared at me. "I swear, I've never touched a child improperly in my life. The thought is disgusting."

"So the children are lying. Every one of them."

Austin looked more sure of himself. "What's the lie? I'm sure they're telling the truth about what happened to them. Their only mistake is in identifying me. And they were led into that. A policeman or someone acting like a policeman comes to them with a photograph, in some instances long after the fact, and tells them, This is the man. You know they'd believe. They'd pick that picture out again even from a later lineup."

"Like they picked Chris Davis," I said.

"Yes." Austin was unapologetic. "That was my doing, I admit that. Once I found out what they were doing I tried to protect myself. But then Chris couldn't bring himself to go through with it. And the delay gave you time to uncover *my* deception, but not my enemies'. I know, Mark, you thought you were doing the right thing when you had me indicted. I trust you. I know you're not in with them."

When I didn't acknowledge the compliment he hurried on.

"You know how these cases are. The little girls can't identify anyone. They're no evidence against me. The boy Kevin Pollard, he's so unsure he couldn't bring himself to testify. Mark, you've had to dismiss three of your four cases. Don't you see, all the cases are weak because they're fabricated."

"But there are other cases that haven't been indicted yet."

"And so haven't been tested," Austin said quickly. "Besides, you know why there are so many. You know when police have one suspect they think they can close every open case they have even if—"

"I know."

He looked at me very openly. "Well, then?"

"What proof do you have of this community center business?"

"Not much, unfortunately," Austin admitted. "I have this." He handed me a much-folded piece of paper. "That's a copy of the original arson report, that describes finding the body. The inspector prepared it to show he was ready to file it."

The document was as Austin had described it, an official report on an official form, with a date four years ago. The box for the name of the report-maker was blank.

I didn't even have to tell Austin the slight value this had. Anyone could have obtained the blank form and filled it out.

"A person, Austin," I said patiently. "Tell me who we suspect. Who were the secret investors?"

His expression didn't flicker. He was looking at me politely, waiting for my question, as if I hadn't spoken.

"Damn it, you expect me to give you a continuance on a trial set less than a week away but you won't give me a crumb of information? Tell me."

"This is why we need the time," Austin said. Now we were a team. "You can imagine how hard this will be to uncover. But I know the guilty parties. I can trap them, perhaps even bargain with them."

"The way you break a conspiracy like this," I said, "is to make the conspirators think the conspiracy's already breaking up. Set them against each other, make each one think the others are setting him up to take the fall. That's when they start talking."

"Yes," Austin said, "and with your help that's what I intend to do."

I sat and thought. I didn't believe Austin's story. I didn't disbelieve it. There were elements of the story that made some things make sense. But there were flaws, too. I pointed one out.

"Why have I been getting all these calls from politicians speaking up for you? If they're all plotting against you—?"

Austin turned a casual hand. The question gave him no trouble. "We're negotiating. They've managed to put me in an even worse position than they're in, and they've offered to free me from the false charges in exchange for my silence. They assume that now I've seen their power I won't dare cross them. And," he continued smoothly, watching me the whole time, "not to put too fine a point on it, but I do have my supporters. Not everyone who's called you knows anything about Pendrake Plaza. Some of them are just old friends genuinely convinced of my innocence. And rightfully so." He sat with his hands folded, waiting for my next question, opening himself to interrogation.

"Tell me the name of just one of the investors," I said. "Give me a starting point." Into the ensuing silence I added, "It will enrich your credibility."

The silence continued. Just as I was about to rise, Austin said, "The mayor."

I raised my eyebrows. "Now that's odd. He called me to plead on your behalf just this week."

"That's because I've been talking to him," Austin said. "I've almost got him believing the others are going to turn on him. He wants to buy us time."

I doubted I could raise a question Austin couldn't answer. Just for practice, I tried.

"Maybe everything you say is true," I said. "Except when you were brought into the scheme. Maybe you were the one who gave the order to burn down the center."

Austin only smiled, in his old self-deprecating way. "I don't give orders. If I did, who would listen? Yes, I make suggestions occasionally. Sometimes they're even followed. But do you think with my training I would suggest a crime? This obvious and unsubtle a crime? No, I was strictly the maid on this occasion. I just tidied up."

He made sense. There was no need for Austin to have been a *secret* investor. He didn't hold public office; there'd have been nothing wrong with his participation in the project. If he'd been involved in the scheme it would have been ahead of time; he would have been a perfectly public investor. I could find that out easily enough.

I stood up. "I can't give you an answer now," I said. "You'd better assume we're still going to trial next week. But I'll start digging into this. If I find anything to corroborate the story, I'll agree to a continuance while we investigate. That's all I can tell you now."

"I'll tell you where to start," Austin said. "Eliot Quinn."

He threw me off stride, as he'd planned.

"Eliot? Was he—?"

"No," Austin said reassuringly. "Eliot wasn't in on the plot. But he knows what happened, he knows what they're trying to do to me now. That's why he tried to help me by bringing Chris Davis to you.

"Eliot knows I'm innocent. Ask him."

He returned my stare as guilelessly as a child.

PART TWO

It is the nature of man to feel as much bound by the favors they do as by those they receive.
Niccolò Machiavelli

11

"IF HE'S TELLING THE TRUTH," BECKY SAID, "THEN the children are lying."

I'd told Becky the story immediately, without giving much thought to whether I should. She was the only confidante I had. There was unresolved tension between us, but when we were working—and we were always working—it expressed itself only in a closer ability to read each other's thoughts.

She added, "And if Kevin Pollard was lying, he's the most convincing liar I've ever seen."

"I know," was all I said. Becky kept watching me as if I were slipping away from her, which in a sense I was. I was falling into the past, into a still-real world where Becky couldn't follow, where my guides were near-strangers to her, but had once been my intimates.

In confirmation that she knew what I was thinking, Becky said, "And if you go see Eliot Quinn like he told you, you can't believe anything Mr. Quinn tells you. I'm sorry, Mark, but you can't."

"I know," I said again. That was why I hadn't run to Eliot immediately after hearing Austin's story. I hated to give Eliot another chance to lie to me. I hated to think he'd use it.

"Why do we have to decide?" Becky said. "Let's just go to trial and let all this come out. See who a jury believes."

When I hesitated she continued, "I don't think a jury would believe his cockamamie story. It's too complicated."

183

"It's not designed to convince a jury. It's designed to convince me."

"And has it?" Becky asked. She sounded curious. She hadn't seen Austin, she couldn't judge his credibility. Or maybe she was curious about me.

"I don't know," I said.

A month earlier, I would have dismissed the story out of hand. Now, through Eliot's stories and the pressure I'd felt myself, I had glimpsed the furtive world of backstage politics. I believed in *it*. Whether Austin was a victim of that kind of maneuvering was another question.

"You don't have much time to get sure," Becky pointed out.

If conspirators had actually framed Austin, they'd picked a hell of a crime. The victims were children, which made it the ugliest crime of all, the one with the longest repercussions, the most pain. But child sexual abuse was also the easiest charge for an innocent man to be caught in. Because children don't know. Adults are an alien race to them. Don't we all look alike?

"Let's just forget it," I said to Becky, as if dismissing the issue.

She stood her ground. "When are you going to see him?" she asked.

"Tonight."

"Hello, Mark. Nice to see you."

A lie, born out of habitual politeness. I'd given Eliot the choice of meeting places and he'd said he'd come to my home. I think Eliot didn't want his own house tainted with the memory of the meeting we were about to have.

"Come in, Eliot. I appreciate you coming. What can I get you? I've got bourbon, club—"

"Do you have tea?" he asked. In Texas tea means iced tea; he made the request more specific. "Hot tea?"

Maybe I looked surprised. He followed me into the kitchen to explain.

"I used to be hot all the time. Well, who isn't, down here? But I must be getting old. Now as soon as the sunlight grows slanted I start feeling chilled. I understand now why all those retired Yankees move down here in the winter."

Indeed, Eliot was wearing a three-piece suit, with the vest tightly buttoned, and a hat, which he'd already removed. He looked dapper as a caricature. He had a gold watch chain dangling across his stomach atop the vest. I know Eliot. He started wearing outfits like this as a costume. He'd made himself into a portrait people embraced, of an elder statesman who hadn't quite let go the reins, who had three times the style of anyone who'd followed. Now he'd become the portrait. Dressing this way to come to our private meeting proved that. Or maybe he expected me to embrace the image too. I always had.

It was six o'clock, the cusp of afternoon and evening. The slanted sunlight was almost gone. It threw a last shaft across my balcony, at the end of the white living room. I let the room grow dim as we talked and waited for his tea water to boil. After a few minutes we crossed into the living room. Eliot carried his cup right beneath his nose, letting the steam perform a facial on him.

"My one sense that's grown stronger with age," he said.

"Well, good," I said. "I need your nose." I sat in an armchair, Eliot settled himself beside me, at right angles, in the end of the sofa. I picked up two remote controls, snapped on the TV; the red power light came on on the VCR. Eliot looked at them as if I were going to show him a modern marvel. "I never knew anyone with a better nose for who was lying than you. Would you mind watching something for me and telling me what you think? It's not long."

"Of course," Eliot said.

Darkness had fallen completely, making my living room a theater. I hit another button and the snow on the screen was replaced by a picture that took a moment to sharpen. It was a young boy, sitting in a big chair that made him look even smaller. It was Kevin Pollard. Karen Rivera's offscreen voice asked him, so kindly, to tell again what had happened to him. Kevin obliged, at first with little feeling as he described a car trip, streets he didn't know, houses disappearing. As he grew lost in the story he grew lost in time. His face changed from that of an uncomfortable but restrained little boy into that of a much younger boy, frightened by darkness and all the unknowns the darkness harbored. When the car reached its destination it was a frightening wood, of shadows and trees both like clutching fingers. Kevin would not be comforted, and the man with him grew impatient. His need was too urgent for him to keep being soft with the boy.

185

Then Kevin jerked, memories of pain and fright still real in his face. He started crying. He cried throughout the rest of the narrative, though he grew less frantic. "We drove away," he finally said. "He kept saying he was sorry. He bought me an ice cream."

I let the tape run out, stopped it, ran it back to the beginning, as if raising a club to strike again. Instead I turned off the TV, let it die in the silence. The silence built. I was staring at the dead screen. I didn't look at Eliot until I turned to snap on a lamp. He looked suddenly captured in the lamplight. His face was crumpled, as Kevin's had grown. Eliot's eyes were wet. His tea was on the coffee table, no longer steaming.

"That's one of Austin's victims," I said unnecessarily. "What do you think? Is he telling the truth?"

Eliot didn't move to wipe his eyes. "What do you want?" he asked. It was the answer to my question.

"I want to tell you another story, and see if you can tell me secondhand whether somebody's lying. You already know the story, but I just heard more of the details yesterday."

I described briefly the meeting with Austin, how Austin had looked, and then relayed to Eliot Austin's explanation of the charges against him. Eliot showed little reaction. A time or two he made a rolling gesture with his hand, telling me to get on with the story, he knew this part. "So that's how Austin became the accused," I concluded. "That's why boys like Kevin and Tommy were induced to make these accusations against him. So the boy you just saw was wrong, or lying, about who raped him."

Eliot jerked his head minutely at my verb, as if he'd argue. I waited, but he didn't.

"So tell me, Eliot. Was Austin telling me the truth?"

In the spaces between my sentences Eliot was forgetting me. His mind was far away. He made an effort to rejoin me. "About the razed community center and the body in the rubble?" he said. "Oh yes, I believe that happened. I'd heard hints. This explains them."

I was surprised. The story was true. I had a lot to do. Austin would cooperate, that was clear. If we hurried we could—

"But it's just a smokescreen," Eliot continued. "It has nothing to do with the cases against Austin."

Eliot was sharp-eyed again, watching me.

"But you tried to help him set up a substitute to take the fall for him. You tried to save him."

"Yes," Eliot said. "I'm very sorry about that. I won't lie to you again. But I still have to save Austin. I'm asking you, Mark. Let him go."

It had been a long time since Eliot was my boss. He didn't speak as if he had any residual authority over me. It was a request. I looked at him sympathetically, but that's all I did.

"Offer him probation, then," Eliot said. "I think he'd take it. He knows he needs help, he hates what he does."

He started to say more about Austin, but I interrupted. "I can't agree to anything without hearing the reason, Eliot. And I can't imagine a reason compelling enough to let him remain free."

Eliot looked at me, glanced over my head, looked back. He'd already decided what he was going to do, but he hated his decision. Finally he forced himself.

"I'm responsible for Austin," he said. "I should be on trial, not him."

"Nothing's going to come out about the old cases against Austin that never reached indictment," I said. "He certainly won't want to bring them up, and I have no reason to, either. I don't see how you'll be mentioned. These are new."

He shook his head. I shut up. Eliot knew he had to tell me or leave, and he couldn't leave.

"This is the hardest thing I've ever had to tell anyone," he finally said. "No one knows, not Mamie, not anyone."

I'd seen Eliot tell many a story. He was Irish, he always took some joy in the telling even when it was a terrible story, even when it was on himself. But in this one there wasn't a trace of pleasure. He spoke woodenly at first, doing his best to be absent while he told the story.

"My best friend in law school was Austin's father," he said. "Pendleton, his name was. Pen and I had met here at St. Mary's. We were nothing alike, I was studious and Pen was casual. He was easygoing, I was intense. So of course we became friends. Which was very flattering to me.

"Did you ever meet Pen?" Eliot asked suddenly. "No, of course not. You're not much older than Austin, are you? And Austin was just a boy when I knew his father. Sometimes—" He shook his head. His eyes were hooded, then brightened.

"Pen was something special. Everybody liked him. He'd gotten on with the professors at law school as if he'd been their friend instead of their student. My standing in school was improved just because he took up with me. Pen had money, and connections. After school he went with the oldest-money private firm, while I went into the district attorney's office.

"Now this seems like such a brief period of my life," Eliot said. He would look sharply at me, gauging me, then let his eyes slide away, almost as if forgetting I was there. "It's easy to forget it. But at the time it seemed to have such permanence. Pen and me, best friends. We'd get together and tell each other what we were discovering the world was like. I was newly married to Mamie, but Pen had married young and already had a young son. Austin," he repeated, but not for my benefit. Eliot said the name softly to himself, as if just then remembering that the story he was telling was about that young boy, or for his sake.

"At first we socialized together, Pen and his wife, Julie, and Mamie and me. We'd have dinner at least once a week. Then that stopped, abruptly, and Pen became a little hard to reach. I'd call him at the office to see if he wanted to meet for a drink and he'd be gone already, but when I'd call him at home he wasn't there, either.

"So it was no great surprise when I learned that he and Julie were divorcing. Pen and I had known each other for four years by then, I suppose I was the best friend he had, so of course I saw it through his eyes. But Mamie and I were family friends, too. His son called me Uncle Eliot."

Eliot picked up his cup of tea but didn't sip from it, just held it in his hands, as if warming them, though the cup couldn't have held much warmth by then.

"Was it a messy divorce?" I asked.

"Very. Pen had some family money, like I say. Julie had nothing, but she liked the life, and she didn't plan to work. His parents had given them the house in Olmos Park, but Julie loved it, too, and every stick of furniture in it. His parents even thought of intervening in the case to reclaim family heirlooms they'd given the couple as gifts. Of course, I was hearing all this filtered through Pen. We were having lunch often. Some days he'd come from just having met Julie and her lawyer and he'd still be red-faced, calling her the vilest names he could

188

think of. Saying he'd see that she never got a dime of his, or the boy either."

"They fought about custody?" I asked, realizing I didn't know a thing about Austin's parents. I'd assumed he came from a moneyed background, he had that air, but the air could have been as false as so much else about Austin. I also thought about myself, growing up in another part of San Antonio. I would have been about ten then, no wonder I knew nothing about all this. But Austin, five years younger, had already been the center of a legal controversy.

"They fought about everything," Eliot said. "The divorce colored all our lives for months. Mamie and I tried to stay neutral, we still met Julie, too, occasionally. If I mentioned Pen to her she would just say I didn't understand, I didn't really know Pen. Of course a bitter woman would say that, but I could have said the same thing back to her with equal justification. Some people live such compartmented lives. I realized Pen had been like that. I knew him well, and his family, but I didn't know his friends, what he did nights after he'd moved out of Julie's house."

"And so?" I asked. Eliot's eyes jerked back to me as if I'd interrupted a private conversation. There was a pause after my question, until Eliot's eyes returned to the carpet, the walls, and my blank TV screen.

"And one day," Eliot said quietly, "all the screaming stopped. Pen grew dead quiet. He tried to concentrate on his law practice again. He wouldn't talk about the divorce at all. But it was still taking its toll on him. He suddenly looked years older—meaning he looked his age. He'd always had that boyish carefreeness, but it was completely extinguished. He started looking nervous. He'd jump if you came up beside him. I kept asking him what was wrong, but he wouldn't tell me."

I was watching Eliot, waiting for him to enter the story. It was a story he'd told no one, he said, not even his wife. I hadn't gotten the impression that was because it was someone else's secret. It was a shameful story for Eliot himself. His eyes studying my carpet reinforced the thought.

He broke his brief silence. "Until one day Pen came into my office in the courthouse with no steam at all, no anger, barely enough strength to walk, it seemed. He came straight into my office and closed the door. I asked him what was wrong, but he wouldn't say anything at first. He walked completely around the room, more than once, running his hands along the walls as if judging how thick they were. I thought he had lost his mind. Maybe he had.

" 'She's going to ruin me,' he finally said. That was how he started, no greeting, no introduction. Of course I knew whom he meant. I could see he was distraught, I tried to tell him it would be okay, he'd make more money, he could remarry and have another family. . . . But Pen just shook his head and glared at me as if I were talking nonsense. 'You don't know what she's going to say,' he finally said.

"He sat in front of me and just stared at me. I asked what his lawyer thought about the latest development, and Pen said no one else knew yet, that Julie had called him, Pen, at home the night before to tell him what she was going to do if he didn't stop fighting her."

"What did she threaten?"

Eliot looked up at me. "Exactly what I asked," he said. "But Pen didn't want to answer me and I was starting to think I didn't want to hear. But finally he said, 'I need your help, Eliot.' Of course I offered to do whatever I could. 'I need to talk to Austin,' he said. 'She won't let me get near him right now. But if I can talk to Austin I can straighten this out. He won't go along with her if I can talk to him first.'

" 'Go along with what?' I asked him. He didn't want to tell me, but he saw he had to if he wanted my help. He stood up and he walked away from me and he laughed, the way a man would laugh just before he shoots himself, and he said, 'She's going to say that I sexually molested my own son.' "

"My God," I said, and Eliot said it along with me, still in his story, quoting himself.

" 'Has she gone crazy?' I asked him. Pen said he thought she had. She'd reached the point where she would say anything to get what she wanted, and this was the worst thing she could think of. Well, I agreed. Wouldn't you, Mark? Can you think of a worse thing a man could be accused of? You must remember, this was the early 1950s. We never even read about such things. I was— It made my skin crawl just to hear Pen say such a thing. All I could think was that Julie must be clinically mad. The divorce had been so bitter already, it had escalated to the point that she would do anything. You see, I didn't even get my mind around the accusation itself. It was like a thick, horrible dose of poison, you'd spit it out the instant it touched your lips. Do you understand?"

"Yes," I said, because he had to hear me say it. I was thinking of Austin.

"When Pen saw I didn't believe it for a second, it didn't even cross my mind to believe it, he was relieved, and he hurried on. He said Austin had been alone with Julie for months by this time, there was no telling what she had filled the boy's head with. No telling what he might say. I told him just to let her make the crazy accusation, no one would believe her. But Pen said he couldn't let Austin be caught in the middle. If Julie convinced the boy to lie for her, it would dog him for the rest of his life. Austin's life. Understand? He was concerned about his son. And he said he couldn't let his parents even hear such a thing. They'd never be able to look at their grandson again."

Eliot stopped talking again. When I'd first turned on the single lamp it had seemed terribly bright, but now the room had grown dim again. There was nothing to be seen through my balcony doors, just the blackness of night. Anyone could be peopling that darkness, any decade. Eliot and I were completely alone, but there seemed to be any number of ghosts just outside the ring of lamplight, an arm's length away.

"What did he convince you to do?" I asked.

I'd said it to allow Eliot to skip that part of the story where he justified what he'd done, to tell him I understood, but Eliot winced momentarily, taking it like a blow.

"To go to Austin's school," he said. "Julie had said she had already told the school authorities not to let Pen see Austin, and had probably convinced Austin to run from him, too. But I could pick up Austin from school. I was a friend of the family. I told Pen it was a bad idea, but he said he knew his son wouldn't betray him if he could only talk to him. His eyes were so tragic I didn't know what he might do if I didn't help him. He kept saying if only he could talk to the boy. So finally I agreed to help."

"How old was Austin?"

"He was six. Just six. This was November, so he'd just begun first grade. I didn't even think much about Austin himself, to tell you the truth. I was only thinking how awful it was of Julie to be using him as a gambit this way. I'd lost sight of Julie, too, by this time. I had forgotten that I'd ever known her. She had just become this horrible, calculating witch in Pen's stories. It was almost a shock to see Austin again, to see him in the flesh, just a normal-looking, handsome little boy. They brought him to me in the principal's office. I wasn't just a family friend, you see, I was an assistant district attorney. I showed them my identification. I told them there was a family crisis, which was true enough, and that I'd been sent to bring the boy home. Austin believed me, too, when they brought him in. He was glad to see me," Eliot said quietly.

"We got into my car and drove away from school and I was talking to Austin the way I always had—"

"What was he like?" I asked.

Eliot shrugged. "He was a six-year-old boy. He was quiet, polite. I'd always liked him, but he didn't occupy much of my thoughts. This was before I had children of my own, and children didn't interest me much. The best thing about Austin was that he didn't get in the way. You could take him to dinner with adults and not even know he was there. But I suppose I'd always been nice to him. I suppose he liked me."

Now the story was disturbing me as well. My eyes were following Eliot's, to the carpet, to the darkness outside.

"A few blocks from the school I stopped the car and Pen got into the back seat beside Austin. The boy didn't say a word. He didn't even greet his father. He slid to the far side of the seat, directly behind me, so I could no longer see him in the rear view mirror. I thought how horrible it was that his mother had done this to him, made him afraid of his own father. Pen just smiled and nodded to me in the mirror."

"Where did you go?"

"A motor lodge. Not a hotel, where we'd have to cross the lobby. A motel, where you could park your car right at the door of your room. Pen had already rented one. There was a string of the places along the Austin Highway then."

There still was, but now the interstate had turned the old Austin Highway into just a wide, decaying road, where the old motels advertised kitchenettes and weekly rates, or water beds and adult movies in the rooms. It was hard to picture the dreary old places when they'd been new, inviting.

"We went into the room, all three of us. Austin stayed as far from his father as possible, but he shrank from me, too. I was talking to him, quietly, telling him it was all right, but he wouldn't even look at me. Pen hadn't said a word. He'd taken off his coat and dropped it over a chair back and sat on the only bed in the room, and after a few minutes he said, 'Why don't you leave us alone now, Eliot, so Austin and I can talk?' "

"And you did," I said, after a long quiet spell.

"Austin was looking at me," Eliot said hoarsely, but he was talking in a rush now, and didn't stop to clear his throat. "He hadn't been before, he wouldn't look at either of us, but when he heard his father say I should leave, his eyes came up and latched on me so hard I could feel them, like hands. They were brimming with tears. His face was white, just white, almost transparent. My God, Mark, I looked at him and I thought—I still didn't think it was true, I couldn't think that, not of Pen— but I thought that Austin believed it. I thought, My God, the woman has hypnotized him."

"Don't tell me you walked out of the room," I said. It was jerked out of me, I hadn't meant to say it. I was thinking, *Don't tell me you left that boy alone with his father.*

"I said—" Eliot was almost mumbling, the way he must have mumbled what he'd said more than thirty-five years earlier, in that room on Austin Highway. "I said I thought I should stay, in case someone tried to make something of the story later. But Pen just smiled. He'd regained his composure so completely it was as if I'd given him a tonic. He said, 'That won't be necessary, old friend.'

"And I couldn't," Eliot continued, "I couldn't stay in that room and let him see I suspected it was true, I couldn't let him believe I suspected him of something so unnatural. He was my friend. I owed him some loyalty. I tore myself away from his son's stare and went outside. I said I'd be nearby, and I left the door ajar, but it closed behind me.

"I walked up and down outside that door, making as much noise as I could. I walked around the whole motor court, to the back window of the room, but it was just a bathroom window, frosted. It was open a fraction, and I could hear a boy crying. And heard Pen say, 'Give me a hug, son.' "

"So finally," I said, and my voice was much harsher than I'd intended.

"So I hurried around and knocked and went in. Nothing had happened, Mark, I'm sure of that. Pen had removed his tie, but he was still fully dressed other than that, and the boy still had his jacket on. There was nothing—in the air, you know what I mean. Pen just smiled at me.

"But Austin wouldn't look at me at all. He didn't run to the door when I came in. I wasn't his savior, you see. I was his kidnapper. I was one of the conspirators."

"But nothing happened," I said.

Eliot was finally looking at me. "Something very important happened. I had helped Pen demonstrate to the boy that there was nowhere Austin could hide from him. That no matter who was protecting him or whom he trusted to keep him safe, his father could always get to him again."

Eliot stopped, the confession ended. "What happened?" I asked.

He sat up straighter on the sofa. "Julie withdrew her threat. You understand why, of course."

Because she couldn't rely on her six-year-old son's testimony any more. Pendleton Paley had taken that from her, with the help of my old boss. Austin would have been too afraid to accuse his father, when he'd learned he couldn't trust anyone in the adult world to believe him or protect him.

"The divorce was settled without trial after that. Both sides grew less demanding. Everyone calmed down."

"Visitation?" I asked. I'd caught Eliot's hoarseness.

"The usual arrangement," Eliot said, staring across the room. "Every other weekend, some holidays. I heard that Julie contrived as often as possible to avoid letting Pen take him, or to see that he went to his grandparents' instead. And Pen didn't press it. But I lost touch. I didn't want— Something—" He shrugged. "The next time I saw Austin Paley was when he was graduating from college. He needed law school recommendations. I was the district attorney by then and he came to see me. You know how Austin is, always friendly, polite to a fault. He was that way to me, too, but he turned away from my handshake to look at the pictures on my wall, and just before he left he looked at me perfectly levelly and unshaken and said, 'It was true, you know.' That was all he said. And he smiled and he nodded and walked out. I gave him his recommendation, of course, and saw that he got others."

But he came to you for a recommendation, I thought. *He wouldn't let you touch him, but he used the connection.*

"And what about his father?" I asked. If Pendleton Paley were still practicing law in San Antonio I would have heard of him. Even if he'd been practicing twenty years ago, when Austin was of law school age and I was a new assistant to Eliot.

"Long dead," Eliot said. "Only a few years after the story I just told you. I saw him very seldom by then. In the back of my mind I think it was a relief to hear—"

"How?"

"By his own hand," Eliot said. An old-fashioned turn of phrase that reminded me how old Eliot was. How old the story was. "He didn't leave a note, but the fact of his suicide itself told me that my suspicion had been true."

I stood up, walked stiffly into the dimness. "Did Austin's mother get Austin some help?" I asked.

Eliot looked pained by the question. "No one went to child psychologists back then. No one specialized in treating cases like this. No one acknowledged that such things happened."

"You never talked to Austin about it," I guessed. Eliot gave me a look as if I were stupid even to ask.

"But you tried to make it up to him."

"Of course I followed his career," Eliot said. "When he graduated from law school I would have given him a job, but he never applied. He didn't try to trade on what had happened. But I did what I could for him. I introduced him to judges, saw that he got some appointments."

After Austin became a defense lawyer, Eliot, the district attorney, would have been in a position to do him any number of favors. "You helped him out," I suggested.

"Once or twice," Eliot said, "I stepped into little cases and gave him a break. It helped his confidence, early on in his career. Little cases that didn't matter to anyone."

While otherwise doing away with the favor system he'd found when he first took office, Eliot had created one favored person. It made sense now, that aura of specialness Austin Paley had always carried. I'm sure Eliot hadn't intervened for him often— I would have heard if he had—but those few little favors had contributed to Austin's sense of himself. I remembered the way he always seemed to move more slowly than everyone else. People would wait for him.

"And later on he did ask you for help."

"A time or two," Eliot repeated. "It was nothing terrible,

195

Mark. A little extra consideration when he had a special client. Just making sure the case got examined more closely."

Giving a case the kind of scrutiny few could bear. Exercising the discretion that was supposed to be for judges or juries alone.

"Until finally," I prompted.

I don't think Eliot had intended to tell me any more. He'd thought the years-old episode explained everything I was supposed to do now on the current cases. Further explanation made the story more sordid. It was in danger of turning ordinary, the old tale of favors growing bigger until the recipient owned the favor-giver.

"Finally he came to tell me he'd been arrested himself," Eliot said, after an audible intake of breath. "For indecency with a child. I think I explained to you before, we didn't—no one took those cases so seriously then as you do now. I investigated, I found the child hadn't been hurt at all. He'd been safe the whole time. It didn't amount to more than touching. I doubt we could even have gotten a conviction. But just an indictment would have ruined Austin. He came to me and cried. He wept like a baby, he swore he could control himself in the future. He was so terrified I was sure nothing like that would ever happen again.

"And he never said that I owed him. Neither of us said that I knew why he was the way he was. He didn't demand anything of me."

I hated to hear the tone that had crept into Eliot's voice. I wanted to turn away from his justifications. I didn't want to hear his implicit plea for my understanding.

Eliot probably understood how he was making me feel, or maybe he suddenly heard his own voice. "I made the case go away," he concluded simply. "I signed the dismissal myself, I didn't have anyone else do it for me."

"By the next time it happened," I said, "Austin could take care of it himself."

"He never asked me for help again," Eliot acknowledged.

This was just wrapping up, avoiding the issue, the request with which Eliot had begun his story, the reason for his confession. To understand all is to forgive all, and as district attorney I was the only person in a position to render Austin Paley concrete forgiveness.

I wondered if Eliot understood— I don't think he intended

it—that implicit in his request that I let Austin off was the understanding that by doing so I would be sparing Eliot, too. Because the story of Austin and his father would certainly be brought out at the punishment phase of trial, if we got that far. And part of the story was that the district attorney of Bexar County—Eliot hadn't been that then, but that was how everyone remembered him—even the toughest DA everyone had ever known had failed to protect the boy Austin. And as a result had derailed child-abuse cases against that grown boy during Eliot's whole subsequent tenure as district attorney. It would change the way people remembered Eliot. It had already changed the way I thought of him, and Eliot realized that, from my outburst question a few minutes earlier. He didn't offer his hand again on his way out. And I didn't make him ask again. But it was not a simple request.

"Eliot," I said. "I'll think about it."

I did, all night, with only occasional interventions of sleep. When I'd wake, I'd find myself in the middle of imaginary conversations. "What do you want me to do, Eliot? Set him loose among the children of this city, assure him he's free to do whatever he wants? I don't hate him, I don't want to see him hurt. Tell me a way to deport him off the planet and I'll do that instead."

Or I'd wake to find myself very small, a boy, alone in the endless dark, listening, on the verge of tears, holding the thin sheet so tight it was in danger of tearing.

When morning finally came I was no longer tearing at the problem. Every answer seemed wrong, but the struggle had left me. The first thing that morning, I went to see Janet McLaren.

It was the first time I had. She had always come to me before, but when I called her at home early that morning she was already gone, and when she finally called me back from her office she said she couldn't get away, but she could squeeze me in between appointments.

Her office was in a twelve-story building out on the northwest Loop, near the medical center. Coming from downtown, I felt as if I'd passed into a different world, one built decades after my own, where the problems of dirt and poverty had been done away with. But in Janet's waiting room was a young girl, five or six, dressed in jeans, with a woman close beside her who glared at me in the fraction of a second before I looked away. I walked stiffly to the receptionist's window and she let me right in. The short hallway had the clinical look of a medical doctor's office, but not the right smells. It smelled of books and paper and the pine cleaner with which the janitors had mopped the linoleum floors overnight.

I found Dr. McLaren in a slightly jumbled office where framed diplomas hung on the wall beside bright, intricate posters of plants, and the heavy, somberly bound tomes on the shelves were bookended by stuffed Eeyores and Madelines. Janet was behind the desk, behind an opened file, but her eyes were closed. She was drinking black coffee as if it had been prescribed. When she opened her eyes she smiled, faintly.

"Hello, Mark. I'm sorry we couldn't have met for breakfast, but I had to rush in this morning. Someone had a bad night."

"Looks like it was you."

"Why, thanks. A child psychiatrist should know better than to stay up late watching a dumb old movie while her patients are having nightmares and waking up crying."

"What was the movie?"

She grimaced. *"The Ghost and Mrs. Muir.* And here you are, looking rather ghostly yourself, as a matter of fact."

I dropped into a chair. "I didn't have much of a night myself."

She looked at me tenderly. "Tell me all your problems. I can give you a minute and forty-eight seconds."

So I talked quickly. "I just wanted to ask you how effective all this is." I gestured around her office. "Take Tommy. Do you think you'll be able to turn Tommy aside, help him be normal?"

She didn't even correct the word. She said, "Psychiatry isn't fortune-telling. I know I can help Tommy. I don't know how much."

"What if you hadn't already started? What if he didn't start getting treatment until years later?"

The weariness had abruptly left Janet's eyes, if not the dark smudges beneath them. "How many years?"

"A man in his forties, who was molested as a young boy, who's been molesting children himself for twenty years, maybe more?"

Janet was watching me closely, obviously fitting each new detail I gave her into a pattern in her head. She realized I wasn't being abstract.

She said slowly, "A man like that, whose whole lifetime has been built around power over children, who doesn't question his values until late in life—I don't know. If he wanted to change—"

"What if he were forced to come see you, if he didn't seek treatment voluntarily?"

She just looked at me. My interjecting the question told her I understood the importance of the detail. After a few seconds she drew a deep breath and said, "What if someone forced you into therapy to make you get over being sexually attracted to women?"

We were asking each other questions that didn't require answers, that *were* answers. I began, "But I—"

"And don't say but your orientation is normal and his is perverted, so it should be easier to change his. The sexual urge doesn't recognize convention."

"That's not what I was going to say. I was going to say I wanted to help him."

Janet looked at me the indulgent way a parent looks at a four-year-old who has offered to help fix the car. "Given what you do," she said, "the only ones you can help are the Tommys who haven't happened yet."

"You mean put this one away where he can't hurt anyone else. But suppose it *were* Tommy we were talking about? It might be, twenty years from now."

She dealt with children all day long, but childishness hadn't rubbed off on her. She was tougher than I. Janet gave me a long look that took only a second. "I'd say the same thing."

She stood up. "And that's all the time I can give you. Come back at lunch time, I'll buy you a tuna sandwich out of the machine." On her way out she squeezed my shoulder, which made me feel better for seconds after she was gone.

I thought about the task she'd given me, the only one I could perform. It was a thankless calling, being the champion of victims-yet-to-be. When I tried to picture them I pictured instead the boy Austin, alone in the dark, wondering if everyone in the house is asleep, if that small sound he hears is a footfall. His horror made unbearable because there was nowhere to turn. He couldn't run to his natural protector for shelter, because that footstep in the dark that made him shudder *was* Daddy's.

But I couldn't picture Austin *as* that boy. Emerging from that wounding helplessness, he had become a man who demanded control, whose whole character was obsessed by the need for it. I could picture the Austin I knew now in therapy, sent there as a condition of his probation: eager to learn, to confess, to change; wooing the therapist as he'd charmed everyone else in his life, but behind his tears and earnestness remaining utterly unchanged, a man who would rule others any way he could, and who viewed the entire world of children as a nation ripe for conquest.

It wasn't a question of blame. If anyone was to blame it might be Austin's father, but he probably had his own history to explain what he'd done. He was long dead, but the damage he'd done was alive in the world. Pain lives, like a radio signal continually received at farther and farther reaches, long after the transmitter has ceased operating.

I was as thoroughly sorry for Austin as I've ever been for anyone, but it wasn't in my power to help him. That he had been a victim didn't change the fact that he was a victimizer. And I was the only person who could stop him. If I didn't, if Austin managed to escape unscathed after I'd brought to bear on him all the heat I could generate, he would emerge assured of his invulnerability.

12

I OWED ELIOT A PERSONAL RESPONSE. HIS OFFICE said he was gone for the day, though it was only early afternoon. Mamie told me yes, he was underfoot at home. I told her I'd drop by.

Eliot and Mamie had lived forever in Olmos Park, an old, expensive neighborhood, but theirs was one of the least grand houses. It was rock, one story, and not rambling at all. It must have bulged at the seams when their three children were teenagers. Now it looked like a grandmother's cottage, with well-tended flower beds bordering the house and an autumn wreath on the dark varnished front door. It made Eliot look rather gnomelike when he answered the door with his vest unbuttoned and his pipe in hand.

"Come in, come in," he said, and Mamie, passing through the hall behind him, called an invitation as well.

"I've just got a minute. Could you come out instead?"

As he passed through the doorway Eliot changed. He left the pipe behind and his face closed down into watchfulness.

"I've already informed his lawyer, but I thought you should know too. We'll be going ahead with Austin's trial Monday morning."

Eliot waited. Absence of expression made his face look hard.

"I can't take the chance, Eliot. My experts say someone like Austin will never change. He'll always be a threat to children.

I can't—" *Neglect my responsibility,* I'd started to say, but I didn't want to sound critical of Eliot himself.

"He's not to blame," Eliot said softly, but he no longer sounded as if he were pleading, the way he had in my home. He sounded as if he were giving *me* my last chance. I didn't understand, but his tone stopped me from feeling apologetic. Eliot tried to continue: "He was just a boy—"

"He's not now. He's a grown man, he's responsible for what he does. It has to stop somewhere. Everybody can't be the victim in this. Somebody has to be the villain."

Eliot's voice was still quiet, and still hard. "I told you, I think with therapy—"

"Therapy wouldn't change him. He doesn't want to change, he just wants to get away with it. For as long as he wants." Eliot didn't offer any more argument. I felt suddenly deflated as I turned away. "I'm sorry, Eliot."

"I am too, Mark."

His voice stopped me. He'd known it would. I waited for his explanation. He didn't look away from me.

"I've agreed to represent him at trial," Eliot said.

If he had punched me I would have been no more immobilized. I don't know if Eliot thought he owed me more explanation or if my face demanded it. "Austin asked me and I agreed," he elaborated. "I hate to oppose you. And I hate like hell how it will look, what it might do to your reelection chances. But I owe that boy so much more.

"And there's one other thing, Mark." He had hold of my arm. "He's innocent. I wish I could show you the evidence, but . . ."

But we were on opposite sides now.

My car drove itself back to the Justice Center. In the DA's offices, I went straight to Jack Pfister's office. He and another investigator had a gin game laid out on a small typing table between their knees. When I went in, the other investigator swiveled away and became very busy with paperwork at his desk, but Jack just looked up at me, raising his eyebrows.

"Did you ever find out what happened to Chris Davis?" I asked.

"Dropped off the planet," Jack said.

Or into it. We knew of one buried body in Austin's past. He claimed not to be responsible for it, but he claimed lots of things.

"Put somebody in Tommy Algren's school," I said. "Don't wait until he gets out. I don't want him alone for a second."

"Already done," Jack said.

I gave him a look. "Why so skittish?" I asked.

"Just being careful. And I thought I'd stick with you."

"Not necessary," I said. "But thanks."

He shrugged.

"What else could he try?" I asked Becky Schirhart an hour later. I was hunched in the one uncomfortable visitor's chair in front of her desk, feeling hemmed in by her cubicle of an office. I was talking about Austin, but I was thinking about Eliot. That's how Becky answered.

She said, "He could get you so distracted with other thoughts that you won't be prepared for trial."

She was favoring me with the kind of warm personal regard one friend gives another while telling him he's being an idiot. "Did you ever see him try a case?" She shook her head. "He's the best, Becky. Everything I know about prosecution I learned from him, and I didn't learn everything *he* knows."

"But this time he's defending. And his defendant is guilty." I nodded, but Becky could see it didn't mean anything. "He's just another lawyer, Mark. Rusty at that."

"Oh, please don't let him make you think that. That's exactly how he'll act, until he sees his opening."

"Where are you going?" she asked.

"Away from here. You do, too. We're all set. Go have yourself a good weekend. Try not to think about the case."

She laughed.

"I know," I said. I touched her lightly on the arm. "See you Monday."

"Mark. Don't you want—?"

"No. Thanks."

I found my investigator in the kitchen, having a sandwich while waiting for Tommy's parents to get home and relieve him from duty. I dismissed him, but I let him take his sandwich with him. Tommy seemed glad to see him go. "What are we going to do?" he asked.

"Let's go outside," I said. "Got a football?" Tommy shook his head. We went out through French doors into the back yard. It was after five, late in October, a seasonless time of day and year. It could have been a summer morning or a winter noon. The sun had declined enough to lose its dominance. It left warmth behind but a chill was creeping in, around our ankles. A breeze encouraged it.

"Have you seen Steve lately?" I asked. Steve was a boy Tommy had mentioned, but only in the past tense. I figured they'd been friends.

My question took him by surprise, as I'd intended. "Steve? No."

"You don't see him at school?"

"We're in different classes," Tommy said.

"Maybe next year."

Tommy looked across his back yard as if it were a foreign place. There was a swing set in his line of vision, but it looked designed for a much younger child. "I'll be in middle school next year."

We talked about middle school, about the pleasure of not being trapped in one room all day. I hinted at the possibilities for change that middle school offered: different friends in different classes, different personality if you wanted. A whole new past and future every fifty minutes.

Tommy had greeted me in his little-man-host role. As we talked in the yard he turned back into himself, the self I knew, the serious boy who could talk about things to come in his life as if he'd already experienced them. I had helped give him that voice. In a few weeks we'd talked about many things—things that might happen in his life; not only about the past.

We didn't talk about the case. I wasn't there to rehearse, I was just fine-tuning the boy, his dependency on me. That's what I wanted, that's what I'd spent weeks trying to accomplish.

If Tommy was telling the truth, he was going to be twice a victim. Seduced and abandoned by Austin, seduced and to be abandoned by me. I wasn't going to spend the rest of my life being his tutor, his friend. Once the case was over he'd be on his own.

That's something prosecutors do sometimes: let the victim think he's their friend, their champion, when in fact the victim is only a necessary element of the case. I wouldn't let myself feel guilty about Tommy. He had to suffer this second victimization so there'd be no other victims.

This time, after what had happened with Kevin Pollard, I'd deliberately set out to bypass Tommy's parents. I wanted to replace them as the authority figure in Tommy's life. I'd put the full court press on Tommy—batting practices, walks in the park, talks about his life—as if to compress years of parenting into one brief month, and I'd succeeded so well that I'd been surprised by the ease of it. There was no one to replace. Tommy's father had abdicated the position years ago.

I didn't hate James Algren. I didn't even dislike him. I understood him perfectly. He was an up-and-coming man, already successful and on the verge of something even better. It didn't take imagination for me to put myself in his place. His work was important to him and he was good at it. It was effortless, compared to raising a son. I could see how easy it had been for Austin to insinuate himself into Tommy's life. I'd only followed the path Austin had blazed for me.

And I wasn't going to let Tommy slip away three days before I needed him.

"What's the matter?" I asked when we went back inside.

Tommy shrugged.

"Nervous?" I asked.

He shook his head.

"You will be," I said. "When you walk into that courtroom and see all those people. But you only need to do one thing. Look at me."

He did. "What?" he said.

"That's it. Just look at me. When you walk in the courtroom I'll stand up. Just ignore everybody else. They're nobody anyway. They're people you'll never see again. They don't know you, they won't care about you two days later. They don't matter. You just look at me. When you get on the witness stand you'll just be talking to me, the way we've always talked. Understand?"

"Yes." He started crying. He looked away from me again. "But I don't want to be there."

"It'll be okay," I said patiently. "We can go practice right now if you want. You've already sat in the chair. You'll—"

"No, no." He shook his head violently. "I mean I don't want to testify. Against Waldo. I don't want to hurt him."

That son of a bitch, I thought. He'd managed to get to him after all. How? I seemed to see Austin Paley's softly smiling face in the room with us. He was inescapable.

"When did you talk to him?" I asked gently.

"I haven't!" Tommy shouted, as if I'd accused him. "I've just been thinking about him. He never hurt me. It wasn't only his fault, what happened. I don't want to hurt him back."

Janet McLaren had warned me to expect this reaction. Austin hadn't just molested the boy, he'd mentored him. Tommy loved him. And he felt a share in the guilt for what had happened.

"Tommy." I waited until he stopped sobbing. He looked at me, scared, understanding the authority he was defying.

"It will be years before you understand how much he hurt you," I said. "I think you're starting to feel it already. You sense it, don't you? Tommy, Austin Paley didn't become your friend and then realize how much he needed to touch you. He stalked you. From the first time you saw him, he was plotting how he could get you alone and get your clothes off. Nothing that happened was your fault. Nothing. Don't let him make you think that."

"I know." Tommy wiped his eyes with the back of his hand. His face looked blurred. "I know about that part. But I still don't want to hurt him."

"And he did the same thing to other boys, too," I continued. "And girls. And some of them *were* hurt. It's not just you. There're others we have to protect. You may think he didn't hurt you, but he might hurt the next boy, very badly. We can't take that chance, can we?"

He shook his head, halfheartedly. I continued talking gently, but now more confidingly. "I like Austin too, Tom. He's been my friend for years. I don't want to hurt him, either. But it's not up to me. Or you. We don't get to decide whether what he did is a crime or not. Other people have already decided that. You and I have jobs we have to do. We can't get out of them, no matter what we think about them. There's a system for deciding these things, and we have to do what they tell us, like it or not."

What bullshit. I *am* the system. I decide whom to go after, and to what extent. I wouldn't let anyone take that decision away from me. Certainly not some damned defendant who'd managed to worm his way into his victim's heart.

"Do you understand, Tom?"

"Yes," he said. He'd stopped crying.

This was the payoff. I had to know now if I'd succeeded or failed. It hadn't just been Tommy's father I'd been struggling to supplant.

"But you can tell the system to go to hell," I said. "You can tell me, too. And I'll just have to go try to find somebody else to tell what Austin did to them."

I wished I could have seen my face. I'd given up sternness. I was trying to look brave but hurt, ready for the worst. Tommy studied me as if he could pluck out all the subtleties of expression, not only what I displayed but the intention behind it.

"No," he finally said. "I'll do it. You can count on me."

"Good boy," I said. I hugged him. It was a spontaneous gesture. I made it brief, then we went into the kitchen and made nachos out of Doritos and processed cheese spread. Tommy loved them. I stayed with him for half an hour after his parents came home. When I left I shook hands with him. He was so little I could have picked him up with one hand. I could have made him do whatever I wanted, but that way wouldn't work. He had to love me. I looked a question at him, and he nodded.

I am not a complete clod. I couldn't miss the comparison. Seeing Tommy with his father was, for me, like looking at old family pictures. Tommy was my son in miniature. His relationship with his father was mine with David in embryo. His father was too busy for him, except in bursts of baffling closeness that were more alarming to the boy than reassuring. The month I'd spent talking with Tommy, taking walks with him, ball tossing, represented just about the same amount of time I'd spent with David during his childhood.

I didn't know whether to expect David to be at home on a Friday night, but he was, and he wasn't alone. Vicky answered the door. "Well, hello," she said, more hearty than I'd ever heard her, pushing wide the door for me.

She was stunning. She was wearing a long white dress that made her fair skin look tanned, and left lots of skin to inspect: shoulders, chest, arms. Her blond hair was loose to her shoulders. She had, I'd never noticed before, a sprinkling of freckles across her nose. Earrings glittered halfway down her neck, it seemed.

"Quiet evening at home?" I asked.

She laughed. "We're going to a *ball*."

In a horse-drawn carriage that had started life as a pumpkin and six white mice, from the looks of her. "I hope you're the guest of honor, because you're going to put everybody else in the shade."

She dimpled, the final touch. "Oh, I'm not even half ready," she said. "Come on in."

I remembered that I had seen Vicky vivacious a time or two before. Usually she was reserved to the point of iciness, as if she were only enduring whatever occasion brought us together. Tonight she looked so happy she made me hopeful for the whole world.

If David had looked happy too I would have made a few minutes of small talk and gone on my way. He was in his den, sitting on the edge of the coffee table, forearms on thighs, holding a drink. The television was on and he was staring in its direction, but he didn't look as if he could have passed a pop quiz on the contents of the show.

"Look who's here," Vicky announced, in a tone of voice I knew well from my own twenty-five years of marriage. It means, *Shape up, Jack, we're not alone any more.*

"Hey, Dad," David said, sounding more puzzled than anything.

I'd never seen him in a tux before. "You look almost handsome enough to be Victoria's escort," I said. I resisted the impulse to straighten his tie and brush off his lapels.

I had to say something else to get the ball rolling. "You're going to a ball?"

David smiled abashedly. "It's for this charity we've gotten involved in."

"I've dragged him into, he means," Vicky said. "I'm sorry, I've got to finish making up or we'll never get there. I'm sorry, Mark."

I turned in time to catch the tail end of a look she'd shot past my back. She smiled at me.

"That's okay, I just dropped by for a minute."

"Offer your father a drink," Vicky called in departure.

David smiled like a little boy, the way he'd been treated, and extended his glass to me. "Just one sip," he said. "It's mine."

I shook my head. "Thanks, I just had some nachos that're still settling.

"So, going out together," I said, in the way I'd speak to an acquaintance met in a theater lobby.

"We do that sometimes," David said. You couldn't put anything past the boy, he was always too alert.

"Glad to hear it," I said. I glanced around the room as if something would give me an idea. Now I was embarrassed I'd come. "I was wondering if you might have a chance to play golf some time," I said off the top of my head.

"Not this weekend, but maybe one day next week."

I had to cough. "Well, that'll be a problem for me, since I've got this trial starting Monday. But as soon as it's over, start looking—"

"And the election," David said. He had a bemused but superior expression, because though my appearance had been a surprise, I was now perfectly following his expectations.

"Oh, the hell with the election," I said. "It's probably over already anyway. But this trial's important."

David didn't take the opportunity to share my burdens. He just nodded as if he already knew everything.

I started shuffling toward the door. "You doing okay, except for the misfortune of having to attend this ball?"

"I don't mind," he said.

"Really? You look pretty tragic about it."

"Would you rather have found me alone?" he asked.

I was close to the wide doorway leading out to the entryway. "I just dropped by, I didn't have anything in mind. I just wanted to see you." As usual, I was making my way out too quickly, fending off attack on the way. Whatever I'd wanted to accomplish, I hadn't. I stopped.

David provided a thin opening. "Why?" he asked, sounding, I'm sure, more vulnerable and hopeful than he would have wanted.

"Because I care about you, David. I love you, and I'm concerned about you. I don't dislike Vicky. But she's not my child. It's you I worry about. If you were happy I'd be happy. But every time I see you you're either alone or unhappy-looking."

"I'm fine," he insisted.

I just looked back at him. He grew angry under my gaze. He waved the hand holding the drink, sloshing it. "Do you care about what I want," he asked, "or just what you want me to be like?" I didn't answer. "I'm *happy*," he insisted.

It was only my expression he kept having to answer. "Look," he said. He waved me over, took my arm, and led me through the kitchen, out the back door onto the patio. There were two tall pecan trees in David's back yard, the shade of which had prematurely killed the grass. A scattering of leaves blew across the bare ground.

"I don't owe you an explanation," David said.

"I don't want one."

"Dad, I am happy. I have just the life I want. Maybe Vicky and I aren't in love, but we're comfortable. We don't pick at each other, we let each other go our own ways."

I was shocked. Not in love? They were too young to have fallen out of love. "But that's not marriage," I said.

David sighed. "Yes it is. It's our kind."

I continued, groping for words. "It's roommates. It's—it's business partners."

David's vulnerable look was gone. He had no trouble looking at me. "That's what I thought marriage was," he said. "People living in the same house, getting along with each other. Smiling over breakfast, then going their own ways."

I took it. I let him see I'd felt it. He looked a trifle scared, the way a boy looks who's punched his opponent and drawn blood, so he suddenly realizes how grim the fight is. I answered him quietly.

"David, you don't know. You don't have the perspective. Your mother and I were in love. My God, we were in love when we were eighteen years old, and there's no love like that. There's no *feeling* like that in this life. We couldn't—" I was struck dumb by images of Lois. Lois young. Her face, over and over, laughing, crying, gazing at me. Green fields, deep woods, the sea. Fighting to get each other's clothes off, buttons popping. Sitting beside each other silently for hours, studying, then looking up at the same moment. "You didn't exist then, David. For you to deny it now—to deny *yourself* that. You've shoved right on past life, David. Why are you in such a hurry? Where do you need to get so fast?"

"I saw you together, Dad. What good is all that wild youthful passion if it disappears so completely that you can spend a whole evening together without speaking to each other?"

"We spent half a lifetime together, David. Longer than you've been alive. Everything fades in that time. That doesn't mean there's nothing left, or that either of us regrets that time. I wouldn't give up those memories—"

"But you see," he said reasonably, "Vicky and I just came to that point sooner, easier, without any bitterness."

I stared at him, appalled. "Some day you'll be forty, David, and you'll explode."

He'd regained his composure and with it his superiority. "I don't think so," he said comfortably.

We went back inside the house, and straight on through the living room. I wasn't going to linger. It was best, when things had gone so badly, to withdraw quickly, not prolong the unpleasantness.

Wasn't that what I'd always thought?

I turned at the door. David almost bumped into me. "I'm going to be around," I told him. "You're going to find me underfoot. When you need me, let me know, okay?"

He didn't look quite so superior. I'd surprised him, which for the moment was about the best I could hope for. I hugged him, too abruptly. He was stiff as a scarecrow made of pipes.

"Tell Vicky I said goodbye," I said.

On the Saturday night of the last weekend before trial, I arrived at a house in Terrell Hills carrying a small, discreet bouquet of flowers. It was a stucco house, big and imposing, but with a friendly bay window. A circular driveway took up most of the front yard, leaving only a small, heavily landscaped plot of earth bristling with flowers hanging on against October. I stood looking at the house, thinking about driving away again.

But at that moment the front door burst open, so I had to start walking as if I'd never been standing there staring. A girl was carrying a hanging bag of clothes. She stayed in the doorway, turned back to call inside. As I drew near she turned abruptly, almost in my face, and said, "Oh! Hi! I forgot Mom was having company."

Dr. McLaren said, "Don't believe it, she's been standing inside that doorway for five minutes, casually holding that bag, peeking out the window."

The girl laughed indulgently. She was about twenty, long-legged, thin—too thin, one would say, if she were a daughter rather than a model in a magazine—with dark hair to her shoulders and sparkling eyes and pale skin. She might have looked rather drab without her smile and her animation, but we would never know for sure.

"Besides which," Janet continued, "she was supposed to be gone this afternoon, until she heard I had—a visitor coming."

The girl stuck out her hand, making me shift the flowers. "I'm Eloise." She had a firm grip. "Mom, would you mind getting that other bag for me? Do you know how to put the top up on one of these?"

Janet smiled a greeting as she withdrew, as I said, "Not really," about the dark green convertible sports car in the circular driveway. Eloise dropped the hanging bag unceremoniously into its miniscule back seat. "Never mind, just pull when I say, okay?"

I set the flowers down, but she immediately snatched them up. "Oh no, not on the hood, they'll wilt. Flowers. That's so—"

"Please don't say sweet."

"—thoughtful. Nobody does that any more."

This was the interrogation I'd planned to do on Dinah's first date: small talk, friendly, but with a maximum of discomfort effect. I steeled myself not to put my hands in my pockets. "Really I'm just here on business. We need to talk about your mother's testimony."

Eloise stepped close to me to return the bouquet. "Right, you just brought the flowers to fool the neighbors."

Her look from under her brows invited confession. "You have your mother's mouth," I said instead.

It quirked into a broader smile. Janet came out of the house carrying a small suitcase. "Is that everything?"

"Ah, the endless parade of beaus," Eloise said. "You did get rid of that last one, didn't you? He's not still upstairs?"

"Get out of here," Janet said. "Go on." Then they flung themselves at each other as if gravity pulled them that way, as if all they had to do was stop resisting and they'd be drawn together from miles apart.

Feeling intrusive, I stepped into the house. I was in a white-tiled-floor entryway lighted by window panels around and above the front door. To my left was a living room with a bleached oak floor and cream-colored wallpaper with a tiny pale blue floral print. And flowers for miles: a large arrangement on a table in the entryway, three more arrangements I could see in the living room. I could have dropped my tiny bouquet into any of them and it would never have been seen again.

"Eloise is on her way back to Austin," Janet said. "She's my youngest, I spoiled her. What can I say? Everyone wonders what a child psychologist's children are like, but I think Eloise would have turned out the same way no matter how we'd raised her. She has a mind of her own."

"Then that must be how you raised her."

Janet smiled. She'd been wiping her cheek as she came inside and I'd given her a moment, standing as if still admiring the entryway. When I turned to look at her completely she said, "I'm not half ready, of course."

"Then I can't wait to see the final result." She was wearing a dark blue dress that displayed her without encasing her, with a thin gold necklace close around her throat. Her hair looked no color at all, the color of elegance, and her eyes were the shade of the dress. She looked even better when her cheeks flushed at my compliment.

"How nice," she said. "I love flowers."

"Gee, really?"

As she led me into that living room I said the obligatory, "Beautiful house."

"Yes. I got it, Ted got to keep his practice."

"He's a lawyer?"

"Doctor. Orthopedic surgeon."

"Ah. You met in medical school."

"No." Janet hesitated. "I didn't go to medical school until years later, sort of to find out what kept Ted so fascinated he could never get home before nine. Then it turned out his fascination wasn't strictly medical."

She realized there was very little I could say to that, so she kept talking. "I should have moved some place smaller years ago. But I wanted the kids to come home to the house they grew up in. Would you like the tour?"

I felt the house spreading around and above me, every foot of it saturated with her memories. The kids' bedrooms, the pictures either displayed or put away in cupboards, the scenes that had happened here, and here, and several here, years jumbled and overlapping, occasions happy and forlorn.

"No," I said.

213

"Good. Maybe some other time. Maybe one room at a time, over several visits. Or—"

"Maybe not," we both said. Janet continued, "Sit down. What would you like to drink? Scotch? Wine?"

She had the makings handy. We talked while she poured. We told each other our children's ages and occupations, then capped that conversation because any more of it would have led to talk of ex-spouses, and it was too early to expose each other to that. Janet sat beside me on the couch but not too close and clinked her glass quietly against mine but without offering a toast. I sipped and cleared my throat.

"We probably won't call you to testify the first day. It probably won't be until—"

"I know," Janet interrupted. "You told me." She hesitated. Hesitation and small talk had comprised our whole conversation so far. "Let's not talk business," she said.

"Right, you're right."

I had the sudden feeling Janet was going to ask me why I'd called her, and I didn't have an answer. A date seemed so juvenile. How could we approach it any way but awkwardly? Linda and I had never dated, we'd fallen into each other when we could no longer stop ourselves. Becky hadn't offered me a date, she'd offered herself.

That's why I was there. I'd grown into a perpetually mournful after-working-hours state, replaying to exhaustion my loss of Linda, of my family, of any personal life. If I'd been noble about Becky, then I needed to do something about the one new person in years who *had* interested me.

So I was there in Janet's lovely living room, feeling sixteen.

"I made a reservation at L'Etoile."

"Oh. Good," she said.

"What's wrong with that?"

"Nothing, it's one of my favorites. Well, it's just that it's almost my neighborhood tavern, I always see half a dozen people I know there—"

"Oh, I didn't realize we were skulking around. Well, I know this great little inn in Fredericksburg, they serve dinner right in your room."

She laughed and put her hand on mine. "It's not that. It's just that people would come up to our table, or I'd feel like I had to stop by theirs, and I don't want us to be interrupted."

No, we wouldn't want anything to sidetrack this scintillating conversation. "How about La Scala?"

"Oh, another favorite. But I happen to know the Tuckers are having a private party there tonight, and everyone—"

"Listen," I said. "On this flood of dates of yours, is there any place you find safe to go?"

"That was just Eloise being an idiot."

"But you go out."

She sized me up. "Is that important to you?"

"No. Why would I—"

"Listen. Mark." She sighed, but she didn't stop looking at me. "When Ted left, or I kicked him out, or whatever happened, I felt very, very low. I'd lost the only man I'd ever loved just because he found someone more—attractive. You know how that makes a woman feel?"

"I know how it feels to lose someone."

"But—" She clenched her fist in the effort to make me understand. "What I did was, after an appropriate interval spent in a vegetative state, I picked myself up, got myself together, and set out to dazzle every male I saw. This was ten years ago, when I worked at it I could still be—"

"Devastating."

She smiled. "Let's just say I was near the top of my form. And I wanted to know it. I don't mean I slept around, that wasn't what I was interested in, I just wanted to feel that response. And I mean, I got dolled up to go to the grocery store. I lowered my voice for waiters. No one was safe. My women friends stopped inviting me to their parties.

"But when I let myself get a little close to a couple of particular men, I found I just didn't want it to go any further. I thought, What's the point? In a few years either he finds somebody new or I get bored with him."

I found it very easy to follow her stories. I could say the punch lines along with her. "So you put away your sequined sheaths and ever since you've lived a life of quiet contemplation."

"Not quite. But this is the first date I've looked forward to in quite a while, and I'm wondering now if I want to try hard to make it work or if I want to deliberately screw it up."

I felt a great ease descend on me. "Ah. Yes."

Her face brightened. "That's how you feel too?"

"I didn't until you described it, but now I think I do. Did. Have been. So which should we do? Work at it, or—?" To cast my vote I stood up, slipped off my suit coat and laid it across a chair, then returned to the couch.

She considered. "I know a good pizza place near here that delivers."

"I know it too. I like their Don Corleone combo."

She widened her eyes at me. "Oh, the heart attack special. How are your arteries? Do you jog?"

"No. I pace."

"Their number's beside the phone in the kitchen," she said. "And I'll permit you to loosen your tie if I can take off this dress."

From my seat I could watch, through the entryway, her legs going up the stairs. I imagined her changing clothes in that room upstairs, and my imagination wasted no effort on what the room looked like.

"What?" she said later, brushing at the collar of the white blouse she'd changed into, along with jeans. "Did I spill?"

The remains of the pizza and salad were back in the kitchen. We were still working on the cabernet. We'd talked about our professions, dipped back into families, talked about books, movies, where we'd been students. We'd never again gotten as personal as Janet had to start the ball rolling, but I felt as if I knew her. She must have realized she'd been more giving in the conversation than I had. "So tell me something awful about yourself," she said abruptly.

And I found that as much as I'd laughed in the last hour, that subterranean river of melancholy was still flowing. Now it was red like the wine. "I've lost everyone I ever cared about," I said, "and I wonder sometimes if that's just the way life happens or if I did it."

Janet sat up straighter. "Whoa, what are you trying to do, top me? Not *every*body, that's just a cliché. Maybe a wife or girl friend or two, but not children. Friends?"

"Go ahead, I'll stop you when you hit one."

"Mark, seriously." She touched my hand again.

"No, not my last good friend," I said slowly. "I'll start that Wednesday."

"You don't lose a friend over every case you try, do you?"

"This is something special. If I ruin his client I'll be ruining Eliot too. Eliot will probably have to bring up Austin's childhood during punishment, what he helped do to him. That will start people wondering what Eliot did *for* Austin later to make it up. And if I don't ruin them both, if I lose, how will I ever forget that Eliot set loose a man who—"

I stopped. I was talking business.

"Mark?"

"This is one of those times when touching would be appropriate," I said.

She wasn't slow about it. She continued flowing toward me and put her arms around me. I clutched her, very tightly at first, then more loosely. We mumbled inarticulate syllables. That was how I found her mouth. After that I felt her fingers on my back. It was no longer a hug of comfort. It could have become painful, in fact, if it hadn't felt so good.

When we drew slightly apart, still holding hands, she smiled, then frowned and again brushed at the front of her blouse. "Are you sure I don't have a stain? You keep looking at my blouse."

"Not at the blouse," I said. She laughed and came to me again.

That part was effortless, thrilling, the touching and tasting and wondering if this skin would become more familiar and more exciting in time. But when my mind became as engaged as my hands, plotting what to do next, I slowed. Next week she would be my witness. I didn't want a closer connection with Janet until after that.

Thinking is a terrible thing.

We talked some more. Even when we stopped holding hands I could still feel her. That feeling was good enough, for both of us, for the time being.

When she walked me to the door I tried to warn her about the week ahead. "The next time you see me, I'll be very different. So will everybody else."

"What do you do, change personalities, like suits?" She laughed.

I found her so appealing I kissed her again, for the last time, before trial.

13

LAWYERS HAVE TRIAL PERSONALITIES. IT'S NOT strictly voluntary. I've seen the nicest man I know turn into a slavering werewolf every time the jury files into the box, then smack himself in the forehead when they were gone and ask himself, "What am I doing?" I've seen laughing, casual women turn into tight-mouthed statisticians. Quiet homebodies turn into shouting idiots. Good trial lawyers can turn it on and off. The best have several personalities they can slip into and out of as the occasion or the witness demands. I waited nervously for Eliot's appearance.

He wasn't on yet when he came in. The three of them entered together, Eliot and Buster Harmony flanking Austin, chatting as if they'd just finished a round of golf.

"He looks nervous," Becky said.

"That's just what he wants you to think. He's ready."

"How long has it been since either of them tried a case?"

"That doesn't matter."

Eliot took the lead defense counsel's chair, near me across the narrow space between the counsel tables. Before sitting he stood over me without offering a handshake.

"I can't wish you luck, Mark. But I wish we were both somewhere else."

"This is my favorite place in the world, Eliot."

Damn it, he'd already made me start sounding stupid. "Easy, big guy," Becky muttered.

*   *   *

When Judge Hernandez took the bench he looked unhappily at us, then motioned us forward with small movements of his fingers, a very subtle gesture for someone of the judge's expansive personality. He looked for the first time like a man who didn't enjoy the spotlight.

"I feel it is my duty," he said quietly when Eliot and Buster and I were at the bench in front of him, "to inquire if there is any chance of a settlement in this case. If a postponement would help you reach agreement, I am prepared to grant one."

He'd made this speech with his eyes downcast, shuffling their way around the objects on his bench. But when he finished he looked closely, almost imploringly, at me.

"We'd be happy to discuss—" Buster began heartily.

"No," I said. "There's no chance."

Judge Hernandez tried to regain his normal bluster. "All right, then," he said snappishly. "Let's get on with it." His hands did the duty of brooms, waving us away.

The judge was in a tight spot and could easily put me in one. He was undoubtedly under a lot of pressure, just as I'd been, from Austin's political cronies. Buster Harmony's presence at the defense table was a constant reminder of that pressure. And Judge Hernandez was in a position to accommodate them. He could wreck my case any number of ways, such as by ruling that my child witness was too young to be qualified to testify. He could cast subtlety to the winds and rule that my evidence wasn't enough to prove guilt, setting Austin free.

And destroying his own career. No matter how many powerful backstage men the judge might please with such a ruling, at the next election voters would remember the judge who so favored a child molester that he let him go without even giving a jury a chance to decide his guilt.

The judge's self-interest was as much on my side as on Austin's. And I thought Judge Hernandez had too much pride to appear so obviously in someone's pocket. From his grumpy, stiff-necked expression that morning I believed I was right.

But there were more subtle ways he could screw me in an attempt to please his friends. He would bear watching.

We were all still rather low-key. The seats behind us held thirty or forty people, reporters and friends and mere spectators, but we were still essentially offstage. The jury panel hadn't been called. I looked at Austin Paley, sitting at the defense table. He turned to me, not offering the comradely smile I knew so well. He just gazed at me rather sorrowfully. He didn't look frightened, just sad, as at watching a friend destroy himself. I returned his gaze for a long time, studying him.

When the prospective jurors entered the courtroom we were facing them, with the judge behind us. I don't know what kind of faces the others put on for the panel. A lot of lawyers smile insipidly. I sat quietly myself, hands folded, glancing neutrally at their faces as the prospective jurors took their seats. They looked back at me nervously or intently or glanced away as if embarrassed to be there, as if they were on trial themselves, which in a way they were.

Like all trial lawyers, I fear and mistrust juries. Who are these strangers who come straggling in off the streets to judge our work, knowing nothing about the law or the history behind the case? But jury *panels* are even more frightening, because of their potential: thirty-two or more people out of whom we choose twelve to judge us. Somewhere there, I knew, were twelve people who would convict anyone I showed them. Also scattered through the panel, the defense hoped, were twelve people who would vote for acquittal if given the chance. But how were we to winnow them out, when they sat there ready to lie to us and disguise their feelings and try like hell to get off the jury or get on? Jury selection is the worst part of trial, the part where you can win your case or hopelessly fuck it up, with no idea which until it's too late.

Becky and I wanted parents on the jury, people who would fear that their own children could fall into the hands of a monster such as we were going to portray. But it soon became clear that the defense might want parents as well.

"How old is your daughter, Mrs. Paglia?" Eliot asked, smiling but in a formal way, not trying to be insidious.

"She's seven," the prospective juror said quickly, the way she'd answered every question, sure of herself.

Eliot tilted his head as if he could see the child in memory. "Has she ever said something to you that you thought might not be strictly true, but that she said just to get your attention?"

The woman appeared to think it over, but was already shaking her head before the question was done. "No, I don't think so."

"No?" Eliot asked incredulously.

And around the woman, other members of the panel were looking skeptical, or smiling in disbelief.

"She's never shaded the truth just a little, or said something for effect, or exaggerated? Goodness, what an honest girl. We need to have her testifying in this trial," Eliot said, drawing laughter.

Buster, beside him, was noting the other members of the panel who shook their heads in disbelief at the idea of a perpetually truthful child.

It's called poisoning the panel. Eliot's questions weren't aimed just at the one prospective juror he was questioning. They were aimed at the whole panel. And they weren't just eliciting information, they were conveying it. Through the questioning of one prospective juror Eliot had ferreted out others on the panel who might be of use, and he'd planted the idea in all their minds that children lie, they can't be trusted.

We did some poisoning of our own, of course. "How do you know when someone's lying to you, Mr. Hendricks?" Becky asked curiously.

"I don't know," the middle-aged service technician said uneasily, "watch his eyes, see how nervous he looks."

"Really? Does that work for you?" Becky asked as if she genuinely wanted to know.

The poor man shrugged. "I don't know. I guess not too many people lie to me."

People around him nodded. Becky nodded too. "Because I'll tell you," she said, "I can't ever tell. I believe everybody. I'm the easiest mark in Texas." Becky was the youngest of the four of us lawyers facing the jury. The jurors smiled at her, at her naïveté. They believed in it instinctively.

"I've made a rule for myself," she went on. "I never make a major purchase the first time I go look. Because when that salesman starts talking, my mouth just goes dry from hanging open. I believe every word he says. I'd buy anything. So I make myself step back, and go home, and then I think, 'Wait a minute, this guy's trying to sell me something.' "

Jurors nodded again. Oh, sure, *salesmen* will lie. We thought you were talking about real people.

"And sometimes," Becky went on, "I've heard other prosecutors in our office talk to Mr. Blackwell here, who's our boss, and they tell him what a wonderful job they just did in a trial, how they asked great questions and argued brilliantly and really kicked some defense lawyer's— Well, you know how people will talk. And I just listen in admiration, hoping I can be that good some day.

"Then later I hear from other people who watched the trial and they say, 'You know, Eddie didn't really do such a hot job at trial, he just got lucky, he just stumbled around and somehow it worked out.'"

Jurors were nodding again. Oh sure, people with something to gain will lie. They'll lie like fiends.

"And what I've learned"—Becky no longer sounded so ingenuous; she appeared to have grown up before the jurors' eyes, grown older and wiser and harder to fool—"is that people with the strongest motive to lie sometimes sound the most sincere. Somebody who just comes forward to tell you his story because he thinks he should, without anything to gain from it, sometimes stumbles a little and seems unsure of himself, but somebody else who really has something to lose, who *has* to make you believe him, he's practiced and he's calm and his face just shines with sincerity. Because he *has* to convince you. Has that been your experience, Mr. Hendricks?"

Mr. Hendricks's answer didn't matter. It was just an opportunity for Becky to explain that if Austin Paley sounded believable when he testified it would be because he was on trial for his life. The jury panel was no longer smiling at Becky. They looked sobered. Several of them glanced at Austin. They knew what we were talking about.

The judge let the prospective jurors go to the bathroom and get drinks for a few minutes, and the opposing lawyers separated. Becky and I made our strikes. We couldn't make sure anyone we wanted would be on the jury, we could only keep off the ones we disliked. We got to strike ten and the defense got ten. The twelve who were left, the ones neither side was sure about, became the jury. I watched them take their seats, certain as I always am that I'd made mistakes in their selection.

". . . We expect the evidence to show that the defendant cultivated a group of children, that he gradually singled out one of them, deliberately got close to this boy. Until the boy came to rely on the defendant, to think Austin Paley was his friend.

And when he'd finally won that trust, Austin Paley violated it in the worst way an adult can harm a child, by raping the boy."

I didn't shake with rage as I made my opening statement, or tremble on the brink of tears. I looked the jurors in their faces and kept the facts I expected to prove short and straightforward—which, Becky and I agreed, was the kind of case we had. I sat back, letting Becky answer Judge Hernandez's order to call our first witness.

That was a nice, competent lady named Maria Alonzo, who testified that Austin Paley had been a licensed realtor for almost twenty years. In answer to Becky's further questions Ms. Alonzo explained to the jury that such a position would allow the defendant access to lockbox combinations on houses for sale.

"So the defendant would have free entry to a large number of vacant houses in San Antonio?" Becky asked.

"Yes."

When Becky passed the witness Eliot said something that troubled me slightly. "No questions," he said, glancing up to smile at our witness. Well, the defense could hardly deny that Austin held a realtor's license.

Next Becky called an officer of a real estate company to testify that a house at a certain address had been vacant during the whole month of May two years ago. Any jurors who had listened very carefully to my opening statement had a chance of understanding where this was leading, but the information was less than scintillating. Again, Eliot asked no questions on cross. Buster Harmony looked bored and impatient, and leaned across to whisper to Eliot.

We hadn't used up half an hour of trial time when Becky called Debby Wesley, a twelve-year-old girl who'd probably been cuter and more pliable two and a half years ago. I wanted to ask for a brief recess to approach the witness and slap the chewing gum out of her mouth.

"Where do you live, Debby?" Becky asked her, smiling.

"Here in San Antonio."

Like pulling teeth. It took another question to elicit the address, 814 Sparrowwood, which the jurors, if they had phenomenal memories, would realize was next door to the vacant house about which they'd just heard testimony.

"How long have you lived there?"

"Since I was little," Debby said, a little irritably, as if offended by the implication that she was one of those flighty types who move all the time.

"More than three years?" Becky asked, still smiling, as if little Debby were the sweetest thing she'd seen in a week.

"Oh yeah."

"Do you remember when the house next door, at 818, was vacant for several months two years ago?"

"Yeah. We didn't think anybody was ever gonna buy it."

Those little unelicited bursts of recollection are nice, they add authenticity. They also make the lawyer doing the questioning cringe with the fear the witness will rattle on and add something else, damaging to the case. Becky's voice grew a little tight.

"Specifically do you remember whether it was vacant in May of 1990?"

"I guess." The near-teen pushed her lank hair back off her cheek and cracked her gum.

"Don't guess, Debby. The jury has to know for sure. That last month of school two years ago, when you were in fourth grade, was the house next door empty?"

"Oh yeah. Yeah, I remember then. I had Miss Jennings, I couldn't wait to get out of her class."

So we had finally pinned down the date. Two or three of the jurors looked as relieved as I felt. A couple of the motherly ones looked as if they wanted to push our witness's face into a sink of soapy water. I scribbled a note to Becky.

"Did something happen with the house next door that month?" Becky asked.

"You mean when he came and started fixing it up?"

Becky used the natural occasion, standing and walking slowly to stand behind Austin. "When you said 'he,' were you pointing at this man?"

"Yeah."

"Your Honor, may the record reflect that the witness has identified the defendant?" Becky took her seat. "Tell us about that," she said. While Debby did, Becky read my note and glanced at me with a small frown. I nodded for emphasis.

". . . we thought he was gonna move in."

"Sit up straight, please, Debby," Becky said, not harshly, but it was such a departure from her earlier tone that Debby looked startled and did indeed rise out of her slouch. One of the women on the jury nodded and one of the men looked satisfied.

I crumpled my note. It's a mistake for a lawyer to think you have to treat every one of your witnesses as if she's your own dear child. Jurors understand that you don't pick your own witnesses. Some of them are criminals and some of them are not too bright and some of them need to be told to sit up straight and spit out their gum.

"How is it you remember the defendant?" Becky asked.

"Well, he was right next door, and he was outside a lot, working on the yard and fixing up the house, and I used to go over and talk to him."

Little flirt, I thought, then grimaced, wondering if anyone else was thinking the same thing.

"Were you the only one of the neighborhood kids who started hanging around the house where the defendant was working?"

"Oh, no, there was a bunch of us. Kids'd ride their bikes by and stop, stuff like that."

"Do you know Tommy Algren?" Becky asked neutrally.

"Yeah, he lives on my street. He's a little kid, though."

Bless you for that, Debby.

"Was he one of the children who started hanging around at the defendant's house?"

"Yeah."

Whew. I doubted that anyone realized how tough this short line of questioning had been, with our little darling continually veering outside the outlines of her testimony as we'd prepared it. It was a relief when she finally said what we needed and Becky could pass her. But Becky didn't relax. She couldn't, not with Eliot now doing the questioning.

Eliot smiled. Debby smiled back.

"You have a remarkable memory, Debby, to remember a man you only saw a few times two and a half years ago."

Debby shrugged, in that charming way she had.

"How many times did the prosecutors show you pictures of Mr. Paley before you identified him?" Eliot still smiled.

"Four or five times," Debby said.

I didn't wince, except internally. Becky rolled her eyes and made a note on the yellow pad in front of her.

"And when you practiced the testimony you were going to give today, did they tell you where Mr. Paley would be sitting in the courtroom?"

"Yeah," darling Debby agreed. Becky made another grimace and another note.

Eliot got down to business. "Now, this man at the house next door, what did you talk with him about?"

Debby frowned. Her remarkable memory took flight. "I don't really remember talking to him much. I'd just go over there 'cause there were other kids there, you know. Mostly I'd just talk to them."

Eliot nodded with a satisfaction that was probably apparent only to me. "So you don't remember him saying anything to you."

"Not really."

"Did he ever ask you to come inside the house?"

Debby wrinkled her nose to help herself think. "Nah, I don't remember going inside."

"There were always other children around?" Eliot emphasized.

"Yeah."

"The man didn't ever make you uncomfortable, did he, Debby? He didn't ever say anything bad to you or touch you in a way that bothered you, did he?"

Debby started shaking her head, then checked herself. "Once I was standing next to him and he was talking to all of us and I started talking to my girl friend and he reached down and squeezed my shoulder to make me shut up. It really hurt, too."

Hah, I thought. At least Debby's flighty memory could offer unpleasantries for the defense to step in, too.

Eliot looked unhurt. "Did he ever take you anywhere in his car?"

"Nah."

He decided to quit there. As soon as the witness was returned to her Becky began asking questions, not bothering to try to charm the witness with a smile first.

"Debby, you said you identified the defendant after we showed you pictures of him four or five times. How did we do that?"

Debby blinked. I was afraid she'd forgotten already. "His picture was mixed in with other people's pictures."

"Yes," Becky confirmed. "And every time we showed you a group of pictures, you picked out the defendant's picture, didn't you?"

"Yeah."

"So it didn't take you four or five times to pick out his picture," Becky made crystal clear. "You picked it out every time we showed you pictures. Isn't that right?"

Debby nodded. Becky had to tell her to answer aloud.

"You also," Becky went on rather grimly, "told Mr. Quinn that Mr. Blackwell and I told you where the defendant would be sitting in the courtroom. What did you mean by that?"

Debby demonstrated with her hands, as if moving doll furniture. "You know, you told me you and Mr. Blackwell would be sitting here, and the jury'd be over there, and the defense table here, and the judge up beside me." She smiled up at the judge, who couldn't decide whether it was more politic to beam at the little tyke or to glare sternly at her, so he gave free rein to his natural inclination and just stared at her as if she were a stain on his witness chair.

"And that there'd be people in the audience," Becky prompted her. Eliot didn't bother to object that she was leading the witness. He sat as if as curious as anyone why the prosecutor was having such trouble making her witness's testimony sound the way the prosecution wanted it to sound.

"Yeah," Debby said blankly.

"Did I ever say anything to you like, 'This is where the man will be sitting you have to identify,' or, 'Be sure to point at the man sitting at the defense table'?"

"You didn't have to tell me, I know it's him."

"But did I? Or did Mr. Blackwell?"

Debby thought she'd already answered. "No."

"No," Becky said firmly. Having worked so hard to clean up two of Debby's answers, Becky didn't elicit any more. Eliot didn't have another go at her either. Debby went traipsing down the aisle and out of our lives.

We hadn't liked Debby much, but she'd been the surest of our child witnesses, because she was the oldest. We put on two more after that, including a boy who *had* gone for a ride to the store with Austin, but hadn't made the final cut. Austin hadn't even touched the boy, a fact Eliot was careful to emphasize on cross-examination. But we'd established that all three children remembered Austin as the friendly man who'd seemed to live in the vacant house on Tommy Algren's street for a month or so around the time of the offense named in the indictment.

Becky and I had debated whether to put on these children as

part of our case in chief or hold them in reserve for rebuttal. The latter might have been better: let Austin testify that he'd never seen Tommy before, then bring on these children to say they remembered the two of them together. We'd decided instead to put them on first because our case would have been so brief otherwise. We had no medical evidence. Tommy showed no signs of scarring, and no medical exam could determine whether he was a virgin. We had no cops. There'd never been a police investigation of this particular accusation. We had essentially nothing but Tommy. We were afraid if we put them head to head, Tommy against Austin, the adult could leave such a strong impression of innocence that our attempts to bolster Tommy's testimony afterward would be hopeless. We wanted to make our case as strong as possible from the beginning, so the jury would already be convinced of Austin's guilt before he took the stand. The children, at least, had been able to corroborate part of Tommy's story. But the burden of our case still rested heavily on Tommy.

I rose to say, "The State calls Tommy Algren," and I remained on my feet, looking back up the aisle, waiting for his entrance.

The defendant enjoys protections no one else in this free land does. Rightfully so, because he is the accused. He has to defend himself. But in trial one of these rights gives the defendant a certain advantage. He has the right to confront the witnesses against him, so he can sit through the whole trial, listening to everything, waiting until last to speak, so that he can tailor his own testimony to conform to everything that's gone before. Other witnesses, including the victim, are excluded from the courtroom except during their own appearances on the witness stand. So Tommy entered the room glancing around furtively, already a little embarrassed, not knowing what had been said about him already, what intimate details of his life these strangers knew before he ever spoke his name.

He was wearing khaki pants, brown loafers, and an open-necked, short-sleeved shirt with blue and white stripes. His blond hair had been slicked down so that the tracks of the comb's teeth were still visible. He looked quite the little man. I hadn't tried to dress him like a young boy, hoping instead that the very formality of his appearance would invite the jury to see through it to the hurt boy beneath.

After his glances around the room Tommy looked straight

ahead, at me. I stood waiting for him, held the gate open when he arrived, and squeezed his shoulder as I directed him toward the witness stand.

"Tell us your name, please, Tommy." A bailiff crossed the front of the room and pushed the microphone down lower, into Tommy's face.

"Tommy Algren."

"How old are you, Tommy?"

"Ten."

"What grade are you in in school?"

"Fifth. Fifth grade."

He looked calm, but he sounded nervous. I continued asking him the easy questions to let him loosen up. "You'll be in middle school next year, is that right?"

"Yes sir."

"Where do you live, Tommy?"

"On Sparrowwood. Number 823."

"With your parents?"

"Yes."

He seemed to be settled down. He was watching me, waiting for my cues. He had, as I'd instructed him, shunted aside everyone else in the room. I was speaking to him as calmly and as reassuringly as I could, nodding occasionally to let him know he was fine.

"I'm going to ask you about some things that happened about two and a half years ago," I said. He looked alert. "Do you remember a house in your neighborhood that was vacant then?"

"Objection," Eliot said. "Leading."

He could have that objection sustained all day long. I'd already told Tommy with the question what we were talking about.

"Do you remember in May 1990, when a new man moved into a house on your block?"

He hesitated. I wondered if my phrasing had confused him. "Yes sir," Tommy finally said.

"Do you remember what he looked like?"

"Yes," he said softly.

"Tom. I want you to look around the courtroom very carefully. Look at people's faces. Take your time, you don't have to hurry. Do you see that man?"

Eliot was on his feet well before I finished. "Objection," he said. "Bolstering."

I rose too, genuinely puzzled. "How can it be bolstering, Your Honor? The witness hasn't even made an identification yet. You can't bolster testimony that hasn't happened."

"It's prebolstering," Eliot said calmly.

"*Prebolstering?*" I said loudly. I was both irritated with Eliot for intruding this novel argument into my important questioning, and unconcerned, because it didn't matter how Judge Hernandez ruled on the silly question. It was just an interruption before Tommy could continue.

I looked at Tommy and saw that while Eliot and I argued, Tommy's gaze had settled on Austin Paley. Tommy didn't look revolted, frightened, or in fact emotionally involved at all. He was just watching. Austin was looking back at him in the same way. There was communication between them, not necessarily antagonistic communication. There in that mutual gaze was the relationship between them, perfectly visible for all to see. There was the hold Austin had had on Tommy. It hadn't just been molesting, it had been mentoring. Tommy's mouth moved a little, ironically. His eyes blinked slowly. He looked like what Austin had made him. He looked sophisticated far beyond his years. It was sad to see that look on the face of a child whose main worry in life should have been not losing his best comic book in a bad trade.

It was also terrifying, to me. Tommy was something more than a child, and Austin was not his enemy. I saw what I'd feared all along, that when the time came to tell his story in public, Tommy would balk. He wouldn't be able to bring himself to hurt his old friend, his hero, Austin. He would exonerate Austin Paley on the witness stand, winning Austin an acquittal when there would no longer be time before the election for me to prepare another case against Austin.

"May I approach the witness, Your Honor?" Without waiting for the judge's permission, I did so. I didn't need to be closer to Tommy, I just wanted to stand between him and Austin. I'd hoped the bond between them was broken, that Tommy hated Austin now, but Janet McLaren had told me otherwise: "The child hates what was done to him but loves the molester." I'd tried to establish my own bond with Tommy, to overcome Austin's power over him, but our friendship was newer and not

remotely as deep. I had only a few minutes to win Tommy over
in spite of his past. After all the pretrial maneuvering, that's
what the case came down to: a direct tug-of-war between Austin
and me over this boy.

And I was mad as hell. God damn Austin Paley, he wasn't
going to steal this case away from me. Even if my own witness
wanted to help him.

"Tommy," I said quietly. "You remember spending time with
other children at the house where the defendant seemed to be
living, on your block?"

Eliot objected to leading again, and was sustained again. I still
didn't care. I couldn't tell Tommy the testimony we'd already
heard that morning—Eliot would have properly objected before
I'd gotten a sentence into it—but Tommy had known who else
was going to testify before him, and what they were going to
say. My phrase *other children* was to remind him of them. He'd
look like a liar if he contradicted them. Even if he were prepared
to lie on Austin's behalf, Tommy didn't want to look like a liar.
He would want to be believed when he denied the essentials of
the crime, the private acts only he and Austin knew about. He
could tell the truth about this without hurting either of them.

"Yes," he said.

"Point out that man, please."

Tommy hesitated, but Austin even obliged by leaning to the
side, so Tommy could see him past me. Thus prompted, Tommy
said, "There."

I moved slightly. Tommy's eyes were on me again. His mouth
was pursed, the tip of his tongue just visible. He looked a little
scared of me.

"Who were some of the other children who played at the
defendant's house?"

The question caught him off stride. "Peter," he said slowly.
I wondered if Peter had been his rival for Austin's attentions.
"Debby, and Jennifer, and Bobby and Dawson and Stevie. A
bunch of kids."

"Where they your friends?"

"Some of them." He shrugged.

"Steve was your friend, wasn't he?"

"Yes." Tommy forgot for a moment to wonder why I was
asking, as memory surged. "Sometimes Stevie would come
over to my house, or I'd go over to his, and we'd get bored and

go to Waldo's, because there was more to do there. Enough kids to have games with."

"Waldo is what you called the defendant?"

Uh-oh, he'd let that slip. Secret name. But again, no harm. "Yes," Tommy admitted.

I put him back on the memory track. "Do you still play with Steve?"

"Not so much," Tommy said.

"Could the prosecutor please take his seat?" Eliot asked behind me. "I can't see the witness."

In San Antonio one of our local rules requires lawyers to question witnesses from our seats at the counsel tables, unless there's some particular reason for standing close to the witness, such as to demonstrate a piece of physical evidence. I had no such legitimate excuse. I walked back to my seat. "Why not?" I asked Tommy, about why he was no longer friends with Steve. I was just shooting in the dark. I didn't know what had come between Tommy and Steve, but there'd been only one major event in Tommy's life that I knew of. I was thinking of what Dr. McLaren had told me, and guessing that Austin had somehow come between Tommy and Steve. Either Tommy had gone along with Austin's scheme and Steve had balked, or Tommy'd no longer felt quite childish enough to have child friends, after what happened to him.

Tommy shrugged again. "We're in different classes this year."

But friendship could survive that, and Tommy's downcast eyes made me think there was something more.

"Remember May twenty-third nineteen-ninety, Tom?"

"I guess."

May 23 was the date alleged in the indictment. Tommy knew it very well, he'd helped us reconstruct just what day it had been. It had been the day of his first sexual encounter with Austin. We'd chosen that day to prosecute, the day Tommy'd been robbed of his virginity, and his childhood, rather than some later occasion when he might be thought a more willing participant. Tommy knew the day I meant. He knew the subject we were edging into. He looked at me with his mouth a thin line, looking defiant. *Go ahead, ask me,* his expression said.

"Do you remember when you came home that night?" I asked.

Eliot said, "Objection. Assumes facts not in evidence." From the corner of my eye I saw him giving me a curious look. I was taking a very roundabout approach.

More important, Tommy was caught a little off guard. He thought I'd asked the wrong question, too.

"Were you playing at Waldo's house that day after school?" I asked.

He hesitated, not sure what he should say, when he should start denying. "I think so," he finally hedged. I didn't care about his uncertainty.

"Do you remember when you came home from his house that night?" I asked.

This was what he didn't understand. I had skipped ahead to *after* the event. "Remember?" I asked quietly.

"Yes," he said.

"Did you tell your parents that anything unusual had happened to you?"

"No."

No, he hadn't. It had been Tommy's secret then—his and Waldo's, but mostly Tommy's. Not a happy secret, a shameful one. He'd still longed for his parents then, his love for them had been stronger than his love for Austin, but he couldn't tell them what had happened because it was something dirty that he'd done. He'd cried himself to sleep that night, not just because he was small and scared, but because he was alone.

I was asking my questions slowly, leaving Tommy time to fill in the gaps from memory.

"Do you remember going to school the next day?"

"Yes." Wondering if it had been a dream, if he could pretend it had never happened. Looking at the children around him and marveling at how young and carefree they were.

"Did you tell anyone there that anything unusual had happened to you the day before?"

"No," Tommy said quietly.

Eliot was openly staring at me now, because I seemed to be asking the questions he would ask, proving that Tommy hadn't made any outcry at the time of the supposed rape. But I wasn't concerned about Eliot. I was concerned with goading Tommy's memory of how he'd felt in the first hot, shameful aftermath of sex with Austin. It hadn't been a happy memory. He hadn't wanted to share it with anyone. Not because it was his special secret, but because telling would reveal to everyone how different he was, what a dirty little boy he was.

"Did you tell your friend Steve?"

"No," Tommy said quietly, remembering, I hoped, that he had still been friends with Steve that day, he did have a friend he could talk to. But not about this new friend in his life. That was when he'd begun losing Steve.

"At lunch and at recess that day, did you play with the other kids like always?"

"Yes," Tommy said, but he was lying. He'd walked apart, feeling unfit to mingle with the other children, as he'd still been walking alone on the days I'd picked him up after school. He had no friends left by then, except Austin. And possibly me.

"After school that next day did you go back to Waldo's house?"

"Yes." Tommy had stopped looking at me, but he wasn't looking at Austin, either. I thought I sensed motion at the defense table as Austin tried to recapture his attention, but Tommy was looking off beyond the jury, into the past.

"Was Waldo there?"

"No."

No. Austin had lain low for a few days, to make sure Tommy hadn't reported what had happened. The vacant house was just a trap that had been sprung. He could walk away from it leaving no trace if he wanted. That was the beauty of his design.

But Tommy had come to the house and found it as abandoned as he felt. After Tommy's long day of secret-keeping on his behalf, Waldo left him alone. If Tommy'd needed final proof that they'd done something shameful, he had it when he found the house empty. It told him something else, too: that his new friend didn't trust him.

"Did you go back the next day looking for him?"

"Yes."

"Was he there?"

"No." Tommy shot a look at Austin. Tommy's eyes looked hot. I couldn't see how Austin looked back at him.

"How did you feel, Tommy, when you kept going back to the house after that day and Waldo wasn't there?"

Tommy shrugged, an adult gesture for his narrow shoulders.

"Did you keep going back?"

He nodded.

"Was he there?"

"No," Tommy said bitterly.

"After you thought he was gone, did you tell your parents what had happened?"

Eliot objected: there'd been no testimony that *anything* had happened. Neither Tommy nor I paid attention to him. Tommy shook his head while Eliot talked. I took that for my answer. Tommy looked very small in the oversized witness chair. I noticed a couple of the jurors were leaning toward him as if to see him better.

"Why didn't you talk to your parents?"

In a very small voice Tommy said, "I was afraid."

It seemed a small breakthrough. He hadn't admitted so far that anything had happened to make him afraid. I didn't press my advantage. "What *did* you do?" I asked.

He shrugged again, like a longtime prisoner describing his daily life. "Ate dinner with Mom and Dad, did my homework, went to bed."

"Did you play with the other kids after school?"

He shook his head.

"Did they miss Waldo too?"

"I don't know."

Idiot, I thought. *Stupid, stupid idiot.* It was suddenly a refrain beating like a pulse in my head. Tommy'd told me what I needed to know and I'd almost missed it, as I had missed it for weeks.

"Tommy. When you went to bed at night, would you go right to sleep?"

Tommy's stare was turned inward. He blinked hard. "Sometimes," he said.

"And sometimes you'd wake up during the night?" I was guessing, but guessing well. I could see it in Tommy's face.

"Yes," he said, softly as a boy not wanting to stir the creatures in his room.

"What would you do?"

"Just laid in bed," Tommy said. I could picture it. In the silence I knew he was picturing it too. That big white house turned dark, with Tommy so far at one end of it that he was completely alone.

"How did you feel?" I asked.

"It was cold," Tommy said, hunching his shoulders. *Cold?* I thought. *In May?* Maybe Tommy's father turned the air conditioning far down at night. Or maybe it had only been Tommy who was cold.

I looked at him in his dress shirt and his neat hair, a little boy all got up as a man. That was how I'd treated him all along, the way Austin had, appealing to the desire in him to grow up fast; trying to seal pacts with a manly squeeze and a knowing look. I'd been wrong, God, all wrong.

"Why didn't you get up and tell your parents?" I asked.

Because the house was cold, and big and dark and what was at the end of it but a man, and Tommy didn't know if any man could be trusted any more.

He didn't answer.

"Did you think about what had happened?" I asked.

Tommy looked up, wildly, frightened. I jumped from my chair and was beside him in a second. I put one arm around his back and he clutched my other hand with both hands. I held them, strongly as I could. "It's all right," I said as he cried. "It's all right."

It was probably the first time he'd cried in front of another person, the first time he'd cried at all since those nights alone in the dark. He'd toughened amazingly since then, but not at the core. It wasn't a friend Tommy needed, it was a father. One who wouldn't betray him by asking him to be an adult too soon.

The image that flashed through my mind was not of Tommy alone in his room, but of David as I'd last seen him, a boy in a tuxedo, not brooding but longing, somewhere deep within him, so deep he probably didn't know it was there; longing to be held, comforted, protected.

I held Tommy against my chest, blocking him not only from Austin but from everyone in the room, shielding him until his sobs were trailing off. Tommy wasn't lost. I could still save him, but only with his help.

"Tommy," I said, squeezing his hand. He looked up at me, lips pressed together, still fearful. "Tell these people what happened," I told him.

"I have to object now, Your Honor," Eliot said quietly behind me. "We cannot see the witness because the prosecutor is blocking him, the defendant is being denied his right of confrontation. And it appears that the district attorney is coercing the witness."

Keen insight, Eliot. Under the cover his voice provided I squeezed Tommy's hand and said, "Tell them the truth." Then I took my seat.

Tommy looked scared still. He watched me, as I'd instructed him to do long ago, last week. I nodded reassuringly. "Was Waldo finally at the house again?"

"Yes," Tommy said clearly. His eyes stayed on me.

"How long later?"

"I don't know."

"A week?" I asked. "A month? A year?"

"Only a few days," Tommy said. But they'd been three or four or five days of painful anxiety, wondering if he was changed forever but also abandoned.

"Were you glad to see him again?"

"Yes." You could see that Tommy remembered the happiness of finding that his friend hadn't left him forever, but he didn't smile now, in the courtroom.

"What did you do together?" I asked.

They'd done the things friends do: gone for a drive, talked, laughed at private jokes. Austin had touched his arm or his leg, giving Tommy momentary scares, but the touches had been fleeting.

"Did anything else happen?"

"No." Tommy said that unthinkingly. It was the truth.

"Did you keep seeing the defendant?"

"Yes."

I took the plunge. "Now let's talk about that other day. You know the one I mean, Tommy. What day was it? The first time."

It didn't take Tommy long to decide. He gulped quietly, but that was only because his voice still wasn't quite steady. He was just watching me, answering my questions.

"May twenty-third," he said. "Nineteen ninety."

"Did you go to the house?"

"Yes."

"Was that the first day you'd gone?"

"Oh, no. I'd been there—lots of times by then."

"You'd already talked to Austin alone?"

"Yes."

"Did you like him, Tommy?"

"Yes," he said. Answering that simple question made his voice give way again, a little.

"How did he treat you?"

Tommy thought. "He talked to me like he cared what I thought. And, and you could tell sometimes when another kid said something, Waldo'd look at me like, Boy, what a dummy. Sometimes we laughed when we were the only two laughing and everybody else wondered what was going on."

Tommy chattered this out like a little child telling you his latest enthusiasm.

"So that day, May twenty-third, when you went to the house, was Waldo outside?"

"No."

"Were there other kids there playing?"

"No." Tommy still sounded a little puzzled about the change in circumstances.

"What did you do?"

"I almost just went home again. But I knocked on the door, just for"—he shrugged—"and he was there, and he said he'd been waiting for me."

"Was anyone else inside the house?"

"No."

"What was it like inside the house?"

Tommy wrinkled his nose. "It wasn't like anybody really lived there. There was a couch and a couple of folding chairs and that was about it. I asked Waldo wasn't he going to get any more furniture and he just laughed."

"What did you do there?"

"We talked, and we played a couple of games. Some other kids knocked on the door but Waldo didn't let them in. We stayed by the door and said, 'Shh,' to each other and laughed about it."

"Why did he say he didn't want them in?"

"Just because we were having so much fun by ourselves."

"Did you go outside at all?"

"Waldo kept saying how hot it was, how it was too hot to do anything outside."

"Was it hot?"

"I guess."

"Do you remember what you were wearing?"

"Shorts, I guess, and a T-shirt. That's what I always wore after school."

"Where were your parents, Tommy?"

"They weren't home from work yet."

"But you were home."

"Usually I'd go to the daycare after school, but sometimes back then we had a maid two days a week and she'd watch me until Mom and Dad got home."

"But she'd let you go outside to play?"

"Yeah."

Tommy's parents were in the audience. I didn't turn around to watch them squirm, and Tommy didn't look past me at them. There were probably any number of parents in the room who might have been having guilty thoughts, maybe some on the jury.

"What was Waldo wearing?" I asked.

"He was— It looked like a suit, I think, but without the coat or tie."

"Did you ever go outside, or anywhere else?"

"After a while Waldo said, 'I know what let's do,' and he jumped up, but he wouldn't tell me what. He went in to the other room and he changed clothes."

"Did you go in with him?"

"No, but it was just in the next room, and he left the door open." Tommy looked uneasy.

"What did he put on?"

"Shorts, and another shirt."

"And what happened?"

"We got in his car, and we drove, and Waldo knew another house, not too far away, and it had a swimming pool."

"Was there anybody else there?"

"No. It had a For Sale sign."

"Did it look like the other house inside?"

"Oh, no," Tommy said. No, Austin wouldn't have introduced him to their new intimacy in the sordid environs of the vacant house, with its bare walls and sagging couch. Tommy still seemed dazzled as he described the other house. "It was pretty. There were gold lamps and glass tables and curtains and the pool."

"Was it the defendant's house?"

"I don't think so. We never went back there again."

"But he knew his way around it."

"Oh yes. He made a drink and got me a Coke and showed me around a little."

Like a tour guide, which Austin was. "Then what did you do?"

Tommy hesitated. I didn't press him. His eyes moved past me, but not toward Austin. Tommy chewed his lip. "He said we should go swimming. I said I didn't have my swim suit, but Waldo said that was okay, since it was just us there."

"And?"

"He went outside and he started taking off his clothes, then he stopped and looked at me like what was wrong?, so I took mine off too." He crossed his arms. "It felt funny to be naked outside like that."

"Weren't there any neighbors?"

"There was a tall fence."

I nodded. "Did you go swimming?"

"Yes."

"Was it fun?"

Tommy looked at me as if the question were unexpected or the answer awkward. I just gave him the same forthright stare I'd worn since resuming my seat. "Yes," he finally said, glancing down. "We swam and floated on air mattresses, and we played tag and submarine races and stuff like that."

"Did he touch you in the water?"

"Yes."

This wasn't the story Tommy had first told me in my office. That one had not been his first sexual encounter with Austin. This story of the first one was remarkably similar, though. Austin had had to reseduce Tommy every time they met. Maybe that was one of the attractions of child molesting. Once the child grew jaded and accepting, it was time to move on. By the time there was no more need for conquest, no fear to overcome, Austin *had* left Tommy behind.

"Did it scare you when he touched you?"

"It just seemed like accidents at first."

"What happened next?"

"I was just floating on an air mattress, resting."

"On your back or your front or your side?"

"On my back."

"Where was Austin?"

"He was swimming around me. He'd swim under my mattress and then come up on the other side. Then once he came up and he seemed real tired, so he put his head and his arms down on my mattress."

"Was it a very big mattress?" I asked. My voice was very level, as if there were no wrong answers and nothing surprised me. Tommy held up his hands about two feet apart. "So he touched you," I said.

Tommy nodded. "His head was right next to my leg and his arms were on top of me."

"On top of you where, Tommy?"

He swallowed. "One was across my legs and the other was sort of up to my waist."

"Were you still naked?"

"Yes."

"So his head and one of his arms were close to your penis," I said.

Eliot objected to leading. Judge Hernandez sustained him. I'd just wanted to be the one to say the word first, giving Tommy permission to do so. "What happened?" I asked.

I didn't think Tommy was going to answer. His mouth was compressed, his lips almost vanished. I could hear the little noises of his fingernails scratching at the rail in front of him. I was on the verge of asking him another question when his voice began:

"He turned his head so he was looking at me, and he smiled at me, and he said my name, and while I looked at his face I felt his hand moving up my leg and then he left it there, right at—right at the top of my leg."

"And then?"

"Then he said something like, 'Oh, what's this?' So I looked where he was looking—I thought there was a bug or something—and he was looking at my penis." Tommy didn't hesitate over the word, he said it in a rush, breathlessly. "Just staring at it, like he'd never seen one before."

I asked questions only when Tommy paused, and when I did he'd rush on, as if my voice released him. "Did he touch it?" I asked then.

"First he just stared, and I got very— I was embarrassed, I started to cover up with my hand, but he stopped me, and then he looked up at me and he stopped smiling, he looked very

241

serious, and he said, 'It's all right. There's nothing to be ashamed of.' Something like that, and I said, 'What do you mean?' and he said, 'Getting excited. It's nothing to be ashamed of, it happens to everyone all the time.' "

"Did you know what he meant?"

"No, not then. But I— But, you know, I knew where he was looking. So I guess I had some idea. Then he said, 'It's perfectly nice.' Not just all right, he said perfectly nice. Then he said . . .''

He stopped. Tommy wasn't looking at anyone else, but he wasn't consistently watching me, either. His eyes would lock on my face, as if undetachable, then suddenly skitter away, drop to the floor, cruise across the legs of the furniture, then dart back to my face. "What?" I asked.

"He said, 'May I touch it?' "

"What did you say?"

"I don't think I said anything, but maybe I nodded or something, because he acted like I had. He held up his hand, very still, like he was trying to catch something, then he brought it down and covered my penis with it."

"Covered it?"

"So you couldn't even see it any more. His whole hand just hid it. Then he—"

"What, Tommy?"

"He just breathed. Just—breathed. I could hear him breathing. That was all I could hear."

In Tommy's pauses, I couldn't hear even that much in the courtroom now. It was Becky's job to watch the jury and keep me apprised of their reactions, but I shot a glance at them as Tommy described listening to his attacker's breathing. One man was looking down at the floor, staring at it, as if concentrating on not being where he was. Two or three other jurors had their hands up to their mouths.

"What did he do next, Tommy?"

"He opened his hand, like he was just taking a peek, and he smiled again. He smiled at me. He told me it was okay again. Then he—he kissed it."

He'd said it so low I was afraid some of the jurors might not have heard. I didn't like to be overly dramatic, but I had to make sure they'd heard. "Kissed what, Tommy?"

"My penis."

Tommy looked down at the interesting twinings his fingers were performing among themselves. I prompted him again. "Then what happened?"

Tommy looked up, apparently glad to have gotten past the beginning. "Then he just stood up, and he smiled again, and he started pulling my air mattress toward the side of the pool."

"How did you feel then, Tommy?"

"I was glad that was over. It made me feel very strange."

"Strange how?"

"Like I didn't know what was going to happen next. I was glad when he stopped."

I couldn't get him to say he'd been afraid. I waited, but Tommy didn't add anything about his emotions. He continued his narrative. "He pulled my air mattress over to the shallow end of the pool, so I figured we were getting out, so I got out, and then Waldo came walking out, up the steps." Tommy paused. His face was a study: Overlaying his expression was the imposed maturity I'd seen so often, but underneath, crawling like a sudden rash spreading, was anxiety so deep it was fear. When he spoke, his voice sounded like an eerie child's impression of Austin's own casual drawl. "And he said, 'See? I told you it happens to everyone.' "

"What was he talking about, Tommy?"

I thought I'd have to prompt him again. But when he spoke the words came quickly: "His penis. It had gotten hard."

"What did he do?"

"He came over and put his arm around me and he said let's dry off. And we went over to where we'd left the towels. They'd been laying in the sun and they were very warm. Waldo picked up one of them and started drying me off. First he was standing next to me, right next to me, and he—"

"So that his penis touched you?" I asked. It was the first time I'd interrupted.

"Yes."

"Where?"

"Here," Tommy said immediately, touching his chest as if the spot were tattooed. "And here. And it ran down my back when he stooped down to dry off my legs."

"What did you do?"

"I just stood there. When I was dry I reached for my shorts and shirt, but he grabbed my arm and said, 'Let's get a little sun first.' And he had me lay down on this wide what-do-you-call-it, like a long beach chair but with a mattress on it. And he laid down next to me. And we just laid there for a while.

"Did Austin lay on his front or his back?"

"His back," Tommy said.

"Did he cover himself?"

"No."

"Did he say anything?"

"He started telling me," Tommy said, "that it was very secret, that only people that were very, very good friends could be together like this. And that he wouldn't ever tell anybody and I shouldn't either. He was holding my hand. And he hugged me, he put his arms around me and squeezed me against his chest."

And Tommy squeezed back, I had no doubt, because he'd never had enough hugs in his life. For a long moment he'd probably thought the worry was past and he finally had someone who loved him and would always be close when Tommy needed him.

"Then he touched me again," Tommy said abruptly. "He ran his hand down my back and he held my behind, and then with both hands. His cheek scraped my face. And he pulled back, and he was still holding me, and he said, 'Look.' "

"At?"

"At his penis. It was right there in front of me, and it was hard again, and it was right in front of me, and he said, 'Wouldn't you like to touch mine?' "

"Did you want to, Tommy?"

He shook his head, back and forth, back and forth. "No. It scared me. It was very red, and it was big, I didn't know it could get so big."

"Did you touch it?"

"Yes."

"Why?"

"Because he wanted me to."

Tommy's voice hadn't faltered very often as he talked. Generally he said things in a rush. He didn't appear on the verge of breaking down as he had earlier, so it may have been very belatedly that I noticed he was crying. There were two shining streaks down his cheeks, and as he talked another tear welled out and slid down the path. He kept talking as if he were somewhere else, watching what he described.

"How did you touch it, Tommy?"

He demonstrated, holding out his index finger, making it as long as he could. "I was just going to tap it, but when I touched it he put his hand around mine and mine was inside and he closed his eyes and I was afraid to move. He didn't move again for a long time, like he'd gone to sleep."

"Did he ever open his eyes?"

"Yes. Then he smiled at me and he said, 'I kissed yours.' "

The story flowed on. Tommy described the oral-genital contact Austin was accused of, and then ejaculation. When I had to intrude questions I did it with a voice so steady I became that voice, detached, nonjudgmental, sympathetic but uninvolved. Tommy sounded similar, but he kept crying, and when he described the shock of climax his head jerked backward and he looked frightened. He sobbed. I didn't return to the witness stand to comfort him. I gave him a moment's respite and a one-sentence reassurance, and he composed himself again. The courtroom was dead silent, as if Tommy's story were a sea that had covered us quietly, flowing in so silently it had taken us unawares, leaving us in a soundless undersea world.

When he was quite, quite done I had him tell about being taken back to his neighborhood and dropped off, left to go home and explain to his parents where he'd been, and to keep Waldo's and his secret that night and for many nights to come, even when Waldo wasn't there to reward his loyalty, when there was only Tommy alone in the dark, alone in the wide world. He was crying again at the end, and I did leave my chair and put my arm around him, and murmured softly to him in front of all those strangers. "I'm proud of you," I said too softly for the microphone to pick up. Tommy nodded and used my handkerchief to wipe his eyes and gradually recovered himself. He smiled at me weakly. I gave him one last warm touch and turned away. I looked at Eliot and said, "I pass the witness."

14

I FELT AN EERIE NERVINESS AS I TOOK MY SEAT. AT first I thought it was the silence ringing in my ears, but it was part of me, it was something running on my skin like ants. Later I realized it was adrenaline, it was the urge to leap up and smash someone. My nerves were rising through my skin with the dread of handing Tommy over to Eliot.

I'd felt Eliot's eyes on me occasionally during my questioning, but as soon as the witness was his he focused on him entirely. Eliot sat straight but at ease, looking at Tommy without a trace of hostility. He looked nothing but compassionate, and disturbed by the story the boy had told.

"Would you like some water, Tommy?" he asked. Tommy shook his head. "Would you like us to stop for a few minutes? All right. My name is Eliot Quinn, Tommy. I'm the lawyer for Austin Paley. I'm helping him the way Mr. Blackwell has helped you. We're trying to find out the truth of what happened a long time ago. To do that, Mr. Blackwell asks you questions and then I do. If you don't understand one of my questions, tell me that, all right?, and I'll try to think of another way to ask it. And you can take your time to think about what you want to answer, all right, Tommy?"

My feet were beneath me. An urge to object kept me on edge, though I don't know what my objection would be. But he was taking too long to get to his questions, he was setting him up. Tommy nodded at him. He'd stopped crying.

"You didn't tell your parents when this happened, Tommy?"

"No."

"Why not?"

"I was afraid," he repeated.

"Afraid of your parents?" Eliot still looked troubled, but now his trouble was in understanding.

Tommy shifted in his seat. "No, I was afraid—because of what had happened."

"But I'm talking about your mother and father, Tommy, not the man. If you were afraid of him, why didn't you tell your parents, so they could protect you from him?"

Tommy struggled to make Eliot understand. "Because it was bad, what I did. I was afraid they'd be mad at me."

"Your own parents?" Eliot asked. "Did they get mad at you a lot?"

"No."

No, I could have explained. They were proud of Tommy, in a distant, abstracted way, and glad in the same way that he caused them so little trouble. Even at eight Tommy must have sensed that, that his parents wouldn't like problems.

"Did they punish you much?" Eliot asked.

"No," Tommy said, then hastened to add, "But I'd never done anything that bad before."

"But it wasn't your fault, was it?"

The language doesn't have enough tenses. I didn't know if Tommy could answer from the precise spot in the past Eliot was talking about. Tommy may have been thinking of the later times when he was Austin's willing accomplice. And those times had convinced him that he'd been at fault from the beginning. He had attracted the grown man. "No," Tommy said slowly, but that was a woefully incomplete answer.

I was still tense in my chair with the urge to intervene. I could feel Eliot closing in on Tommy, the way I'd seen him trap a hundred witnesses. *Restraint,* I thought, *restraint.* I had to let Eliot do his work. *But how,* I thought, *can you hurt this boy, when you're acting out of guilt over what you once helped do to the onetime boy beside you?*

"Then why didn't you tell your parents?" Eliot asked insistently.

Tommy sat silent. Eliot let him. When it seemed Tommy

couldn't come up with an answer, he finally said, "I didn't want them to think I'd been bad."

Eliot regarded Tommy quietly. Eliot was a grandfatherly presence in the trial, and he knew it. He wasn't going to press too hard. Eliot spoke as if moving on to something else. "Who *was* the first person you told about what had happened?"

"Mom and Dad," Tommy said.

Eliot looked baffled. He even said aloud, "Hmf." Then asked, "You didn't tell anyone else?"

"No. Not at first."

"You didn't tell any of your friends?"

"No."

"All these children who used to hang around at Austin's house with you, you didn't warn any of them, you didn't tell them just a little bit of what had happened to you?"

"No."

"Not the whole thing, Tommy. I mean didn't you just say something like, 'I didn't like the way he touched me,' or, 'He made me feel funny,' or even just, 'I don't want to go play there any more'?"

"No," Tommy insisted.

"In fact, you *did* keep going back there to play, didn't you?"

"Yes," Tommy admitted.

"When did you tell your parents?" Eliot asked.

"This summer."

"*This* summer? Two months ago, three months ago?"

"Yes."

"How long was that after it had happened, Tommy?"

"Two years."

"*More* than two years, yes, from May nineteen-ninety to August or so of this year?"

Tommy shrugged.

"Why did you tell them then?" Eliot asked, adding before Tommy could answer, "Were they asking you if something like that had happened?"

"No," Tommy said.

"Had you been acting like something was wrong? Were your mom and dad worried about you?"

"Objection," I said, finally having found a spot for it. "He can't testify what was in someone else's mind."

Eliot was on his feet, too. "He would know if his parents acted worried about him, Your Honor."

"Phrase it that way," Judge Hernandez said neutrally.

"Tommy." Eliot was making his transition now. Not quite so kindly, a little more stern. He was leaning toward Tommy, a constant small frown shaping his features as he struggled to understand. "At the time you told your parents what had happened, were they acting concerned about you? Did they seem to be worried about the way you were acting?"

Tommy's eyes were downcast as he searched his memory for a time when his parents had seemed concerned about him. "No," he said.

"What was the occasion, what was happening, when you did tell them? Were they talking to you?"

"No. We were watching TV."

"TV. What were you watching?"

Bingo. *Say it, Tommy.* Eliot had read Tommy's written statement, he knew he'd picked out Austin from television news. I'd hoped Eliot would ask him about that, because it was such a fluky ID. Eliot had to broach it. And when he did, Tommy could say what *hadn't* been in his written statement:

"The news," Tommy said. "And I saw him, I saw Austin on TV. They said other children had been molested. So I knew he'd done it to other kids too," Tommy concluded.

Good boy. I couldn't offer evidence of the other child-molesting cases against Austin, but if Eliot accidentally elicited the information himself, well, that couldn't be helped, could it?

When I turned toward him Eliot was still looking at Tommy, showing no sign that he'd just been hurt.

"But Austin wasn't accused of those crimes, was he, Tommy? He was representing someone who was accused. Isn't that what the story on TV said?"

"I think. But I knew it was him who'd done it to them," Tommy said, true to the program. But I didn't like the way he looked as he made his accusation. He had lost the hurt-little-boy look; now he looked like a little man again. He even shot a look at Austin as he mentioned the other children, a look that spoke of very adult jealousy and sense of betrayal. Maybe there *is* nothing adult about our emotions. Maybe children feel them as strongly as we. But what was important at that moment was that Tommy no longer looked childish enough. Eliot sat silent for a few seconds, letting the jury study Tommy's expression before he asked another question.

"So what you told your parents—correct me if I don't have this right—was, 'Me, too. I was molested too.' Was that what you said, Tommy?"

"Yes." Tommy saw nothing wrong with that.

"And what did your parents do?" Eliot asked. "Did they call the police, did they take you to a doctor?"

"No. Not—"

"No?" Eliot stared at him. "Did they bring you the next day to see the district attorney?"

"No," Tommy tried to explain. "Not at first."

"Did they do anything at first?"

"Just talked to me," Tommy said.

"How *did* you get to see a doctor and the police and these prosecutors?"

"I told my teacher at school the next day."

"Your teacher. This was August," Eliot said.

"And the nurse," Tommy added, nodding.

"The nurse. Had you talked to her very often?"

"I think I saw her in third grade," Tommy said, "when my stomach hurt and I had to go home."

Eliot nodded at the recollection. I saw exactly where Eliot had led him. I assumed everyone else did, too.

"I have no more questions," Eliot said.

Which startled me. I'd expected Eliot to challenge Tommy's identification of Austin, which would have allowed me on cross-examination to expand my inquiry in order to show the jury how long Tommy and Austin had known each other, therefore how sure Tommy must be of his molester's identity. Eliot hadn't given me that opening. Without it, I wasn't sure I'd even be allowed to introduce Austin's subsequent continuing sexual assaults on Tommy. They would be considered extraneous offenses, irrelevant to the one assault that was the subject of this trial.

I felt Eliot close beside me as the witness was mine again.

"Tommy," I said, speaking slowly, "why did you tell your parents about this man molesting you?"

"Because I thought he'd done it to other kids, too," Tommy said earnestly. "And I thought—"

"Objection," Eliot said, on his feet at once. "This is pure speculation on this boy's part, based on nothing. It introduces the idea of extraneous offenses, to the defendant's extreme prejudice, and is completely unfounded."

"Your Honor, the defense inquired into the witness's motive for his accusation. That makes my question—"

"Motive?" Eliot said to me, throwing up one hand. "All I asked was when he finally told someone, after years of silence. What does that—?"

"Now I object to this speaking objection," I said. "Defense counsel can make a speech when the time comes—"

"Stop arguing with each other," Judge Hernandez snapped. "The objection is sustained. Ladies and gentlemen," he added to the jury, "ignore that last answer. As defense counsel said, it has no basis in the evidence at all. You are concerned with only one accusation in this case."

I shook my head and sat down, not as displeased as I appeared. The jurors understood, I hoped, that if they had a question about Tommy's motive it wasn't my fault that it wouldn't be answered for them. It was the defense that was determined to cut off any mention of those other children. The jurors wouldn't forget.

"Tommy," I continued. "Was that day that he took you to the swimming pool the last time you saw Austin Paley?"

Tommy shook his head.

"Did he come back to the vacant house in your neighborhood?"

"Yes," Tommy said softly. He appeared a little frightened by the exchange Eliot and I had had over his testimony. I liked the effect on him. He looked small and scared again. I wasn't going to waste that emotion.

"Did the defendant come to find you?"

Now it was Eliot who was tense, ready to object. I could feel him coiled beside me. I tried to ask questions that would keep him poised just that way, anxious to spring to his feet but with no objection to make.

"Yes," Tommy said.

"More than once?"

He nodded.

"Speak up, please, Tommy. Did he come find you more than once after that day by the pool?"

"Yes."

"Twice, three times?"

"More," Tommy said. "Lots more."

"Total, Tommy. Between that day by the pool and the day you saw Austin on television and said, 'That's him,' how much time did you spend with him, total? A few minutes?"

"Hours," Tommy said.

I think Eliot was going to object then, that my questions and Tommy's answers were implying other crimes his client had committed. But I was the one who rose to my feet. I walked behind Eliot, inches from his back. He ignored me. Buster Harmony looked up, his mouth falling open.

I stood behind Austin Paley. He didn't turn to me. I couldn't tell from his posture if he was even nervous.

"Forget television, Tommy," I said loudly. "Look here, now. Think about those times, and particularly that first day beside the swimming pool. Is this the man who was with you that day?"

Tommy was staring at him as instructed. He looked sad, sorry, a victim of violated trust. "Yes," he said.

"Is this the man who put his penis in your mouth?"

"Objection," Eliot said. "This has been asked and answered. The district attorney is just straining for effect."

I don't think anyone was listening to him. Because I had achieved my effect. Tommy's face was closing in on itself. His eyes turned wet again.

"Sustained," said the judge.

"Do you have any doubts?" I asked Tommy.

He shook his head. The movement started a tear down his cheek.

Eliot was still on his feet, right beside me. He was looking at me without hostility. I felt a strange intimacy in his almost-blank expression.

"Your witness," I said.

Tommy, on the witness stand, had his hand in front of his mouth. He was no longer looking directly at Austin. He was trying to stop crying but couldn't. His crying was soft and undemonstrative, but that only made him more pitiful. Eliot looked at him and saw only damage to be done to the defense case. "No more questions," he said.

I walked to the witness stand to help Tommy down. "Don't

worry," I said softly, and put my arm around him. He kept his head down as I walked him to the railing. "You did fine."

"We reserve the right to recall the witness," Eliot was saying.

Karen Rivera was waiting at the railing to take Tommy off my hands. She frowned at me before she led Tommy out of the room. Mrs. Algren, halfway back among the spectators, struggled out to the aisle to join them. Mr. Algren remained where he was, watching me.

"Call your next witness," Judge Hernandez said.

I didn't let him hurry me. I resumed my seat and leaned close to Becky. "Do we need somebody now?" I asked softly.

"We need everybody we can get," she said.

"Yeah. You're right." I reflected that it was the first conversation I'd had with Becky since the trial had begun. It seemed like days. She looked at me seriously, offering her best advice, not a smile of encouragement or intimacy. I nodded and stood up. Judge Hernandez was regarding me as if I were an inept waiter too slow to take his order.

I said, "The State calls—"

And stopped. I looked down at Eliot, in the chair on my left. He was leaning the other way to confer quietly with his client and co-counsel, but when my voice stopped he glanced up at me. I had a sudden fear that I was doing something wrong. My case was essentially done, only the filigree work left. But anything I added gave Eliot another chance to hurt me. I'd planned to save this witness for rebuttal. This last-minute rearrangement made me feel I was being pushed into making a mistake.

"Who?" the judge asked ironically.

But Becky had agreed, and she was watching the trial from the side, less emotionally involved than I. She thought our case needed help now.

"Dr. Janet McLaren," I said.

Judge Hernandez nodded to one of the bailiffs, who started toward the gate in the railing that opened to the courtroom's aisle. I stopped him.

"Dr. McLaren isn't here," I told the judge. "We need a few minutes to bring her from her office."

He frowned at me. "You didn't know you were going to need her testimony?" he asked loudly.

"Your Honor, maybe a doctor will spend all afternoon waiting in *your* waiting room, but I can't get any to do it for me. We'll need a few minutes."

Judge Hernandez didn't like the knowing chuckles my explanation received. He looked at his watch, an ornate gold affair heavy on his wrist. "We'll take fifteen minutes," he decided. "Be back at four-thirty. Sharp. Bailiff, see if the jurors need anything." He wouldn't let them escape his benevolence. They were voters.

I was surprised by the time. It was almost the end of the first day, and we were about to call our last witness. I couldn't believe it had gone so fast.

"I'll go call her office," Becky said, and was gone. I sat alone at the State's table with no notes to peruse, nothing to do but worry. I had an urge to turn to Eliot and discuss the case with him. It wouldn't be unprecedented. Prosecutors and defense lawyers often chat together during breaks in trials, each more interested in his opponent's opinion of his performance than in the feelings of laymen such as the jury and the defendant. But when I turned toward Eliot he was deep in quiet conversation with Austin and Buster. Buster was the one doing the talking, animatedly. The few words I picked up were angry: ". . . hit him harder . . ." I couldn't hear Eliot.

It was Wednesday, October 30. Election day was Tuesday, six days away. Three days should be enough to finish the trial. By the weekend I'd know whether I still had a career. No: I'd know if I *didn't*. Losing the trial would almost certainly lose me the election. I'd look as if I'd engaged in malicious prosecution for devious reasons, and induced children to lie, to try to convict an innocent man. I wasn't sure that winning the trial would win me the election. Maybe I was too far behind. I was sure only that losing the trial would set Austin free, and leave him so sure of his power that he would never restrain himself again.

I looked at him across the narrow space of the front of the courtroom. He was facing my direction, head inclined toward Eliot beside him, nodding at his instructions. Then Austin began speaking, in an intimate undertone, but he looked not at his lawyers but at me. In Austin's eye was his familiar sparkle and I swear his mouth shaped itself into a wry smile as he spoke. It was the same look he'd given me a hundred times in the past. Now it seemed to say, *I'm not worth all this trouble.*

What I thought in return, staring back at him, was, *I may have to kill you, Austin, my old friend.* If I lost this trial, and lost my office as well, how could I retire to private life with the picture of Austin unbridled, no one to check him? How could I sleep at night knowing he was out in the same night, planning, stalking, perhaps with his hand at that moment on a child's shoulder, smiling charmingly?

I came to myself with a start, as if awakening from a nightmare of falling. Austin was no longer looking at me, but I thought I detected the residue of a satisfied smile on his face, as if he knew what I'd been imagining, because he'd been picturing the same scene himself, with relish.

I looked in his face for traces of the boy who had been molested by his father. Eliot must have seen them; if he didn't see Austin as a victim he could never have agreed to defend him. But all I saw was the man who had used Eliot Quinn's guilt feelings to cover his own crimes. All I saw was the victimizer. It was strange I had never seen that in Austin's face all these years. It seemed so plain now.

"I wish there were some land mines we could lay in your testimony, but I don't know of any—unless there's something you haven't told me, like you once happened to stumble upon Austin Paley fondling Tommy?"

Janet McLaren shook her head.

"Too bad. Then we're just going to ask you questions until they stop us. We're just going to pound you as far as we can."

"Like a battering ram," she said.

"Exactly. And when they do cut us off I want you to look like there's lots more juicy stuff you could tell the jury if not for these darned rules."

She nodded, accepting her instructions without demur, but with an ironic cast to her mouth. Janet looked like a completely professional woman, but not one trying to be a man. She wore a dark green suit that made me aware of the flash of her eyes, and the silky blouse beneath the jacket made it clear she was flesh, not animated fabric. I had greeted her with pleasure, but while instructing her made sure not to touch her or smile.

"Tommy's telling the truth, and there are damned good reasons why he didn't speak up sooner. He's a frightened little boy, abused by a man who took advantage of him. By that particular man." I pointed downward, to the courtroom two floors below my office, where the three of us stood. Janet looked poised and ready. Becky stood beside her, arms folded, head bent slightly, staring at me as if she too were accepting instructions. "Right?" I asked.

Janet McLaren nodded, but too slowly; too judiciously, I thought. "You have to come across as a detached professional," I said, "who has coolly evaluated the evidence and come to conclusions. But I hope that's not what you are. I hope you don't feel neutral and impartial about this case." She started to speak and I stopped her. "Don't answer that, Eliot might ask you if you've ever expressed a personal opinion about this case. But we understand each other?"

She nodded.

"Good. And, Doctor? They're going to hit back. You have to take whatever Eliot hits you with and shrug it off, as if he's just not bright enough to understand. Don't let him get to you. Your personal feelings aren't involved. If he makes you testy, or flustered, you'll be that much less use to me. And to Tommy. Just sit quietly and let the questions roll off you. Take your time to think about your answer; don't blurt anything out in the heat of the moment. And never, ever, ever give him one word more than he asks for. Don't give him even that if you can avoid it."

She began to let her exasperation show. "This isn't my first time to testify."

I laughed harshly. "Tell me that again in an hour. *I* just made you visibly annoyed in less than a minute. And you *are* going to wear some expression other than that supercilious smirk you have on now, aren't you?"

Janet turned to Becky. "Is he always like this during trial?"

"We all are," Becky said.

"How many children have you examined, Dr. McLaren, during your ten years working in this field?"

"Hundreds. Perhaps as many as a thousand."

"All boys, all girls, or a mix?"

Janet took her time answering. The jurors were to her left, within a few feet of her. I looked in their direction. Janet showed no reaction to my glance. "I'd say a slight majority have been girls," she said.

"But you've examined hundreds of boys who had been sexually abused?"

Now she turned toward the jurors. She looked them over swiftly but individually, as if under other circumstances she'd like to get to know them better. "Yes," she said.

"Have your examinations been limited to verbal interviews?"

"No. I also examine the children physically."

"You are a medical doctor, I believe you testified?" We had already established Janet's professional qualifications. She explained for the jury's benefit that she insisted on doing physical exams of the children before starting her psychological evaluations, in order to gain the children's confidence, to reassure them they were still physically normal. She didn't tell the jury, as she'd told me weeks ago, in what a small percentage of cases she found physical evidence of abuse.

"Do you continue treating these children for some time, Dr. McLaren?"

"In most cases, yes. On the average I treat a child for three or four years."

Good answer. It told the jury not only that Janet knew what she was talking about, from long examination of abused children, but that such children *required* lengthy treatment to recover from the effects of sexual abuse.

"Do you have a pretty good cure rate?"

She smiled, slightly and sadly. "I'll never know. We make progress, the children and I. I help them reconcile what happened to them with how they feel about themselves. Often when they leave my care I feel their self-esteem has recovered enough to allow them to find happiness—or at least to give them as good a chance as anyone else has. But the literature tells us that in children who've been sexually abused problems recur years later, sometimes decades later. So I can't use a word like *cured*."

I paused as if I were absorbing this sad truth. Then, "What are some of the long-term effects on children who have been sexually assaulted by adults?" I asked.

Again Janet paused for reflection. She was taking my advice seriously. She appeared both knowledgeable and thoughtful. But this time her pause gave Eliot time to stand.

"Objection, Your Honor. This is irrelevant. There is only one alleged victim in this case. Case studies on other children are irrelevant."

I started to rise too, but Judge Hernandez said, "Sustained," before I could even push back my chair.

"Then let's just talk about Tommy Algren," I said. "Have you treated him professionally, Doctor?"

"Yes. But only for the last two months, since he came forward with what happened to him."

"Have you had enough sessions with him to form professional opinions about him?"

"Oh, yes," Janet said. Careful. A little too eager.

"He's told you what happened to him?"

"Yes."

"Do you have an opinion about the psychological effect on him?"

"Yes."

"Has he been damaged?"

"Quite definitely." Janet glanced at me, she didn't want to jump the gun, but when I nodded slightly she began speaking quickly, to the jury. "Tommy Algren is ten years old. I had to keep reminding myself of that while treating him, because he gives an appearance of much greater maturity. He comes across as a little man. I can tell Tommy's modeled himself after his abuser, who must be a man of some—"

She had turned to look directly at Austin, who stared back at her as if she were a faintly amusing movie but he was about to go to the lobby for popcorn.

"Objection," Eliot said exasperatedly. "It strains credulity to believe that Dr. McLaren can give a profile of someone based on her examination of someone *else*."

"I believe that's a question for the jury, Your Honor," I interjected quickly, hoping I could nudge the judge aside from his ruling.

"Not when it's a question of law," Eliot said. "The doctor hasn't been qualified as an expert on anyone except children."

"Sustained," the judge said laconically.

"What about Tommy, Doctor?" I asked.

She lifted her stare from Austin. She pursed her lips. "Sometimes," she began slowly, then spoke with increasing urgency, "a child comes to me just shattered. We have to start from zero to build a personality. The child has retreated so far inside in response to the abuse that there's nothing left, no visible signs of responsiveness. In other cases, I learn from questioning others that the child has undergone a complete change in personality—has become, perhaps, more aggressive. Constantly acts out inappropriate behavior."

Janet wasn't glancing at Eliot as if putting one over on him, but it was patently obvious that she was now giving the testimony to which Eliot had successfully objected: detailing the various reactions of child rape victims. *I* looked at Eliot, who was watching my witness closely, not at all caught napping. I frowned. Something— I tried to put myself in Eliot's position. Why was he letting this happen?

"A case like Tommy's is the most difficult, in many ways," Janet was continuing. She was talking directly to the jury and they were watching her with absorption. "Because he seems at first untouched. But what I've discovered is that his maturity is a thin shell, over a personality much too young for its age. Once you pierce that shell—once you make him question whether he's really found the right way to behave—you break through to a very, very young boy who has no idea *how* to act. He doesn't know how to be a child and he doesn't know how to be an adult. Tommy is ten years old, he'll be an adolescent soon. But he's not ready. He's hopelessly muddled about sex, of course, but it goes deeper than that. He's only passing as a child, and not very successfully. For example, he has no friends. He's cut himself off from the few he had, because it's too difficult for him to try to behave normally with them. He doesn't know what normal is. He's a very isolated, very troubled little boy."

I did not nod in sympathy. "It sounds, Doctor, as if you're describing a typically confused boy on the verge of being a teenager. Aren't even normal kids 'hopelessly muddled' at Tommy's stage of life?"

She shook her head emphatically. "Not to this degree. Normal children—we don't use that word, so let's say untraumatized children—have *some* place where they can be themselves. School may scare them but they're all right with their families. Or with their friends. Or they *like* school, and they're okay there. Or in church, or with me—often it's with me. But Tommy has no place to be himself comfortably. He *has* no self. He's putting up a front for everyone, and inside he's just scared to death. I'm very concerned about him."

I expected that expression of personal feeling to draw another objection from Eliot, but again there was only ominous silence from the defense table.

"Dr. McLaren, Tommy didn't report this sexual assault on him for a long time, two years or more. And then he blurted it out while watching television with his parents. Doesn't that sound to you like a story he might have just made up on the spot to draw attention?"

"Objection, Your Honor. No matter how expert the witness is, she can't testify whether someone else is telling the truth. The jurors must decide that for themselves."

I almost stepped on the end of Eliot's last sentence in my eagerness to dissuade the judge from ruling in his favor. "I'm sure the court understands," I said smoothly, "that I'm not asking the witness to tell the jury whether Tommy was telling the truth. I'm asking her whether his behavior is consistent or inconsistent with the many hundreds of patients she's examined. Of course," I added, in a tone that said the judge and I understood this well, I was only speaking for the benefit of less astute minds, "that's what being an expert witness is all about."

Judge Hernandez nodded. "Overruled," he said.

I hurried on with my questioning. "Doesn't it sound like a lie, Doctor?"

Janet spoke as if I were the one who needed educating; or as if I were trying to trip her up with subtle questions. "Of course it could be a lie," she said, "from the bare facts you've given me. But it's also consistent with Tommy's telling the truth. Again, children react differently. Many of them do make an immediate outcry right after the abuse. But many others conceal it, sometimes for years. They feel guilty. And of course the child is afraid of what people will think about him when they find out.

"The way Tommy told what had happened, when he sees the man again after some time, but he's safe at home with his parents at the time, and finally he can't suppress his anger and his hurt any more, I find that consistent with the behavior of a sexually abused child."

Janet turned from the jury to me. It was probably my imagination—I'm sure I was the only person who saw it—that her expression seemed to challenge me. *See? I told you I could do this.* From the corner of my eye I saw Eliot watching her intently.

Janet continued, "The way Tommy's behaved since his revelation also convinces me he was telling the truth. A lying child will break down any number of times, change the story, back off from it. The way Tommy's persisted through telling the story to teachers, police officers, people in your office, and of course me, over the course of weeks of treatment, makes me very much doubt he's lying."

That seemed a good assertion with which to stop. "Thank you, Doctor. I"—Becky was scribbling me a note—"pass the witness."

Becky moved the note toward me. It said, "medical evidence."

"I'll clean that up on redirect," I whispered.

There are so many subtleties to questioning a witness, and everyone has a different style. I had meant to bring up the subject of what Janet's medical exam of Tommy had uncovered. But her answers had led me away from the subject, and I thought it more important to stop when I had, rather than return to, and end with, the weakest feature of my case. I try to hand a witness over to the opposition just when the witness has made her strongest statement on my behalf, when she sounds most credible and, I hope, the jury is most in sympathy with her. Janet had made a very good impression. Let Eliot start attacking her while the jurors were still nodding to themselves over Janet's sincerity and professionalism.

Eliot didn't shy away from the job. "Dr. McLaren," he said, without introduction or preamble. "You said you also gave Tommy a medical examination. What was the result of that exam?"

Shit. This is why *I* should have broached the subject first, to take the sting out of it. By neglecting it I'd given Eliot a weapon.

"The physical exam was consistent with a child who has been sexually abused," Janet said calmly.

Oh, no, no, no. Janet thought she was being clever, but she was giving Eliot exactly the answer he wanted, the one I would have wanted if I'd been on the defense team.

"Let me be more specific," Eliot said. "Did you find physical evidence of sexual abuse?"

"Not definitive evidence," Janet said, "but indications that told me—"

"Any scarring in the anal area?"

"No."

"Or redness?"

"Of course, redness wouldn't have persisted long enough for me—"

"Yes or no, Doctor, redness."

"No."

"Any enlargement of the rectum?"

"No," Janet said coldly. "Of course, from Tommy's descriptions of the sexual assaults, there wouldn't have been."

I caught the plurals. Janet was fighting back. I wanted to call a time out to tell her to calm down. This was my fault. I'd handed my witness over to Eliot with a target plastered on her chest.

"Was there any scarring in the mouth, then?" Eliot asked reasonably. "Or the genitals?"

"No," Janet said. "There wouldn't necessarily—"

"In other words," Eliot concluded, "you found *no* physical evidence of sexual abuse; yet you conclude that that is consistent with sexual assault. Wasn't that your testimony?"

"What I *found*," Janet said firmly, "was that Tommy was familiar with male sexual physiology in a way no ten-year-old, physically immature boy could be without having experienced—"

"What I asked, Doctor, was whether you had found any *physical* evidence. I didn't ask for your psychological conclusions."

"It's not psychology—" Janet began.

I interrupted. "Objection, Your Honor. This is argumentative. Defense counsel is badgering the witness."

And very effectively. I was speaking more to Janet than to the judge. *Don't argue with him. I'll straighten this out when I get you back.* Janet drew a deep breath while Judge Hernandez overruled my objection. She looked at the jury again, gave them a tight smile.

Eliot had changed personalities like putting on a new hat. Janet wasn't a child. He treated her as if he were as professionally qualified as she, and had no faith in Janet's diagnoses.

"Let's discuss the various reactions you said abused children have. I believe you said if a child is very withdrawn, overly shy with strangers, that tends to indicate the child has been abused."

"I don't believe I said overly shy, but yes, those are common symptoms of sexual abuse. Having been molested by one, of course the child withdraws from other strangers, or even from family members."

Eliot nodded. "And if a child is overly aggressive, that can be a sign as well. What did you call it?"

" 'Acting out.' Meaning a child acting aggressively toward other children, especially sexually aggressive." Janet seemed to want to say more, but perhaps she remembered my advice to give Eliot nothing extra.

Eliot seemed satisfied. "Then you have a case like Tommy's, where he seems perfectly normal, even mature for his age, but that's only a mask for deep insecurity."

"It can be," Janet said carefully, with perhaps an inkling of where Eliot was going. "Of course, there are some perfectly happy-seeming children who actually *are*—"

"So in other words," Eliot said again. I hated that phrase so much that I stood to object to it.

"He's putting words in the witness's mouth, Your Honor."

"Not so far," Eliot answered. "I haven't even finished my sentence yet."

Judge Hernandez motioned for him to continue.

"So," Eliot continued, "if a child is shy, that can be a sign of sexual abuse. If a child is *not* shy, is in fact outgoing, *that* can be a sign of sexual abuse. Or a child who is neither too shy nor too aggressive lights up a signal in your mind that he has been sexually abused."

Janet didn't let Eliot get to her. "There is a wide range of reactions," she said.

"I'm afraid you're going to scare the parents on this jury to death," Eliot said calmly. "Every one of them can go home after hearing your testimony and find signs that their own children have been sexually abused."

"Objection, objection," I was saying well before he finished. "He's not questioning the witness, he's making an argument."

"You have a question?" Judge Hernandez asked Eliot mildly.

"Yes, I have a question. Doctor"— Eliot used the title in a tone that made clear he extended it to the witness only out of politeness—"you said you've examined hundreds of sexually abused children. Have you ever examined any who *haven't* been sexually abused?"

Janet didn't understand. "Of course I treat children who have other problems. My field of specialization is sexually abused children, but I have other types of patients."

Eliot was shaking his head. "I mean, out of the thousand children who've come to you claiming to be sexually abused, have you ever concluded that *any* of them was lying?"

"Of course," Janet said.

"How many?" Eliot asked. "Out of the thousand you've interviewed, how many did you not believe?"

"Objection," I said, with no idea what I was going to say next. I fell back on the standard. "This is irrelevant. We're only concerned here with one child."

Eliot turned to me with a look of surprise, because my objection sounded so familiar. "I believe we talked about a great many children during the witness's *direct* examination," he said innocently.

"Overruled," Judge Hernandez agreed. He looked at me as he would have at a virgin trial lawyer appearing in his court for the first time, making rookie mistakes. "You opened the door, counsel," he added to me, gratuitously.

"How many?" Eliot urged my witness.

"Several," Janet said, and immediately corrected herself. "Quite a few. I can't give you a number—"

"Several?" Eliot said unbelievingly. "Out of a thousand children? What does 'several' mean? Five, six?"

"Many more than that," Janet said hastily. "But you have to understand, the children aren't brought to me until they've convinced other people that something actually happened to them. I'm not—"

"Particularly their parents, who would naturally be very concerned if their children said they'd been sexually attacked by a stranger," Eliot said. He appeared very cool. It was Janet who seemed nervous, or at least pressed, eager to explain everything she said.

"Yes, of course," she said, "but usually they've convinced other people, too. Teachers, their pediatricians, sometimes police officers."

"But you're the professional, Doctor. You're the one who evaluates the children based on your years of experience"—his tone gently mocked the phrase—"and you believe them *all*, don't you, Doctor? You *never* think a child is lying when he claims to have been sexually abused, do you?"

"That's not true," Janet insisted.

"How often? In what percentage of your cases do you decide the child is lying?"

"A small percentage," Janet admitted.

"*Very* small, wouldn't that be more accurate?"

Janet was straining. She wanted very much to be understood.

"Children come to me very, very hurt. Very troubled. It would be hard to say, 'No, this child isn't damaged. This child is just making up stories.' "

"Well," Eliot responded, " 'troubles' can arise for any number of reasons, can't they? A child could have been damaged in many other ways than by being sexually abused. Ways that could result in lying, couldn't they, Doctor?"

"Yes. Certainly."

"Some children lie every time they open their mouths, isn't that true, Doctor? Have you encountered any pathological liars in your practice, Doctor?"

"Yes. One or two. Genuine pathological liars, rather than the way laypersons throw the term around, are very rare."

"At least *you* don't uncover any very often, do you, Dr. McLaren?" There was no good answer for that. Janet made none. Eliot continued, "If a child immediately reports the sexual attack, that's evidence of truthfulness, isn't it? If the child is still in the immediate grip of the pain and the fear, he or she is believable, isn't he?"

"Yes. Most of us—"

"But if he puts off telling anyone for a week or two, struggling with guilt, or the fear the stranger will return, that's consistent with truthfulness in your evaluation too, isn't it, Doctor?"

"That *is* the way some children react."

"And if he waits more than *two years*, passing up many, many good opportunities, many occasions when he's alone with his parents, safe as he can be, but he doesn't tell them until they're all sitting in front of the television, with a news announcer talking about other children, and the boy's parents paying more attention to those children's stories than to him, and *that's* when the boy tells his story, you find *that* consistent with truthfulness too," Eliot said harshly, almost out of breath from the length of his statement.

"In this case, yes," Janet said, having regained her composure. "I've treated many children who kept silent for months or longer without telling anyone they'd been abused. It's consistent."

"Is there *any* possibility in the timing of when Tommy told his story that would arouse your suspicion?" Eliot asked, as if on the verge of giving up.

Janet struggled to come up with an answer. Eliot let her struggle. So did I, because I couldn't think of any way to help. Long seconds passed. "Many children don't tell for a long time," Janet finally reiterated weakly.

Eliot sat for a moment, tapping a pencil. Buster was tugging at his sleeve, but Eliot ignored him. "Dr. McLaren, you testified that you're concerned about Tommy."

"Yes."

Eliot nodded. "And of course you're trying to help him. You believe what he's told you, don't you?"

This was a question I couldn't have asked without objection. Whether Tommy was telling the truth was, as Eliot had pointed out, for the jury to decide, not any other witness. It worried me that Eliot was asking the question.

"Yes, I believe him," Janet told the jury.

"In spite of the delay, in spite of the complete absence of physical evidence to corroborate his story."

"As I said, those are explainable."

"Yes," Eliot said, "because you believe him you can excuse any inconsistencies."

"Objection. Argumentative."

"Sustained," Judge Hernandez said. "Don't argue with the witness. Disregard that last remark," he added to the jury. As if they could.

"Let's help the *jury* decide how to evaluate Tommy's testimony," Eliot said. Feeling me stir, he added quickly, "Based on your years of experience and hundreds of patients. What did you say are some of the things that would make you think a child was lying?"

"Well, changing his story, for example. Not sticking by it when challenged."

"Like Tommy," Eliot said suddenly.

Janet frowned. "No," she said.

"I mean," Eliot said earnestly, as if just trying to jog the doctor's memory, "there *have* been occasions when he's backed off his story, said it wasn't true."

Janet shook her head, still frowning.

"He's *never* denied the story to you, even once? Never said it was all a lie, nothing actually happened between Austin Paley and him?"

"Never," Janet said firmly.

Eliot sat staring at Janet, with a puzzled look. The back of my neck went cold. Eliot did not ask questions at random. He knew something.

After letting the jury see his surprise, Eliot seemed to recover himself. "What else, then?" he asked. "What else would indicate to you that the child was lying?"

Janet thought carefully. I wanted to help her, but I couldn't object. This followed exactly my own line of questioning to her.

"Inconsistencies," she said finally. "If the child couldn't keep significant aspects of the story straight, that would certainly be some indication that it wasn't true."

"Changing the story," Eliot said helpfully. "Forgetting details."

"Well, of course, no one's memory is perfect, and often children repress—"

"Doctor," Eliot said gently, "you're making excuses for him again."

"Objection."

"Sustained. Please disregard."

"I mean major details, Doctor," Eliot continued. "Where the assault happened, when, that sort of thing. The identity of the attacker. A child who says this person assaulted me, no, that person did it, no, the first one again, tends to invite suspicion, doesn't he, Doctor?"

"Yes. Of course. But children do get confused about details more easily than adults," Janet said.

"And sometimes they lie, don't they, Doctor?"

She had to say yes. If she said no, children never lie, she'd destroy her own believability. But if she said yes she was admitting the possibility that Tommy had lied. "Yes," Dr. McLaren said.

Eliot didn't give her right up to me. He sat silently for several beats, letting us all think about lying children and the damage they can do. When he finally passed the witness I spoke quickly.

"But you don't think Tommy is lying, do you, Dr. McLaren?"

"No."

"This lack of physical evidence," I asked, frowning as if it troubled me, too. "Is that rare?"

"No, it's common. It's the norm." Janet became more authoritative again as she described how seldom she found physical evidence that children had been raped. I let her speak at some length, until the subject was thoroughly exhausted.

I think my next question surprised her. "Are children naturally suspicious of adults, Doctor?"

"Not in my experience," she said. I didn't like to hear her equivocate that way. I think she heard the doubt in her voice herself, and continued more surely, "Children tend to equate all adults with their parents. They look up to them, literally and figuratively. When he's frightened or hurt, a child looks around to any adult for comfort. That trust seems to be instinctive, until someone violates it."

"Which would confuse the child?"

"It can wreck his entire view of the world," Janet said simply.

"So once that child's trust has been abused, he no longer knows whom he *can* trust, is that right?"

"Yes. Exactly. He has nowhere to turn."

I had no more questions. Neither did Eliot. It was after five-thirty, the jurors looked tired. I was surprised when Janet was excused and Judge Hernandez looked at me inquiringly. I leaned over to Becky. "What have I messed up?"

She showed me her copy of the indictment, on which she'd checked off all the elements of the crime as we'd elicited testimony covering them. We had proven our case, if the jury believed us. That "if" made me very reluctant to rise and say what I had to say.

"The State rests, Your Honor."

The judge nodded briskly as he turned to Eliot. "You'll be prepared to begin in the morning, Mr. Quinn? That is, if you have any witnesses to offer?"

"I do, Your Honor. And we will be ready."

"I'm going to excuse you now. . . ." Judge Hernandez droned his instructions at length before letting the jurors file out. "Well, shit," I said. Becky shot her eyes sidelong at Eliot. As if I were telling a secret, as if Eliot didn't know the damage he'd done.

"I need to apologize to the doctor," I added.

Janet was still in the courtroom. I swept her up with a word and a hand on her arm. There were reporters to get past, of course, but their eyes began to glaze over after only a minute or two of my variation of "This guy's gonna be sorry he ever pulled this nastiness in *this* God-fearing county, by golly," and we were on our way, Becky and the good doctor and I.

"I'm sorry," I said to Janet on our way up the stairs. *"I* should have asked you about the physical evidence first. And I should have given you a better idea how he was going to come at you."

"Hey," she said casually, "I told you this wasn't my first time. I didn't expect him to take it easy on me."

Oh, right. I gave her a look that said it was easy to act nonchalant about the ordeal of cross-examination now, but I'd seen her sweating on the stand. I put my arm around her and she touched my hand. Just for a moment, as we went professionally side by side up the stairs. Just a touch.

We were in my office before I turned to Becky. "He knows something," I said of Eliot. Becky didn't have to ask. "But what?" I added.

"What *can* he know?" Becky answered. "What *is* there to know?"

"What are you talking about?" Janet asked.

"Tommy's denied the story to me," I said. "Who else has he told it didn't happen?"

Becky shrugged. "His parents, probably? Teacher, maybe someone at the daycare center?"

I addressed the doctor: "Tommy's never told you it was someone else who molested him, not Austin?"

Janet shook her head. "I swear," she said, which may have been ironic, since I was asking her in effect if she'd just lied under oath. She smiled at me.

"That was just smoke," Becky opined. "He just wants the jury to start wondering."

"Maybe," I said. "But I hate to leave it at that." Eliot was perfectly capable of that, in fact it was almost required—scattershooting doubt through our witnesses' testimony—but I'd be very surprised if he didn't have some evidence to back up at least some of the questions he'd asked. He'd as good as told me so, when he'd claimed Austin was innocent. He must have some proof.

"There's not much we can do about it tonight," Becky said, but when I looked at her her stance belied her expression of resignation. She looked eager to do something, question somebody. I realized how little Becky had done in the trial so far, and what a disappointment that must have been to her, a good trial lawyer. But I couldn't stand to give up any of the weight of the trial. I didn't believe its outcome could be as important to anyone in the world as it was to me.

"How was Tommy?" Janet asked. The rule that excludes witnesses from the courtroom had kept her from watching his testimony.

"He was fine," I said briefly.

But Becky contradicted me. "Not at first. He was so weak when he first took the stand I thought we'd lost him."

"You thought so too?" I said with relief, as Janet asked, "What do you mean?"

"Mark broke him down," Becky said admiringly. "If he hadn't started with how Tommy felt about what had happened, if he hadn't reminded him of how scared he'd been, the rest of his testimony would have been terribly bland. You know how Tommy talks, like he's talking about something that happened to someone else. But he was a sobbing little boy by the time he finished today."

Janet was looking at me with something other than the admiration Becky was expressing. "I hope it didn't look contrived," I said.

"*I* believed him," Becky said. That's all we can ever know. Jurors, if they talk to us at all after trials, tell us such bizarre details on which their decisions turned, things we never noticed, that we've learned not to try to predict them.

"We almost didn't call you today," Becky continued to Janet. "We thought we needed to explain Tommy's delay. But from the way Eliot went after you"—Becky turned to me—"you would have thought Dr. McLaren was our main witness."

Whenever Eliot's name came up they both turned to me, as if I knew everything our opponent was thinking. "Yes," I said slowly. "Because Janet *was* bolstering Tommy's testimony. So if Eliot demolished Janet it would leave Tommy standing alone."

"But he hardly went after Tommy at all," Becky said.

Yes. Eliot had avoided the problem I had seen in his path. I had laid the trap for him and he had sidestepped it, as casually as if he hadn't known it was there.

Janet was looking back and forth between Becky and me, left out. She turned to me alone.

"Will you need to recall me, do you think? If so, perhaps we should go some place where we can—"

I felt Becky watching us. "I'll call you," I said to Janet. "But first, I have another appointment." I resisted their questions.

It was late for my surprised hosts, but they let me in. I answered their questions, which they interrupted each other to ask, but I didn't stop walking, through the elegant foyer, into the white living room, and through it. "May I?" I asked. They nodded. Mrs. Algren reached for her husband's hand and he looked down at hers, with a surprised expression, as I turned my back on them and went into Tommy's room.

It was dark, except for light through the miniblinds that threw a railroad-track pattern on the carpet leading toward the bed. Tommy wasn't asleep. As I stopped in the center of the room I realized he'd been waiting for me.

"I came to tell you you did fine today."

There was enough light that I could see his head turning back and forth on the pillow in denial.

"Yes you were," I said. There was a desk across the room, with a straight-backed chair. I took it and sat beside the narrow bed, right next to Tommy. He made such a short mound under his covers that he looked like an amputee.

He stopped shaking his head, but not because I'd convinced him. "I'm sorry," he whispered.

"You don't have anything to be sorry for. Anything."

"I wasn't going to—" Tommy said. "I almost didn't—"

"That wasn't your fault either," I told him. I put my hand on his arm that was lying atop the covers. He sighed. "Did Austin ask you to?" I asked quietly.

Tommy nodded. "He called me."

"While my investigator was here with you?"

He nodded again. "But I answered the phone and I told him it was somebody else."

Austin needed Tommy's help to get to him, and Tommy had provided it. "It's all right," I said.

Tommy's voice was so faint I knew he'd lost control of it. "He told me he'd go to prison. He told me what they'd do to him in prison."

"Whatever happens to Austin, he's brought on himself," I said. "You were too young, Tommy, you had nothing to do with it. He planned it all. And with lots of other children. We had to stop him."

There was no response. I wondered how long Tommy had been lying in the dark waiting for me to come, and how long he'd lie there awake after I left. I squeezed his arm again. "He won't bother you any more, ever," I said.

Tommy started crying. Maybe from relief, maybe from the thought of never seeing Austin again, never having a private moment with him.

I hugged him, half-lifting him from the bed. He felt like a much younger boy than he was, like a long-ago memory of my own tiny children, years ago when I'd felt I could encompass their whole lives in my arms. I held him tightly, because the hug had to last Tommy a long, long time. All night.

His tears were wetting my shoulder. After a while he said, "Mr. Quinn knows."

"Don't worry about him," I said. "He's done with you. You're done. You don't even have to go back to the court."

Tommy shook his head against my neck. "He knows," he said again.

I let him back down on the pillow. "What does he know?"

He just shook his head.

"That you wanted to help Austin? That doesn't matter. He won't tell anyone that."

We talked in the dark a while longer. I led our conversation from the past, through today, to tomorrow, to school, to the long future when other things would capture all his concern, and he'd forget all this as surely as we all forget how it is to be a child, guilty but helpless. When Tommy's answers grew short and the silences long, I covered him and pushed aside the hair on his forehead and kissed him there.

"Good night," I said from the doorway, and there was only a faint murmur in reply.

15

COMING BACK INTO THE COURTROOM AFTER HAVING rested his case racks a prosecutor's nerves. I've spent my case, put on everything, but then have to walk back in and sit in front of that jury and wait for what the defense will do. The first part of trial is not so tense for the defense, because the State's case is not a surprise. The prosecution lists its witnesses on the indictment, and the defense lawyer has had access to the State's file. Perhaps the defense doesn't know everything a prosecution witness will say, but for the most part the State's case is straightforward and unsurprising.

The prosecutors, by contrast, do not get to review the defense case. That *will* be a surprise. You just have to sit there and take it, hoping you'll have material for cross-examination, hoping inspiration will come when you need it.

One opportunity I felt sure of was that of cross-examining Austin. Eliot and I know what the presumption of innocence is worth. A defendant who sits mum in front of the jury, offering no alternative to the State's story, is just asking to be convicted. Eliot would have to call Austin to testify in his own defense.

When Eliot entered the courtroom he was in close conference with Austin and Buster. Buster was doing the talking. That had often been the case during breaks in the trial. Buster must have been frustrated at being allowed to do so little in such a highly publicized trial, but Eliot would not have let him take over the defense, and Austin would have supported Eliot: he knew who

273

was the better trial lawyer. But Buster was getting his licks in among the three of them. Today he seemed to be upsetting Eliot, and Austin was nodding sober agreement to whatever Buster was saying.

I took my seat. Becky was beside me, but we didn't speak. There was nothing to say. We didn't know what we had to be ready for.

A few minutes later, the jury in the box and the judge on the bench, Eliot still seemed to be in charge of the defense. He rose to say, "The defense calls Martin Reese."

Becky and I gave each other raised eyebrows. Martin Reese was a stranger to us. I turned and saw him coming up the aisle, a pudgy man who'd bought his suit when he was fifteen pounds lighter. He had heavy cheeks, a thick black mustache, and several strands of brown hair combed from one ear to the other. He glared at me as if I were the one who'd made him out of breath.

Becky shook her head when I looked back at her. She didn't know him. "Me," she said softly.

I was the lead prosecutor. Normally that would mean I'd question our victim and cross-examine the defendant if he testified, and the second chair prosecutor could handle the lesser witnesses. But this wasn't a normal case. I'd taken almost everyone during our case in chief. And as I stared at this stranger taking the oath and the witness stand I was already studying him for weaknesses.

"Me," Becky said more emphatically, still too softly for anyone but me to hear.

I looked down at her hand on my wrist. I took a breath. I let my own grip relax slightly. "Yours," I muttered.

She turned away from me at once, pulling a pad toward her, uncapping her pen, and staring at the witness, as did I. Who was Martin Reese?

He didn't want to let us know. Eliot's second question to him, after he'd stated his name, was, "Where do you live, Mr. Reese?"

"I'd rather not say," the witness said. And again he glared at me.

"Do you live in Texas?" Eliot asked.

It appeared he wasn't going to answer. After a few beats he

burst out, "I don't want anyone involved in this trial to know where I live. I've already been harassed enough."

By whom? As some members of the jury followed Mr. Reese's glare to me, I strove to look innocent and perplexed. It wasn't hard.

"Let's put it this way, then," Eliot said consolingly. "Where did you live two years ago?"

"I lived on Sparrowwood Drive, here in San Antonio."

Ping. The first blip of distant alarm sounded in my mind. Martin Reese had been Tommy's neighbor. But how could he refute Tommy's story? Had he stared through his window and seen something *not* happen between Austin and Tommy? I turned and saw that Mr. and Mrs. Algren were again in the audience. Mrs. Algren was pressed as far back against her bench as she could be, as if she were trying to leave the room without moving. Her face was white.

"I'll be right back," I whispered to Becky, and stepped quickly to the gate and through. As I approached the Algrens I gestured to them, restrained but in a way that would not brook refusal. They turned guilty eyes toward me and followed me out of the courtroom.

I ushered Tommy's parents into one of the small conference rooms by the entrance to the courtroom and closed the door behind us. "Who is he?" I asked.

Mrs. Algren was clutching her husband's hand again. He edged subtly between us, but if he was trying to look like his wife's fierce defender, he was failing.

"He was our neighbor," he said. "He moved away about a year ago."

"And?" I didn't want the slow buildup.

"This is why we didn't believe Tommy at first," Mrs. Algren said, imploring me to understand.

I felt cold all over. It was hard for me to move. I turned only my eyes, to her husband.

"Tommy accused Mr. Reese of molesting him," he confirmed.

"Oh, Jesus." I put a hand to my forehead.

"It wasn't true," Mrs. Algren said hastily, as if this news were helpful. "We looked into it and it just wasn't so. Tommy admitted after a while that he'd made it up."

"We were damned lucky the man didn't sue us," Mr. Algren

275

said. "He *would* have, if we hadn't managed to keep the whole thing quiet."

"Even from me," I said quietly. My mind was racing.

"We didn't think anyone else could have known," Algren was saying. "And we didn't dare let a peep of it leak out. He still could have—"

"Go up to my office," I said quietly, disagreement not to be tolerated.

"What are you going to do about it? Can't we—?"

"I don't know yet," I said very quietly. "Be in my office when I come. Whenever I get there."

I felt everyone staring at me as I walked back up the aisle. But they weren't. They were watching the witness.

I didn't have to ask Becky how it was going. She didn't glance at me. Her attention was divided between Martin Reese and the notes she was writing.

As I sat she stood. "Objection," she said. "Calls for hearsay."

Eliot said pedantically, "We're certainly not offering the statement as the truth. We intend to show, to the contrary, that it was not true. Mr. Reese is only going to testify that he heard it made."

"*If* he heard it," Becky insisted. "I thought he was about to testify that someone else told him the statement was made."

"We will show indicia—" Eliot began, but Judge Hernandez was tired of the argument, and he wasn't going to take the chance of excluding important defense evidence.

"Overruled," he said.

"What did Tommy Algren's parents tell you?" Eliot asked.

"That Tommy had told them I'd molested him," Reese said, in a quiet but fierce voice, a restrained bellow. He was so dark in the face I feared he'd have a stroke before Becky could cross-examine him.

"Could you be more specific?" Eliot asked.

I wrote quickly on my own pad, "It wasn't true. Tommy took it back." Becky glanced at the note with no reaction. She'd already figured that out.

"They said he said I'd lured him over into my yard one day before they got home from work and that I—I *did* things to him. Disgusting things. Made him take off his clothes. Made him do things."

"Was that true?" Eliot asked.

"No!" This time the bellow wasn't restrained. "It was a damned lie! I've got kids of my own. I never—*never*—did anything like that in my life. Never *thought* about it. I'd kill someone who did."

"What happened?"

"The Algrens said they were going to call the cops. I told them they'd better make goddamned sure what they were doing before they made a public fuss of it. I think that took them back a little."

"What did you do?"

"I told them I'd take a polygraph test, and they could get their lying kid to take one, too."

"Did you take such a test?" Eliot asked.

"Objection." Becky was on her feet quickly. "The results of polygraph tests are of course not admissible."

"I didn't ask him for the result," Eliot said easily, not even bothering to stand.

But even mention of having taken a polygraph test is objectionable. The judge sustained Becky's objection. But one of the nice things about being on the defense side is that there's no fear of asking improper questions. The defense doesn't fear a reversal.

"Did you take a lie detector test?" Eliot asked his witness.

"I did," he said, and everyone heard it, over Becky's objection. "And I passed it," he added vehemently, after the judge's ruling. He glared at Becky and she stared back. I was impressed by her coolness, knowing she had nothing to back it up.

Equally coolly, as if he and his witness had done nothing wrong, Eliot asked, "Were the police called?"

"Not after that," Reese said self-righteously, folding his arms.

"Did Tommy ever make this accusation to your face, Mr. Reese?"

"No. I said I wanted to talk to him, with his parents there, but they wouldn't let me near him. When I *would* see him he'd turn his head, he couldn't look at me."

"What finally happened?"

"I kept asking them if they'd made the kid take a lie detector test yet, but they never—"

"Objection," Becky said. "Hearsay." She was sustained, but the witness continued.

"They started avoiding me, but I wouldn't let it drop. I told them they owed me an apology or I was going to sue. Course, I probably wouldn't have, because *I* didn't want it all aired in public either, but I think it scared them when I said it. They finally admitted it'd all been a lie. They said—"

"Objection. Hearsay."

"Sustained."

"Did you get your apology, Mr. Reese?"

"Yeah."

"From Tommy's parents?"

"Yes sir. I told them they needed to make the boy come tell me himself he was sorry, but he never showed up. A few months later I was offered a transfer and I was glad to take it, since the neighborhood didn't appeal to me any more. It should've been them that had to move, though."

Eliot probably realized his witness was less than appealing, no matter how damaging his testimony was. He didn't keep him talking long. When he was passed to our side, Becky began without formalities.

"Mr. Reese," Becky said. "You never heard Tommy accuse you himself?"

"No. He wouldn't face me."

"So everything you've testified about that has just been something you heard from someone else." She shot a glance at the judge. He looked back at her imperturbably.

"I never heard him say it."

Becky nodded. She hesitated. I sensed her nervousness. That's the problem with cross-examining surprise defense witnesses. Too often you have to violate the rule that warns not to ask a question to which you don't know the answer.

"How long were you a neighbor of the Algrens, Mr. Reese?"

He exhaled rather noisily as he thought. "I don't know, five years. Six."

"What kind of relationship did you have with Tommy before this accusation you heard about?"

"What relationship? He was a kid. I didn't have anything to do with him. Maybe he played with my kids, I don't know, but I hardly even noticed him."

"Never any unpleasantness between you?" I knew Becky was groping in the dark, but I admired her tone. She sounded as if she had something she was about to spring on the fat blowhard.

"He was a *kid*," Reese insisted. "What'm I going to do, get in a fight with him?"

"Did you?"

"No!"

"I don't mean a fistfight, Mr. Reese. Did you ever order Tommy out of your yard, or yell at him for doing something you didn't approve of?"

Reese looked baffled. "Who knows? Maybe."

Becky stared at him as if deciding whether to drop the bomb. Wisely—since there *was* no bomb—she withheld it. "I pass the witness."

Eliot efficiently cleared up the tiny stain Becky had sought to cast on his witness's motives. "Mr. Reese, did you agree to testify today because you have something against Tommy Algren?"

Reese's face darkened again. "You think I'd come here because I'm mad at some kid? You think I like being here? I didn't want to come at all. But when I heard that lying kid was wrecking somebody *else's* life, I knew I had to come."

"Thank you, Mr. Reese."

Good public citizen, he nodded to the jury before he left. We reserved the right to recall him to the stand, hoping we could dig up some dirt on him by the end of the day, but I doubted that. Eliot would have already checked him out thoroughly.

I was thinking of leaving the next witness to Becky as well, and going to confront the Algrens in my office, but when Judge Hernandez told Eliot to call his next witness he surprised me.

"The defense calls Austin Paley."

It seemed too soon. One other witness and then—boom!—the defendant on the stand. But I suppose it made sense. Eliot had already softened up the jury's faith in Tommy's story. Now Austin could kill it completely.

Austin was very formal taking the oath. He looked as if he were being sworn into office. He held his right hand high and looked the bailiff in the eye as he swore. When he took his seat he relaxed slightly, looked at the jurors without smiling but without looking frightened of them, either.

He was, of course, the best-dressed person in the room, in a gray pinstripe suit, a pale yellow shirt, and a blue and gray patterned tie. Sometimes it was considered best for the defendant to dress down for trial, but there was no reason in this case. Austin wasn't charged with theft. Still, a man with a fashion sense is suspect, isn't he? A man who considers his appearance too carefully? I watched him as coldly as I could, trying to be objectively analytical. Austin was no longer my friend of many years. Nor was he the monster I'd come to picture him. He was a defendant about to testify. I had to destroy him.

"Austin Roberts Paley," he said clearly.

"What do you do for a living, Mr. Paley?"

"I'm a lawyer."

"Are you a native of San Antonio?"

"All my life," Austin said. He was answering the questions in a precise voice, louder than his normal, and without a trace of his usual irony.

"You understand what you're charged with?" Eliot asked.

"Yes," Austin said, with a hint of distaste, and growing more steely.

"Did you do it? Did you sexually molest Tommy Algren?"

"No," Austin said firmly.

Well, we were getting right into it. Austin didn't babble in faked outrage that he'd never touched a boy improperly. That would have allowed me to put on evidence of the other cases against him. He only made a simple denial of the crime with which he was charged in this trial. Austin was a lawyer, and in danger of having his carefully cultivated life stripped from him. He wouldn't misstep.

"Do you *know* Tommy?" Eliot asked next.

"Yes."

What? I thought the jurors stirred, but maybe it was me doing so. I'd expected Austin to deny ever meeting Tommy.

"*How* do you know him?" Eliot asked.

"Very slightly, and quite some time ago. In addition to my law practice, I make some investments in real estate from time to time. I was looking over a house in Tommy Algren's neighborhood a couple of years ago, thinking about buying it. I spent a few hours there several different days, because I was afraid the house had some structural problems and couldn't be remodeled the way I wished. While I was working around the house, some neighborhood children took to dropping by. One of them was Tommy."

"You remember him in particular?" Eliot asked, dangerously.

Austin nodded. He looked troubled. "Because he was the one

who came most frequently. Sometimes when I arrived Tommy was there waiting for me. He seemed—"

I rose. "Objection, Your Honor. He can't testify what was in someone else's mind."

Eliot was standing beside me, looking only at the judge. "He can certainly testify to his impressions, Your Honor. He was there, he can say what he saw."

"Objection is overruled." I sat down slowly, wondering if any of my objections would be sustained. Now that it was Austin himself on the stand, was the judge determined to cut him as many breaks as possible, to appease Austin's friends?

"How did Tommy seem, Mr. Paley?"

"He seemed like a lonely little boy. I wondered why he never stayed at home, or played with the other children."

"Did you talk to him?"

Austin shrugged. "No more than to any of the others. Well, that's not true. Necessarily I talked to him more, because he spent more time there. But not about anything consequential. It wasn't my place."

"Did you ever take him inside the house with you?"

"No. I never let any of the children inside. It wasn't my house. I didn't want them damaging anything."

"Did you ever take Tommy anywhere else with you?"

"Never."

Austin was looking at the jury, not at me. He was looking from face to face with absolute sincerity. I studied him as scientists study a virus. Was he convincing? Was he believable to strangers who knew nothing about him but what they'd heard in this trial? I saw him as the most careful of liars. It was almost as if he'd planned this day in court, years ago. He'd never been alone with Tommy when someone else could know it. Inside the house, they'd hidden and laughed when other children rang the doorbell. Then he'd driven Tommy to another empty house, and afterward let him out again, unseen, near Tommy's house. No one could deny what Austin was saying now except Tommy, whose testimony had suddenly been rendered suspect by the prior witness. I was coldly frightened as I watched Austin on the witness stand.

Eliot looked at his client sternly. "Austin, did you ever touch Tommy in a sexual way?"

"I don't remember ever touching him at all. *No,* to answer

your question. I never felt sexual desire for Tommy. I never touched him that way."

"Did you have occasion?" Eliot asked.

Austin shook his head. "We were never alone together. We never had a private moment, except outdoors in front of the whole neighborhood. The boy and I were never alone."

Eliot looked at him with complete confidence. "Why would he accuse you like this?"

"Objection, Your Honor. He's testified he hardly knows Tommy, he's certainly not qualified to guess what he was thinking."

"He can testify to what he observed, Your Honor, and let the jurors draw their own conclusions." Judge Hernandez, I thought, appeared grateful to Eliot for giving him a good reason for overruling my objection, which he did.

"Why do you think Tommy brought this false charge against you?" Eliot put it this time.

Austin looked as if he'd given the question some thought. "As I said, he appeared to me a lonely little boy who didn't have much of a home life. I assumed it was a bid for his parents' attention."

Eliot nodded: that sounded reasonable to him. After a thoughtful pause he said the words a prosecutor eagerly waits to hear in that situation. "I pass the witness."

There is nothing sweeter for a prosecutor than having the defendant handed over for cross-examination. So many of them are such obvious liars. So many have criminal records that can be brought out on cross. So many have poorly-thought-out defenses, and contradict themselves with only slight aid from the questioner.

But Austin was far from an ordinary witness, and his lawyer was close to being the best in the business. They hadn't rambled while presenting their defense. They hadn't strayed into secondary material. They had not, in short, given me very much to work with. The legal pad before me was almost clean.

"Hello, Austin," I said.

He nodded politely. "Mark," he said.

"You and I have known each other for a long time, haven't we?"

"Yes. Quite a few years."

"I'd say we've been friends. Would you?"

Eliot stood to ask, "Could we get to something relevant, Your Honor?" Judge Hernandez sustained him, so I didn't get to hear how Austin would have answered the question.

"You've told us a little bit about your background," I hurried on. "Tell us a little more. Are you married?"

"No."

"Have you ever been?"

"I fail to see the relevance of anyone's marital history," Eliot said.

"You really can't understand why the jury would want to know that?" I asked him. Eliot didn't return my look. He scrupulously kept his eyes toward the bench.

"Sustained," said the judge.

"Any serious romantic involvements with grown women?" I returned quickly to Austin.

"Same objection."

"I'll answer that," Austin said. He was looking at me, not at the jury. "Of course I've been seriously involved in committed relationships with women. But I'm not going to drag those women up here so you can attack them. This isn't their problem, and I'm not going to embarrass them with it."

"How noble," I said. I thought it and I said it. There was no pause for reflection.

"Objection to the sidebar," Eliot said just as quickly.

"Sustained. Keep your remarks to yourself," Judge Hernandez ordered me. I didn't even glance at him.

I said to Austin, "So you knew Tommy Algren but not in the biblical sense."

"I knew him slightly," Austin said carefully. "Very slightly, for a very short period of time. But I never molested him."

"Not as short a time as most people would expect, under the circumstances. You spent quite a long time at that vacant house, didn't you? How many days did you go there?"

Austin shrugged. "Maybe seven times. Maybe eight."

"For several hours each time?"

"For one or two hours, perhaps. I'm very careful about my investments. I don't make many. I try not to make mistakes."

"Don't you find it surprising that these children remember you more than two years later, after you made only a few brief appearances in their neighborhood?"

"Three of the children *say* they remember," Austin said icily.

"I'm sure their recollections have been assisted. After people started questioning them about it, it must have seemed important to them that they identify me, no matter how little importance they'd attached to my appearances at the time."

"But you remember *them*, too. At least, you remember Tommy."

There was ever so slight a pause, while Austin thought how to answer that, or perhaps swallowed the first answer that had sprung to his lips. "I've always had a good memory for faces," he said. "That helps, in my business."

I gave the jury a pause to consider that answer. Which of them would remember a child he'd seen a few times two years ago?

"Since you were there only a few times, the children must have started playing at the house—in its yard—as soon as you appeared."

"It was a vacant house," Austin said casually. "I'm sure they'd already been playing there, before I came and after I stopped coming. Children do like empty houses, don't they?"

"Do they? But they're usually frightened of strangers."

"Not—" Austin stopped himself. "Not in my experience," I'm sure he'd been about to say. "Always," he concluded smoothly.

"No," I said. "Certainly not in your case. They came to your house and they remember you playing with them."

"I didn't hear anyone say that," Austin said. He was shifting a bit in his seat. He made himself sit still. "I was inspecting the house. I stayed outside *with* them, sometimes, but I didn't join in the play."

"The children just gathered around you, without your doing anything to encourage them?"

"Children flock to me," Austin said, a trace of wonderment in his voice. "They always have. The Sunday school class I teach at St. Michael's—"

"Objection, Your Honor," I said harshly. "This is unresponsive and self-serving."

"You asked for explanation, counsel," the judge said. "Overruled."

"I was just going to say it's a popular class," Austin concluded with an offhand shrug.

"And I'm sure you enjoy teaching it. Are you a Cub Scout pack leader, as well?"

For a moment Austin forgot to be warm and poised. Then he remembered. His eyelids fell for a moment over the angry glare he'd directed at me. When he opened his eyes again he was looking at the jury, almost apologetically. He gave them again a few seconds of study, and the chance to study him, at ease and sincere. "No," he said quietly.

"You deny the story Tommy told this jury."

"I certainly do," Austin said firmly.

"How much of it did he get wrong? Did he go inside the house with you?"

"No. I already testified, I never let any of the children inside."

"Was the house furnished the way Tommy said, with an old sofa and some folding chairs?"

"No. It was completely vacant."

"With all the empty houses you've been inside with your realtor's license, you remember particularly that this one was completely empty?"

He blinked, but only for an instant. "I spent more time than usual in this one, because I was thinking of buying it."

"So you remember this particular house vividly. It stands out in your memory."

"I wouldn't say vividly."

"But Tommy remembers it vividly, doesn't he, Austin?"

"With Tommy it's his imagination that's vivid," Austin snapped.

I wanted to keep him talking about Tommy. It seemed to me that Austin's voice had an intimate quality when he mentioned the boy. "He remembers seeing you change clothes," I said. "Did that happen?"

Austin shook his head impatiently. "I didn't keep clothes at the house."

"So if anyone saw you arrive at the house wearing a suit and leave wearing casual clothes, they'd be wrong too?" I had no witness to this, but Austin didn't know that.

He frowned in memory. "I suppose once I might have taken a change of clothes, if I was going to play tennis or something after stopping at the house."

"So Tommy might have been right about that."

"Not about watching me change. I told you—"

"But he could have gotten that detail right. What about the drive? Did you ever take him anywhere in your car?"

"No."

"What kind of car did you drive then, Austin?"

His eyes flickered. He saw the trap. "I believe then I had a Continental." He glanced at the jury. "The economy was better back then," he told them. No one chuckled for his benefit.

"What color was it?"

"White. Maybe the children would remember it. It was a very gaudy machine." He rubbed his lips together briefly.

"What about the interior? What color was it?"

"Oh, I don't remember very well." That was a poor answer. He thought better of it. "Maroon. It was maroon leather inside."

"Bench seat or bucket seats in the front?"

"I think everything has bucket seats now, doesn't it?"

"So it had bucket seats."

"Yes."

"Anything distinctive about the interior?"

He blinked again. He'd lost a bit of his composure. No matter how debonair you are, the witness stand makes you sweat. Especially if you're lying. "I don't think so," he said.

"What was between the front seats? A hand brake? A storage compartment?"

Austin leaned toward me. "If you plan to pass these details on to your complainant, in hopes of convincing this jury—"

"Don't you want to describe the car?" I shot back. "Or do you think Tommy will remember it better than you?"

"Objection," Eliot said sternly, as if putting a stop to a spat between children. He not only stood up, he moved out into the narrow space between us, toward his client. "I object to the prosecutor badgering the witness and arguing with him. This isn't a duel."

Eliot was only giving his client time to recover himself. Austin was quietly drawing a breath, regaining his calmness. I didn't want to give him any more time.

"I'll sustain the objection," Judge Hernandez said easily.

Eliot took his time taking his seat. I started speaking again before he did. "What was between the front seats of your car, Austin?"

"A storage compartment," he said.

"What did you keep inside it?"

"I object to this as irrelevant," Eliot ventured.

I stood to argue the point. "This is to test the witness's memory, Your Honor. As opposed to the victim's memory. That's precisely what's at issue here."

I stared at the judge. I needed this. He looked back at me with a stare that said he owed me nothing. "Test it on something more relevant, counsel. Objection sustained."

I sat down, with no time to seethe, and asked quickly, "So Tommy's wrong about the car. Is he wrong about the house you took him to?"

"Yes," Austin said.

"It didn't have a pool?"

"There was no house," Austin said calmly, not remotely falling for that.

"It didn't have white furnishings, and pastel prints on the walls? There wasn't a bar from which you made a drink, and gave him a Coke?"

"I never took him to any such house."

I sat back, staring at him. After a few moments I said, "You heard Mr. Reese's testimony."

"Yes," Austin said vigorously, nodding. It was nice of me to remind the jury of it.

"That Tommy falsely accused him of sexually assaulting him?"

"Yes. Just as he's falsely accused me."

"Then why didn't you settle the problem as easily as Mr. Reese did?"

"What?"

"Why didn't you take a lie detector test?"

"Objection," Eliot said. "The prosecutor knows this is a completely improper question, Your Honor."

"So the defense has learned some law between this witness and the previous one," I said. "It was the defense who opened this door, Your Honor."

Judge Hernandez hesitated. Austin, who had had a few moments to think, saved him from making a ruling. "I don't mind answering that, Your Honor," Austin said easily. And just as easily, he turned back to me confidently and said, "I *did* offer to take a polygraph exam."

"What?" I was outraged. "To *whom* did you make such an offer?" Austin had cornered himself. He must have known that whatever name he said next, I'd find that person and put him or her on the witness stand to contradict him.

"I told my attorney I'd take one, if it would clear this thing up," Austin said. He looked directly at Eliot.

If Eliot was surprised, he didn't show it. He looked straight back at his client. His eyes didn't widen. His mouth, perhaps, hardened slightly. I know lawyers who, in that situation, would nod in support of their client, or turn to the jury or opposing counsel with a knowing look and smile of assurance. Eliot didn't do that. He sat stock still, giving nothing away. But I knew. I knew, from his lack of response either way, that Austin was lying. But there was nothing I could do about it. He had picked the one person I couldn't call as a witness to refute him. The attorney-client privilege wouldn't let me.

"But Eliot said there was no point," Austin continued smoothly, looking at him. "He said since the result couldn't be admitted in court anyway, it wouldn't solve anything. I decided—"

"Oh, stop it!" I snapped. "This is self-serving hearsay, and you know very well I can't call him to contradict you."

"Objection, Your Honor," Eliot said. His voice was cool as iced tea. "Counsel should address his objections to the court, not the witness."

"Don't argue," the judge said noncommittally.

I hadn't let my attention stray from Austin. "Go take one now," I told him. "We'll take a recess. I won't—"

"Objection," Eliot said again, exasperation creeping into his tone. "Counsel isn't even asking questions. And he knows this is an irrelevant line of inquiry."

"I won't object," I said, holding out my hands in a gesture of reasonableness.

"Move along, counselor," the judge ruled.

I sat for a long time, as if his ruling had defeated me. I was trying to project my entire mistrust of the defendant. I glanced at Becky. On the legal pad in front of her were a series of questions she'd thought of, then crossed out as I'd asked them on my own. Only two sentences remained.

I looked back at Austin, who waited for me, more warily than when he'd first sat down. "Did you buy the house on Sparrowwood?" I asked.

He shook his head. "It wasn't suitable."

"After you'd used the house to spring your trap," I continued, "after you'd found Tommy and raped him, you wanted to stay well clear of the neighborhood, didn't you?"

Austin sighed, unreasonably maligned. "After I'd decided the house wouldn't do, I had no reason to go back."

"Did you ever contact Tommy again?"

"No. I never contacted him at all."

I nodded. I held Austin's stare. He didn't drop his eyes. "No more questions," I said.

Eliot had a few, mainly reiteration of Austin's claim of complete innocence where Tommy was concerned. His redirect examination was brief and offered nothing new. I didn't take up the witness again. Austin stood and walked back to the defense table, walking a little stiffly in his desire to appear unruffled. I had shaken him, but that was only a personal satisfaction. It didn't help the case. It was hard for me to evaluate his performance. There was no way he could have appeared credible to me. I'd have to wait for the jury's reaction. I was afraid of what their answer would be. For a jury to take a child's word over a grown man's, the disparity in their honesty has to be obvious. Austin hadn't been an obvious liar by any means. And the defense had Martin Reese on their side. Two grown men against Tommy.

"Call your next witness," Judge Hernandez said. He was sitting up alertly, expecting Eliot to rest his case. Traditionally the defendant is the last defense witness, the one who will leave the strongest impression on the jury. But it wasn't Eliot who stood in response to the judge's order. It was Buster Harmony, looking self-satisfied at finally getting an official word in.

"The defense calls Mamie Quinn," he said.

I turned to stare at Eliot. He sat with his eyes downcast as if he hadn't heard. But then he stood too, along with Austin, and I looked up the aisle and saw Mamie Quinn, Eliot's wife of forty years, walking serenely toward us. Mamie was a lady of grandmotherly proportions, today wearing a flowered dress and without, for once, her traditional campaign-function hat. I stood, automatically, as she neared us. She smiled at me in greeting. The round lenses of her glasses magnified her blue eyes, making her appear a wide-eyed innocent. There was nothing troubled in her expression.

I turned toward Eliot as I sat down, but he had already reseated himself and didn't look up. Buster Harmony made harumphy noises of greeting as Mamie was sworn in.

So Mamie did know. She knew the old story—she and Eliot had already been married then—of when Eliot had failed to protect Austin, and she felt the family obligation toward him extended to her, too.

I looked at Austin. He didn't look smug, or even relieved. He sat stiffly, his mouth compressed, like a ventriloquist being very careful not to move his lips.

Since sitting down again I'd remained stock still. I hadn't even drawn a legal pad toward me as Buster began questioning Mamie about her name and background. Becky touched my wrist. When I looked at her she mouthed, "Me."

I shook my head, and did reach for a pad. "I have to do it," I whispered.

Becky shook her head minutely but more urgently than I had. "I'll take her," she said, very quietly. "I don't owe her anything."

I looked at Mamie, listening intently to Buster's routine question, then returned my gaze to Becky. "Very, *very* gently," I said. "She's mistaken, not lying."

Becky nodded at once. She turned her attention to the witness. I looked again at Eliot. He was aware of my gaze, I was sure, but he just stared straight ahead, making notes, watching the witness as if she were a stranger to him. I chewed my knuckle and watched Mamie's performance, wondering if anyone could possibly disbelieve her.

"Mrs. Quinn, do you know this man beside me?" Buster was asking her.

"Of course. Austin Paley. Hello, Austin."

"What is your relationship to him?" Buster asked.

"He's a longtime family friend," Mamie said, smiling at him, "of Eliot's and mine."

"So you see him socially."

"Oh, more than that. We rely on him."

Buster smiled in satisfaction, but he didn't want to lay on the friendship angle so thick that people might think Mamie would lie to save Austin. So Buster cut to the facts. "Do you remember what you were doing May twenty-third, nineteen-ninety, Mrs. Quinn?" Naming the date Tommy had testified he'd spent the afternoon with Austin.

"Yes."

"Where were you?"

"I was at home, all day."

"Was your husband home with you?"

"No. Eliot was working."

"He was retired by that time, wasn't he?" Buster asked officiously.

"He was retired from public office," Mamie corrected him gently. "But he still maintains a private practice. He was in his office that day, I believe."

In those few words Mamie left Eliot out of the picture. She was protecting him from perjury as well as from his past. I looked at him again and whispered to Becky, "Eliot won't testify either way, I'm pretty sure. Play it that way." Becky nodded. She might need the information for her cross-examination, and I knew Eliot much better than she. He wouldn't commit perjury, even for this. But he sat there condoning it.

"Were you alone all day?" Buster asked Mamie. Buster had fallen into his own trial personality, in which he sat up very straight in his chair, frowning slightly with each question, and speaking in a loud, overenunciated voice as if he were addressing a crowd of foreigners.

"No. At about noon I received a call from Austin. He called to confirm another appointment we had, and then we just chatted, as we often did."

"How did you feel that day?" Buster asked.

"I was not at my best," Mamie said slowly. "I'd awakened that morning feeling rather oppressed by the heaviness of the air. It was hard for me to catch my breath. By lunchtime I had a cough."

"Did Austin notice that when you were talking on the phone to him?"

"Yes. He acted very concerned, of course. When he heard me having trouble drawing a breath he said I should call my doctor. But I said I'd be fine. He said then he was going to come and sit with me. I told him don't be silly, that wouldn't be necessary, but before I could say any more he'd hung up.

"Well." Mamie laughed gently, rolling her eyes at the jury. "I felt like a silly old woman. But I was happy when Austin arrived at my door a little while later. He was very sweet, made me tea and made sure I was comfortable, and we just sat like old friends in a nursing home for the rest of the afternoon, talking and laughing and watching some of the silly shows on the television."

Did this sound believable? It did to me. I could picture it: Mamie the gracious old lady from another era, who missed the tea parties she'd once had and was glad to host another; Austin rather time-displaced himself, happy to play the gentleman caller. I could see them gabbing away the afternoon, sometimes laughing and leaning forward to touch each other's knees, gossiping about everyone they knew with that friendly maliciousness of small town southern ladies.

"Did he stay late?" Buster asked.

Mamie nodded. "Until after seven. Eliot was running late, and Austin stayed until Eliot called to say he was on his way home. I kept telling Austin he shouldn't waste his whole day on me, but he wouldn't hear of leaving me alone. He insisted he had nothing better to do—which I didn't believe for a minute," Mamie added, smiling, as if speaking fondly of a nephew she knew got into mischief when she didn't have her eye on him.

Buster asked, "Did he ever leave, even for a few minutes?"

"Leave the house?" Mamie asked. "No. I don't believe he even made any phone calls. He was keeping rather a close eye on me, as if I were a critical case."

I looked at Eliot. Mamie Quinn was throwing herself into her role, acting as if she'd never been asked these questions before and as if she didn't understand the significance of her answers. She sounded quite sincere. Eliot was doing his own job, making notes, nodding along with the testimony. But his face was rather lifeless.

"Thank you, Mrs. Quinn," Buster said, with a valedictory lighter-toned flourish. "I pass the witness."

Mamie turned to me. She'd seen many trials, she knew what happened next. She gave me a disarming smile but settled herself for my attack. I looked back at her, not angrily, but not with any sympathy, either. Mamie looked surprised when it was the girl next to me who spoke up.

"Mrs. Quinn, my name is Rebecca Schirhart. I'm going to ask you a few questions now, all right?"

"Certainly."

"Please, if I don't make myself clear, just ask me to rephrase. Now, you said Austin Paley has been your friend for many years."

"Yes."

"And he must be a very good friend, to have rushed to your side the way you've described."

"He is," Mamie said. She was more subdued than she'd been under Buster's questioning. She was watchful.

"Have you spent many social occasions with him?" Becky asked.

"Very many."

Becky nodded. "Mrs. Quinn, we've been talking about a day more than two years ago. Not a particularly eventful day, from what you've said. Nothing out of the ordinary, just one of many visits from your good friend. How can you be so sure of the date?"

Mamie smiled at her, prepared for the question. "I probably wouldn't have," she said, "but I keep a medical diary. I've had a few problems over the years, and my doctor suggested I keep a diary, so we could trace my symptoms that recur. As I said, I was very short of breath that day in May. I kept a record of that, and that helped me place the date exactly."

Becky smiled at her admiringly. "Do you have the diary with you? Or could you bring it for us to see?"

No, Mamie wasn't going to provide us with documentary evidence with which to impeach her. She laughed lightly. "Oh, my dear, I threw it away some time ago. It's not a personal diary, just a medical one. There's no need to keep it long after each doctor visit. I usually start anew each year."

"So you threw that one away at the end of nineteen-ninety?" Becky asked. "But that's been almost two years. So you *haven't* been able to consult it recently to be sure of the date."

Mamie had been ad-libbing about the medical diary, I was sure, and as extemporizing witnesses usually do, she'd messed up. She looked flustered. "No, I kept it past the end of the year," she said, contradicting herself. "I came across it again recently, and it was only then I threw it away."

"After first leafing through it to see which afternoon you'd spent with the defendant," Becky said gently. Mamie frowned but didn't answer. "If you *could* bring us the diary," Becky continued, "wouldn't it show that May twenty-first of nineteen-ninety wasn't the only day you were short of breath? Wasn't that a common symptom of yours, if you kept a diary to record it?"

"Of course it did happen now and again," Mamie said. "But not often as severely as that day. And of course, I remember the day for other reasons."

"Such as the TV shows you watched with the defendant?" Becky asked.

Mamie laughed again. "Oh, they were nothing memorable. Just silly things, you know, old reruns and game shows. Nothing that would stick in my mind for two years."

"You can't tell us one television show you watched and enjoyed with Austin on May twenty-fifth?" Becky asked. I winced at the question, but then, I had the indictment in front of me. Mamie didn't seem to notice anything amiss.

"Andy Griffin, I think," she said, concentrating. "And what's that ridiculous one about the people lost on the island?"

"Do you remember the particular episode you saw on May sixth?"

"Could anyone?" Mamie asked the jury, reasonably. None of them responded even by gesture. Jurors have a way of keeping their feelings to themselves, as if it would be cheating to nod or smile.

"Have you talked to Austin Paley about what date it was?" Becky asked gently.

"No," Mamie said quickly, then realized that was unbelievable. "Well, of course we discussed it, to be sure I was right. But *I* was the one who remembered the day. I came to him to tell him I could"—she didn't want to use the word *alibi*, which sounded like something a criminal needed—"vouch for where he'd been that day."

"So the date of May twenty-fourth, nineteen-ninety, was pretty firmly fixed in your mind by the time you talked to him?"

"Yes." Mamie nodded, sure of herself. Eliot stirred, finally, pulled his file toward him and found a document, then hastily leaned over and whispered to Buster, who looked back at him blankly. Eliot whispered again, more urgently.

Becky was asking, "And when your good friend needed help to place himself somewhere other than in a house where a young boy was being raped on that day, you came forward?"

Mamie looked at her interrogator with conviction. "I knew he was innocent as soon as I heard. I was very glad later when I realized I could help."

Becky let her get away with the testimonial. The jury could

see the bias behind it. "Help him by establishing an alibi for him on the date of the crime," Becky said. "Which was that?" she asked suddenly, as if she'd forgotten herself. "What day have we been talking about?"

"May twenty-fourth," Mamie said confidently. Silence greeted her answer. She heard it. "Of nineteen-ninety," she added, "not this year." More silence. Mamie looked at the jury.

"Are you sure?" Becky finally asked.

"Objection, Your Honor," Buster said, standing and leaning forward on the defense table. "The prosecutor has obscured the date by injecting incorrect ones into her questions, without foundation in the evidence. The witness has already testified that the date was May—"

"Objection to counsel leading the witness!" Becky shouted quickly. "Especially as he's not even examining the witness at the moment."

I think Buster had said the correct date, but I hadn't heard him over Becky's raised voice, so I'm sure Mamie hadn't either, so much farther away. She looked puzzled to the point of fright. She shot a helpless glance at Austin, but he could do nothing to help. I watched him, as I'm sure did at least a couple of the jurors, to see if he was giving his witness a signal. Austin sat with his hands in his lap, looking sad for Mamie. His mouth still didn't move.

"Overruled," Judge Hernandez snapped. "Both objections overruled. Take your seats."

As she did, Becky asked immediately, "What date was it, Mrs. Quinn?"

"The same date you've been talking about," Mamie said. She pointed toward us, toward the notes and documents on the table in front of us. "The date the boy says—says . . ."

"But what date was that?" Becky asked gently.

Mamie stared at her, not glaring, but very intently, as if Becky's face would give her a clue if Mamie watched it hard enough.

"May," she said slowly, then quietly took her shot: "twenty-first. Nineteen ninety."

At the defense table, Austin winced, but by now Mamie wasn't watching him. She was looking to Becky for reaction, to see if she'd gotten it right.

"Are you sure?" Becky asked quietly.

"I think so. I'm sure it was the same day. I made sure of that."

"Then what you're sure of is the date your old friend Austin Paley needed help with, not the date you actually saw him."

"No." Mamie shook her head vigorously. "I told you, I came to him. I was sure before I talked to him."

"Perhaps your husband could confirm the date," Becky said. "Perhaps he kept his business appointment book."

"I told you, Eliot wasn't there," Mamie said firmly. She was probably glad to shift away from the subject of dates.

"That's right," Becky said as if she'd just remembered. "Austin Paley came to your house when you were alone and he left before your husband returned, even though he didn't want you to be alone."

"He'd been there a long time by then," Mamie said, "and he knew Eliot would be home momentarily."

"But the timing was such that only you can say he was there that day," Becky said, an unnecessary remark. Sometimes we say unnecessary things to make sure everyone in the courtroom is thinking them at the same time.

"Yes," Mamie said.

Becky looked at her indulgently. "I pass the witness," she said.

Buster gave Mamie the chance to repeat again her certainty of the date Austin had been at her house, and offered Mamie the chance to say that she hadn't been confused about the date at all until the prosecutor's misleading questions. When Buster passed the witness again Mamie turned her staunch gaze on Becky, ready, but Becky, as if forbearing to mistreat an old woman, simply smiled at her and said she had no more questions. This time Austin rose to assist Mamie through the gate as she made her way past us. She favored him with a smile and a touch on the arm. Her concern and affection for him were obvious, and unfeigned.

Eliot was on his feet in response to Judge Hernandez's command to call his next witness. There was a pause. I knew that pause, the fearful one when the defense lawyer is certain he hasn't fully done his job, that there is some obvious witness he's forgotten to call.

"The defense rests," Eliot said.

Judge Hernandez's eyes went up to the clock above the courtroom entrance. It was after eleven-thirty. "Both sides approach," he said, drawing us with his fingers.

When Eliot and I stood before him he leaned forward, hand covering his microphone, and asked me, "You have rebuttal witnesses?"

"Yes."

"Who are they?" he asked.

I scowled. He was being too blatant. "I don't have to tell you that. Certainly not in the presence of the defense."

The judge sighed as if I'd wronged him. "Don't get your back up, Blackie. I'm simply thinking of my schedule. How soon can you have them here, and how long will you take?"

"Soon. We should take the afternoon."

He nodded. "Step back."

He released the jury, and all of us, for lunch. That gave me about an hour and a half to take apart Eliot's well-constructed defense. I started by taking apart the parents of my victim.

"Why the hell did we first hear about this in the middle of trial and not before?" Becky was already interrogating Mr. and Mrs. Algren when I walked into my office. I stayed to the side and let her.

Again Mr. Algren was the one who spoke up. "We didn't think anyone else knew. We wanted it kept quiet."

"Mr. Algren, you try to keep things quiet from the other side, not from your own lawyers," Becky explained. "Did you think we'd pass the news on to the media if you shared it with us? Did you think we'd want *any*one to know?"

"He almost sued us," Algren explained quietly. "If word had gotten out about what Tommy'd said about him, he probably *would* have sued us. This is a big office, we didn't want anyone to know. Besides, we didn't think it would hurt your case. No one knew except the Reeses and us. We didn't think anyone would find out."

"Well, they did," I said, stepping forward. "The defense in this case is very, very thorough. There were probably rumors around the neighborhood. They tracked them down."

As we should have done. *I* should have learned this long before trial. I'd spent my investigational resources on the defendant; I hadn't investigated my own primary witness closely enough. I hadn't realized his damned parents would try to hide information from me.

"What can we do now?" James Algren said. "How can we make up for it?"

That's what I'd been thinking about, ever since Reese had testified. What I'd realized was not only what had to be done, but how I could again lead my opponent to the edge of the pitfall he'd avoided once.

Becky was waiting for my answer too. She saw that I had one. "We need your wife's help," I said to James Algren. Mrs. Algren tilted her head, surprised to be singled out.

"And Tommy's," I said sadly.

16

I HAD FOUND IN MY MIND A PLAN. IT HAD FORMED there without conscious effort, but with a certainty that it was the only thing to be done. In fact, I marveled at the beauty of it: an opportunity to betray both my "client"—for if a prosecutor has a client in a case it is the victim—and my old mentor.

Then, sitting at this intersection of my life, a spectator to the imminent collision, I saw my son.

The Algrens had left when Becky and I emerged from my office, and David was sitting there, his legs jutting out from the plastic visitor's chair, quietly waiting his turn to see me. I said his name, with the surprise I felt. He stood and was introduced to Becky, who quickly left us alone.

"I came to watch a little," David said. He must have realized the inadequacy of that explanation; he hadn't come to watch me in trial since he was thirteen. He smiled awkwardly. "I know you don't have time for lunch. Want me to get you a sandwich or something?"

"I have time," I said. Judge Hernandez did not skimp on lunch breaks, and I had nothing else to do before trial resumed.

David and I walked across Main Plaza, past the *raspa* vendor and through the noise of the five-man band in the square, to a Mexican restaurant dense with smells and close-packed tables populated by courthouse regulars. Judge Hernandez occupied one, with a courtier or two. There were even a few jurors, wearing the bright blue badges that identified them as unapproach-ables to the participants in the trial.

David and I got a booth, as private as lunch got that close to the courthouse. I ordered light, flautas and rice, but David got the special that came on two plates. He seemed to absorb the food without filling his mouth, because he still did most of the talking.

"How's it going?" he asked. "The papers make your case sound airtight."

"Wait 'til you read about this morning's developments."

He asked what they'd been, but I dismissed the subject briefly. I found David's presence touching. And, as always, touchy. He knew the importance of this case to me, but I didn't believe he'd come to offer his support. But with David I couldn't question him openly.

"Were you in the neighborhood?" I asked instead.

"Sort of. Well, really I was just wandering." He took a breath. "I'm leaving the company."

It didn't sound like good news to me, after what he'd told me of his corporate life. Had he grown too uncomfortable work-ing with people, or had they finally found him too hard to work with? I didn't know how David got along at work, except by his own account, which hadn't made the workday sound like fun for anyone.

"Really?" I said, concerned. "You think maybe the company's not doing well?"

"The company's doing great," he said, around a mouthful of *chalupa compuesta.* "I think I can do better."

I nodded. "You're responsible for a larger share of the com-pany's success than you're getting paid for," I guessed, smiling as I said it.

He shook his head impatiently. "It's not just that. I'm tired of running everything I think through three layers of foot-draggers. By the time we get around to doing it it's not worth doing any more."

"Tired of having bosses. I understand that."

There was a pause, for me to express an opinion or question his loss of security or nervously ask about his other prospects. I didn't. David looked up at me, waited, then went on with a note of relief. "I'm going into business for myself."

I smiled again. "That's the only thing to do if you don't want bosses. Are you looking for backers?"

Lines appeared above his nose as he shook his head quickly. "I'd rather lose a bank's money."

"I know you're a good risk," was all I said. Modest as his accounts of his working life were, I thought I'd detected that most of the computer software company's new product ideas were David's.

He was still waiting, as if he'd be plagued by his own doubts until he'd fended off mine. I was thinking of Tommy. The night before I'd tucked him in, something I would never do again for my own son. I had done it often, years ago. Often the tucking in was the first time I'd seen David that day. It didn't seem that long ago, and maybe David was here because it didn't seem very far in the past to him, either. He was still, I realized, waiting for me to play the coda of his day.

But I wouldn't do it. I wouldn't pick at his plans. As I'd realized that I must loosen my grip on the trial, set its participants free, I had realized the same thing about my son. "David," I said, putting my hand over his, "I hope it will be a great success. If there's any way I can help, just tell me. And if you need any advice, you know what mine will be worth. Because I haven't even figured out how to turn on a computer yet."

He looked at me suspiciously. My laissez-faire approach to his affairs was new. He was waiting for me to drop it and begin meddling.

I was still remembering him as a baby, maybe one year old. There'd been moments then, before he could talk, when David would look at me with such perfect comprehension that I was sure he would remember the moment for the rest of his life. I'd told myself to take note of them, so we could compare memories some day, but I had forgotten. Looking at David grown, I was sure he *had* remembered everything. He was giving me the same look of perfect understanding. I tried to remember the good moments of his childhood, the baseball advice, the walks. Had I forgotten some, good or bad, some moment so poignant for him it had shaped our whole relationship without my knowing? "David?"

"Uh-huh."

But it wasn't his burden, for me to ask for that interpretation.

Maybe some day he'd have a son of his own who could ask him about those times he'd spent with his father, and David could pass on those important memories to *him*. That's how memories should pass, not *up* the generational stream.

I said, "Did you know it's considered good luck, after telling someone you're starting a new business, to buy his lunch?"

He grinned.

As I began my rebuttal case, a phrase from the war in Vietnam stayed in my mind: "We had to destroy the village in order to save it." That's what I was about to do to the family that was the centerpiece of my case. Because the case wasn't about them. They were only there to represent all of Austin Paley's victims, past and potential. As symbols they were necessary. As actual people, they were expendable.

"The State calls Pamela Algren." I'd had to ask her her first name in my office during the lunch break. Pamela. Pretty name. A girl's name. She'd probably been a pretty little girl, devoted to her parents. Her first name reminded me that Mrs. Algren had a life much larger and longer than the part this trial would touch. But she could be injured here in a fundamental aspect of her character, an injury she would reexamine for the rest of her life.

"You have a son?" I asked her before she was quite settled in the witness stand.

"Yes, Tommy. He's ten years old," Pamela Algren shifted, trying to make herself comfortable. She glanced at the judge and the jury and looked away again. I waited until she was looking at me, which she did with a little start, because she'd just remembered her instructions, which were to watch me. She'd failed already.

"The Tommy Algren who was sexually assaulted by this man here," I said, pointing.

All I wanted was to turn Mrs. Algren's attention toward Austin. She studied him with appalled curiosity. I don't think he'd been real to her until that moment.

"Yes," she said, looking down at her hands. I waited.

When she looked up at me I said, "Austin Paley isn't the first man Tommy's accused of sexually abusing him, is he?"

"No," Mrs. Algren said in a small voice.

"Who *was* the first?"

She was very quiet. She didn't want to say the name, even now. "Martin Reese," she said, "a neighbor of ours."

"Was he a friend, as well as a neighbor?"

"No. Just neighbors. You know, we'd wave. I don't think he was ever in our house."

"Did Tommy play at Mr. Reese's house?"

"Once in a while, I think," Mrs. Algren said, after hesitating. "The Reeses had a boy close to Tommy's age."

"Did Tommy like Mr. Reese?"

The question took her by surprise. "I don't suppose Tommy knew him any better than we did. At least before."

"Before Tommy accused him."

"Yes," she said softly.

"How did that happen? What did Tommy tell you?"

"He told us during dinner one night. He said he'd been playing in the back yard and Mr. Reese had leaned over the fence and called him over and asked Tommy to come help him with something, then he just lifted him right over the fence and Tommy saw that he wasn't wearing any pants."

"You must have been surprised," I offered.

"We were stunned," Pamela Algren said, forgetting her nervousness in front of the crowd in the courtroom as she fell back into that amazing scene. "We just—couldn't even move for a minute. We couldn't think what to do."

"Did Tommy say anything more?"

"Yes. He described it all. He said—" She stopped, self-conscious again. I nodded to her. "He said Mr. Reese made him take off his clothes, too. He said no one else was home, and they went inside, and Mr. Reese—abused him."

"Did you believe Tommy?" I asked.

"Of course."

"So what did you do?"

"We were going to call the police that night, but James—my husband—said we should confront Mr. Reese ourselves first. So we waited until the next day and James went to see him, but it turned out Mrs. Reese had been home too, inside the house, the day before when Tommy said Mr. Reese had abused him. Well, of course, we figured she might say that anyway, but we did more checking—"

"You confronted Tommy."

"Well, that too, and it turned out not to be true. It just didn't—match up."

"Tommy lied," I said briskly.

"Yes."

"Did you ever call the police?"

"No. There was no need."

"Did you have Tommy examined?"

She looked surprised. "By a psychologist?"

"By a medical doctor."

"Oh. No. There was no point. It was over too quickly."

"The case never came to trial."

"Oh, no," she said in a horrified tone. "Nothing like that. It never went outside our two houses. We told Mr. Reese we were sorry and that was that. He moved away later, to our relief."

I paused to study her. So did everyone else in the courtroom. Finally I said, "You said Tommy told you Martin Reese had abused him. Is that how he said it?"

"No. I don't think he ever used that word."

"Did he say Mr. Reese had touched him in a bad way?"

Pamela Algren's denial came in a rush. "Oh, no. It was much more explicit than that. That's why we believed him." She appealed to us all to understand their mistake. "Tommy told us things he couldn't have just heard on TV, or at school. He described it in great detail."

"What did he say?"

She gave me a disapproving glance. Wasn't "great detail" enough for decent people? I returned her stare absolutely blankly. I wasn't pretending to be her friend.

"He described the man naked," she said.

"What, in particular, did he describe?"

She was blushing. "An erect penis," she said clearly, so she wouldn't have to repeat it.

"To your satisfaction? So you were convinced he'd seen it?"

"Yes," she said tightly, still red.

"And what else?"

She was speaking in a voice that tried for firmness but didn't have much breath behind it. "He said Mr. Reese took off his clothes, Tommy's clothes, and ran his hands over him."

"Again, did he go into detail?"

"Yes, very much. He said he put his finger between Tommy's buttocks."

"And what else?" I asked relentlessly.

She was looking at me as if she hated me, which was neither here nor there. "He said the man kissed his penis. Tommy's penis. And made Tommy kiss his."

"Anything else?"

"And he said white fluid came out. Tommy said it looked like Elmer's Glue when it starts to dry."

I hoped the jury found that accurate. I thought it had the ring of authenticity. It had obviously made an impression on Mrs. Algren, because she'd remembered it.

"How long ago did this happen, Mrs. Algren?"

"About a year ago."

"No more than that?"

She did some calculating. "A year ago last month."

The questions about dates had given her a moment to recover her composure. She looked relieved. She was taking deeper breaths.

"Before that time, had Tommy ever seen you and your husband making love?"

She gasped. It was audible to me. Her blush returned instantly. "No."

"Are you certain?"

She turned her embarrassment to anger, glaring at me. "I absolutely am. We close our door."

"Had Tommy had any other occasion to see representations of sex? Have you or your husband ever had X-rated videocassettes in the house?"

"No," she almost shouted. "Not even *Playboy*. Never. Nothing like that at all."

I nodded. I paused for so long that she must have thought her ordeal was over. "Mrs. Algren," I asked softly, "what kind of relationship do you and your husband have with Tommy?"

She looked confused. "We're his parents. Tommy's our only child, so I think we're closer than other parents and children."

I nodded as if I believed her. "Do you pick him up from school?"

"Yes."

"Immediately after school lets out?" I clarified.

"Oh. No, we can't do that. He used to go to a daycare after school. Now he stays right at the school until we come get him."

"Which is what time?"

"Five. Or as soon after that as we can make it."

"Sometimes later?"

"Yes," she said. She wasn't defensive. She was describing a normal life.

"Do you and your husband both work?"

"Yes. I'm a special accounts manager at First Security Trust. James is a vice president at Quantco Equipment Corporation."

"Vice president in charge of what?" I asked.

"Sales, basically. Quantco holds several smaller companies, and James is primarily in charge of sales for all of them. Particularly in expanding their markets."

I wondered if she was aware of the pride that had crept into her voice and posture. "Does that involve travel?" I asked, sounding suitably impressed.

"Yes. Usually a couple of trips a month."

"And your job, Mrs. Algren, what does it entail?"

"I help clients make investment decisions, particularly long-range investments."

"You're a stockbroker."

"It involves much more than that," she said, as if I'd insulted her. "Stocks are only a small part of what I deal with. Government bonds—of all kinds—mutual funds, real estate, sometimes more exotic opportunities such as motion pictures, or private companies that aren't listed on the stock exchanges."

"You put together movie deals?" I asked, glamour-struck.

"I have," she said. "I mean, the investor-package portion of the deal."

I asked, "Is that a nine-to-five, Monday-through-Friday sort of job?"

"Well, it can't be," Mrs. Algren said. She had completely recovered herself. She was assured again. She turned toward the jurors. "Many of my clients are busy people who can only meet on a weekend or an evening."

"So where's Tommy when you're meeting with a client and his father's out of town?"

The question jarred her. I hoped the jury could see that in the pleasure of describing her job she'd forgotten, momentarily, her son, the object of this trial.

"We have a couple of regular sitters," she said.

"When's Tommy's birthday, Mrs. Algren?"

"In March."

"Do you remember what you got him for his last birthday?"

She was ready for me. She took pride in her gifts. "His main present was a computer game he'd been wanting. It teaches geography while making a game. He goes all around the world trying to find stolen objects. He knows things now that I don't think I ever knew. He amazes me."

"Exactly how do you play the game?" I asked.

"Objection," Eliot said. "I question the relevance."

I stood. "It goes to the victim's motivation to lie, Your Honor, an issue the defense raised."

Eliot was looking at me oddly. He knew I must have a goal with this line of questioning, but he couldn't see it. Judge Hernandez overruled his objection, probably because he thought I was doing myself more harm than good.

"How do you play this computer game, Mrs. Algren?"

"You'd have to ask Tommy," she said indulgently. "He's the expert."

"He plays the game by himself."

"Yes," she said. "Usually."

"When was your last family vacation, Mrs. Algren?"

She looked puzzled. "James and I managed a weekend—was that this summer? No, it—"

"Family, Mrs. Algren. All three of you."

She hesitated. Then, realizing how it sounded that she didn't have a ready answer, she began explaining. "It's very hard for us to get our schedules together to get time off. James doesn't have a slack season, and I never know when I'm going to be able to take some time."

I waited patiently. She didn't have an answer.

"I suppose Tommy plays with his friends," I said. "Who's his best friend, Mrs. Algren?"

"Stevie," she said promptly. "Steve Petersen. He—"

"Tommy hasn't talked to Stevie in more than a year, Mrs. Algren," I said quietly. Eliot objected to my testifying, but it didn't matter, Pamela Algren was looking at me startled, assuming I was telling her the truth. "What's the name of Tommy's best friend *now*?" I asked her.

Her eyes scoured my face for the answer, didn't find it. "There's another boy in his class," she said slowly, improvising as much as remembering. "Tommy talks about him. Jason. He's mentioned him. I don't know if that's his *best* friend. I'm not sure he has one particular boy now. He plays with several."

"At your house?" I asked.

"Well, no. But there're neighborhood children. Sometimes I see Tommy with them, riding bicycles or . . ."

I let her wind down, and just sat watching her, a specimen I had studied long enough to label. I was sure everyone else could, too.

"I pass the witness," I finally said in the silence of the high-ceilinged, closely packed courtroom.

Eliot was studying Mrs. Algren too, but he didn't ask a question immediately. I doubted he knew what to do with her. She already seemed thoroughly demolished by *my* questions.

"You didn't believe Tommy when he accused Austin Paley of having molested him, did you, Mrs. Algren?" he finally asked, going right to the heart.

"Not at first," Mrs. Algren hedged.

"Not for a long time," Eliot insisted. "You didn't call the police, did you?"

"No."

"You didn't take him to a doctor."

"Not then."

"Not until a doctor contacted *you*, in fact."

"Yes," we heard from a doctor first. Tommy had told the nurse at school—"

"Even then, when you heard he'd gone to strangers with his story, you didn't believe him, did you? You thought he was just letting you in for more embarrassment. Didn't you?"

Eliot had to add the little question at the end because it didn't look as if Mrs. Algren was going to answer. She hesitated even longer, the silence growing threatening.

"We weren't sure," she said.

"Because you knew he'd lied once before," Eliot insisted.

"Yes," Pamela Algren said in a small voice.

Eliot looked at her rather more compassionately than I had questioned her. But I suspect he was thinking about me, not about Pamela Algren.

"Pass the witness," Eliot said.

"But the first time Tommy accused someone," I said immediately, "he recanted the story almost as soon as he was confronted, is that right?"

308

"Yes," Mrs. Algren said. She was turning a little robotic, distancing herself from all of us.

"He didn't stick to the story even for a day."

"No."

"But *this* time, when he accused Austin Paley, he's persisted, even in the face of your and your husband's disbelief, hasn't he?"

"Yes," Mrs. Algren said. "He wouldn't let it go." I thought she still showed a tinge of embarrassment that Tommy *had* persisted; a faint, lingering wish that he'd let the whole thing drop. That was a good image with which to end: the cost to the family of *this* accusation.

"No more questions."

Eliot shook his head. "I have none either."

Pamela Algren kept her head down as she left the stand. I thought she might stumble into my table. She had one moment, though, just before she reached us, when she looked up, to the side, at Austin. She stopped where she was and stared at him. Her face turned bleak; not as if she was afraid of him, but as if she had just realized she had a terrible job to perform. Austin didn't see her expression. He wouldn't look at her.

Becky leaned close to me and said, "Are you sure?" At the same time, Judge Hernandez asked loudly if I had another witness. I stood and answered them both.

"We recall Tommy Algren," I said.

He was standing by. I'd had Tommy brought from school when I'd realized I was going to need him again, but I hadn't briefed him very much on why he was back. He took his place on the altar of truth ignorant of the use I planned to make of him. He looked nervous. His eyes traveled around the room, and questioningly over the faces of the jurors, as if they were keeping something from him.

"Tommy." My voice seemed to startle him. I pointed. "Is this the man who molested you? Austin Paley?"

Tommy glanced only once along the path my finger indicated, then back at me. "Yes."

"When did that happen?"

"In May, two years ago," he said quietly. He was leaning forward, his shoulders hunching.

"But about *one* year ago," I said, "you told your parents a

309

different man had sexually assaulted you. Do you remember that?"

"Yes."

"Who was that?"

"Mr. Reese, our neighbor." Tommy was still speaking softly, but clearly, with a trace of defiance. He was prepared to be stubborn, as if someone had accused him.

I softened my tone. "Was that true, Tommy?"

"No," he said.

"Not at all?"

"He—" Tommy began quickly, then drooped. "No. Nothing about that was true."

"Why did you say it?"

There is always an explanation. For children, for adults; everyone has a good reason. The man who breaks into a home and strangles five strangers can tell you why they had it coming. Tommy was no different. As soon as he began explaining he became more animated.

"I shouldn't have said it, I know, but Mr. Reese was mean to me first. One time I was playing a game with Ronnie—his son— where we were trying to hit a volleyball back and forth over the fence, from my back yard into his and like that, and Mr. Reese came out and told us to knock it off, we were going to hurt the fence. Like we were going to knock down the fence with a ball! And Mr. Reese picked up the ball and took it inside his house. And it was my ball! And I told him, very nice, I said, 'Mr. Reese, that's my ball.' And he just kept walking, he didn't even turn around."

"Did he ever give the ball back?"

"No. I asked Ronnie for it the next day and he said his dad still had it."

"So that's why you made up a story about what Mr. Reese had done to you?"

"Not just that," Tommy said quickly. "Another time, I was coming home from school, running, and I cut across their yard, and I didn't see that Mr. Reese had some string laid out because he was going to build something there, and I tripped over the string, and Mr. Reese got mad and yelled and he *swatted* me."

"Swatted you?"

"He hit me on the—on the behind with his hand, and he told me to go home."

I was glad I had parents on the jury, but it was important to have people who could remember what it was like to be children, who could understand how large these offenses could remain in a child's mind; a child, who still expected the world to be just.

"So that's why you told your parents what you did about Mr. Reese?"

"Yes," Tommy said, a little sullenly, as if *he* felt justified, no matter what anyone else might think.

I sat silently for a long moment, until several pairs of eyes turned toward me. Then I did what I'd put Tommy on the stand to do.

"Pass the witness," I said.

There had been stirrings at the defense table ever since I'd announced Tommy's name, whispered consultation that had grown almost loud enough for me to protest. But one likes to hear consternation in the enemy ranks. Now I saw the end of the argument. Both defense lawyers were looking at Austin, who inclined his head toward Buster. Eliot sat back, composed as always, but his face was a tight mask of composure. Buster Harmony leaned forward eagerly, glanced down through his half-glasses at his notes, and glared sternly at my witness.

"Did you realize, Tommy," he asked, "how seriously grown-ups would take this accusation you made?"

Tommy looked as if he thought about it now for the first time. "I don't know," he said.

"You don't know? You didn't think about it at all before you told this lie about your neighbor? You didn't think about how much trouble you could get him in?"

"Well, I knew my parents would get mad, but I was mad, too."

"Why didn't you just tell your parents what had really happened? Why didn't you ask your father to get your ball back for you?"

Tommy screwed up his face in preparation for a lengthy explanation, then fell back on, "I don't know."

I think defendants have a hard time during moments like that. Austin knew how crucial this testimony could be. If his lawyer managed to destroy the victim's credibility, the case against Austin would be destroyed as well. But you don't want your defendant to sit there like a vulpine cheering section, his face

exclaiming, "Yeah! Get the kid!" As a defense lawyer I've instructed people how to look during moments like that in front
of a jury: stern but sympathetic, as if you're sorry for the victim
but he or she brought it on himself. It requires a fine range of
expression.

By leaning back I could look past Eliot's back and get a pretty
good view of Austin. As I would have expected, he was in good
control of his face. He stared at Tommy as if he were sitting in
judgment of the boy. There was no one in the courtroom better
able to sympathize with Tommy, but Austin wasn't putting himself in Tommy's place. He was thinking about where Tommy
had put him.

"Tell us, Tommy," Buster said. "Didn't you think your father
would get the ball back if you asked him to?"

"I don't know," Tommy insisted.

Buster was equally insistent. "You must have thought about
it. Did you think your dad would side with Mr. Reese if you
just told him about the ball?"

Becky looked at me, concern forming a crease between her
eyebrows. I sat still.

"I thought—" Tommy hesitated, "maybe it wouldn't be
important enough to him to make a fuss about."

"But it was important to you, wasn't it, Tommy?"

Tommy shrugged.

"Well, it must have been, for you to make up this story about
your neighbor."

"And he hit me, too," Tommy whined. "It wasn't just because
of the ball."

"Why didn't you tell your parents about that? Did you think
that wouldn't be important to them, either?"

"No."

"No, what? It wouldn't have been important?"

"Not as much as it was to me," Tommy said.

"Didn't you think your dad would go over and say something
to Mr. Reese about it, tell him not to touch you any more?"

Tommy made a face as if he'd said something ridiculous.
Buster wouldn't let even that silent expression pass. "Why do
you make that face, Tommy? What does that mean?"

Becky touched my wrist with her fingers. I ignored her,
watching Tommy.

Buster had started out trying to tone his questions down to a child's level, but by now he was no longer treating Tommy like anything but a hostile witness. That, I was sure, was what the defense argument had been about. Eliot had been too soft on the boy the first day. Buster had convinced Austin that a firmer hand was needed. Buster had won the argument, and now he had to prove he'd been right.

"My dad doesn't like trouble," Tommy said.

His dad was in the audience. I didn't turn to look at him, but I could imagine his reactions. Tommy didn't search the crowd for him, either, but he knew he was there.

"He wouldn't want to make a scene," Tommy continued explaining, "over something like a ball or a little—" He moved his hand in demonstration of a tap on the bottom.

"So to get your dad to pay attention to what really bothered you, you had to make up something much worse than what had happened," Buster said, not bothering to lift his voice into a question at the end.

"Yes," Tommy said quietly.

If Buster had spoken softly to him at that point, he might have started crying. Buster maintained the same firm tone. "But it didn't work very long, did it, Tommy?"

"What?"

"Well, you told your parents the story, but all they did was talk to Mr. Reese and he said he didn't do it and they believed him instead of you. And that was it, right?"

"They wanted me to tell him I was sorry," Tommy added.

"And then things went back to just the way they'd been, right? Your father out of town half the time and both of them busy all the time and neither of them paid any attention to you."

Tommy shrugged. He looked understanding, but I could see through it to the miserable child within, and I was sure others could see it as well. "They have a lot of things they have to do," Tommy said.

I glanced again at Austin. He had taken on some of his attorney's hard look as he stared at Tommy.

"So time went by and things were just the same and you had to do something again to get your parents' attention, didn't you, Tommy?" Buster said relentlessly.

Tommy looked puzzled. "I tried," he said hesitantly. "I always made good grades and they always said they were proud of me. And I—I was good for them."

"But that wasn't enough, was it?" Buster's tone was growing harder. Becky was looking at me again.

Tommy shrugged. He was looking down, as if there were something in the witness stand with him.

"You never got enough of their attention, did you, Tommy?"

In a small voice, after a pause, Tommy said, "I wish . . ."

He trailed off. Buster didn't pursue it. He had his own program. "So after a while you had to make them pay attention again, didn't you?" Tommy looked up at him. "You heard about other children being sexually abused, and then you saw this man on television and you told your parents he'd molested you."

"Yes," Tommy said.

For a moment Buster thought he'd achieved his victory. But he quickly realized there wasn't yet a contradiction.

"Did you remember him from when he'd been looking over the vacant house in your neighborhood?"

"I remembered him from lots of times," Tommy said.

Buster veered quickly away from that. "So you lied again, to get your parents' attention?"

"No," Tommy said.

"Didn't you want your parents to pay attention to you? Isn't that why you told them?"

"No."

"You *didn't* want their attention?" Buster asked sharply. Now even Judge Hernandez was looking at me. I could weather his stare, too. "Isn't that what you just told us?"

"Yes, I did," Tommy said. "But I didn't lie."

"You *did* lie," Buster said, "the first time, about Mr. Reese."

"Yes," Tommy admitted. He glanced at me, but Buster's voice reclaimed him.

"And when that didn't work you lied again."

"No." Tommy kept shaking his head. He even looked at Austin, as if Austin would back him up, but Austin was giving him that judgmental stare, cold as an old painting's.

"And they *still* didn't pay any attention to you, did they? They didn't even believe you for a second."

"No," Tommy said. The pain of that rejection was perfectly visible on his face, as if it had just happened.

"So you had to do more this time. Is that why you went to your teacher, and the school nurse? You wanted them to help you get through to your parents?"

"I had to tell somebody else," Tommy said.

"Because if you didn't it would all just fall apart again, the way it did the first time? You needed other people to help you reach your parents."

"If they didn't believe me I had to tell somebody else," Tommy said.

Buster nodded. "So you got caught in the lie, because people who didn't know you as well as your parents believed it."

"It wasn't a lie!" Tommy's voice went shrill.

"When, Tommy? You've already told us you lied. You admitted it."

"I didn't lie about him." Tommy jerked his head at Austin. The movement seemed to draw tears into Tommy's eyes. He was suddenly blinking.

"You didn't realize how you'd be hurting him, did you, Tommy? He was just somebody you'd seen in the neighborhood."

Tommy shook his head. That movement, too, made his eyes grow more moist.

Tommy's misery was blood in the water to Buster. He bored in relentlessly. Like him, his client was leaning forward, resting one arm on the defense table as if gaining leverage to leap over the table and get at the boy. Eliot was still in his initial position, having nothing to do with them. Buster's voice remained hard. "You didn't know all this would happen, did you, Tommy? The first time you lied it all went away without much trouble, didn't it? You didn't expect this second accusation to come to trial, did you?"

"I did," he said softly. "I thought that's what would happen."

"You were prepared from the beginning to tell this story in front of these people?"

"If I had to."

"To lie again?" Buster insisted.

"I'm not lying." He began crying, softly.

"—and again, and again, as long as it took to get your parents to notice you?"

"No." Tommy shook his head over and over, past making his

315

point. He might have been on the verge of hysteria. "I wouldn't lie about this."

"Tommy," Buster said, moderating his tone as if Tommy had convinced him. Tommy stopped shaking his head and looked at him. "It's okay. It wasn't so terrible to lie about what happened before. It wasn't very bad. But lying here, after you've sworn to tell the truth, when this man could go to prison if you keep it up—lying here is very, very bad."

"I know that," the boy said solemnly.

Buster sensed a breakthrough. "Then don't. Tell us the truth now."

Tommy didn't hesitate. "I have," he said.

"Tommy." Buster was about to lose his patience with him. "You expect us to believe you lied once about the same thing, but you're telling the truth now?"

"I am," he said. Something in his face quivered. His nose, his lips.

"No. It was a lie. You lied about going inside the house with this man—"

"No."

"You lied about riding in his car, you lied about the other house. You made it all up, didn't you, Tommy?"

"No."

"Look at him and say that, please."

Buster and Austin were both staring at Tommy as if they could reach inside him and pull out what they wanted; as if they wanted the chance to try, anyway.

Tommy looked up. The quivering grew worse. It was apparent he was crying. Becky had hold of my arm again.

I didn't think Tommy was going to be able to break the silence. He was staring at Austin Paley, without a trace of hatred. His expression held sorrow and loneliness and longing. Austin looked back at him as if Tommy were someone he didn't want to be seen with.

"He did," Tommy said, softly at first. "He took me to that house, and he took my clothes off, and he hugged me, and he touched me, and he made me touch him." He kept looking at Austin. His eyes were liquid. "He told me he loved me."

"No!" Buster slapped his hand on the table. "Tell the truth."

"I am," Tommy said. His voice had grown firmer.

Buster should have known he had lost the moment, but he

wouldn't let go. "Did it get you what you wanted?" he asked. "Did it make your parents pay attention? Was *this* lie good enough?"

I shook off Becky's hand and stood up at last. "I object, Your Honor. I believe defense counsel has hammered at the witness as long as he should be allowed to. He's growing repetitious."

At the defense table, Austin seemed to come to himself. He shot a glance at the jurors and saw that some of them were staring at him, rather than at Tommy. Austin touched Buster Harmony's arm.

"Sustained," Judge Hernandez said. Even he seemed relieved that I'd finally punctuated the interrogation with an objection.

When I sat down Buster was shaking his head, at something his client had told him. But he did as he was told.

"Pass the witness."

"Tommy," I said gently. He remembered his long-ago instructions to watch me, and he fastened his eyes on me. He swiped one forearm across his eyes. "You said you used to call this defendant Waldo. How did you find out his real name?"

Tommy himself seemed surprised by this turn of questioning. He sat up straighter. "When I was riding in his car," he began. I interrupted him.

"What kind of car was it?"

"Big and white," Tommy said. "A—what do you call it?"

"I don't know."

"Continental," he remembered.

"What color was it inside? The seats and the rest of the interior."

"Red," Tommy said. "Dark red."

"And how did you find his name?"

"There was a box between the front seats. Built in, like an extra glove compartment. I opened it and I found some papers with his name on them. Letters he'd gotten."

"What did they say?"

"Austin Paley."

"Did they say anything else, that you remember?"

"They said—" At first Tommy kept staring at me, just trying to see what I wanted. Then his eyes lifted, into the past. He was seeing an envelope in his hands. "They said 'attorney,' " he said.

"Thank you, Tommy. No more questions."

Buster's eyes were half-lidded. He stared at Tommy as if he could see the lever with which to open him up. But Austin's hand was on his arm. "I'm done too," Buster said.

Once again I escorted Tommy down from the witness stand. I put my arm around his shoulder, but before we reached the counsel tables I moved around him, so that I was between him and the defense table when we passed it. Karen Rivera met me to take the boy from me. I didn't even look at her. Halfway down the aisle Tommy broke away from her and darted into a row of spectator seats, where his father was sitting. Tommy lunged against him, clamped himself to his father's side, and James Algren hugged him with both arms, covered him up, hid him away from all the rest of us.

Everyone in the courtroom watched this reunion, except Austin and his lawyers, who sat in their different attitudes staring forward, waiting for the trial to resume.

While I'd stood watching Tommy and his dad, Judge Hernandez had said something, undoubtedly asking me to call my next witness. I leaned down to Becky, we exchanged a sentence apiece, and I straightened and said, "The State closes, Your Honor."

Eliot huddled with his client. Buster half-leaned toward them too, his job done. Eliot rose stiffly and said, "The defense closes too."

"Both sides rest and close," the judge said with satisfaction. He looked at the clock, then at the jury. "It is late and the attorneys and I still have work to do," he began. I stopped listening. I looked at Eliot. His chin was high. He was watching the jurors.

There'd been a potential trap for the defense in cross-examining Tommy. He was a child, you couldn't hammer him too hard, you'd lose the jury's sympathy for your own client. Eliot had avoided the pitfall the first time around. He'd been stern but not harsh with Tommy, almost grandfatherly.

But the case had still been close. I'd offered the temptation again. I'd given Tommy to the defense, first providing them with the fuel about his home life, his too-busy parents, that seemed to create a motive for him to lie, then I'd brought Tommy on again and offered him up.

Eliot hadn't gone for it, but Austin had. Buster had. He'd seen how he could open the boy up, and Austin had given him his head. But in trying relentlessly to break Tommy down, Buster had finally looked vindictive. With Austin beside him giving Tommy that same icy stare, the jury had seen, right before their eyes, adult men abusing that boy. I was counting on their imaginations to picture the different form of abuse to which one of those adults had subjected Tommy.

I'd also counted on Tommy, on his bearing up under the cross-examination. Because I believed in him. I was certain he was telling the truth. So I'd given Buster a free hand, sitting silent sometimes when I should have objected to spare my witness, hoping like hell he could take it. And he had. I hadn't prepared him for what was coming, I'd let him look confused and vulnerable in front of the jury, because that was best for my case. Even so, Tommy had stuck by his story. Under the relentless defense cross-examination, Tommy's insistence had looked even more truthful. That had been my hope. After the case Eliot had put on, I'd had to do something, and all I'd had to offer the jury, again, was Tommy.

"We will see you at ten o'clock tomorrow morning," Judge Hernandez was concluding his remarks to the jury. "Remember my instructions."

It took a while for the courtroom to clear. I wanted to see Tommy but found that he was gone. His father had whisked him away before anyone could get to him. In doing so Mr. Algren had violated my instructions to remain available at the end of the day. I was proud of him for that.

Becky and I waited around the court's office to pick up copies of the proposed jury instructions. It was a way of avoiding people. By the time we came back into the courtroom even the press had left. But there was one person I knew still waiting.

Becky stood undecided for a moment, then said, "I'll take these upstairs."

I accompanied her as far as the railing, where Janet was waiting. Waiting for me, apparently, but she didn't speak immediately.

"Did you watch? You shouldn't have, I might have needed to call you again and I couldn't have if you—"

"I wanted to see Tommy," Dr. McLaren said. She had that look that people get, weary but alert, when a crisis is well advanced. I wanted to ask her how her day had been, but she continued.

319

"Was it really necessary to bring him back, to ask him the same questions again, to let that despicable lawyer abuse him all over again?"

It was worse than she thought. I could have spared Tommy some of the abuse by objecting to the repetitive questions. But I'd needed him to look helpless; needed the jury to see him suffer.

"I thought so."

Her gaze went around the stark, empty courtroom and she hugged herself, hands holding her upper arms. I wanted to hold her myself, but my exquisite sense of timing told me the moment wasn't right. When she looked at me again I saw there was anger behind her sadness.

"You don't make my job any easier. This public carving up. He'll remember this after he's put aside the trauma of the rape. If he ever does."

"You told me I couldn't help Tommy. I could only try to prevent its happening to other kids. This was the best way I knew how. My best shot at conviction."

"I know what I said. I just—don't like seeing my advice acted out."

I heard the unspoken rest of the sentence, the part where she added that she didn't want anything to do with the kind of man who could put the theory into practice in the brutal realm of a criminal trial, where the victim often suffers more than the accused.

"Janet, could we—"

She made a negative sound and held up her hand to block me. She must have thought of more to say, but kept it to herself. She just walked away. In the echoing confines of the empty courtroom the rhythm of her heels came back to me with the staccato insistence of a message in telegraph code. She went out the door without ever looking back.

I perfectly agreed with her.

17

I SHOULD TALK ABOUT THE LIE RIGHT OFF," BECKY said. "Take it out of the case if I can, so the jury can have their minds made up about it before they even get to argue it."

"No. I need to talk about that. If I don't, it'll look as if it scares me. It's their strongest weapon, I've got to address it last."

I was speaking by rote, abstracted, already lost in the arguments I was going to make to the jury this morning, the arguments that had filled my head all night, making sleep only a thin, thin layer of cotton laid over my racing thoughts.

Becky snapped me out of it momentarily. "Damn it, Mark!" I was surprised to see that she was completely exasperated with me. "You want it all," she said.

She was right. I did want it all. I was scared to death. I had never wanted so badly to convince a jury.

What was this look of concern on Becky's face, underlying the anger? She looked as if she had worries, too.

After a moment I said, "I see. You want part of this."

"Yes!" She laughed, but the laughter didn't eradicate the anger, or the worry. Her worry, I saw, was not just for the case.

So I made myself do what a good manager is supposed to do—delegate. We divided the arguments more equitably, but it didn't calm either of us. We were sunk in silence when we walked out of my office.

* * *

I had the hardest role. I had to sit and watch the other arguments, waiting for my turn, feeling my burden grow heavier and heavier as I tried to remember everything I had to say, every response I had to make. Becky was luckier. She came quickly to her feet as soon as Judge Hernandez finished reading his instructions to the jury.

"These are the elements of this offense," she told the jury. She'd written them on a large tablet standing on an easel in front of the witness stand. "If you find that these things happened, then you will find the defendant guilty of aggravated sexual assault." She read off the elements she'd numbered. "This defendant penetrated the mouth of a child with the defendant's sexual organ, *or* caused the child's sexual organ to contact the defendant's mouth, and the child was younger than fourteen years old. That's all. That's all you have to decide. They're listed in the charge the judge will give you. You can look at them now, you can read them over and over again in the jury room, and one thing you will not find is anything about consent. In an adult rape case consent is an issue. In rape of a child—this kind of case—it is not. The legislature has decided that children *can't* consent to have sex with an adult. Children aren't mature enough to make a decision like that. The adult has to bear the responsibility, no matter what. So you don't have to decide in this case whether Tommy was physically forced to do what he did, or whether he was psychologically coerced, or whether he was seduced rather than raped. When a child is the victim, there's no such thing as seduction. There is only rape."

She walked along the railing in front of the jury box, making eye contact with each juror. She ended at the corner of the box closest to the witness stand. Becky turned and pointed at its chair.

"You will never see," she said, "a witness sit in that chair and tell you he's lying. They come here to tell you their story, whether it's the truth or a lie, and they're going to stick to it.

"But something almost as unusual happened in this case," Becky continued. "Our victim told you that he *had* lied. He sat here in front of you and admitted that he lied about someone else a year ago. He didn't have to admit that to you. He could have persisted in his lie, he could have tried to make you believe it.

"But as Tommy's mother told you, Tommy *never* persisted in

that lie. As soon as he was confronted about it, he admitted he wasn't telling the truth. And that was the end of it. The lie never left the neighborhood. It barely left the house. When he wasn't telling the truth, Tommy couldn't keep it up. He didn't even try."

Becky paused. The jurors gave her nothing but their attention; no hint of their leanings.

"How different was what happened in this case," she continued. "This time, when Tommy saw the man who really had raped him, he wouldn't let it go. He couldn't. When he told his parents what had happened, and they doubted, like they had before, did Tommy break down and say he was lying? No. He went to someone else. This time he *had* to tell his story until it was believed. Because it was the truth. He went to his teacher, he went to the school nurse, he went to a doctor, he went to the police, he came to *us*. He never faltered. He never backed down."

Again Becky studied the jurors. "Do you think what you saw on this witness stand was a boy who was lying?" She shook her head. "You know better. You saw a boy who wouldn't break down, who insisted on his story in the face of devastating cross-examination. A boy who knew all the details of the story, who never contradicted himself. You know that." She had slowly backed up, until she was in front of the defense table. She pointed. Austin should have been expecting that, but nonetheless he looked startled for a moment. "This man knows it," Becky said.

She held her arm for long moments. When she dropped it she stayed in the vicinity of the defense table. She didn't want the jury forgetting Austin Paley. She wanted the crime very real to them. She wanted them to picture it, and she wanted Austin in the picture.

"There's one other way you can be sure Tommy Algren was telling you the truth," Becky said. "The proof is in the pudding, as they say. This truth is in the details of the story itself. Did it sound to you like something made up? No. Tommy knows every detail of what it's like to have sexual intercourse with a grown man. He described it to you. He described it to his mother a year ago. Because it had already happened by then. Tommy didn't say, 'He touched me in a bad place.' He didn't just drop a few phrases he'd heard somewhere. No. He described the sex act in such detail that his mother was horrified. She was convinced it had happened to him."

Becky gave the jury one last long stare. "It did," she concluded simply.

There was a long silence while she stood a moment longer, a silence that continued while she took her seat beside me. I laid a hand on her arm. I knew what she was thinking, what every lawyer thinks when she sits down again: There was something else I should have said.

I heard Eliot's voice before I knew he had come to his feet. "Yes," he said, "you know what it's like to see Tommy lie. You watched it happen."

And *he* had the jury's attention. "The prosecutor would have you believe the boy overcame great odds to bring you his story. But that's not true, is it? It was easy for Tommy. It was *too* easy.

"To whom did he tell this story? Whom did he manage to convince? His teacher, first of all. But remember when this happened. A few months ago, in August. August! School had just started. The teacher didn't know Tommy. She'd had him in class how long? A week, two? Barely time to learn the names of all her students. So when Tommy told her his story, she believed him. She had no reason not to, and with the hysteria that prevails now about child sexual abuse, she knew she'd better pay attention to his story, or her job would be in jeopardy."

"Objection," I said, without much force. "That's outside the record."

"Sustained," Judge Hernandez said. "Please ignore that argument."

Eliot wasn't thrown off stride. I had never seen him argue on behalf of a defendant before. He used that novelty to his advantage. He seemed to be appearing out of a concern for impartial justice. He spoke quietly but forcefully; reason was on his side. "Then Tommy told his story to the school nurse, who perhaps gave him aspirin two years ago. Again, a stranger. Next to a doctor, then to police officers who had never seen the boy before, whose job it is to take statements from people who claim to be victims, and pass them on. They didn't investigate Tommy's background, they didn't find out if there were reason to believe him or not. They just passed on what he'd told them. To these people." Now it was Eliot's turn to point at us, at Becky and me. "These people have a job to do: to present claims of crime to you. Not to question the supposed victim's story. They *represent* the victim. That's what they're supposed to do. That's how I trained one of them. And he did a fine job here. But again, Tommy was a stranger to the district attorney. He had no reason not to believe him."

I didn't feel a stranger to Tommy, not by this time, but that offered no basis for objection. I sat stolidly, waiting.

"So put no stock in the unquestioning acceptance of all these strangers. You heard the only real evidence about whether Tommy deserves to be believed. Out of all the people in this world, who knows Tommy best? His parents. And they were the only ones, out of this world of strangers, who did *not* believe him. They knew he had lied before, they knew he had told them the exact same story about someone else, and that it was a lie. They knew their son couldn't be believed. That's a sad fact for them, but it's even sadder for Austin Paley, who is here in front of you today because people who didn't know any better believed a lying boy, when his own parents could have told them Tommy couldn't be trusted to tell the truth."

Austin looked suitably saddened at his own predicament. I couldn't read at all what he was really thinking. His gleam of irony was completely suppressed. He was pure facade.

Eliot's head was lowered. When he spoke again his voice sounded troubled. "But the second time he persisted," he said, as if asking why. "Shouldn't we believe Tommy because this time he took the story much further?" He lifted his head. "Or did the story take *him?*"

He moved closer to the jury. "We have seen what Tommy's life with his parents is like. It's a common story: too little time to go around. His parents give him things, but not what Tommy craves most, their attention. After a while he took extraordinary steps to gain their notice." He was choosing his words carefully. "He lied. He told them the worst thing he could think of that had happened to him.

"And the first time, the lie worked wonderfully well. Tommy got exactly what he wanted, his parents' undivided attention. That first night, the whole household revolved around him exclusively. So when Tommy's parents suggested the scary idea of his actually facing the man he'd accused, Tommy could afford to back down. He could let go of the lie. It had already accomplished what he wanted.

"But then time passed, and things went back to the way they had been. Tommy lost the parental attention he craved so desperately. So he tried again. Tommy saw a story on television about children being molested, he imagined the attention those children were receiving, and he told the same story."

Eliot moved along the front of the jury box. He was being very careful not to sound as if he were attacking Tommy. He sounded sympathetic toward him, but removed. It was a sad story, but not of Eliot's making.

"This time, though, it didn't work. His parents didn't believe him. Tommy had to do more this time. He had to go to strangers to help him win his parents' attention. You saw Tommy. He is a smart little boy. He knew if he enlisted other adults on his side, his parents would have to take notice, too.

"And it worked beautifully. He got attention. You can imagine, Tommy's had more of his parents' time in the last three months than he had in three years before now."

I was watching the side of Eliot's face, cheek seamed with years of experience but still with a jaw muscle that tightened at the end of sentences as if he couldn't bear to let anything go. When he turned toward my end of the jury box I saw his eyes, which could be piercing but now were deeply concerned, wells of potential tragedy in which jurors could see a drowning innocent.

"And do you know what made it so much easier this time?" Eliot asked the jurors. He waved a hand at his client. "This time no one suggested Tommy might have to face the man he'd accused. Oh, no. He was perfectly sheltered. The man he accused this time wasn't a flesh-and-blood next-door neighbor, it was a man Tommy had picked at random off a TV screen, because he remembered him vaguely from having seen him a few times at a vacant house in the neighborhood. The man was anonymous to Tommy, and he stayed anonymous. Tommy never had to see him, never had to think about the pain he might be causing with his lie. By the time he did have to face the man, here in court, it was too late to turn back. The lie had become the whole basis for Tommy's newfound closeness to his parents. This time he could not give it up. Even if it means sending a stranger to prison."

Eliot walked a few steps, thinking. I knew the pressure on him. He was responding to Becky's argument, but he also had to answer my final one, without having heard it yet. The prose-cution would get two chances, but Eliot only had this one. He had to remember everything.

"The proof is in the details, the prosecutor has told you. And she would have you believe there is only one possible source for those details. But you know better. Some of you are parents. You know how children have changed. Today's children are nothing like what we were like growing up. They have some amazing details at their fingertips. They know things that astound us. That disgust us sometimes. And what is the first thing a child, particularly a close-to-teenager like Tommy, does when he learns something new and sordid and terrible?"

A lady on the front row of the jury knew the answer. Eliot spotted her knowing look and focused on her. "He runs to share it with other children," Eliot answered his own question, and the lady on the front row looked satisfied, as if she'd given the answer herself. "Especially if it's something grown-up and nasty, that you know you shouldn't be allowed to know, it *has* to be shared. If one child in the fifth grade learns some secret facet of adult behavior, soon they all know."

Eliot shrugged. "Perhaps this is how Tommy learned the de-tails he passed on to his parents. Perhaps he once saw some-thing himself. We can't know. We can only guess. But your verdict cannot be based on a guess. You must be certain *beyond a reasonable doubt*. That is not possible.

"Now," he said, "having talked about what is wrong with the State's case, I will remind you of the defense. The State's case is inherently flawed, but once your also consider the de-fense's testimony, your verdict is certain.

"Consider Austin Paley himself. He is not an ordinary defen-dant. He's not a multitime loser who comes to you already tainted by past convictions and brushes with the law. He is a grown man, and his record is unblemished. If it were otherwise, *they* could have told you about it."

Since I was the "they" referred to, I stood up for myself. "Objection, Your Honor. 'Brushes with the law' wouldn't be admissible except under certain circumstances that didn't arise in this case."

"Overruled," said the judge, and I wondered if any lay per-sons knew what we were talking about.

"Do you think a man reaches this defendant's age being the

kind of lustful creature the prosecution has described, and never before been brought to trial for any sort of crime?" Eliot continued instantly. "No. You know better. Austin Paley is an innocent man caught in the most terrible accusation of which a man can be accused. He sat here before you and told you, without mistakes, without contradictions, that he had nothing to do with this boy. And the State has brought you no witness, except the admittedly lying boy, to contradict him.

"But the *defense* had another witness. Austin was very lucky in this case, after the terrible bad luck of being caught up in a boy's lie. He was lucky because he had a friend. How many of us can prove where we were on any given day? Our days blend so easily into one another, and we spend so much time alone, going from one place to another. But Austin was lucky because he has a friend who remembered that particular day, because it was unusual. You heard her testimony. Normally now I would speak in glowing terms of the character of this witness, but modesty prevents me. I've been married to her for more than forty years, and that should be testimonial enough to how I feel about her." The jury smiled along with him. "So I won't praise her character, but I will point out what you have not heard from the other side: a reason why Mamie Quinn would lie. The prosecution did not even suggest that she did. Austin Paley is an old friend of Mamie's, but he isn't her son. He isn't close enough that she would commit perjury on his behalf. Mrs. Quinn was as close to an impartial witness as you will ever see in a trial."

Eliot waved away what he was about to say next. "Yes, the prosecutor managed to confuse her momentarily about the date when Austin was at our house all afternoon, by throwing at her a string of different dates. Those are just numbers. But Mamie remembers the *day*. She had no uncertainty about that."

Thin ice. Eliot looked down so that his eyes were hooded. I was touched to hear him speak of Mamie. I couldn't stand the thought of attacking her. Eliot remained quiet. He had brought his hands up in front of his chest and folded them. His voice when it came was terribly sad.

"There may be no more horrible a crime than the one with which Austin Paley is charged. We recoil from it. We can't even look rationally at a man who would do that to a child. It is perhaps the oldest human instinct. When we hear that a lion is loose among the flock, we rush to the defense of the lambs with clubs and stones." He nodded as if he would lead the mob himself.

"*But*," he said, suddenly changing course, "this is also one of the easiest accusations to make. The State doesn't have to support it at all. They don't have to show you a corpse, they don't have to bring you other witnesses, they don't have to present medical evidence or *any* other physical evidence at all! They haven't, in this case. Only the word of a troubled, confused, lying boy.

"I know you feel sorry for that boy, as we all do. But you must look critically at the State's evidence. Because while this is a terrible crime, it is also terrible to be accused of it falsely. *This* man's life will be ruined if you make the wrong decision. How could he ever live down the stigma of it? You owe him a critical examination of the State's case."

He sounded short of breath. He was wrapping up. "And when you do look at it critically you will see on one side two adults, one of them completely impartial, sure of their facts, with completely unsullied backgrounds. On the other side you will find a confused child who is an admitted liar, whose own parents did not believe him. When you weigh those two sides, you cannot fail to have a reasonable doubt."

With all the trial's evidence boiled down to that uneven balancing, he was right. If I hadn't known what I knew about the case, I think Eliot would have convinced me. And the jurors didn't know what I knew.

He was returning to his seat very slowly, looking enormously troubled. One would have thought he was the accused himself. I crossed quickly between Eliot's retreating back and the jurors' faces.

"*He* doesn't want you to do the job you're here to do," I said quickly. "He doesn't want to give you the chance to weigh the evidence."

Eliot hadn't even sat down. "Objection, Your Honor!" he cried. "That is a complete mischaracterization of my argument. It is striking at the defendant through an attack on his counsel."

"Sustained," said Judge Hernandez. "Ladies and gentlemen of the jury, disregard that argument of the prosecutor's."

I had been watching the jury throughout this exchange. I took up the thread of my argument as if it hadn't been interrupted.

"He wants you to do it by the numbers. Two witnesses on one side against one on the other means you have to find his client not guilty. But that's not the way life works, is it? We have all seen in our lifetimes big lies that have lots of adherents, and sometimes only one small voice opposing them. And we know that sometimes the one small voice is right."

I was moving. I felt shot through with energy. I seemed to have grown a foot taller, so that twitches became gestures. I knew I had to restrain myself.

"Mr. Quinn wants you to believe that Tommy got caught in a lie, that the lie took on a life of its own so that he couldn't escape it, he was forced to repeat it to you in this courtroom. That's not his history, that's not how we know he behaves when he's confronted with a lie, but the defense would have you believe that it happened this one time, when he accused *their* client.

"But that's not what you saw happen here. Yes, Tommy told his story to strangers. He had to, to find someone to believe him, because his parents were understandably skeptical. But he didn't tell a bunch of credulous, naïve innocents. He told professionals, people trained to spot lies.

"And finally"—I put a hand on my chest—"the story came to me. Defense counsel has implied that I presented the story to you just because it's my job to do so. But do you think I want to put a reluctant witness on the witness stand? Do you think I want to risk losing a case like this by having it depend on someone I think is lying? Tommy could have called a halt to this at any time—*any* time—simply by telling me it was a lie, that this man never harmed him. A lie doesn't have that kind of momentum. It was the truth that carried Tommy through the ordeal of testifying."

I took a turn in front of the box, pacing as if thinking. My steps brought me close to the defense table. "And now for the defense evidence. I want you to do what defense counsel asked you to do. I want you to think about the defendant." I knelt beside Austin with my hand on the back of his chair, my arm almost around him. Austin looked sidelong at me, appalled at this family portrait opportunity. "Think about the predicament he found himself in. Put yourself in his place. Accused of raping a child. Caught. Imagine it. A successful attorney with a good life, good friends, nice car, money to buy houses for investments. All that suddenly at risk. What would you do? What would you do in his place?"

I stood up, putting space between Austin and myself again. "Anything," I said. "You would do whatever it took to save yourself. You would hire the best lawyer you could think of, you would investigate the hell out of the case, you would find anything you could to discredit the boy, you would lie with all the sincerity you could muster, you would do what*ever* you could think to do.

"Including looking for an alibi witness. In this case, because the boy's story is true, that meant *inventing* an alibi witness. And that's how Mamie Quinn was brought to you. I don't for a second accuse Mrs. Quinn of lying to this jury. She remembers that day. It *was* an unusual day, when Austin Paley spent the whole afternoon and early evening with her—exactly, conveniently, the time for which he needed an alibi.

"But Mrs. Quinn doesn't know the date. You heard her say the wrong one, and then guess at which one she meant. Because one day is much like another for Mamie Quinn. She doesn't keep business appointments, she doesn't have deadlines to meet. So when her old friend Austin Paley came to her and said"—I put my own hands together in prayer—" 'Please, God, Mamie, I'm in trouble, terrible trouble, you're the only one who can help me,' and he told her that the day she remembered happened on the date on which he was sexually assaulting Tommy Algren, Mrs. Quinn took him at his word. Mamie Quinn wants to help her friend, and that's admirable, but the only date she knows is the date Austin Paley told her."

I pointed at the defense table. "They could have pinned down the date. They could have brought you Mrs. Quinn's diary, but it's been discarded. They could have brought you Mamie Quinn's husband if they'd really wanted to be certain about the date. Because *Eliot* Quinn *does* have appointments to keep. He would have calendars to consult to pin down that date. But the defense didn't offer *his* testimony."

I didn't look at Eliot. I was fixed on the jury.

But I still felt the force of his argument. He had gotten to the jurors first. Their minds might already be made up. I had to break them down.

"And that's the last time I'm going to ask you to put yourself in the defendant's place," I said. "Because ultimately, you can't.

You and I cannot understand him. The forces that drive him. The desire that won't let him lead a normal life, that compels him to trap a boy like Tommy. The defense has told you Austin Paley shouldn't even be here, but it's *Tommy* who should never have been here. Tommy's life should never have taken this turn. He should still be an innocent ten-year-old boy. But a house went vacant in his neighborhood and a man appeared, trolling for children, for a lonely, neglected boy just like Tommy Algren."

I had lost my manic energy. My shoulders slumped. I returned, as I've been trained to do, to the weakest part of my case.

"Yes, Tommy lied once. Martin Reese made him mad, and Reese didn't know what he was messing with in Tommy, did he? Because by that time, a year ago, Tommy was no ordinary little boy. Yes, Tommy lied, but look at the ammunition he had for that lie. He knew precisely what it was like to be sexually abused. He could describe it to his parents step by step, every detail, what everything looked like, all the textures, all the feelings. It wasn't something abstract, something he heard. He knew exactly what it was like to be raped. And he knew the man who'd done it to him. He knew the house where he met him, he knew what the inside of the man's car looked like, he knew his face. He knew his name."

I was backing up, but I wasn't creeping up on anyone. Everyone knew where I was headed. When I came abreast of Austin he was looking at me stubbornly, his shoulders slightly hunched. I looked at him, too, looking for the trace of what I knew must be there.

Everyone boasts a guilty heart. We can't live five years without acquiring one. Even Tommy, the only complete innocent in the case, felt guilty about betraying Austin. Even Eliot, who'd done nothing worse than a favor for a friend, felt guilty toward Austin as a result.

I felt guilty over the way I'd raised David, by hit and miss and crucial absences. David probably felt guilty that he hadn't lived up to the ideas he'd imagined I'd had of a son.

Everyone appeared to feel guilty but Austin. He seemed to feel it was his due to live as he wanted, at anyone's expense; that the world could never pay off its debt to him for his anguished childhood.

But I could not believe that. If there was anguish in Austin's past it lived in him still, no matter with how nonchalant a face he hid it. It is the mark of humankind that we feel guilt toward those we have hurt, and guilt for having been victimized, as well.

"Think of that boy," I said. "No one can help him. He thinks no one *will*. He can't even trust his own parents. His father isn't there for him. Think about that boy alone in the dark at night. No one to comfort him.

"Is it any wonder he didn't tell anyone? Is it any wonder he lied? Imagine how the world appears to him. He thought he'd found one true friend, a new father, big enough to protect him, to explain the world to him. And then that man violated him. Raped him. Imagine the effect. Not just the physical horror and pain, but the confusion. Nothing in the world can be trusted any more."

There was one person in the room who understood perfectly what I was saying, for whom it took no leap of imagination to empathize with the victim. I was directing my argument at him. Austin looked back at me blank-faced. *You will not touch me,* he seemed to say. But he didn't take his eyes off me as I continued to address him.

"Then some time later, after he's begun to sort things out, after he thinks he understands a little how the world is, Tommy is deeply offended by something a neighbor does to him and he strikes back, with the rage that's been in him for a long time. He *uses* what happened to him, the pain he can describe with such horrible exactness. Do you blame him?"

Are you proud of the boy you made, Austin? It was akin to the transformation he had experienced himself. From victim to user. He understood the venting of pain. I hoped he understood, too, how he had made a legacy of his injury, hurt someone else exactly as he'd been hurt. I knew I could make him see, if not the jury. Austin was still watching me. His expression hadn't softened, but it was as if he had retreated behind the mask of his face. His eyes, I thought, were moist. A boy's eyes, still bright, eager, often confused.

I turned back to the jury. "Yes, Tommy used his pain to try to punish someone who'd offended him. But the pain was already there for him to tap. He lied about who had molested him, but he didn't lie about what had happened. He described it so vividly that his parents knew it was the truth. You know it too, don't you? An eight-year-old boy doesn't know those details unless he's experienced them. Unless he's been raped.

"And when he came in here and told you who had really done it, you recognized the truth, didn't you? You heard the sound of true, anguished memory. And you know that Tommy, try as he might, can never forget the man who raped him."

My voice sounded loud. The silence that followed it was equally loud. There were no rustlings from the jury, or murmurs in the crowd. Or maybe I had just grown deaf to them, as I'd grown blind, for just a moment, to every face in that crowded courtroom but one.

"I'd like Tommy to be here for the verdict," James Algren said. His face was stiff as he talked, as if he were a ventriloquist's dummy being inexpertly operated. "Well, to tell you the truth, he insisted on being here."

Algren probably disliked me as much as he did anyone else involved in his son's tragedy. I'd put on the evidence that told the world what a lousy father he was. But I was his only contact in the sordid world of criminal law, and he had questions.

"Will they handcuff him and take him to jail after the verdict?" There was an undisguised vindictiveness in the question.

I shook my head. "I'm sure the judge will continue him on bond until the entire trial's over. After all, he might get only probation. Anyway, I wouldn't count too heavily on the verdict. It might be one you don't want to hear."

"You think they might not convict him?"

"I think it's likely he'll be found not guilty."

"How?" James Algren asked.

Weren't you watching? I wanted to ask him. Didn't you hear the testimony that *you* didn't even believe Tommy? Instead I said, "It's very hard for a jury to take the word of a child against an adult's. In a case like this, with an emphatic denial and an alibi, it's almost impossible not to have a doubt."

"And that would be it?" Mr. Algren spat out. "Could you try him again?"

Sometimes I'm amazed by intelligent laypersons' ignorance of the law. "Not for this," I said. "You could file a civil suit against him, try to win damages. That would be easier, you'd be on an

equal footing, you wouldn't have the burden of proving it beyond a reasonable—"

Mr. Algren sneered. "I wouldn't put Tommy through this
again for money." He paused. His eyes slid away from me.
"That's not what I was thinking of doing."

I took his arm. "Keep to yourself what you're thinking. I'm
still the district attorney."

For another two months or so, I thought as I ushered him out.
He stopped at the door. "Tommy and I'll be down in the
courtroom."

"It might be a long wait."

"We'll be there."

He left me alone in my office. I stood beside my desk for a
long moment, looking at the wall behind it, where my plaques
and diplomas and pictures hung. The office already looked unfamiliar, as if I were returning to it only in memory, long after
departing. I turned toward the corner where my view lay, the
five-story drop to the city streets and a large slice of the old red
stone courthouse across the street where I'd grown up. Soon
I'd be dislodged from this perch. The television news had been
on the night before while I'd paced my condo, rehearsing my
argument. It had been interrupted by a commercial for Leo Mendoza, a newly made one in which he sat on the edge of a desk
much like the one in my office, with crossed flags behind it.
Leo had spoken confidently, already with the air of authority to
which my job would entitle him.

There would be no more polls before the election. The most
recent one showed Leo with the allegiance of almost half the
people who claimed they'd be voting, me with the loyalty of
only about a third of the prospective voters. A gap like that
could be closed, but not in only a week, not by a well-publicized
trial loss. The news this week seemed to focus on the trial I'd
been conducting rather than on the election. I had no idea what
citizens thought about that trial, but I was pretty sure what they
would think if Austin was acquitted and began trumpeting his
victory over my unjust prosecution of him.

Curiously, though, I couldn't keep my attention on the consequences of the trial. I kept returning to Austin himself. After it
was over he would be free. His friends would embrace him, his
practice would continue, his influence might even be extended.
He would be more cautious than ever, perhaps for a long while,

but not forever. Some day he would appear again in a new neighborhood, in the vicinity of a school where he'd never been seen, in an apartment complex teeming with children whose parents were too busy for them. By the time that happened I would be a private citizen, as powerless as James Algren. But I still felt the responsibility. I knew that weight would only grow heavier once I was out of office. Perhaps I would linger close to Austin's life, to let him know he wasn't forgotten. Perhaps I might even have to take some action.

The jury had been out for almost an hour. In a case like this, a quick verdict would have been bad, it would have signaled a rapid agreement among jurors that they couldn't possibly decide who was telling the truth, so they must make a finding of not guilty. The time for a verdict like that was passing. If the jury continued deliberating too long, though, they would arrive back at the same point. Too much talk meant dissension, and dissension was good for the defense. They only needed one juror holding out for acquittal. I needed all of them voting guilty.

Without warning the office door opened and Becky walked in. She carried a paper sack, its top gathered and wrinkled as if it had been opened and closed again several times.

Gone was the deference Becky had shown me early in our partnership. We stared at each other like battlefield veterans meeting in a tent we would soon have to pack up or abandon. Becky dropped the paper sack on my coffee table. "Someone was nice enough to bring me a sandwich," she said. "I thought I'd share it with you."

I leaned over the sack, loosened its top with a finger. Inside was a barbecued beef sandwich that had been only loosely re-wrapped in its waxy paper. The sandwich had been cut in half, and its filling was spilling out between the halves, as if the sandwich had vomited it out. White veins of fat gleamed amid the dark lumps of meat. No steam rose from it.

"You're too kind," I said.

Becky dropped onto the couch. For a moment she slumped there, her knees on a level with her waist, looking like a TV-stunned child late on a Saturday morning. The next moment she underwent a remarkable transformation. She pulled herself up straight, put her hands on her thighs, and looked up at me as if she were well rested and just beginning her preparations for trial. I don't think I ever had that resilience.

336

"Think we need to put Tommy on again at punishment?" she asked seriously.

I laughed, a burst of surprise.

"No, really," Becky said, frowning with concentration. "To testify about how this has affected his life. That's relevant to punishment. This time we can really let out all the stops. Bring in the other times it happened, have the psychological testimony about how he'll never recover from it even with—"

"Becky." When she stopped I just drew a hand across the air, a cavalry officer canceling a charge.

"We have to be ready," she said stubbornly.

"I know." But I didn't mean by it what she had, and she knew it. I sat in the chair next to her and leaned forward so our heads were close. "Listen," I said, looking at the floor. "I don't know how much Leo will clean house here. I think you could hang in if you try, but I don't know what your prospects for advancement would be. Maybe if you stayed on for a few months, so it wouldn't look like you were being kicked out, you could catch on with a civil firm. But if you want to get out right away, or have to, I know a few people who'd hire you, I'm sure. It wouldn't be one of the big firms, but—"

"What would *you* do?" Becky asked. Still optimistic, she spoke of possibilities, while I'd been discussing what *was* going to happen.

I shrugged. Go back to defense work, I started to say, but I heard the phrase in my mind and didn't like the sound of it. I left my answer at a shrug.

Becky was giving my face one long moment of close study. Then I saw a lessening of intensity in her look, a shade going down far back in her eyes. She gave me the knowing but benevolent look that passes between friends.

"Let's talk about the case," she said.

I smiled. We fell silent, but the subject of the silence had changed. We sat waiting for a verdict.

They took their damned time about it. Juries. What was there to discuss? Either they believed our boy or they believed the defense, or they threw up their hands and decided they couldn't decide. How could they keep hashing over those simple choices for hours?

At midafternoon, when the jury had been out for more than four hours, James Algren reappeared in my office.

"Listen, uh, I had no idea it was going to take this long," he said apologetically. "I need to run by the office just for a minute. It's not far, I'll be right back. Client's been waiting for me since one."

"Okay," I said. "If it's been this long, there's no telling."

"Tommy wants to stay," Algren continued. "Could I leave him with you? I promise it won't be—"

"Sure," I said simply. Tommy should have been sitting with Becky and me all along. The three of us were the trial team.

Mr. Algren looked relieved. He brought Tommy into the office, spoke to him quietly for a minute, then left, trailing more apologies. Even before his father was out the door, Tommy gave me a look. Here was the pattern of his life reasserting itself already. But Tommy's expression was indulgent. He was a little adult again, so much so that he showed an adult understanding of the demands on his father.

"Tom," I said, "I don't think things are going our way."

He nodded, lips pursed. I wondered which would be harder on him, a verdict of guilty or not guilty: seeing Austin off to prison, or learning that he was going to remain at large.

Tommy tried to reassure *me*. "I'll be all right," he said.

Becky and I glanced at each other. Tommy joined our circle of silence.

The jury seemed just to have been waiting for James Algren to leave the building. He hadn't been gone half an hour when my phone buzzed. Becky and I knew what that meant, because I'd told Patty I didn't want to receive any calls except the one from the court. Becky looked, for just a moment, panicked, as if we'd been caught together in a compromising position. I felt the same way. They'd tracked me down. I'd been in hiding from this verdict.

This was one I would have liked to receive privately, in a small office, where I could stand near the door. Instead it would be one of the most public verdicts of my career.

"I think it would be better if you wait here, Tommy," I heard myself saying. "I'll come back and tell you what happened as soon as we find out."

He was shaking his head. "I want to hear it."

I couldn't deny him. In the outer office I asked Patty if Karen Rivera was around. Patty pressed four buttons on her phone and, a few seconds later, shook her head. "Get Jack, then," I said, "or one of the other investigators. Have him bring Tommy down to the court. Tell him to get him out of the courtroom as soon as the verdict's announced, whatever it is. We don't want him being interviewed. I've got to head down."

I knelt to speak face to face to Tommy. "Whatever happens," I said, gripping his arms, "you don't have to be afraid. He'll never come near you again."

Tommy nodded, an ambiguous reply, but his mouth was a firm line.

I left him waiting for my investigator while Becky and I hurried down the stairs. Only one television reporter tried to elicit a statement from me outside the courtroom doors. The other reporters were already inside, jammed among a throng of spectators. It looked like the headquarters of a successful candidate on election night. I took Becky's hand to be sure she made it through the crowd with me.

Inside the railing, relative calm prevailed. The bench and the jury box were vacant. A bailiff lounged behind his desk opposite the jury box. "We have a verdict?" I asked him, and he nodded calmly.

Eliot was already seated, his client beside him. He looked up at me with very little expression: no hostility, no smile, no obvious nervousness. Just an acknowledgment, I thought, that we knew each other, that we'd been in this position hundreds of times. In a few minutes one of us would be elated, the other stricken. For a moment it seemed to me that Eliot wished me well, in that shared anxiety.

Beside him, Austin didn't look up. He was staring straight ahead, rigid in his effort to appear calm. If nothing else, I had the satisfaction of finally seeing him utterly robbed of his omnipresent devil-may-care sparkle. That didn't feel like a victory, though. I felt as if I'd seen an old friend transformed into congealed dust.

I scanned the crowd, looking for Tommy. He didn't seem to be there. Then a flutter of motion caught my eye. Tommy was waving from a seat in the far back corner of the courtroom. I waved back, and caught the eye of my investigator Jim Lewis, kneeling beside Tommy in the narrow aisle. I gave him a significant look, glancing at Tommy again, and Jim nodded.

When I turned back the judge was just taking his seat.

"I am told we have a verdict," he said with great detachment, and nodded at the bailiff, who sauntered across the room and out the door behind the judge's bench.

I hate that moment. Even when I am confident of the verdict, I don't like to sit and wait to hear it from a stranger's lips, because any half-smart trial lawyer has learned that you can *never* be confident. Juries always find a way to surprise us. They hear things in testimony none of the rest of us hears, they find significance in details the lawyers didn't deliberately elicit, that just slipped out in a witness's offhand maundering. Sometimes juries seem to have based their verdict on the essential evidence, but just as often they offer us after trial an explanation for their verdict so bizarre it cannot be the truth, they must be covering up something flawed and ugly in their decision-making. I'd hate to have my life in the hands of a jury.

The bailiff reappeared, and behind him the jurors. They blinked as they walked single file into the courtroom, as if they'd spent the last few hours trapped in a dark hole. They didn't look at all familiar to me. The bailiff could have brought back the wrong jury for all I could tell. Then I recognized a middle-aged Mexican-American man with dark-rimmed glasses, whom I'd wanted on the jury because he had children and he'd looked so serious during jury selection. Behind him came an overweight Anglo woman who'd worn the same yellow dress every day of trial. She had trouble negotiating the step up into the jury box and the man I'd recognized turned to help her. They spoke briefly to each other and even exchanged quick smiles.

Now I recognized other members of the jury. Something had happened to them, though. They were no longer the stiff faces I'd watched covertly during testimony and intently during final argument. They had become a group of living people, moving, looking over their shoulders at one another, speaking hurriedly in asides, even in the glare of the attention they knew was focused on them. They seemed affected by the hostages' syndrome that binds people held at gunpoint for a daylong bank robbery.

They were moving too slowly for Judge Hernandez. "Have you reached a verdict?" he asked with an edge.

Another man stood, a very thin one wearing a short-sleeved white shirt on this dank, cool November day. "Yes, Your Honor," he said stiffly.

Judge Hernandez said, "Read your verdict." He moved his head fractionally and Austin and Eliot stood to receive the verdict.

The foreman unfolded the paper, as if his memory of their decision wouldn't do. He never looked up again as he read laboriously:

"We find the defendant, Austin Paley, guilty of aggravated sexual assault, as charged in the indictment."

For a second I didn't look up. If I did I'd see Austin smiling and shaking Eliot's hand and realize I'd heard an illusion. But Becky grabbed my wrist and I could feel in her grip that I'd heard right. We had a guilty verdict.

Never let the jury see you exult. To any normal citizen the sight of a happy lawyer is offensive. If I gave vent to my feelings, screamed "Yessss!" or even just smiled broadly, I might make the jurors feel I'd put one over on them. Instead I only looked at them. My lips tightened and I nodded slightly, as if they'd done their simple duty, as I'd expected them to do. Inside, I was jumping up and down.

The judge was beckoning me forward. There was noise from the spectators, but he didn't subdue it. The jury foreman was still standing as I walked forward. "Thank you," Judge Hernandez said to him, and I said the same thing.

"It would be nice to be done with this," the judge said quietly when Eliot and I stood before him. "You have many punishment witnesses?"

Though I'd thought it hypothetical, Becky and I had discussed it. "Two, Your Honor. Maybe three," I said.

The judge didn't even turn to Eliot. "And of course the defense will," the judge said. "All right. Let's do it Monday." He motioned us away. "It is late on Friday and this jury has worked hard enough today," he announced to the room. "We will begin the punishment phase Monday morning at nine o'clock. Sharp."

When I turned away from the bench I had my first good look at Austin Paley since the verdict. He had collapsed into his chair, collapsed inside his suit as if all his air were gone. For the first time he looked like that portrait he must have kept in his attic. He looked old, older than Eliot Quinn, older than a man on his deathbed. His chest was fluttering. He was breathing in quick, shallow gasps. At first I thought he was having an attack. Then I dismissed what I was seeing as a carefully rehearsed performance, designed to tell the jury they'd made a terrible mistake, so they'd go easy on him at punishment.

By the time I reached my chair there was pandemonium in the courtroom. People were pouring in through the gate in the railing. Some of them were reporters, thrusting microphones and questions at me. I lifted Becky to her feet beside me. I would have tried to shield her from defeat, but she deserved to share in the victory.

I heard myself, with heartfelt sincerity, mouthing stupid, shopworn phrases like, ". . . remarkably intelligent jury. And they worked very hard."

"And after the evidence we present at punishment," Becky added, "the jury will have no doubts about what should be done with this defendant." I turned to her, surprised at the hardness of her tone. *Yes, Monday*, I thought. Monday would seal Austin's fate. Monday the city would hear about his abused childhood, and I would try to convince the jury to send him to prison in spite of that sad background.

Monday would be the day before the election, too.

There is a back way out of the courtroom, which leads into a hall open only to lawyers and court personnel. We used that exit, to give ourselves a moment of respite. Becky and I looked at each other, grinned matching goofy grins, and threw our arms around each other, which after a few seconds was a little awkward, so we pulled apart, still smiling, and shook hands. I put my arm around her shoulders in another congratulatory squeeze as we started down the hall. "Punishment Monday," she said.

I laughed. "You're a killer. Give yourself a few minutes to be happy."

The hall was narrow and white and had an experimental look, as if at its end I'd be confronted with a choice of three unmarked doors. Instead I turned a corner and found myself face to face with Eliot. He was just coming out of the court's office.

He looked even neater than when the trial had ended, in his gray suit with a yellow vest, but he looked as if his heart wasn't in it, as if he was just wearing the clothes he'd found laid out this morning. There were deep lines in his cheeks. When he saw me he waited. Becky and I sobered immediately. Eliot took my hand.

"Congratulations, Mark."

Becky was excusing herself, but Eliot stopped her before she could turn away. "Young lady," he said, "I first used that trick of mixing other dates into a cross-examination before you were born. And it was taught to me by a man who used it before *I* was born. It's so old I didn't even think to warn my wife against it."

He spoke admiringly, as if to an apt student. Becky smiled slightly. "Really," she said. "I thought I'd invented it."

She left us, and Eliot turned his attention to me. "Powerful closing, Mark. You—were convincing."

"Thank you."

"I can't offer wholehearted congratulations on the verdict," he added.

"I know, Eliot."

"But I can't— I wanted you to know I bear you no ill will, either. You made a decision I . . ."

He couldn't say that, either. "I still owe him," he concluded softly.

"You didn't do anything wrong, Eliot. All you did was believe a friend. There's nothing wrong with that."

Of course, to make up for the guilt of that mistake, he *had* done something wrong years later. He'd killed cases against Austin Paley. He'd let him think he was immune to the law. He'd as good as put innocent children in Austin's path. I don't know how I could have lived with such knowledge.

"You put on a hell of a case," I said. It was a most oblique question, but Eliot heard it.

"Mamie went to Austin and Buster before I ever agreed to be part of the case," he said quietly. "I wouldn't have let them call her if I hadn't believed her. I don't think for a moment—"

"No."

"On the other hand," Eliot went on quickly, looking down, "your child was quite convincing himself. Quite." I wished I could see his eyes. Eliot clapped me on the arm, but he wasn't looking at me. "But it's not our job to decide who's telling the truth, is it, Mark?"

After a quiet moment I said, "Austin may get lucky on punishment, after you—"

Put on your evidence, I'd started to say, then realized Eliot himself was the witness to Austin's childhood abuse, maybe the only witness other than Austin himself. And Eliot still felt he owed him everything he could do for him. Come Monday, I might be cross-examining my old boss.

"A lot of people in this town are fretting about what Austin will do now," Eliot said. "They're wondering if now that he has nothing to lose Austin will decide to take everyone else down with him. He holds a lot of dirty secrets, Mark, and he has nothing more to fear if he spills them.

"Don't think anybody will forget your part, either," Eliot went on. "If you'd done what they asked you to do there'd be no occasion for Austin to smear them. It's going to come down on you like the wrath of God, if they can manage it. The squirming, the pleas for probation, the lust for revenge." Eliot had recovered himself. He sounded almost jovial, talking about the wrecked lives just ahead. "Going to be a hell of a weekend," he said.

My office windows had gone gray by the time I returned from the courtroom and realized how weary I was. Becky was gone, Patty was standing beside her desk with her purse in her hand. I would have liked to call Janet, but in our last meeting in the empty courtroom I thought I'd heard that door firmly close. I wondered if there was anyone in the world who would have a drink with me, the winner.

I had on my coat, and was turning off my office light, when the phone rang. I shook my head at Patty, but she had already picked it up, in an automatic response. I trudged past her.

"Mark?"

Patty was holding the phone toward me. "It's Mr. Algren," she said. "He's down in the courtroom."

Instantly I felt guilty for having forgotten Tommy. I should have talked to him as soon as he heard the guilty verdict, but I'd been trapped in my own affairs. I knew I should run down and speak to him before his father took him away.

"Tell him I'll be right down."

"Mark." Patty stopped me with only that. She was still extending the phone toward me, stiffly. I suppressed a shudder, but it spread across my shoulders and down my back like melting ice.

James Algren was no longer unhappy with me. "Congratulations!" he shouted happily. "I heard the news on the radio. Listen, I'm down in the hall outside the court and it's locked, everybody's gone. I was wondering where you've got Tommy."

"He's with one of my investigators," I said with unfelt assurance. Patty was already on the phone at another desk. But she wasn't speaking. She shook her head at me. "Why don't you come on up?" I added to Algren, and hung up.

"Where's Jim?" I asked sharply.

Patty had gotten hold of somebody. While she listened she spoke to me. "They haven't seen him since he went down to the courtroom."

"Idiot," I said. Patty knew I wasn't speaking to her. She was already making another call. I started calling too. I couldn't find the man *I* was looking for. I even called Eliot. He hadn't seen his client since two minutes after the verdict.

We were expecting James Algren when the hall door swung open. Instead Jim Lewis was standing there. His face announced permission to panic.

"Is he here?" he asked loudly.

We found a few people still at their desks. We called others at home. When Algren came in we tried to keep the news from him, but he quickly realized what was up. The investigator had brought Tommy back to the offices right after the verdict. Jim had left Tommy with a secretary while Jim went to the bathroom. When we tracked the secretary down she said Tommy had gone down to the basement to get a Coke. Nobody'd told her she had to stay with him. When Tommy didn't come back she figured he'd found his father, or Jim.

We scoured the building, which was almost empty by that time on a Friday afternoon. While others looked for Tommy I was continuing my own search, which proved equally fruitless.

By six we were standing staring at each other, forced to admit that Tommy was no longer in the building.

No one knew where Austin Paley was, either.

18

------◆------

FOR THE FIRST TIME IN TOO LONG I REMEMBERED Chris Davis, Austin's youthful lover, who had vanished off the face of this earth after he became a threat to Austin. He'd drifted to the back of my mind because he'd fallen out of the case, but now his disappearance seemed a foreshadowing, an announcement of what Austin could do when desperate.

We had no evidence that Austin Paley had kidnapped Tommy, but as the quarter-hours crawled by with no sign of either of them, it began to seem certain. Police were poring over the neighborhood around the courthouse complex, anywhere Tommy might have wandered, but they found no one. Mrs. Algren, at home, hadn't heard from him. I sent an investigator— it was Jim Lewis, anxious to atone—to Austin's office and his home. Jim called me from Austin's house—I didn't ask how he'd gotten inside—to report there'd been no one at either place. Jim started trying to trace Austin's friends. Other investigators, and cops, were doing the same.

The DA's offices began to grow as congested as on a working day, though it was by now early evening. I wasn't surprised to see anyone. Becky was there, and Janet McLaren. The Algrens must have called her, in their panic. Janet stopped me as I paced past.

"Mark—" She lowered her voice, glancing at James Algren sitting stunned in my outer office. "It may not be as bad as it seems. Tommy may have gone with him willingly. Tommy feels guilty, you know. And he still loves Austin. He may want to help him."

"I've already thought of that. But Tommy's willingness doesn't have anything to do with Austin's intentions. Austin doesn't love Tommy."

"Maybe he's trying to talk Tommy into recanting."

"Could be," I said, to let Janet retain that hope. I didn't. I'd seen Austin in court after the guilty verdict. I realized now his breakdown hadn't been an act. And his collapse hadn't been only physical. If he thought he could save himself by holding Tommy hostage, he'd lost his mind. Nor could the Austin Paley I'd known, the cool, efficient attorney for important clients, hold any rational hope that any of us would believe a new story he might force Tommy to tell. Austin couldn't hope to accomplish anything sane by snatching Tommy. That left me trying to fathom a madman's motives.

Seven o'clock took three or four hours to become seven-thirty. I had a sip of the coffee someone had made, felt it drop unimpeded into my stomach and begin burrowing into the lining, and tried to remember when I'd last eaten.

I have a private line in my office. Only four or five people know its number. When, sitting in the outer office in order to be closer to the lack of action, I heard the phone on my desk begin ringing, I knew something was about to happen. I sprinted past a blur of statues, paused with my hand on the phone to draw a breath, and answered.

"I've been calling you at home, like a fool," the man said. "Your answering machine will have a lot of hang-ups on it when you check it."

I was so expecting to hear Austin Paley's voice that I thought I was. It took that second sentence for me to identify the caller.

"Eliot?"

"I can tell you where he is, Mark. But he wants you to go alone, and *now*. Right away, so you don't have time to plan anything."

I thought of all those people in my outer office, some of whom were now crowding through my doorway to listen to my end of the call. "I don't know if I can manage the alone part," I said.

Eliot didn't respond. "Here's the address." He gave it to me. "It's south of downtown, you exit 37 at—"

"I know where it is."

"Yes, he said you would. Good luck, Mark."

"Eliot. Does he have Tommy? Is Tommy all right?"

Silence, as if our connection were bad. I hated his hesitation. Maybe it was because I'd asked two questions at once, which they teach you in law school not to do. "Eliot!"

"Yes," Eliot Quinn said quickly, and the line went dead.

I didn't even *drive* alone to the battered old house in the little cul-de-sac neighborhood. Two cops went with me, one a negotiator trying to give me the ten-minute course in talking a crazy out of his hostage. I wasn't paying much attention. His voice was just background noise to my thoughts.

When I'd first realized Austin had taken Tommy I'd been livid. If I'd seen Austin in that moment I could have strangled him. But rage is hard to sustain for hours. I'd had time to sit and think. I knew I was partly mad at myself, because I'd abandoned Tommy as soon as I no longer needed him. I'd allowed Austin to take him. I remembered the way Tommy had stared at me from the witness stand, looking to me at every moment of uncertainty. I'd told him to put himself in my hands and he had. My feigned friendship of the last few months had been effective. I'd beaten Austin for Tommy's trust. Then betrayed that trust at every step.

We'd given Tommy a hell of a preparation for manhood; his father, Austin, me. I remembered how quickly, it seemed to me, Tommy had responded to the role model I'd offered him. I'd straightened out his life as easily as I'd straightened out his batting swing. But Tommy must have realized by now why I'd grown close to him. I'd dropped him like a hot coal as soon as I no longer needed him. As Austin had. If Tommy was still alive, he had learned there was no one he could count on; no one motivated by uncalculated affection for Tommy.

My rage had given way to cold resolve. I would take Tommy from Austin again. Or if that was no longer possible, I'd have the revenge to which a father is entitled.

Sawhorses blocked the entrance to the short street. They didn't say POLICE, they said CITY PUBLIC SERVICE. Very subtle. Around the corner, barely out of sight of the house, was a squadron of cars: police cruisers, ambulances, a fire truck, and, pulling up just as I did, the *Eyewitness News* van. Not quite a circus, more like an open-air carnival whose power has just failed. There were no spotlights or flashing lights. We were all in the dark.

I met Lieutenant Paul Romano, whom I'd known slightly since he was a patrolman and I an assistant DA using him as a witness on a DWI. He took me to the corner, from which we could just see the house where I'd met Austin two months ago. Its porch light was burning, making it look like Grandma's house when company is expected.

"We got men in back," Lieutenant Romano said without preliminaries, "we got this end blocked off, we got a spotter in the culvert at the dead end of the street. He's not going anywhere. But we don't move 'til we know what's up. We don't even know who's in there. There's two cars in the driveway, and a garage in back, so he could have twenty men in there. We don't know if the boy's there or not. We're going to try to send in a negotiator—"

"He won't let anybody in. Except maybe me." It had been obvious that Eliot had spoken to me with permission. Austin wanted me to know where he was.

Lieutenant Romano was looking down. He rubbed a thumb on an eyebrow. He'd been waiting for me to say it, unwilling to make the suggestion himself. He wouldn't even endorse it. "I wouldn't recommend it," he said. "Trading one hostage for another never works. He'll end up with both of you."

"But I'll be inside."

Romano nodded. He'd exhausted his opposition. "We'll put a wire on you," he said. "If you can just get up to the door and talk to him, maybe he'll let slip who else's in the house with him. While you've got him distracted, we might ease up closer. And we'll have shooters across the street. If he even opens the front door with a gun in his hand—"

I felt strangely like a traitor while listening to these plans, even as I nodded and approved them. While ready to kill Austin myself, it seemed cowardly to serve as the bait to lure him to a spot where he'd be vulnerable.

"Let's get you ready," the lieutenant said. "Then—" He handed me a cordless telephone.

* * *

Ten minutes later I was dressed again. My tailors assured me the wire under my shirt was invisible, but I could feel it. The adhesives holding it in place itched. They warned me not to scratch, which made scratching the most desirable sensation on earth.

I stepped away from the others to dial the phone number they'd told me. It rang three, four times. I was beginning to think they'd given me the wrong number, or that Austin didn't want to talk. I was disappointed, but it would also be a relief to step back and let the SWAT team take over.

Then a voice answered, a slow, calm voice with its irony restored. "Hello, Mark."

"Hello, Austin. I'm here, right outside."

"With all your friends," his voice drawled.

"They don't matter. It's me you want to talk to, isn't it?"

There was only slight hesitation. "Yes. Come on in, Mark. Um—" He paused, as if he were going to ask me to pick up a bag of ice for the party, but didn't like to impose. "Naked, please," he said.

"What?"

He was smiling. I could hear it. "I'm not going to let you come in here armed, or broadcasting. So just take off your clothes, please."

"Like hell. Austin, if you brought me here to humiliate me *and* kill me, I'm not going to give you both satisfactions. If that's what you want, you can go fuck yourself."

I was surprised to hear myself arguing about this. The wire was already gone as an idea. Austin would frisk me and disconnect it as soon as I got inside. But I was the district attorney and he was a criminal. I was damned if I was going to let him make me look ridiculous. I knew that if I gave up the upper hand to Austin I would never recover it.

We compromised. After I'd disconnected the call, I walked back to Lieutenant Romano.

"Give me a chance to work it out peacefully," I told him. "See if I can get the boy out of there. But if anybody fires a shot it will be him, Austin. It'll be too late to help me then. If you hear a shot, one shot, come in blasting. Shoot every man in the room. There won't be time to make distinctions. Everybody over five feet tall, kill them."

A lieutenant is a high-ranking police officer. He reports to a captain, to assistant chiefs, to the chief of police. I was nowhere in that chain of command. But I was an elected public official, to whom he could legitimately pass the buck for whatever might happen. He looked at me as if he hadn't calculated all that, as if making a personal promise.

"All right," he said.

A few minutes later I stood in the street in front of Austin's rental house, wearing my pants and holding my shirt in my outstretched hand. My chest was bare in the cool night. The marks where the technicians had stripped off the wire were already fading. Down the street, a spotlight sprang into life. I knew I was being videotaped. But the spotlight served to assure Austin of my harmlessness, too. No one made the cameraman shut it off. There was no longer a pretense that I was alone.

I turned to display my bare back to the house as well. Then I walked up to it, up the three steps onto the creaking wooden porch. I didn't knock. A voice called, assuming the role of hearty host, "It's open."

I went in. After standing on the well-lighted porch, I was blind momentarily in that dim living room. My skin felt icy. I was certain I was about to be shot, or stabbed, or struck.

So when a hand did touch me, I jumped. "Relax," Austin said. "I just need to check. If you'd taken off your pants, like I asked, this wouldn't be necessary."

He frisked me briefly but thoroughly. By the time he finished my eyes had adjusted. I found myself looking not at Austin but at Eliot Quinn. He sat in the old damask-covered armchair directly in front of me, under a fringed floor lamp. Thank God he nodded when I looked at him. For a moment I'd thought he was dead.

Eliot was fully dressed in a suit and tie, but he was missing his traditional hat. His bare head, with a faint gleam of skull through the white hair, made him look vulnerable. He was sitting in front of the large front window of the living room. I didn't think his position accidental. Gunfire from outside would find Eliot as its first target.

But Eliot didn't look like a hostage. He looked like an adviser, even a cohort. He watched me sadly.

I turned to Austin. He had stepped back away from me, well out of reach, but he still held the silver-plated automatic pistol pointed at me. Austin, too, was formally dressed, in the suit he'd been wearing in court. He wore his old smile, too, the self-deprecating one that contemplated the possibility he'd made a social blunder. But the smile didn't touch his eyes, which were perfectly self-satisfied and looked me over coldly. I drew on my white shirt. Austin's hand twitched, as if that small self-protective gesture of mine were justification enough for him to kill me.

"Where's Tommy?" I said. Austin continued to regard me amusedly. I took a step toward him, anger my only protection. Austin made a small gesture toward the back of the house. That was with the hand holding the gun. With the other he made a calming gesture toward me. But I was not to be calmed. Rage had owned me since I'd stepped into the house, certain I was going to die.

"That boy loves you, Austin," I said. "After everything you've done to him, you're still the most important person in the world to him. If you've hurt him I'll kill you. I'll find some way, believe me."

"This isn't about Tommy," Austin said.

"He's all right," Eliot Quinn said, the first words he'd spoken since I'd arrived. But the nervous glance he gave Austin as he said it scared me.

I heard a faint sound from the back of the house that made me think someone was back there. That calmed me slightly. Calmness was not my friend. It meant I had to think my way out of this, instead of doing something crazy.

"This isn't about Tommy," Austin repeated. "Who was Tommy to you? Nobody, you'd never heard of him. But you and I were friends, Mark. We'd been friends a long time. But when I needed your help, you preferred some strange boy to me."

"You never came to me for help, Austin. You just tried to trick and intimidate me. I want to help you. What can I do?"

He told me, very explicitly. "I want you to dismiss the case. I want you to join in a motion for a new trial and then dismiss the case, all the cases. I want you to announce, very publicly, that you've uncovered new evidence that conclusively proves my innocence."

He wanted, in other words, to go on being the person he'd always been, not some vile convicted felon. His demands were insane. How long did he think he could hold a gun on me? I studied him as if I were thinking it over. I asked a question, remembering the police negotiator's suggestion that talk might be all a man holding a hostage wanted to do.

"Why didn't you just quit, Austin? You seem to have been inactive for a few years. Why didn't you just stop while you were safe?"

"Why don't you?" Austin replied. "You're a single man now, you don't have a readily available sexual partner. You have to go looking. Why don't you just throw it over, declare celibacy, stay home with a good book? Wouldn't it make life simpler?" He looked at me as if he knew everything about me. He could see the answer. *Yes, but.* Austin smiled. "It's no different with me, my friend. The urge doesn't die. The urge is the same, even if the object is different. Maybe my urge is stronger, even, because it's forbidden. Why should I stop?"

"Because it's illegal."

Austin shook his head. "Not for me."

"Because it's wrong, then," I said, watching him closely. "Because it scares the children. Who can know better than you how it hurts them?"

He stopped bantering. Austin's expression grew more intense. His gaze held me. He could make me see. "The children never resisted, Mark. I've never raped anyone. They knew it wasn't wrong. They knew it was natural as swimming. Just another skill to learn. Have you ever really thought about it? You're not one of these robots, you don't think with your gag reflex. Think about it. That soft skin, their clear eyes. Completely unsullied by experience. Utterly open. You don't have to worry about why they're doing this, do they want something from you, are they out to get you? Children are full of love, and curiosity, and they are hungry for any gesture of affection. No one gets enough affection, Mark, no one's capacity is ever filled. Especially children, especially today. Have you ever walked into a daycare center and seen all their eyes light up, seen them all come running to the stranger, begging for attention, pleading for love? They'll come up and stroke your legs, just to say, Look at me, touch me. Love me.

"Where are their parents?" Austin held out a helpless hand to me, forgetting it was the hand that held the gun. "Where are the aunts and uncles and grandparents who should be lavishing love on them? All working, all too busy. Too busy for the children they've spawned and set loose in the world. I try to take up some of the slack. I love them, Mark. I do. And they love me."

I felt chilled, not because he was raving, but because he was telling the truth. I *had* been to daycare centers recently, enough to see that Austin was right. And I believed he loved them. I didn't try to argue with him, partly because I didn't want to antagonize him; partly because I had no response.

Eliot cleared his throat. We looked at him. He was looking down at the floor, his face red.

"Why don't you go, Eliot?" I said, then to Austin, "He doesn't have to stay, does he?"

Austin looked at Eliot with no sympathy. "Not on my account," he said. Eliot just shook his head, still not looking at us. It was obvious he hadn't been brought here, he had come on his own, still feeling responsible. "We have a history in my family of involving old friends in our crises," Austin said, just to watch Eliot grow more miserable.

There was another sound from the back of the house. I couldn't make it out, but I believed it was Tommy. Austin would have him close. What was keeping Tommy back there?

"I'm going to get Tommy," I said. Austin stood up straighter in my path. "There's no reason he has to be here." Austin shook his head. "Austin, think of him. He's scared, he's a boy. He needs our help." Silently I was thinking, expecting him to hear the thought as well, *I can save him, Austin. I can't save you.*

Maybe he did hear me, but he wasn't willing to give Tommy up. For all I knew, Tommy wasn't alone in the back of the house. Perhaps Chris Davis was with him, or someone like Chris Davis. The idea restored my fear, and fear renewed my anger. And I didn't believe in Austin's threat with the gun. With all I'd uncovered about him, I'd never heard he was violent. I didn't believe he could bring himself to shoot me.

"I'm going back there," I said quietly, "and get Tommy. If he's all right I'll take him out of here. If he's not, you'd better start running now."

Austin moved, toward Eliot, so that he was no longer blocking the far doorway with its beaded curtain, but he kept the gun leveled at me. He was sweating, I saw for the first time, and it terrified me. "I can't let you do that," Austin said.

His answer scared me even more. *Why* couldn't he let me see Tommy? I turned away from Austin, starting to run. Flight made me feel safer. But before I got halfway to the doorway the gun went off. I thought I'd been hit. Instinct threw me aside, almost knocked me off my feet. Instinct was stupid. It killed my momentum, left me standing. I looked back and saw Eliot Quinn on his feet, struggling with Austin. The gun was pointed toward the ceiling. Eliot's hand was on Austin's wrist, but Austin was a much younger, stronger man. He was already turning the gun.

My first instinct was to leave Eliot to his fate while I ran to find Tommy, but I didn't want to leave this maniac with a gun at my back. I ran back to them. The gun was swinging wildly, pointing at me, then to the side, then back at me. I had no time to make distinctions. I just gave both struggling men a shove, the momentum of my run behind it. I hoped to throw them both to the ground and grab the gun as they scrambled up.

But I was stronger than I knew, crazed by adrenaline, and my push was desperate. We all careened toward the window. Eliot and Austin crashed through the flimsy curtain and the old glass and fell out onto the porch. I pulled up just in time. The porch light was still burning, spotlighting the two of them in the black night. Eliot lay where he'd fallen. Blood was starting from half a dozen cuts on his face.

Austin was dazed but still conscious. And the gun had gone out the window with him. He looked down at Eliot, who was no longer struggling, then back at me. There was a wild but perfectly aware look in his eye. He looked down, saw the gun, and picked it up, and started to his feet.

I dived to the side, away from the open window, down to the floor. In the next second, in the time it would have taken Austin to rise, the gunfire came. Rifle shots, both remote and piercing. They came in a burst, too many to count, and died as abruptly as they'd begun.

I stood, with some trouble. I was shaking. I didn't go near that shattered window, but I got a sidelong glimpse of two bodies on the ground. I ran the other way, through the beaded curtain, skidding on a scarred kitchen floor.

"Tommy!" I screamed.

A voice answered. Behind the kitchen was a short hallway with a dark hardwood floor and peeling print wallpaper on the walls. I burst through a closed paneled door with an old glass doorknob.

Tommy was on the antique brass bed. He was still wearing the dress slacks and shirt I'd last seen him wearing in court. He was sitting up on the bed. Nothing bound him to it. I grabbed him, ran my hands over his arms and legs. "Are you okay?" I was asking, more than once, too loudly for him to interrupt with an answer. I remembered to look around the room, and saw no one else.

"I'm fine," Tommy said, and he seemed to be, except that I was scaring him. I made myself calm down.

"He didn't hurt you?" I asked.

Tommy shook his head. "I just wanted to talk to him," Tommy said. "I just wanted to tell him I was sorry."

I looked at him sharply. Tommy didn't look or act like a kidnapping victim. He might have arranged this meeting himself.

"Is Waldo all right?" Tommy asked.

I pulled him to me and held him. I couldn't lie to him, but it didn't seem like the moment to tell him the truth, either.

I felt a gathering tension, as if the whole house were leaning in above me. There was no sound from the front room. The police might still be afraid to rush the house, not having seen me or Tommy.

I picked Tommy up, along with a blanket and pillow off the bed. Tommy was light, too light to be the almost-grown boy he was. I carried him back through the kitchen. Sure enough, the living room was still empty. By the front door, I set Tommy on his feet for a moment, but kept him facing me, the broken window behind him. I opened the front door of the house and held the white pillow out through it. When gunfire didn't tear it out of my hand I stepped into the open doorway and waved. No one shot at me, either. I heard running footsteps.

I stepped back in and picked Tommy up again. He was looking curiously at the window. From that angle I didn't think he could see anything outside. After he was in my arms I draped the blanket over his head. "Cold out here," I said.

I stepped out onto the porch carrying him. Tommy's face was covered, but *I* could see the two men lying on the porch. Eliot's eyes were still closed. As I watched, an EMS technician ran up and knelt beside him. He didn't even bother with Austin, who was lying a few feet away. Blood had turned his white shirtfront black in the glare of night. Austin's eyes were open, but there was no question that he was alive. The bullets had left his face unmarked. It was smoothed in death, his unnatural youthfulness regained. I didn't stare at him. I hurried down off the porch with Tommy. I was aware that there was plenty of light now. The headlights and flashing lights of the various official vehicles and the lights of the television cameras lit the scene like day. A man ran toward me and tried to take Tommy away from me. I resisted until I saw that it was James Algren. He lifted Tommy out of my arms. "Don't let him see," I said. Algren shot me a look so compounded of emotions it looked like hatred, the way all colors blended together make black. He looked as if he were grateful to me but didn't like it. I didn't blame him.

Without the warmth of Tommy's body against me I felt suddenly cold. My shirt was thin. Someone handed me a jacket. It wasn't my suit coat, it was a police windbreaker. I was glad to have it, especially as I thought it had started raining. My face was wet. When I reached to wipe it off I discovered another EMS technician beside me. "Don't touch it," he said authoritatively. He turned a bright flashlight on my face and probed at a spot on my temple with a cold bit of metal. "Ow," I said.

"I don't think the glass is still in there," he said, "but we'll need to look again. Just hold this on it for right now." He pressed a clean piece of cloth to my temple, put my hand on it like a child's, and ran off to attend to someone else. From the bustle and the number of people spreading through the night one would have thought a dozen hostages had been held.

Lieutenant Romano took my arm. "I'll have someone drive you to a hospital," he said.

I resisted automatically. "I'm not leaving 'til it's over."

He shrugged. "What's left to do?"

He had a point. "You did our work for us," Romano added. I looked back the way I'd come. Tommy was gone. His father must have hustled him away, avoiding the postcrisis interview. On the porch of the house, someone had draped a jacket over Austin Paley's face. A medical examiner's investigator was kneeling over him, pulling back the jacket. The porch was otherwise empty. A uniformed police officer stood inside the broken window, talking on a portable phone.

A television cameraman was filming the carnage. At his side, the reporter turned and saw me, and started down off the porch. The cameraman needed a dead body for maximum impact, but the reporter needed a live one.

"Where's Eliot?" I asked Romano. He nodded toward the ambulance, which stood thirty yards away, its light off and its loading doors standing open.

"Why isn't it taking off?" I asked. I knew the answer. There was no rush.

But Romano shrugged and said, "It's not that serious. Few cuts from flying glass, I think that's it."

I grabbed his arm. "He's alive?"

The lieutenant looked offended. "Nobody shot him. He stayed on the ground. Nobody'd've shot the crazy one, if he'd stayed down. What kind of men you think I give rifles to out here?"

I started toward the ambulance. But that was where the majority of the reporters were congregated. A technician stepped out of the ambulance and waved them away. One or two, discouraged, turned and saw me. Romano pulled me back again. "You want to give a press conference here?"

He was right. I could talk to Eliot later. I could avoid reporters' pointed questions until there was an official version of what had happened here tonight.

Voices called my name as I turned away. "In the morning," I muttered.

As it became clear I wasn't going to stop, questions replaced my name. As I ignored them, too, the questions grew uglier. "What happened inside?" "Are you glad he's dead?" "Do you think this will improve your reelection chances?" I didn't turn.

Until Jenny Lord's voice pierced the buzzing of the others. "Why was your old boss here?" she asked.

I stopped. The clamor died. "Was he trying to continue the cover-up?" Jenny Lord asked softly.

I turned. There were four of them, with eager or patient or knowing expressions. A camera flash glared in my face as I looked at them.

"Eliot Quinn was here to try to defuse the situation and help out two old friends," I said. "That was all."

Jenny shook her head. "We know, Mark. About the old cases. Austin Paley went back a long way."

"What happened to the old cases?" asked the hairdo from channel 4. I just looked at him for a moment.

"That was before my time."

"But you know how the system works," Jenny said, and the other newspaper reporter added, with the smugness of someone who only writes about the slime and doesn't have to step in it, "Were you part of the corruption or were you trying to stop it?"

It was Eliot's reputation they were talking about shredding. He had already connected himself to Austin by defending him. That had made someone start digging. I wasn't going to give them anything they didn't have, except maybe the right perspective.

"This isn't about corruption," I said. "What happens isn't always because of money, or sleaze. Sometimes, even when something bad comes of it, it started just from trying to help. To do the best you could. Our judicial system is no more corrupt than, say"—I groped for analogy, gazed around at all the official vehicles around us—"the auto parts business. The trouble is, we're entrusted with something precious—justice—but we run the system the same way the auto parts business is run: You treat some customers preferentially because they're your friends, or because they can do you some favor in return. You make do with the stock you have when you don't have the right part. You try to make a living."

I felt myself growing taller, rising above the scene, into the starry sky. I'd forgotten to keep the cloth pressed against my head, and blood was trickling down my cheek again.

"But our stock is human lives. People count on us. When we make do, someone's life could be ruined. A prosecutor gives away a case because it's too much trouble to pursue it, or would step on someone's toes; so a criminal is loose in the world. And a little respect for the law dies. The hope of ever achieving justice withers. People say there's no point in trying to do the right thing. And everybody suffers."

Jenny Lord was looking at me thoughtfully, not writing. But the TV hairdo just wanted to keep me babbling. "So you're saying covering up somebody's crimes is just part of the game?"

I hated his self-righteousness. He was maybe twenty-five years old. If he'd ever been confronted by an ethical dilemma, he probably hadn't noticed. "Have you ever killed a story as a favor to someone?" I asked him hotly. "Maybe you did it because you thought you could get a better story later in return. So does that make it just business, or corruption—or just a favor for a friend?"

He looked alarmed. "I've never done that."

"Oh no?" I asked quietly, staring at him. He shut up.

But there's always someone with another question. "So does that still go on?" the *Eyewitness News* reporter asked. "Do *you* do favors for friends?"

I raised my chin, indicating the old house behind them. "What do you think?" I said. "Austin Paley was my friend."

19

T HE NEWS COVERAGE OF THE EVENING'S ADVENTURE
was interesting, not for the divergence of angles, but for the
similar spin all the news outlets put on what had happened.
I'm sure the reporters hadn't colluded. But practicalities dictated
the outcome. My light-headed speech didn't make it intact into
print or on the air. It was too wordy for TV, and didn't fit the
print stories.

They all made me the hero, because that's the image that fit
the footage they had: the district attorney going in half-naked
to face an armed madman and emerging with the child victim
in his arms. The images were striking. Without too closely examining the background, they made a good story.

Jenny Lord's piece had a quiet tone that didn't match the
vivid photos, one of which was a shot of Austin's body on the
porch, with the caption, THE DA'S FRIEND. There was no mention of a possible cover-up in the dead man's past. I wondered,
but never asked, if Jenny had omitted that as a favor to me or
because *she* had understood my implied threat to the bubblehead
TV reporter. We had all known each other long enough to harbor secrets. I *knew* stories they'd all killed, or favors done. And
so it continued. The web of favors can take a hit from a cannon-
ball, and by morning the spiders will have repaired it
completely.

Leo Mendoza was in the news too, commenting on the end
of the strange case in which he had declared the defendant

innocent—the defendant a jury had found guilty of child rape just before his crazed death. Asked for his reaction, Leo sounded huffy: "I'm certain voters are tired of Mark Blackwell's brand of cowboy justice, that ends in a shootout rather than in a courtroom."

He spoke like an upholder of legal order, and I'm sure Leo was confident he was still riding high in the polls, but a lot of voters prefer cowboy justice to any other kind. Before the weekend was over I'd received four invitations to speak to citizens' groups. People I'd never met greeted me on the street and shook my hand. I decided I was the darling of the lunatic fringe.

Monday night, election day eve, I had my long-deferred dinner with David and Vicky. We ate in a Chinese restaurant where we'd all been before, but never together, never while I was still married to Lois. We ordered sesame beef and kung pao chicken and a pupu platter and ate family style. Vicky was gorgeous, in a tossed-back way that as a young man I'd thought indicated effortlessness. Her blond hair was freer than usual, swept back from her face. Her eyes and cheekbones and lips were prominent, but when I greeted her she was cool as ever, as if she'd come under duress.

David wasn't wearing a tie, but he looked as if he'd just rushed into the house, torn it off, and rushed out again. "Tough day?" I asked, and he only nodded.

So we all had a drink, then wine with dinner. "Good luck tomorrow," David said dutifully. I shrugged.

"You do want to win, don't you?"

"Sure," I said. "But it wouldn't be so terrible if I didn't. It would be nice to have a life again, not see everything I do on videotape the next day."

"But you have to win," Vicky said. "What if one of us gets in trouble again?"

I just looked at the girl. Either she was a complete dullard or she had a quirkier sense of humor than I'd ever realized.

We didn't talk about me after that, we talked about David's business venture and Vicky's job and their latest charity involvement. I noticed that they left things out of the conversation, they glanced at each other and mutually, silently agreed to skip ahead; once she even nudged David's arm and they snickered in unison. "What?" I asked, but they wouldn't say.

Vicky and I reached for the last piece of sesame beef simultaneously, I with a fork, she with chopsticks. "Go ahead," I said, "I don't need it," patting my stomach.

"Hey, I saw you on TV and you didn't look bad," she answered. "And they say TV adds ten pounds."

"Only if you have clothes on," I said.

She said to David, "See, I told you it was only his clothes that make him look like that."

"Like what?" I asked, glancing down at what I was wearing. "You think I need help?"

"Doesn't David look better since I started going with him to buy clothes?" Vicky replied.

I looked at David. He *did* look better. Even rumpled as he was at the end of the day, his shirt was not only nice-looking but did something to his face that diminished his habitual paleness. And his jacket didn't hang awkwardly on him as if he'd taken it from someone else's closet. I tried to remember when he'd stopped dressing like a teenager. It wasn't just his clothes, either. David seemed at ease. He leaned back in his chair, stepping into the conversation only when he had something to say. He didn't feel responsible for it. This ease was a recent addition to David's personality. He had an adult assuredness. Maybe David was growing old enough to put aside his adolescent resentments, or at least to view them more critically. You don't have to be adult very long to realize *you* can make mistakes too.

The food was gone, but we had another round of wine. I was in no hurry to get back to my barren condo. David and Vicky didn't seem to mind staying with me.

After the check was already on the table, David leaned forward and said, with his old hesitancy returning, "You haven't asked about Mom."

"I have my sources, David. I have a whole staff of investigators, you don't have to be one of them."

He grew easier in his manner again after I relieved him of the duty of reporting. "She's good," he said, "she seems happy."

"I'm glad."

David was watching me to see how I took the news, then he and Vicky exchanged another of those looks. I couldn't see what she was telling him, but after the exchange David added, "But I'm not sure if she's happy because things are going well or because they're not."

"What?" I directed the question as much at Vicky as at David. It was David who answered.

"With the new boyfriend. Sometimes when she seems to be spending a lot of time with him you can see her draw back, like she doesn't want to get too involved too fast."

"Well, I guess that's—"

"I think she enjoys keeping him off balance," Vicky said confidentially.

I looked at her, then decided, what the hell, to say what I was thinking. "Oh, you know something about the pleasure of that, Vicky?"

It could have been a bad blunder, ending a pleasant evening. But Vicky's smile broadened. She laughed. I laughed with her. "I have my memories," she said, putting a hand on David's shoulder. He rolled his eyes. "Me, too."

Damn, I thought. *I could get to like this woman.* David seemed to have discovered that he liked her too. Amazing thing, how their lives seemed to be blossoming, with no help from me.

On election day I went to work, but I didn't spend much time in my office. I roamed around the old courthouse and the new Justice Center in a valedictory way, reminiscing with acquaintances of long standing or sitting in empty courtrooms alone. Here was where I'd tried my first case. Here was my old office. Here were the stairs down which I'd thrown my briefcase after an especially bitter loss. I'd left my marks on the buildings, and they on me, even if I'd never have an official position in them again. That was what hurt most about the prospect of losing the election, the thought of being exiled from this world I knew best, by strangers who didn't know it at all.

I stayed until after six, then walked a few blocks across downtown to the old Menger Hotel, where Tim Scheuless had rented a suite for me and, optimistically, a ballroom for my supporters. Avoiding the latter, I went straight upstairs, where I found a small group of campaign organizers whose quiet cheer at my appearance was rather dispiriting. I joined them in a drink.

At seven o'clock the polls closed and, a few minutes later, the first results were announced. It was a presidential election year, my race came well down the ballot. The screen showed the numbers while the commentator read them. I was leading 53 percent to 47.

No one said anything, so I said it. "Not enough," I said. These first figures showed only the absentee voting, which had already been counted. The conservative north side of San Antonio, which should have been my most solid base of support, votes disproportionately heavily in the absentee voting period. I should have had a very big lead in that first announcement, which would be whittled down gradually throughout the evening as the rest of the city's votes were counted. Six percentage points were not enough of a lead to endure that whittling.

An hour later I had retired to the inner bedroom, and no one disturbed me there. Oddly enough, I couldn't keep my thoughts on the election. I was standing at the window, staring down at the narrow street that ran between the hotel and the grounds of the Alamo next door, thinking of Austin Paley. I don't like to view the body at a funeral. I'm always afraid that last glimpse of the departed will overlay all my memories of him, so that I will never remember him any other way. That had been happening to my memories of Austin: It wasn't that last view of him on the porch that had been superseding everything else, it had been the last weeks, when he'd been a defendant and I a prosecutor. But Austin and I had had twenty years before that. We hadn't been close friends—I wondered now if anyone had really shared Austin's life—but he'd had a gift for making me feel close to him in a few snatched moments. It wasn't only me on whom he'd exercised this gift. I remembered an occasion ten or twelve years ago, long enough ago that Austin had been representing a DWI defendant and I'd been a defense lawyer, when I'd overheard Austin talking to the prosecutor of the case. Austin never made what he did sound like plea bargaining, but that's what it was, and the prosecutor was being a hard-ass, insisting on some jail time. Austin started talking about the number of drinks the defendant had had—too many, but not enough to justify nights in jail. Then he'd leaned closer to the prosecutor. "Confidentially," he'd said, "I was at the same party. I'm lucky it wasn't me arrested afterwards."

The prosecutor had smiled with him. In a few words Austin had turned the courtroom into a confessional and the discussion of the crime into a reminiscence of a social occasion. The threat of jail time had gone away. And when he'd seen me watching Austin had winked, out of the prosecutor's sight, taking me alone into his confidence. Austin's life was layers of confidences, none of them real. Or maybe all of them real. He was a complex man. I didn't like the simple creature he'd been made in his obituaries.

The door opened behind me. It seemed quite natural that the man behind me was here, as if my thoughts had conjured him. "Hello, Eliot," I said before I turned.

"If I'd known you were psychic," he said, "I'd have never tried to put anything over on you."

I indicated the window. "I saw you in the glass."

He glanced past me and shrugged as if he were turning stupid. He still looked rather battered. He had a Band-Aid on his forehead and another on his cheek; other cuts were healed enough to remain uncovered, but they still marked him.

"I just came to say good luck."

"Thanks." Eliot knew where the luck lay in this campaign, and he must have seen the first returns and known what they meant, so I appreciated his appearance. He showed no inclination to leave. A minute later I was saying, "I watched him, Eliot. He was never unconscious. He knew exactly what he was doing. He knew who was out there watching his every move. And he knew what picking up the gun would do."

Eliot sat silent for a moment, as if even now he felt bound by some confidence of Austin's. But then he said, "I knew he had no designs on the boy. That was just a way to get you there. And he knew you wouldn't come alone."

"You're saying—"

"He wasn't going to prison, Mark. There was no way he could let that happen."

In the silence that followed, Austin Paley seemed to be in the room with us, smiling silently, as we tried to fathom his mind. "But he still might have gotten probation," I finally said. "He was an ideal candidate."

"The conviction was all that mattered to Austin," Eliot said. "Having his life spread before the whole city like that. He could never have been what he was again. In the end he just couldn't face it."

"Like his friend Chris Davis," I said.

Eliot's lips tightened again; he had the secret-holding habit, even after the cause was gone.

"Chris volunteered to fade the heat for Austin," I said, and I waited long enough that Eliot answered.

"Yes. Because he loved Austin. And he thought it didn't matter where he spent his last days anyway." Eliot looked at me. "You realized Chris was dying?"

"It crossed my mind. He looked worse every time I saw him."

After a moment Eliot said, "But he couldn't go through with the plea. And I don't know if Austin would have let him in the end. He loved Chris, you know. He loved—"

He stopped. Putting Austin into words was too painful for Eliot.

"Mark?" It was one of the campaign workers at the door, a Young Republican type whose name, I was proud of myself for remembering, was Jesse. "Could you come out here for a minute?"

I followed him out to the living room, which seemed brighter than it had been. Tim Scheuless waved me over to where they had the traditional three televisions set up. "Quick, quick," he said, and as I joined him, "They're about to show it on Channel 4. They just showed it on 5."

I didn't have to ask what he meant. The new numbers. I wondered if this was the round that would drop me below 50 percent. It must be nerve-racking for Leo Mendoza to watch this, sure he was going to win but starting from behind.

"And in the race for Bexar County District Attorney," the newsreader intoned, then waited for the numbers on the screen to flip, "latest returns indicate the incumbent, Mark Blackwell, leading with fifty-five percent of the votes."

"Fifty-*five?*" I said.

"It's true," Tim assured me. "That's what the other channel just reported too."

My lead was growing, not shrinking. "Cowboy justice," I muttered, but no one heard me. The half-dozen people in the room were clapping.

I looked back at Eliot, in the doorway of the bedroom, who wore a little smile. I wondered if he was thinking what I was thinking. In an ugly case like Austin's, the public couldn't really be satisfied unless the defendant ended up dead, and immediately. Screw all the official support I didn't have, the political kingmakers who were furious with me. I'd not only prosecuted a monster, I'd killed him. Good job, the voters were replying.

* * *

The numbers continued to climb through the short evening. With the new electronic ballot counting no one has to stay up all night any more to know who's won a local race. It was only nine-thirty when my percentage of the vote hit 57 percent and the rumors began that Leo had already conceded. It was clear that I had won when other elected officials began showing up in the hotel suite and the ballroom below was reported to be filling. Tim told me, laughing, that the bumper stickers and yard signs we couldn't give away a week ago were suddenly in demand. Tomorrow morning everyone would look like one of my lifelong supporters. I laughed with him. Let everybody climb aboard.

They let me go into the bedroom alone to straighten up and prepare a few remarks—ones I hadn't expected to deliver. Jesse tried to shoo out the old man in the chair who was the last person in the bedroom. "Please, sir, the district attorney needs a few moments alone."

"It's okay, Jesse," I said. He looked at me puzzledly—he had no idea who the old man was—but left, shutting the door.

It seemed fitting that I be alone for a minute with Eliot. Paradoxically, he was still one of the few people I trusted.

He came up to me and clapped me on the arms, exactly like a father congratulating a son. "I will leave you alone," he said. "I just wanted to remind you of one thing. Everybody's on your team now, because you're a winner. But don't you ever forget who your real friends were, when you needed them."

I stumbled over the words. "I know, Eliot. I—"

"Nobody," Eliot said firmly. "Nobody turned a finger to help you. Everybody was against you. And that's still who you're going to have on your side in a crunch. Nobody. The ones who come up and shake your hand, they're the ones you can trust the least. Unless—" He studied me. "What are you going to do with what Austin told you? The recreation center, the dead man in the basement?"

"Dig," I said. "Find where the body's buried, to start. Get enough on somebody to make him turn on the others. See how far I can take it. Prosecute the ones who should be."

I was sure of my answer, but I couldn't tell from Eliot's face that it was the right one. "Austin's dead," he reminded me needlessly. "*You* could be the man with the secrets now. Something like this, you keep it in your pocket, it'll be better than money in the bank for years to come."

It was a strange speech from Eliot, so much so that I thought I was being tested. I just shook my head. Eliot looked at me sadly. "Then I've got nothing to tell you," he said. "I wish I could offer you some advice, but there's none that would do you any good. I'm not even sure which of the people in power will be after your hide. But they will be. You're what they hate most: a loner with popular support. You watch your back."

And he was gone, in his black suit, knowing he would be a troubling specter at the feast. I thought about what he'd said to me for two minutes, until the mob came in and started carrying me down to my beloved friends in the ballroom. As I laughed and shook hands and recognized faces I was startled to see there, smiling at me, I was rehearsing in my mind my victory speech: *Well, I won for the wrong reasons, but I still won. I got very, very lucky. And some people are going to be very sorry about it.*

When I found myself at the podium, in front of a serpent's tangle of microphones, I looked out on a crowd of hundreds of people, so many I couldn't see individual faces, all beaming at me. I opened my mouth and said:

"Well, children, we did it."

They went nuts. When the noise died down I put on a more serious expression and said, "We got our message out to the people, and the people liked what they heard. They heard that this is an administration committed to one thing: the truth. They heard . . ."

It was a ridiculous speech. You don't want to hear any more of it. It went over very big.

If I could have asked for one person to come congratulate me on my victory the next morning, it would have been the one Patty ushered into my office without warning. I thought I'd seen her for the last time the night of Tommy's kidnapping.

Janet even came in person rather than phoning, which was delightful. She was pleasing to eyes that had had only three or four hours' sleep. She took my hands for a moment but let me go.

"I should have come last night," she said.

"No, you shouldn't have. It would've made you sick." Not

like a criminal trial, but a political campaign victory party is in its way just as disgusting.

"I did see you on the news, with Tommy." She was scrutinizing me closely—trying to see, I imagined, if I'd acted out of concern for Tommy or in order to look like a hero in the last days of my reelection campaign. I didn't say anything. I was sure I couldn't convince her of anything she didn't already believe.

"No one else could have saved him," Janet said. Then I realized it was my forehead she was studying. She reached up to almost touch it. "It looked like you were hurt."

"I'm all right."

She looked at her own hands. "Mark, let's make an agreement. Let's not ever see each other again," she said, looking troubled, "professionally."

Thank God for the last word. "Absolutely," I said seriously. "Because let me tell you, you were a great flaming pain in the ass to work with." I liked the way her eyes went wide and her mouth came open and color rushed into her face. "Sashaying around here the way you did while we were supposed to be having a professional consultation," I went on. "Flirting with me like a schoolgirl, doing those things with your eyes and the way your voice would drop when you looked at me, like I was the most wonderful—"

She rolled her eyes. "You have a rich fantasy life."

"Oh, you mean you did it all unconsciously? You know what Freud would say about that."

"No, and neither do you," she said. "And he was probably wrong."

"It may take some study, but I'll find it. You have a professional library, don't you? Maybe if I browsed through it . . ."

We were standing close. Janet turned serious again. "But one thing," she said. "Have you been to see Tommy yet?"

I felt reproached by the question. "I've tried to call him a couple of times, but—"

"Good. Don't go see him. Not yet, maybe not ever. Don't keep being part of his life. They're trying to put their lives together. They don't need you there to remind them what they've been through. Or to compete for Tommy's attention just when James Algren is finally trying to be a real father."

"Is he? That's great. I wish—"

I didn't finish. I'd almost said I wished David and I had had a tragedy like that earlier in our lives, something to make me stop and question what was important in my life.

Janet didn't ask me to finish the thought. She finally gave me a smile. Business was done.

"And if this advice leaves you with a lot of free time you don't know what to do with," she smiled, "I have another suggestion."

I stood lost in contemplation of her, as if her voice were speaking my thoughts aloud. When she stepped forward and held me I relaxed for the first time in days. No, weeks.

She left too soon. She was a busy person, after all, a doctor. She had sanities to save.

Her departure left me free to renew my study of the single sheet of paper on my desk. It was handwritten, on the stationery of my own office. Two crisp sentences, following a formal salutation.

"Patty?" I asked the intercom, "Is Becky Schirhart by any chance waiting to see me?"

"She's not out here."

"Find her and ask her to come in, would you?"

It seemed so strange to be sitting behind my own desk, in the office of the district attorney, with no boxes in sight, no packing to do. Everything felt brand new. I couldn't wait to get started.

When Becky arrived she walked briskly into the office, as if I'd taken her away from something important. There was an assurance about her movements I hadn't seen before. She didn't feel called on to speak first. She came up to the desk and looked at me, questioningly, then a little more intently, with a touch of concern.

"I had a hard night," I said.

"You had a great night."

"I didn't see you there."

"I wasn't there," she said, not dropping her eyes or explaining further.

"I'm glad to hear it," I said. "It confirms my opinion of you."

She looked questioning again at that, but I changed the subject, pushing her letter of resignation toward her across the desk. "I wish you'd take this back," I said, "and tear it up, or maybe keep it until you need it."

"I think I need it now," she said slowly.

"Found a good job?"

"I haven't started looking yet." She frowned, disliking to say more. She'd wanted it to be cleaner. "But after what happened between us"—she laughed slightly, not smiling—"or *didn't* happen, it would be too uncomfortable for me to go on working here. For both of us."

"Not—"

She continued doggedly, "I don't think you could get over the lingering suspicion that I did it to gain an advantage, when I had the chance."

I shook my head. "You obviously didn't do it to advance yourself at work." I touched her letter of resignation again. "This proves that."

Becky's mouth moved. She didn't want to argue. "Maybe I'm just being sly."

"If you're that cunning, I want you on my side. Becky, winning another term was the first shot in a war. Things could get ugly around here. I have to be very careful now to have around me only people I completely trust."

Her eyebrows went up. "And that's me?"

"That's you."

She finally picked up the letter, read it, and tore it in half. She glanced at me and away. She was happy and didn't like to let me see it, or maybe didn't like to let herself feel it.

"Sentimental old fool," she said.

Amazonia

James Rollins

WM

WILLIAM MORROW

An Imprint of HarperCollins*Publishers*

Amazonia

Plant drawings provided and copyrighted by Raintree Nutrition, Inc. All rights reserved. http://www.rain-tree.com used by permission of Leslie Taylor.

FIRST EDITION

Designed by Gretchen Achilles
Maps by Jeffrey L. Ward

Printed on acid-free paper

Library of Congress Cataloging-in-Publication Data

Rollins, James, 1961–
    Amazonia / by James Rollins.
      p. cm.
    ISBN 0-06-000248-4 (hc.)
    1. Amazon River Region—Fiction.   2. Prion diseases—Fiction.   I. Title.

PS3568.O5398 A83   2002
813'.54—dc21

                          2001044049

02 03 04 05 06 QW 10 9 8 7 6 5 4 3 2 1

To John Petty and Rick Hourigan
friends and co-conspirators

ACKNOWLEDGMENTS

Special thanks to all those who helped in the research of this novel, especially Leslie Taylor of Raintree Nutrition, Inc., for the use of her wonderful plant diagrams in this book and for her valuable knowledge of the medicinal applications of rainforest botanicals. I would also be remiss not to acknowledge two resources of utmost value: Redmond O'Hanlon's *In Trouble Again: A Journey Between the Orinoco and the Amazon* and the book that inspired my own, Dr. Mark Plotkin's *Tales of a Shaman's Apprentice*. For more specific help, I most heartily thank my friends and family who helped shape the manuscript into its present form: Chris Crowe, Michael Gallowglas, Lee Garrett, Dennis Grayson, Susan Tunis, Penny Hill, Debbie Nelson, Dave Meek, Jane O'Riva, Chris "The Little" Smith, Judy and Steve Prey, and Caroline Williams. For help with the French language, my Canadian friend Dianne Daigle; for assistance on the Internet, Steve Winter; and for her arduous moral support, Carolyn McCray. For the maps used here, I must acknowledge their source: *The CIA World Factbook 2000*. Finally, the three folks who remain my best critics and most loyal supporters: my editor, Lyssa Keusch; my agent, Russ Galen; and my publicist, Jim Davis. Last and most important, I must stress that any and all errors of fact or detail fall squarely on my own shoulders.

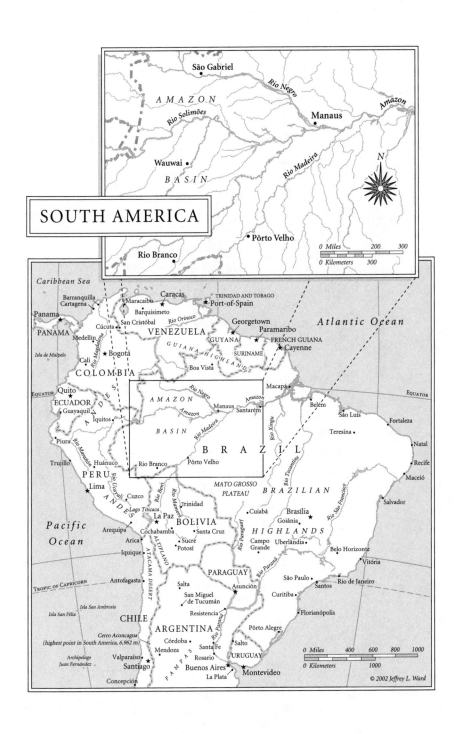

SOUTH AMERICA

São Gabriel

Rio Negro

A M A Z O N

Amazon

Rio Solimões

Manaus

Wauwai

B A S I N

Rio Madeira

N

Pôrto Velho

0 Miles   200   300
0 Kilometers   300

Rio Branco

Caribbean Sea

Barranquilla
Cartagena   Maracaibo   Caracas   TRINIDAD AND TOBAGO
Panama   Barquisimeto Port-of-Spain   *Atlantic Ocean*
PANAMA   Cúcuta San Cristóbal   *Rio Orinoco*   Georgetown Paramaribo
       Medellín   **VENEZUELA**   **GUYANA** FRENCH GUIANA
Isla de Malpelo   Bogotá   *G U I A N A*   SURINAME   Cayenne
       Cali   *H I G H L A N D S*
       COLOMBIA   Boa Vista
EQUATOR Quito   *Rio Negro*   Macapá   *EQUATOR*
       ECUADOR   *A M A Z O N*   *Amazon*
       Guayaquil   Manaus Santarém   Belém
       Iquitos   *Amazon*   São Luís   Fortaleza
       Piura   *B A S I N* *Rio Madeira*   Teresina
                                                                        Natal
       Trujillo   Huánuco   Rio Branco Pôrto Velho   **B R A Z I L**
       PERU   Cuzco   Recife
       Lima   *MATO GROSSO* **B R A Z I L I A N**   Maceió
Pacific   *Lago Titicaca* *Rio Mamoré* *PLATEAU*   Salvador
Ocean   La Paz Trinidad   Cuiabá Brasília
       Arequipa   **BOLIVIA** Santa Cruz   Goiânia **H I G H L A N D S**
       Arica Cochabamba Sucre   Campo Uberlândia   Belo Horizonte
       Iquique   Potosí   Grande   Vitória
TROPIC OF CAPRICORN Antofagasta Salta **PARAGUAY**   São Paulo
       CHILE   San Miguel   Asunción Curitiba   Santos Rio de Janeiro
Isla San Ambrosio   de Tucumán
Isla San Félix   Resistencia   Florianópolis
                 ARGENTINA   Pôrto Alegre
Cerro Aconcagua   Córdoba   Santa Fe Salto
(highest point in South America, 6,962 m) Mendoza   **URUGUAY**
Archipélago   Valparaíso Rosario   0 Miles   400   600   800 1000
Juan Fernández Santiago Buenos Aires Montevideo   0 Kilometers   1000
       Concepción   La Plata

© 2002 Jeffrey L. Ward

Prologue

Padre Garcia Luiz Batista was struggling with his hoe, tilling weeds from the mission's garden, when the stranger stumbled from the jungle. The figure wore a tattered pair of black denim pants and nothing else. Bare-chested and shoeless, the man fell to his knees among rows of sprouting cassava plants. His skin, burnt a deep mocha, was tattooed with blue and crimson dyes.

Mistaking the fellow for one of the local Yanomamo Indians, Padre Batista pushed back his wide-brimmed straw hat and greeted the fellow in the Indians' native tongue. "*Eou, shori,*" he said. "Welcome, friend, to the mission of Wauwai."

The stranger lifted his face, and Garcia instantly knew his mistake. The fellow's eyes were the deepest blue, a color unnatural among the Amazonian tribes. He also bore a scraggled growth of dark beard.

Clearly not an Indian, but a white man.

"*Bemvindo,*" he offered in Portuguese, believing now that the fellow must be one of the ubiquitous peasants from the coastal cities who ventured into the Amazon rain forest to stake a claim and build a better life for themselves. "Be welcome here, my friend."

The poor soul had clearly been in the jungle a long time. His skin was stretched over bone, each rib visible. His black hair was tangled, and his body bore cuts and oozing sores. Flies flocked about him, buzzing and feeding on his wounds.

1

When the stranger tried to speak, his parched lips cracked and fresh blood dribbled down his chin. He half crawled toward Garcia, an arm raised in supplication. His words, though, were garbled, unintelligible, a beastly sound.

Garcia's first impulse was to retreat from the man, but his calling to God would not let him. The Good Samaritan did not refuse the wayward traveler. He bent and helped the man to his feet. The fellow was so wasted he weighed no more than a child in his arms. Even through his own shirt, the padre could feel the heat of the man's skin as he burned with fever.

"Come, let us get you inside out of the sun." Garcia guided the man toward the mission's church, its whitewashed steeple poking toward the blue sky. Beyond the building, a ragtag mix of palm-thatched huts and wooden homes spread across the cleared jungle floor.

The mission of Wauwai had been established only five years earlier, but already the village had swelled to nearly eighty inhabitants, a mix of various indigenous tribes. Some of the homes were on stilts, as was typical of the Apalai Indians, while others built solely of palm thatch were home to the Waiwai and Tiriós tribes. But the greatest number of the mission's dwellers were Yanomamo, marked by their large communal roundhouse.

Garcia waved his free arm to one of the Yanomamo tribesmen at the garden's edge, a fellow named Henaowe. The short Indian, the padre's assistant, was dressed in pants and a buttoned, long-sleeved shirt. He hurried forward.

"Help me get this man into my house."

Henaowe nodded vigorously and crossed to the man's other side. With the feverish man slung between them, they passed through the garden gate and around the church to the clapboard building jutting from its south face. The missionaries' residence was the only home with a gas generator. It powered the church's lights, a refrigerator, and the village's only air conditioner. Sometimes Garcia wondered if the success of his mission was not based solely on the wonders of the church's cool interior, rather than any heartfelt belief in salvation through Christ.

Once they reached the residence, Henaowe ducked forward and yanked the rear door open. They manhandled the stranger through the dining room to a back room. It was one of the domiciles of the mission's acolytes, but it was now unoccupied. Two days ago, the younger mission-

Alone in the dim room, Garcia felt a chill in the air that didn't come from the air-conditioning. He had heard whispers of the Ban-ali, one of the mythic ghost tribes of the deep forest. A frightening people who mated with jaguars and possessed unspeakable powers.

Garcia kissed his crucifix and cast aside these fanciful superstitions. Turning to the bucket and medicines, he soaked a sponge in the tepid water and brought it to the wasted man's lips.

"Drink," he whispered. In the jungle, dehydration, more than anything, was often the factor between life and death. He squeezed the sponge and dribbled water across the man's cracked lips.

Like a babe suckling at his mother's teat, the stranger responded to the water. He slurped the trickle, gasping and half choking. Garcia helped raise the man's head so he could drink more easily. After a few minutes, the delirium faded somewhat from the man's eyes. He scrabbled for the sponge, responding to the life-giving water, but Garcia pulled it away. It was unhealthy to drink too quickly after such severe dehydration.

"Rest, senhor," he urged the stranger. "Let me clean your wounds and get some antibiotics into you."

The man did not seem to understand. He struggled to sit up, reaching for the sponge, crying out eerily. As Garcia pushed him by the shoulders to the pillow, the man gasped out, and the padre finally understood why the man could not speak.

He had no tongue. It had been cut away.

Grimacing, Garcia prepared a syringe of ampicillin and prayed to God for the souls of the monsters that could do this to another man. The medicine was past its expiration date, but it was the best he could get out here. He injected the antibiotic into the man's left buttock, then began to work on his wounds with sponge and salve.

The stranger lapsed between lucidity and delirium. Whenever he was conscious, the man struggled mindlessly for his piled clothes, as if he intended to dress and continue his jungle trek. But Garcia would always push his arms back down and cover him again with blankets.

As the sun set and night swept over the forests, Garcia sat with the Bible in hand and prayed for the man. But in his heart, the padre knew his prayers would not be answered. Kamala, the shaman, was correct in his assessment. The man would not last the night.

As a precaution, in case the man was a child of Christ, he had performed the sacrament of Last Rites an hour earlier. The fellow had stirred as he marked his forehead with oil, but he did not wake. His brow burned feverishly. The antibiotics had failed to break through the blood infections.

Resolved that the man would die, Garcia maintained his vigil. It was the least he could do for the poor soul. But as midnight neared and the jungle awoke with the whining sounds of locusts and the *cronk*ing of myriad frogs, Garcia slipped to sleep in his chair, the Bible in his lap.

He woke hours later at a strangled cry from the man. Believing his patient was gasping his last breath, Garcia struggled up, knocking his Bible to the floor. As he bent to pick it up, he found the man staring back at him. His eyes were glassy, but the delirium had faded. The stranger lifted a trembling hand. He pointed again to his discarded clothes.

"You can't leave," Garcia said.

The man closed his eyes a moment, shook his head, then with a pleading look, he again pointed to his pants.

Garcia finally relented. How could he refuse this last feverish request? Standing, he crossed to the foot of the bed and retrieved the rumpled pair of pants. He handed them to the dying man.

The stranger grabbed them up and immediately began pawing along the length of one leg of his garment, following the inner seam. Finally, he stopped and fingered a section of the cotton denim.

With shaking arms, he held the pants out to Garcia.

The padre thought the stranger was slipping back into delirium. In fact, the poor man's breathing had become more ragged and coarse. But Garcia humored his nonsensical actions. He took the pants and felt where the man indicated.

To his surprise, he found something stiffer than denim under his fingers, something hidden under the seam. A secret pocket.

Curious, the padre fished out a pair of scissors from the first-aid kit. Off to the side, the man sank down to his pillow with a sigh, clearly content that his message had finally been understood.

Using the scissors, Garcia trimmed through the seam's threads and opened the secret pocket. Reaching inside, he tugged out a small bronze coin and held it up to the lamp. A name was engraved on the coin.

"Gerald Wallace Clark," he read aloud. Was this the stranger? "Is this you, senhor?"

He glanced back to the bed.

"Sweet Jesus in heaven," the padre mumbled.

Atop the cot, the man stared blindly toward the ceiling, mouth lolled open, chest unmoving. He had let go the ghost, a stranger no longer.

"Rest in peace, Senhor Clark."

Padre Batista again raised the bronze coin to the lantern and flipped it over. As he saw the words inscribed on the opposite side, his mouth grew dry with dread.

United States Army Special Forces.

George Fielding had been surprised by the call. As deputy director of Central Intelligence, he had often been summoned to urgent meetings by various division heads, but to get a priority one call from Marshall O'Brien, the head of the Directorate Environmental Center, was unusual. The DEC had been established back in 1997, a division of the intelligence community dedicated to environmental issues. So far in his tenure, the DEC had never raised a priority call. Such a response was reserved for matters of immediate national security. What could have rattled the Old Bird—as Marshall O'Brien had been nicknamed—to place such an alert?

Fielding strode rapidly down the hall that connected the original headquarters building to the new headquarters. The newer facility had been built in the late eighties. It housed many of the burgeoning divisions of the service, including the DEC.

As he walked, he glanced at the framed paintings lining the long passageway, a gallery of the former directors of the CIA, going back all the way to Major General Donovan, who served as director of the Office of Strategic Services, the World War II–era counterpart of the CIA. Fielding's own boss would be added to this wall one day, and if George played his cards smartly, he himself might assume the directorship.

With this thought in mind, he entered the New Headquarters Building and followed the halls to the DEC's suite of offices. Once through the main door, he was instantly greeted by a secretary.

She stood as he entered. "Deputy Director, Mr. O'Brien is waiting for you in his office." The secretary crossed to a set of mahogany doors, knocked perfunctorily, then pushed open the door, holding it wide for him.

"Thank you."

Inside, a deep, rumbling voice greeted him. "Deputy Director Fielding, I appreciate you coming in person." Marshall O'Brien stood up from his chair. He was a towering man with silver-gray hair. He dwarfed the large executive desk. He waved to a chair. "Please take a seat. I know your time is valuable, and I won't waste it."

Always to the point, Fielding thought. Four years ago, there had been talk that Marshall O'Brien might assume the directorship of the CIA. In fact, the man had been deputy director before Fielding, but he had bristled too many senators with his no-nonsense attitude and burned even more bridges with his rigid sense of right and wrong. That wasn't how politics were played in Washington. So instead, O'Brien had been demoted to a token figurehead here at the Environmental Center. The old man's urgent call was probably his way of scraping some bit of importance from his position, trying to stay in the game.

"What's this all about?" Fielding asked as he sat down.

O'Brien settled to his own seat and opened a gray folder atop his desk.

Someone's dossier, Fielding noted.

The old man cleared his throat. "Two days ago, an American's body was reported to the Consular Agency in Manaus, Brazil. The deceased was identified by his Special Forces challenge coin from his old unit."

Fielding frowned. Challenge coins were carried by many divisions of the military. They were more a tradition than a true means of identification. A unit member, active or not, caught without his coin was duty-bound to buy a round of drinks for his mates. "What does this have to do with us?"

"The man was not only ex–Special Forces. He was one of my operatives. Agent Gerald Clark."

Fielding blinked in surprise.

O'Brien continued, "Agent Clark had been sent undercover with a research team to investigate complaints of environmental damage from gold-mining operations and to gather data on the transshipment of Bolivian and Colombian cocaine through the Amazon basin."

Fielding straightened in his seat. "And was he murdered? Is that what this is all about?"

"No. Six days ago, Agent Clark appeared at a missionary village deep in the remote jungle, half dead from fever and exposure. The head of the mission attempted to care for him, but he died within a few hours."

"A tragedy indeed, but how is this a matter of national security?"

"Because Agent Clark has been missing for four years." O'Brien passed him a faxed newspaper article.

Confused, Fielding accepted the article. "Four years?"

EXPEDITION VANISHES IN AMAZONIAN JUNGLE
Associated Press

MANAUS, BRAZIL, MARCH 20— The continuing search for millionaire industrialist Dr. Carl Rand and his international team of 30 researchers and guides has been called off after three months of intense searching. The team, a joint venture between the U.S. National Cancer Institute and the Brazilian Indian Foundation, vanished into the rain forests without leaving a single clue as to their fate.

The expedition's yearlong goal had been to conduct a census on the true number of Indians and tribes living in the Amazon forests. However, three months after leaving the jungle city of Manaus, their daily progress reports, radioed in from the field, ended abruptly. All attempts to contact the team have failed. Rescue helicopters and ground search teams were sent to their last known location, but no one was found. Two weeks later, one last, frantic message was received: "Send help . . . can't last much longer. Oh, God, they're all around us." Then the team was swallowed into the vast jungle.

Now, after a three-month search involving an international

team and much publicity, Commander Ferdinand Gonzales, the rescue team's leader, has declared the expedition and its members "lost and likely dead." All searches have been called off.

The current consensus of the investigators is that the team either was overwhelmed by a hostile tribe or had stumbled upon a hidden base of drug traffickers. Either way, any hope for rescue dies today as the search teams are called home. It should be noted that each year scores of researchers, explorers, and missionaries disappear into the Amazon forest, never to be seen again.

"My God."

O'Brien retrieved the article from the stunned man's fingers and continued, "After disappearing, no further contact was ever made by the research team or our operative. Agent Clark was classified as deceased."

"But are we sure this is the same man?"

O'Brien nodded. "Dental records and fingerprints match those on file."

Fielding shook his head, the initial shock ebbing. "As tragic as all this is and as messy as the paperwork will be, I still don't see why it's a matter of national security."

"I would normally agree, except for one additional oddity." O'Brien shuffled through the dossier's ream of papers and pulled out two photographs. He handed over the first one. "This was taken just a few days before he departed on his mission."

Fielding glanced at the grainy photo of a man dressed in Levi's, a Hawaiian shirt, and a safari hat. The man wore a large grin and was hoisting a tropical drink in hand. "Agent Clark?"

"Yes, the photo was taken by one of the researchers during a going-away party." O'Brien passed him the second photograph. "And this was taken at the morgue in Manaus, where the body now resides."

Fielding took the glossy with a twinge of queasiness. He had no desire to look at photographs of dead people, but he had no choice. The corpse in this photograph was naked, laid out on a stainless steel table, an emaciated skeleton wrapped in skin. Strange tattoos marked his flesh. Still, Fielding recognized the man's facial features. It *was* Agent Clark—but with one notable difference. He retrieved the first photograph and compared the two.

O'Brien must have noted the blood draining from his face and spoke up. "Two years prior to his disappearance, Agent Clark took a sniper's bullet to his left arm during a forced recon mission in Iraq. Gangrene set in before he could reach a U.S. camp. The limb had to be amputated at the shoulder, ending his career with the army's Special Forces."

"But the body in the morgue has both arms."

"Exactly. The fingerprints from the corpse's arm match those on file prior to the shooting. It would seem Agent Clark went into the Amazon with one arm and came back with two."

"But that's impossible. What the hell happened out there?"

Marshall O'Brien studied Fielding with his hawkish eyes, demonstrating why he had earned his nickname, the Old Bird. Fielding felt like a mouse before an eagle. The old man's voice deepened. "That's what I intend to find out."

The Mission

CURARE

FAMILY: *Menispermaceae*

GENUS: *Chondrodendron*

SPECIES: *Tomentosum*

COMMON NAME: *Curare*

PARTS USED: *Leaf, Root*

PROPERTIES/ACTIONS: *Diuretic, Febrifuge, Muscle Relaxant, Tonic, Poison*

ONE

Snake Oil

The anaconda held the small Indian girl wrapped in its heavy coils, dragging her toward the river.

Nathan Rand was on his way back to the Yanomamo village after an early morning of gathering medicinal plants when he heard her screams. He dropped his specimen bag and ran to her aid. As he sprinted, he shrugged his short-barreled shotgun from his shoulder. When alone in the jungle, one always carried a weapon.

He pushed through a fringe of dense foliage and spotted the snake and girl. The anaconda, one of the largest he had ever seen, at least forty feet in length, lay half in the water and half stretched out on the muddy beach. Its black scales shone wetly. It must have been lurking under the surface when the girl had come to collect water from the river. It was not unusual for the giant snakes to prey upon animals who came to the river to drink: wild peccary, capybara rodents, forest deer. But the great snakes seldom attacked humans.

Still, during the past decade of working as a ethnobotanist in the jungles of the Amazon basin, Nathan had learned one important rule: if a beast were hungry enough, all rules were broken. It was an eat-or-be-eaten world under the endless green bower.

Nathan squinted through his gun's sight. He recognized the girl. "Oh, God, Tama!" She was the chieftain's nine-year-old niece, a smiling, happy child who had given him a bouquet of jungle flowers as a gift upon his arrival in the village a month ago. Afterward she kept pulling at the hairs on his arm, a rarity among the smooth-skinned Yanomamo, and nicknamed him *Jako Basho*, "Brother Monkey."

Biting his lip, he searched through his weapon's sight. He had no clean shot, not with the child wrapped in the muscular coils of the predator.

"Damn it!" He tossed his shotgun aside and reached to the machete at his belt. Unhitching the weapon, Nathan lunged forward—but as he neared, the snake rolled and pulled the girl under the black waters of the river. Her screams ended and bubbles followed her course.

Without thinking, Nathan dove in after her.

Of all the environments of the Amazon, none were more dangerous than its waterways. Under its placid surfaces lay countless hazards. Schools of bone-scouring piranhas hunted its depths, while stingrays lay buried in the mud and electric eels roosted amid roots and sunken logs. But worst of all were the river's true man-killers, the black caimans—giant crocodilian reptiles. With all its dangers, the Indians of the Amazon knew better than to venture into unknown waters.

But Nathan Rand was no Indian.

Holding his breath, he searched through the muddy waters and spotted the surge of coils ahead. A pale limb waved. With a kick of his legs, he reached out to the small hand, snatching it up in his large grip. Small fingers clutched his in desperation.

Tama was still conscious!

He used her arm to pull himself closer to the snake. In his other hand, he drew the machete back, kicking to hold his place, squeezing Tama's hand.

Then the dark waters swirled, and he found himself staring into the red eyes of the giant snake. It had sensed the challenge to its meal. Its black maw opened and struck at him.

Nate ducked aside, fighting to maintain his grip on the girl.

The anaconda's jaws snapped like a vice onto his arm. Though its bite was nonpoisonous, the pressure threatened to crush Nate's wrist. Ignoring the pain and his own mounting panic, he brought his other arm around, aiming for the snake's eyes with his machete.

At the last moment, the giant anaconda rolled in the water, throwing Nate to the silty bottom and pinning him. Nate felt the air squeezed from his lungs as four hundred pounds of scaled muscle trapped him. He struggled and fought, but he found no purchase in the slick river mud.

The girl's fingers were torn from his grip as the coils churned her away from him.

No . . . Tama!

He abandoned his machete and pushed with his hands against the weight of the snake's bulk. His shoulders sank into the soft muck of the riverbed, but still he pushed. For every coil he shoved aside, another would take its place. His arms weakened, and his lungs screamed for air.

Nathan Rand knew in this moment that he was doomed—and he was not particularly surprised. He knew it would happen one day. It was his destiny, the curse of his family. During the past twenty years, both his parents had been consumed by the Amazon forest. When he was eleven, his mother had succumbed to an unknown jungle fever, dying in a small missionary hospital. Then, four years ago, his father had simply vanished into the rain forest, disappearing without witnesses.

As Nate remembered the heartbreak of losing his father, rage flamed through his chest. Cursed or not, he refused to follow in his father's footsteps. He would *not* allow himself simply to be swallowed by the jungle. But more important, he would *not* lose Tama!

Screaming out the last of the trapped air in his chest, Nathan shoved the anaconda's bulk off his legs. Freed for a moment, he swung his feet under him, sinking into the mud up to his ankles, and shoved straight up.

His head burst from the river, and he gulped a breath of fresh air, then was dragged by his arm back under the dark water.

This time, Nathan did not fight the strength of the snake. Holding the clamped wrist to his chest, he twisted into the coils, managing to get a choke hold around the neck of the snake with his other arm. With the beast trapped, Nate dug his left thumb into the snake's nearest eye.

The snake writhed, tossing Nate momentarily out of the water, then slamming him back down. He held tight.

C'mon, you bastard, let up!

He bent his trapped wrist enough to drive his other thumb into the snake's remaining eye. He pushed hard on both sides, praying his basic training in reptile physiology proved true. Pressure on the eyes of a snake should trigger a gag reflex via the optic nerve.

He pressed harder, his heartbeat thudding in his ears.

Suddenly the pressure on his wrist released, and Nathan found himself flung away with such force that he half sailed out of the river and hit the riverbank with his shoulder. He twisted around and saw a pale form float to the surface of the river, facedown in midstream.

Tama!

As he had hoped, the visceral reflex of the snake had released both prisoners. Nathan shoved into the river and grabbed the child by the arm, pulling her slack form to him. He slung her over a shoulder and climbed quickly to the shore.

He spread her soaked body on the bank. She was not breathing. Her lips were purple. He checked her pulse. It was there but weak.

Nathan glanced around futilely for help. With no one around, it would be up to him to revive the girl. He had been trained in first aid and CPR before venturing into the jungle, but Nathan was no doctor. He knelt, rolled the girl on her stomach, and pumped her back. A small amount of water sloshed from her nose and mouth.

Satisfied, he rolled Tama back around and began mouth-to-mouth.

At this moment, one of the Yanomamo tribesfolk, a middle-aged woman, stepped from the jungle's edge. She was small, as were all the Indians, no more than five feet in height. Her black hair was sheared in the usual bowl cut and her ears were pierced with feathers and bits of bamboo. Her dark eyes grew huge at the sight of the white man bent over the small child.

Nathan knew how it must look. He straightened up from his crouch just as Tama suddenly regained consciousness, coughing out gouts of river water and thrashing and crying in horror and fright. The panicked child beat at him with tiny fists, still in the nightmare of the snake attack.

"Hush, you're safe," he said in the Yanomamo dialect, trying to snare her hands in his grip. He turned to the woman, meaning to explain, but the small Indian dropped her basket and vanished into the thick fringe at the river's edge, whooping with alarm. Nathan knew the call. It was raised whenever a villager was under attack.

"Great, just great." Nathan closed his eyes and sighed.

When he had first come to this particular village four weeks ago, intending to record the medicinal wisdom of the tribe's old shaman, he had been instructed by the chief to stay away from the Indian women. In the past, there had been occasions when strangers had taken advantage of the tribe's womenfolk. Nathan had honored this request, even though some of the women had been more than willing to share his hammock. His six-foot-plus frame, blue eyes, and sandy-colored hair were a novelty to the women of this isolated tribe.

In the distance, the fleeing woman's distress call was answered by others, many others. The name *Yanomamo* translated roughly as "the fierce people." The tribes were considered some of the most savage warriors. The *huyas,* or young men of the village, were always contesting some point of honor or claiming some curse had been set upon them, anything to warrant a brawl with a neighboring tribe or another tribesman. They were known to wipe out entire villages for so slight an insult as calling someone a derogatory name.

Nathan stared down into the face of the young girl. And what would these *huyas* make of this? A white man attacking one of their children, the chieftain's niece.

At his side, Tama had slowed her panic, swooning back into a fitful slumber. Her breathing remained regular, but when he checked her forehead, it was warm from a growing fever. He also spotted a darkening bruise on her right side. He fingered the injury—two broken ribs from the crushing embrace of the anaconda. He sat back on his heels, biting his lower lip. If she was to survive, she would need immediate treatment.

Bending, he gently scooped her into his arms. The closest hospital was ten miles downstream in the small town of São Gabriel. He would have to get her there.

But there was only one problem—the Yanomamo. There was no way he could flee with the girl and expect to get away. This was Indian territory, and though he knew the terrain well, he was no native. There was a proverb spoken throughout the Amazon: *Na boesi, ingi sabe ala sani.* In their jungle, the Indian know everything. The Yanomamo were superb hunters, skilled with bow, blowgun, spear, and club.

There was no way he could escape.

Stepping away from the river, he retrieved his discarded shotgun from the brush and slung it over his shoulder. Lifting the girl higher in his arms, Nathan set off toward the village. He would have to make them listen to him, both for his sake and Tama's.

Ahead, the Indian village that he had called home for the past month had gone deathly quiet. Nathan winced as he walked. Even the constant twitter of birds and hooting call of monkeys had grown silent.

Holding his breath, he turned a corner in the trail and found a wall of Indians blocking his way, arrows nocked and drawn, spears raised. He sensed more than heard movement behind him. He glanced over his shoulder and saw more Indians already in position, faces daubed with crimson.

Nate had only one hope to rescue the girl and himself, an act he was loath to do, but he had no choice.

"*Nabrushi yi yi!*" he called out forcefully. "I demand trial by combat!"

AUGUST 6, 11:38 A.M.
OUTSIDE SÃO GABRIEL DA COCHOERIA

Manuel Azevedo knew he was being hunted. He heard the jaguar's coughing grunt coming from the forest fringes as he ran along the trail. Exhausted, soaked in sweat, he stumbled down the steep trail from the summit of the Mount of the Sacred Way. Ahead, a break in the foliage opened a view upon São Gabriel. The township lay nestled in the curve of the Rio Negro, the northern tributary of the great Amazon River.

So close . . . perhaps close enough . . .

Manny slid to a stop and faced back up the trail. He strained for any sign of the jaguar's approach: the snap of a twig, the rustle of leaves. But no telltale sign revealed the jungle cat's whereabouts. Even its hunting cough had gone silent. It knew it had run its prey to exhaustion. Now it crept in for the kill.

Manny cocked his head. The buzz of locusts and distant trill of birds were the only sounds. A rivulet of sweat dribbled down his neck. He tensed, ears straining. His fingers instinctively went to the knife on his belt. His other hand settled on the strap of his short whip.

Manny searched the dappled jungle floor around him. Chokes of ropy vines and leafy bushes clogged the path to both sides. Where would it come from?

Shadows shifted.

He spun on a heel, crouching. He tried to see through the dense foliage. *Nothing.*

Farther down the trail, a section of shadow lurched toward him, a sleek mirage of dappled fur, black on orange. It had been standing only ten feet away, lying low to the ground, haunches bunched under it. The cat was a large juvenile male, two years old.

Sensing it had been spotted, it whipped its tail back and forth with savage strokes, rattling the leaves.

Manny crouched, ready for the attack.

With a deep growl, the great cat leaped at him, fangs bared.

Manny grunted as its weight struck him like a crashing boulder. The pair went rolling down the trail. The wind was knocked out of Manny's thin frame as he tumbled. The world dissolved down to flashes of green, splashes of sunlight, and a blur of fur and teeth.

Claws pierced his khakis as the great cat wrapped Manny in its grip. A pocket ripped away. Fangs clamped onto his shoulder. Though the jaguar had the second strongest jaws of any land animal, its teeth did no more than press into his flesh.

The pair finally came to a stop several yards down the trail where it leveled off. Manny found himself pinned under the jaguar. He stared into the fiery eyes of his adversary as it gnawed at his shirt and growled.

"Are you done, Tor-tor?" He gasped. He had named the great cat after the Arawak Indian word for *ghost*. Though presently, with the jaguar's bulk seated on his chest, the name did not seem particularly apt.

At the sound of its master's voice, the jaguar let loose his shirt and stared back at him. Then a hot, coarse tongue swiped the sweat from Manny's forehead.

"I love you, too. Now get your furry butt off me."

Claws retracted, and Manny sat up. He checked the condition of his clothes and sighed. Training the young jaguar to hunt was quickly laying waste his wardrobe.

Standing up, Manny groaned and worked a kink from his back. At thirty-two, he was getting too old to play this game.

The cat rolled to its paws and stretched. Then, with a swish of the tail, it began to sniff at the air.

With a small laugh, Manny cuffed the jaguar on the side of its head. "We're done hunting for today. It's getting late. And I have a stack of reports still waiting for me back at the office."

Tor-tor rumbled grumpily, but followed.

Two years back, Manny had rescued the orphaned jaguar cub when it was only a few days old. Its mother had been killed by poachers for her pelt, a treasure that still brought a tidy sum on the black market. At current estimate, the population of wild jaguars was down to fifteen thousand, spread thin across the vast jungles of the Amazon basin. Conservation efforts did little to dissuade peasants who eked out a subsistence-level existence from hunting them for profit. A hungry belly made one shortsighted to efforts of wildlife preservation.

Manny knew this too well himself. Half Indian, he had been an orphan on the streets of Barcellos, along the banks of the Amazon River. He had lived hand to mouth, begging for coins from passing tourist boats and stealing when his palm came up empty. Eventually he was taken in by a Salesian missionary and worked his way up to a degree in biology at the University of São Paulo, his scholarship sponsored by the Brazilian Indian foundation, FUNAI. As payback for his scholarship, he worked with local Indian tribes: protecting their interests, preserving their ways of life, helping them claim their own lands legally. And at thirty, he found himself posted here in São Gabriel, heading the local FUNAI office.

It was during his investigation of poachers encroaching on Yanomamo lands that Manny discovered Tor-tor, an orphan like himself. The cub's right hind leg had been fractured where he had been kicked by one of the poachers. Manny could not abandon the tiny creature. So he had collected the mewling and hissing cub in a blanket and slowly nursed the foundling back to health.

Manny watched Tor-tor pace ahead of him. He could still see the slight tweak to his gait from his injured leg. In less than a year, Tor-tor would be sexually mature. The cat's feral nature would begin to shine, and it would be time to loose him into the jungle. But before that happened Manny wanted Tor-tor to be able to fend for himself. The jungle was no place for the uninitiated.

Ahead, the trail curved through the last of the jungled slopes of the Mount of the Sacred Way. The city of São Gabriel spread open before him, a mix of hovels and utilitarian cement-block structures bustled up against the Negro River. A few new hotels and buildings dotted the landscape, built within the last half decade to accommodate the growing flood of tourists to the region. And in the distance lay a new commercial airstrip. Its tarmac was a black scar through the surrounding jungle. It seemed even in the remote wilds there was no stopping progress.

Manny wiped his damp forehead, then stumbled into Tor-tor when the cat suddenly stopped. The jaguar growled deep in its throat, a warning.

"What's the matter?" Then he heard it, too.

Echoing across the blanket of jungle, a deep *thump-thump*ing grew in volume. It seemed to be coming from all around them. Manny's eyes narrowed. He recognized the sound, though it was seldom heard out here. A helicopter. Most travelers to São Gabriel came by riverboat or by small prop planes. The distances were generally too vast to accommodate helicopters. Even the local Brazilian army base had only a single bird, used for rescue and evacuation missions.

As Manny listened and the noise grew in volume, he realized something else. It was more than just *one* helicopter.

He searched the skies but saw nothing.

Suddenly Tor-tor tensed and dashed into the surrounding brush.

A company of three helicopters flashed overhead, sweeping past the Mount of the Sacred Way and circling toward the small township like a swarm of wasps. *Camouflaged* wasps.

The bulky choppers—UH-1 Hueys—were clearly military.

Craning up, Manny watched a fourth helicopter pass directly above him. But unlike its brethren, this one was sleek and black. It whispered over the jungle. Manny recognized its characteristic shape and enclosed tail rotor from his short stint in the military. It was an RAH-66 Comanche, a reconnaissance and attack helicopter.

The slender craft passed close enough for Manny to discern the tiny

American flag on its side. Above him, the jungle canopy rattled with its rotor wash. Monkeys fled, screaming in fright, and a flock of scarlet macaws broke like a streak of fire across the blue sky.

Then this helicopter was gone, too. It descended toward the open fields around the Brazilian army base, circling to join the other three.

Frowning, Manny whistled for Tor-tor. The huge cat slunk from its hiding place, eyes searching all around.

"It's all right," he assured the jaguar.

The *thump-thump*ing noise died away as the helicopters settled to the fields.

He crossed to Tor-tor and rested one hand on the great cat's shoulder, which trembled under his touch. The jaguar's nervousness flowed into him.

Manny headed downhill, settling a palm on the knobbed handle of the bullwhip hitched to his belt. "What the hell is the United States military doing here in São Gabriel?"

Nathan stood, stripped to his boxers, in the middle of the village's central plaza. Around him lay the Yanomamo *shabano,* or roundhouse, a circular structure half a football field wide with the central roof cut away to expose the sky. Women and older men lay sprawled in hammocks under the banana leaf roof, while the younger men, the *huyas,* bore spears and bows, ensuring Nathan did not try to flee.

Earlier, as he had been led at spearpoint back to camp, he had tried to explain about the attack by the anaconda, baring the bite marks on his wrist as proof. But no one would listen. Even the village chieftain, who had taken the child from his arms, had waved his words away as if they offended him.

Nathan knew that his voice would not be heard by those around him until the trial was over. It was the Yanomamo way. He had demanded combat as a way to buy time, and now no one would listen until the battle was over. Only if the gods granted him victory would he be heard.

Nathan stood barefoot in the dirt. Off to the side, a group of *huyas* argued over who would accept his challenge and what weapons would be used in the battle. The traditional duel was usually waged with *nabrushi,* slender, eight-foot-long wooden clubs that the combatants used to beat each other. But in more serious duels, deadly weapons were used, such as machetes or spears.

Across the plaza, the throng parted. A single Indian stepped forth. He was tall for a tribesman, almost as tall as Nathan, and wiry with muscle. It was Tama's father, Takaho, the chieftain's brother. He wore nothing but a braided string around his waist into which was tucked the foreskin of his penis, the typical garb of Yanomamo men. Across his chest were slash lines drawn in ash, while under a monkey-tail headband his face had been painted crimson. His lower lip bulged with a large tuck of tobacco, giving him a belligerent look.

He held out a hand, and one of the *huyas* hurried forward and placed a long ax in his palm. The ax's haft was carved of purple snakewood and ended in a pikelike steel head. It was a wicked-looking tool and one of the most savage dueling weapons.

Nate found a similar ax thrust into his own hands.

Across the way, he watched another *huya* hurry forward and hold out a clay pot full of an oily liquid. Takaho dipped his axhead into the pot.

Nate recognized the mixture. He had assisted the shaman in preparing this batch of *woorari,* in English *curare,* a deadly paralyzing nerve poison prepared from a liana vine of the moonseed family. The drug was used in hunting monkeys, but today it was intended for a more sinister purpose.

Nathan glanced around. No one came forth to offer a similar pot to anoint his blade. It seemed the battle was not to be exactly even.

The village chief raised a bow over his head and sounded the call for the duel to begin.

Takaho strode across the plaza, wielding the ax with practiced skill.

Nathan lifted his own ax. How could he win here? A single scratch meant death. And if he did win, what would be gained? He had come here to save Tama, and to do that, he would have to slay her father.

Bracing himself, he lifted the ax across his chest. He met the angry eyes of his opponent. "I didn't hurt your daughter!" he called out fiercely.

Takaho's eyes narrowed. He had heard Nate's words, but mistrust shone in his eyes. Takaho glanced to where Tama was being ministered to by the village shaman. The lanky elder was bowed over the girl, waving a smoking bundle of dried grass while chanting. Nathan could smell the bitter incense, an acrid form of smelling salts derived from hempweed. But the girl did not move.

Takaho faced Nate. With a roar, the Indian lunged forward, swinging his ax toward Nate's head.

Trained as a wrestler in his youth, Nate knew how to move. He dropped under the ax and rolled to the side, sweeping wide with his own weapon and knocking his opponent's legs out from under him.

Takaho fell hard to the packed dirt, smacking his shoulder and knocking loose his monkey-tail headband. But he was otherwise unharmed. Nate had struck with the blunt side of his ax, refusing to go for a maiming blow.

With the man down, Nate leaped at him, meaning to pin the Indian under his larger frame. *If I could just immobilize him* . . .

But Takaho rolled away with the speed of a cat, then swung again with a savage backstroke of his ax.

Nate reared away from the weapon's deadly arc. The poisoned blade whistled past the tip of his nose and slammed into the dirt between his hands. Relieved at the close call, Nathan was a second too late in dodging the foot kicked at his head. Ears ringing from the blow, he tumbled across the dirt. His own ax bounced out of his stunned hand and skittered into the crowd of onlookers.

Spitting out blood from his split lip, Nathan stood quickly.

Takaho was already on his feet.

As the Indian tugged his embedded ax from the dirt, Nathan noticed the shaman over his shoulder. The elder was now exhaling smoke across Tama's lips, a way of chasing off bad spirits before death.

Around him, the other *huyas* were now chanting for the kill.

Takaho lifted his ax with a grunt and turned to Nate. The Indian's face was a crimson mask of rage. He rushed at Nate, his ax whirling in a blur before him.

Without a weapon, Nate retreated. *So this is how I die* . . .

Nate found himself backed against a wall of spears held by other Indians. There was no escape. Takaho slowed for the kill, the ax high over his head.

Nathan felt the prick of spearheads in his bare back as he instinctively leaned away.

Takaho swung his weapon down with the strength of both shoulders.

"*Yulo!*" The sharp cry burst through the chanting *huyas.* "Stop!"

Nathan cringed from the blow that never came. He glanced up. The ax trembled about an inch from his face. A dribble of poison dripped onto his cheek.

The shaman, the one who had called out, pushed past other tribesmen into the central plaza. "Your daughter wakes!" He pointed to Nate. "She speaks of a giant snake and of her rescue by the white man."

All faces turned to where Tama was sipping weakly at a gourd of water held by a tribeswoman.

Nathan stared up into Takaho's eyes as the Indian faced him again. Takaho's hard expression melted with relief. He pulled away his weapon, then dropped it to the dirt. An empty hand clamped onto Nate's shoulder, and Takaho pulled him to his chest. "*Jako,*" he said, hugging him tight. "Brother."

And just like that, it was over.

The chieftain pushed forward, puffing out his chest. "You battled the great *susuri,* the anaconda, and pulled our tribe's daughter from its belly." He removed a long feather from his ear and tucked it into Nate's hair. It was the tail feather of a harpy eagle, a treasured prize. "You are no longer a *nabe,* an outsider. You are now *jako,* brother to my brother. You are now Yanomamo."

A great cheer rose all around the *shabono.*

Nathan knew this was an honor above all honors, but he still had a pressing concern. "My sister," he said, pointing toward Tama. It was taboo to refer to a Yanomamo by his or her given name. Familial designations, real or not, were used instead. Tama moaned softly where she lay. "My sister is still sick. She has suffered injuries that the healers in São Gabriel can help mend. I ask that you allow me to take her to the town's hospital."

The village shaman stepped forward. Nathan feared he would argue that his own medicine could heal the girl. As a whole, shamans were a prideful group. But instead, the Indian elder agreed, placing a hand on Nate's shoulder. "Our little sister was saved from the *susuri* by our new *jako.* We should heed the gods in choosing him as her rescuer. I can do no more for her."

Nathan wiped the poison from his cheek, careful to keep it away from any open cuts, and thanked the elder. The shaman had done more than enough already. His natural medicines had been able to revive the girl in time to save him. Nathan turned next to Takaho. "I would ask to borrow your canoe for the journey."

"All that is mine is yours," Takaho said. "I will go with you to São Gabriel."

Nathan nodded. "We should hurry."

In short order, Tama was loaded on a stretcher of bamboo and palm fronds and placed in the canoe. Takaho, now dressed in a tank top and a pair of Nike shorts, waved Nathan to the bow of the dugout canoe, then shoved away from the shore with his oar and into the main current of the Negro River. The river led all the way to São Gabriel.

They made the ten-mile journey in silence. Nathan checked on Tama frequently and recognized the worry in her father's eyes. The girl had slipped back into a stupor, trembling, moaning softly now and then. Nathan wrapped a blanket around her small form.

Takaho wended the small canoe with skill through small rapids and around tangles of fallen trees. He seemed to have an uncanny skill at finding the swiftest currents.

As the canoe sped downriver, they passed a group of Indians from a neighboring village fishing in the river with spears. He watched a woman sprinkle a dark powder into the waters from an upstream canoe. Nate knew what she was doing. It was crushed *ayaeya* vine. As it flowed downstream, the dissolved powder would stun fish, floating them to the surface where they were speared and collected by the men. It was an ancient fishing method used throughout the Amazon.

But how long would such traditions last? A generation or two? Then this art would be lost forever.

Nathan settled into his seat, knowing there were certain battles he could never win. For good or bad, civilization would continue its march through the jungle.

As they continued along, Nate stared out at the walls of dense foliage that framed both banks. All around him, life buzzed, chirped, squawked, hooted, and grunted.

On either side, packs of red howler monkeys yelled in chorus and bounced aggressively atop their branches. Along the shallows, white-feathered bitterns with long orange beaks speared fish, while the plated snouts of caimans marked nesting grounds of the Amazonian crocodiles. Closer still, in the air around them, clouds of gnats and stinging flies harangued every inch of exposed skin.

Here the jungle ruled in all its forms. It seemed endless, impenetrable, full of mystery. It was one of the last regions of the planet that had yet to be fully explored. There were vast stretches never walked by man. It was this mystery and wonder that had attracted Nathan's parents to spend their lives here, eventually infecting their only son with their love of the great forest.

Nathan watched the jungle pass around him, noting the emerging signs of civilization, and knew that they neared São Gabriel. Small clearings made by peasant farmers began to appear, dotting the banks of the river. From the shore, children waved and called as the canoe whisked past. Even the noises of the jungle grew muted, driven away by the noisome ruckus of the modern world: the grumble of diesel tractors in the fields, the whine of motor boats that sped past the canoe, the tinny music of a radio blaring from a homestead.

Then, from around a bend in the river, the jungle ended abruptly. The small city of São Gabriel appeared like some cancer that had eaten away the belly of the forest. Near the river, the city was a ramshackle mix of rotting wooden shacks and cement government buildings. Away from the water, homes both small and large climbed the nearby hills. Closer at hand, the wharves and jetties were crowded with tourist boats and primer-scarred river barges.

Nathan turned to direct Takaho toward a section of open riverbank. He found the Indian staring in horror at the city, his oar clutched tightly to his chest.

"It fills the world," he mumbled.

Nathan glanced back to the small township. It had been two weeks since his last supply run to São Gabriel, and the noise and bustle were a rude shock to him. What must it be like for someone who had never left the jungle?

Nathan nodded to a spot to beach the canoe. "There is nothing here that a great warrior need fear. We must get your daughter to the hospital."

Takaho nodded, clearly swallowing back his shock. His face again settled into a stoic expression, but his eyes continued to flit around the wonders of this other world. He guided the canoe as directed, then helped Nathan haul out the stretcher on which Tama's limp form lay.

As she was shifted, the girl moaned, and her eyelids fluttered, eyes rolling white. She had paled significantly during the ride here.

"We must hurry."

Together, the two carried the girl through the waterfront region, earning the gawking stares of the townies and a few blinding flashes from camera-wielding tourists. Though Takaho wore "civilized" clothes, his monkey-tail headband, the sprouts of feathers in his ears, and his bowl-shaped haircut marked this fellow as one of the Amazon's indigenous tribespeople.

Luckily, the small single-story hospital was just past the waterfront region. The only way one could tell it was a hospital was the flaking red cross painted above the threshold, but Nathan had been here before, consulting with the doctor on staff, a fellow from Manaus. They were soon off the streets and guiding their stretcher through the door. The hospital reeked of ammonia and bleach, but it was deliciously air-conditioned. The cool air struck Nate like a wet towel to the face.

He crossed to the nurse's station and spoke rapidly. The pudgy woman's brow wrinkled with a lack of understanding until Nathan realized he had been speaking in the Yanomamo dialect. He switched quickly to Portuguese. "The girl has been attacked by an anaconda. She's suffered a few broken ribs, but I think her internal injuries might be more severe."

"Come this way." The nurse waved them toward a set of double doors. She eyed Takaho with clear suspicion.

"He's her father."

The nurse nodded. "Dr. Rodriguez is out on a house call, but I can ring him for an emergency."

"Ring him," Nathan said.

"Maybe I can help," a voice said behind him.

Nathan turned.

A tall, slender woman with long auburn hair rose from the wooden folding chairs in the waiting room. She had been partially hidden behind a pile of wooden crates emblazoned with the red cross. Approaching with calm assurance, she studied them all intently.

Nathan stood straighter.

"My name is Kelly O'Brien," she said in fluent Portuguese, but Nate heard a trace of a Boston accent. She pulled out identification with the familiar medical caduceus stamped on it. "I'm an American doctor."

"Dr. O'Brien," he said, switching to English, "I could certainly use your help. The girl here was attacked—"

Atop the stretcher, Tama's back suddenly arched. Her heels began to beat at the palm fronds, then her thrashing spread through the rest of her body.

"She's seizing!" the woman said. "Get her into the ward!"

The pudgy nurse led the way, holding the door wide for the stretcher.

Kelly O'Brien rushed alongside the girl as the two men swung the stretcher toward one of the four beds in the tiny emergency ward. Snatching a pair of surgical gloves, the tall doctor barked to the nurse, "I need ten milligrams of diazepam!"

The nurse nodded and dashed to a drug cabinet. In seconds, a syringe of amber-colored fluid was slapped into Kelly's gloved hand. The doctor already had a rubber tourniquet in place. "Hold her down," she ordered Nate and Takaho.

By now, a nurse and a large orderly had arrived as the quiet hospital awakened to the emergency.

"Get ready with an IV line and a bag of LRS," Kelly said sharply. Her fingers palpated a decent vein in the girl's thin arm. With obvious competence, Kelly inserted the needle and slowly injected the drug.

"It's Valium," she said as she worked. "It should calm the seizure long enough to find out what's wrong with her."

Her words proved instantly true. Tama's convulsions calmed. Her limbs stopped thrashing and relaxed to the bed. Only her eyelids and the corner of her lips still twitched. Kelly was examining her pupils with a penlight.

The orderly nudged Nate aside as he worked on Tama's other arm, preparing a catheter and IV line.

Nate glanced over the orderly's shoulder and saw the fear and panic in her father's eyes.

"What happened to her?" the doctor asked as she continued examining the girl.

Nathan described the attack. "She's been slipping in and out of consciousness most of the time. The village shaman was able to revive her for a short time."

"She's sustained a pair of cracked ribs and associated hematomas, but I can't account for the seizure or stupor. Did she have any seizures en route here?"

"No."

"Any familial history of epilepsy?"

Nate turned to Takaho and repeated the question in Yanomamo.

Takaho nodded. *"Ah-de-me-nah gunti."*

Nate frowned.

"What did he say?" Kelly asked.

"Ah-de-me-nah means electric eel. *Gunti* is disease or sickness."

"Electric eel disease?"

Nate nodded. "That's what he said. But it makes no sense. A victim of an electric eel attack will often convulse, but it's an immediate reaction. And Tama hasn't been in any water for hours. I don't know . . . maybe 'electric eel disease' is the Yanomamo term for epilepsy."

"Has she been treated for it? On medication?"

Nate got the answer from Takaho. "The village shaman has been treating her once a week with the smoke of the hempweed vine."

Kelly sighed in exasperation. "So in other words, she's been unmedicated. No wonder the stress of the near drowning triggered such a severe attack. Why don't you take her father out to the waiting room? I'll see if I can get these seizures to cease with stronger meds."

Nate glanced to the bed. Tama's form lay quiet. "Do you think she'll have more?"

Kelly glanced into his eyes. "She's still having them." She pointed to the persistent facial twitches. "She's in status epilepticus, a continual seizure. Most patients who suffer from such prolonged attacks will appear stuporous, moaning, uncoordinated. The full grand mal events like a moment ago will be interspersed. If we can't stop it, she'll die."

Nate stared at the little girl. "You mean she's been seizing this entire time?"

"From what you describe, more or less."

"But the village shaman was able to draw her out of the stupor for a short time."

"I find that hard to believe." Kelly returned her attention to the girl. "He wouldn't have medication strong enough to break this cycle."

Nate remembered the girl sipping at the gourd. "But he did. Don't discount tribal shamans as mere witch doctors. I've worked for years with them. And considering what they have to work with, they're quite sophisticated."

"Well, wise or not, we've stronger medications here. Real medicine." She nodded again to the father. "Why don't you take her father out to the waiting room?" Kelly turned back to the orderly and nurses, dismissing him.

Nate bristled, but obeyed. For centuries, the value of shamanism had been scorned by practitioners of Western medicine. Nate coaxed Takaho out of the ward and into the waiting room. He guided the Indian to a chair and instructed him to stay, then headed for the door.

He slammed his way out into the heat of the Amazon. Whether the American doctor believed him or not, he had seen the shaman revive the girl. If there was one man who might have an answer for Tama's mysterious illness, he knew where to find him.

Half running, he raced through the afternoon heat toward the southern outskirts of the city. In about ten blocks, he was skirting the edge of the Brazilian army camp. The normally sleepy base buzzed with activity. Nate noted the four helicopters with United States markings in the open field. Locals lined the base's fences, pointing toward the novelty of the foreign military craft and chattering excitedly.

He ignored the oddity and hurried to a cement-block building set amid a row of dilapidated wooden structures. The letters FUNAI were painted on the wall facing the street. It was the local office for the Brazilian Indian Foundation and represented the sole source of aid, education, and legal representation for the local tribes, the Baniwa and Yanomamo. The small building housed both offices and a homeless shelter for Indians who had come in search of the white man's prosperity.

FUNAI also had its own medical counselor, a longtime friend of the family and his own father's mentor here in the jungles of the Amazon.

Nate pushed through the anteroom and hurried down a hall and up a set of stairs. He prayed his friend was in his office. As he neared the open door, he heard the strands of Mozart's Fifth Violin Concerto flowing out.

Thank God!

Knocking on the door's frame, Nate announced himself. "Professor Kouwe?"

Behind a small desk, a mocha-skinned Indian glanced up from a pile of papers. In his mid-fifties, he had shoulder-length black hair that was graying at the temples, and he now wore wire-rimmed glasses when reading. He took off those glasses and smiled broadly when he recognized Nate.

"Nathan!" Resh Kouwe stood and came around the desk to give him a hug that rivaled the coils of the anaconda he had fought. For his compact frame, the man was as strong as an ox. Formerly a shaman of the Tiriós tribe of southern Venezuela, Kouwe had met Nate's father three decades ago, and the two had become fast friends. Kouwe had eventually left the jungle with his father's help and was schooled at Oxford, earning a dual degree in linguistics and paleoanthropology. He was also one of the pre-eminent experts in the botanical lore of the region. "My boy, I can't believe you're here! Did Manny contact you?"

Nathan frowned as he was released from the bear hug. "No, what do you mean?"

"He's looking for you. He stopped by about an hour ago to see if I knew which village you were conducting your current research in."

"Why?" Nathan's brow wrinkled.

"He didn't say, but he did have one of those Tellux corporate honchos with him."

Nathan rolled his eyes. Tellux Pharmaceuticals was the multinational corporation that had been financing his investigative research into the practices of the region's tribal shamans.

Kouwe recognized his sour expression. "It was you who made the pact with the devil."

"Like I had any choice after my father died."

Kouwe frowned. "You should not have given up on yourself so quickly. You were always—"

"Listen," Nathan said, cutting him off. He didn't want to be reminded of that black period in his life. He had made his own bed and would have to lie in it. "I've got a different problem than Tellux." He quickly explained about Tama and her illness. "I'm worried about her treatment. I thought you could consult with the doctor."

Kouwe grabbed a fishing tackle box from a shelf. "Foolish, foolish, foolish," he said, and headed for the door.

Nathan followed him down the stairs and out into the street. He had to hurry to keep up with the older man. Soon the two were pushing through the hospital's front doors.

Takaho leaped to his feet at the reappearance of Nathan. "*Jako . . .* Brother."

Nathan waved him back down. "I've brought someone who might be able to help your daughter."

Kouwe did not wait. He was already shoving into the ward beyond the doors. Nathan hurried after him.

What he found in the next room was chaos. The slender American doctor, her face drenched with sweat, was bent over Tama, who was again in a full grand mal seizure. Nurses were scurrying to and fro at her orders.

Kelly glanced over the girl's convulsing body. "We're losing her," she said, her eyes frightened.

"Maybe I can help," Kouwe said. "What medications has she been given?"

Kelly ran down a quick list, wiping strands of hair from her damp forehead.

Nodding, Kouwe opened his tackle box and grabbed a small pouch from one of the many tiny compartments. "I need a straw."

A nurse obeyed him as quickly as she had Dr. O'Brien. Nathan could guess that this was not the first visit Professor Kouwe had made to the hospital here. There was no one wiser on indigenous diseases and their cures.

"What are you doing?" Kelly asked, her face red. Her loose auburn hair had been pulled back in a ponytail.

"You've been working under a false assumption," he said calmly as he packed the plastic straw with his powder. "The convulsive nature of electric eel disease is not a manifestation of a CNS disturbance, like epilepsy. It's due to a hereditary chemical imbalance in the cerebral spinal fluid. The disease is unique to a handful of Yanomamo tribes."

"A hereditary metabolic disorder?"

"Exactly, like favism among certain Mediterranean families or 'cold-fat disease' among the Maroon tribes of Venezuela."

Kouwe crossed to the girl and waved to Nathan. "Hold her still."

Nathan crossed and held Tama's head to the pillow.

The shaman positioned one end of the straw into the girl's nostril, then blew the straw's powdery content up her nose.

Dr. O'Brien hovered behind him. "Are you the hospital's clinician? Dr. Rodriguez?"

"No, my dear," Kouwe said, straightening. "I'm the local witch doctor."

Kelly looked at him with an expression of disbelief and horror, but before she could object, the girl's thrashing began to calm, first slowly, then more rapidly.

Kouwe checked Tama's eyelids. The sick pallor to her skin was already improving. "I've found the absorption of certain drugs through the sinus membranes is almost as effective as intravenous administration."

Kelly looked on in amazement. "It's working."

Kouwe passed the pouch to one of the nurses. "Is Dr. Rodriguez on his way in?"

"I called him earlier, Professor," a nurse answered, glancing at her wristwatch. "He should be here in ten minutes."

"Make sure the girl gets half a straw of the powder every three hours for the next twenty-four, then once daily. That should stabilize her so her other injuries can be addressed satisfactorily."

"Yes, Professor."

On the bed, Tama slowly blinked open her eyes. She stared at the strangers around her, confusion and fright clear in her face, then her eyes found Nathan's. "*Jako Basho,*" she said weakly.

"Yes, Brother Monkey is here," he said in Yanomamo, patting her hand. "You're safe. Your papa is here, too."

One of the nurses fetched Takaho. When he saw his daughter awake and speaking, he fell to his knees. His stoic demeanor shattered, and he wept with relief.

"She'll be fine from here," Nate assured him.

Kouwe collected his fishing tackle box and retreated from the room. Nathan and Dr. O'Brien followed.

"What was in that powder?" the auburn-haired doctor asked.

"Desiccated *ku-nah-ne-mah* vine."

Nate answered the doctor's confused expression. "Climbing hemp-weed. The same plant the tribal shaman burned to revive the girl back at the village. Just like I told you before."

Kelly blushed. "I guess I owe you an apology. I didn't think . . . I mean I couldn't imagine . . ."

Kouwe patted her on her elbow. "Western ethnocentrism is a common rudeness out here. It's nothing to be embarrassed about." He winked at her. "Just outgrown."

Nate did not feel as courteous. "Next time," he said harshly, "listen with a more open mind."

She bit her lip and turned away.

Nathan instantly felt like a cad. His worry and fear throughout the day had worn his patience thin. The doctor had only been trying her best. Knowing he shouldn't have been so hard on her, he opened his mouth to apologize.

But before he could speak, the front door swung open and a tall red-headed man dressed in khakis and a beat-up Red Sox baseball cap stepped into the lobby. He spotted the doctor. "Kelly, if you've finished delivering the supplies, we need to be under way. We've a boat that's willing to take us upriver."

"Yes," she said. "I'm all done here."

She then glanced at Nathan and Kouwe. "Thank you."

Nathan recognized the similarities between this newcomer and the young doctor: the splash of freckles, the same crinkle around the eyes, even their voices had the same Boston lilt. Her brother, he guessed.

Nathan followed them out of the hospital and into the street. But what he found there caused him to take an involuntary step backward, bumping into Professor Kouwe.

Aligned across the road was a group of ten soldiers in full gear, including M-16s with collapsible butt stocks, holstered pistols, and heavy packs. Nate recognized the shoulder insignia common to them all. Army Rangers. One spoke into a radio and waved the group forward toward the waterfront. The pair of Americans joined the departing group.

"Wait!" someone called from beyond the line of Rangers.

The military wall parted, and a familiar face appeared. It was Manny

Azevedo. The stocky black-haired man broke through the ranks. He wore scuffed trousers and the pocket of his shirt had been ripped to a hanging flap. His characteristic bullwhip was wound at his waist.

Nathan returned Manny's smile and crossed to him. They hugged briefly, patting each other on the back. Then Nathan flicked the torn bit of his khaki shirt. "Playing with Tor-tor again, I see."

Manny grinned. "The monster's gained ten kilos since the last time you saw him."

Nathan laughed. "Great. Like he wasn't big enough already." Noting that the Rangers had stopped and were staring at the pair, as were Kelly O'Brien and her brother, Nathan nodded to the military party and leaned closer. "So what's all this about? Where are they heading?"

Manny glanced at the group. By now, a large crowd of onlookers had gathered to gawk at the line of stiff Army Rangers. "It seems the U.S. government is financing a recon team for a deep-jungle expedition."

"Why? Are they after drug traffickers?"

By now, Kelly O'Brien had stepped back toward them.

Manny acknowledged her with a nod, then waved a hand to Nathan. "May I introduce you to Dr. Rand? Dr. Nathan Rand."

"It seems we've already met," Kelly said with an embarrassed smile. "But he never offered his name."

Nathan sensed something unspoken pass between Kelly and Manny. "What's going on?" he asked. "What are you searching for upriver?"

She stared him straight in the eyes. Her eyes were the most striking shade of emerald. "We came to find you, Dr. Rand."

TWO

Debriefing

Nate crossed the street from Manny's offices at FUNAI and headed toward the Brazilian army base. He was accompanied by the Brazilian biologist and Professor Kouwe. The professor had just returned from the hospital. Nate was relieved to hear that Tama was recuperating well.

Freshly showered and shaved, his clothes laundered, Nathan Rand felt nothing like the man who had arrived here only hours before with the girl. It was as if he had scraped and scrubbed the jungle from his body along with the dirt and sweat. In a few hours, he went from a newly anointed member of the Yanomamo tribe back to an American citizen. It was amazing the transformational power of Irish Spring deodorant soap. He sniffed at the residual smell.

"After being so long in the jungle, it's nauseating, isn't it?" Professor Kouwe said, puffing on a pipe. "When I first left my home in the Venezuelan jungle, it was the bombardment upon my senses—the smells, the noises, the furious motion of civilization—that took the longest to acclimatize to."

Nathan dropped his arm. "It's strange how quickly you adapt to the simpler life out in the wilds. But I can tell you one thing that makes all the hassles of modern civilized life worth it."

"What's that?" Manny asked.

"Toilet paper," Nathan said.

Kouwe snorted with laughter. "Why do you think I left the jungle?"

They crossed toward the gate of the illuminated base. The meeting was scheduled to start in another ten minutes. Maybe then he'd have some answers.

As they walked, Nathan glanced over the quiet city and studied this little bastion of civilization. Over the river, a full moon hung, reflected in the sleek surface, blurred by an evening mist spreading into the city. Only at night does the jungle reclaim São Gabriel. After the sun sets, the noises of the city die down, replaced by the echoing song of the nightjar in the surrounding trees, accompanied by the chorus of honking frogs and the vibrato of locusts and crickets. Even in the streets, the flutter of bats and whine of blood-hungry mosquitoes replace the honk of cars and chatter of people. Only as one passes an open cantina, where the tinkling laughter of late-night patrons flows forth, does human life intrude.

Otherwise, at night, the jungle rules.

Nathan kept pace with Manny. "What could the U.S. government possibly need with me?"

Manny shook his head. "I'm not sure. But it somehow involves your financiers."

"Tellux Pharmaceuticals?"

"Right. They arrived with several corporate types. Lawyers, by the look of them."

Nate scowled. "Aren't there always when Tellux is involved?"

Kouwe spoke around the stem of his pipe. "You didn't have to sell Eco-tek to them."

Nate sighed. "Professor . . ."

The shaman raised his hands in submission. "Sorry. I know . . . sore subject."

Sore wasn't the word Nathan would have used. Established twelve years ago, Eco-Tek had been his father's brainchild. It was a niche pharmaceutical firm that had sought to utilize shamanic knowledge as the means to discover new botanical drugs. His father had wanted to preserve the wisdom of the vanishing medicine men of the Amazon basin and to insure that these local tribes profited from their own knowledge through intellectual property rights. Not only had it been his father's dream and purpose in life, but also the culmination of a promise to Nate's mother, Sarah.

While working as a medical doctor for the Peace Corps, she had dedicated her life to the indigenous people here, and her passion was contagious. Nate's father had promised to continue on in her footsteps and, years later, Eco-Tek was the result, a fusion of razor-sharp business models and non-profit advocacy.

But now all that was left of his parents' legacy was gone, dismantled and swallowed by Tellux.

"Looks like we're getting an escort," Manny said, breaking through Nate's thoughts.

At the gate's guard station, two Rangers in tan berets stood stiffly behind a nervous-looking Brazilian soldier.

Nathan eyed their holstered sidearms warily and wondered again at the nature of this meeting.

As they reached the gates, the Brazilian guard checked their identifications. Then one of the two Rangers stepped forward. "We're to take you to the debriefing. If you'll please follow." He turned sharply on his heel and strode away.

Nathan glanced to his friends, then proceeded through the gates. The second Ranger took up a strategic position behind them. Ushered along by their escorts, with a view of the four military helicopters resting on the camp's soccer field, Nathan felt a distinct sense of dread in his belly.

None of this seemed to concern Professor Kouwe. He simply puffed on his pipe and strode casually after their armed escort. Manny also appeared more distracted than alarmed.

They were marched past the corrugated Quonset huts that served as barracks for the Brazilian troops and led to a derelict timber-framed warehouse on the far side with the few windows painted black.

The Ranger in the lead opened the rusted door. Nathan was the first through. Expecting to find a gloomy, spider-infested interior, he was surprised to find the large warehouse brightly lit with halogen poles and overhead fluorescents. The cement floor was crisscrossed with cables, some as thick around as his wrist. From one of the three offices lining the back half of the warehouse, a generator could be heard chugging away.

Nathan gaped at the level of sophisticated hardware positioned throughout the room: computers, radio equipment, televisions, and monitors.

Amid all the organized chaos, a long conference table had been set up, strewn with printouts, maps, graphs, even a pile of newspapers. Men and women in both military garb and civilian clothes were busy throughout the room. Several were poring over reams of paper at the table, including Kelly O'Brien.

What's going on here? Nathan wondered.

"I'm afraid there's no smoking inside," their escort said to Professor Kouwe, indicating the lit pipe.

"Of course." Kouwe tapped out his pipe's bowl onto the threshold's dirt floor. The Ranger used his boot heel to squash the burning tobacco. "Thank you."

From across the way, one of the office doors opened and the tall red-headed man who appeared to be Dr. O'Brien's brother stepped out. At his side was a man Nate knew well enough to dislike immensely. He was dressed in a navy blue suit with the jacket slung over one arm, a coat Nate was sure bore the Tellux logo. As usual, his dark brown hair was oiled and combed into perfect place, as was his smartly trimmed goatee. The smile he wore as he approached Nathan and his two friends was just as oily.

On the other hand, his redheaded companion crossed with an arm extended and a more genuine expression of welcome. "Dr. Rand, thank you for coming. I think you know Dr. Richard Zane."

"We've met," Nathan said coldly, then shook the redhead's hand. The man had a grip that could crush stone.

"I'm Frank O'Brien, the head of operations here. You've already met my sister." He nodded over to Kelly, who glanced up from the table. She lifted a hand in greeting. "Now that you're all here we can get this meeting under way."

Frank guided Nate, Kouwe, and Manny toward the table, then waved an arm, signaling the others to take their seats.

A hard-faced man with a long pale scar across his throat settled himself across the table from Nathan. At his side sat one of the Rangers, his two silver bars suggesting he was the captain of the military forces here.

At the head of the table, Richard Zane sat between Kelly and Frank, who remained standing. To the left was another Tellux employee, a small Asian woman in a conservative blue pantsuit. Her eyes glinted with intelligence and seemed to soak in everything around her. Nate caught her gaze. She gave him the faintest of smiles and nodded her head.

Once everyone else was settled, Frank cleared his throat. "First, Dr. Rand, let me welcome you to the command center for Operation Amazonia, a joint operation between the CIA's Environmental Center and Special Forces Command." He gave a short nod to the silver-barred captain. "We're also supported by the Brazilian government and are assisted by Tellux Pharmaceutical's research division."

Kelly interrupted her brother, raising a hand. She clearly read the confusion on Nathan's face. "Dr. Rand, I'm sure you've many questions. Foremost being, why you've been sought as a partner in this venture."

Nathan nodded.

Kelly stood. "The main objective of Operation Amazonia is to discover the fate of your father's lost expedition."

Nate's jaw dropped and his vision blackened at the edges. He felt as if he'd just been sucker-punched. He stammered for half a moment until he found his voice. "But . . . but that was over four years ago."

"We understand that, but—"

"No!" He found himself on his feet, his chair skittering across the cement behind him. "They're dead. All dead!"

Professor Kouwe reached to place a restraining hand on his elbow. "Nathan . . ."

He shook his arm free. He remembered that call as if it were yesterday. He had been finishing up his doctoral thesis at Harvard. He had taken the next plane down to Brazil and joined the search for the vanished team. Memories flowed through him as he stood in the warehouse—the blinding fear, the anger, the frustration. After the searches were called off, he had refused to give up. He couldn't! He had pleaded with Tellux Pharmaceuticals to help continue the search privately. Tellux had been a co-sponsor, along with Eco-tek, in this venture. The ten-year goal: to conduct a census of the current populations of indigenous tribes and begin a systematic cataloging of their medicinal knowledge before such information was lost forever. But Tellux had refused Nate's request for assistance. The corporation had supported the conclusion that the team either had been killed by a tribe of hostile Indians or had stumbled upon a camp of drug traffickers.

Nate had not. Over the next year, he spent millions continuing the search, beating the bush for any sign, clue, inkling of what had become of his father. It was a financial black hole into which he poured Eco-tek's assets, further destabilizing his father's company. Eco-tek had already taken a devastating hit on Wall Street, its stock value plummeting after the loss of its CEO in the jungle. Eventually, the well ran dry. Tellux made a run for his father's company in a hostile takeover bid. Nate was too wounded, tired, and heartsore to fight. Eco-tek and its assets, including Nathan himself, became beholden to the multinational corporation.

What followed was an even blacker period of his life, a hazy blur of alcohol, drugs, and disillusionment. It was only with the help of friends like Professor Kouwe and Manny Azevedo that he had ever found himself again. In the jungles, he found the pain was less severe. He discovered he could survive a day, then another. He plodded his way as best he could, continuing his father's work with the Indians, financed on a pittance from Tellux.

Until now. "They're dead!" he repeated, sagging toward the table. "After so long, there's no hope of ever discovering what happened to my father."

Nathan felt Kelly's penetrating emerald eyes on him as she waited for him to compose himself. Finally, she spoke. "Do you know Gerald Wallace Clark?"

Opening his mouth to say no, Nathan suddenly recognized the name. He had been a member of his father's team. Nathan licked his lips. "Yes. He was a former soldier. He headed the expedition's five-man weapons team."

Kelly took a deep breath. "Twelve days ago, Gerald Wallace Clark walked out of the jungle."

Nate's eyes grew wide.

"Damn," Manny said beside him.

Professor Kouwe had retrieved Nate's toppled chair and now helped guide him down to his seat.

Kelly continued, "Unfortunately, Gerald Clark died at a missionary settlement before he could indicate where he had come from. The goal of our operation is to backtrack this latest trail to find out what happened.

We were hoping that as the son of Carl Rand, you'd be interested in cooperating with our search."

A silence descended over the table.

Frank cleared his throat, adding, "Dr. Rand, not only are you an expert on the jungle and its indigenous tribes, but you also knew your father and his team better than anyone. Such knowledge could prove an asset during this deep-jungle search."

Nathan was still too stunned to speak or answer. Professor Kouwe was not. He spoke calmly. "I can see why Tellux Pharmaceuticals is invested in this matter." Kouwe nodded to Richard Zane, who smiled back at the professor. "They were never one to pass up a chance to profit from another's tragedy."

Zane's smile soured.

Kouwe continued, now turning his attention to Frank and Kelly. "But why is this matter of interest to the CIA's Environmental Center? And what's the rationale for assigning an Army Ranger unit to the mission?" He turned to the military man, raising a single eyebrow. "Would either of you two or the captain here wish to elaborate?"

Frank's brow wrinkled at the quick and piercing assessment from the professor. Kelly's eyes sparked.

She answered. "Besides being an ex-soldier and a weapons expert, Gerald Clark was also a CIA operative. He was sent along with the expedition to gather intelligence on the cocaine shipment routes through the rain forest basin."

Frank glanced quickly at Kelly, as if this bit of information were given a bit too freely.

She ignored her brother and continued. "But any further elaboration will only be given if Dr. Rand agrees to join our operation. Otherwise, additional details will be restricted."

Kouwe, his eyes bright with warning, glanced to Nathan.

Nate took a deep breath. "If there's any hope of finding out what happened to my father, then I can't pass up this chance." He turned to his two friends. "You both know I can't."

Nathan stood and faced the table. "I'll go."

Manny shoved out of his chair. "Then I'm going with him." He faced the others and continued before anyone could object. "I've already talked to my superiors in Brasilia. As chief representative of FUNAI here, I have the power at my discretion to place any restrictions or qualifications on this mission."

Frank nodded. "So we were informed an hour ago. It's your choice. Either way, you'll have no objection from me. I read your file. Your background as a biologist could prove useful."

Next, Professor Kouwe stood up and placed a hand on Nate's shoulder. "Then perhaps you could use an expert in linguistics also."

"I appreciate your offer." Frank waved to the small Asian woman. "But we do have that covered. Dr. Anna Fong is an anthropologist with a specialty in indigenous tribes. She speaks a dozen different dialects."

Nathan scoffed, "No offense to Dr. Fong, but Professor Kouwe speaks over a hundred and fifty. There is no better expert in the field."

Anna spoke up, her voice soft and sweet. "Dr. Rand is most correct. Professor Kouwe is world renowned for his knowledge of the Amazon's indigenous tribes. It would be a privilege to have his cooperation."

"And it seems," Kelly added with a respectful nod toward the older man, "the good professor is also a distinguished expert on botanical medicines and jungle diseases."

Kouwe bowed his head in her direction.

Kelly turned to her brother. "As the expedition's medical doctor, I wouldn't mind having him along either."

Frank shrugged. "What's one more?" He faced Nathan. "Is this acceptable to you?"

Nathan glanced to his right and left. "Of course."

Frank nodded and raised his voice. "Let's all get back to work then. Discovering Dr. Rand here in the city has accelerated our schedule. We've a lot to accomplish in order to be under way at the crack of dawn tomorrow." As the others began to disperse, Frank turned to Nathan. "Now let's see if we can't get a few more of your questions answered."

He and his sister led the way toward one of the back offices.

Nate and his two friends followed.

Manny glanced over his shoulder to the bustling room. "Just what the hell have we volunteered for?"

"Something amazing," Kelly answered from ahead, holding open the office door. "Step inside and I'll show you."

Nathan clutched the photos of Agent Clark and passed them around to the others. "And you're telling me this man actually grew his arm back?"

Frank stepped around the desk and took a seat. "So it would seem. It's been verified by fingerprints. The man's body was shipped today from the morgue in Manaus back to the States. His remains are due to be examined tomorrow at a private research facility sponsored by MEDEA."

"MEDEA?" Manny asked. "Why does that name sound familiar?"

Kelly answered from where she was studying topographic maps tacked on the wall. "MEDEA's been active in rain forest conservation since its inception back in 1992."

"What is MEDEA?" Nathan asked, placing the photos on the desk.

"Back in 1989, there were congressional hearings on whether or not the classified data gathered by the CIA through its satellite surveillance systems might be useful in studying and monitoring global environmental changes. As a result, MEDEA was formed in 1992. The CIA recruited more than sixty researchers in various environmental-related fields into a single organization to analyze classified data in regard to environmental concerns."

"I see," Nathan said.

Frank spoke up, "Our mother was one of the original MEDEA founders, with a background in medicine and hazardous-waste risks. She was hired by my father when he was deputy director of the CIA. She'll be overseeing the autopsy of Agent Clark."

Manny frowned. "Your father is the deputy director of the CIA?"

"*Was,*" Frank said bitterly.

Kelly turned from the maps. "He's now director of the CIA's Environmental Center. A division that was founded by Al Gore in 1997 at the behest of MEDEA. Frank works in this division, as well."

"And you?" Nathan asked. "Are you CIA, too?"

Kelly waved away his question.

"She's the youngest member of MEDEA," Frank said with a bit of pride in his voice. "Quite the distinguished honor. It was why we were chosen to head this operation. I represent the CIA. She represents MEDEA."

"Nothing like keeping it all in the family," Kouwe said with a snort.

"The fewer who know about the mission the better," Frank added.

"Then how does Tellux Pharmaceuticals play a role in all this?" Nathan asked.

Kouwe answered before either of the O'Brien siblings. "Isn't it obvious? Your father's expedition was financed by Eco-tek and Tellux, which are now one and the same. They own any proprietary intelligence gained from the expedition. If the team discovered some compound out there with regenerative properties, Tellux owns the majority rights to it."

Nathan glanced to Kelly, who stared at her toes.

Frank simply nodded. "He's right. But even at Tellux, only a handful of people know the true purpose of our mission here."

Nate shook his head. "Great, just great." Kouwe placed a sympathetic hand on his shoulder.

"All that aside," Manny said, "what's our first step?"

"Let me show you." Kelly turned once again to the maps on the back wall. She pointed to the centermost one. "I'm sure Dr. Rand is familiar with this map."

He stared at it and did indeed recognize it like the lines on his own palm. "It's the recorded route my father's team took four years ago."

"Exactly," Kelly said, tracing her finger along the dotted course that led in haphazard fashion from Manaus south along the Madeira River until it reached the town of Pôrto Velho, where it angled north into the heart of the Amazon basin. From there, the team crisscrossed the area until they bridged into the little-explored region between the southern and northern tributaries of the Amazon. Her finger stopped at the small cross at the end of the line. "Here is where all radio contact with the team ceased. And where all searches originated—both those sponsored by the Brazilian government and those financed privately." She glanced significantly at Nathan. "What can you tell us about the searches?"

Nate circled around the desk to stare at the map. A familiar creeping despair edged through the core of his being. "It was December, the height of the rainy season," he whispered dully. "Two major storm systems had moved through the region. It was one of the reasons no one was initially concerned. But when an update from the team grew to be almost a week late and the storms had abated, an alarm went up. At first, no one was really that worried. These were people who had lived their lives in the jungle. What could go wrong? But as search teams began tentatively looking, it was realized that all trace of the expedition was gone, erased by the rains and the flooded forests. This spot"—Nathan placed a finger on the black X—"was found to be underwater when the first team arrived."

He turned to the others. "Another week went by, then another. Nothing. No clues, no further word . . . until one last frantic signal. 'Send help . . . can't last much longer. Oh, God, they're all around us.' " Nate took a deep breath. The memory of those words still haunted him deeply. "The signal was so full of static that it was impossible to discern who even spoke. Maybe it was this Agent Clark." But in his heart, Nathan knew it had been his father. He had listened over and over to that last message. The last words of his father.

Nathan stared at the photos and documents strewn across the desktop. "For the next three months, the searchers swept throughout the region, but storms and floods made any progress difficult. There was no telling in which direction my father's team had headed: east, west, north, south." He shrugged. "It was impossible. We were searching a region larger than the state of Texas. Eventually everyone gave up."

"Except you," Kelly said softly.

Nathan clenched a fist. "And a lot of good that did. No further contact was ever heard."

"Until now," Kelly said. She gently drew him around and pointed to a small red circle he had not noticed before. She pointed to it. It lay about two hundred miles due south of São Gabriel, near the river of Jarurá, a branch of the Solimões, the mighty southern tributary of the Amazon. "This is the mission of Wauwai, where Agent Clark died. This is where we're heading tomorrow."

"And what then?" Manny asked.

"We follow Gerald Clark's trail. Unlike the earlier searches, we have an advantage."

"What is that?" Manny asked.

Nathan spoke up, leaning close to the wall map. "We're at the end of the dry season. There hasn't been a major storm through here in a month." He glanced over his shoulder. "We should be able to track his movements."

"Hence, the urgency and speed of organizing this mission." Frank stood. He leaned one hand on the wall and nodded to the map. "We hope to follow any clues before the wet season begins and the trail is washed away. We're also hoping Agent Clark was sound enough in mind to leave some evidence of his route—marks on a tree, piles of rock—some way to lead us back to where he had been held these past four years."

Frank turned back to the desk and slid out a large folded sheet of sketch paper. "In addition, we've employed Anna Fong so we can communicate with any natives of the region: peasants, Indians, trappers, whoever. To see if anyone has seen a man with these markings pass by." Frank unfolded and smoothed the paper. A hand-sketched drawing was revealed. "This was tattooed across Agent Clark's chest and abdomen. We hope that we'll find isolated folk who might have seen a man with this marking."

Professor Kouwe flinched.

His reaction did not go unnoticed by those in the room.

"What is it?" Nathan asked.

Kouwe pointed to the sketch paper. It delineated a complex serpentine pattern that spiraled out from a single stylized handprint.

"This is bad. Very bad." Kouwe fumbled in his pocket and pulled out his pipe. He lifted a questioning eye at Frank.

The redheaded man nodded.

Kouwe slipped out a pouch and tamped some locally grown tobacco into the pipe, then lit it with a single match. Nathan noted his uncharacteristically trembling fingers.

"What is it?"

Kouwe puffed on his pipe and spoke slowly. "It's the symbol for the Ban-ali. The Blood Jaguars."

"You know this tribe?" Kelly asked.

The shaman blew out a long stream of smoke and sighed, then shook his head. "No one *knows* this tribe. It is what's whispered among village elders, stories passed from one generation to another. Myths of a tribe that mates with jaguars and whose members can vanish into thin air. They bring death to all who encounter them. It is said they are as old as the forest and that the very jungle bends to their will."

"But I've never heard of them," Nathan said, "and I've worked with tribes throughout the Amazon."

"And Dr. Fong, the Tellux anthropologist," Frank said. "She didn't recognize it either."

"I'm not surprised. No matter how well you're accepted, a non-tribesman will always be considered *pananakiri*, an alien to the Indians of the region. They would never speak of the Ban-ali to you."

Nate couldn't help but feel a bit insulted. "But I—"

"No, Nathan. I don't mean to slight your own work or abilities. But for many tribes, names have power. Few will speak the name Ban-ali. They fear to draw the attention of the Blood Jaguars." Kouwe pointed to the drawing. "If you take this symbol with you, it must be shown with care. Many Indians would slay you for possessing such a paper. There is no greater taboo than allowing that symbol into a village."

Kelly frowned. "Then it's doubtful Agent Clark passed through any villages."

"If he did, he wouldn't have walked out alive."

Kelly and Frank shared a concerned look, then the doctor turned to Nathan. "Your father's expedition was cataloging Amazonian tribes. If he had heard of these mysterious Ban-ali or had found some clue of their existence, perhaps he sought them out."

Manny folded the sketched drawing. "And perhaps he found them."

Kouwe studied the glowing tip of his pipe. "Pray to God he did not."

A little later, with most of the details settled, Kelly watched the trio, escorted by a Ranger, cross the room and exit the warehouse. Her brother Frank was already at the portable satellite uplink to report the day's progress to his superiors, including their father.

But Kelly found her gaze following Nathan Rand. After their antagonistic exchange in the hospital, she was still slightly put off by his demeanor. But he was hardly the same oily-haired, foul-smelling wretch she had seen hauling the girl on a stretcher. Shaved and in clean clothes, he was certainly handsome: sandy-blond hair, dark complexion, steel-blue eyes. Even the way one eyebrow would rise when he was intrigued was oddly charming.

"Kelly!" her brother called. "There's someone who'd like to say hi."

With a tired sigh, Kelly joined her brother at the table. All around the room, final preparations and equipment checks were being finished. She leaned both palms on the table and stared into the laptop's screen. She saw two familiar faces, and a warm smile crossed her face.

"Mother, Jessie's not supposed to be up this late." She glanced to her own wristwatch and did a quick calculation. "It must be close to midnight."

"Actually after midnight, hon."

Kelly's mother could have been her sister. Her hair was as deep an auburn as her own. The only sign of her age was the slightly deeper crinkles at the corners of her eyes and the small pair of glasses perched on her nose. She had been pregnant with Kelly and Frank when she was only twenty-two, still in med school herself. Giving birth to fraternal twins was enough of a family for the med student and the young navy surveillance engineer. Kelly's mother and father never had any more children.

But that didn't stop Kelly from following in her mother's footsteps, getting pregnant in her fourth year of medical school at Georgetown. Yet unlike her mother, who remained married to the father of her children, Kelly divorced Daniel Nickerson when she found him in bed with a fellow residency student. He at least had enough decency not to contest Kelly's demand for custody of their one-year-old daughter, Jessica.

Jessie, now six years old, stood at her grandmother's shoulder, dressed in a yellow flannel nightgown with Disney's Pocahontas on the front. Her tousled red hair looked as if she had just climbed out of bed. She waved at the screen. "Hi, Mommy!"

"Hi, sweetheart. Are you having a good time with Grandma and Grandpa?"

She nodded vigorously. "We went to Chuck E. Cheese's today!"

Kelly's smile broadened. "That sounds like fun. I wish I could've been there."

"We saved a piece of pizza for you."

In the background, her mother's eyes rolled with the exasperation of all grandparents who've had encounters with the giant Chuck E. Cheese's rodent.

"Did you see any lions, Mommy?"

This earned a chuckle. "No, hon, there are no lions here. That's Africa."

"How about gorillas?"

"No, that's Africa, too—but we did see some monkeys."

Jessica's eyes grew round. "Can you catch one and bring one home? I always wanted a monkey."

"I don't think the monkey would like that. He has his own mommy here."

Her mother placed an arm around Jessica. "And I think it's time we let your mommy get some sleep. She has to get up early like you do."

Jessica's face fell into a pout.

Kelly leaned closer to the screen. "I love you, Jessie."

She waved at the screen. "Bye, Mommy."

Her mother smiled at her. "Be careful, hon. I wish I could be there."

"You've got enough work of your own. Did the . . . um . . ." Her eyes flicked to Jessie. ". . . *package* arrive safely?"

Her mother's face drifted to a more serious demeanor. "It cleared customs in Miami about six o'clock, arrived here in Virginia about ten, and was trucked to the Instar Institute. In fact, your father's still over there, making sure all is in order for tomorrow's examination."

Kelly nodded, relieved Clark's body had arrived in the States safely.

"I should get Jessie to bed, but I'll update you tomorrow night during the evening uplink. You be careful out there."

"Don't worry. I've got a crack team of ten Army Rangers as bodyguards. I'll be safer than on the streets of downtown Washington."

"Still, you two watch each other's backs."

Kelly glanced to Frank, who was talking to Richard Zane. "We will."

Her mother swept her a kiss. "I love you."

"Love you too, Mom." Then the screen went dead.

Kelly closed the laptop, then slumped to a chair by the table, suddenly exhausted. She stared at the others. Her gear was already packed and stored on the Huey. Free from any responsibilities for the moment, her mind drifted back to the red serpentine tattoo wrapped around a blue palm, the symbol of the Ban-ali, the ghost tribe of the Amazon.

Two questions nagged her: Did such a tribe exist, a tribe with these mythic powers? And if so, would ten armed Rangers be enough?

THREE

The Doctor and the Witch

Louis Favre was often described as a bastard and drunkard, but never to his face. *Never.* The unfortunate sot who had dared now sat on his backside in the alley behind the Hotel Seine, a great decaying colonial edifice that sat on a hill overlooking the capital city of French Guiana.

A moment ago, in the hotel's dark bar, the miscreant at his feet had been hassling a fellow regular, a man in his eighties, a survivor of the dreaded penal colony of Devil's Island. Louis had never spoken to the old man, but he had heard his tale from the barkeep. As with many of the prisoners shipped here from France, he had been doubly sentenced: for every year spent in the island hellhole ten miles off the coast, the fellow was forced to spend an equal number of years in French Guiana afterward. It was a way to ensure a French presence in the colony. And as the government had hoped, most of these pitiable souls ended up staying here. What life did they have back in France after so long?

Louis had often studied this fellow, a kindred soul, another exile. He would watch the man sip his neat bourbons, reading the lines in his aged and despairing face. He valued these quiet moments.

So when the half-drunk Englishman had tripped and bumped into the old man's elbow, knocking over his drink, and then simply tottered on past without the courtesy of apology or acknowledgment, Louis Favre had gained his feet and confronted the man.

"Piss off, Frenchie," the young man had slurred in his face.

Louis continued to block the man's exit from the bar. "You'll buy my dear friend another drink, or we'll have it out, monsieur."

"Bugger off already, you drunk wanker." The man attempted to shove past.

Louis had sighed, then struck out with a fist, bashing the man's nose bloody, and grabbed him by the lapels of his poor suit. Other patrons turned their attention to their own drinks. Louis hauled the rude young man, still dazed from the blow and a night of heavy drinking, through a back door into the alley.

He set to work on earning an apology from the man, not that he could really talk with a mouthful of bloody teeth. By the time Louis was done kicking and beating the man, he lay in a ruin of piss and blood in the alley's filth. He gave the man one final savage kick, hearing a satisfying crack of ribs. With a nod, Louis retrieved his white Panama hat from atop a rubbish bin and straightened his linen suit. He stared at his shoes, ivory patent leather. Frowning, he plucked out a pristine handkerchief and wiped the blood from the tip of his shoes. He scowled at the Englishman, thought about kicking him one last time, but then studied his newly polished shoes and decided better.

Positioning his hat in place, he reentered the smoky bar and signaled the barman. He pointed to the old gent. "Please refresh my friend's drink."

The Spanish barkeep nodded and reached for a bottle of bourbon.

Louis met his gaze and wagged a finger at him.

The barman bit his lip at the faux pas. Louis always went for the best, even when buying drinks for friends. Duly admonished, the man reached for a bottle of properly aged Glenlivet, the best in the house.

"*Merci.*" With matters rectified, Louis headed for the entrance to the hotel's lobby, almost running into the concierge.

The small-framed man bowed and apologized profusely. "Dr. Favre! I was just coming to find you," he said breathlessly. "I have an overseas call holding for your attention." He passed Louis a folded note. "They refused to leave a message and stressed the call was urgent."

Louis unfolded the slip and read the name, printed neatly: *St. Savin*

Biochimique Compagnie. A French drug company. He refolded the paper and tucked it into his breast pocket. "I'll take the call."

"There is a private salon—"

"I know where it is," Louis said. He had taken many of his business calls down here.

With the concierge in tow, Louis strode to the small cubicle beside the hotel's front desk. He left the man at the door and sat in the small upholstered chair that smelled of mold and a mélange of old cologne and sweat. Louis settled to the seat and picked up the phone's receiver. "Dr. Louis Favre," he said crisply.

"*Bonjour,* Dr. Favre," a voice spoke on the other end of the line. "We have a request for your services."

"If you have this number, then I assume you know my pricing schedule."

"We do."

"And may I ask what class of service you require?"

"*Première.*"

The single word caused Louis's fingers to tighten on the receiver. First class. It meant a payment over six figures. "Location?"

"The Brazilian rain forest."

"And the objective?"

The man spoke rapidly. Louis listened without taking notes. Each number was fixed in his mind, as was each name, especially *one.* Louis's eyes narrowed. He sat up straighter. The man finished, "The U.S. team must be tracked and whatever they discover must be obtained."

"And the other team?"

There was no answer, just the static of the other line.

"I understand and accept," Louis said. "I'll need to see half the fee in my usual account by close of business tomorrow. Furthermore, any and all details of the U.S. team and its resources should be faxed to my private line as soon as possible." He gave the number quickly.

"It will be done within the hour."

"*Très bon.*"

The line clicked dead, the business settled.

Louis slowly replaced the receiver in its cradle and sat back. The thoughts of the money and the thousand details in setting up his own team were pushed back for now. At this moment, one name shone like burning magnesium across his mind's eye. His new employer had glossed over it, unaware of the significance. If he had been, St. Savin's offer probably would have been considerably less. In fact, Louis would have taken this job for the cost of a cheap bottle of wine. He whispered the name now, tasting it on his tongue.

"Carl Rand."

Seven years ago, Louis Favre had been a biologist employed by the Base Biologique Nationale de Recherches, the premier French science foundation. With a specialty in rain forest ecosystems, Louis had worked throughout the world: Australia, Borneo, Madagascar, the Congo. But for fifteen years, his specialty had been the Amazon rain forest. He had journeyed throughout the region, establishing an international reputation.

That is, until he ran into the damnable Dr. Carl Rand.

The American pharmaceutical entrepreneur had found Louis's methods of research to be a bit suspect, after stumbling upon Louis's interrogation of a local shaman. Dr. Rand had not believed cutting off the man's fingers, one by one, had been a viable way of gleaning information from the stubborn Indian, and no amount of money would convince the simpering American otherwise. Of course, the pile of endangered black caiman carcasses and jaguar pelts found in the village had not helped matters. Dr. Rand seemed incapable of understanding that supplementing one's work with black market income was simply a lifestyle choice.

Unfortunately, Carl and his Brazilian forces had outnumbered his own team. Louis Favre was captured and incarcerated by the Brazilian army. Luckily, he had connections in France and enough money to ply the palms of a few corrupt Brazilian officials in order to slip away with no more than a slap on the wrist.

However, it was the figurative slap to his face that had stung worse. The incident had blackened his good name beyond repair. Penniless, he was forced to flee Brazil for French Guiana. There, always resourceful and with previous contacts in the black market, he scrounged together a mercenary jungle force. During the past five years, his group had protected drug shipments from Colombia, hunted down various rare and endangered animals for private collectors, eliminated a troublesome Brazilian government regulator for a gold-mining operation, even wiped out a small peasant village whose inhabitants objected to a logging company's intrusion onto their lands. It was good business all around.

And now this latest offer: to track a U.S. military team through the jungle as they searched for Carl Rand's lost expedition and steal whatever they discovered. All in order to be the first one to obtain some regenerative compound believed to have been discovered by Rand's group.

Such a request was not unusual. In the past few years, the race for new rain forest drugs had become more and more frantic, a multibillion-dollar industry. The search for "green gold," the next new wonder drug, had spurred a new "gold rush" here in the Amazon. And in the trackless depths of the forest, where millions of dollars were cast into an economy of dirt-poor farmers and unschooled Indians, betrayals and atrocities were committed daily. There were no spying eyes and no one to tell tales. Each year, the jungle alone consumed thousands from disease, from attack, from injuries. What were a few more—a biologist, an ethnobotanist, a drug researcher?

It was a financial free-for-all.

And Louis Favre was about to join the game, championed by a French pharmaceutical company. Smiling, he stood up. He had been delighted when he heard about Carl Rand's disappearance four years ago. He had gotten drunk that night, toasting the man's misfortune. Now he would pound the final nail in the bastard's coffin by stealing whatever the man had discovered and laying more lives upon his grave.

Unlocking the salon's door, Louis stepped out.

"I hope everything was satisfactory, Dr. Favre," the concierge called politely from his desk.

"Most satisfactory, Claude," he said with a nod. "Most satisfactory indeed." Louis crossed to the hotel's small elevator, an antique cell of wrought iron and wood. It hardly fit two people. He pressed the button for the sixth floor, where his apartment suite lay. He was anxious to share the news.

The elevator clanked, groaned, and sighed its way up to his floor. Once the door was open, Louis hurried down the narrow hall to the farthest room. Like a handful of other guests who had taken up permanent residence in the Hotel Seine, Louis had a suite of rooms: two bedrooms, a cramped kitchen, a broad sitting room with doors that opened upon a wrought-iron balcony, and even a small study lined with bookshelves. The suite was not elaborate, but it suited his needs. The staff was discreet and well accustomed to the eccentricities of the guests.

Louis keyed open his door and pushed inside. Two things struck him immediately. First, a familiar and arousing scent filled the room. It came from a pot on the small gas stovetop, boiling ayahuasca leaves that produced the powerful hallucinogenic tea, *natem.*

Second, he heard the whine of the fax machine coming from the study. His new employers were certainly efficient.

"Tshui!" he called out.

He expected no answer, but as was customary among the Shuar tribespeople, one always announced one's presence when entering a dwelling. He noticed the door to the bedroom slightly ajar.

With a smile, he crossed to the study and watched another sheet of paper roll from the machine and fall to the growing stack. The details of the upcoming mission. "Tshui, I have marvelous news."

Louis retrieved the topmost printout from the faxed pile and glanced at it. It was a list of those who would comprise the U.S. search team.

10:45 P.M. UPDATE from Base Station Alpha

I. Op. AMAZONIA: Civilian Unit Members
    (1) Kelly O'Brien, M.D.—MEDEA
    (2) Francis J. O'Brien—Environmental Center, CIA
    (3) Olin Pasternak—Science and Technology Directorate, CIA
    (4) Richard Zane, Ph.D.—Tellux Pharmaceutical research head
    (5) Anna Fong, Ph.D.—Tellux Pharmaceutical employee

II. Op. AMAZONIA: Mil. Support: 75th Army Ranger Unit
    CAPTAIN: Craig Waxman
    STAFF SERGEANT: Alberto Kostos
    CORPORALS: Brian Conger, James DeMartini, Rodney Graves, Thomas Graves, Dennis Jorgensen, Kenneth Okamoto, Nolan Warczak, Samad Yamir

III. Op. AMAZONIA: Locally Recruited
  (1) **Manuel Azevedo—FUNAI, Brazilian national**
  (2) **Resh Kouwe, Ph.D.—FUNAI, Indigenous Peoples Representative**
  (3) **Nathan Rand, Ph.D.—Ethnobotanist, U.S. citizen**

Louis almost missed the last name on the list. He gripped the faxed printout tighter. *Nathan Rand,* the son of Carl Rand. Of course, it made sense. The boy would not let this team search for his father without accompanying them. He closed his eyes, savoring this boon. It was as if the gods of the dark jungle were aligning in his favor. The revenge he had failed to mete upon the father would fall upon the shoulders of the son. It was almost biblical.

As he stood there, he heard a slight rustle coming from the next room, the master bedroom. He let the paper slip from his fingers back to the pile. He would have time later to review the details and formulate a plan. Right now, he simply wanted to enjoy the serendipity of the moment.

"Tshui!" he called again and crossed to the bedroom door.

He slipped the door open and found the room beyond lit with candles and a single incense burner. His mistress lay naked on the canopy bed. The queen-sized bed was draped in white silk with its mosquito net folded back. The Shuar woman reclined upon pillows atop the ivory sheets. Her deep-bronze skin glowed in the candlelight. Her long black hair was a fan around her, while her eyes were heavy-lidded from both passion and *natem* tea. Two cups lay on the small nightstand, one empty, the other full.

As usual, Louis found his breath simply stolen from him at the sight of his love. He had first met the beauty three years ago in Equador. She had been the wife of a Shuar chieftain, until the fool's infidelity had enraged her. She slew him with his own machete. Though such acts—both the infidelity and the murder—were common among the brutal Shuar, Tshui was banished from the tribe, sent naked into the jungle. None, not even the chieftain's kinsmen, would dare touch her. She was well known throughout the region as one of the rare female shamans, a practitioner of *wawek,* malevolent sorcery. Her skill at poisons, tortures, and the lost art of *tsantza,* head-shrinking, were both respected and feared. In fact, the only article of adornment she had worn as she left the village was the shrunken head of her husband, hung on a twined cord and resting between her breasts.

This was how Louis found the woman, a wild, beautiful creature of the jungle. Though he had an estranged wife back in France, Louis had taken the woman as his own. She had not refused, especially when he and his mercenaries slew every man, woman, and child in her village, marking her revenge.

Since that day, the two had been inseparable. Tshui, an accomplished interrogator and wise in the ways of the jungle, accompanied him on all his missions. She continued to collect trophies from each venture.

Around the room, aligned on shelves on all four walls, were forty-three *tsantza,* each head no more than a wizened apple—the eyes and lips sewn closed, the hair trailing over the shelf edges like Spanish moss on trees. Her skill at shrinking heads was amazing. He had watched the entire process once.

Once was enough.

With the skill of a surgeon, she would flay the skin in one piece from the skull of her victim, sometimes while he or she was still alive and screaming. She truly was an artist. After boiling the skin, hair and all, and drying it over hot ashes, she used a bone needle and thread to close the mouth and eyes, then filled the inside with hot pebbles and sand. As the leathery skin shrank, she would mold its shape with her fingers. Tshui had an uncanny ability to sculpt the head into an amazing approximation of the victim's original face.

Louis glanced to her latest work of art. It rested on the far bedside table. It was a Bolivian army officer who had been blackmailing a cocaine shipper. From his trimmed mustache to the straight bangs hanging over his forehead, the detail of her work was amazing. The collection was worthy of the finest museum. In fact, the staff of the Hotel Seine thought Louis was a university anthropologist, collecting these specimens for just such a museum. If any thought otherwise, they knew to keep silent.

"*Ma chérie,*" he said, finding his breath again. "I have wonderful news."

She rolled toward him, reaching in his direction. She made a small sound, encouraging him to join her. Tshui seldom spoke. A word here or there. Otherwise, like some jungle cat, she was all eyes, motions, and soft purrs.

Louis could not resist. He knocked off his hat and slipped from his jacket. In moments, he was as naked as she. His own body was lean, muscled, and crisscrossed with scars. He swallowed the draught of *natem* laid out for him while Tshui lazily traced one of his scars down his belly to his inner thigh. A shiver trembled up his back.

As the drug swept through him, heightening his senses, he fell upon his woman. She opened to him, and he sank gratefully into her warmth. He kissed her deeply, while she raked his back with sharpened nails.

Soon, colors and lights played across his vision. The room spun slightly from the alkaloids in the tea. For a moment, it seemed the scores of shrunken heads were watching their play, the eyes of the dead upon him as he thrust into the woman. The audience aroused him further. He pinned Tshui under him, his back arching as he drove into her again and again, a scream clenched in his chest.

All around him were faces staring down, watching with blind eyes.

Louis had one final thought before being consumed fully by his passion and the exquisite pain. A final trophy to add to these shelves, a memento from the son of the man who had ruined him: *the head of Nathan Rand.*

ACT TWO

Under the Canopy

PERIWINKLE

FAMILY: *Apocynaceae*

GENUS: *Vinca*

SPECIES: *Minor, Major*

COMMON NAMES: *Periwinkle, Cezayirmeneksesi, Common Periwinkle, Vincapervinc*

PARTS USED: *Whole Plant*

PROPERTIES/ACTIONS: *Analgesic, Antibacterial, Antimicrobial, Antiinflammatory, Astringent, Cardiotonic, Carminative, Depurative, Diuretic, Emmenagogue, Febrifuge, Hemostat, Hypotensive, Lactogogue, Hepatoprotective, Sedative, Sialogogue, Spasmolytic, Stomachic, Tonic, Vulnerary*

FOUR

Wauwai

Nathan stared out the helicopter's windows. Even through the sound-dampening earphones, the roar of the blades was deafening, isolating each passenger in his own cocoon of noise.

Below, a vast sea of green spread to the horizon in all directions. From this vantage, it was as if the entire world were just forest. The only breaks in the featureless expanse of the continuous canopy were the occasional giant trees, the emergents, that poked their leafy crowns above their brethren, great monsters of the forest that served as nesting sites for harpy eagles and toucans. The only other breaks were the half-hidden dark rivers, snaking lazily through the forest.

Otherwise, the jungle remained supreme, impenetrable, endless.

Nathan leaned his forehead against the glass. Was his father down there somewhere? And if not, were there at least answers?

Deep inside, Nathan felt a seed of anxiety, bitter and sour. Could he handle what he discovered? After four years of not knowing, Nate had learned one thing. Time did indeed heal all wounds, but it left a nasty, unforgiving scar.

After his father's disappearance, Nate had isolated himself from the world, first in the bottom of a bottle of Jack Daniel's, then in the embrace of stronger drugs. Back in the States, his therapists had used phrases such as *abandonment issues, trust conflicts, and clinical depression*. But Nate experienced it as a faithlessness in life. With the exception of Manny and Kouwe, he had formed no deep friendships. He had become too hard, too numb, too scarred.

Only after returning to the jungle had Nate found some semblance of peace. But now this . . .

Was he ready to reopen those old wounds? To face that pain?

The earphone radio clicked on with a rasp of static, and the pilot's voice cut momentarily through the rotor's roar. "We're twenty klicks from Wauwai. But there's smoke on the horizon."

Nathan peered ahead, yet all he could see was the terrain below and to the side. Wauwai would serve as a secondary field base for the search team, a launching-off point from which to supply and monitor those trekking through the forest. Two hours ago, the three Hueys, along with the sleek black Comanche, had set off from São Gabriel, carrying the initial supplies, gear, armament, and personnel. After the expedition proceeded into the jungle later today, the Hueys would serve as a flying supply chain between Wauwai and São Gabriel, ferrying additional supplies, men, and fuel. Meanwhile, the Comanche would remain at Wauwai, a black bird reserved in case of an emergency. Its armament and long-range capabilities would help protect the team from the air if necessary.

That had been the plan.

"The smoke appears to be coming from our destination," the pilot continued. "The village is burning."

Nathan pulled away from the window. *Burning?* He glanced around the cabin. In addition to the two O'Briens, he shared the space with Professor Kouwe, Richard Zane, and Anna Fong. The seventh and final passenger was the hard-faced man who had sat across the conference table from Nathan during the debriefing, the one with the ugly scar across his neck. He had been introduced this morning as Olin Pasternak, another CIA agent, one associated with the administration's Science and Technology division. He found the man's ice-blue eyes staring right back at him, his face an unreadable stoic mask.

To his side, he watched Frank pull a microphone up to his lips. "Can we still land?"

"I can't be sure from this distance, sir," the pilot answered. "Captain Waxman is proceeding ahead to survey the situation."

Nathan watched one of the helicopters break formation and speed forward as their own craft slowed. As they waited, the Huey banked around, and Nathan spotted a column of smoke rising from the blanket of greenery near the horizon. It climbed high into the blue skies. The other passengers shifted closer to peer out the port-side windows.

Kelly O'Brien leaned near his shoulder, eyes on the smoke. He watched her lips move, but the noise and the earphones blocked her words. She pulled back and caught him staring at her.

Her eyes flicked away, and a slight blush reddened her cheeks.

The pilot came on over the radio. "Folks, it looks like we have an okay to proceed from the captain. The landing field is upwind of the fires. Please ready yourselves for landing."

Everyone settled back into their seats and snapped their buckles into place. In short order, the bevy of helicopters was circling the village. Each pilot was careful to keep the wash from his rotor from blowing the smoke toward the landing field. Though still unable to see the source of the flames, Nathan watched a chain of people passing buckets from the river as the helicopter aligned for landing.

As they descended, a clapboard church with a whitewashed steeple came into view. The source of the fire was on its far side, and someone stood on the church's roof, soaking down its shingles.

Then the skids of the helicopter settled to the ground with a slight bump, and Frank signaled for everyone to disembark.

Nathan tugged off his earphones and was assaulted by the growl of the rotors. He unbuckled his shoulder harness and climbed from the helicopter. Once clear of the rotors, he stretched and surveyed the area. The last of the Hueys settled to earth on the far side of the field. The tilled soil and barren rows were telltale signs that the landing field must once have been the village's garden.

Across the yard, the Rangers were already busy. A handful were offloading gear and supplies, while most of the others trotted toward the front of the church to help with the fires.

Slowly, the noise of the helicopters dissipated, and voices could be heard again: shouted orders, yells from beyond the church, the chatter of soldiers hauling equipment.

Kelly stepped to Nathan's side with Frank in tow. "We should see if we can find the padre who found Agent Clark. Interview him, so we can be on our way."

Frank nodded, and the two headed for the rear door of the church.

Someone clapped Nate on the shoulder. It was Professor Kouwe. "Let's go help," the older man said, pointing toward the smoke.

Nathan followed the professor through the fields and around the side of the church. What he found on the far side was chaos: people running with buckets and shovels, smoke billowing in every direction, flames rampant.

"My God," Nate said.

A village of a hundred or so small homes lay between the church and the river. Three-quarters of them were burning.

He and the professor hurried forward, adding the strength of their backs to the water brigade. Working around them were a mix of brown-skinned Indians, white missionaries, and uniformed Rangers. After about an hour of laboring, they all looked the same, just soot-covered rescuers choking and coughing on the smoke.

Nathan ran with buckets, dousing flames, concentrating on maintaining a fire break around the burning section of the village. It was up to them to hold the flames at bay. Inside the fire zone, the blaze consumed all the palm-thatched structures, turning homes into torches in mere seconds. But with the additional men, the fire was contained at last. The conflagration quickly died down as all the homes were consumed within the fire zone. Only a few glowing embers dotted the smoky ruined landscape.

During the crisis, Nate had lost track of the professor and now found himself resting beside a tall, broad-shouldered Brazilian. The man looked close to tears. He mumbled something in Portuguese that sounded like a prayer. Nate guessed he was one of the missionaries.

"I'm sorry," Nate said in Portuguese, tugging away the scrap of cloth that had been shielding his nose and mouth. "Was anyone killed?"

"Five. All children." The man's voice cracked. "But many others were sickened by the smoke."

"What happened here?"

The missionary wiped the soot from his face with a handkerchief. "It was m . . . my fault. I should've known better." He glanced over his shoulder to the steepled church. Aside from being stained with ash and smoke, it stood unharmed. He covered his eyes, and his shoulders shook. It took him another moment to speak. "It was my decision to send the man's body to Manaus."

Nathan suddenly realized to whom he was speaking. "Padre Batista?" It was the mission's leader, the one who had found Gerald Clark.

The tall Brazilian nodded. "May God forgive me."

Nate guided Garcia Luiz Batista away from the blackened ruins of the village and into untouched green fields. He quickly introduced himself as he led the man back to his church. En route, he passed one of the Rangers, covered in soot and sweat, and asked him to send the O'Briens to the church.

With a sharp nod, the Ranger took off.

Nate walked the padre up the wooden steps and through the double doors. The interior was dark and cool. Varnished wooden pews lined the way to the altar and giant mahogany crucifix. The room was mostly empty. A few Indians lay sprawled, exhausted, both on the floor and on pews. Nate led the church's leader toward the front and settled him in the first pew.

The man sagged into his seat, his eyes fixed on the crucifix. "It's all my fault." He bowed his head and lifted his hands in prayer.

Nathan remained quiet, giving the man a private moment. The church door swung open, and he spotted Frank and Kelly. Professor Kouwe was with them. All three were covered in ash from head to toe. He waved them over.

The arrival of the other three drew Padre Batista's attention from his prayers. Nathan made introductions all around. Once done, he sat beside the padre. "Tell me what happened. How did the fires start?"

Garcia glanced around at the others, then sighed heavily and looked at his toes. "It was my own shortsightedness."

Kelly sat on the man's other side. "What do you mean?" she asked softly.

After a moment more, the padre spoke again. "On the night the poor man stumbled out of the forest, a shaman of the Yanomamo tribe scolded me for taking the man into the mission. He warned me that the man's body must be burned." The padre glanced to Nathan. "How could I do that? He surely had family. Maybe he was even a Christian."

Nathan patted his hand. "Of course."

"But I should not have so easily dismissed the Indians' superstitions. I had put too much faith in their conversion to Catholicism. They'd even been baptized." The padre shook his head.

Nate understood. "It's not your fault. Some beliefs are too ingrained to be washed away in a single baptism."

Padre Batista sagged. "At first, all seemed well. The shaman was still angered at my decision not to burn the body, but he accepted that at least it was gone from the village. This seemed to appease him."

"What changed that?" Kelly asked.

"A week later, a couple of children in the village developed fevers. It was nothing new. Such ailments are commonplace. But the shaman decided these illnesses were the sign of a curse from the dead man."

Nate nodded. He had seen firsthand such assessments himself. In most Indian tribes, illness was considered not only due to injury or disease, but often to a spell cast by the shaman of another village. Wars had broken out over such accusations.

"There was nothing I could do to dissuade him. In another few days, three more children fell ill, one of them from the Yanomamo *shabano*. The whole village grew tense. In fear, entire families packed up and left. Every night, drums beat and chanting could be heard." Garcia closed his eyes. "I radioed for medical assistance. But when a doctor arrived from Junta four days later, none of the Indians would let the man examine their children. The Yanomamo shaman had won them over. I tried to plead, but they refused any medical help. Instead, they left the little ones in the care of that witch doctor."

Nathan bristled at this term. He glanced to Professor Kouwe, who gave a small shake of his head, indicating Nate should remain silent.

The padre continued. "Then last night, one of the children died. A great wailing consumed the village. To cover up his failure, the shaman declared the village cursed. He warned that all should leave here. I tried my best to calm the panic, but the shaman had the others under his spell. Just before dawn, he and his fellow Yanomamo tribesmen set fire to their own roundhouse, then fled into the jungle." Garcia was now openly weeping. "The . . . the monster had left the sick children inside. He burned them all alive."

The padre covered his face with his hands. "With so few still in the village to help fight the fire, the flames spread through the huts. If you all had not come and helped, we could have lost everything. My church, my flock."

Nathan placed a hand on the man's shoulder. "Don't despair. We can help you rebuild." He glanced over to Kelly's brother for confirmation.

Frank cleared his throat. "Of course. A contingent of Rangers and researchers are going to remain here after we head into the jungle. As guests here, I'm sure they'll be more than willing to haul in supplies with their helicopters and lend you manpower to rebuild the village out of the ashes."

The man's words seemed to strengthen the padre. "God bless you." He wiped his eyes and nose with his handkerchief.

"We'll do all we can," Kelly assured him. "But, padre, time is of the essence for us, too. We hope to begin tracking the dead man's trail before it grows any colder."

"Of course, of course . . ." Garcia said in a tired voice, and stood. "I'll tell you all I know."

It was a short talk. The padre explained as he led them past the altar to the common rooms of the church. The dining room had been converted into a makeshift hospital for smoke-inhalation victims, but no one appeared seriously injured. Garcia related how he had convinced a few Indians to track the dead man's trail, in case the fellow had any companions out there. The trail led to one of the tributaries of the Jarurá River. No boat was found, but the tracks seemed to follow the offshoot's course, heading west into the most remote sections of the rain forest. The Indian trackers feared going any farther.

Kelly leaned on a window overlooking the rear garden. "Can someone show us this tributary?"

Garcia nodded. He had washed his face and seemed to have collected himself. Steel had entered his voice and demeanor as the initial shock wore away. "I can get my assistant, Henaowe, to show you." He pointed to a small Indian.

Nathan was surprised to see the man was Yanomamo.

"He was the only one of the tribe who remained behind," Garcia said with a sigh. "At least the love of our Lord Jesus was able to save one of them."

The padre waved his assistant over and spoke rapidly in Yanomamo. Nathan was surprised at how fluent the priest was in the dialect.

Henaowe nodded, agreeing, but Nathan saw the fear in his eyes. Saved or not, deep-seated superstitions still ruled the man.

The group proceeded back outside, the damp heat falling upon them like a wet wool blanket. They skirted around the helicopters to find the Rangers had been busy. A line of rucksacks, heavily packed, lay in the dirt. A Ranger was positioned behind each one.

Captain Waxman was inspecting both his men and their gear. He spotted the group and straightened. "We're ready to head out whenever you give the go." Waxman, in his forties, was pure military: stone-faced, broad-shouldered, his field uniform crisp with pressed creases. Even his brown hair had been shaved to a stubble atop his head.

"We're ready now," Frank said. "We've got someone here to set us on the right trail." He nodded to the small Indian.

The captain nodded and turned sharply. "Load up!" he called to his men.

Kelly led their group to another row of backpacks, each about half the size of the Rangers' rucksacks. There, Nathan found the last members of the expedition. Anna Fong was in deep conversation with Richard Zane, both in matching khaki outfits with the Tellux logo emblazoned on the shoulders. To their side stood Olin Pasternak, sporting a clean but clearly well-worn set of gray coveralls with black boots. He bent down to pick up the largest of the packs. Nate knew it contained their satellite communication gear. But as he hoisted the pack, the man's attention was not on the fragile gear, but on the expedition's final member . . . or rather *members*.

Nate smiled. He had not seen Manny since they had left from São Gabriel. The Brazilian biologist had been on one of the other Hueys. The reason for the separate flight was clear. Manny waved to Nate, a whip in one hand, the other holding a leather leash.

"So how did Tor-tor handle the flight?" Nathan asked.

Manny patted the two-hundred-pound jaguar with the side of his whip. "Like a kitten. Nothing like the wonders of modern chemistry."

Nathan watched the cat wobble a little from the aftereffects of the tranquilizer. Stretching forward to sniff at Nate's pant leg, Tor-tor seemed to recognize his scent, and nuzzled him half drunkenly.

"The big fellow's always had a thing for you," Manny said with a chuckle.

Nate bent to one knee and rubbed the cat's jowls, cuffing him lightly under the chin. This earned him a growled purr of appreciation. "God, he is so much bigger than the last time I saw him."

Olin Pasternak scowled at the beast, then mumbled under his breath and turned away, clearly unimpressed by the newest addition to the team.

Nathan straightened. Tor-tor's inclusion had been a hard sell, but Manny had persisted. Tor-tor was close to being sexually mature and needed to log more jungle time. This trek would be of benefit to the cat. Additionally, the jaguar had been well trained by Manny and could prove of use—both in protection and in tracking.

Nathan had added his own support. If the team wished to convince any Indians into cooperating, the presence of Tor-tor could go a long way toward winning them over. The jaguar was revered by all Indians. To have one accompany the expedition would give the team instant validity.

Anna Fong had agreed.

Slowly Frank and Captain Waxman had been worn down, and Tor-tor was allowed to join the expedition.

Kelly eyed the cat from a safe distance. "We should gear up."

Nathan nodded and picked up his own small pack. It contained only the essential supplies: hammock, mosquito netting, a bit of dry rations, a change of clothes, machete, water bottle, and filter pump. He could travel months in the jungle with little else. What with the wealth of the forest readily available—from various fruits and berries to roots and edible plants to abundant game and fish—there was little need to haul additional food.

Still, there was one other essential piece of equipment. Nathan hooked his own short-barreled shotgun over a shoulder. Though the team was backed by the Rangers' weaponry, Nate preferred to have a little firepower of his own.

"Let's get going," Kelly said. "We've already lost the morning putting out the fires." The slender woman hefted her own pack to her shoulders, and Nate couldn't help but stare at her long legs. He forced his gaze upward. Her pack had a large red cross printed on its back, marking the team's medical supplies.

Frank ran down the line of civilian team members, making sure all was in readiness. He stopped in front of Nate, pulled out a faded baseball cap from a back pocket, and tugged it in place.

Nate recognized it as the same one from when he had first seen the man at São Gabriel's hospital. "Fan?" he asked, pointing to the Boston Red Sox logo.

"And a good-luck charm," Frank added, then turned to the group. "Let's set out!"

In short order, the eighteen-man team tromped into the jungle, led for the moment by a small, wide-eyed Indian.

Kelly had never been in a jungle. In preparation for this trip, she had scanned books and articles, but the first sight of the rain forest was not what she had expected.

As she followed the four Rangers in the lead, she craned around in wonder. Contrary to old movies, the understory of the Amazon rain forest was not a clotted mass of clinging vines and overgrown vegetation. Instead, it was more like they were marching through a green cathedral. A dense canopy of woven tree branches arched overhead, absorbing most of the sunlight and casting everything in a greenish glow. Kelly had read that less than 10 percent of the sun's light pierced through the unbroken green tent to reach the jungle floor. Because of this, the lowest level of the forest, where they walked now, was surprisingly clear of vegetation. Here the jungle was a world of shadow and decomposition, the domain of insects, fungi, and roots.

Still, the lack of green vegetation didn't necessarily make trekking through the pathless forest an easy journey. Rotted logs and branches lay everywhere, frosted with yellow mold and white mushrooms. Under her boots, a slick mulch of decaying black leaves threatened her footing, while buttress roots that supported the gigantic trees in the thin soil snaked under the leaves and added to the risk of a twisted ankle.

And though the vegetation down at this level was scant, it was not nonexistent. The floor was festooned with fan-tailed ferns, thorny bromeliads, graceful orchids, and slender palms, and everywhere around were draped the ubiquitous ropelike vines called lianas.

The sound of a slap drew her attention around.

Her brother rubbed at his neck. "Damn flies."

Kelly reached into a pocket and passed a plastic bottle of insect repellent to Frank. "Put more on."

He doused his exposed limbs and rubbed some on his neck.

Nathan stepped beside her. He had donned an Australian bush hat, and looked like some cross between Indiana Jones and Crocodile Dundee. His blue eyes sparkled with amusement in the jungle gloom. "You're wasting your time with that repellent," he said to Frank. "Anything you put on will be sweated off your skin in minutes."

Kelly couldn't argue with that. After just fifteen minutes of trekking, she felt damp everywhere. The humidity under the canopy had to be close to a hundred percent. "Then what do you suggest for the bugs?"

Nathan shrugged, wearing a crooked grin. "You surrender. You ignore them. It's a battle you can't win. Here it's an eat-or-be-eaten world, and sometimes you have to simply pay the price."

"With my own blood?" Frank asked.

"Don't complain. That's getting off cheap. There are much worse insects out there, and I don't just mean the big ones, like bird-eating spiders or footlong black scorpions. It's the little ones that'll get you. Are you familiar with the assassin bug?"

"No, I don't think so," Frank said.

Kelly shook her head, too.

"Well, it has the unpleasant habit of biting and defecating at the same time. Then when the victim scratches the wound, he drives the feces loaded with the protozoan *Tripanozoma crusii* into the bloodstream. Then in anywhere from one to twenty years you die due to damage to the brain or heart."

Frank paled and stopped scratching at the fly bite on his neck.

"Then there are the blackflies that transmit worms to the eyeball and cause a disease called river blindness. And sand flies that can trigger Leishmaniasis, a leprosy type of disease."

Kelly frowned at the botanist's attempt to shake her brother. "I'm well familiar with the transmittable diseases out here. Yellow fever, dengue fever, malaria, cholera, typhoid." She hiked her medical pack higher on her shoulders. "I'm prepared for the worst."

"And are you prepared for the candiru?"

Her brow crinkled. "What type of disease is that?"

"It's not a disease. It's a common little fish in the waters here, sometimes called the toothpick fish. It's a slender creature, about two inches long, and lives parasitically in the gills of larger fish. It has the nasty habit of swimming up the urethras of human males and lodging there."

"Lodging there?" Frank asked, wincing.

"It spreads its gill spines and embeds itself in place, blocking the bladder and killing you most excruciatingly in about twenty-four hours."

"How do you get rid of it?"

By now, Kelly had recognized the little fish's description and nasty habits. She had indeed read about them. She turned to her brother and said matter-of-factly, "The only cure is to cut the victim's penis off and extract the fish."

Frank flinched, half covering himself. "Cut his penis off?"

Nate shrugged. "Welcome to the jungle."

Kelly scowled at him, knowing the man was only trying to spook them. But from his grin, she could tell it was mostly all in good fun.

"Then there are the snakes . . ." Nate continued.

"I think that's enough," Professor Kouwe said behind them, rescuing the siblings from Dr. Rand's further lecturing. He stepped forward. "While the jungle must be respected as Nathan has suggested so eloquently, it's as much a place of beauty as danger. It contains the ability to cure as well as sicken."

"And that's why we're all out here," a new voice said behind them.

Kelly turned. It was Dr. Richard Zane. Over his shoulder, she noticed Anna Fong and Olin Pasternak deep in conversation. And beyond them, Manuel Azevedo stalked with his jaguar alongside the Rangers at the rear.

She turned around and saw that the grin on Nate's face had vanished. His expression had hardened at the intrusion by the Tellux representative. "And what would you know of the jungle?" Nate asked. "You've not set foot out of the main offices of Tellux in Chicago in over four years . . . about the time my father vanished, as I recall."

Richard Zane rubbed his small trimmed goatee and maintained his casual countenance, but Kelly had not missed the flash of fire in the man's eyes. "I know what you think of me, Dr. Rand. It was one of the reasons I *volunteered* for this expedition. You know I was a friend of your—"

Nathan took a fast step in the man's direction, one hand balled into a fist. "Don't say it!" he spat out. "Don't say you were a *friend* of my father! I came to you, begged you to continue the search after the government stopped. And you refused. I read the memo you dispatched from Brasília back to the States: 'I see no further benefit in extending Tellux's financial resources in a futile search for Dr. Carl Rand. Our monies are better spent in new endeavors.' Do you remember those words, words that damned my father! If you had pressed the corporate office—"

"The result would've been the same," Zane said between clenched teeth. "You were always so naive. The decision was made long before I gave my report."

"Bullshit," Nathan said.

"Tellux was hit by over three hundred separate lawsuits after the expedition's disappearance. From families, from underwriters, from insurance companies, from the Brazilian government, from the NSF. Tellux was under assault from all sides. It was one of the reasons we had to merge Eco-tek's assets. It helped insulate us from other rapacious pharmaceutical companies. They were circling like sharks around our financially bleeding carcass. We could not continue funding a search that seemed hopeless. We had a bigger fight on our hands."

Nathan continued to glower.

"The decision *had* already been made."

"You'll excuse me if I don't shed tears for Tellux."

"If we had lost our battle, thousands of families would have lost their jobs. Hard decisions had to be made, and I won't apologize for them."

Nate and Zane continued to stare each other down.

Professor Kouwe attempted to mediate. "For now, let the past lie in the past. If we're to succeed here, I suspect we'll all need to work together. I suggest a truce."

After a pause, Zane held out a hand.

Nathan glanced to the open palm, then turned away. "Let's go."

Zane shook his head and lowered his hand. He met the professor's eyes. "Thanks for trying."

Kouwe watched Nate's departing back. "Give him time. Though he tries to hide it, he's still in a lot of pain."

Kelly stared after Nathan. He walked stiffly, shoulders back. She tried to imagine losing her mother, then her father, but it was a loss she could not comprehend. It was a well of pain from which she didn't know if she could have emerged. Especially alone.

She glanced to her brother, suddenly glad he was here.

A call rang out from far ahead. One of the Rangers. "We've reached the river!"

As the team continued along, paralleling the river, Nathan found himself lagging behind the others. To his right, glimpses of the river peeked from the tangle of vegetation that bordered the small brown tributary. They had been following it now for almost four hours. Nathan estimated they had traveled about twelve miles. The going was slow while one of the Rangers, a corporal named Nolan Warczak, a skilled tracker, kept them on the proper trail.

An Indian guide could have moved with more assurance and set a faster pace. But after reaching the tributary, the small Yanomamo tribesman from Wauwai had refused to go any farther. He had pointed to clear footprints in the loam that led deeper into the forest, following the watercourse.

"You go," he had mumbled in stilted Portuguese. "I stay here with Padre Batista."

So they had set off, determined to cover as much distance as possible before nightfall. But Corporal Warczak was a cautious tracker, proceeding at a snail's pace. This left much time for Nathan to review his heated outburst with Richard Zane. It had taken him this long to cool off and consider the man's words. Maybe he had been narrow-minded and had not considered all the factors involved.

Off to his left, the crackle of dead twigs announced Manny's approach. He and Tor-tor had kept a bit of distance between themselves and the rest. When the large cat was nearby the Rangers were edgy, fingering their M-16s. The only one of the unit who showed curiosity about the jaguar was Corporal Dennis Jorgensen. He accompanied Manny now, asking questions about the cat.

"So how much does he eat in a day?" The tall corporal took off his slouch hat and swiped the sweat from his brow. He had shockingly white hair and pale blue eyes, clearly of some Nordic descent.

Manny patted the cat. "Somewhere around ten pounds of meat, but he's been living a pretty sedentary life with me. Out in the wild, you almost have to double that amount."

"And how are you going to keep feeding him out here?"

Manny nodded to Nathan as he joined him. "He'll have to hunt. It was the reason I brought him along."

"And if he fails?"

Manny glanced to the soldiers behind them. "There's always other sources of meat."

Jorgensen's face paled a bit, then realized Manny was joking and nudged him with an elbow. "Very funny." He fell back to join the others in his unit.

Manny turned his attention to Nate. "So how're you holding up? I heard about that row with Zane."

"I'm fine," he said with a long sigh. Tor-tor nudged his leg with a furry muzzle, and Nate scratched the jaguar behind the ear. "Just feeling damn foolish."

"Nothing to feel foolish about. I trust that guy about as far as it would take Tor-tor to run his sorry ass down. Which, believe me, wouldn't be far." He pointed a hand forward. "Did you see that dandy outfit he's wearing? Has he ever been in the real jungle?"

Nate smiled, cheered by his friend.

"Now that Dr. Fong. She looks damn fine in her outfit." Manny glanced to him with one eyebrow raised. "I wouldn't kick her out of my hammock for eating crackers. And Kelly O'Brien—"

A commotion ahead interrupted Manny. Voices were raised, and the group was stopped, gathered near a bend in the river. Manny and Nate hurried forward.

As Nate stepped into the throng, he found Anna Fong and Professor Kouwe bent near a dugout canoe that had been pulled fully onto the bank and clumsily covered with palm fronds.

"The trail led here," Kelly said.

Nathan glanced at her. The doctor's face, covered in a sheen of sweat, was almost aglow. Her hair had been pulled back with a rolled green hand-kerchief that served as a headband.

Professor Kouwe stood with a palm frond in his hand. "These were torn from a *mwapu* palm." He flipped to show the ragged end of the branch. "Not cut, torn."

Kelly nodded. "Agent Clark had no knives with him when he was found."

Professor Kouwe ran a finger along the dried and yellowing tips of the fronds. "And from the rate of decay, this was torn from the living plant around two weeks ago."

Frank bent closer. "Around the time when Gerald Clark stumbled into the village."

"Exactly."

Kelly's voice grew excited. "Then there's no doubt he must have used this boat to get here."

Nathan stared out at the small river. Both banks were thick with dense walls of vegetation: vines, palms, bushes, mosses, stranglers, and ferns. The river itself was about thirty feet across, a featureless silty brown flow. Near the shores, the waters were clear enough to see the muddy, rocky riverbed, but within a few feet visibility vanished.

Anything could be lurking under the water: snakes, caimans, piranhas. There were even catfish so large that they were known to bite the feet off unsuspecting swimmers.

Captain Waxman shoved forward. "So where do we go from here? We can airlift boats to our position, but then what?"

Anna Fong raised a hand. "I think I might be able to answer that." She shoved off more of the palm fronds. Her small fingers ran along the inside of the canoe. "From the pattern in which this canoe was chopped, and from the painted red edges, this had to come from a Yanomamo tribe. They're the only ones who construct canoes in such a manner."

Nate knelt down and ran his own hands along the interior of the canoe. "She's right. Gerald Clark must have obtained or perhaps stolen this canoe from the tribe. If we travel upriver, we can ask any of the Yanomamo Indians if they've seen a white man pass through or if any of their canoes have gone missing." He turned to Frank and Kelly. "From there, we can begin tracking again."

Frank nodded and turned to Captain Waxman. "You mentioned boats."

He nodded sharply. "I'll radio in our position and have the Hueys airlift in the pontoons. It'll eat up the remaining daylight, so we might as well set up an early camp for today."

With a plan in place, everyone began to busy themselves setting up their homestead a short distance from the river. A fire was started. Kouwe collected a few hogplums and sawari nuts from the nearby forest, while Manny, after sending Tor-tor into the jungle to hunt, used a pole and net to catch a few jungle trout.

Within the course of the next hour, the roar of helicopters rattled the forest, causing birds and monkeys to screech and holler, flitting and leaping through the canopy. Three large crates were lowered into the water and pulled to shore by ropes. Packed inside were self-inflating pontoons with small outboard motors, what the Rangers called "rubber raiders." By the time the sun had begun to set, the three black boats were tethered to shoreside trees, ready for tomorrow's travel.

As the Rangers worked, Nathan had set up his own hammock and was now skillfully stretching his mosquito netting around it. He saw Kelly having trouble and went to her aid.

"You want to make sure the netting is spread so that none of it touches the hammock, or the night feeders will attack you right through the fabric."

"I can manage," she said, but her brow was furrowed in frustration.

"Let me show you." He used small stones and bits of forest flotsam to pin her netting away from her hammock, creating a silky canopy around her bed.

Off to the side, Frank was fighting his own netting. "I don't know why we can't just use sleeping bags. They were fine whenever I went camping."

"This is the jungle," Nate answered. "If you sleep on the ground, you'll find all sorts of nasty creatures sharing your bed by morning. Snakes, lizards, scorpions, spiders. But be my guest."

Frank grumbled but continued to wrestle with his own bed site. "Fine, I'll sleep in the damn hammock. But what's so important about the netting anyway? We've been plagued by mosquitoes all day."

"At night, they're a thousand times worse. And if the bugs don't bleed you dry, the vampire bats will."

"Vampire bats?" Kelly asked.

"They're all over the place here. At night, you want to be careful even sneaking off to the latrine. They'll attack anything warm-blooded."

Kelly's eyes grew wide.

"You're vaccinated against rabies, right?" he asked.

She nodded slowly.

"Good."

She glanced over the bed he had helped make, then turned to him, her face only inches from his as he straightened from his crouch. "Thanks."

Nathan was again struck by her eyes, an emerald green with a hint of gold. "Y . . . You're welcome." He turned to the fire and saw that others were gathering for an early evening meal. "Let's see what's for dinner."

Around the campfire, the flames were not the only thing heating up. Nathan found Manny and Richard Zane in midargument.

"How could you possibly be against placing constraints on the logging industry?" Manny said, stirring his filleted fish in the frying pan. "Commercial logging is the single largest destroyer of rain forests worldwide. Here in the Amazon we're losing one acre of forest every *second*."

Richard Zane sat on a log, no longer wearing his khaki jacket. His sleeves were rolled up, seemingly ready to fight. "Those statistics are greatly exaggerated by environmentalists. They're based on bad science and generated more by a desire to scare than to educate. More realistic evidence from satellite photography shows that ninety percent of the Brazilian rain forest is still intact."

Manny was near to blustering now. "Even if the rate of deforestation is exaggerated as you claim, whatever is lost is lost forever. We're losing over a hundred species of plants and animals every single day. Lost forever."

"So you say," Richard Zane said calmly. "The idea that a cleared rain forest can't grow back is an outdated myth. After eight years of commercial logging in the rain forests of Indonesia, the rate of recovery of both native plants and animals far exceeded expectations. And here in your own forests, the same is true. In 1982, miners cleared a large tract of forest in western Brazil. Fifteen years later, scientists returned to find that the rejuvenated forest is virtually indistinguishable from the surrounding forest. Such cases suggest that sustainable logging is possible, and that man and nature can coexist here."

Nate found himself drawn into the discussion. *How can the jackass actually advocate rain forest destruction?* "What about peasants burning forestland for grazing and agriculture? I suppose you support that, too."

"Of course," Zane said. "In the forests of western America, we think it's healthy for fires to burn periodically through a mature forest. It shakes things up. Why is it any different here? When dominant species are removed by either logging or burning, it allows for the growth of what are termed 'suppressed species,' the smaller shrubs and plants. And it is in fact these very plants that are of the most medicinal value. So why not allow a little burning and logging? It's good for all concerned."

Kelly spoke into the stunned silence. "But you're ignoring the global implications. Like the greenhouse effect. Aren't the rain forests the proverbial 'lungs of the planet,' a major source of oxygen?"

" 'Proverbial' is the key word, I'm afraid," Zane said sadly. "Newest research from weather satellites shows that the forests contribute little if any to the world's oxygen supply. It's a closed system. While the greenery of the canopy produces abundant oxygen, the supply is totally consumed by the fire of decomposition below, resulting in no net oxygen production. Again, the only real areas of positive production are in those regions of secondary forest growth, where new young trees are producing abundant oxygen. So in fact, controlled deforestation is beneficial to the world's atmosphere."

Nathan listened, balanced between disbelief and anger. "And what of those who live in the forest? In the past five hundred years, the number of indigenous tribes has dwindled from over ten million to under two hundred thousand. I suppose that's good, too."

Richard Zane shook his head. "Of course not. That's the true tragedy here. When a medicine man dies without passing on his experience, then the world loses great volumes of irreplaceable knowledge. It's one of the reasons I kept pushing for funds to finance your own research among the fading tribes. It's invaluable work."

Nathan narrowed his eyes with suspicion. "But the forest and its people are intertwined. Even if what you say is true, deforestation does destroy some species. You can't argue against that."

"Sure, but the green movement exaggerates the true number lost."

"Still, even a single species can be significant. Such as the Madagascan periwinkle."

Zane's face reddened. "Well, that surely is a rare exception. You can hardly think that such a discovery is common."

"The Madagascan periwinkle?" Kelly asked, confusion in her eyes.

"The rosy periwinkle of Madagascar is the source of two potent anti-cancer drugs—vinblastine and vincristine."

Kelly's brows rose with recognition. "Used in the treatment of Hodgkin's disease, lymphomas, and many childhood cancers."

Nate nodded. "These drugs save thousands of children every year. But the plant that generated this life-saving drug is now extinct in Madagascar. What if these properties of the rosy periwinkle hadn't been discovered in time? How many children would have needlessly died?"

"Like I said, the periwinkle is a rare finding."

"And how would you know? With all your talk of statistics and satellite photography, it comes down to one fact. Every plant has the potential to cure. Each species is invaluable. Who knows what drug could be lost through unchecked deforestation? What rare plant could hold the cure to AIDS? To diabetes? To the thousands of cancers that plague mankind?"

"Or perhaps even to cause limbs to regenerate?" Kelly added pointedly.

Richard Zane frowned and stared into the flames. "Who can say?"

"My point exactly," Nate finished.

Frank stepped up to the flames, seemingly oblivious to the heated debate that had been waged over the campfire. "You're burning the fish," the tall man said, pointing to the black smoke rising from the forgotten frying pan.

Manny chuckled and pulled the pan off the fire. "Thank goodness for the practical Mr. O'Brien, or we'd be eating dry rations tonight."

Frank nudged Kelly. "Olin almost has the satellite feed hooked to the laptop." He checked his watch. "We should be able to connect stateside in another hour."

"Good." Kelly glanced over to where Olin Pasternak was busy around a compact satellite dish and computer equipment. "Perhaps we'll have some answers from the autopsy on Gerald Clark's body. Something that will help."

Nate listened. Maybe it was because he was staring into the flames, but he had a strange foreboding that maybe they all should have heeded the Yanomamo shaman and burned the man's body. As Richard Zane has said just a moment ago, the Indians were wiser than anyone in the ways and dark paths of the jungle. *Na boesi, ingi sabe ala sani.* In the jungle, the Indian knows everything.

He glanced to the darkening forest as the sun sank away.

Here, with the jungle awakening in a chorus of echoing hoots and lonely calls, the myths of the deep forest gained substance and form. Anything could be possible in the lost tracts of the jungle.

Even the curse of the Ban-ali.

FIVE

Stem Cell Research

AUGUST 7, 5:32 P.M.

INSTAR INSTITUTE, LANGLEY, VIRGINIA

Lauren O'Brien sat hunched over her microscope when the call came from the morgue. "Damn it," she mumbled at the interruption. She straightened, slipped her reading glasses from her forehead to the bridge of her nose, and hit the speaker phone.

"Histology here," she said.

"Dr. O'Brien, I think you should come down and see this." The voice belonged to Stanley Hibbert, the forensic pathologist from Johns Hopkins and a fellow member of MEDEA. He had been called in to consult on the post mortem of Gerald Clark.

"I'm somewhat busy with the tissue samples. I've just started reviewing them."

"And was I right about the oral lesions?"

Lauren sighed. "Your assessment was correct. Squamous cell carcinoma. From the high degree of mitosis and loss of differentiation, I'd grade it a type one malignancy. One of the worst I've ever seen."

"So the victim's tongue had *not* been cut out. It had rotted away from the cancer."

Lauren suppressed a nonprofessional shudder. The dead man's mouth had been rank with tumors. His tongue had been no more than a friable bloody stump, eaten away by the carcinoma. And this was not the extent of the man's disease. During the autopsy, his entire body was found to be riddled with cancers in various stages, involving lungs, kidneys, liver, spleen, pancreas. Lauren glanced to the stack of slides prepared by the histology lab, each containing sections of various tumors or bone marrow aspirates.

"Any estimate of the onset of the oral cancer?" the pathologist asked.

"It's hard to say with certainty, but I'd estimate it started between six to eight weeks ago."

A whistle of appreciation sounded over the line. "That's damn fast!"

"I know. And so far, most of the other slides I've reviewed show a similar high degree of malignancy. I can't find a single cancer that looks older than three months." She fingered the stack before her. "But then again, I've still got quite a few slides to review."

"What about the teratomas?"

"They're the same. All between one to three months. But—"

Dr. Hibbert interrupted. "My God, it makes no sense. I've never seen so many cancers in one body. Especially teratomas."

Lauren understood his consternation. Teratomas were cystic tumors of the body's embryonic stem cells, those rare germ cells that could mature into any bodily tissue: muscle, hair, bone. Tumors of these cells were usually only found in a few organs, such as the thymus or testes. But in Gerald Clark's body, they were everywhere—and that wasn't the oddest detail.

"Stanley, they aren't just terato*mas*. They're terato*carcinomas*."

"What? All of them?"

She nodded, then realized she was on the phone. "Every single one of them." Teratocarcinomas were the malignant form of the teratoma, a riotous cancer that sprouted a mix of muscle, hair, teeth, bone, and nerves. "I've never seen such samples. I've found sections with partly formed livers, testicular tissue, even ganglia spindles."

"Then that might explain what we found down here," Stanley said.

"What do you mean?"

"Like I said when I first called, you really should come and see this for yourself."

"Fine," she said with an exasperated sigh. "I'll be right down."

Lauren ended the connection and pushed away from the microscope table. She stretched the kink out of her back from the two hours spent stooped over the slides. She considered calling her husband, but he was surely just as busy over at CIA headquarters. Besides, she'd catch up with him in another hour when they conferenced with Frank and Kelly in the field.

Grabbing her lab smock, Lauren headed out the door and descended the stairs to the institute's morgue. A bit of trepidation coursed through her. Though she was a doctor and had worked as an ER clinician for ten years, she still grew queasy during gross necropsies. She preferred the clean histology suite to the morgue's bone saws, stainless steel tables, and hanging scales. But she had no choice today.

As she crossed down the long hall toward the double doors, she distracted herself with the mystery of the case. Gerald Clark had been missing for four years, then walked out of the jungle with a new arm, undoubtedly a miraculous cure. But contrarily, his body had been ravaged by tumors, a cancerous onslaught that had started no more than three months prior. So why the sudden burst of cancer? Why the preponderance of the monstrous teratocarcinomas? And ultimately, where the hell had Gerald Clark been these past four years?

She shook her head. It was too soon for answers. But she had faith in modern science. Between her own research and the fieldwork being done by her children, the mystery would be solved.

Lauren pushed into the locker room, slipped blue paper booties over her shoes, then smeared a dab of Vicks VapoRub under her nose to offset the smells and donned a surgical mask. Once ready, she entered the lab.

It looked like a bad horror movie. Gerald Clark's body lay splayed open like a frog in biology class. Half the contents of his body cavities lay either wrapped in red-and-orange hazardous-waste bags or were resting atop steel scales. Across the room, samples were being prepped in both formaldehyde and liquid nitrogen. Eventually Lauren would see the end result as a pile of neatly inscribed microscope slides, stained and ready for her review, just the way she preferred it.

As Lauren entered the room, some of the stronger smells cut through the mentholated jelly: bleach, blood, bowel, and necrotic gases. She tried to concentrate on breathing through her mouth.

Around her, men and women in bloody aprons worked throughout the lab, oblivious to the horror. It was an efficient operation, a macabre dance of medical professionals.

A tall man, skeletally thin, lifted an arm in greeting and waved her over. Lauren nodded and slipped past a woman tilting a hanging tray and sliding Gerald Clark's liver into a waste bag.

"What did you find, Stanley?" Lauren asked as she approached the worktable.

Dr. Hibbert pointed down, his voice muffled by his surgical mask. "I wanted you to see this before we cut it out."

They stood at the head of the slanted table holding Gerald Clark's body. Bile, blood, and other bodily fluids flowed in trickles to the catch bucket at the other end. Closer at hand, the top of Gerald Clark's skull had been sawed open, exposing the brain beneath.

"Look here," Stanley said, leaning closer to the purplish brain.

With a thumb forceps, the pathologist carefully pulled back the outer meningeal membranes, as if drawing back a curtain. Beneath the membranes, the gyri and folds of the cerebral cortex were plainly visible, traced with darker arteries and veins.

"While dissecting the brain from the cranium, we found this."

Dr. Hibbert separated the right and left hemispheres of the cerebrum. In the groove between the two sections of the brain lay a walnut-size mass. It seemed to be nestled atop the corpus callosum, a whitish channel of nerves and vessels that connected the two hemispheres.

Stanley glanced at her. "It's another teratoma . . . or maybe a teratocarcinoma, if it's like all the others. But watch this. I've never seen anything like this." Using his thumb forceps, he touched the mass.

"Dear God!" Lauren jumped as the tumor flinched away from the tip of his forceps. "It . . . it's moving!"

"Amazing, isn't it? That's why I wanted you to see it. I've read about this property of some teratomic masses. An ability to respond to external stimuli. There was one case even of a well-differentiated teratoma that had enough cardiac muscle to beat like a heart."

Lauren finally found her voice. "But Gerald Clark's been dead for two weeks."

Stanley shrugged. "I imagine, considering where it's located, that it's rich with nerve cells. And a good portion of them must still be viable enough to respond weakly to stimulation. But I expect this ability will quickly fade as the nerves lose juice and the tiny muscles exhaust their reserve calcium."

Lauren took a few deep breaths to collect her thoughts. "Even so, the mass must be highly organized to develop a flinch reflex."

"Undoubtedly . . . quite organized. I'll have it sectioned and slides assembled ASAP." Stanley straightened. "But I thought you'd appreciate personally seeing it in action first."

Lauren nodded. Her eyes shifted from the tumor in the brain to the corpse's arm. A sudden thought rose in her mind. "I wonder," she mumbled.

"What?"

Lauren pictured how the mass had twitched. "The number of the teratomas and the mature development of this particular tumor could be clues to the mechanism by which Clark's arm grew back."

The pathologist's eyes narrowed. "I'm not following you."

Lauren faced him, glad to find something else to stare at than the ravaged body. "What I'm saying is—and this is just a conjecture, of course—what if the man's arm is just a teratoma that grew into a fully functioning limb?"

Stanley's brows rose high. "Like some form of controlled cancer growth? Like a living, functioning tumor?"

"Why not? That's pretty much how we all developed. From one fertilized cell, our bodies formed through rapid cellular proliferation, similar to cancer. Only this profusion of cells differentiated into all the proper tissues. I mean, isn't that the goal of most stem cell research? To discover the mechanism for this controlled growth? What causes one cell to become a bone cell and its neighbor a muscle cell and the one after that a nerve cell?" Lauren stared at the splayed corpse of Gerald Clark, not in horror any longer but in wonder. "We may be on our way to answering that very mystery."

"And if we could succeed in discovering the mechanism . . ."

"It would mean the end of cancer and would revolutionize the entire medical field."

Stanley shook his head and swung away, returning to his bloody work. "Then let's pray your son and daughter succeed in their search."

Lauren nodded and retreated back across the morgue. She checked her watch. Speaking of Frank and Kelly, it was getting close to the designated conference call. Time to compare notes. Lauren glanced back one last time to the ruin that was left of Gerald Wallace Clark. "Something's out in that jungle," she mumbled to herself. "But what?"

Kelly stood off from the others, trying her best to assimilate the news her mother had reported. She stared out into the jungle, serenaded by the endless chorus of locusts and river frogs. Firelight failed to penetrate more than a few yards into the shadowed depths of the forest. Beyond the glow, the jungle hid its mysteries.

Closer at hand, a group of Rangers knelt, setting up the camp's perimeter motion-sensor system. The laser grid, rigged a few feet off the ground and established between the jungle and the camp, was meant to keep any large predator from wandering too near without being detected.

Kelly stared beyond their labors to the dark forest.

What had happened to Agent Clark out there?

A voice spoke near her shoulder, startling her. "Gruesome news indeed."

Kelly glanced over and found Professor Kouwe standing quietly at her side. How long had he been there? Clearly the shaman had not lost his innate abilities to move noiselessly across the forest floor. "Y . . . Yes," she stammered. "Very disturbing."

Kouwe slipped out his pipe and began stoking it with tobacco, then lit it with a fiery flourish. The pungent odor of smoky tobacco welled around them. "And what of your mother's belief that the cancers and the regenerated arm might be connected?"

"It's intriguing . . . and perhaps not without merit."

"How so?"

Kelly rubbed the bridge of her nose and gathered her thoughts. "Before I left the States to come here, I did a literature search on the subject of regeneration. I figured it might better prepare me for anything we find."

"Hmm . . . very wise. When it comes to the jungle, preparation and knowledge can mean the difference between life and death."

Kelly nodded and continued with her thoughts, glad to express them aloud and bounce them off someone else. "While conducting this research, I came across an interesting article in the *Proceedings of the National Academy of Sciences*. Back in 1999, a research team in Philadelphia raised a group of mice with damaged immune systems. The mice were to be used as a model to study multiple sclerosis and AIDS. But as they began working with the immune-compromised creatures, an odd and unexpected phenomenon developed."

Kouwe turned to her, one eyebrow raised. "And what was that?"

"The researchers had punched holes in the mice's ears, a common way of marking test animals, and discovered that the holes healed amazingly fast, leaving no trace of a wound. They had not just scarred over, but had regenerated cartilage, skin, blood vessels, even nerves." Kelly let this news sink in, then continued. "After this discovery, the lead researcher, Dr. Ellen Heber-Katz, tried a few experiments. She amputated a few mice's tails, and they grew back. She severed optic nerves, and they healed. Even the excision of a section of spinal cord grew back in less than a month. Such phenomenal regeneration had never been seen in mammals."

Kouwe removed his pipe, his eyes wide. "So what was causing it?"

Kelly shook her head. "The only difference between these healing mice and ordinary mice was their defective immune systems."

"And the significance?"

Kelly suppressed a grin, warming to the subject, especially with such an astute audience. "From the study of animals with the proven ability to regenerate limbs—starfish, amphibians, and reptiles—we do know their immune systems are rudimentary at best. Therefore, Dr. Heber-Katz hypothesized that eons ago, mammals made an evolutionary trade-off. To defend against cancers, we relinquished the ability to regenerate bodily limbs. You see, our complex immune systems are designed specifically to eliminate inappropriate cell proliferation, like cancers. Which is beneficial, of course, but at the same time, such immune systems would also block a body's attempt to regenerate a limb. It would treat the proliferation of poorly differentiated cells necessary to grow a new arm as cancerous and eliminate it."

"So the complexity of our immune systems both protect and damn us."

Kelly narrowed her eyes as she concentrated. "Unless something can safely turn off the immune system. Like in those mice."

"Or like in Gerald Clark?" Kouwe eyed her. "You're suggesting something turned off his immune system so he was able to regenerate his arm, but this phenomenon also allowed multiple cancers to sprout throughout his body."

"Perhaps. But it has to be more complicated than that. What's the mechanism? Why did all the cancers arise so suddenly?" She shook her head. "And more important, what could trigger such a change?"

Kouwe nodded toward the dark jungle. "If such a trigger exists, it might be found out there. Currently three-quarters of all anticancer drugs in use today are derived from rain forest plants. So why not one plant that does the opposite—one that *causes* cancer?"

"A carcinogen?"

"Yes, but one with beneficial side effects . . . like regeneration."

"It seems improbable, but considering Agent Clark's state, anything might be possible. Over the next few days, at my request, the MEDEA researchers will be investigating the status of Gerald Clark's immune system and examining his cancers more closely. Maybe they'll come up with something."

Kouwe blew out a long stream of smoke. "Whatever the ultimate answer is, it won't come from a lab. Of that I'm certain."

"Then from where?"

Instead of answering, Kouwe simply pointed the glowing bowl of his pipe toward the dark forest.

Hours later, deeper in the forest, the naked figure crouched motionless in the murk of the jungle, just beyond the reach of the firelight. His slender body had been painted with a mix of ash and *meh-nu* fruit, staining his skin in a complex pattern of blues and blacks, turning him into a living shadow.

Ever since first dark, he had been spying upon these outsiders. Patience had been taught to him by the jungle. All *teshari-rin*, tribal trackers, knew success depended less on one's actions than on the silence between one's steps.

He maintained his post throughout the night, a dark sentinel upon the camp. As he crouched, he studied the giant men, stinking with their foreignness, while they circled around and around the site. They spoke in strange tongues and bore clothing most odd.

Still, he watched, spying, learning of his enemy.

At one point, a cricket crawled across the back of his hand as his palm rested in the dirt. One eye watched the camp, while the other watched the small insect scratch its hind legs together, a whisper of characteristic cricket song.

A promise of dawn.

He dared wait no longer. He had learned all he could. He rose smoothly to his feet, the motion so swift and silent that the cricket remained on the back of his steady hand, still playing its last song of the night. He raised the hand to his lips and blew the surprised insect from its perch.

With a final glance to the camp, he fled away into the jungle. He had been trained to run the forest paths without disturbing a single leaf. None would know he had passed.

Moreover, the tracker knew his ultimate duty.

Death must come to all but the Chosen.

SIX

The Amazon Factor

AUGUST 11, 3:12 P.M.

AMAZON JUNGLE

Nate kept one finger fixed to his shotgun's trigger, the muzzle pointed ahead. The caiman had to be almost twenty feet long. It was a huge specimen of *Melanosuchus niger*, the black caiman, the king of the giant crocodilian predators of the Amazon rivers. It lay atop the muddy bank, sunning in the midafternoon heat. Black armored scales shone dully. Its maw gaped slightly open. Jagged yellow teeth, longer than Nate's own palm, lined the cavity. Its bulging, ridged eyes were solid black, cold and dead, the eyes of a prehistoric monster. Stone still, it was impossible to tell if the great beast even acknowledged the trio of approaching boats.

"Will it attack?" Kelly whispered behind him.

Nate shrugged without looking back. "They're unpredictable. But if we leave it alone, it should leave us alone."

Nate crouched in the prow of the middle pontoon boat. He shared the craft with the two O'Briens, Richard Zane, and Anna Fong. A single soldier, Corporal Okamoto, manned the small outboard engine in the boat's stern. The stocky Asian corporal had developed the habit of whistling almost nonstop, which after four days of motoring up the wide tributary had grown to be excruciating. But at least the giant monster lounging on the bank had squelched the man's tuneless noise.

Ahead, the lead boat puttered past the beast, sticking close to the opposite shore. The starboard pontoon bristled with M-16s, all pointing toward the black caiman.

Each boat held a complement of six team members. The lead boat carried three soldiers and the rest of the civilians: Professor Kouwe, Olin Pasternak, and Manny, who lounged with his pet jaguar in the center of the boat. Tor-tor had been on boats before and seemed to enjoy this means of transportation, tail lazily flicking, ears pricked for noises, eyes mostly in a half-lidded drowse.

The rear boat held the other six Rangers, anchored by Captain Waxman.

"They should just shoot the damn thing," Frank said.

Nate glanced to the man. "It's an endangered species. In the last century, they were poached to near extinction. Only lately have their numbers grown."

"And why does this news not please me?" Frank muttered, glancing to the waters around them. He tugged the bill of his baseball cap lower as if he were trying to hide behind it.

"The caimans kill hundreds every year," Zane mumbled, hunched down beside his pontoon. "They've swamped boats, attacking anything. I read about a black caiman found dead with two outboard motors in its belly, swallowed whole. I'm with Mr. O'Brien. A few well-placed shots . . ."

By now, the lead boat was past the beast's sunning spot, and Nate's boat followed next, moving slowly against the sludgy current as it passed the caiman, motor rumbling.

"Marvelous," Nate said. He faced the creature, no farther away than thirty yards. It was monstrous, a creature from another time. "It's bloody beautiful."

"A male, isn't it?" Anna Fong asked, staring avidly.

"From the ridge lines and shape of the nostrils, I'd agree."

"Shh!" Frank hissed at them.

"It's moving!" Kelly yelped, shifting from her seat to the far side of the boat. She was quickly followed by Richard Zane.

The armored head swung slowly, now following their boat.

"It's waking up," Frank said.

"It was never asleep," Nate corrected as they glided safely past. "It's just as curious about us as we are about it."

"I'm sure as hell *not* curious," Frank said, clearly glad to be past the monster. "In fact, it can just kiss my hairy—"

The giant caiman suddenly lunged, lightning quick, diving smoothly across the slick mud to vanish under the brown water. The third boat had just been drawing abreast of it. A few shots were fired by the soldiers aboard. But the crocodile's speed and sudden movement had caught them all by surprise. It was already gone by the time the few shots peppered the muddy bank.

"Stop!" Nate called out. "It's just running!" With nothing to protect, the caiman's first reaction was to flee from the unknown—that is, unless aroused . . . or threatened.

One of the Rangers, a tall black corporal named Rodney Graves, stood halfway up in the boat, searching the waters, gun pointed. "I don't see—"

It happened fast. The rear boat jarred about three feet in the air. Nate caught the barest glimpse of the thick scaled tail. The soldier who had been standing tumbled headfirst into the water. The others grabbed rubber handholds and held tight. The boat slammed back to the river.

Captain Waxman crouched by the outboard motor. "Graves!"

The fallen corporal suddenly popped out of the water, ten meters downstream from the trio of boats, carried by the current. The man's hat was gone, but he still had his gun. He began to kick and swim toward the nearest boat.

Behind him, like a submarine rising, the head of the caiman crested the waters, its eyes two periscopes.

The Rangers scrambled to bring their weapons to bear. But before a single shot was fired, the caiman had sunk away again.

Nate imagined the giant creature slashing its thick tail, sweeping through the muddy depths toward the kicking soldier, drawn by the man's thrashing. "Damn it," he said under his breath, then yelled with all his lungs. "Corporal Graves! *Don't move!* Stop kicking!"

He was not heard. By now, everyone was yelling for the man to hurry. His panicked thrashing grew worse. Captain Waxman motored the boat backward, trying to meet the frantic swimmer.

Nate yelled again, "Stop swimming!" Finally, more in frustration at not being heard than any true bravery, Nate tossed his gun aside and dove into the river. He glided smoothly, eyes open. But the murky depths hid everything beyond a few feet. He gave one solid kick and sweep of his arms, then simply let his momentum and the current propel him forward. Under the water, he heard the motor of the rear boat pass off to the left.

Arching up, his head broke the surface. Rodney Graves was only a yard to his right. "Corporal Graves! Quit kicking! You've gotta play dead." Nate kept his own limbs unmoving. He half floated on his back.

The soldier turned to him, his eyes wide with panic. "Fuck . . . that!" he screamed between gasping breaths. He continued to thrash and kick. The rescue boat was now only three yards away. Already others were stretching out to grab him up.

Nate sensed movement nearby, a sudden surge against the current. It swept between him and the corporal. Something large and swift.

Oh, God . . .

"Graves!" he cried out one last time.

One of the Rangers—Nate recognized him as the swimmer's brother, Thomas Graves—leaned far over the pontoon. He was supported by two others holding his belt. Tom lunged out with both arms, straining with every muscle in his body, his face a mask of fear for his brother.

Rodney kicked and reached, fingers scrambling out.

Tom caught his hand. "Got him!" he yelled. The muscles of his forearm bulged like corded iron.

The two soldiers yanked Tom back as he hauled Rodney forward. With his free arm, Tom snatched a handful of his brother's soaked field jacket for extra purchase, then fell backward, yanking his brother over the pontoon.

Rodney flew up out of the water, landing belly-first onto the pontoon. He laughed in relief. "Goddamn crocodile!"

He twisted to pull his feet out of the water when giant jaws, already gaped wide open, shot out of the water and swallowed both booted legs up to his thighs. The jaws clamped over their captured prey, then fell back into the river. The ton of armored beast could not be fought. Rodney was torn out of his brother's hands, a cry on his lips.

Rodney disappeared under the water, but his last scream echoed over the river. Soldiers, on their knees, had rifles pointed toward the river, but no one shot. Any blind round could take out their fellow unit member rather than the caiman. Yet from their expressions, Nate knew they all understood the truth. Corporal Rodney Graves was gone. They all had seen the size of the monster, had seen the jaws snap him away.

And Nate knew they were right.

The caiman would take its prey deep and merely hold it clamped until the waters drowned its victim. Then it would either eat or store the body in the submerged mangrove roots where it would rot and be easier to tear apart.

There was no way to rescue the man.

Nate remained floating in the water, keeping his limbs still. The caiman was probably content with its meal, but where there was one, there might be other predators, especially once the blood flowed down the current. He took no chances. He rolled to his back and floated quietly until he felt hands grab him and haul him back aboard the boat.

He found himself staring into the stricken face of Tom Graves. The corporal was staring at his hands, as if blaming them for not being strong enough to hold his brother.

"I'm sorry," Nate said softly.

The man glanced up, and Nate was shocked to see the flash of anger in the man's eyes, *anger* that Nate had survived, *anger* that his brother had been taken instead. Tom turned away stiffly.

Another of the unit was not so reticent. "What in God's name were you trying to do?" It was Captain Waxman, his face almost purple with rage. "What sort of asinine stunt was that? You trying to get yourself killed, too?"

Nate swept the wet locks of hair out of his eyes. It was the second time in a week he had dived into the Amazon's waters to rescue someone. Without doubt, it was becoming a bad habit. "I was trying to help," he mumbled.

The fire in Captain Waxman's voice burned down to dull coals. "We were sent to protect *you*. Not the other way around."

By now, Nate's own boat had drawn abreast of the Rangers'. He clambered over the pontoons to resume his original seat.

Once settled, Captain Waxman waved an arm for them to continue forward. The pitch of the motors rose.

Nathan heard a protest raised by Tom Graves. "Captain . . . my brother . . . his body."

"Gone, Corporal. He's gone."

So the trio of boats continued on. Nate caught Professor Kouwe's gaze across the waters from the other boat. Kouwe shook his head sadly. In the jungle, no amount of military training or arsenal could completely protect you. If the jungle wanted you, it was going to take you. It was called the Amazon Factor. All who traveled the mighty green bower were at the jungle's mercy and whim.

Nate felt a touch on his knee. He turned and saw Kelly seated beside him. She sighed, staring forward, then spoke. "That was a stupid thing to do. It really was, but"—she glanced at him—"I'm glad you tried."

After the sudden tragedy, Nate didn't have the strength to muster more than a simple nod, but her words helped warm the cold hollowness inside him. She took her hand from his knee.

The rest of the day's journey was made in silence. There was no more whistling by Corporal Okamoto as he manned the craft's outboard motor. They traveled until the sun was near the horizon, as if trying to put as much distance as possible between them and the death of Rodney Graves.

As the camp was prepared, the news was passed back to the base at Wauwai. The somber mood stretched through a dinner of fish, rice, and a platter of jungle yams Professor Kouwe had found near the campsite.

The only topic of discussion was the sugary yams. Nathan had asked from where such an abundance had come. "It's unusual to find so many plants." The professor had returned with an efficiently constructed backpack of palm leaves filled to the brim with wild yams.

Kouwe nodded toward the deeper forest. "I suspect the site where I found these was an old Indian garden. I saw a few avocado trees and stumpy pineapple plants in the same area."

Kelly straightened with a fork half-raised. "An Indian garden?"

For the past four days, they had not encountered a single soul. If Gerald Clark had obtained his canoe from a Yanomamo village, they had no clue where he got it.

"It was long abandoned," Kouwe said, dashing the hope that had briefly shone in Kelly's eyes. "Such sites dot the riverways throughout the Amazon. Tribes, especially the Yanomamo, are nomadic. They plant gardens, stay a year or two, then move on. I'm afraid a garden's presence here does not mean anything significant."

"Still, it's at least something," Kelly said, refusing to dismiss this bit of hopeful news. "Some sign that others are out there."

"And besides, these yams are damn good," Frank added, munching a mouthful. "I was already getting sick of the rice."

Manny grinned, running his fingers through his jaguar's ruff. Tor-tor had feasted on a large catfish and lay stretched by the fire.

The Rangers had set up a second campfire a short distance away. At sunset, they held a short service for their fallen comrade. Now they were sullen. Only a few muttered words were shared among them. It was unlike the previous nights when the soldiers were full of ribald jokes and loud guffaws before settling to their own hammocks and posts. Not this night.

"We should all get to sleep," Kelly finally said, pushing to her feet. "We have another long day tomorrow."

With murmured assents and a few groans, the party dispersed to their separate hammocks. When returning from the latrine, Nate found Professor Kouwe smoking near his hammock.

"Professor," Nate said, sensing Kouwe wanted to speak to him in private.

"Walk with me a moment. Before the Rangers activate the motion sensors." The shaman led the way a short distance into the forest.

Nate followed. "What is it?"

Kouwe simply continued until they were deep within the jungle's gloom. The camp's two fires were only greenish glows through the bushes. He finally stopped, puffing deeply on his pipe.

"Why did you bring me out here?"

Kouwe flicked on a small flashlight.

Nate stared around. The jungle ahead was clear of all but a few trees: short breadfruit palms, oranges, figs. Bushes and low plants covered the forest floor, unnaturally dense. Nate realized what he was seeing. It was the abandoned Indian garden. He even spotted a pair of bamboo poles, staked among the plantings and burned at the top. Normally these torches were filled with *tok-tok* powder and lit during harvest times as a smoky repellent against hungry insects. Without a doubt, Indians had once labored here.

Nate had seen other such cultivations during his journeys in the Amazon, but now, here at night, with the patch overgrown and gone wild, it had a haunted feeling to it. He could almost sense the eyes of the Indian dead watching him.

"We're being tracked," Kouwe said.

The words startled Nate. "What are you talking about?"

Kouwe led Nate into the garden. He pointed his flashlight toward a passion fruit tree and pulled down one of the lower branches. "It's been picked bare." Kouwe turned to him. "I'd say about the same time as when we were hauling and securing the boats. Several of the plucked stems were still moist with sap."

"And you noticed this?"

"I was watching for it," Kouwe said. "The past two mornings, when I've gone off to gather fruit for the day's journey, I noticed some places that I'd walked the night before had been disturbed. Broken branches, a hogplum tree half empty of its fruit."

"It could be jungle animals, foraging during the night."

Kouwe nodded. "I thought so at first, too. So I kept silent. I could find no footprints or definite proof. But now the regularity of these occurrences has convinced me otherwise. Someone is tracking us."

"Who?"

"Most likely Indians. These are their forests. They would know how to follow without being seen."

"The Yanomamo."

"Most likely," Kouwe said.

Nate heard the doubt in the professor's voice. "Who else could it be?"

Kouwe's eyes narrowed. "I don't know. But it strikes me as odd that they would not be more careful. A true tracker would not let his presence be known. It's almost too sloppy for an Indian."

"But you're an Indian. No white man would've noticed these clues, not even the Army Rangers."

"Maybe." Kouwe sounded unconvinced.

"We should alert Captain Waxman."

"That's why I pulled you aside first. Should we?"

"What do you mean?"

"If they are Indians, I don't think we should force the issue by having an Army Ranger team beating the bushes in search of them. The Indians, or whoever is out there, would simply vanish. If we wish to contact them, maybe we should let them come to us. Let them grow accustomed to our strangeness. Let them make the first move rather than the other way around."

Nate's first instinct was to argue against such caution. He was anxious to forge ahead, to find answers to his father's disappearance after so many years. Patience was hard to swallow. The wet season would begin soon. The rains would start again, washing away all hopes of tracking Gerald Clark's trail.

But then again, as he had been reminded today by the caiman's attack, the Amazon was king. It had to be taken at its own pace. To fight, to thrash, only invited defeat. The best way to survive was to flow with the current.

"I think it's best if we wait a few more days," Kouwe continued. "First to see if I'm correct. Maybe you're right. Maybe it's just jungle animals. But if I'm right, I'd like to give the Indians a chance to come out on their own, rather than scare them away or force them here at gunpoint. Either way, we'd get no information."

Nate finally conceded, but with a condition. "We'll give it another two days. Then we tell someone."

Kouwe nodded and flicked off his flashlight. "We should be getting to bed."

The pair hiked the short distance back to the glowing campfires. Nate pondered the shaman's words and insight. He remembered the way Kouwe's eyes had narrowed, questioning if it was Indians out there. *Who else could it be?*

Arriving back at the site, Nate found most of the camp already retired to their hammocks. A few soldiers patrolled the perimeter. Kouwe wished him good night and strode to his own mosquito-netted hammock. As Nate kicked out of his boots, he heard a mumbled moan from Frank O'Brien in a nearby hammock. After today's tragedy, Nate expected everyone would have troubled dreams.

He climbed into his hammock and threw an arm over his eyes, blocking out the firelight. Like it or not, there was no fighting the Amazon. It had its own pace, its own hunger. All you could do was pray you weren't the next victim. With this thought in mind, it was a long time until sleep claimed Nate. His final thought: Who *would* be next?

———

Corporal Jim DeMartini was quickly growing to hate this jungle. After four days traveling the river, DeMartini was sick of the whole damned place: the eternal moist air, the stinging flies, the gnats, the constant screams of monkeys and birds. Additionally, closer to home, mold seemed to grow on everything—on their clothes, on their hammocks, on their rucksacks. All his gear smelled like sweaty gym socks abandoned in a locker for a month. And this was after only *four* days.

Pulling patrol, he stood in the woods near the latrine, leaning on a tree, his M-16 resting comfortably in his arms. Jorgensen shared this shift with him but had stopped to use the latrine. From only a few yards away, DeMartini could hear his partner whistling as he zipped down.

"Fine time to take a shit," DeMartini groused.

Jorgensen heard him. "It's the damn water . . ."

"Just hurry it up." DeMartini shook out a cigarette, his mind drifting back to the fate of his fellow unit member Rodney Graves. DeMartini had been in the lead boat with a few of the civilians, but he had been close enough to see the monstrous caiman rise out of the river and rip Graves from the other boat. He gave an involuntary shudder. He was no plebe. He had seen men die before: gunshots, helicopter crashes, drowning. But nothing compared to what he had witnessed today. It was something out of a nightmare.

Glancing over his shoulder, he cursed Jorgensen. *What's taking the bastard so long?* He took a deep drag on the cigarette. *Probably jerking off.* But then again, he couldn't blame Jorgensen if he was. It was distracting with the two women among them. After setting up camp, he had covertly spied upon the Asian scientist as she had stripped out of her khaki jacket. Her thin blouse beneath had been damp from sweat and clung invitingly to her small breasts.

He shoved back these thoughts, ground out his smoke, and stood straighter. In the dark, the only light came from the flashlight taped on the underside of his rifle. He kept it pointed forward, toward the nearby river.

Deeper in the woods, past the laser motion sensors, small lights winked and flitted. Fireflies. He had been raised in southern California, where there were no such insects. So the blinking of the bugs kept him further on edge. The flashes kept drawing his eye, while around him the jungle sighed with the rustle of leaves. Larger branches creaked like old men's joints. It was as if the jungle were a living creature and he was swallowed inside it.

DeMartini swung his light all around. He firmly believed in the buddy system—and even more so right now in this cursed black jungle. There was an old adage among the Rangers: *The buddy system is essential to survival—it gives the enemy somebody else to shoot at.*

Slightly spooked for his buddy's company, he called back to the latrine. "C'mon, Jorgensen!"

"Give me half a break," his partner snapped irritably from a few yards away.

As DeMartini turned back around, something stung his cheek. He slapped at the insect, squashing it under his palm. An even fiercer sting struck his neck, just under the line of his jaw. Grimacing, he reached to brush the fly or mosquito away, and his fingers touched something still clinging to his neck. Startled, he batted it away in horror.

"What the fuck!" he hissed, stepping back. "Goddamn bloodsuckers!"

Jorgensen laughed from nearby. "At least you aren't bare-assed!"

Staring around the jungle with distaste, he pulled the collar of his jacket higher, offering less of a target to the bloodthirsty insects. As he turned, the splash of his flashlight revealed something bright in the mud at his feet. He bent to pick it up. It was a tied bunch of feathers around a pointed dart. The tip was wet with blood, his own blood.

Shit!

He dropped into a crouch and opened his mouth to shout a warning, but all that came out was a silent gurgle. He tried to take a deep breath but realized he couldn't seem to get his chest to move. His limbs grew leaden. Suddenly weak, he fell onto his side.

Poisoned . . . paralyzed, he realized with panic.

His hand still had enough motor control to scrabble like a spider over the stock of his rifle, struggling to reach the trigger. If he could fire his M-16 . . . warn Jorgensen . . .

Then he sensed someone standing over him, watching him from the dark jungle. He couldn't turn his head to see, but the prickle of some primal instinct sent warnings through his body.

Further panicked, he strained for the M-16's trigger, praying, wordlessly begging. His finger finally reaching the trigger guard. If he could have gasped, he would have done so in relief. As darkness blackened the edges of his sight, he fed all his remaining energy into his single finger—and pulled the trigger.

Nothing happened.

In despair, he realized the rifle's safety was still on. A single tear of defeat rolled down his cheek as he lay in the mud. Paralyzed, he could not even close his eyelids.

The lurker finally stepped over his prone body. In the glow of his weapon's light, he saw a sight that made no sense.

It was a woman . . . a naked woman, a sleek creature of wondrous beauty, with long smooth legs, gentle curves leading to full hips, firm and rounded breasts. But it was her large, dark eyes—full of mystery, full of hunger—that held his attention as he slowly suffocated. She leaned over him, a cascading fall of black hair over his slack face.

For a moment, it felt as if she were breathing into him. He felt something course through him, something warm and smoky.

Then he was gone, darkness swallowing him away.

Kelly startled awake. Voices shouted all around her. She sat up too quickly and tumbled out of her hammock, crashing to her knees. "Damn it!" She glanced up.

More branches had been tossed on the two campfires. Flames climbed higher, spreading smoke and a fiery light all around. In the distance, flashlights bobbled through the forests, clearly searching. Shouts and orders echoed out of the jungle.

Gaining her feet, Kelly struggled to find her way through the tangled mosquito netting. She spotted Nate and Manny nearby. Both men were barefooted, dressed in boxers and T-shirts. The large jaguar sat between them. "What's going on?" she called, finally freeing herself of the netting.

The other civilians were now all beginning to gather in various states of undress and confusion. Kelly quickly noticed that all the green canvas hammocks of the Rangers were empty. A single corporal stood between the two fires. His rifle was held at ready.

Nate answered her question, bending down to tug on his boots. "One of the soldiers on patrol has gone missing. We're to stay here until the others secure the area."

"Missing? Who? How?"

"Corporal DeMartini."

Kelly remembered the man: slick black hair, wide nose, eyes that constantly squinted with suspicion. "What happened?"

Nate shook his head. "No one knows yet. He simply vanished."

A sharp shout arose from near the river. Most of the bobbling flashlights converged toward the site.

Professor Kouwe joined them. Kelly noticed an odd look pass between the two men. Something unspoken, something they shared.

Frank suddenly appeared on the far side of the camp. Flashlight in hand, he rushed toward them. He arrived out of breath, the freckles on his cheeks standing out against his ashen face. "We've found the missing man's weapon." His eyes flicked between Nate, Manny, and Kouwe. "You all know more about the jungle than anyone. There's something we could use your opinion about. Captain Waxman has asked for you to come take a look."

The whole group of civilians stepped toward Frank, intending to follow.

He held up a hand. "Just these three."

Kelly pushed forward. "If the man was injured, I may be of help, too."

Frank hesitated, then nodded.

Richard Zane moved to follow, his mouth open to protest, but Frank shook his head. "We don't want the site trampled any more than necessary."

With the matter settled, the group hurried past the fires toward the river. The jaguar kept to its master's side, padding silently with them. They crossed into the dense growth that fringed the tributary. Here was the true mythic jungle: a tangle of vines, bushes, and trees. Single file, the group trekked into the thick growth, approaching the glow of many flashlights ahead.

Kelly followed behind Nate. For the first time, she noticed the spread of his shoulders—and how well he moved through the woods. For such a tall man, he slipped under liana vines and around bushes with a casual ease. She trod in his steps and tried to mimic his moves, but she kept stumbling in the dark.

Her heel slid on something slippery. Her feet went out from under her. She fell sideways, hands out to break her fall.

Then Nate's arms were around her, catching her. "Careful."

"Th . . . thanks." Blushing, she reached toward a vine to pull herself up, but before she could grip it, Nate yanked her away. Only her fingers brushed the vine.

"What are you—*ow!*" Her fingertips began to burn. She rubbed them on her untucked blouse, but the sting grew even worse. It felt as if her fingers were on fire.

"Hold still," Professor Kouwe said. "Rubbing will spread it." He snatched a handful of thick leaves from a slender tree. Crushing them in his hands, he grabbed Kelly's wrist and smeared the oily moisture over her fingers and hand.

Instantly the sting faded. Kelly stared in wonder at the crushed leaves.

"*Ku-run-yeh,*" Nate said behind her. "Of the violet family. A potent analgesic."

Kouwe continued to rub her fingers until the pain was gone.

In the glow of her brother's flashlight, she saw that a couple of blisters had formed on the tips of her fingers.

"Are you okay?" Frank asked.

She nodded, feeling stupid.

"Keep applying the *ku-run-yeh* and you'll heal faster," Kouwe said, giving her arm a fatherly squeeze.

Nate helped her to her feet. He pointed to the grayish vine. "It's named 'fire liana.' And not without reason." The vine draped from a tree and lay tangled near the trunk's base. She would've fallen into the nest of vines if Nate hadn't caught her. "The vine exudes a potent irritant to keep insects away."

"A form of chemical warfare," Kouwe added.

"Exactly." Nate nodded for Frank to continue ahead, then waved an arm. "It's going on all around you all the time here. It's what makes the jungle such a potent medicinal storehouse. The ingenuity and variety of chemicals and compounds waged in this war far outwit anything human scientists could invent in a lab."

Kelly listened, not feeling particularly appreciative of being a casualty in this chemical war.

After a few more yards, they reached the Rangers, gathered in a ring around one section of forest. A couple of men stood off to the side, weapons on their shoulders, night-vision goggles in place over their faces.

Corporal Jorgensen stood at attention before the unit's captain. "Like I said, I was just using the latrine. DeMartini was standing guard by a nearby tree."

"And this?" Captain Waxman held up the butt of a cigarette under the man's nose.

"Okay, I heard him light up, but I didn't think he left. When I zipped and turned around, he was gone. He didn't say a word that he was going to wander over to the river."

"All for a goddamn smoke," Captain Waxman grumbled, then waved an arm. "Dismissed, corporal."

"Yes, sir."

After taking a deep breath, Captain Waxman crossed to them, fire still in his eyes. "I need your expertise on this," he said, his gaze sweeping over Nate, Kouwe, and Manny. Turning, he swung his lights toward an area of trampled jungle grasses. "We found DeMartini's weapon abandoned here, and this stubbed cigarette, but no sign of what happened to his body. Corporal Warczak has searched for any prints leading from here. There aren't any. Just this trampled and shredded area of grasses that leads back to the river."

Kelly saw that the disturbed area did indeed lead all the way to the water's edge. The tall green reeds lining the bank were parted and crushed.

"I'd like to examine this more closely," Professor Kouwe said.

Captain Waxman nodded, passing Kouwe his flashlight.

Nate and Kouwe moved forward. Manny followed, but his pet jaguar stopped at the edge of the area, growling deep in the back of his throat as it sniffed at the grasses.

Hand on his whip, Manny tried to coax the cat to follow. "C'mon, Tortor." The jaguar refused, even retreated a step.

Kouwe glanced back to them. The professor had stopped to crouch at a spot, examining something near the reeds. He sniffed at his fingers.

"What is it?" Nate asked.

"Caiman feces." He wiped his hand clean on some grasses, then nodded to the growling jaguar. "I think Tor-tor agrees."

"What do you mean?" Kelly asked.

Manny answered, "Wild cats have the ability to sense the size of an animal from just the smell of its excrement or urine. In fact, elephant urine is sold throughout the western United States as a repellent against bobcats and cougars. They won't go near a site marked with elephant urine, freaked by the smell of such a huge animal."

Kouwe clambered through the reeds to the river's edge. He was careful to pluck aside a few broken stalks, then waved Captain Waxman over. Kelly followed.

Kouwe shone his light on a spot of muddy bank. Clawed prints were clear in the riverbank mud. "Caiman."

Kelly heard an odd note of relief in Kouwe's voice. Again Nate and the professor shared a secretive glance.

Straightening, Kouwe explained, "Caimans will often hunt the riverbanks, snatching tapir and wild pigs as they come to drink. Your corporal must have come too close to the river and was grabbed."

"Could it be the same one that attacked Corporal Graves?" Waxman asked.

Kouwe shrugged. "Black caimans are fairly intelligent. After learning that our boats are a source of food, it might have followed the rumble of our motors, then lay in wait until nightfall."

"Goddamn that motherfucker!" Waxman spat, a fist clenched. "Two men in one day."

Staff Sergeant Kostos stepped forward. The tall swarthy Ranger wore a tight expression. "Sir, I can call for reinforcements. The Hueys could be here by morning with two more men."

"Do it," he snapped. "And from here on out, I want two patrols every shift. Two men in each patrol! I don't want anyone—civilian or soldier—walking this jungle alone. Ever! And I want the river side of every camp set up with motion sensors, not just the jungle."

"Yes, sir."

Captain Waxman turned to them. There was no warmth in his words, only dismissal. "Thank you for your assistance."

The group wound back through the forest. As they marched, Kelly felt numb. Another man gone . . . so suddenly. She hiked past the nest of fire liana vines and eyed them warily. It wasn't only chemical warfare going on out here, but a savage feeding frenzy, where the strong consumed the weak.

Kelly was glad to reach the campsite with its roaring fires—the warmth, the light. In a small way, the flames were reassuring, temporarily driving back the dark heart of the forest.

She found the eyes of the other teammates upon them. Anna Fong stood with Richard Zane. Frank's fellow operative, Olin Pasternak, stood near the fires, warming his hands.

Manny quickly explained what they had found. As he talked, Anna covered her mouth with her hand and turned away. Richard shook his head. And as usual, Olin remained his stoic self, staring into the flames.

Kelly barely noticed their reactions. Standing by the campfire, her attention remained focused on Nate and Kouwe. The pair had moved to the side, near Nate's hammock. From the corner of her eye, she watched them. No words were exchanged between the two men, but she caught the inquiring look on Kouwe's face. An unspoken question.

Nate answered with a small shake of his head.

With some secret settled between them, Kouwe reached to his pipe and moved a few steps away, clearly needing a moment alone.

Kelly turned, giving the older man his privacy, and found Nate staring at her.

She glanced back to the fires. She felt foolish and oddly frightened. She swallowed and bit her lower lip, remembering the man's strong arms catching her, saving her. She sensed Nate still staring at her, his gaze like the sun's heat on her skin. Warm, deep, and tingling.

Slowly the feeling faded.

What was he hiding?

SEVEN

Data Collection

Lauren O'Brien was going to be late for work. "Jessie!" she called as she nestled an orange beside a peanut-butter-and-jelly sandwich in a lunch box. "Hon, I need you down here . . . *now.*" The day-care center was a twenty-minute drive out of her way, followed by the usual fight through morning traffic into Langley.

She checked her watch and rolled her eyes. "Marshall!"

"We're coming," a stern voice answered.

Lauren leaned around the corner. Her husband was leading their granddaughter down the stairs. Jessie was dressed, though her socks didn't match. *Close enough,* she thought to herself. She had forgotten what it was like to have a child in the house again. Patterns and schedules had to be altered.

"I can take her to day care," Marshall said, reaching the bottom stairs. "I don't have a meeting until nine o'clock."

"No, I can do it."

"Lauren . . ." He crossed and gave her a quick peck on the cheek. "Let me help you."

She returned to the kitchen and snapped shut the lunch box. "You should get into the office as soon as possible." She tried to keep the tension out of her voice.

But Marshall heard it anyway. "Jessie, why don't you get your sweater?"

" 'Kay, Grandpa." The girl skipped toward the front door.

Marshall turned back to Lauren. "Frank and Kelly are fine. If there was any change, we would know it right away."

Lauren nodded, but she kept her back toward him. She did not want Marshall to see the threatening tears. Last night, they had heard about the first Army Ranger being attacked by a crocodile. Then, a few hours past midnight, the phone had rung. From Marshall's tone as he spoke, Lauren had known it was more bad news. A call this late could only mean one thing—something horrible had happened to either Frank or Kelly. She was sure of it. After Marshall had hung up the phone and explained about the second dead soldier, Lauren had cried with selfish relief. Still, deep inside, a seed of dread had been planted that she could not shake. *Two dead . . . how many more?* She had been unable to sleep the rest of the night.

"Another two Rangers are being airlifted to their campsite as we speak. They have plenty of protection."

She nodded and sniffed back tears. She was being foolish. She had spoken with the twins last night. They were clearly shaken by the tragedy, but both were determined to continue onward.

"They're tough kids," Marshall said. "Resourceful and cautious. They're not going to take any foolish chances."

With her back still turned to her husband, she mumbled, "Foolish chances? They're out there, aren't they? That's foolish enough."

Marshall's hands settled on her shoulders. He brushed aside the hair from the back of her neck and kissed her gently. "They'll be fine," he whispered in her ear calmly.

At fifty-four, Marshall was a striking man. His black-Irish hair was going to silver at the temples. He had a strong jaw, softened by full lips. His eyes, a bluish hazel, caught her and held her.

"Kelly and Frank will be fine," he said succinctly. "Let me hear you say it."

She tried to glance down, but a fingertip moved her chin back up.

"Say it . . . please. For me. I need to hear it, too."

She saw the glimmer of pain in his eyes. "Kelly and Frank . . . will be fine." Though her words were muttered, speaking them aloud was somehow reassuring.

"They will be. We raised them, didn't we?" He smiled at her, the pain fading in his eyes.

"We sure did." She slipped her arms around her husband and hugged him.

After a moment, Marshall kissed her on the forehead. "I'll take Jessie to day care."

She didn't object. After giving her grandchild a long hug by the front door, she allowed herself to be guided to her BMW. The forty-minute drive to the Instar Institute was a blur. When she arrived, she was glad to grab her briefcase and head through the cipher-locked doors into the main building. After such a disturbing night, it was good to be busy again, to have something to distract her from her worries.

She crossed to her offices, greeting familiar faces in the hall. The complete immunology report was due today, and she was anxious to test Kelly's theory about an alteration to Gerald Clark's immune status. Preliminary results, coming piecemeal, were not terribly helpful. With the degree of cancerous processes ravaging the body, assessment was difficult.

Reaching her office, Lauren found a stranger standing by her door.

"Good morning, Dr. O'Brien," the man said, holding out a hand. He was no older than twenty-five, slender, with a shaved head, and dressed in blue scrubs.

Lauren, as head of the MEDEA project, knew everyone involved on the research, but not this man. "Yes?"

"I'm Hank Alvisio."

The name rang a bell. Lauren shook his hand while racking her brain.

"Epidemiology," he said, clearly reading her momentary confusion.

Lauren nodded. "Of course, I'm sorry, Dr. Alvisio." The young man was an epidemiologist out of Stanford. She had never met him in person. His field of expertise was the study of disease transmission. "How can I help you?"

He lifted a manila folder. "Something I'd like you to see."

She checked her watch. "I have a meeting with Immunology in about ten minutes."

"All the more reason you should see this."

She unlocked her office door with a magnetic ID card and ushered him inside. Switching on the lights, she crossed to her desk and offered Dr. Alvisio a seat on the other side. "What have you got?"

"Something I've been working on." He fiddled through his folder. "I've turned up some disturbing data that I wanted to run past you."

"What data?"

He glanced up. "I've been reviewing Brazilian medical records, looking for any other cases similar to Gerald Clark's."

"Other people with strange regenerations?"

He grinned shyly. "Of course not. But I was trying to put together an epidemiological assessment of cancers among those living in the Brazilian rain forests, with particular concentration in the area where Gerald Clark died. I thought maybe, by tracking cancer rates, we could indirectly track where the man had traveled."

Lauren sat up. This was an intriguing angle, even ingenious. No wonder Dr. Alvisio had been hired. If he could discover a cluster of similar cancers, then it might narrow the search parameters, which in turn could shorten the time Kelly and Frank would need to trek the jungle on foot. "And what did you find?"

"Not what I expected," he said with a worried look in his eyes. "I contacted every city hospital, medical facility, and jungle field clinic in the area. They've been sending me data covering the past decade. It's taken me this long to crunch the information through my computer models."

"And did you discover any trends in cancer rates in the area?" Lauren asked hopefully.

He shook his head. "Nothing like the cancers seen in Gerald Clark. He seems to be a very unique case."

Lauren hid her disappointment but could not keep a touch of irritation from entering her voice. "Then what did you discover?"

He pulled out a sheet of paper and passed it to Lauren. She slipped on her reading glasses.

It was a map of northwestern Brazil. Rivers snaked across the region, all draining toward one destination—the Amazon River. Cities and towns dotted the course, most sticking close to channels and waterways. The black-and-white map was dotted with small red X's.

The young doctor tapped a few of the marks with the tip of a pen.

"Here are all the medical facilities that supplied data. While working with them, I was contacted by a staff doctor at a hospital in the city of Barcellos." His pen pointed to a township along the Amazon, about two hundred miles upriver from Manaus. "They were having a problem with a viral outbreak among the city's children and elderly. Something that sounded like some form of hemorrhagic fever. Spiking temperatures, jaundice, vomiting, oral ulcerations. They had already lost over a dozen children to the disease. The doctor in Barcellos said he had never seen anything like it and asked for my assistance. I agreed to help."

Lauren frowned, slightly irked. The epidemiologist had been hired and flown here to work specifically and solely on this project. But she kept silent and let him continue.

"Since I already had a network of contacts established in the region, I utilized them, sending out an emergency request for any other reports of this outbreak." Dr. Alvisio pulled out a second sheet of paper. It appeared to be the same map: rivers and red X's. But on this map, several of the X's were circled in blue, with dates written next to them. "These are the sites that reported similar cases."

Lauren's eyes widened. There were so many. At least a dozen medical facilities were seeing cases.

"Do you see the trend here?" Dr. Alvisio said.

Lauren stared, then slowly shook her head.

The epidemiologist pointed to one X with a blue circle. "I've dated each reported case. This is the earliest." He glanced up from the paper and tapped the spot. "This is the mission of Wauwai."

"Where Gerald Clark was found?"

The doctor nodded.

She now recalled reading the field report from the expedition's first day. The Wauwai mission had been razed by superstitious Indians. They'd been frightened after several village children had become inexplicably sick.

"I checked with local authorities," Dr. Alvisio continued. He began to tap down the line of blue-circled X's. "The small steamboat that transported Clark's body stopped at each of these ports." The epidemiologist continued to tap the riverside towns. "Every site where the body passed, the disease appeared."

"My God," Lauren mumbled. "You're thinking the body was carrying some pathogen."

"At first. I thought it was one of several possibilities. The disease could have spread out from Wauwai through a variety of carriers. Almost all transportation through the region is by river, so *any* contagious disease would've followed a similar pattern. The pattern alone wasn't conclusive evidence that the body was the source of the contagion."

Lauren sighed, relieved. "It couldn't be the body. Before being shipped from Brazil, my daughter oversaw the disposition of the remains. It was tested for a wide variety of pathogens: cholera, yellow fever, dengue, malaria, typhoid, tuberculosis. We were thorough. We checked for every known pathogen. The body was clean."

"But I'm afraid it wasn't," Dr. Alvisio said softly.

"Why do you say that?"

"This was faxed this morning." He slid a final paper out of his folder. It was a CDC report out of Miami. "Clark's body was inspected in customs at Miami International. Now three cases of the disease have been reported in local children. All of them from families of airport employees."

Lauren sank into her chair as the horror of the man's words struck her. "Then whatever the disease is, it's here. We brought it here. Is that what you're saying?" She glanced over to Dr. Alvisio.

He nodded.

"How contagious is it? How virulent?"

The man's voice became suddenly mumbled. "It's hard to say with any certainty."

Lauren knew the man, even at such a young age, was a leader in his field or he wouldn't be here. "What is your cursory assessment? You have one, don't you?"

He visibly swallowed. "From the initial study of transmission rates and the disease's incubation period, it's a bug that's a hundredfold more contagious than the common cold . . . and as virulent as the Ebola virus."

Lauren felt the blood drain from her face. "And the mortality rate?"

Dr. Alvisio glanced down and shook his head.

"Hank?" she said hoarsely, her voice hushed with fear.

He lifted his face. "So far no one has survived."

Louis Favre stood at the edge of his camp, enjoying the view of the river at sunrise. It was a quiet moment after a long night. Kidnapping the corporal from under the other camp's nose had taken hours to prepare and execute, but as usual, his team had performed without fail.

After four days, the job of shadowing the other team was reduced to a routine. Each night, runners would slip ahead of the Rangers' team, trekking through the deep jungle to set up spy positions in well-camouflaged roosts in emergent trees that towered above the forest canopy. While spying, they maintained contact with the mercenary team via radio. During the day, Louis and the bulk of his forces followed in a caravan of canoes, trailing ten kilometers behind the others. Only at night had they crept any nearer.

Louis turned from the river and crossed into the deeper wood. Hidden among the trees, the camp was hard to spot until you were on top of it. He stared around while his forty-man team began to break camp. It was a motley group: bronze-skinned Indians culled from various tribes, lanky black Maroons out of Suriname, swarthy Colombians hired from the drug trade. Despite their differences, all the men had one thing in common: they were a hardened lot, marked by the jungle and forged in its bloody bower.

Rifles and guns, wrapped in sailcloth, lay in an orderly spread beside sleeping sites. The armament was as varied as his crew: German Heckler & Koch MP5s, Czech Skorpions, stubby Ingram submachine guns, Israeli-manufactured Uzis, even a few obsolete British Sten guns. Each man had his favorite. Louis's weapon of choice was his compact Mini-Uzi. It had all of the power of its bigger brother but measured only fourteen inches long. Louis appreciated its efficient design, small but deadly, like himself.

In addition to the munitions, a few men were sharpening machetes. The scrape of steel on rock blended with the morning calls of waking birds and barking monkeys. In hand-to-hand combat, a well-turned blade was better than a gun.

As he surveyed the camp, his second-in-command, a tall black Maroon tribesman named Jacques, approached. At the age of thirteen, Jacques had been exiled from his village after raping a girl from a neighboring tribe. The man still bore a scar from his boyhood journey through the jungle. One side of his nose was missing from an attack by a piranha. He nodded his head respectfully. "Doctor."

"Yes, Jacques."

"Mistress Tshui indicates that she is ready for you."

Louis sighed. *Finally.* The prisoner had proven especially difficult.

Reaching into a pocket, Louis pulled free the dog tags and jangled them in his palm. He crossed to the lone tent set near the edge of the camp. Normally the camouflaged tent was shared by Louis and Tshui, but not this past night. During the long evening, Tshui had been entertaining a new guest.

Louis announced himself. "Tshui, my dear, is our visitor ready for company?" He pulled back the flap and bowed his way through the opening.

It was intolerably hot inside. A small brazier was burning in a corner. His mistress knelt naked before the small camp stove, lighting a bundle of dried leaves. Aromatic smoke spiraled upward. She rose to her feet. Her mocha skin shone with a sleek layer of sweat.

Louis stared, drinking her in. He longed to take her then and there, but he restrained himself. They had a guest this morning.

He turned his attention to the naked man staked spread-eagle on the bare-earth floor. The only bit of clothing he wore was a ball gag. Louis kept his eyes diverted from the bloody ruin of the corporal's body.

Still holding the man's dog tags, Louis crossed to a folding camp chair and sat down. He glanced to the name etched on the tags. "Corporal James DeMartini," he said in crisp English, reading the name, then looking up. "I've heard it from good authority that you're ready to cooperate."

The man moaned, tears flowed from his eyes.

"Is that a yes?"

The Ranger, a beaten and tortured dog, nodded with a pained wince. Louis studied the man. *What hurt more,* he wondered, *the torture? Or the actual moment you finally broke?*

With a tired sigh, he pulled the man's gag free. Louis needed information. Over the years, he had learned that the difference between success and failure lay in the details. He had reams of facts on the opposing team—not only information supplied directly by St. Savin, but also timely intelligence gained from a closer source.

Still Louis hadn't been satisfied.

He had kidnapped the young corporal because his other resources had proved woefully lacking in specific details about the Army Ranger unit: their firepower, their radio codes, their timetables. Furthermore, there was always the unspoken military objective, orders meant only for military ears. And last, Louis had arranged the abduction simply as a challenge, a small test of his forces.

The maneuver had gone flawlessly. Equipped with night-vision glasses, a small team had snuck in via the river. Once the chance arose, they had poisoned one of the Rangers with a special curare dart prepared by Tshui. Afterward, they had covered their tracks, setting up a false trail beside the river with caiman dung and prints. His mistress had then kept the kidnapped man alive by breathing mouth-to-mouth until he could be revived back at their camp with a special antidote.

But Tshui's true talents were proven during the long night. Her art of torture was without equal, plying pain and pleasure in a strange hypnotic rhythm until finally her prey's will broke.

"Please kill me," the man begged, hoarse, blood dribbling from his lips.

"Soon enough, *mon ami* . . . but first a few questions." Louis leaned back as Tshui walked around the corporal, waving her smoking bundle of dried leaves through the air. He noticed the broken soldier flinch from the woman, his terrified eyes following her every move.

Louis found this extremely arousing, but he kept himself focused. "Let's first go over a few numbers." Over the next few minutes, he extracted all the codes and time schedules of the army unit. He did not have to write any of it down, setting all the frequencies and numbers to memory. The information would greatly facilitate eavesdropping on the other team's communications. Next, he collected the details on the Ranger force's strength: number and types of weapons, skill levels, weaknesses, means of air support.

The man proved most talkative. He babbled on and on, giving out more information than requested. ". . . Staff Sergeant Kostos has a secret stash of whiskey in his rucksack . . . two bottles . . . and in Captain Wax-man's boat, there's a crate that holds a cradle of napalm minibombs . . . and Corporal Conger has a *Penthouse* mag—"

Louis sat up. "Hold on, monsieur. Let's back up. Napalm bombs?"

"Minibombs . . . an even dozen . . ."

"Why?"

The corporal looked confused.

"James," he said sternly.

"I . . . I don't know. I suppose if we need to clear a section of jungle. Something that blocks our way."

"How large a region would one of those bombs clear?"

"I . . ." The man choked back a sob. "I'm not sure . . . maybe an acre . . . I don't know."

Louis leaned his elbows on his knees. "Are you telling me the truth, James?" He wiggled a finger for Tshui, who had grown bored with the conversation and sat cross-legged, busy laying out a new set of tools.

On his signal, she rose from her work and crawled like some jungle cat toward the naked soldier.

"No," the corporal cried, mewling, "no, I don't know anything more."

Louis shifted back in his seat. "Do I believe you?"

"Please . . ."

"I think I will believe you." Standing, he turned to his mistress. "We're done here, *ma chérie*. He's all yours."

She slid smoothly to her feet, offering a cheek to be kissed as he passed.

"No," the man on the ground moaned, pleading.

"Don't dawdle," he said to Tshui. "The sun is almost up, and we'll need to be under way shortly."

She smiled, smoky and full of hidden lusts. As he stepped to the tent's threshold, he saw her bend down and collect her bone needle and thread from the spread of tools. Lately, Tshui had been trying a new approach in preparing her specimens for head-shrinking. She now liked to sew her victims' eyelids closed while they were yet alive. To better capture their essence, he supposed. The Shuar shamans placed special significance in the eyes, a path to the spirit.

A sharp scream arose behind him.

"Tshui, don't forget the man's gag," Louis scolded. He made the mistake of glancing over his shoulder.

Tshui squatted above the face of Corporal James, her thighs on either side of his head, holding the squirming man in place as she busied herself with her needle and thread. He lifted an eyebrow in surprise. It seemed Tshui was trying something new.

"*Pardon, ma chérie,*" he said, bowing out of the tent. Apparently he had scolded her too soon. The gag truly wasn't necessary.

Tshui was already sewing the corporal's lips shut.

Survival of the Fittest

BRAZIL NUT

FAMILY: *Lecythidaceae*

GENUS: *Bertholletia*

SPECIES: *Excelsa*

COMMON NAMES: *Brazil Nut, Castanheiro do Para, Para-Nut, Creamnut, Castana-de-Para, Castana-de-Brazil*

PARTS USED: *Nut, Seed Oil*

PROPERTIES/ACTIONS: *Emollient, Nutritive, Antioxidant, Insecticide*

EIGHT

Village

Frowning, Nate caught the line and secured it to a mangrove tree. "Careful," he warned his boat mates. "It's swampy here. Watch your footing." He helped Kelly climb over the pontoon and onto the firmest section of the bank. He himself was muddy up to his knees and soaked everywhere else.

He lifted his face to the drizzle of rain from the cloudy skies. A storm had blown in overnight, starting with a fierce downpour, then fading into a steady misty drizzle within the last hour. The day's journey so far had been dreary. They had taken turns with a hand pump to bilge the water out of the boat all morning. Nate was glad when Captain Waxman had called a halt for lunch.

After helping everyone off their boats, Nate climbed the muddy bank onto higher ground. The jungle wept all around him, dripping, sluicing, and trickling from the leafy canopy overhead.

Professor Kouwe seemed unperturbed. With a pack hastily constructed of palm leaves, he was already heading out into the forest to forage for edibles, accompanied by a sodden Corporal Jorgensen. From the sour expression on the soldier's face, the tall Swede seemed little interested in a jungle trek. But Captain Waxman insisted that no one, not even the experienced Kouwe, walk the jungles alone.

Around the camp, the mood of the entire group remained sullen. Word of a possible contagion associated with Gerald Clark's body had reached them yesterday. Quarantines had been set up in Miami and around the institute where the body was being examined. Additionally, the Brazilian government had been informed and quarantine centers were being established throughout the Amazon. So far only children, the elderly, and those with compromised immune systems were at risk. Healthy adults seemed resistant. But much was still unknown: the causative agent, modes of transmission, treatment protocols. Back in the States, a Level Four containment had been set up at the Instar Institute to research these questions.

Nate glanced over to Frank and Kelly. Frank had his arm around his sister. She was still pale. Their entire family, including Kelly's daughter and the families of other scientists and workers at Instar, had been put into quarantine at the institute. No one was showing any symptoms, but the worry etched in Kelly's face was clear.

Nate turned away, giving them their privacy, and continued on.

The only bright spot in the last forty-eight hours was that no additional members of their party had fallen prey to the jungle. After losing Corporal DeMartini two days ago, everyone had kept alert, minding Nate's and Kouwe's warnings about jungle hazards, respecting their native lore. Now, before disembarking from a boat or bathing, everyone checked the shallows for buried stingrays in the mud or hidden electric eels. Kouwe gave lessons on how to avoid scorpions and snakes. No one put on a boot in the morning without first thoroughly shaking it out.

Nate checked the camp, walking the periphery, searching for any other hazards: fire liana, ant nests, hidden snakes. It was the new routine.

He spotted the two new members of the team, replacements for those lost. They were gathering wood. Both were ranked private first class, newly commissioned Rangers: a battle tank of a man with a thick Bronx accent, Eddie Jones, and, surprisingly, a woman, one of the first female Rangers, Maria Carrera. Special Forces had only started accepting women applicants six months before, after an amendment to Title 10 restrictions had passed Congress. But these new female recruits were still limited from front-line combat, assigned to missions like this one.

The morning after the nighttime attack, the two soldiers had been flown in from the field base at Wauwai, sliding down ropes from a hovering Huey. Afterward, small tanks of fuel and additional supplies were lowered.

It was a critical shipment, their last one. From that morning on, the team would be motoring beyond the range of the Hueys, beyond the range of air support. In fact, as of today, they had traveled close to four hundred miles. The only craft with enough range to reach them now was the black Comanche. But the sleek attack helicopter would only be utilized in case of emergency, such as the evacuation of an injured team member or in case an aerial assault was needed. Otherwise from here on out, they were on their own.

Finished with his survey, Nate crossed back to the center of the camp. Corporal Conger was hunched over a pile of twigs. With a match, he was trying to light a pile of dead leaves under a steeple of twigs. A drip of water from overhead doused his flame. "Damn it," the young Texan swore, tossing the match aside in disgust. "Everything's friggin' waterlogged. I could break out a magnesium flare and try to light it."

"Save them," Captain Waxman ordered from a step away. "We'll just make a cold camp for lunch."

Manny groaned from nearby. He was soaked to the skin. The only team member who looked even more dejected was Tor-tor. The jaguar stalked sullenly around its master, fur dripping water, ears drooped. Nothing was more piteous than a wet cat, even a two-hundred-pound one.

"I think I might be able to help," Nate said.

Eyes glanced to him.

"I know an old Indian trick."

He crossed back to the forest, searching for a particular tree he had noted during his survey of the campsite. He was followed by Manny and Captain Waxman. He quickly found the tall tree with characteristic bumpy gray bark. Slipping out his machete, he pierced the bark. A thick rusty resin flowed out. He fingered the sap and held it toward Waxman's nose.

The captain sniffed it. "Smells like turpentine."

Nate patted the tree. "It's called *copal,* derived from the Aztec word for resin, *copalli.* Trees in this family are found throughout the rain forests of Central and South America. It's used for a variety of purposes: healing wounds, treating diarrhea, alleviating cold symptoms. It's even used today in modern dentistry."

"Dentistry?" Manny asked.

Nate lifted his sticky finger. "If you ever had a cavity filled, you have some of this stuff in your mouth."

"And how is this all supposed to help us?" Waxman asked.

Nate knelt and pawed through the decaying leaves at the base of the tree. "Copal is rich in hydrocarbons. In fact, there has been some research recently into using it as a fuel source. Copal poured into a regular engine will run cleaner and more efficiently than gasoline." Nate found what he was searching for. "But Indians have known of this property for ages."

Standing, Nate revealed a fist-sized hardened lump of sap. He speared it atop a sharp stick like a marshmallow. "Can I borrow a match?"

Captain Waxman removed one from a waterproof container.

Nate struck the matchhead on the bark and held the flame to a corner of the resin ball. Immediately it ignited into a bright blue flame. He held it out and marched toward the site of the failed campfire. "Indian hunters have been using this sap for centuries to light campfires during rainstorms. It'll burn for hours, acting as a starter to light wet wood."

Other eyes were drawn to the flame. Frank and Kelly joined the group as Nate settled the flaming resin ball into a nest of leaves and twigs. In a short time, the tinder and wood took the flame. A decent blaze arose.

"Good job," Frank said, warming his hands.

Nate found Kelly staring at him with a trace of a smile. It was her first smile in the past twenty-four hours.

Nate cleared his throat. "Don't thank me," he mumbled. "Thank the Indians."

"We may be able to do just that," Kouwe said suddenly from behind them.

Everyone turned.

The professor and Corporal Jorgensen crossed quickly toward them.

"We found a village," Jorgensen said, his eyes wide. He pointed in the direction that the pair had gone in search of foodstuffs. "Only a quarter mile upstream. It's deserted."

"Or appears to be," Kouwe said, staring significantly at Nate.

Nate's eyes grew wide. *Were these the same Indians who had been secretly dogging their trail?* Hope surged in Nate. With the rainstorm, he had been worried that any trail left by Gerald Clark would be washed away. This storm was but the first to mark the beginning of the Amazonian wet season. Time grew short. *But now . . .*

"We should investigate immediately," Captain Waxman said. "But first, I want a three-man Ranger team to recon the village."

Kouwe raised an arm. "It might be better if we approached less aggressively. By now, the Indians know we're here. I believe that's why the village is deserted."

Captain Waxman opened his mouth to disagree, but Frank held up a hand. "What do you suggest?"

Kouwe nodded to Nate. "Let the two of us go first . . . alone."

"Certainly not!" Waxman blurted. "I won't have you going in unprotected."

Frank took off his Red Sox cap and wiped his brow. "I think we should listen to the professor. Swarming in with heavily armed soldiers will only make the Indians fear us. We need their cooperation. But at the same time, I share Captain Waxman's concern about the two of you going in on your own."

"Then only one Ranger," Nate said. "And he keeps his gun on his shoulder. Though these Indians may be isolated, most are well aware of rifles."

"I'd like to go, too," Anna Fong said. The anthropologist's long black hair lay plastered to her face and shoulders. "A woman among the group may appear less hostile. Indian raiding parties don't bring women with them."

Nate nodded. "Dr. Fong is right."

Captain Waxman scowled, clearly not keen on letting civilians lead the way into an unknown encampment.

"Then perhaps I should be the one to go as their backup." Gazes turned to Private Carrera, the female Ranger. She was strikingly beautiful, a dark-skinned Latina with short-cropped black hair. She faced Captain Waxman. "Sir, if women are viewed as less hostile, I would be best suited for this mission."

Waxman finally agreed grudgingly. "Fine. I'll trust Professor Kouwe's assessment for now. But I want the rest of my forces set within a hundred yards of their position. And I want constant radio contact."

Frank glanced to Nate and Kouwe.

They nodded.

Satisfied, Frank cleared his throat. "Then let's move."

Kelly watched the camp fracture into various units. Nate, Kouwe, Anna Fong, and Private Carrera were already motoring their pontoon boat into the current, while Captain Waxman selected three of his men and led them to a second rubber raider. They would paddle a hundred yards behind the first boat, keeping a safe distance away yet close enough for a rapid response. Additionally, three more Rangers would travel overland with Corporal Jorgensen in command. This team would take up a position a hundred yards from the village. In preparation, they painted their faces in jungle camouflage.

Manny had attempted to join this last party, but he'd been rebuffed by Captain Waxman. "All other civilians stay here."

With the matter settled, Kelly could only watch as the others set off. Two Rangers—the newly arrived Private Eddie Jones and Corporal Tom Graves—remained at the camp as bodyguards. Once the others were launched and on their way, Kelly overheard Jones grumble to Graves, "How did we end up minding the friggin' sheep?"

Corporal Graves did not respond, staring dully into the drizzle, clearly grieving for his brother Rodney.

Alone now, Kelly crossed to Frank's side. As the nominal leader of this operation, her brother had the right to insist on joining either of the departing groups, but he had chosen to remain behind—not out of fear, she knew, but concern for his twin sister.

"Olin has the satellite link hooked up," Frank said, taking his sister under his arm. "We can reach the States when you're ready."

She nodded. Not far from the fire, under a rain tarp, Olin sat hunched before a laptop and a satellite dish. He tapped busily at the keyboard, his face scrunched in concentration. Richard Zane stood over his shoulder watching him work.

Finally, Olin glanced to them and nodded. "All set," he said. Kelly heard the trace of his Russian accent. It was easy to miss unless one's ears were tuned for it. Olin was ex-KGB, once a member of their computer surveillance department before the fall of the communist regime. He had defected to the States only months before the Berlin Wall tumbled. His background in technology and his knowledge of Russian systems earned him a low-level security position in the CIA's Directorate of Science and Technology.

Frank guided Kelly to a camp chair before the laptop computer. Since learning of the contagion, Kelly had insisted they be updated twice daily now. Her excuse was to keep both sides fully apprised, but in reality, she had to know her family was still okay. Her mother, her father, her daughter. All three were at ground zero.

Kelly sat on the camp chair, eyeing Olin askance as he moved aside. She was never fully at ease around the man. Maybe because he was ex-KGB and she had grown up with a father in the CIA. Or maybe it was that ropy scar that stretched from ear to ear across his throat. Olin had claimed to be no more than a Russian computer geek for the KGB. But if that were true, how had he obtained that scar?

Olin pointed to the screen. "We should be uplinked in thirty seconds."

Kelly watched the small timer on the computer screen count downward. When it reached zero, her father's face blinked onto the screen. He was dressed casually, his tie half undone, no jacket.

"You look like a drowned rat" were his first words from the flickering image.

With a small smile, Kelly lifted a hand to her wet hair. "The rains have started."

"So I see." Her father returned her grin. "How are things out there?"

Frank leaned forward into the view. He gave a quick overview of their discovery.

As he talked, Kelly listened to the echoing whine of Nate's boat. The waters here and the overhanging jungle played tricks with acoustics. It sounded like the boat was still nearby, but then the noise suddenly choked off. They must have reached the village already.

"Watch out for your sister, Frank," her father said, finishing their talk.

"Will do, sir."

Now it was Kelly's turn. "How're Mother and Jessie?" she asked, holding her fists clenched in her lap.

Her father smiled reassuringly. "Both in the pink of health. We all are. The entire institute. So far no cases have been reported in the area. Any risk of contamination has been successfully quarantined, and we've converted the west wing of the institute into temporary family housing. With so many MEDEA members here, we've got around-the-clock doctors."

"How's Jessie handling it?"

"She's a six-year-old," he said with a shrug. "At first she was a bit scared at being uprooted. But now she's having a ball with the other staff's children. In fact, why don't you ask her yourself?"

Kelly sat straighter as her daughter's face came into view, a small hand waving. "Hi, Mommy!"

Tears welled. "Hi, sweetheart. Are you having fun?"

Her daughter nodded vigorously, climbing into her grandfather's lap. "We had chocolate cake, and I rode a pony!"

Choking back a laugh, her father spoke over the top of his granddaughter's head. "There's a small farm nearby, in the quarantine zone. They brought a pony over to entertain the kids."

"That sounds like fun, honey. I wish I could've been there."

Jessie squirmed in her seat. "And you know what else? A clown is coming over and is gonna make animal balloons."

"A clown?"

Her father whispered to the side. "Dr. Emory from histopathology. He's damn good at it, too."

"I'm gonna ask him to make me a monkey," Jessie said.

"That's wonderful." Kelly leaned closer, soaking up the view of both her father and her daughter.

After a bit more elaboration on clowns and ponies, Jessie was lifted off her grandfather's knee. "It's time for Ms. Gramercy to take you back to class."

Jessie pouted but obeyed.

"Bye, honey," Kelly called. "I love you!"

She waved again, using her entire arm. "Bye, Mommy! Bye, Uncle Frankie!"

Kelly had to restrain herself from touching the screen.

Once Jessie was gone, her father's face grew grim. "Not all the news is so bright."

"What?" Kelly asked.

"It's why your mother isn't here. While we seem to have things contained, the outbreak in Florida is spreading. Overnight, there's been another six cases reported in Miami hospitals, and another dozen in outlying county hospitals. The quarantine zone is being widened, but we don't think we secured the area in time. Your mother and others are monitoring reports from across the country."

"My God," Kelly gasped.

"In the last twelve hours, the number of cases has now climbed to twenty-two. The fatalities to eight. Scenarios calculated by the best epidemiologists in the country have these numbers doubling every twelve hours. In fact, along the Amazon, the death toll is already climbing toward the five hundred mark."

As Kelly calculated in her head, her face blanched. Frank's hand on her shoulder tightened. In just a few days, the number in the U.S. could climb into the tens of thousands.

"The president has just signed an order to mobilize the National Guard in Florida. The official story is an outbreak of a virulent South American flu. Specifics on how it got here are being kept under wraps."

Kelly leaned back, as if distance would lessen the horror. "Has any protocol for treatment been established?"

"Not as of yet. Antibiotics and antivirals don't seem to be of any help. All we can offer is symptomatic care—intravenous fluids, drugs to combat fever, and pain relievers. Until we know what is causing the disease, fighting it's an uphill battle." Her father leaned closer to the screen. "That's why your work out in the field is so critical. If you can find out what happened to Agent Clark, you may discover a clue to this disease."

Kelly nodded.

Frank spoke, his voice a hoarse whisper. "We'll do our best."

"Then I'd better let you all get back to your work." After a sober goodbye, her father signed off.

Kelly glanced to her brother. She saw that Manny stood to one side of him, Richard Zane to the other.

"What have we done?" Manny asked. "Maybe someone should have listened to that Indian shaman back in Wauwai. Burned Clark's body after he died."

Zane shook his head and mumbled, "It wouldn't have mattered. The disease would've eventually broken out of the forest. It's just like AIDS."

"What do you mean?" Kelly asked, turning in her seat.

"AIDS started after a highway was built into the African jungle. We come disturbing these ancient ecosystems, and we don't know what we stir up."

Kelly pushed out of the camp chair. "Then it's up to us to stop it. The jungle may have produced AIDS, but it also offered our best treatments against the disease. Seventy percent of AIDS drugs are derived from tropical plants. So if this new disease came out of the jungle, why not the cure, too?"

"That's if we can find it," Zane said.

Off to the side, Manny's jaguar suddenly growled. The great cat swung around and crouched, ears pricked, eyes fixed on the jungle behind them.

"What's wrong with him?" Zane asked, backing a step away.

Manny squinted at the shadowed rain forest as Tor-tor continued a deep warning growl. "He's caught a scent . . . something's out there."

Nate crossed down the narrow trail toward the small Indian village, which consisted of a single large roundhouse, open to the sky in the middle. As he approached the structure, he heard none of the usual noises coming from the *shabano*. No arguing *huyas*, no women yelling for more plantains, no laughter of children. It was ghostly quiet and unnerving.

"The construction is definitely Yanomamo," Nathan said softly to Kouwe and Anna Fong. "But small. It probably houses no more than thirty villagers."

Behind them marched Private Carrera, her M-16 held in both hands, muzzle pointed at the ground. She was whispering into her radio's microphone.

Anna stared wide-eyed at the *shabano*.

Nate stopped her from continuing through the roundhouse's small doorway and into the village proper. "Have you ever been among the Yanomamo?"

Anna shook her head.

Nate cupped his mouth. "*Klock, klock, klock*," he yelled. Then softer to Anna, he explained, "Whether it seems deserted or not, you never approach a Yanomamo village without first announcing yourself. It's a good way to get an arrow in your back. They have the tendency to shoot first and ask questions later."

"Nothing wrong with that policy," Carrera mumbled behind him.

They stood near the entrance for a full minute, then Kouwe spoke. "No one's here." He waved an arm behind him. "No canoes by the river, no nets or fishing gear either. No *yebis* squawking in alarm."

"*Yebis?*" their Ranger escort asked.

"The gray-winged trumpeter," Nate said. "Sort of an ugly chicken really. The Indians use them like feathered guard dogs. They raise a ruckus when anyone approaches."

The Ranger nodded. "So no chickens, no Indians." She turned in a slow circle, surveying the forest around them. The woman refused to let down her guard. "Let me go first."

Lifting her weapon higher, she paused near the short entrance. Bowing low, she ducked her head through. After a moment, she slid through the bamboo-framed entrance, sticking close to the banana-leaf wall, then barked to them, "All clear. But stick behind me."

Carrera moved toward the center of the circular structure. She kept her weapon ready, but as Nate had suggested, she kept the rifle's muzzle pointing at the ground. Among the Yanomamo, an arrow nocked and aimed at a fellow tribesman was a call to war. Since Nate didn't know how familiar these particular Indians were with modern weapons, he wanted no misinterpretations on this point.

As a group, Nate, Kouwe, and Anna entered the *shabano*.

Around them, the individual family units were sectioned off from their neighbors by drapes of tobacco leaves, water gourds, and baskets. Woven hammocks, all empty, hung from the roof beams. A pair of stone bowls lay toppled in the central clearing beside a grinding stone, manioc flour spilled onto the dirt.

A sudden burst of color startled them all as a parrot took wing. It had been roosting atop a pile of brown bananas.

"I don't like this," Kouwe said.

Nate knew what he meant and nodded.

"Why?" asked Carrera.

"When the Yanomamo migrate to a new site, they either burn the old *shabano* or at least strip it of all useful items." Kouwe pointed around him. "Look at all these baskets, hammocks, and feather collections. They wouldn't leave these behind."

"What could make them leave so suddenly?" Anna asked.

Kouwe slowly shook his head. "Something must have panicked them."

"Us?" Anna stared around her. "Do you think they knew we were coming?"

"If the Indians had been here, I'm sure they would've been well aware of our approach. They keep a keen watch on their forest. But I don't think it was our party that made them abandon this *shabano* so quickly."

"Why do you say that?" Nate asked.

Kouwe crossed around the edge of the living sites. "All the fires are cold." He nudged the pile of bananas upon which the parrot had been feeding. "They're half rotten. The Yanomamo would not have wasted food like this."

Nate understood. "So you think the village was abandoned some time ago."

"At least a week, I'd estimate."

"Where did they go?" Anna asked.

Kouwe stood in place and turned in a slow circle. "It's hard to say, but there's one other detail that may be significant." He glanced to Nate to see if he had noticed it, too.

Frowning, Nate studied the dwellings. Then it dawned on him. "All the weapons are gone." Among the abandoned wares, there was not a single arrow, bow, club, or machete.

"Whatever spooked them to run," Kouwe said, "they were scared for their lives."

Private Carrera edged closer to them. "If you're right, if this place is long deserted, I should call in my unit."

Kouwe nodded.

She stepped away, mumbling into her radio.

Kouwe silently waved Nate aside so they could speak privately. Anna was busy examining an individual dwelling, picking through the goods left behind.

Kouwe whispered. "It was not these Yanomamo who were tracking our party."

"Then who?"

"Some other group . . . I'm still not sure it was even Indians. I think it's time we informed Frank and Captain Waxman."

"Are you thinking that whatever spooked the Indians is what's now on our trail?"

"I'm not sure, but whatever could frighten the Yanomamo from their homes is something we should be wary of."

By now, the constant drizzle had stopped. The cloud banks began to break apart, allowing cracks of afternoon sunlight to pierce through in dazzling rays. After so long in the misty murk, the light was bright.

In the distance, Nate heard a single engine roar to life. Captain Waxman and his Rangers were coming.

"You're certain we should tell them?" Nate asked.

Before Kouwe could answer, Anna had wandered over. She pointed to the skies off to the south. "Look at all those birds!"

Nate glanced to where she pointed. With the rains dying away, various birds were rising from the canopy to dry their wings and begin the hunt for food again. But a half mile away, a huge flock of black birds rose from the canopy like a dark mist. Thousands of them.

Oh, God. Nate crossed quickly to Private Carrera. "Let me have your binoculars."

The Ranger's eyes were on the strange dance of black birds, too. She unsnapped a compact set of binoculars from her field jacket and passed them to Nate. Holding his breath, he peered through the glasses. It took him a moment to focus on the birds. Through the lenses, the flock broke down to individuals, a mix of large and small birds. Many were fighting among themselves in the air, tearing at each other. But despite their differences, the various birds all shared one common trait.

"Vultures," Nate said, lowering the binoculars.

Kouwe edged nearer. "So many . . ."

"Turkey vultures, yellow-heads, even king vultures."

"We should investigate," Kouwe said. In his eyes, Nate saw the worry shared by all. The missing Indians . . . the vultures . . . It was a dire omen.

"Not until the unit gets here," Private Carrera warned.

Behind them, the roaring of the other boat drew abreast of their location and choked out. In a few minutes, Captain Waxman and another three Rangers were entering the *shabano*. Private Carrera quickly updated the others.

"I've sent the Rangers stationed in the woods back to camp," Captain Waxman said. "They'll gather everyone here. In the meantime, we'll scout what lies out there." He pointed to three of his unit: Private Carrera, Corporal Conger, and Staff Sergeant Kostos.

"I'd like to go with them," Nate said. "I know this jungle better than anyone."

After a short pause, Captain Waxman sighed. "So you've proven." He waved them off. "Keep in radio contact."

As they left, Nate heard Kouwe approach Waxman. "Captain, there is something I think you should be made aware of . . ."

Nate ducked out of the *shabano*'s low door, glad to escape. He imagined Captain Waxman would not be pleased that he and Kouwe had kept hushed about the nighttime prowlers around their campsites. Nate was more than happy to leave such explanations to the diplomatic professor.

Out in the woods, the two men, Conger and Kostos, took the point, leaving Private Carrera to dog Nate's steps and maintain a rear guard.

They half trotted through the wet woods, careful of the slippery mud and dense layers of sodden leaves. A small stream that drained toward the river behind them seemed to be heading in the same direction. They found an old game trail paralleling it and made better time.

Nate noticed footprints along the trail. Old prints almost obscured by the rain. *Barefooted.* He pointed one out to Private Carrera. "The Indians must've fled this way."

She nodded and waved him onward.

Nate pondered this oddity. *If panicked, why flee on foot? Why not use the river?*

The scouting party climbed the trail, following the streambed. Despite the hard pace, Nate kept up with the Rangers in the lead. The forest around them was unusually quiet, almost hushed. It was eerie, and suddenly Nate regretted leaving his shotgun back at camp.

So occupied was he with keeping his footing and watching for any hidden dangers that Nate almost missed it. He stumbled to a stop with a gasp.

Private Carrera almost collided into him. "Damn it. Give some warning."

The other two Rangers, failing to notice the pair had halted, continued up the trail.

"Need a rest?" Carrera asked with a bit of playful disdain.

"No," Nate said, panting heavily to catch his breath. "Look."

Soaked and pinned to a small branch was a scrap of faded yellow material. It was small, half the size of a standard playing card and roughly square. Nathan pulled it free.

"What is it?" Carrera peered over his shoulder. "Something from the Indians?"

"No, not likely." He fingered the material. "It's polyester, I think. A synthetic." He checked the branch upon which the scrap had been impaled. The thin limb had been cut, not naturally broken. As he examined the end, crude markings on the tree's trunk caught his attention. "What's this?"

He reached and brushed rainwater from the trunk. "My God . . ."

"What?"

Nathan stood clear so his escort could see. Deeply inscribed into the bark of the tree's trunk was a coded message.

Private Carrera whistled appreciatively and leaned closer. "This *G* and *C* near the bottom . . ."

"Gerald Clark," Nathan finished her thought. "He signed it. The arrow must indicate where he had come from . . . or at least where his next marker might lie."

Carrera checked her wrist compass. "Southwest. It's pointing the right way."

"But what about the numbers? Seventeen and five."

The Ranger scrunched up her face. "Maybe a date, done the military way. The day, followed by the month."

"That would make it May seventeenth? That's nearly three months ago." Turning, Nate started to question her assessment, but Carrera had a palm raised toward him. Her other hand pressed her radio earpiece more firmly in place.

She spoke into her radio. "Roger that. We're on our way."

Nate raised an inquiring eyebrow.

"Conger and Kostos," she said. "They've found bodies ahead."

Nate felt a sickening lurch in his belly.

"Come on," Carrera said stiffly. "They want your opinion."

Nodding, Nate continued up the trail. Behind him, as they marched, Private Carrera reported their discovery to her captain.

As Nate hurried, he glanced down and realized he still held the bit of faded yellow material. He remembered Gerald Clark had stumbled out of the jungle barefoot, wearing only pants. Had the man used the scraps of his own shirt to flag these sites? Like a trail of bread crumbs back to wherever he had come from?

Nate rubbed the bit of cloth between his fingers. After four years, here was the first tangible bit of proof that at least some of his father's team had survived. Up to this point, Nate had not entertained any hope that his father was still alive. In fact, he had refused even to contemplate that possibility, not after so long, not after coming to some semblance of peace with his father's death. The pain of losing his father a second time would be more than he could handle. Nate stared at the scrap in his hand for a second longer, then stuffed it into a pocket.

As he trekked up the trail, he wondered if there were more such flags out there. Though he had no way of knowing, Nate knew one thing for certain. He would not stop looking, not until he discovered the truth of his father's fate.

Carrera swore behind him.

Nathan glanced back. Carrera had an arm over her nose and mouth. Only then did Nate notice the stench in the air. Rancid meat and offal.

"Over here!" a voice called out. It was Staff Sergeant Kostos. The older Ranger stood only ten yards farther down the trail. In full camouflage, he blended well with the dappled background.

Nate crossed to him and was immediately assaulted by a horrible sight.

"Jesus Christ," Carrera gasped behind him.

Corporal Conger, the young Texan, was farther down the trail, a handkerchief over his face, in the thick of the slaughterhouse. He waved off vultures with his M-16 as swarms of flies rose around him.

Bodies lay sprawled everywhere: on the trail, in the woods, some draped halfway in the stream. Men, women, children. All Indians from the look of them, but it was difficult to say for sure. Faces had been chewed away, limbs gnawed to bone, entrails ripped from bellies. The carrion feeders had made quick work of the bodies, leaving the rest to flies, other insects, and burrowing worms. Only the diminutive sizes of the corpses suggested they were Yanomamo, the missing villagers. And from the number, probably the *entire* village.

Nathan closed his eyes. He pictured the villagers with whom he had worked in the past: little Tama, noble Takaho. With a sudden burst, he rushed off the trail and hunched over the stream. He breathed deeply, fighting in vain the rising gorge. With a sickening groan, his stomach spasmed. Bile splattered into the flowing water, swelled by the recent rains. Nate remained crouched, hands on his knees, breathing hard.

Kostos barked behind him. "We don't have all day, Rand. What do you think happened here? An attack by another tribe?"

Nate could not move, not trusting his stomach.

Private Carrera joined him, placing a sympathetic hand on his shoulder. "The sooner we get this done," she said softly, "the sooner we can leave."

Nathan nodded, took a final deep breath, and forced himself to climb back within view of the slaughter. He studied the area from a few steps away, then moved closer.

"What do you think?" Carrera asked.

Gulping back bile, Nate spoke quietly. "They must've fled during the night."

"Why do you say that?" Kostos asked.

Nate glanced to the sergeant, then nudged a stick near one of the corpses. "A torch. Burned to char at the end. The village took flight in full darkness." He studied the bodies, recognizing a pattern to the carnage. He pointed an arm as he spoke. "When the attack came, the men tried to protect the women and children. When they failed, the women were a second line of defense. They tried to run with the children." Nate indicated a woman's corpse deeper in the woods. In her arms rested a dead child. He turned away.

"The attack came from across the stream," Nate continued. His hand shook as he pointed to the number of male bodies piled near or in the stream. "They must have been caught by surprise. Too late to put up an adequate defense."

"I don't care in what order they were killed," Kostos said. "Who the hell killed them?"

"I don't know," Nate said. "None of the bodies are pierced by arrows or spears. But then again, the enemy might have collected their weapons after the attack—to conserve their arsenal and to leave no evidence behind. With the bodies so torn apart, it's impossible to tell which wounds are from weapons and which from the carrion feeders."

"So in other words, you have no damn clue." Kostos shook his head and swung around. From a few steps away, he spoke into his radio.

Nate wiped his damp forehead and shivered. What the hell *had* happened here?

Finally, Kostos stepped forward, raising his voice. "New orders everyone. We're to collect a body for Dr. O'Brien to examine—one that's chewed up the least—and return it to the village. Any volunteers?"

No one answered, which earned a mean snicker from the sergeant. "Okay," Kostos said. "I didn't think so." He pointed to Private Carrera. "Why don't you take our fragile little doctor back to camp? This is *men's* work."

"Yes, sir." Carrera waved Nate to the path, and together they continued down toward the village. Once out of earshot, Carrera grumbled under her breath. "What an asshole . . ."

Nate nodded, but truthfully, he was only too glad to leave the massacre site. He couldn't care less what Sergeant Kostos might think. But he understood Carrera's anger. Nate could only imagine the hassles the woman had to endure from the all-male force.

The remainder of the journey down the trail was made in silence. As they neared the *shabano,* voices could be heard. Nathan's pace quickened. It would be good to be among the living again. He hoped someone had thought to light a fire.

Circling around the *shabano,* Nathan approached Private Eddie Jones, who stood guard by the entrance. Beyond him, limned against the water, a pair of Rangers was posted by the river.

As he and Carrera reached the roundhouse's door, Eddie Jones greeted them and blurted out the news. "Hey, you guys ain't gonna fuckin' believe what we fished out of the jungle."

"What?" Carrera asked.

Jones thrust a thumb toward the door. "Go see for yourselves."

Carrera waved her rifle's barrel for Nate to go first.

Within the *shabano,* a small congregation was clustered in the roundhouse's open central yard. Manny stood somewhat to the side with Tor-tor. He lifted an arm when he spotted Nate, but there was no greeting smile.

The voices from the others were raised in argument.

"He's my prisoner!" Captain Waxman boomed. He stood with three Rangers, who all had their weapons on their shoulders pointing at someone out of sight behind the group of civilians.

"At least remove the cuffs on his wrists," Kelly argued. "His ankles are still bound. He's just an old man."

"If you want cooperation," Kouwe added, "this is no way to go about it."

"He'll answer our questions," Waxman said with clear menace.

Frank stepped in front of Waxman. "This is still my operation, Captain. And I won't tolerate abuse of this prisoner."

By now, Nate had crossed the yard and joined them. Anna Fong glanced to him, her eyes scared.

Richard Zane stood slightly to the side, a satisfied smirk on his face. He nodded to Nathan. "We caught him lurking in the jungle. Manny's big cat helped hunt him down. You should have heard him screaming when the jaguar had him pinned against a tree."

Zane stepped aside, and Nate saw who had been captured. The small Indian lay in the dirt, his ankles and wrists bound in strips of thick plastic zip ties. His shoulder-length white hair clearly marked him as an elder. He sat before the others, mumbling under his breath. His eyes flicked between the rifles pointed at him and Tor-tor pacing nearby.

Nate listened to his muttered words. *Yanomamo.* He moved closer. It was a shamanic prayer, a warding against evil. Nate realized the prisoner must be a shaman. *Was he from this village? A survivor of the slaughter?*

The Indian's eyes suddenly flicked to Nate, his nostrils flaring. "Death clings to you," he warned, in his native dialect. "You know. You saw."

Nate realized the man must smell the stench of the massacre on his clothes and skin. He knelt nearer and spoke in Yanomamo. "*Haya*. Grandfather. Who are you? Are you from this village?"

He shook his head with a deep scowl. "This village is marked by *shawari*. Evil spirits. I came here to deliver myself to the Ban-ali. But I was too late."

Around Nate, the arguing had stopped as they watched the exchange. Kelly whispered behind him. "He's not spoken a word to anyone, not even Professor Kouwe."

"Why do you seek the Blood Jaguars, the Ban-ali?"

"To save my own village. We did not heed their ways. We did not burn the body of the *nabe*, the white man marked as a slave of the Ban-ali. Now all our children sicken with evil magic."

Nate suddenly understood. The white man marked by the Ban-ali had to be Gerald Clark. If so, that meant . . . "You're from Wauwai."

He nodded and spit into the dirt. "Curse that name. Curse the day we ever set foot in that *nabe* village."

Nate realized this was the shaman who had tried to heal the sick mission children, then burned their village down in an attempt to protect the others. But by his own admission, the shaman must have failed. The contagion was still spreading through the Yanomamo children.

"Why come here? How did you get here?"

"I followed the *nabe*'s tracks to his canoe. I saw how it was painted. I know he came from this village, and I know the trails here. I came to seek the Ban-ali. To give myself to them. To beg them to lift their curse."

Nate leaned back. The shaman, in his guilt, had come to sacrifice himself.

"But I was too late. I find only one woman still alive." He glanced toward the site of the massacre. "I give her water, and she tells me the tale of her village."

Nate sat up straighter.

"What is he saying?" Captain Waxman asked.

Nate waved off his question. "What happened?"

"The white man was found by hunters three moons ago, sick and bony. They saw his markings. In terror, they imprisoned the man, fearing he would come to their village. They stripped him of all his belongings and tethered him in a cage, deep in the woods, intending to leave him for the Blood Jaguars to collect. The hunters fed and cared for him, fearing to harm what belonged to the Ban-ali. But the *nabe* continued to sicken. Then, a moon later, one of the hunter's sons grew ill."

Nate nodded. The contagious disease had spread.

"The shaman here declared them cursed and demanded the death of the *nabe*. They would burn his body to appease the wrath of the Ban-ali. But that morning when the hunters reached the cage, he was gone. They thought the Ban-ali had claimed him and were relieved. Only later that day would they discover one of their canoes was missing. But by then it was too late."

The Indian grew quiet. "Over the next days, the hunter's child died, and more in the village grew ill. Then a week ago, a woman returning from gathering bananas from the garden found a marking on the outer wall of the *shabano*. No one knew how it got there." The Indian nodded to the southwest section of the roundhouse. "It is still there. The mark of the Ban-ali."

Nate stopped the story and turned to the others. He quickly recounted what the Indian shaman had told him. Their eyes grew wide with the telling. Afterward, Captain Waxman sent Jorgensen to check that section of the outer wall.

As they waited for him to return, Nate convinced Captain Waxman to slice the wrist bindings off the prisoner. He agreed, since the man was clearly cooperating. The shaman now sat in the dirt with a canteen in hand, sipping from it gratefully.

Kelly knelt beside Nathan. "His story makes a certain sense from a medical standpoint. The tribe, when they kept Clark isolated in the jungle, almost succeeded in quarantining him. But as Clark's disease progressed, either the man became more contagious . . . or perhaps the hunter, whose son got sick, had somehow contaminated himself. Either way, the disease leaped here."

"And the tribe panicked."

Behind them, Jorgensen ducked back into the *shabano*, his face grim. "The old guy's right. There's a scrawled drawing on the wall. Just like the tattoo on Agent Clark's body." His nose curled in distaste. "But the damn thing smells like it was drawn with pig shit or something. Stinks something fierce."

Frank frowned and turned back to Nate. "See if you can find out what else the shaman knows."

Nate nodded and turned back to the shaman. "After finding the symbol, what happened?"

The shaman scrunched up his face. "The tribe fled that same night . . . but . . . but something came for them."

"What?"

The Indian frowned. "The woman who spoke to me was near to death. Her words began to wander. Something about the river coming to eat them. They fled, but it followed them up the little stream and caught them."

"What? What caught them? The Ban-ali?"

The shaman gulped from the canteen. "No, that's not what the woman said."

"Then what?"

The shaman stared Nate in the eye to show he spoke truthfully. "The jungle. She said the jungle rose out of the river and attacked them."

Nathan frowned.

The shaman shrugged. "I know no more. The cursed woman died, and her spirit went to join her tribe. The next day, this day, I hear you coming up the river. I go to see who you are." He glanced over to Manny's jaguar. "But I am found. Death scent clings to me, like it does to you."

Nathan sat back on his heels. He stared over at Manny. The biologist had Tor-tor on a leash, but the cat was clearly agitated, pacing around and around with his hackles raised. Spooked.

Kouwe finished translating for the others. "That's all he knows."

Waxman waved for Jorgensen to slice the shaman's ankle restraints, too.

"What do you make of his story?" Kelly asked, still kneeling at his side.

"I don't know," he mumbled, picturing the spread of bodies up the trail. He had thought something had attacked from the stream's far side, but if the woman's story was true, the attack had come from the stream itself.

Kouwe joined them. "The story is consistent with the myths of the Ban-ali. They're said to be able to bend the very jungle to their will."

"But what could come from the river and kill all those tribesmen?" Kelly asked.

Kouwe slowly shook his head. "I can't even imagine."

A commotion near the *shabano*'s door drew their attention. Staff Sergeant Kostos pushed inside, dragging a travois behind him. A dead body lay atop it. One of the massacred.

Behind them, the shaman let out a piercing cry.

Nate swung around.

The Indian, his eyes wide with terror, backed away. "Do not bring the cursed here! You will call the Ban-ali upon us!"

Jorgensen tried to restrain the man, but even at his age, the Indian was wiry with muscle. He slipped out of the Ranger's grip, fled to one of the dwellings, then, using a hammock as a ladder, scrambled to the encircling roof of the *shabano*.

One of the Rangers raised his rifle.

"Don't shoot!" Nathan called.

"Lower your weapon, Corporal," Waxman ordered.

The shaman paused atop the roof and turned to them. "The dead belong to the Ban-ali! They will come to collect what is theirs!" With these final words, the shaman dove off the roof and into the surrounding jungle.

"Go fetch him," Waxman ordered two of the Rangers.

"They'll never find him," Kouwe said. "As scared as he is, he'll vanish into these jungles."

The professor's words proved prophetic. The Yanomamo shaman was never found. As afternoon closed toward evening, Kelly ensconced herself in a corner of the *shabano* and worked to discover what had killed the tribesman. Nate took Captain Waxman and Frank over to the tree with the carved directions left behind by Gerald Clark.

"He must have written this just before being captured," Frank said. "How awful. He was so close to reaching civilization, then was captured and imprisoned." Frank shook his head. "For almost three months."

As they returned to the *shabano*, the rest of the team prepared to set up for the night: lighting fires, setting up guard shifts, preparing food. The plan tomorrow was to leave the river and to begin the overland journey, following Gerald Clark's trail.

With the sun setting and a meal of fish and rice being prepared, Kelly finally left her makeshift morgue. She settled to a camp chair with a long, tired sigh and stared into the flames as she gave her report. "As near as I can tell, he was poisoned by something. I found evidence of a convulsive death. Tongue chewed through, signs of contracted stricture of spine and limbs."

"What poisoned him?" Frank asked.

"I'd need a tox lab to identify it. I couldn't even tell you how it was delivered. Maybe a poisoned spear, arrow, or dart. The body was too macerated by the carrion feeders to judge adequately."

Watching the sun set, Nate listened as the discussions continued. He remembered the words of the vanished shaman—*they will come to collect what is theirs*—and pondered the massacre up the nearby trail and the disease spreading here and through the States. As he did so, Nate could not escape the sinking sensation that time was running out for them all.

NINE

Night Attack

Kelly woke from a nightmare, bolting up from her hammock. She didn't remember the specifics of her dream, only a vague sense of corpses and a chase. She checked her watch. The glowing dial put the time after midnight.

All around the *shabano,* most of the others were asleep. A single Ranger stood by the fire; his partner was guarding the door. Kelly knew another pair patrolled outside the roundhouse. Otherwise, the rest were snuggled in their hammocks after the long, horrible day.

It was no surprise she had nightmares: the massacre, the ravaged body she had examined, the ongoing tension. All of it overshadowed by the ever-present fear for her family back in Virginia. Her subconscious had plenty of fodder to mull through during her REM sleep.

Yesterday's evening report from the States had not been any cheerier than the lunchtime update. Another twelve cases had been reported in the U.S., and another three deaths—two children and an elderly matron from Palm Beach. Meanwhile, across the Amazon basin, disease and death were spreading like fire through dry tinder. People were barricading themselves indoors or leaving cities. Bodies were being burned in the streets of Manaus.

Kelly's mother had reported that so far no cases had yet arisen among the research team at Instar. But it was too soon to say they were out of the woods. The newest data, gathered mostly from cases in the Amazon, where the disease had a longer track record, suggested that the incubation period could be as short as three days or as long as seven. It all depended on the initial health of the victim. Children with poorer nutrition or parasitic conditions became sick faster.

As to the cause of the disease, a bacterial pathogen had been firmly ruled out by the CDC, but various viral assays were still continuing. So far, the culprit had not yet been identified.

Still, even as grim as the report was, there was worse news. Her mother had looked pale as she had spoken over the satellite link. "We now know that the transmission of the disease can be strictly airborne. It does not require physical contact." Kelly knew what this meant. With such ease of transmission, a pathogen like this was one of the hardest to quarantine. And with the mortality rates so high . . .

"There's only one hope," her mother had said at the end. "We need a cure."

Kelly reached to her canteen beside her hammock and took a long slow drink. She sat for a moment and knew sleep would not come. Moving quietly, she climbed from her hammock.

The guard by the fire noticed her movement and turned toward her. Still in the clothes she had worn yesterday—a gray T-shirt and brown trousers—she simply slipped on her boots. She pointed toward the entrance, wanting to stretch her legs but not wishing to disturb the others sleeping.

The Ranger nodded.

Kelly walked quietly to the *shabano*'s entrance. Ducking through, she found Private Carrera standing guard.

"Just needed some fresh air," Kelly whispered.

The female Ranger nodded and pointed her weapon toward the river. "You're not the only one."

Kelly saw a figure standing a few yards down the path by the river. From his silhouette, Kelly knew it was Nathan Rand. He was alone, except for two Rangers positioned a short distance upriver, easily spotted by their flashlights.

"Keep a safe distance from the water," Private Carrera warned. "We didn't have enough motion sensors to secure the perimeter and the river."

"I will." Kelly remembered too well what had happened to Corporal DeMartini.

Walking down the path from the roundhouse, Kelly listened to the jungle hum of locust song, accompanied by the soft croaking of countless frogs. It was a peaceful sound. In the distance, fireflies danced in the branches and zipped in graceful arcs over the river.

The lone spectator heard Kelly's approach. Nathan turned. He had a cigarette hanging from his lips, its tip a red spark in the night.

"I didn't know you smoked," Kelly said, stepping next to him and staring at the river from atop the bank.

"I don't," he said with a grin, puffing out a long stream of smoke. "At least not much. I bummed it from Corporal Conger." He thumbed in the direction of the pair on patrol. "Haven't touched one in four or five months, but . . . I don't know . . . I guess I needed an excuse to come out here. To be moving."

"I know what you mean. I came out here for the proverbial fresh air." She held out her hand.

He passed his cigarette.

She took a deep drag and sighed out the smoke, releasing her tension. "Nothing like fresh air." She passed the cigarette back to him.

He took one last puff, then dropped it and stamped it out. "Those things'll kill you."

They stood in silence as the river quietly flowed by. A pair of bats glided over the water, hunting fish, while somewhere in the distance, a bird cried out a long mournful note.

"She'll be okay," Nate finally said, almost a whisper.

Kelly glanced to him. "What?"

"Jessie, your daughter . . . she'll be okay."

Stunned for a moment, Kelly had no breath to reply.

"I'm sorry," Nate mumbled. "I'm intruding."

She touched his elbow. "No, I'm grateful . . . really. I just didn't think my worry was so plain."

"You may be a great physician, but you're a mother first."

Kelly remained quiet for a bit, then spoke softly. "It's more than that. Jess is my only child. The only child I'll ever have."

"What do you mean?"

Kelly couldn't say exactly why she was discussing this with Nate, only that it helped to voice her fears aloud. "When I gave birth to Jessie, there were complications . . . and an emergency surgery." She glanced to Nate, then away. "Afterward, I couldn't bear any more children."

"I'm sorry."

She smiled tiredly. "It was a long time ago. I've come to terms with it. But now with Jessie threatened . . ."

Nate sighed and settled to a seat on a fallen log. "I understand all too well. Here you are in the jungle, worrying about someone you love deeply, but having to continue on, to be strong."

Kelly sank beside him. "Like you, when your father was first lost."

Nate stared at the river and spoke dully. "And it's not just the worry and fear. It's guilt, too."

She knew exactly what he meant. With Jessie at risk, what was she doing here, traipsing through the jungle? She should be searching for the first flight home.

Silence again fell between them, but it grew too painful.

Kelly asked a question that had been nagging her since she had first met Nate. "Why are you here then?"

"What do you mean?"

"You lost both your mother and your father to the Amazon. Why come back? Isn't it too painful?"

Nate rubbed his palms together, staring down between his toes, silent.

"I'm sorry. It's none of my business."

"No," he said quickly, glancing to her, then away. "I . . . I was just regretting stamping out that cigarette. I could use it right now."

She smiled. "We can change the subject."

"No, it's okay. You just caught me by surprise. But your question's hard to answer, and even harder to put into words." Nate leaned back. "When I lost my father, when I truly gave up on ever finding him, I *did* leave the jungle, vowing to never come back. But in the States, the pain followed me. I tried to drown it away in alcohol and numb it away with drugs, but nothing worked. Then a year ago, I found myself on a flight back here. I couldn't say why. I walked into the airport, bought a ticket at the Varig counter, and before I knew it, I was landing in Manaus."

Nathan paused. Kelly heard his breath beside her, heavy and deep, full of emotion. She tentatively placed a hand on his bare knee. Without speaking, he covered it with his own palm.

"Once back in the jungle, I found the pain less to bear, less all-consuming."

"Why?"

"I don't know. Though my parents died here, they also *lived* here. This was their true heartland." Nate shook his head. "I'm not making any sense."

"I think you are. Here is where you still feel the closest to them."

She felt Nate stiffen beside her. He remained silent for the longest time. "Nate?"

His voice was hoarse. "I couldn't put it into words before. But you're right. Here in the jungle, they're all around me. Their memories are strongest here. My mother teaching me how to grind manioc into flour . . . my father teaching me how to identify trees by their leaves alone . . ." He turned to her, his eyes bright. "This is my home."

In his face, she saw the mix of joy and loss. She found herself leaning closer to him, drawn by the depth of his emotion. "Nate . . ."

A small explosion of water startled them both. Only a few yards from the bank, a narrow geyser shot three feet above the river's surface. Where it blew, something large hunched through the water and disappeared.

"What was that?" Kelly asked, tense, half on her feet, ready to bolt.

Nate put his arm around her shoulders and pulled her back down. "It's nothing to be afraid of. It's just a *boto*, a freshwater dolphin. They're abundant, but pretty shy. You'll mostly find them in remote areas like this, traveling in small packs."

Proving his point, another pair of geysers blew, casting spray high into the air. Ready this time, and less panicked, Kelly spotted small dorsal fins arcing through the water, then diving back down. They were moving swiftly.

"They're fast," she said.

"Probably hunting."

As they settled back to their log, a whole procession of dolphins sped by, arcing, spraying. Frantic clicks and whistles echoed out eerily. Soon it seemed the whole river was full of dolphins racing down the current.

Nate frowned and stood.

"What's wrong?" Kelly asked.

"I don't know." A single dolphin shot through the shallows near their feet. It struck the mud bank, almost beaching itself, then, with a flip of its tail, fled to deeper waters. "Something's panicking them."

Kelly got up and joined him. "What?"

Nate shook his head. "I've never seen them display this behavior before." He glanced over to where the two patrolling Rangers stood guard. They also stared at the parade of dolphins. "I need more light."

Nate hurried along the top of the bank toward the soldiers. Kelly followed, her blood beginning to race. The guards were positioned where a small stream emptied into the river.

"Corporal Conger, could I borrow your flashlight?" Nate asked.

"They're just dolphins," said the other soldier. It was Staff Sergeant Kostos. The swarthy man scowled at them. "We've seen lots of the damned things while patrolling at night. But, oh yeah, that was while you all were sleeping in your beds, all tucked away."

The younger Ranger was more cooperative. "Here, Dr. Rand," Corporal Conger said, passing his flashlight.

With a mumbled thanks, Nathan accepted the light. He moved down the bank, shining the light upriver. Dolphins continued to pass but not in as great a number. As Kelly looked on, Nate widened the cone of the light, splashing it down the river.

"Damn," Nate said.

Almost at the reach of his light, the river's surface seemed to be churning, like white-water rapids over sharp rocks, frothing and gurgling. Only these rapids were moving toward them, flowing down the current.

"What is that?" Kelly asked.

Another dolphin bumped into the shallows, bellying into the mud, but this one didn't quickly flip away. It rolled against the bank, squealing a high-pitched wail. Nate swung the light. Kelly gasped and took a couple steps back.

The tail end of the dolphin was gone. Its belly had been ripped open. Intestines trailed. The current rolled the pitiful creature back into the river.

Nathan swung his light back upstream. The churning white water was already much closer.

"What is it?" Corporal Conger asked, his Texas drawl thicker. "What's happening?"

From up the river, the piercing squeal of a pig woke the night. Nesting birds took wing. Monkeys, startled awake, barked in irritation.

"What's going on?" the Texan repeated.

"I need your night-vision goggles," Nate ordered.

Kelly stood behind his shoulder. "What is it?"

Nate grabbed the Ranger's glasses. "I've seen rivers churn like this a few times before—but *never* this much."

"What's causing it?" Kelly asked.

Nate lifted the goggles. "Piranhas . . . in a feeding frenzy."

Through the night-vision lenses, the world both brightened and dissolved into a monochrome green. It took Nate a moment to focus on where the waters churned. He fingered the telescopic lenses to bring the image closer. Within the roiling waters, he spotted flashes of large fins—dolphins caught by the razor-toothed predators—and in brief flickers, the silvery flash of the deadly fish themselves as they fought over their meal.

"What's the threat?" Kostos said with thick disdain. "Let the dumb fucks chew up the dolphins. They ain't gonna get us on dry land."

The sergeant was right, but Nate remembered the bodies of the massacred Indians . . . and their fear of the river. Was this the threat? Were the waters here so thick with piranhas that the Indians themselves feared to travel the rivers at night? Was that why they had fled on foot? And this behavior, attacking dolphins . . . it made no sense. Nate had never heard of such a slaughter.

Motion at the edge of his goggles drew his eye. He turned from the churning water, and spotted a carcass lying on the bank. It appeared to be a peccary, a wild pig. Was it the same one that had screamed a moment ago? Something smaller, several of them, hopped around the carcass, like huge bullfrogs, except these seemed to be tearing into the dead pig and dragging it toward the water.

"What the hell . . ." Nate mumbled.

"What?" Kelly asked. "What do you see?"

Nate clicked the telescopic lenses up a few notches, zeroing in. He watched more of the bullfroglike creatures leap out of the water and attack the carcass. Others joined it, flying high over the bank to disappear into the riverside foliage. As he watched, a large capybara burst from the jungle and ran along the muddy bank. It looked like a hundred-pound guinea pig racing beside the river. Then it suddenly fell as if tripping over its own feet. Its body began to convulse. From the waters, the creatures flopped and hopped, leaping at this new meal.

Nate suddenly knew what he was seeing. It was what the village Indians must have seen. He remembered the shaman's words. *The jungle rose out of the river and attacked them.* Down the bank, the capybara ceased writhing as death claimed it. Hadn't Kelly mentioned something about the corpse she had examined showing signs of a convulsive event?

He ripped off the goggles. The line of white water was now only thirty yards away. "We need to get everyone away from the river! Away from all waterways."

Sergeant Kostos scoffed. "What the hell are you talking about?"

Corporal Conger retrieved his glasses. "Maybe we should listen to Dr.—" Something knocked the corporal's helmet askew, hitting with a wet plop. "Jesus Christ."

Nathan shone his light down. Sitting in the mud was a strange creature, slightly stunned. It looked like a monstrous tadpole, but in the stage where its muscular hind legs had developed.

Before anyone could react, the creature leaped again, latching onto Conger's thigh with its jaws. Gasping, the corporal bludgeoned it away with the stock of his rifle and took a few shaky steps away. "Damn thing has teeth."

Kostos slammed his boot heel atop the creature, squashing it and shooting entrails down the bank. "Not any longer it doesn't."

As a group, they scurried away from the river. Conger fingered the pant leg of his fatigues, hopping along. A hole had been torn in the fabric, and when he lifted his hand, Nate spotted blood on the corporal's fingertips. "Practically tore a chunk out of me," Conger said with a nervous laugh.

In no time, they were back at the *shabano*'s entrance.

"What's going on?" Private Carrera asked.

Nate pointed back to the river. "Whatever got the Indians is coming our way. We need to clear out of here."

"For now, maintain your post," Kostos ordered Carrera. "Conger, you get that leg looked at while I go report to Captain Waxman."

"My med pack is inside," Kelly said.

Conger leaned against a beam of bamboo. "Sarge, I'm not feeling so good."

All eyes turned to the man.

"Everything's gone sort of blurry."

Kelly reached to help him. Nathan saw ropes of drool begin to flow from the corner of the man's lips. Then his head fell back, followed by his body, already convulsing.

Sergeant Kostos caught him. "Conger!"

"Get him inside!" Kelly snapped, ducking through the entrance.

The Ranger hauled the soldier toward the *shabano*'s door, but was having difficulty as the man thrashed. Private Carrera shouldered her rifle and bent to help. "Maintain your post, soldier!" Kostos barked, then turned to Nate. "Grab his goddamn legs!"

Nate dropped and hooked Conger's ankles under his arms. It was like holding the end of a downed power line as the man's body snapped and seized. "Go!"

As a team, they hauled the soldier through the narrow doorway.

Others came rushing up, awakened by the yelling.

"What happened?" Zane asked.

"Stand out of the way!" Kostos hollered, bowling the man over as he ran with the fallen soldier.

"Over here!" Kelly called. She already had her pack open and a syringe in hand. "Lay him down and hold him still."

After lowering Conger to the dirt, Nate was elbowed aside. Two Rangers took his place, pinning the soldier's legs to the ground.

Kostos knelt on the corporal's shoulders, holding him in place. But the man's head continued to bang up and down as if he were trying to knock himself unconscious. Froth foamed from his lips, bloody from where he half chewed through his own lip. "Jesus Christ! Conger!"

Kelly sliced open the man's right sleeve with a razor blade, then quickly slid a needle into Conger's arm. She injected the syringe's contents and knelt back to watch their effect, holding his wrist clamped in her fingers. "C'mon . . . c'mon . . ."

Suddenly the man's contorted form relaxed.

"Thank God," Kostos sighed.

Kelly's reaction wasn't as relieved. "Damn it!" She pounced on his form, checking his neck for a pulse, then pushed the soldiers aside as she began CPR on his chest. "Someone start mouth-to-mouth."

The Rangers were too stunned for a moment to move.

Nathan bumped Kostos aside, wiped the bloody froth from Conger's mouth, then began to breathe in sync with Kelly's labors. Nate's focus narrowed down to the rhythm of their work. He vaguely heard the concerned chatter of the others.

"Some damn frog thing or fish," Kostos explained. "It hopped out and bit Conger on the leg."

"Poisoned!" Kelly huffed as she worked. "It must have been venomous."

"I've never heard of such a creature," Kouwe said.

Nathan wanted to agree, but was too busy breathing for the dying soldier.

"There were thousands," Kostos continued, "chewing their way downstream toward here."

"What are we going to do?" Zane asked.

Captain Waxman's voice drowned everyone else out. "First of all, we're not going to panic. Corporal Graves and Private Jones . . . join Carrera in securing the perimeter."

"Wait!" Nate gasped between breaths.

Waxman turned on him. "What?"

Nate spoke in stilted breaths between attempts to resuscitate Conger. "We're too close to the stream. It runs right past the *shabano.*"

"So?"

"They'll come for us from the stream . . . like the Indians." Nate was dizzy from hyperventilating. He breathed into Corporal Conger's mouth, then was up again. "We have to get away. Away from the waterways until daybreak. Nocturnal . . ." Down he went to breathe.

"What do you mean?"

Professor Kouwe answered. "The Indians were attacked at night. Now this assault. Nathan believes these creatures may be nocturnal. If we could avoid their path until sunrise, we should be safe."

"But we have shelter and a secure area here. They're just fish or frogs or something."

Nate remembered the black-and-white view through the night-vision goggles: the creatures leaping from the river, bounding high into the trees. "We're not secure here!" he gasped out. He bent down again, but he was stopped by a hand on his shoulder.

"It's useless," Kelly said, pulling him up. "He's gone." She faced the others. "I'm sorry. The poison spread too quickly. Without an antivenom . . ." She shook her head sadly.

Nate stared at the still form of the young Texan. "Damn it . . ." He stood up. "We have to get away. Far away from the waters. I don't know how far from the streams and rivers these creatures can travel, but the one I saw had gills. They probably can't stay out of the water for long."

"What do you suggest?" Frank asked.

"We travel to higher ground. Avoid the river and the little stream. I think the Indians believed it was just the river they needed to fear, but the predators followed the stream and ambushed them."

"You're speaking as if the creatures are intelligent."

"No, I can't imagine they are." Nate remembered the way the dolphins were fleeing, while none of the larger river fish were bothered. He pictured the attack on the pig and the capybara. A theory slowly jelled. "Maybe they're simply focused on warm-blooded creatures. I don't know . . . maybe they can zone in on body heat or something, scouring both the water and the river's edges for prey."

Frank turned to Waxman. "I say we heed Dr. Rand."

"So do I," Kelly said, standing. She pointed to Corporal Conger. "If a single bite can do this, we can't take the risk."

Waxman turned on Frank. "You may be the head of operations, but in matters of security, my word is law."

Private Carrera ducked her head through the roundhouse's doorway. "Something's happening out here. The river is frothing something fierce. One of the boats' pontoons just blew."

Beyond the walls of the *shabano*, the jungle awoke with monkey howls and screeching birds.

"We're running out of options," Nate said fiercely. "If they come up the stream and flank us, cutting us off from higher ground, many more will die like Conger . . . like the Indians."

Nate found support in the most unlikely of places. "The doctor's right," Sergeant Kostos said. "I saw those buggers. Nothing'll stop them from attacking." He waved an arm. "Definitely not this flimsy place. We're sitting ducks in here, sir."

After a pause, Waxman nodded. "Load up the gear."

"What about the motion sensors outside?" Kostos asked.

"Leave 'em. Right now, I don't want anyone out there."

Kostos nodded and turned to obey.

In short order, everyone was shouldering packs. Two Rangers dug a shallow grave for Corporal Conger's body.

Carrera stood crouched by the doorway. She wore night-vision goggles and stared out toward the river and jungle. "The commotion by the river's died down, but I hear rustling in the brush."

Beyond the walls, the jungle had grown silent.

Nate crossed to the door and knelt on one knee beside Carrera. He was already packed and ready, his stubby-nosed shotgun clutched in his right hand. "What do you see?"

Carrera adjusted her goggles. "Nothing. But the jungle is too dense to see far."

Nate leaned out the door. He heard a branch snap. Then a small forest deer, a spotted fawn, shot out of the jungle and dashed past where Nate and the Ranger crouched. Both gasped and ducked inside before realizing there was no danger.

"Christ," Carrera said with a choked laugh.

The deer paused near the edge of the roundhouse, ears pricked.

"Shoo!" the Ranger called, waving her M-16 threateningly.

Then something dropped out of the trees and landed on the fawn's back. The deer suddenly squealed in pain and terror.

"Get inside!" Nate ordered Carrera.

As she rolled through the door, Nate covered her with his shotgun. Another creature pounced from the jungle's edge toward the deer. A third leaped from the underbrush. The fawn skittered a few steps, then fell on its side, legs kicking.

A single motion sensor blared from the direction of the side stream.

"They're here," Nathan mumbled.

By his side, Carrera had torn off her night-vision goggles and clicked on her flashlight. The brightness spread down the jungle trail to the river. The jungle to either side remained dark, blocking the light. "I don't see—"

Something plopped into the trail, only a few yards away.

From this angle, the creature appeared to be all legs with a long finned tail dragging behind it. It took a small hop toward them. From under two globular black eyes, its mouth gaped open. Teeth glinted in the bright light, like some cross between a tadpole and a piranha.

"What the hell is it?" Carrera whispered.

It leaped toward her voice.

Nate pulled the trigger of his shotgun. The spray of pellets shredded the creature, blowing it backward. That's what Nate appreciated about a shotgun in the jungle. It didn't require precision aim. Perfect for small threats—poisonous snakes, scorpions, spiders—and apparently against venomous amphibians, too.

"Get back," he said and swung the small door shut. It was no more than a woven flap of banana leaves, but it would temporarily block the creatures.

"That's the only way out," Carrera said.

Nate stood and unhooked his machete with his left hand. "Not in a *shabano*." He pointed the blade toward the far wall, the side opposite both river and stream. "You can make a doorway wherever you want."

Frank and Captain Waxman joined him as he crossed to the central yard. Waxman was folding a field map.

"They're already out there," Nate said. He reached the far wall, raised his machete, and began hacking through the woven palm and banana leaves. "We have to leave now."

Waxman nodded, then shouted and waved an arm in the air. "We're hauling out! Now!"

Nate cleared a ragged hole through the rear wall, kicking debris aside.

Waxman waved Corporal Okamoto to take the point. Nate saw an unusual weapon in the soldier's hands. "Flamethrower," Okamoto explained, hefting the weapon. "If necessary we'll burn a way through the bastards." He pressed the trigger and a steam of orange fire shot from the muzzle like the flickering tongue of a snake.

"Excellent." Nate patted the corporal's shoulder. After so many days on the river, Nate had grown fond of his boat's motorman, although the Asian corporal's off-tune whistling still drove him crazy.

With a wink to Nathan, Okamoto ducked through the arch without hesitation. As he passed, Nate spotted the small fuel tank strapped to the corporal's back.

Another four Rangers followed: Warczak, Graves, Jones, and Kostos. All had outfitted their M-16s with grenade launchers. They spread to the right and left of their point man. New alarms blared as the Rangers tripped the perimeter's motion-sensor lasers.

"Now the civilians," Waxman ordered. "Stay close. Always keep a Ranger between you and the forest."

Richard Zane and Anna Fong hurried through. Next Olin and Manny followed, trailed by Tor-tor. Last, Kelly, Frank, and Kouwe passed.

"C'mon," Kelly said to Nate.

He nodded, glancing back to the *shabano*. Waxman oversaw the last of the Rangers, who would guard their rear. Two soldiers were gathered over something in the middle of the yard.

"Let's move, ladies!" Waxman ordered.

The Rangers stood. One, a corporal named Samad Yamir, gave a thumbs-up sign to Waxman. The corporal seldom spoke, and when he did, his voice was thick with a Pakistani accent. There was only one other fact Nate knew about Yamir. He was the unit's demolitions expert.

Nate eyed the device left in the yard with suspicion.

Waxman found Nate staring. The captain pointed his rifle toward the opening. "Waiting for a personal invitation, Dr. Rand?"

Nate licked his lips and followed after Frank and Kelly.

Again he found Private Carrera marching behind him. She was now outfitted with a flamethrower, too. She studied the dark forest with narrowed eyes. Beyond her, Waxman and Yamir were the last to leave the *shabano*.

"Stay close!" Waxman yelled. "Frag or fry anything that moves."

Carrera spoke at Nate's shoulder. "We're going to make for a knoll about five klicks ahead."

"How do you know it's there?"

"Topographic map." Her voice sounded unsure.

Nate glanced over his shoulder questioningly.

Carrera lowered her voice and nodded to the side. "The stream wasn't on the map."

Kelly glanced over, looking sick, but she remained silent.

Nate sighed. He was not surprised at the inaccuracy of the map. The waterways through the deep jungle were unpredictable. While the boundaries of lakes and swamps varied according to the rainfall, the smaller rivers and streams were even more changeable. Most remained unnamed and uncharted. But at least the knoll was on the map.

"Keep moving!" Waxman ordered behind them.

As a group, the team fled into the jungle. Nate stared around him, his ears pricked for any suspicious rustle. In the distance, he heard the babble of the small stream. He imagined the Indian villagers racing up the nearby footpath, unaware of the danger lurking so close, oblivious of the death that lay ahead.

Nate tromped after Frank and Kelly. A flicker of flame lit up the jungle ahead as Corporal Okamoto led the way. Few words were shared as the group scaled up the gentle slope away from the river. All eyes watched the jungle around them.

After about twenty minutes of climbing, Waxman spoke to the soldier at his side. "Light the candle, Yamir."

Nate turned. Samad Yamir swung around and faced the way they had come. He shouldered his M-16 and loosened a handheld device.

"Radio transmitter," Carrera explained.

Yamir raised the device and pressed a button, triggering a red light to blink rapidly.

Nate frowned. "What is—?"

A soft *boom* sounded. A section of forest blew upward in a ball of fire. Flames shot high into the night sky and mushroomed through the surrounding forest.

Stunned, Nate stumbled back. Shouts of surprise arose from the other civilians. Nate watched the sphere of flames die away, collapsing in on itself, but leaving a good section of the forest burning. Through the hellish red glow, a scorched hole in the forest was evident, every tree stripped of leaf and branch. At least an acre. There was no sign of the *shabano*. Even the motion-sensor alarms had gone silent, fried by the explosion.

Nate was too dumbstruck to speak—but his eyes, furious, met Waxman's gaze.

The captain waved them all on. "Keep moving."

Carrera urged Nate forward. "Fail-safe method. Burning everything behind us."

"What was that?" Kouwe asked.

"Napalm bomb," the corporal explained dourly. "New jungle munition."

"Why weren't we told . . . at least warned?" Frank asked loudly, walking half backward.

Captain Waxman answered, marching and waving them on. "It was my call. My order. I wanted no arguments about it. Security is my priority."

"Which I appreciate, captain," Richard Zane called back from up ahead. "I, for one, commend your actions. Hopefully you've annihilated the venomous bunch."

"That doesn't appear to be the case," Olin said with narrowed eyes. Their Russian teammate pointed to the stream, now visible due to the blaze. A section of the waterway on their side of the fires frothed with the leaping, racing bodies of thousands of small creatures. A roiling stampede climbed up the stream, like salmon spawning.

"Get moving!" Waxman yelled. "We need to reach higher ground!"

The pace of the party accelerated. They scrambled up the slope, less concerned with watching the forest than with speed. The creatures were flanking them off to the right.

Flashes of fire marked the point man ahead. "I've got water here!" Okamoto called.

The group converged toward him.

"Dear Lord," Kelly said.

Fifty yards ahead, another stream cut across their path. It was only ten yards wide, but was dark and still. Beyond it, the land continued to rise toward the knoll, their destination.

"Is this the same stream?" Frank asked.

One of the Rangers, Jorgensen, pushed out of the forest. He had his night-vision glasses in his hand. "I've scouted down a ways. It's an offshoot of the other stream. This one feeds into the other."

"Fuck," Waxman swore. "This place is a goddamn water maze."

"We should cross while we still can," Kouwe said. "The creatures will surely come this way soon."

Waxman stared at the slowly flowing water with clear trepidation. He moved beside Okamoto. "I need some light."

The Ranger fired his flamethrower across the waters. It did little to reveal what lay in the murky depths.

"Sir, I'll go across first," Okamoto volunteered. "See if it can be crossed safely."

"Careful, son."

"Always, sir."

Taking a deep breath, Okamoto kissed a crucifix around his neck, then stepped into the water. He waded into it, his weapon held chest high. "Current's sluggish," he said softly, "but deep." Halfway across, the waters had climbed to his waist.

"Hurry up," Frank mumbled. He had a fist clenched to his belly.

Okamoto climbed to the far side and out of the water. He turned with a grin. "It appears to be safe."

"For now," Kouwe said. "We should hurry."

"Let's go!" Waxman ordered.

As a group, they splashed through the waters. Frank held Kelly's hand. Nate helped Anna Fong. "I'm not a good swimmer," Anna said to no one in particular.

The Rangers followed, guns held above their heads.

On the far side, the party climbed the steep slope. With wet boots and the mud still slick from the rains yesterday, trekking was treacherous. Their progress slowed. The tight group began to stretch apart.

Jorgensen appeared out of the gloom, night scope in hand. "Captain," he said, "I've checked the other stream. The waters seem to have calmed. I don't see any more of the creatures."

"They're out there," Nate said. "They're just not in a frenzy any longer."

"Or maybe now that the fires have died down, they fled back to the main river channel," Jorgensen offered hopefully.

Waxman frowned. "I don't think we should count—"

A sharp cry interrupted the captain. Off to the left, a body slid down the slick, muddy slope. It was a Ranger. Eddie Jones. His limbs flailed as he tried to break his fall. "Fuck!" he screamed in frustration. He tried to grasp a bush, but its roots ripped out of the thin soil. Then he hit a bump in the slope, and went cartwheeling, his weapon flying from his fingers, and landed in the stream.

A pair of Rangers—Warczak and Graves—ran to his aid.

He popped out, coughing water and choking. "Goddamn it!" He clambered to the stream's edge. "Fuck this jungle!" As he straightened his helmet, more colorful obscenities flowed. He climbed out of the stream.

"Smooth, Jones . . . very smooth," Warczak said, running his flashlight up and down the man's soaked form. "I'd give you a perfect ten in the jungle slalom."

"Cram it up your ass," Jones said, bending to finger a rope of sticky algae from his pant leg. "Ugh."

Corporal Graves was the first to spot it: something moving atop the other man's pack. "Jones . . ."

Still half crouched, the man glanced up. "What?"

The creature leaped, latching onto the soft flesh under Jones's jaw. He jerked. "What the hell!" He tore the creature from his neck, blood spurting. "Ahhhhh . . ."

The small stream suddenly frothed and burst forth with another dozen of the creatures. They leaped at the man, attacking his legs. Jones fell backward, his face twisted in agony. He hit the stream with a loud splash.

"Jones!" Warczak stepped nearer.

Another of the creatures leaped from the water and plopped in the wet mud at the corporal's feet, gill flaps vibrating. Warczak scrambled backward, as did Graves.

In the shallow stream, Jones writhed. It was as if he had been thrown in boiling water. His body jerked and spasmed.

"Get back!" Waxman yelled. "Everyone uphill!"

Warczak and Graves were already running. From the stream, more of the creatures leaped and bounded in pursuit.

The group tossed caution aside and scrambled up the slope, some half crawling on hands and knees. Kelly's legs suddenly went out from under her. Her muddy hand slipped out of her brother's grip. She began a deadly slide.

"Kelly!" Frank called out.

But Nate was a couple yards behind her. He caught her one-handed by the waist, falling on top of her, holding his shotgun in his other arm. Manny came to their aid, hauling both back to their feet. Tor-tor paced anxiously back and forth behind him.

The Brazilian waved the jaguar ahead. "Move your furry ass."

By now, the three were the last of the group. Frank waited a few yards up.

Only Private Carrera was still with them. She stood and sprayed a jet of fire behind them, her flamethrower roaring dully. "Let's pick up the pace," she said tensely, backing up the slope, herding them upward.

"Thanks," Kelly said, her eyes swiveling to encompass the entire group.

Frank met them and took his sister in hand. "Don't do that again."

"I'm not planning on it."

Nate kept a watch behind them. He met Carrera's gaze. He saw the fear in her eyes. This momentary distraction was all it took. One of the creatures sprang at the Ranger from the surrounding underbrush. It had slipped past her firewall.

Carrera fell backward, fire spitting into the sky.

The creature had latched onto her belt, but squirmed for a meatier purchase.

Before anyone else could react, a sharp *crack* split the night. The creature was flung away, the two halves of its body sailing high. Both Carrera and Nate turned to see Manny snapping his short bullwhip back into ready position.

"Are you just gonna sit there gawking?" Manny asked.

Carrera scrambled up with Nate's help. The group sped up the hill. At last they reached the summit. Nate hoped putting the rise between them and the amphibious creatures would be enough.

He found the others gathered on top.

"We should keep moving," Nate said. "Keep as much land between us and them as possible."

"That's a good theory," Kouwe said. "But putting it into practice is another thing altogether." The shaman pointed down the knoll's far side.

Nathan stared. From this height, the stream below shone silver in the moonlight. Groaning, he realized it was the same stream they had been avoiding all along. Nate turned in a slow circle, recognizing their predicament. They had made a fatal error.

The small waterway they had crossed a few minutes ago was not a feeder draining into the larger stream, but actually a *part* of the same stream.

"We're on an island," Kelly said with dismay.

Nate stared upstream and saw that the flow of the waterway split and ran around both sides of the knoll. Once past the hill, it joined to become a single stream again. The party indeed stood on an island, in the middle of the deadly stream, water all around.

Nate felt sick. "We're trapped."

2:12 A.M.
WEST WING OF THE INSTAR INSTITUTE
LANGLEY, VIRGINIA

Lauren O'Brien sat at the small table in the communal galley, hunched over a cup of coffee. At this late hour, she had the place to herself. All the other quarantined MEDEA members were either asleep in their makeshift bedrooms or working in the main labs.

Even Marshall had retired to their room with Jessie hours ago. He had an early morning conference call with the CDC, two Cabinet heads, and the director of the CIA. He had eloquently described the meeting as "a preemptive strike before the political shitstorm hits the fan." Such were the ways of government. Rather than attacking the problem aggressively, everyone was still pointing fingers and running for cover. Marshall's goal tomorrow was to shake things up. A decisive plan of action was needed. So far, the fifteen outbreak zones were being managed fifteen different ways. It was chaos.

Sighing, Lauren stared at the reams of papers and printouts spread atop her table. Her team was still struggling with one simple question. *What was causing the disease?*

Testing and research were ongoing in labs across the country—from the CDC in Atlanta all the way to the Salk facility in San Diego. But the Instar Institute had become scientific ground zero for the disease.

Lauren pushed away a report from a Dr. Shelby on utilizing monkey kidney cells as a culture medium. He had failed. *Negative response.* Up to this point, the contagious agent continued to thwart all means of identification: aerobic and anaerobic cultures, fungal assays, electron microscopy, dot hybridization, polymerase chain reaction. As of today, no progress had been made. Each study ended with similar tags: *negative response, zero growth, indeterminate analysis.* All fancy ways of saying failure.

Her beeper, resting beside her now-cold cup of coffee, began to buzz and dance across the Formica countertop. She snatched it before it fell off the table.

"Who the heck is paging me at this hour?" she mumbled, glancing at the beeper's screen. The Caller ID feature listed the number as *Large Scale Biological Labs.* She didn't know the facility, but the area code placed it somewhere in northern California. The call was probably just some technician requesting their fax number or submission protocol. Still . . .

Lauren stood, pocketed her beeper, and headed over to the phone on the wall. As she picked up the receiver, she heard a door open behind her. Over her shoulder, she was surprised to see Jessie standing in her pajamas, rubbing at her eyes blearily.

"Grandma . . ."

Lauren replaced the receiver and crossed to the child. "Honey, what are you doing up? You should be in bed."

"I couldn't find you."

She knelt before the girl. "What's wrong? Did you have another scary dream?" The first few nights here, Jessie had awoken with nightmares, triggered by the quarantine and the strange environment. But the child had seemed to adjust rapidly, making friends with several of the other kids.

"My tummy hurts," she said, her eyes sheening with threatening tears.

"Oh, honey, that's what you get for eating ice cream so late." Lauren reached out and pulled the girl into a hug. "Why don't I get you a glass of water, and we'll get you tucked back into—"

Lauren's voice died as she realized how warm the child was. She reached a palm to Jessie's forehead. "Oh, God," she mumbled under her breath.

The child was burning up.

2:31 A.M.

AMAZON JUNGLE

Louis stood by his tent as Jacques strode up from the river. His lieutenant carried something wrapped in a sodden blanket under his arms. Whatever it was, it appeared no larger than a watermelon.

"Doctor," the Maroon tribesman said stiffly.

"Jacques, what did you discover?" He had sent the man and two others to investigate the explosion that had occurred just after midnight. The noise had woken his own camp mere minutes after they had settled in for the night. Earlier, at sunset, Louis's had learned of the discovery of the Indian *shabano* and the fate of the villagers. Then hours later the explosion . . .

What was going on over there?

"Sir, the village has been incinerated . . . as has much of the surrounding forest. We could not get too close due to the remaining fires. Maybe by morning."

"And the other team?"

Jacques glanced to his toes. "Gone, sir. I dropped Malachim and Toady ashore to scout after them."

Louis clenched a fist and cursed his overconfidence. After the successful abduction of one of their soldiers, he had grown complacent with his prey. But now this! One of his team's trackers must have been spotted. Now that the fox had been alerted to the hounds, Louis's mission was far more complicated. "Gather the other men. If the Rangers are running from us, we don't want them to get too far away."

"Yes, sir. But, Doctor, I'm not sure the others are fleeing from us."

"What makes you think that?"

"As we paddled up to the fire zone, we saw a body float out from a side stream."

"A body?" Louis feared it was his mole, dispatched and sent downriver as a message.

Jacques unrolled the sodden blanket in his arms and dropped its content to the leafed floor of the jungle. It was a human head. "We found it floating near the remains."

Frowning, Louis knelt and examined the head, what little there was of it. The face had been all but chewed away, but from the shaved scalp, it was clearly one of the Rangers.

"The body was the same," Jacques said, "gnawed to the bone."

Louis glanced up. "What happened to him?"

"Piranhas, I'd say, from the bite wounds."

"Are you sure?"

"Pretty damn sure." Jacques fingered the scarred half of his nose, reminding Louis that, as a boy, his lieutenant had had intimate experience with the voracious river predators.

"Did they feed on him after he was dead?"

Jacques shrugged. "If he wasn't, I pity the poor bastard."

Louis climbed to his feet. He stared out toward the river. "What the hell is happening out there?"

TEN

Escape

AUGUST 14, 3:12 A.M.

AMAZON JUNGLE

Atop the island knoll, Nate stood with the other civilians, ringed by the Ranger team, which was now down to eight members. *One for each of the civilians*, Nate thought, *like personal bodyguards.*

"How about using another of your napalm bombs to clear a path through the buggers?" Frank asked, standing near Captain Waxman. "Roll it down the slope, then duck for cover."

"We'd all be dead. If the heat blast didn't fry us, then we'd be pinned down between a burning forest and the poisonous bastards."

Frank sighed, staring out into the dark forests. "How about your grenades? We could lob them in series, creating a swath through them."

Waxman frowned. "It'd be risky to deploy them so close to us, and no guarantee that it would kill enough of the bastards among all these tree trunks. I say we hold the hill, try to last until daybreak."

Frank crossed his arms, little pleased with this plan.

Around the knoll, occasional fiery blasts from the flamethrowers ignited the night as Corporal Okamoto and Private Carrera maintained sentry posts on either slope. Though it had been half an hour since sighting one of them, the beasts were still out there. The surrounding forests had gone deathly quiet, no monkey calls, no birdsong. Even the insects seemed to have died down to a whispery buzz and whine. But beyond the reach of their flashlights, the leaves still rustled as unseen lurkers crept through the underbrush.

Night scopes focused on the surrounding waters revealed creatures still hopping into and out of the stream. Nathan's earlier assessment seemed to be accurate. The creatures, gill-breathers, needed to return to the waters occasionally to revive themselves.

Nearby, Manny knelt in the leaf-strewn dirt, working by flashlight. Kelly and Kouwe stood behind his shoulder. Earlier, Manny had risked his life to dash into the forest's fringe to collect one of the beasts stunned by a blast of flame. Though partially charbroiled, it was a decent specimen. The creature was about a foot long from the tip of its tail to its razor-toothed mouth. Large black eyes protruded, giving it a nearly 360-degree view of its surroundings. Strong articulated limbs ended in webbed and suckered toes almost as long as the body itself.

As the others watched, Manny was performing a rapid dissection. The Brazilian biologist worked deftly with a scalpel and forceps from Kelly's med kit.

"This thing is amazing," Manny finally mumbled.

Nate joined Kelly and Kouwe as the biologist explained.

"It's clearly some form of chimera. An amalgam of more than one species."

"How so?" Kelly asked.

Manny shifted aside and pointed with his thumb forceps. "Nathan was right. Though its skin is not scaled like a fish, it definitely has the breathing system of an aquatic species. Gills, no lungs. But its legs—notice the banding on the skin—are definitely amphibious. The striping pattern is very characteristic of *Phobobates trivittatus,* the striped poison-dart frog, the largest and most toxic member of the frog family."

"So you're saying it's some mutated form of this species?" Nate asked.

"I thought so at first. It looks almost like a tadpole whose growth was arrested at the stage where gills were still present and only its hind legs had formed. But as I dissected further, I became less convinced. First, and most obvious, is that its size is way out of proportion. This thing must weigh close to five pounds. Monstrously gigantic for even the largest species of dart frog."

Manny rolled the dissected creature over and pointed to its eyes and teeth. "Additionally, its skull structure is all misshapen. Rather than flattened horizontally like a frog's, the cranium is flattened vertically, more like a fish's. In fact, the skull conformation, jaw, and teeth are almost identical in size and shape to a common Amazonian river predator—*Serrasalmus rhombeus*." Manny glanced up from his handiwork. "The black piranha."

Kelly leaned away. "That's impossible."

"If this thing weren't right in front of me, I'd agree." Manny sat back. "I've worked with Amazonian species all my life, and I've seen nothing like it. A true chimera. A single creature that shares the biological features of both frog and fish."

Nate eyed the creature. "How could that be?"

Manny shook his head. "I don't know. But how does a man regenerate a limb? I think the presence of such a chimera suggests we're on the right trail. Something is out there, something your father's expedition discovered, something with a distinct mutating ability."

Nate stared at the dissected ruins. *What the hell was out there?*

A call arose from Private Carrera. Her sentry post faced the northern slope of the knoll. "They're on the move again!"

Nate straightened. The rustling from her side of the forest had grown louder. It sounded as if the entire jungle were stirring.

Carrera flamed the lower slope. Her fiery jets pushed back the darkness. Reflected in the fire were hundreds of tiny eyes, covering both the forest floor and the trees. One of the creatures sprang from its perch on the limb of a palm tree and bounded into the fire zone. There was a short chatter of automatic rifle fire, and the creature was shredded to a bloody mush.

"Everybody back!" Carrera called. "They're coming!"

From the trees and underbrush, small bodies started to leap and bound toward them, oblivious to the fire and bullets. The creatures were determined to overrun them with their sheer numbers.

Nate flashed back on the Indian massacre site. It was happening all over again. He swung his shotgun from his shoulder, aimed, and blasted a creature in midair as it leaped from a branch over Carrera's head. Gobbets of flesh rained down.

As a group, they were forced to vacate the knoll's summit and retreat down the southern face. Gunfire and flames lit the night. Flashlights danced, making every shadow shift and jerk.

Leading the charge down the southern slope, Corporal Okamoto swathed jets of fire before them. "It still looks clear this way!" he called out.

Nate risked a peek his way. Distantly through the forest, he could make out the other fork of the stream below as it swept around the southern flank of the hill.

"Why aren't any of the creatures on this side of the hill?" Anna asked, her face flushed.

Zane answered, his eyes wide as he kept glancing behind him. "They probably rallied all their numbers on the far side for this final assault."

Nate stared toward the stream below. It was wide, smooth, and quiet, but he knew better. He remembered the large capybara rodent flushed from the forest and racing along the river, where it was set upon by the predators. "They're herding us," he mumbled.

"What?" Kelly asked.

"They want us close to the water. The pack is driving us to the river."

Manny heard him. "I think Nate's right. Despite their ability to move on land for short distances, they're basically aquatic. They'd want their meal as close to water as possible before taking it down."

Kelly looked behind her to the line of Rangers flaming and firing along their back trail. "What choice do we have?"

Down the slope, Okamoto slowed as they neared the river, clearly suspicious of the water, too. The corporal turned to Captain Waxman behind him. "Sir, I'll try to cross first. Like last time."

Waxman nodded. "Careful, corporal."

Okamoto headed for the stream.

"No!" Nate called. "I'm sure it's a trap."

Okamoto glanced to him, then to his captain, who waved him forward again.

"We have to get off this island," Waxman said.

"Wait," Manny said, stepping forward, his voice pained. "I . . . I can send Tor-tor instead."

The others were now all gathered around.

Waxman stared at the jaguar, then nodded. "Do it."

Manny guided his jaguar toward the dark waters.

Nate's mind spun. It was suicide to enter those waters. He knew this as certainly as he knew the sun would rise tomorrow. But Waxman was right. They had to find a way across. He ran through various scenarios in his head.

A rope bridge over the stream. He quickly ruled that out. Even if they could somehow string a bridge up, the aquatic creatures were adept at leaping great heights. They'd all just be so much bait strung on a line.

Maybe grenades tossed in the water to stun them. But the stream was long. Any creatures killed by the concussion would be quickly replaced by those upstream. They would sweep down the sluggish current, attacking the team as they tried to rush across. No, what was needed was something that could strip this entire fork of the creatures—but what could do that?

Then it dawned on him. He had seen the answer demonstrated just a few days back.

By now, Manny and Tor-tor were only a couple of yards from the stream. Okamoto was with them, flames lighting the way.

"Wait!" Nate called. "I have an idea!"

Manny paused.

"What?" Waxman asked.

"According to Manny, these things are basically fish."

"So?"

Nate ignored the captain's glare and turned to Kouwe. "You have powdered *ayaeya* vine in your medicine kit, don't you?"

"Certainly, but what—?" Then the professor's eyes grew rounder with understanding. "Brilliant, Nate. I should've thought of that."

"What?" Waxman asked, growing frustrated.

Behind them, up the slope, the line of Rangers held the creatures momentarily at bay with rifles and fire. Down slope, Okamoto stood ready by the river.

Nate quickly explained. "Indians use crushed *ayaeya* vine to fish." He remembered the small fishing scene he had witnessed as he canoed with Tama and Takaho to São Gabriel: a woman dusting the river with a black powder, while downstream the men gathered stunned fish with spears and nets. "The vine contains a potent rotenone, a toxin that literally chokes and suffocates the fish. The effect is almost instantaneous."

"So what are you proposing?" Waxman asked.

"I'm familiar with the compound. I'll take the satchel upstream and poison the stream. As the toxin flows down this fork, it should stun any and all of the creatures in the river."

Waxman's eyes narrowed. "This powder will do this?"

Kouwe answered, digging in his pack. "It should. As long as the creatures are true gill-breathers." The professor glanced to Manny.

The biologist nodded, clear relief in his eyes. "I'm sure of it."

Sighing, Waxman waved Okamoto and Manny away from the stream. As the captain turned back to Nate, an explosion sounded behind them.

Dirt, leaves, and branches blew high into the air. Someone had fired a grenade. "They're breaking through!" Sergeant Kostos yelled.

Waxman pointed to Nate. "Move!"

Nate turned.

Professor Kouwe pulled a large leather satchel from his pack and tossed it to Nate. "Be careful."

Nate caught the bag of powder one-handed, swinging around with his shotgun in the other.

"Carrera!" Waxman called and pointed to Nate. "Cover him."

"Yes, sir." The private backed down the slope with her flamethrower, leaving her post to Okamoto.

"When you first start to see fish float to the surface," Nate instructed the others, "haul ass across. Though the current here is slow, I'm not sure how long the effect will last before the toxin is swept away."

"I'll make sure we're ready," Kouwe said.

Nate glanced around the group. Kelly's eyes met his, a fist clutched to her throat. He offered her a small, confident smile, then turned away.

Together, he and Private Carrera sprinted upstream, keeping a wary distance from the water.

Nate trailed behind the soldier as she strafed the way ahead with continual bursts from her flamethrower. They crashed through the smoking underbrush and raced ahead. Nate searched behind. The encampment of his fellow teammates had dwindled down to a green glow in the forest.

"The buggers must know something's up," Carrera said, gasping with exertion. She pointed a free arm toward the stream. A couple splashes marked where creatures were beginning to hop out of the water in pursuit of the pair.

"Keep moving," Nate urged. "It's not much farther."

They rushed on, accompanied by tiny splashes and the sound of crashing bodies hitting the underbrush.

At last they reached the place where the main stream forked into the northern and southern branches, encircling the knoll. Here the channel was narrower, the current swifter, rumbling over rocks in a frothy white foam. More of the creatures leapt from the current, slick bodies glistening in the glow of the firelight.

Nate stopped as Carrera laid down a protective spray of flame. Creatures sizzled in the muddy bank, some fleeing back into the river, skin smoking. "Now or never," Carrera said.

Shouldering his shotgun, Nate slipped in front of her, the satchel of powder in hand. He quickly loosened the pouch's leather tie.

"Just lob the whole thing in," the Ranger recommended.

"No, I have to make sure it disperses evenly." Nate took another step nearer the river.

"Careful." Carrera followed, jetting bursts of flame around them to discourage the predators.

Nate reached the edge of the stream, standing now only a foot away.

Carrera half knelt and strafed fire over the water's surface, ready to incinerate anything that dared pop out. "Do it!"

With a nod, Nate leaned over the stream, extending his arm, his fingers clutching the satchel. Attracted by the movement, something sprang from the water. Nate jerked his arm back in time to miss getting bitten. Instead, the creature latched its razored teeth into the cuff of his shirt sleeve, hanging there.

Nate whipped his arm back, fabric ripped, and the creature went flying far into the woods. "Damn it!" Not waiting, Nate quickly powdered the river with the crushed *ayaeya* vine, sprinkling it slowly, ensuring a good spread.

Behind him, Carrera was busy protecting their rear. The beasts from the stream were now converging on them.

Nate shook the last of the powder from the satchel, then tossed it into the stream. As he watched the pouch drift downstream rapidly, he prayed his plan would work. "Done," he said, turning.

Carrera glanced over to him. Past her shoulder, Nate spotted bodies leaping from branches in the deeper jungle. "We have a problem," the Ranger said.

"What?"

The Ranger lifted her flamethrower and shot a jet of fire toward the jungle. As he watched, the line of fire drizzled back to the weapon's muzzle, like a hose draining after the spigot had been turned off.

"Out of fuel," she said.

Frank O'Brien stood by his twin sister, guarding her. At times, he swore that he could read her mind. Like now. Kelly stared at the river, watching with Kouwe and Manny for any sign that Rand's plan might work. But he noticed how she kept peering into the jungle, her eyes drawn to the path the ethnobotanist and soldier had taken. He also saw the glint in her eyes.

An explosion momentarily drew his attention around. Another grenade. The rain of debris rattled through the canopy. Gunfire was now almost continuous, all around them. The line of Rangers was slowly being driven back to the cluster of civilians. Soon they would have no choice but to retreat toward the stream and closer to whatever skulked in its watery depths.

Nearby, Anna Fong stood with Zane, guarded by Olin Pasternak, who stood with a 9mm Beretta pistol in hand. It was a poor weapon against such small, fast-moving targets, but it was better than nothing.

A growl suddenly rumbled behind him, from Manny's jaguar.

"Look!" Kelly called out.

Frank turned. His sister stood with her flashlight pointed toward the stream. Then he saw it, too, lit by the reflection of her flashlight. Small glistening objects began to bob up from the water's depths, floating, drifting with the current.

"Nate did it!" Kelly said, a smile on her face.

At her side, Professor Kouwe stepped nearer the streambed. One of the piranha-frogs burst from the water toward him, but landed on its side in the mud. It flopped for a couple seconds, then lay still. Stunned. Kouwe glanced to Frank. "We must not lose this chance. We must cross now."

Frank turned and spotted Captain Waxman a short distance up the slope. He yelled to be heard above the gunfire. "Captain Waxman! Rand's plan is working!" Frank waved an arm. "We can cross! Now!"

Waxman acknowledged his words with a nod, then his voice boomed. "Bravo unit! Retreat toward the stream!"

Frank touched the brim of his lucky baseball cap and stepped to Kelly. "Let's go."

Manny hurried past them. "Tor-tor and I'll still go first. It was my dissection upon which this plan was based." He didn't wait for a reply. He and his pet stepped to the stream's edge. He paused for half a breath, then waded into the stream. This fork was clearly deeper. Midstream, the water reached Manny's chest. Tor-tor had to swim.

But shortly the biologist was climbing out the far side. He turned. "Hurry! It's safe for the moment!"

"Move it!" Waxman ordered.

The civilians crossed together, strung along the current.

Frank went with Kelly, holding her hand. By now, hundreds of creatures bobbed in the water. They had to wade through the deadly forms, bumping them aside, avoiding sharp teeth that glistened from slack mouths. Horrified, Frank held his breath, praying for them to remain inert.

They reached the far side and scrambled, half panicked, out of the water. The Rangers followed next, rushing across in full gear, oblivious to what floated around them. As they clambered up to dry land, the first of the advancing creatures began to appear on the far side of the stream, hurtling out of the jungle. A couple piranha-frogs approached the stream but stopped at the water's edge, gill flaps trembling.

They must sense the danger, Frank thought. But they had no choice. On land they were suffocating. As if obeying some silent signal, the mass of mutated piranhas fled into the water.

"Back away!" Waxman ordered. "We can't count on the water still being tainted."

The group fled from the stream into the jungle-covered heights. Flashlights remained fixed on the water and banks. But after several minutes, it was clear the pursuit was over. Either the waters were still toxic to the beasts or they had given up their chase.

Frank sighed. "It's over."

Kelly remained quietly focused beside him, using her flashlight to scan the far bank of the stream. "Where's Private Carrera?" she asked softly, then turned to Frank. "Where's Nate?"

Upriver, a blast sounded, echoing through the forest.

Kelly's eyes widened as she stared at Frank. "They're in trouble."

Nate raised his shotgun and blasted another of the creatures that ventured too close. Carrera had shrugged off her weapon's fuel canister and was bent over it. "How much longer?" Nate asked, eyes wide, trying to watch everything at once.

"Almost done."

Nate glanced to the stream at his back. In the glow from Carrera's flashlight, he saw that the poison in the water was working. Downstream, bodies floated to the surface, but the current was rapidly carrying them away. The narrow streambed behind them was empty of bodies and could not be trusted. The current, as swift as it was, had surely swept the powdered poison away from here and down the length of the stream. It was not safe. They needed to backtrack along the trailing toxin in the water and seek a secure place to cross, where the current was more sluggish, somewhere where the poison was still active—but between them and safety lay a small legion of the creatures, entrenched in the forest, blocking their way.

"Ready," Carrera said, standing.

She hauled her handiwork from the jungle floor and tightened the canister's lid, leaving a primer cord draping from it. The tank contained only a bit of fuel, not enough to service the weapon, but enough for their purposes. At least he hoped.

Nate held his position with his shotgun. "Are you sure this will work?"

"It had better."

Her words were not exactly the vote of confidence Nate was seeking.

"Point out the target again," she said, moving beside him.

He shifted his shotgun's muzzle and pointed at the gray-barked tree about thirty yards downstream.

"Okay." Carrera lit the end of the primer cord with a butane lighter. "Get ready." She swung her arm back and, using all the strength in her body, lobbed the canister underhanded.

Nate held his breath. It arced end-over-end—and landed at the foot of the targeted tree.

"All those years of women's softball finally paid off," Carrera mumbled, then to Nate: "Get down!"

Both dropped to the leafy floor. Nate fell, keeping his shotgun pointed ahead of him. And he was lucky he did. One of the creatures leaped from a bush, landing inches from his nose. Nate rolled and batted it away with the stock of his shotgun. He rolled back to his belly and glanced to the Ranger beside him. "Varsity baseball," he mumbled. "Senior year."

"Down!" Carrera reached and smashed his head to the dirt.

The explosion was deafening, shrapnel ripped through the canopy overhead. Nate glanced over. Carrera's trick had indeed worked. She had transformed the near-empty fuel tank into a large Molotov cocktail. Flames lit the night.

Carrera got to her knees. "What about—?"

Now it was Nate's turn to tug her down.

The second explosion sounded like a lightning strike: splintering wood accompanied by a low *boom*. The nearby jungle was shredded apart, followed by a rain of flaming copal resin.

"Damn it!" Carrera swore. Her sleeve was on fire. She patted it out in the loam.

Nate stood, relieved to see that the plan had worked. The tree, their target, was now just a blasted wreck, bluish flames dancing atop the stump. As Nate expected, the sap, rich in hydrocarbons, had acted as fuel, causing the makeshift Molotov cocktail to turn the tree into a natural bomb, and torch the entire riverbank as well.

"C'mon!" Nate called, bounding up with Carrera.

Together, they ran along the flaming and shredded section of the forest, paralleling the stream until they overtook the poison trailing through the water. Bodies of the creatures and other fish filled the channel.

"This way!" Nate ran into the river, half swimming, half clawing his way across. Carrera followed.

In no time, they were scrambling up the far bank.

"We did it!" the Ranger said with a laugh.

Nate sighed. Off in the distance, he spotted the shine of the others' flashlights. The team had made it across, too. "Let's go see if everyone else is okay."

They helped each other up and stumbled away from the stream, aiming for the other camp.

When they marched out of the forest, a cheer went up. "Way to go, Carrera," Kostos said, a true smile on his lips.

Nate's greeting was no less earnest. As soon as he arrived, Kelly threw her arms around his neck and hugged him tight. "You made it," she mumbled in his ear. "You did it."

"And not a minute too soon," Nate said with a nod.

Frank patted him on the back.

"Well done, Dr. Rand," Captain Waxman said stoically, and turned to organize his troops. No one wanted to remain this close to the stream, poisoned or not.

Kelly dropped her arms, but not before planting a soft kiss on his cheek. "Thanks . . . thanks for saving us. And thanks for returning safely."

She swung away, leaving Nate somewhat bewildered.

Carrera nudged him with an elbow and rolled her eyes. "Looks like someone made a friend."

10:02 A.M.

AMAZON JUNGLE

Louis stood in the center of the blasted region near the river's edge. He could still smell the acrid tang of napalm in the air. Behind him, his team was offloading the canoes and loading up backpacks. From here, the journey would be on foot.

With the dawn, clouds had rolled in, and a steady drizzle fell from the sky, dousing the few fires that still smoldered. A smoky mist clung to the dead pocket of jungle, ghostly white and thick.

Off to the side, his mistress wandered around the site, a wounded expression on her face, as if the damage to the forest were a personal injury. She slowly circled a pole planted in the ground with a speared creature impaled on it. It was one of the strange beasts that had attacked the other group. Louis had never seen anything of its ilk before. And from Tshui's expression, neither had she. Tshui eyed the beast, cocking her head like a bird studying a worm.

Jacques stepped up behind Louis. "You have a radio call . . . on your coded frequency."

"Finally," he sighed.

Earlier, just before dawn, one of his two scouts had returned, badly frightened and wild-eyed. He had reported that his partner, a squat Colombian who went by the name of Toady, had been attacked by one of these beasts and died horribly. Malachim had barely made it back alive. Unfortunately, the man's report of the other team's whereabouts was thready at best. It seemed the Rangers' group, chased across a tributary stream, had fled these same beasts, and were now heading in a southwesterly direction. But toward where?

Louis had a way of finding out. He accepted the radio from Jacques. It was a direct link to a tiny scrambled transmitter held by a member of the opposing team, a little mole planted under the Rangers' noses at significant expense.

"Thank you, Jacques." Radio in hand, Louis stepped a few yards away. He had already had one previous call this morning, from his financiers, St. Savin Pharmaceuticals in France. It seemed some disease was spreading across the Amazon and the United States, something associated with the dead man's body. Stakes were now higher. Louis had argued to raise his own fee, on the grounds that his work was now more hazardous. St. Savin had accepted, as he knew they would. A cure to this disease would be worth billions to his employer. What were a few more francs tossed his way?

Louis lifted the radio. "Favre here."

"Dr. Favre." The relief was clear in the other's voice. "Thank God, I reached you."

"I've been awaiting your call." A bit of menace entered Louis's tone. "I lost a good man last night because someone did not have the foresight to inform us of these venomous little toads."

There was a long pause. "I . . . I'm sorry. In all the commotion, I could hardly sneak off and place a call. In fact, this is the first chance I've had to slip away to the latrine alone."

"Fine. So tell me about this *commotion* last night."

"It was horrible." His spy blathered in his ear for the next three minutes, giving Louis an overview of what happened. "If it wasn't for Rand's use of some powdered fish toxin, we would all have surely died."

Louis's fingers gripped the radio tighter at the mention of Rand's name. The family name alone bristled the small hairs on his neck. "And where are you all now?"

"We're still heading in a southwesterly direction, searching for Gerald Clark's next marker."

"Very good."

"But—"

"What is it?"

"I . . . I want out."

"Pardon, mon ami?"

"Last night I was almost killed. I was hoping that you could . . . I don't know . . . pick me up if I wandered off. I would be willing to pay for my safe delivery back to civilization."

Louis closed his eyes. It seemed his mole was getting cold feet. He would have to warm the little mouse up. "Well, if you vacate your post, I will certainly find you."

"Th . . . thank you. I would—"

He interrupted. "And I'd be sure, when I found you, that your death would be long, painful, and humiliating. If you're familiar with my dossier, I'm sure you know how *creative* I can be."

There was silence on the other end. Louis could imagine his little spy blanching and quivering with fear.

"I understand."

"Excellent. I'm glad we've settled this matter. Now on to more important matters. It seems our mutual benefactor in France has placed a request upon our services. Something, I'm afraid, you'll have to accomplish."

"Wh . . . what?"

"For security purposes and to ensure their proprietary rights to what lies ahead, they wish to choke off the team's communication to the outside world, preferably as soon as possible without raising suspicion."

"How am I supposed to do that? You know I was supplied the computer virus to degrade the team's satellite uplink, but the Rangers have their own communication equipment. I wouldn't be able to get near it."

"No *problème*. You get that virus planted and leave the Rangers to me."

"But—"

"Have faith. You are never alone."

The line was silent again. Louis smiled. His words had not reassured his agent.

"Update me again tonight," Louis said.

A pause. "I'll try."

"Don't try . . . *do*."

"Yes, Doctor." The line went dead.

Louis lowered the radio and strode to Jacques. "We should be under way. The other team has a good start on us."

"Yes, sir." Jacques retreated to gather and organize his men.

Louis noticed that Tshui still stood by the impaled creature. If he wasn't mistaken, there was a trace of fear in the woman's eyes. But Louis wasn't sure. How could he be? He had never seen such an emotion displayed by the Indian witch. He crossed to her and pulled her into his arms.

She trembled ever so slightly under his hand.

"Hush, *ma chérie*. There is nothing to fear."

Tshui leaned against him, but her eyes flicked to the stake. She pulled tighter to him, a slight moan escaping her lips.

Louis frowned. Maybe he should heed his lover's unspoken warning. From here, they should proceed with more caution, more stealth. The other team had almost been destroyed by these aquatic predators, something never seen before. A clear sign they were probably on the right path. *But what if there are more hidden dangers out there?*

As he pondered this risk, he realized his team possessed a certain inherent advantage. Last night, it had taken all his opponents' cunning and ingenuity to survive the assault—a battle which inadvertently had opened a safer path for Louis's group to follow. So why not again? Why not let the other team flush out any other threats?

Louis mumbled, "Then we'll waltz in over their dead bodies and collect the prize." Pleased once again, he leaned and kissed the top of Tshui's head. "Fear not, my love. We cannot lose."

Lauren O'Brien sat beside the bed, a book forgotten in her lap. Dr. Seuss's *Green Eggs and Ham,* Jessie's favorite. Her grandchild was asleep, curled on her side. Her fever had broken with the rising of the sun. The cocktail of antiinflammatories and antipyretics had done the job, slowly dropping the child's temperature from 102 back to 98.6. No one was sure if Jessie had contracted the jungle contagion—childhood fevers were common and plentiful—but no one was taking any chances.

The ward in which her granddaughter now slept was a closed system, sealed and vented against the spread of any potential germ. Lauren herself wore a one-piece disposable quarantine suit, outfitted with a self-breathing mask. She had refused at first, fearing the garb would further alarm Jessie. But policy dictated that all hospital staff and visitors wear proper isolation gear.

When Lauren had first entered the room, all suited up, Jessie had indeed appeared frightened, but the clear faceplate of the mask and a few reassuring words calmed her. Lauren had remained bedside all morning as Jessie was examined, blood samples collected, and drugs administered. With the resilience of the young, she now slept soundly.

A slight *whoosh* announced a newcomer to the room. Lauren awkwardly turned in her suit. She saw a familiar face behind another mask. She placed the book on a table and stood. "Marshall."

Her husband crossed to her and enveloped her in his plastic-clad arms. "I read her chart before coming in," he said, his voice sounding slightly tinny and distant. "Fever's down."

"Yes, it broke a couple of hours ago."

"Any word yet on the lab work?" Lauren heard the fear in his voice.

"No . . . it's too soon to tell if this is the plague." Without knowing the causative agent, there was no quick test. Diagnosis was made on a trio of clinical signs: oral ulcerations, tiny submucosal hemorrhages, and a dramatic drop in total white blood cell counts. But these symptoms typically would not manifest until thirty-six hours after the initial fever. It would be a long wait. Unless . . .

Lauren tried to change the subject. "How did your conference call go with the CDC and the folks in the Cabinet?"

Marshall shook his head. "A waste of time. It'll be days until all the politicking settles and a true course of action can be administered. The only good news is that Blaine at the CDC supported my idea to close Florida's border. That surprised me."

"It shouldn't," Lauren said. "I've been sending him case data all week, including what's happening in Brazil. The implications are pretty damn frightening."

"Well, you must have shaken him up." He squeezed her hand. "Thanks."

Lauren let out a long rattling sigh as she stared at the bed.

"Why don't you take a break? I can watch over Jessie for a while. You should try to catch a nap. You've been up all night."

"I'll never be able to sleep."

Marshall put his arm around her waist. "Then at least get some coffee and a little breakfast. We have the midday call with Kelly and Frank scheduled in a couple hours."

Lauren leaned against him. "What are we going to tell Kelly?"

"The truth. Jessie has a fever, but it's nothing to panic about. We still don't know for sure if it's the disease or not."

Lauren nodded. They remained silent for a bit, then Marshall guided her gently to the door. "Go."

Lauren passed through the air-locked doors and crossed down the hall to the locker room, where she stripped out of the suit and changed into scrubs. As she left the locker room, she stopped by the nurses' station. "Did any of the labs come back yet?"

A small Asian nurse flipped a plastic case file to her. "These were faxed just a minute ago."

Lauren flipped the file open and thumbed to the page of blood chemistries and hematology results. Her finger ran down the long list. The chemistries were all normal, as expected. But her nail stopped at the line for the total white blood cell count:

TWBC: 2130 (L)   6,000–15,000

It was low, significantly low, one of the trio of signs expected with the plague.

With her finger trembling, she ran down the report to the section that detailed the different white blood cell levels. There was one piece of news that the team's epidemiologist, Dr. Alvisio, had mentioned to her late last night, a possible pattern in the lab data that his computer model for the disease had noted: an unusual spike of a specific line of white blood cells, *basophils,* that occurred early in the disease as the total white blood cell levels were dropping. Though it was too soon to say for certain, it seemed to be consistent in all cases of the disease. It was perhaps a way to accelerate early detection.

Lauren read the last line.

Basophil count: 12 (H)   0–4

"Oh, God." She lowered the chart to the nurses' station. Jessie's basophil levels were spiked above normal, well above normal.

Lauren closed her eyes.

"Are you okay, Dr. O'Brien?"

Lauren didn't hear the nurse. Her mind was too full of a horrifying realization: Jessie had the plague.

11:48 A.M.

AMAZON JUNGLE

Kelly followed the line of the others, bone tired but determined to keep moving. They had been walking all night with frequent rest breaks. After the attack, they had marched for a solid two hours, then made a temporary camp at dawn while the Rangers contacted the field base in Wauwai. They had decided to push on until at least midday, when they would use the satellite link to contact the States. Afterward, the team would rest the remainder of the day, regroup, and decide how to proceed.

Kelly glanced at her watch. Noon approached. *Thank God.* Already she heard Waxman grumbling about choosing a site for the day's camp. "Well away from any waterways," she heard him warn.

All day long, the team had been wary of streams and pools, skirting them or crossing in a mad rush. But there were no further attacks.

Manny had offered a reason. "Perhaps the creatures were local to just that small territory. Maybe that's why the buggers were never seen before."

"If so, good riddance," Frank had voiced sourly.

They had trudged onward, the morning drizzle drying slowly to a thick humid mist. The moisture weighed everything down: clothes, packs, boots. But no one complained about the march. All were glad to put distance between them and the horror of the previous night.

From up ahead, a Ranger scout called back. "A clearing!" It was Corporal Warczak. As the unit's tracker, his scouting served double duty. He was also watching for any physical evidence of Gerald Clark's passage. "The spot looks perfect for a campsite!"

Kelly sighed. "About time."

"Check it out!" Waxman said. "Make sure there are no close streams."

"Yes, sir! Kostos is already reconnoitering the area."

Nate, just a couple steps ahead of her, called forward, "Be careful! There could be—"

A pained shout rose from ahead.

Everyone froze, except Nate who rushed forward. "Damn it, doesn't anyone listen to what I tell them?" he muttered as he ran. He glanced back to Kelly and Kouwe and waved an arm. "We'll need your help! Both of you."

Kelly moved to follow. "What is it?" she asked Kouwe.

The Indian professor was already slinging his pack forward and working the straps loose. "*Supay chacra,* I'd imagine. The devil's garden. C'mon."

Devil's garden? Kelly did not like the sound of that.

Captain Waxman ordered the bulk of his Rangers to remain with the other civilians. He and Frank joined in following Nate.

Kelly hurried forward and saw a pair of Rangers on the ground ahead. They seemed to be fighting, one rolling in the dirt, the other striking him with the flat of his hand.

Nate ran toward them.

"Get these goddamn shits off me!" the Ranger on the ground yelled, rolling through the underbrush. It was Sergeant Kostos.

"I'm trying," Corporal Warczak replied, continuing to slap at the man.

Nate knocked the corporal aside. "Stop! You're only making them angrier." Then to the soldier on the ground, he ordered, "Sergeant Kostos, lie still!"

"They're stinging me all over!"

Kelly was now close enough to see that the man was covered with large black ants, each about an inch long. There had to be thousands of them.

"Quit moving and they'll leave you alone."

Kostos glanced to Nate, eyes burning and angry, but he did as told. He stopped thrashing in the brush and lay panting.

Kelly noticed the blistered welts all over his arms and face. It looked as if he had been attacked with a burning cigarette butt.

"What happened?" Captain Waxman asked.

Nate held everyone away from Kostos. "Stand back."

Kostos trembled where he lay. Kelly saw the tears of pain at the corners of the man's eyes. He must be in agony. But Nate's advice proved sound. As he lay, unmoving, the ants stopped biting and crawled from his arms and legs, disappearing into the leafy brush.

"Where are they going?" Kelly asked.

"Back home," Kouwe said. "They were the colony's soldiers." He pointed past a few trees. A few yards ahead opened a jungle clearing, so empty and bare it looked as if someone had taken a broom and hedge clippers to the area. In the center stood a massive tree, its branches spread through the space, a solitary giant.

"It's an ant tree," the professor continued to explain. "The ant colony lives inside it."

"Inside it?"

Kouwe nodded. "It's just one of the many ways rain forest plants have adapted to animals or insects. The tree has evolved with special hollow branches and tubules that serve the ants, even feeding the colony with a special sugary sap. The tree in turn is serviced by the ants. Not only does the colony's debris help fertilize the tree, but they're active in protecting it, too—from other insects, from birds and animals." Kouwe nodded to the clearing. "The ants destroy anything that grows near the tree, trimming away stranglers or climbers from the branches themselves. It's why such spots in the jungle are called *supay chacra,* or a devil's garden."

"What a strange relationship."

"Indeed. But the relationship is mutually beneficial to both species— tree and insect. In fact, one cannot live without the other."

Kelly stared toward the clearing, amazed at how intertwined life was out here. A few days back, Nate had shown her an orchid whose flower was shaped like the reproductive parts of a certain species of wasp. "In order to lure the insect over to pollinate it." Then there were others that traded sugary nectars to lure different pollinators. And such relationships weren't limited to insect and plant. The fruit of certain trees *had* to be consumed by a specific bird or animal and pass through its digestive tract before it could root and grow. So much strangeness, all life dependent and twined to its neighbors in a complex evolutionary web.

Nate knelt beside the sergeant, drawing back her attention. By now, the ants had vacated the soldier's body. "How many times have I warned you to watch what you lean against?"

"I didn't see them," Kostos said, his voice pained and belligerent. "And I needed to take a leak."

Kelly saw the man's zipper was indeed down.

Nate shook his head. "Against an ant tree?"

Kouwe explained as he rummaged through his pack. "Ants are tuned to chemical markers. The man's urine would have been taken as an assault on the colony living in the tree."

Kelly broke out a syringe of antihistamine, while Kouwe removed a handful of leaves from his own pack and began to rub them together. She recognized the leaves and the scent of the oily compound. "*Ku-run-yeh?*" she asked.

The Indian smiled at her. "Very good." It was the same medicinal plant that Kouwe had used to treat her blistered fingers when she had touched the fire liana vine. A potent analgesic.

The two doctors began to work on their patient. As Kelly injected a combination of an antihistamine and a steroidal antiinflammatory, Kouwe smeared some of the *ku-run-yeh* extract on the soldier's arm, showing him how to apply it.

The sergeant's face reflected the immediate soothing relief. He sighed and took the handful of leaves. "I can do the rest myself," he said, his voice hard with embarrassment.

Corporal Warczak helped his sergeant stand.

"We should skirt around this area," Nate said. "We don't want to camp too near an ant tree. Our food might draw their scouts."

Captain Waxman nodded. "Then let's get going. We've wasted enough time here." His glance toward the limping sergeant was not sympathetic.

Over the next half hour, the group wound again under the forest canopy, accompanied by the hoots and calls of capuchin and wooly monkeys. Manny pointed out a tiny pigmy anteater nestled atop a branch. Frozen in place by fear, it looked more like a stuffed animal with its large eyes and silky coat. And of more menace, but appearing just as artificial due to its fluorescent-green scales, was a forest pit viper, wrapped and dangling from a palm frond.

At last, a shout arose from up ahead. It was Corporal Warczak. "I've found something!"

Kelly prayed it wasn't another ant tree.

"I believe it's a marker from Clark!"

The group converged toward the sound of his voice. Up a short hill, they found a large Brazil nut tree. Its bower shaded a great area littered with old nuts and leaves. Upon the trunk, a small strip of torn cloth hung, soaked and limp.

The others approached, but Corporal Warczak waved them all away. "I've found boot tracks," he said. "Don't trample them."

"Boot tracks?" Kelly said in a hushed voice as the soldier slowly circled the tree, then stopped on the far side.

"I see a trail leading here!" he called back.

Captain Waxman and Frank crossed over to him.

Kelly frowned. "I thought Gerald Clark came out of the forest barefooted."

"He did," Nate answered as they waited. "But the Yanomamo shaman we captured mentioned that the Indian villagers had stripped Clark of his possessions. They must have taken his boots."

Kelly nodded.

Richard Zane pointed toward the tree. "Is there another message?"

They all waited for the okay to enter the area. Captain Waxman and Frank returned, leaving Corporal Warczak crouched by the trail.

The group was waved forward. "We'll camp here," Waxman declared.

Sounds of relief flowed, and the team approached the tree, decaying nuts crackling underfoot. Kelly was one of the first to the trunk. Again, deeply incised in the bark were clear markings.

"G. C.: Clark again," Nate said. He pointed in the direction of the arrow. "Due west. Just like the boot trail Warczak found. Dated May seventh."

Olin leaned against the tree. "May seventh? That means it took Clark ten days to reach the village from here? He must have been moving damn slowly."

"He probably didn't make a beeline like we did," Nate said. "He probably spent a lot of time searching for some sign of habitation or civilization, tracking back and forth."

"Plus he was getting sick by this time," Kelly added. "According to my mother's examination of his remains, the cancers would've been starting to spread through his body. He probably had to rest often."

Anna Fong sighed sadly. "If only he could've reached civilization sooner . . . been able to communicate where he'd been all this time."

Olin shoved away from the tree. "Speaking of communication, I should get the satellite uplink set up. We're due to conference in another half hour."

"I'll help you," Zane said, heading off with him.

The rest of the group dispersed to string up hammocks, gather wood, and scrounge up some local fruits. Kelly busied herself with her own campsite, spreading her mosquito netting like a pro.

Frank worked beside her. "Kelly . . . ?" From her brother's tone, she could tell he was about to tread on cautious ground.

"What?"

"I think you should go back."

She stopped tugging her netting and turned. "What do you mean?"

"I've been talking to Captain Waxman. When he reported the attack this morning to his superiors, they ordered him to trim nonessential personnel after a safe camp had been established. Last night was too close. They don't want to risk additional casualties. Plus the others are slowing the Rangers down." Frank glanced over his shoulder. "To expedite our search, it's been decided to leave Anna and Zane here, along with Manny and Kouwe."

"But—"

"Olin, Nate, and I will continue with the Rangers."

Kelly turned fully around. "I'm *not* nonessential, Frank. I'm the only physician here, and I can travel just as well as you."

"Corporal Okamoto is a trained field medic."

"That doesn't make him an M.D."

"Kelly . . ."

"Frank, don't do this."

He wouldn't meet her eyes. "It's already been decided."

Kelly circled to make him look at her. "*You* decided this. You're the leader of this operation."

He finally looked up. "Okay, it was my decision." His shoulders sagged, and he swung away. "I don't want you at risk."

Kelly fumed, trembling with frustration. But she knew the decision was indeed ultimately her brother's.

"We'll send out a GPS lock on our current position and leave two Rangers as guards. Then a team will evacuate you as soon as a Brazilian supply helicopter with the range to reach camp can be coordinated. In the meantime, the remaining party—the six Rangers and the three of us—will strike out from here."

"When?"

"After a short rest break. We'll leave this afternoon. March until sundown. Now that we're on Clark's trail, a smaller party can travel faster."

Kelly closed her eyes, huffing out a sigh. The plan was sound. And with the contagion spreading here and in the States, time was essential. Besides, if something was found, a scientific research team could always be airlifted to the site to investigate. "I guess I have no choice."

Frank remained silent, cinching his hammock for his short rest break.

A call broke the tension. Olin, busy establishing the satellite uplink, shouted, "We're ready here!"

Kelly followed Frank to the laptop, again protected under a rain tarp.

Olin hunched over the keyboard, tapping rapidly. "Damn it, I'm having trouble getting a solid feed." He continued working. "All this dampness . . . ah, here we go!" He sat up. "Got it!"

The ex-KGB agent slid to the side. Kelly crouched with Frank. A face formed on the screen, jittering and pixellating out of focus.

"It's the best I can manage," Olin whispered from the side.

It was their father. Even through the interference, his hard face did not look pleased. "I heard about last night," he said as introduction. "It's good to see you're both safe."

Frank nodded. "We're fine. Tired but okay."

"I read the report from the army, but tell me yourselves what happened."

Together Frank and Kelly quickly related the attack by the strange creatures.

"A chimera?" her father said as they finished, eyes narrowed. "A mix of frog and fish?"

"That's what the *biologist* here believes," Kelly said pointedly, glancing to Frank, stressing that even Manny had proven useful to the expedition.

"Then that settles matters," her father said, straightening and staring directly at Kelly. "An hour ago I was contacted by the head of Special Forces out of Fort Bragg and was informed of the revised plan."

"What revised plan?" Zane asked behind them.

Frank waved away his question.

Their father continued, "Considering what's happening with this damn disease, I totally concur with General Korsen. A cure must be found, and time has become a critical factor."

Kelly thought about protesting her expulsion, but bit her lip, knowing she would find no ally in her father. He had not wanted his little girl to come out here in the first place.

Frank leaned closer to the screen. "What's the condition in the States?"

Their father shook his head. "I'll let your mother answer that." He slid aside.

She looked exhausted, her eyes shadowed with fatigue. "The number of cases . . ." Lauren coughed and cleared her throat. "The number of cases has trebled in the last twelve hours."

Kelly cringed. *So fast . . .*

"Mostly in Florida, but we're now seeing cases in California, Georgia, Alabama, and Missouri."

"What about in Langley?" Kelly asked. "At the Institute?"

A glance was shared between her parents.

"Kelly . . ." her father began. His tone sounded like Frank's from a moment ago, cautionary. "I don't want you to panic."

Kelly sat up straighter, her heart already climbing into her throat. Don't panic? Did those words *ever* calm someone? "What is it?"

"Jessie's sick—"

The next few words were lost on Kelly. Her vision darkened at the corners. She had been dreading hearing those words since first learning of the contagion. *Jessie's sick . . .*

Her father must have noticed her falling back in her seat, pale and trembling. Frank put his arm around her, holding her.

"Kelly," her father said. "We don't know if it's the disease. It's just a fever, and she's already responding to medications. She was eating ice cream and chattering happily when we came to make this call."

Her mother placed a hand on her father's shoulder, and they exchanged a look. "It's probably not the disease, is it, Lauren?"

Their mother smiled. "I'm sure it's not."

Frank sighed. "Thank God. Is anyone else showing symptoms?"

"Not a one," her father assured them.

But Kelly's eyes were fixed on her mother. Her smile now looked sickly and wan. Her gaze slipped down.

Kelly closed her own eyes. *Oh, God . . .*

"We'll see you soon," her father concluded.

Frank nudged her.

She nodded. "Soon . . ."

Zane again spoke behind her. "What did your father mean that he'd see you soon? What's this about revised plans? What's going on?"

Frank gave Kelly a final squeeze. "Jessie's fine," he whispered to her. "You'll see when you get home." He then turned to answer Zane's question.

Kelly remained frozen before the laptop as the arguments began to rage behind her. In her mind's eye, she again saw her mother's smile fade, her eyes lower in shame. She knew her mother's moods better than anyone, possibly even better than her father did. Her mother had been lying. She had seen the knowledge hidden behind the reassuring words.

Jessie had the disease. Her mother believed it. Kelly knew this with certainty. And if her mother believed it . . .

Kelly could not stop the tears. Busily arguing about the change in plans, the others failed to notice her.

She covered her face with her hand. *Oh, God . . . no . . .*

ELEVEN

Aerial Assault

Nate could not sleep. As he lay in his hammock, he knew he should be resting for the next leg of the journey. In only another hour, his group was due to depart, but questions still persisted. He stared around the campsite. While half the camp napped, the other half were still quietly arguing about the split-up.

"We can just follow them," Zane said. "What are they going to do, shoot us?"

"We should mind their orders," Kouwe said calmly, but Nate knew the older professor was no more pleased with being abandoned than the Tellux rep.

Nate turned his back on them, but he understood their frustration. If he had been one of those left behind, they would've had to hog-tie him to stop him from continuing on his own.

From this new vantage, he spotted Kelly lying in her hammock. She was the only one who had not protested. Her concern for her daughter was clearly foremost in her mind. As he watched, Kelly rolled over and their gazes met. Her eyes were puffy from tears.

Nate gave up trying to nap and slid from his hammock. He crossed to her side and knelt. "Jessie will be fine," he said softly.

Kelly stared at him in silence, then spoke through her pain, her voice small. "She has the disease."

Nate frowned. "Now that's just your fear talking. There's no proof that—"

"I saw it in my mother's eyes. She could never hide anything from me. She knows Jessie has the disease and is trying to spare me."

Nate didn't know what to say. He reached through the netting and rested a hand on her shoulder. He quietly comforted her, willing her strength, then spoke with his heart, softly but earnestly, "If what you say is true, I'll find a cure out there somewhere. I promise."

This earned a tired smile. Her lips moved, but no words came out. Still, Nate read those lips easily. *Thank you.* A single tear rolled from her eyes before she covered her face and turned away.

Nate stood, leaving her to her grief. He noticed Frank and Captain Waxman conferring over a map splayed across the ground and headed toward them. With a glance back at Kelly, he silently repeated his promise. *I will find a cure.*

The map the two were surveying was a topographic study of the terrain. Captain Waxman drew a finger across the map. "Following due west of here, the land elevates as it approaches the Peruvian border. But it's a broken jumble of cliffs and valleys, a veritable maze. It'll be easy to get lost in there."

"We'll have to watch closely for Gerald Clark's signposts," Frank said, then looked up to acknowledge Nate's presence. "You should get your pack ready. We're gonna head out shortly and take advantage of as much daylight as we can."

Nate nodded. "I can be ready in five minutes."

Frank stood. "Let's get moving then."

Over the next half hour, the team was assembled. They decided to leave the Rangers' SATCOM radio equipment with the remaining party, who needed to coordinate the retrieval effort by the Brazilian army. The group heading out would continue to use the CIA's satellite array to maintain contact.

Nate hoisted his shotgun to one shoulder and shifted his backpack to a comfortable spot. The plan was to move swiftly, with few rest breaks, until sunset.

Waxman raised an arm and the group headed off into the forest, led by Corporal Warczak.

As they left, Nate looked behind him. He had already said good-bye to his friends, Kouwe and Manny. But behind the pair stood the two Rangers who would act as guards: Corporal Jorgensen and Private Carrera. The woman lifted her weapon in farewell. Nate waved back.

Waxman had originally slated Corporal Graves to remain behind, to be evacuated out, on account of the death of his brother Rodney. But Graves had argued, "Sir, this mission cost my brother's life along with my fellow teammates. With your permission, I'd like to see it through to the end. For the honor of my brother . . . for all my brothers."

Waxman had consented.

With no further words, the group set off through the jungle. The sun had finally broken through the clouds, creating a steam bath under the damp canopy. Within minutes, everyone's face shone with sweat.

Nate marched beside Frank O'Brien. Every few steps, the man slid off his baseball cap and wiped the trickling dampness from his brow. Nate wore a handkerchief as a headband, keeping the sweat from his own eyes. But he couldn't keep the black flies and gnats, attracted by the salt and odor, from plaguing him.

Despite the heat, humidity, and constant buzzing in their ears, they made good progress. Within a couple of hours, Nathan estimated they had covered over seven miles. Warczak was still finding bootprints in the bare soil as they headed west into the jungle. The prints were barely discernable, pooled with water from yesterday's rains.

Ahead of him marched Corporal Okamoto, whistling his damn tune again. Nate sighed. *Didn't the jungle offer enough aggravations?*

As they continued, Nate kept wary watch for any perils: snakes, fire liana, ant trees, anything that might slow them down. Each stream was crossed with caution. But no sign of the piranha-frogs appeared. Overhead, Nate saw a three-toed sloth amble along a branch high in the canopy, oblivious to the intrusion. He watched its passage, glancing over his shoulder as he walked under it. Sloths seemed slow and amiable, but when injured, they were known to gut those who came too close. Their climbing claws were dagger-sharp. But this great beast just continued its arboreal journey.

Turning back around, Nate caught the barest flicker of something reflecting from high in a tree, about half a mile back. He paused to study it.

"What is it?" Frank asked, noticing Nate had stopped.

The flickering reflection vanished. He shook his head. Probably just a wet leaf fluttering in the sunlight. "Nothing," he said and waved Frank on. But throughout the remainder of the afternoon, he kept glancing over his shoulder. He could not escape the feeling that they were being watched, spied upon from on high. The feeling grew worse as the day wore on.

Finally, he turned to Frank. "Something's bothering me. Something we neglected to address after the attack back at the village."

"What?"

"Remember Kouwe's assessment that we were being tracked?"

"Yeah, but he wasn't a hundred percent sure. Just some picked fruit and bushes disturbed during the night. No footprints or anything concrete."

Nate glanced over his shoulder. "Let's say the professor was correct. If so, who's tracking us? It couldn't have been the Indians at the village. They were dead before we even entered the jungle. So who was it?"

Frank noticed the direction of Nate's stare. "You think we're still being tracked. Did you see something?"

"No, not really . . . just an odd reflection in the trees a while back. It's probably nothing."

Frank nodded. "All the same, I'll let Captain Waxman know. It wouldn't hurt to be on extra guard out here." Frank dropped back to speak with the Rangers' leader, who was marching with Olin Pasternak.

Alone, Nate stared into the shadowy forest around him. He was suddenly less sure that leaving the others behind was such a wise move.

5:12 P.M.

Manny ran a brush through Tor-tor's coat. Not that the bit of hygiene was necessary. The jaguar did a good enough job with his own bristled tongue. But it was a chore that both cat and human enjoyed. Tor-tor responded with a slow growl as Manny groomed the cat's belly. Manny wanted to growl himself, but not in contentment and pleasure.

He hated being left behind by the others.

Hearing a rustle at his side, Manny glanced up. It was the anthropologist, Anna Fong. "May I?" She pointed to the jaguar.

Manny lifted an eyebrow in mild surprise. He had noticed the woman eyeing the cat before, but he had thought it was with more fear than interest. "Sure." He patted the spot next to him. She knelt, and he handed her the brush. "He especially likes his belly and ruff worked over."

Anna took the brush and bent over the sleek feline. She stretched her arm, cautiously wary as Tor-tor watched her. She slowly lowered the brush and drew it through his thick coat. "He's so beautiful. Back at home, in Hong Kong, I watched the cats stalk back and forth in their cages at the zoo. But to raise one of them yourself, how wonderful that must be."

Manny liked the way she talked, soft with a certain stilted diction, oddly formal. "Wonderful, you say? He's been eating through my household budget, chewed through two sofas, and shredded I don't know how many throw rugs."

She smiled. "Still . . . it must be worth it."

Manny agreed, but he was reluctant to speak it aloud. It was somehow unmanly to express how much he loved the great big lug. "I'll have to release him soon."

Though he tried to hide it, she must have heard the sorrow in his words. Anna glanced up to him, her eyes supportive. "I'm sure it's still worth it."

Manny grinned shyly. *It sure was.*

Anna continued to massage the cat with the brush. Manny watched her from the side. One fall of her silky hair was tucked behind an ear. Her nose crinkled ever so slightly as she concentrated on the cat's grooming.

"Everyone!" a voice called out, interrupting them.

They both turned.

Nearby, Corporal Jorgensen lowered the radio's receiver and shook his head. He turned and faced the camp. "Everyone. I've got good news and bad news."

A universal grumbling met the soldier's attempt at joviality.

"The *good* news is that the Brazilian army has rousted up a helicopter to fly us out of here."

"And the bad?" Manny asked.

Jorgensen frowned. "It won't be here for another two days. With the plague spreading through the region, the demand for aircraft is fierce. And for the moment, our evac is a low priority."

"Two days?" Manny spoke up, accepting the brush back from Anna. Irritation entered his voice. "Then we could've traveled with the others until then."

"Captain Waxman had his orders," Jorgensen said with a shrug.

"What about the Comanche helicopter stationed at Wauwai?" Zane asked. He had been lounging in his hammock, quietly fuming.

Private Carrera answered from where she was cleaning her weapon. "It's a two-seater attack chopper. Besides, the Comanche's held in reserve to back up the other team as necessary."

Manny shook his head and furtively glanced at Kelly O'Brien. She sat in her hammock, eyes tired, dull, defeated. The waiting would be the worst for her. Two more days lost before she could join her sick daughter.

Kouwe spoke from near the large Brazil nut tree. He had been examining the crude markings knifed in the bark by Clark, and now had his head cocked questioningly. "Does anyone else smell smoke?"

Manny sniffed, but the air seemed clear.

Anna crimped her brow. "I smell something . . ."

Kouwe swung around the base of the large Brazil nut tree, nose half raised. Though long out of the forests, the professor's Indian senses were still keen. "There!" he called out from the far side.

The group followed after him. Carrera quickly slapped her M-16 back together, hauling it up as she stood.

To the south of their camp, about a hundred feet into the forest, small flames flickered in the shadows, low to the ground. Through breaks in the canopy, a thin column of gray smoke drifted skyward.

"I'll investigate," Jorgensen said. "The rest hang back with Carrera."

"I'm going with you," Manny said. "If anyone's out there, Tor-tor will scent them."

As answer, Jorgensen unstrapped the M-9 pistol from his belt and passed it to Manny. Together they cautiously passed into the deeper jungle. Manny signaled with his hand, and Tor-tor trotted ahead of them, taking the point.

Back behind them, Carrera ordered everyone together. "Keep alert!"

Manny followed after his cat, walking abreast of Corporal Jorgensen. "The fire's burning on the ground," Manny whispered.

As they neared the spot, the corporal signaled for silence.

Both men's senses were stretched, watching for any shift of shadows, listening for the telltale snap of a twig, searching for any sign of a hidden threat. But with the twittering of birds and mating calls of monkeys, it was difficult work. Their steps slowed as they neared the smoldering glow.

Ahead Tor-tor edged closer, his natural feline curiosity piqued. But once within a few yards of the smoky fire, he suddenly crouched, growling. He stared at the flames and slowly backed away.

The men stopped. Jorgensen lifted a hand, a silent warning. *The jaguar sensed something.* He motioned for Manny to sink lower and take up a guard position. Once set, Jorgensen proceeded ahead. Manny held his breath as the corporal moved silently through the forest, stepping carefully, weapon ready.

Manny kept watch all around them, unblinking, ears straining. Tor-tor backed to his side, now silent, hackles raised, golden eyes aglow. Beside him, Manny heard the cat chuffing at the air. Manny remembered the cat's reaction to the caiman urine beside the river. *He smells something . . . something that has him spooked.*

With adrenaline doped in Manny's blood, his own senses were more acute. Alerted by the jaguar, Manny now recognized an odd scent to the smoke: metallic, bitter, acrid. It was not plain wood smoke.

Straightening, Manny wanted to warn Jorgensen, but the soldier had already reached the site. As the soldier eyed the burning patch, Manny saw the man's shoulders jerk with surprise. He slowly circled the smoldering fire, rifle pointed outward. Nothing came out of the forest to threaten. Jorgenson maintained his watch for a full two minutes, then waved Manny over.

Letting out his held breath, Manny approached. Tor-tor hung back, still refusing to approach the fire.

"Whoever set this must have run off," Jorgensen said. He pointed at the fire. "Meant to scare us."

Manny moved close enough to see the spread of flames on the forest floor. It was not wood that burned, but some thick oily paste painted atop a cleared section of dirt. It cast a fierce brightness but little heat. The smoke rising from it was redolent and cloying, like some musky incense.

But it was not the smoke nor the strange fuel of this fire that sent icy chills along Manny's limbs—it was the pattern.

Painted and burning on the jungle floor was a familiar serpentine coiled symbol—the mark of the Ban-ali, burning bright under the canopy's gloom.

Jorgensen used the tip of his boot to nudge the oily substance. "Some combustible paste." He then used his other foot to kick dirt over the spot, smothering the flames. He worked along the burning lines, and with Manny's help, they doused the fire. Once they were done, Manny stared up, following the smoke into the late afternoon sky.

"We should get back to camp."

Manny nodded. They retreated back to the bower under the large Brazil nut tree. Jorgensen reported what they discovered. "I'll radio the field base. Let them know what we found." He crossed to the bulky radio pack and picked up the receiver. After a few moments, the soldier swore and slammed the receiver down.

"What is it?" Manny asked.

"We've missed SATCOM's satellite window by five minutes."

"What does that mean?" Anna asked.

Jorgensen waved an arm at the radio unit, then at the sky overhead. "The military's satellite transponders are out of range."

"Until when?"

"Till four o'clock tomorrow morning."

"What about reaching the other team?" Manny asked. "Using your personal radios?"

"I already tried that, too. The Sabers only have a range of six miles. Captain Waxman's team is beyond our reach."

"So we're cut off?" Anna asked.

Jorgensen shook his head. "Just until morning."

"And what then?" Zane paced nervously, eyes on the forest. "We can't stay here for two more days waiting for that damned helicopter."

"I agree," Kouwe said, frowning deeply. "The village Indians found the same mark on their *shabano* the very night they were assaulted by the piranha creatures."

Private Carrera turned to him. "What are you suggesting?"

Kouwe frowned. "I'm not sure yet." The professor's eyes were fixed on the smoggy smudge in the sky. The forest still reeked of the bitter fumes. "But we've been marked."

Frank was never happier to see the sun sink toward the horizon. They should be stopping soon. Every muscle ached from so many hours of hiking and so little sleep. He stumbled in step with the Ranger ahead of him, Nate marching behind.

Someone yelled a short distance away. "Whoa! Check this out!"

The straggling team members increased their pace. Frank climbed a short rise and saw what had triggered the startled response. A quarter mile ahead, the jungle was flooded by a small lake. Its surface was a sheet of silver from the setting sun to the west. It blocked their path, spreading for miles in both directions.

"It's an *igapo*," Nate said. "A swamp forest."

"It's not on my map," Captain Waxman said.

Nate shrugged. "Such sections dot the Amazon basin. Some come and go according to the rainfall levels. But for this region still to be so wet at the end of the dry season suggests it's been here a while." Nate pointed ahead. "Notice how the jungle breaks down here, drowned away by years of continual swamping."

Frank indeed noticed how the dense canopy ended ahead. What remained of the jungle here were just occasional massive trees growing straight out of the water and thousands of islands and hummocks. Otherwise, above the swamp, the blue sky was open and wide. The brightness after so long in the green gloom was sharp and biting.

The group cautiously hiked down the long, low slope that headed toward the swamp. The air seemed to grow more fecund and thick. Around the swamp, spiky bromeliads and massive orchids adorned their view. Frogs and toads set up a chorus, while the chattering of birds attempted to drown out their amphibious neighbors. Near the water's edges, spindly-limbed wading birds, herons and egrets, hunted fish. A handful of ducks took wing at their noisy approach.

Once within fifty feet of the water's edge, Captain Waxman called a halt. "We'll search the bank for any sign of a marker, but first we should make sure the water is safe to be near. I don't want any surprises."

Nate moved forward. "We may be okay. According to Manny, those predatory creatures were part piranha. Those fish don't like standing water like this. They prefer flowing streams."

Captain Waxman glanced to him. "And the last time I checked, piranhas didn't chase their prey onto dry land either."

Frank saw Nate blush slightly and nod.

Waxman sent Corporal Yamir forward toward the swamp's edge. "Let's see if anything stirs up."

The Pakistani soldier raised his M-16 and shot a grenade from its attached launcher toward the shallows off to the side. The explosion geysered water high into the air, startling birds and monkeys from their perches. Water and bits of lily pads rained down upon the forest.

The party waited for ten minutes, but nothing responded. No venomous predators fled the assault or attacked from the water's edge.

Captain Waxman waved his men forward to begin the search for another tree marker. "Be careful. Stay away from the water's edge and keep your eyes open!"

They didn't have long to wait. Again Corporal Warczak, the team's tracker, raised his voice. "Found it!" He stood only ten yards to the right, not far from the sludgy water.

Upon the bole of a palm that leaned over the water was the now familiar strip of polyester cloth, nailed to the tree with a thorn. The markings were almost identical to the last one. The initials and an arrow pointing due west again, right toward the swamp. Only the date was different. "May fifth," Olin read aloud. "Two days from the last marker."

Warczak stood a few paces away. "It looks like Clark came from this way."

"But the arrow points across the water," Frank said. He tipped the bill of his baseball cap to shadow his eyes and stared over the water. Distantly, beyond the swamp, he could see the highlands that Captain Waxman had shown him on the topographic map: a series of red cliff faces, broken with jungle-choked chasms and separated into tall forest-crowned mesas.

At his side, Corporal Okamoto passed him a set of binoculars. "Try these."

"Thanks." Frank fitted the scopes in place. Nate was also offered a pair. Through the lenses, the cliffs and mesas grew clearer. Small waterfalls tumbled from the towering heights into the swampy region below, while thick mists clung to the lower faces, obscuring the forested chasms that stretched from the swamp and up into the highlands.

"Those small streams and falls must feed the swamp," Nate said. "Keeping the area wet year round."

Frank lowered his glasses and found Captain Waxman studying a compass.

Nate pointed to the tree. "I wager that this marker points to Clark's next signpost. He must have had to circle around the swamp." Nate stared at the huge boggy spread of the water. "It would've taken him weeks to skirt the water."

Frank heard the despair in Dr. Rand's voice. To hike around the swamp would take them just as long.

Captain Waxman lifted his eyes from the compass and squinted across the swamp. "If the marker lies straight across, that's where we'll go." He pointed an arm. "It'll only take us a day to raft across here, rather than losing a week hiking."

"But we have no rubber raiders," Frank said.

Waxman glanced to him condescendingly. "We're Army Rangers, not Boy Scouts." He waved to the forest. "There are plenty of downed logs, acres of bamboo, and with the rope we have with us and the vines around us, we should be able to lash together a couple of rafts. It's what we're trained to do—improvise with the resources available." He glanced to the distant shore. "It can't be more than a couple miles to cross here."

Nate nodded. "Good. We can shave days off the search."

"Then let's get to work! I want to be finished by nightfall, so we're rested and ready in the morning to cross." Waxman assembled various teams: to roll and manhandle logs to the swamp's edge, to go out with axes and hack lengths of bamboo, and to strip vines for lashing material.

Frank assisted where needed and was surprised how quickly the building material accumulated on the muddy shore. They soon had enough for a flotilla of rafts. The assembling took even less time. Two matching logs were aligned parallel and topped with a solid layer of bamboo. Ropes and vines secured it all together. The first raft was shoved through the slick mud and into the water, bobbing in the shallows.

A cheer rose from the Rangers. Nate grinned approvingly as he sculpted paddles from bamboo and dried palm fronds.

A second raft was soon finished. The entire process took less than two hours.

Frank watched the second raft drift beside its mate. By now, the sun was setting. The western sky was aglow with a mix of reds, oranges, and splashes of deep indigo.

Around him, the camp was being set up. A fire lit, hammocks strung, food being prepared. Frank turned to join them when he spotted a dark streak against the bright sunset. He pinched his eyebrows, squinting.

Corporal Okamoto was passing Frank with an armful of tinder. "Can I borrow your binoculars?" Frank asked.

"Sure. Grab 'em from my field jacket." The soldier shifted his burden.

Frank thanked him and took the glasses. Once Okamoto had continued past, Frank raised the binoculars to his eyes. It took him a moment to find the dark streak rising in the sky. *Smoke?* It rose from the distant highlands. A sign of habitation? He followed the curling black line.

"What do you see?" Nate said.

"I'm not sure." Frank pointed to the sky. "I think it's smoke. Maybe from another camp or village."

Nate frowned and took the glasses. "Whatever it is," he said after a moment, "it's drifting this way."

Frank stared. Even without the binoculars, he could see that Nate was correct. The column of smoke was arching toward them. Frank lifted a hand. "That makes no sense. The wind is blowing in the opposite direction."

"I know," Nate said. "It's not smoke. Something is flying this way."

"I'd better alert the captain."

Soon everyone was outfitted with binoculars, staring upward. The ribbon of darkness had become a dense black cloud, sweeping directly toward them.

"What are they?" Okamoto mumbled. "Birds? Bats?"

"I don't think so," Nate said. The smoky darkness still appeared to be more cloud than substance, its edges billowing, ebbing, flowing as it raced toward them.

"What the hell are they?" someone mumbled.

In a matter of moments, the dark cloud swept over the campsite, just above tree level, blocking the last of the sunlight. The team was immediately flooded by a high-pitched droning. After so many days in the jungle, it was a familiar sound—but *amplified*. The tiny hairs on Frank's body vibrated to the subsonic whine.

"Locusts," Nate said, craning upward. "Millions of them."

As the cloud passed overhead, the lower edges of the swarm rattled the leafy foliage. The team ducked warily from the creatures, but the locusts passed them without pausing, sweeping east.

Frank lowered his binoculars as the tail end of the cloud droned over them. "What are they doing? Migrating or something?"

Nate shook his head. "No. This behavior makes no sense."

"But they're gone now," Captain Waxman said, ready to dismiss the aerial show.

Nate nodded, but he glanced to the east, one eye narrowed. "Yes, but *where* are they going?"

Frank caught Nate's glance. Something did lie to the east: *the other half of their party*. Frank swallowed back his sudden fear. *Kelly . . .*

7:28 P.M.

As the day darkened into twilight, Kelly heard a strange noise, a sharp whirring or whine. She walked around the Brazil nut tree. Squinting her eyes, she tried to focus on its source.

"You hear it, too?" Kouwe asked, meeting her on the far side of the trunk.

Nearby, the two Rangers stood with weapons raised. Others stood by the camp's large bonfire, feeding more dry branches and bamboo to the flames. With the threat of someone stalking around their camp, they wanted as much light as possible. Stacked beside the fire was a large pile of additional fodder for the flames, enough to last the night.

"That noise . . . it's getting louder," Kelly mumbled. "What is it?"

Kouwe cocked his head. "I'm not sure."

By now, others heard the noise, too. It rose quickly to a feverish pitch. Everyone started glancing to the sky.

Kelly pointed to the rosy gloaming to the west. "Look!"

Cast against the glow of the setting sun, a dark shadow climbed the skies, a black cloud, spreading and sweeping toward them.

"A swarm of locusts," Kouwe said, his voice tight with suspicion. "They'll do that sometimes in mating season, but it's the wrong time of the year. And I've never seen a swarm this big."

"Is it a threat?" Jorgensen asked from a few steps away.

"Not usually. More a pest for gardens and jungle farms. A large enough cloud of locusts can strip leaf, vegetable, and fruit from a spot in mere minutes."

"What about people?" Richard Zane asked.

"Not much of a threat. They're herbivorous, but they can bite a little when panicked. It's nothing more than a pinprick." Kouwe eyed the swarm. "Still . . ."

"What?" Kelly asked.

"I don't like the coincidence of such a swarm appearing after finding the Ban-ali mark."

"Surely there can't be any connection," Anna said at Richard's side.

Manny approached with Tor-tor. The great cat whined in chorus with the locusts, edgy and padding a slow circle around his master. "Professor, you aren't thinking the locusts might be like the piranha creatures? Some new threat from the jungle, another attack?"

Kouwe glanced to the biologist. "First there was the mark at the village, then piranhas. Now a mark here, and a strange swarm rises." Kouwe strode over to his pack. "It's a coincidence that we shouldn't dismiss."

Kelly felt a cold certainty that the professor was right.

"What can we do?" Jorgensen asked. His fellow soldier, Private Carrera, kept watch with him. The front edge of the swarm disappeared into the twilight gloom overhead, one shadow merging with another.

"First shelter . . ." Kouwe glanced up, his eyes narrowing with concentration. "They're almost here. Everyone into their hammocks! Close the mosquito netting tight and keep your flesh away from the fabric."

Zane protested. "But—"

"Now!" Kouwe barked. He began to dig more purposefully in his pack.

"Do as he says!" Jorgensen ordered, shouldering his useless weapon.

Kelly was already moving. She ducked into her tent of mosquito netting, glad that they had set up camp earlier. She closed the opening and positioned a stone atop the flap to hold the cheesecloth netting in place. Once secure, she clambered onto her hammock, tucking her legs and arms tight around herself, keeping her head ducked from the tent's top.

She glanced around her. The rest of her party were digging in, too, each hammock a solitary island of shrouded material. Only one member of the camp was still outside.

"Professor Kouwe!" Jorgensen called from his spot. The soldier began to clamber out of his netted tent.

"Stay!" Kouwe ordered as he rummaged in his pack.

Jorgensen froze with indecision. "What're you doing?"

"Preparing to fight fire with fire."

Suddenly, from clear skies, it began to rain. The canopy rattled with the familiar sounds of heavy drops striking leaves. But it was not water that cascaded from the skies. Large black insects pelted through the dense canopy and dove earthward.

The swarm had reached them.

Kelly saw one insect land on her netting. It was three inches long, its black carapace shining like oil in the firelight. Trebled wings twitched on its back as it fought to keep its perch. She balled her limbs tighter around herself. She had seen locusts and cicadas before, but nothing like this monstrous bug. It had no eyes. Its face was all clashing mandibles, gnashing at the air. Though blind, it was not senseless. Long antennae probed through the netting's mesh, swiveling like a pair of divining rods. Other of its brethren struck the netting with little smacks, clinging with segmented black legs.

A cry of pain drew her attention to Kouwe. The professor stood five yards away, still crouched by the fire. He swatted a locust on his arm.

"Professor!" Jorgensen called out.

"Stay where you are!" Kouwe fought the leather tie on a tiny bag. Kelly saw the blood dripping from his arm from the locust's bite. Even from here, she could tell it was a deep wound. She prayed the bugs were not venomous, like the piranhas. Kouwe crouched closer to the fire, his skin ruddy and aglow. But the flames' intense heat and smoke seemed to keep the worst of the swarm at bay.

All around the forest, locusts flitted and whined. With each breath, more and more filled the space.

"They're chewing through the netting!" Zane cried in panic.

Kelly turned her attention to the bugs closer at hand. The first attacker had retracted its antennae and was indeed gnashing at the netting, slicing through with its razored jaws. Before it could burrow inside, Kelly struck out with the back of her hand and knocked it away. She didn't kill it, but her netting was protected from further damage. She went to work on the other clinging insects.

"Smack them loose!" she yelled back to the others. "Don't give them a chance to bite through!"

Another yelp erupted from nearby. "Goddamn it!" It was Manny. A loud slap sounded, followed by more swearing.

Kelly couldn't get a good look at his position since his hammock was behind hers. "Are you okay?"

"One crawled under the netting!" Manny called back. "Be careful! The buggers pack a vicious bite. The saliva burns with some type of digestive acid."

Again she prayed the insects weren't toxic. She twisted around to get a look at Manny, but all she could make out was Tor-tor pacing at the edge of his master's tent. Clusters of the black insects crawled across the cat's fur, making it look as if his spots were squirming. The jaguar ignored the pests, its dense coat a natural barrier. One landed on the cat's nose, but a paw simply batted it away.

By now, the area buzzed with wings. The constant whine set Kelly's teeth on edge. In moments, the swarm thickened. It grew difficult to see much outside her tent. It was as if a swirling black fog had descended over them. The bugs coated everything, chewing and biting. Kelly focused her attention on knocking the insects off her netting, but it quickly became a losing battle. The bugs crawled and skittered everywhere.

As she struggled, sweat dripped down her face and into her eyes. Panicked, she batted and swung at the clinging insects and began to lose hope.

Then in her mind's eye, she pictured Jessie in a hospital bed, arms stretched out for her missing mother, crying her name. "Damn it!" She fought the insects more vigorously, refusing to give up.

I won't die here . . . not like this, not without seeing Jessie.

A sharp sting flamed from her thigh. Using the flat of her hand, she crushed the insect with a gasp. Another landed on her arm. She shook it away in disgust. A third scrabbled in her hair.

As she fought, a scream built like a storm in her chest. Her tent had been breached. Cries arose from other spots in the camp. They were all under assault.

They had lost.

Jessie . . . Kelly moaned, striking a locust from her neck. *I'm sorry, baby.* New stings bloomed on her calves and ankles. She futilely kicked, eyes weeping in pain and loss.

It soon became hard to breathe. She coughed, choking. Her eyes began to sting worse. A sharp smell filled her nostrils, sweet with resins, like green pine logs in a hearth. She coughed again.

What was happening?

Through her tears, she watched the dense swarm disperse as if blown by a mighty gust. Directly ahead, the camp's bonfire grew clearer. She spotted Kouwe standing on the far side of the flames, waving a large palm frond over the fire, which had grown much smokier.

"*Tok-tok* powder!" Kouwe called to her. His body was covered with bleeding bites. "A headache medicine and, when burned, a powerful insect repellent."

The locusts clinging to her netting dislodged and winged away from the odor. Kelly vaguely remembered Nate telling her how the Indians would stake their gardens with bamboo torches and burn some type of powder as an insect repellent to protect their harvest. She silently thanked the Indians of the forest for their ingenuity.

Once the locusts had dwindled to only a few stragglers, Kouwe waved to her, to all of them. "Come here!" he called. "Quickly!"

She climbed from her hammock, and after a moment's hesitation, she slipped through her netting, now ragged and frayed. Ducking low, she crossed to the fire. Others followed in step behind her.

The smoke was choking and cloying, but the insects held back. The locusts had not dispersed. The swarm still whined and whirred overhead in a dark cloud. Occasional bombers would dive toward them and away, chased off by the fire's smoke.

"How did you know the smoke would work?" Jorgensen asked.

"I didn't. At least not for sure." Kouwe panted slightly and continued to waft his palm frond as he explained. "The flaming Ban-ali symbol in the jungle . . . the amount of smoke and the strong scent of it. I thought it might be some sort of signal."

"A smoke signal?" Zane asked.

"No, more of a *scent* signal," Kouwe said. "Something in the smoke drew the locusts here specifically."

Manny grunted at this idea. "Like a pheromone or something."

"Perhaps. And once here, the little bastards were bred to lay waste to anything in the area."

"So what you're saying is that we were marked for death," Anna commented. "The locusts were sent here on purpose."

Kouwe nodded. "The same could be true with the piranha creatures. Something must have drawn them specifically to the village, maybe another scent trace, something dribbled in the water that guided them to the *shabano*." He shook his head. "I don't know for sure. But for a second time, the Ban-ali have called the jungle down upon us."

"What are we going to do?" Zane asked. "Will the powder last till dawn?"

"No." Kouwe glanced to the dark swarm around them.

8:05 P.M.

Nate was tired of arguing. He, Captain Waxman, and Frank were still in the midst of a debate that had been going on for the past fifteen minutes. "We have to go back and investigate," he insisted. "At least send one person to check on the others. He can be there and back before dawn."

Waxman sighed. "They were only locusts, Dr. Rand. They passed over us with no harm. What makes you think the others are at risk?"

Nate frowned. "I have no proof. Just my gut instinct. But I've lived all my life in these jungles and something was unnatural about the way those locusts were swarming."

Frank initially had been on Nate's side, but slowly he had warmed to the Ranger's logic of wait-and-see. "I think we should consider Captain Waxman's plan. First thing tomorrow morning, when the satellites are overhead, we can relay a message to the others and make sure they're okay."

"Besides," Waxman added, "now that we're down to six Rangers, I'm not about to risk a pair on this futile mission—not without some sign of real trouble."

"I'll go myself." Nate balled a fist in frustration.

"I won't allow it." Waxman shook his head. "You're just jumping at shadows, Dr. Rand. In the morning, you'll see they're okay."

Nate's mind spun, trying to find some way past the captain's obstinate attitude. "Then at least let me head out with a radio. See if I can get close enough to contact someone over there. What's the range on your personal radios?"

"Six or seven miles."

"And we traveled roughly fifteen miles. That means I would only have to hike back eight miles to be within radio range of the others. I could be back before midnight."

Waxman frowned.

Frank moved a step closer to Nathan. "Still . . . it's not a totally foolhardy plan, Captain. In fact, it's a reasonable compromise."

Nate recognized the pained set to Frank's eyes. It was his sister out there. So far the man had been balancing between fear for his sister and Waxman's reasonable caution, trying his best to be a logical operations leader while reining in his own concern.

"I'm sure the others *are* okay," Nate pressed. "But it doesn't hurt to be a little extra wary . . . especially after the last couple of days."

Frank was now nodding.

"Let me take a radio," Nate urged.

Waxman puffed out an exasperated breath and conceded. "But you're not going alone."

Nate bit back a shout. *Finally . . .*

"I'll send one of the Rangers with you. I won't risk two of my men."

"Good . . . good." Frank seemed almost to sag with relief. He turned to Nate, a look of gratitude in his eyes.

Captain Waxman turned. "Corporal Warczak! Front and center!"

8:23 P.M.

Manny and the others stood by the fire, smoke billowing around them. The pall from the powder kept the locusts in check. All around, the swarm swirled, a black cocoon, holding them trapped. Manny's eyes stung as he studied the flames. How long would the professor's *tok-tok* powder last? Already the smoke seemed less dense.

"Here!" Kelly said behind him. She passed him a two-foot length of bamboo from the pile of tinder beside the fire, then returned to work, kneeling with Professor Kouwe. The Indian shaman was packing a final piece of bamboo with a plug of *tok-tok* powder.

Manny shifted his feet nervously. The professor's plan was based on too many assumptions for his liking.

Finished with the last stick of bamboo, Kelly and Kouwe stood. Manny stared around the fire. Everyone had packs in place and was holding a short length of bamboo, like his own.

"Okay," Jorgensen said. "Ready?"

No one answered. Everyone's eyes reflected the same mix of panic and fear.

Jorgensen nodded. "Light the torches."

As a unit, each member reached and dipped the ends of their bamboo in the bonfire's flames. The powder ignited along with the dry wood. As they pulled the bamboo free, smoke wafted in thick curls up from their makeshift torches.

"Keep them close, but held aloft," Kouwe instructed, demonstrating with his own torch. "We must move quickly."

Manny swallowed. He eyed the whirring wall of locusts. He had been bitten only twice. But the wounds still ached. Tor-tor kept close to his side, rubbing against him, sensing the fear in the air.

"Keep together," Kouwe hissed as they began to walk away from the sheltering fire and toward the waiting swarm.

The plan was to use the tiki torches primed with *tok-tok* powder to breach the swarm while holding the locusts at bay. Under this veil of smoky protection, the team would attempt to flee the area. As Kouwe had explained earlier, "The locusts were drawn specifically *here* by the scent from the burning Ban-ali symbol. If we get far enough away from this specific area, we might escape them."

It was a risky plan, but they didn't have much choice. The shaman's supply of powder was meager. It would not keep the bonfire smoking for more than another hour or two. And the locusts seemed determined to remain in the area. So it was up to them—they would have to vacate the region.

"C'mon, Tor-tor." Manny followed after Corporal Jorgensen. Behind and to the side, the group moved in a tight cluster, torches held high. Manny's ears were full of the swarm's drone. As he walked, he prayed Kouwe's assumptions were sound.

No one spoke . . . no one even breathed. The group trod slowly forward, heading west, in the direction the other team had taken. It was their only hope. Manny glanced behind him. The comforting light of their bonfire was now a weak glow as the swarm closed in behind them.

Underfoot, Manny crushed straggling locusts on the ground.

Silently, the group marched into the forest. After several minutes, there was still no end to the cloud of insects. The team remained surrounded on all sides. Locusts were everywhere: buzzing through the air, coating the trunks of trees, scrabbling through the underbrush. Only the smoke kept them away.

Manny felt something vibrating on his pantleg. He glanced down and used his free hand to swat the locust away. The bugs were getting bolder.

"We should be through them by now," Kouwe muttered.

"I think they're following us," Anna said.

Kouwe slowed, and his eyes narrowed. "I believe you're right."

"What are we going to do?" Zane hissed. "These torches aren't gonna last much longer. Maybe if we ran. Maybe we could—"

"Quiet . . . let me think!" Kouwe scolded. He stared at the swarm and mumbled. "Why are they following us? Why aren't they staying where they were summoned?"

Carrera spoke softly at the rear of the group. She held her torch high. "Maybe they're like those piranha creatures. Once drawn here, they caught *our* scent. They'll follow us now until one or the other of us is destroyed."

Manny had a sudden idea. "Then why don't we do what the Ban-ali do?"

"What do you mean?" Kelly asked.

"Give the buggers something more interesting than our blood to swarm after."

"Like what?"

"The same scent that drew the locusts here in the first place." Words tumbled from Manny in his excitement. He pictured the flaming symbol of the Blood Jaguars. "Corporal Jorgensen and I doused the flames that produced the smoky pheromone or whatever—but the fuel is still there! Out in the forest." He pointed his arm.

Jorgensen nodded. "Manny's right. If we could relight it . . ."

Kouwe brightened. "Then the fresh smoke would draw the swarm away from us, keep it here while we ran off."

"Exactly," Manny said.

"Let's do it," Zane said. "What are we waiting for?"

Jorgensen stepped in front. "With our torches burning low, time is limited. There's no reason to risk all of us going back."

"What are you saying?" Manny asked.

Jorgensen pointed. "You all continue on the trail after the others. I'll backtrack and light the fire on my own."

Manny stepped forward. "I'll go with you."

"No. I won't risk a civilian." Jorgensen backed away. "And besides, I can travel faster on my own."

"But—"

"We're wasting time and powder," the corporal barked. He turned to his fellow Ranger. "Carrera, get everyone away from here. Double time. I'll join up with you after I've lit the motherfucker."

"Yes, sir."

With a final nod, Jorgensen turned and began to trot back toward the camp, torch held high. In moments, his form was swallowed away as he dove through the swarm. Just the bobbing light of his torch illuminated his progress, then even that vanished amid the dense mass of swirling insects.

"Move out!" Carrera said.

The group turned and once again headed down the trail. Manny prayed the corporal succeeded. With a final glance behind him, Manny followed the others.

Jorgensen rushed through the swarm. With only his single torch protecting him, the swarm grew tighter. He was stung a few times by bolder bugs, but he ignored the discomfort. A Ranger went through vigorous training programs across a multitude of terrains: mountains, jungles, swamps, snow, desert.

But never this . . . never a goddamn cloud of carnivorous bugs!

With his weapon on his shoulder, he shrugged his pack higher on his back, both to make it easier to run and to shield him from the swarm overhead.

Though he should have been panicked, an odd surge of zeal fired his blood. This was why he had volunteered for the Rangers, to test his mettle and to experience balls-out action. How many farm boys from the backwaters of Minnesota had a chance to do this?

He thrust his torch forward and forged ahead. "Fuck you!" he yelled at the locusts.

Focusing on the abandoned campfire as a beacon, Jorgensen worked across the dizzying landscape of whirling bugs. Smoke from his torch wafted around him, redolent with the burning powder. He circled around the Brazil nut tree and headed toward where the Ban-ali's burning signature had been set in the forest.

Half blind, he ran past the site before realizing it and doubled back. He fell to his knees beside the spot. "Thank God."

Jorgensen planted his torch in the soft loam, then leaned over and swept free the dirt and scrabbling bugs from the buried resinous compound. Locusts lay thick over this site. Several bites stung his hand as he brushed them away. Leaning close, the residual fumes from the oil filled his nostrils, bitter and sharp. The professor was right. It certainly attracted the buggers.

Working quickly, Jorgensen continued to uncover the original marker.

He didn't know how much of the black oil should be lit to keep the swarm's attention here, but he wasn't taking any chances. He didn't want to have to return a second time. Crawling on his knees, his hands sticky with the black resin, he worked around the site. He soon had at least half of the serpentine pattern exposed.

Satisfied, he sat back, pulled free a butane lighter, and flicked a flame. He lowered the lighter to the oil. "C'mon . . . burn, baby."

His wish was granted. The oil caught fire, flames racing down the twists and curls of the exposed symbol. In fact, the ignition was so fiercely combustible that the first flames caught him off guard, burning his fingers.

Jorgensen dropped the lighter and pulled his hand away, his fingers on fire. "Shit!" The smattering of sticky oil on his hand had caught the flames. "*Shit!*"

He rolled to the side and shoved his hands into the loose dirt to stanch the fire. As he did so, his elbow accidentally struck the planted bamboo torch, knocking it into a nearby bush, casting embers in a fiery arc. Jorgensen swore and snatched at the torch—but he was too late. The powder stored in the hollow top of the bamboo had scattered into the dirt and bush, sizzling out. The top of the torch still glowed crimson, but it was no longer smoking.

Jorgensen sprang to his feet.

Behind him, the symbol of the Ban-ali flamed brightly, calling the swarm to its meal.

"Oh, God!"

Kelly heard the first scream, a horrible sound that froze everyone in place.

"Jorgensen . . ." Private Carrera said, swinging around.

Kelly stepped beside the Ranger.

"We can't go back," Zane said, shifting further down the trail.

A second scream, bone-chilling, garbled, echoed from the forest.

Kelly noticed the swarm of locusts whisk from around them, retreating back toward the original campsite. "They're leaving!"

Professor Kouwe spoke at her shoulder. "The corporal must have succeeded in relighting the symbol."

By now, the agonized cries were constant, prolonged, bestial. No human could scream like that.

"We have to go help him," Manny said.

Carrera clicked on a flashlight in her free hand. She pointed it back toward the campsite. Fifty yards away, the condensed swarm was so thick, the trees themselves were invisible, swallowed by the black cloud. "There's not enough time," she said softly and lifted her own bamboo torch. It was already sputtering. "We don't know how long a distraction Jorgensen has bought us."

Manny turned to her. "We could at least still try. He might be alive."

As if hearing him, the distant cries died away.

Carrera glanced to him and shook her head.

"Look!" Anna called out, pointing her arm.

Off to the left, a figure stumbled out of the swarm.

Carrera pointed her flashlight. "Jorgensen!"

Kelly gasped and covered her mouth.

The man was impossible to identify, covered from crown to ankle with crawling locusts. His arms were out, waving, blind. His legs wobbled, and he tripped in the underbrush, falling to his knees. All the while, he remained eerily silent. Only his arms stretched out for help.

Manny took a step in the man's direction, but Carrera held him back.

The swarm rolled back over the kneeling man, swallowing him.

"It's too late," Carrera said. "And we're all running out of time." Punctuating her statement, her own torch cast a final sputter of fiery ash, then dimmed. "We need to get as far from here as possible before we lose our advantage."

"But—" Manny began.

He was cut off by a hard stare from the Ranger. Her words were even harder. "I won't have Jorgensen's sacrifice be meaningless." She pointed toward the deeper wood. "Move out!"

Kelly glanced back as they headed away. The swarm remained behind them, a featureless black cloud. But at its heart was a man who had given his life to save them all. Tears filled her eyes. Her legs were numb with exhaustion and despair, her heart heavy.

Despite the loss of the corporal, one thought, one face remained foremost in Kelly's mind. Her daughter needed her. Her mind roiled with flashes of her child in bed, burning with fever. *I'll get back to you, baby,* she promised silently.

But deep in her heart, she now wondered if it was a pact she could keep. With each step deeper into the forest, more men died. *Graves, DeMartini, Conger, Jones . . . and now Jorgensen . . .*

She shook her head, refusing to give up hope. As long as she was alive, putting one foot in front of the other, she would find a way home.

Over the next hour, the group forged through the forest, following the path the other half of their team had taken the previous afternoon. One by one, their torches flickered out. Flashlights were passed around. So far, no sign of renewed pursuit by the swarm manifested. Maybe they were safe, beyond the interest of the blind locusts, but no one voiced such a hope aloud.

Manny marched close to the Ranger. "What if we miss the other team?" he asked softly. "Jorgensen had our radio equipment. It was our only way of contacting the outside world."

Kelly hadn't considered this fact. With the radio gone, they were cut off.

"We'll reach the others," Carrera said with a steely determination.

No one argued with her. No one wanted to.

They marched onward through the dark jungle, concentrating on just moving forward. As hours ticked by, the tension blended into a blur of bone-weary exhaustion and endless fear. Their passage was marked with hoots and strange cries. Everyone's ears were pricked for the telltale buzz of the locusts.

So they were all startled when the small personal radio hanging from Private Carrera's field jacket squawked with static and a few scratchy words. "This is . . . if you can hear . . . radio range . . ."

Everyone swung to face the Ranger, eyes wide. She pulled her radio's microphone from her helmet to her mouth. "This is Private Carrera. Can you hear me? *Over.*"

There was a long pause, then . . . "Read you, Carrera. Warczak here. What's your status?"

The Ranger quickly related the events in a dispassionate and professional manner. But Kelly saw how the soldier's fingers trembled as she held the microphone to her lips. She finished, "We're following your trail. Hoping to rendezvous with the main team in two hours."

Corporal Warczak responded, "Roger that. Dr. Rand and I are already under way to meet you. Over and out."

The Ranger closed her eyes and sighed loudly. "We're gonna be okay," she whispered to no one in particular.

As the others murmured in relief, Kelly stared out at the dark jungle.

Out here in the Amazon, they were all far from okay.

Blood Jaguars

HORSETAIL

FAMILY: *Equisetaceae*

GENUS: *Equisetum*

SPECIES: *Arvense*

COMMON NAME: *Field Horsetail*

ETHNIC NAMES: *At Quyroughi, Atkuyrugu, Chieh Hsu Ts'Ao, Cola de Caballo, Equiseto Menor, Kilkah Asb, Prele, Sugina, Thanab al Khail, Vara de Oro, Wen Ching*

PROPERTIES/ACTIONS: *Astringent, Antiinflammatory, Diuretic, Antihemorrhagic*

TWELVE

Lake Crossing

Lauren slid the magnetic security card through the lock on her office door and entered. It was the first chance she'd had to return to her office in the past day. Between stretches in the institute's hospital ward visiting Jessie and meetings with various MEDEA members, she hadn't had a moment to herself. The only reason she had this free moment was that Jessie seemed to be doing very well. Her temperature continued to remain normal, and her attitude was growing brighter with every passing hour.

Cautiously optimistic, Lauren began to hope that her initial diagnosis had been mistaken. Maybe Jessie did *not* have the jungle disease. Lauren was now glad she had kept silent about her fears. She could have needlessly panicked Marshall and Kelly. Lauren may have indeed placed too much confidence in Alvisio's statistical model. But she could not fault the epidemiologist. Dr. Alvisio *had* indeed warned her his results were far from conclusive. Further data would need to be collected and correlated.

But then again, that pretty much defined all the current levels of investigation. Each day, as the disease spread through Florida and the southern states, thousands of theories were bandied about: etiological agents, therapeutic protocols, diagnostic parameters, quarantine guidelines. Instar had become the nation's think tank on this contagion. It was their job to ferret through the maze of scientific conjecture and fanciful epidemiological models to glean the pearls from the rubbish. It was a daunting task as data flowed in from all corners of the country. But they had the best minds here.

Lauren collapsed into her seat and flicked on her computer. The chime for incoming mail sounded. She groaned as she slipped on a pair of reading glasses and leaned closer to the screen. *Three hundred and fourteen messages waited.* And this was just her private mailbox. She scrolled down the list of addresses and skimmed the subject lines, searching through the little snippets for anything important or interesting.

Inbox	
From	**Subject**
jpcdvm@davis.uc.org	re: simian biosimilarities
trent_magnus@scriabs.com	call for sample standardization
systematica@cdc.gov	prog. report
xreynolds@largebio.com	large scale biological labs
synergymeds@phdrugs.com	pharmacy question
gerard@dadecounty.fl.gov	quarantine projection
hrt@washingtonpost.org	request for interview

As she scrolled down, one name caught her eye. It was oddly familiar, but she could not remember exactly why. She brought her computer's pointer to the name: *Large Scale Biological Labs.* She crinkled her nose in thought, then it came to her. The night Jessie's fever developed, she had been paged by this same outfit. Well after midnight, she recalled. But the sick child had distracted her from following up on the page.

It probably wasn't important, but she opened the e-mail anyway, her curiosity now aroused. The letter appeared on the screen. *Dr. Xavier Reynolds.* She smiled, instantly recognizing the name. He had been a grad student of hers years ago and had taken a position at some lab in California, perhaps this same lab. The young man had been one of her best students. Lauren had attempted to recruit him into the MEDEA group here at Instar, but he had declined. His fiancé had accepted an associate professorship at Berkeley, and he had naturally not wanted to be separated.

She read his note. As she did, the smile on her lips slowly faded.

From: xreynolds@largebio.com
Date: 14 Aug 13:48:28

To: lauren_obrien@instar.org
Subject: Large Scale Biological Labs

Dr. O'Brien:

Please excuse this intrusion. I attempted to page you last night, but I assume you're very busy. So I'll keep this brief.

As with many labs around the country, our own is involved in researching the virulent disease, and I think I've come across an intriguing angle, if not a possible answer to the root puzzle: *What is causing the disease?* But before voicing my findings, I wanted to get your input.

As head of the proteonomic team here at Large Scale Biological Labs, I have been attempting to index mankind's protein genome, similar to the Human Genome Project for DNA. As such, my take on the disease was to investigate it backward. Most disease-causing agents—bacteria, viruses, fungi, parasites—do not cause illness by themselves. It is the *proteins* they produce that trigger clinical disease. So I hunted for a unique protein that might be common to all patients.

And I found one! But from its folded and twisted pattern, a new thought arose. This new protein bears a striking similarity to the protein that causes bovine spongiform encephalopathy. Which in turn raises the question: *Have we been chasing the wrong tail in pursuing a viral cause for this disease?*

Has anyone considered a *prion* as the cause?

For your consideration, I've modeled the protein below.

Title: unknown prion (?)
Compound: folded protein w/ double terminal alpha helixes
Model:

Exp. Method: X-ray diffraction

EC Number: 3.4.1.18

Source: Patient #24-b12, Anawak Tribe, lower Amazon

Resolution: 2.00   **R-Value:** 0.145

Space Group: P21 20 21

   Unit cell:

      dim: a 60.34   b 52.02   c 44.68

      angles: *alpha* 90.00   *beta* 90.00   *gamma* 90.00

Polymer chains: 156L   **Residues:** 144

Atoms: 1286

So there you have the twisted puzzle. As I value your expertise, Dr. O'Brien, I would appreciate your thoughts, opinions, or judgments before promoting this radical theory.

    Sincerely,

    Xavier Reynolds, Ph.D.

"A prion." Lauren touched the diagram of the molecule. *Could this indeed be the cause?*

She pondered the possibility. The word *prion* was scientific shorthand for "proteinaceous infectious particle." The role of prions in disease had only been documented within the last decade, earning a U.S. biochemist the 1997 Nobel Prize. Prion proteins were found in all creatures, from humans down to single-celled yeast. Though usually innocuous, they had an insidious duality to their molecular structure, a Jekyll-and-Hyde sort of thing. In one form, they were safe and friendly to a cell. But the same protein could fold and twist upon itself, creating a monster that wreaked havoc on cellular processes. And the effect was cumulative. Once a twisted prion was introduced into a host, it would begin converting the body's other proteins to match, which in turn converted its neighbors, spreading exponentially through the host's systems. Worse, this host could also pass the process to another body, a true infectious phenomenon.

Prion diseases had been documented both in animals and man: from scabies in sheep to Creutsfeldt-Jacob disease in humans. The most well-known prion disease to date was one that *crossed* between species. Dr. Reynolds had mentioned it in his letter: bovine spongiform encephalopathy, or more commonly, mad cow disease.

But these human diseases were more of a degenerative nature, and none were known to be transmitted so readily. Still, that did not rule out prions as a possibility here. She had read research papers on prions and their role in genetic mutations and more severe manifestations. Was something like that happening here? And what about airborne transmission? Prions were particulate and subviral in size, so since certain viruses could be airborne, why not certain prions?

Lauren stared at the modeled protein on the computer screen and reached for her desk phone. As she dialed, an icy finger ran up her spine. She prayed her former student was mistaken.

The phone rang on the other end, and after a moment, it was answered. "Dr. Reynolds, proteonomics lab."

"Xavier?"

"Yes?"

"This is Dr. O'Brien."

"Dr. O'Brien!" The man began talking animatedly, thanking her, thrilled.

She cut him off. "Xavier, tell me more about this protein of yours." She needed as much information from him as possible, the sooner the better. If there was even a minute possibility that Dr. Reynolds was correct . . .

Lauren bit back a shudder as she stared at the crablike molecule on her computer monitor. There was one other fact she knew about prion-triggered diseases.

There were no known cures.

Nate looked over Olin Pasternak's shoulder. The CIA's communications expert was growing ever more frustrated with the satellite computer system. Beads of sweat bulleted his forehead, both from the morning's steaming heat and his own consternation.

"Still no feed . . . goddamn it!" Olin chewed his lower lip, eyes squinting.

"Keep trying," Frank urged on the other side.

Nate glanced to Kelly, who stood beside her brother. Her eyes were haunted and dull. Nate had heard various versions of last night's attack: the strange swarm of giant locusts attracted to the camp by the burning Ban-ali marker. It was too horrible to imagine, impossible, but Jorgensen's death made it all too real.

Once the entire group had been reassembled at the swamp-side camp last night, the Ranger team had remained on guard. The group kept a posted watch throughout the night, in and around the surrounding forest, alert for any danger, watchful for any flare of flames, ears keened for the whine of locusts. But nothing happened. The few hours until dawn had been uneventful.

As soon as the communication satellite was in range, Olin had set about trying to reach the States and to relay messages to the Wauwai field base. It was vital to radio the change in plans to all parties. With unknown hunters dogging their trail, it was decided to continue with the goal of rafting across the swamp. Captain Waxman hoped to get a couple of days' jump on his pursuers, leave their trackers traipsing around the swamp on foot. Once across, Waxman would keep a constant watch on the waters for any Ban-ali canoes and keep the group intact on the far shore until the evac helicopter could arrive. He planned to trade each civilian with another Ranger from the field base at the mission. With these new forces, he would continue on Gerald Clark's trail.

There was only one problem with his plan.

"I'm gonna have to rip the laptop down to the motherboard," Olin said. "Something is damnably fritzed. Maybe a faulty chip or even a loose one knocked out of place by the manhandling these past two days. I don't know. I'll have to tear it down and check it all."

Waxman had been speaking with his staff sergeant, but he overheard Olin. The captain stepped nearer. "We don't have time for that. The third raft is ready, and it'll take a good four hours to cross the waters. We need to get moving."

Nate glanced to the swamp's edge and saw four Rangers positioning the newly constructed raft so that it floated beside the two prepared last night. The additional raft was necessary to carry everyone in their expanded party.

Olin hovered over his computer and satellite dish with a small screwdriver. "But I've not been able to reach anyone. They won't know where we are." He wiped his forehead with the back of his wrist. His features were pale.

Zane stood, shifting his feet uneasily and rubbing at a Band-Aid on his cheek that covered a locust bite. "We could send someone back and retrieve Jorgensen's pack with the military radio," he suggested.

Everyone began talking at once, arguing both sides.

"We'd lose another day waiting." "We'd risk more of our people." "We need to reach *someone*!" "Who knows if his radio will even work, what with all those locusts. They could've chewed through the wiring and—"

Waxman interrupted, his voice booming. "There is no reason to panic!" He directed his comment to all of them. "Even if we can't raise the outside, the field base knows our rough location from yesterday's report. When the Brazilian evac copter comes tomorrow as previously arranged, we'll hear it—even from across the swamp. We can send up orange smoke flares to draw their attention to our new location."

Nate nodded. He had not participated in the argument. In his mind, there was only one way to go—*forward*.

Waxman pointed to Olin. "Pack it up. You can work on the problem once we're on the far side."

Resigned, Olin nodded. He returned his tiny screwdriver to his repair kit.

With the matter settled, the others dispersed to gather their own gear, readying for the day's journey.

"At least we won't have to walk," Manny said, patting Nate on the shoulder as he passed on his way to wake Tor-tor. The jaguar was asleep under a palm, oblivious to the world after last night's trek.

Nate stretched a kink from his neck and approached Professor Kouwe. The Indian shaman stood near the swamp, smoking his pipe. His eyes were as haunted as Kelly's had been. When Nate and Corporal Warczak had met the fleeing group on the trail, the professor had been unusually quiet and somber, more than could be attributed to the loss of Jorgensen.

Nate stood silently beside his old friend, studying the lake, too.

After a time, Kouwe spoke softly, not looking at Nate. "They sent the locusts . . . the Ban-ali . . ." The shaman shook his head. "They wiped out the Yanomamo tribe with the piranha creatures. I've never seen anything like it. It's as if the Blood Jaguar tribe could indeed control the jungle. And if that myth is true, what else?" He shook his head again.

"What's troubling you?"

"I've been a professor of Indian Studies for close to two decades. I grew up in these jungles." His voice grew quiet, full of pain. "I should have known . . . the corporal . . . his screams . . ."

Nate glanced to Kouwe and placed a hand on the man's shoulder. "Professor, you saved everyone with the *tok-tok* powder."

"Not everyone." Kouwe drew on his pipe and exhaled. "I should've thought to relight the Ban-ali symbol before we left the camp. If I had, the young corporal would be alive."

Nate spoke sharply, trying to cut through the man's remorse and guilt. "You're being too hard on yourself. No amount of study or experience could prepare you to deal with the Ban-ali and their biological attacks. Nothing like it has ever been documented before."

Kouwe nodded, but Nate sensed that the man was hardly convinced.

Captain Waxman called from near the water's edge. "Let's load up! Five to a raft!" He began assigning Rangers and dividing the civilians accordingly.

Nate ended up with Kouwe and Manny, along with Tor-tor. Their two mates were Corporal Okamoto and Private Carrera. The group was forced to wade through the shallows to reach the bamboo-and-log constructions. As Nate heaved himself onboard, he appreciated its sturdy construction. Reaching out, Nate helped Manny guide the large cat atop the bobbing raft.

Tor-tor was not pleased about getting wet. As the cat shook the swamp water from its pelt, the rest of the group mounted their own boats.

On the neighboring raft, Kelly and Frank stood with Captain Waxman, along with corporals Warczak and Yamir. The last five teammates climbed onto the farthest raft. Olin was careful to carry his pack with the satellite gear high above his head. Richard Zane and Anna Fong helped him aboard, flanked by a stoic Tom Graves and a scowling Sergeant Kostos.

Once everyone was mounted, lengths of bamboo were used as poles to push away from shore and through the shallows. But the swamp's banks dropped steeply. Within a hundred feet of the shore, the poles no longer touched bottom, and the paddles were taken up. With four paddles per raft, it allowed one person to rotate out and rest. The goal was to continue straight across without a break.

Nate manned the raft's starboard side as the tiny flotilla slowly drifted toward the far bank. Out on the waters, the distant roar of multiple waterfalls, muffled and threatening, echoed over the swamp lake. Nate stared, shading his eyes. The highlands across the way remained shrouded in mist: a mix of green jungle, red cliffs, and a fog of heavy spray. Their goal was a narrow ravine between two towering, flat-topped mesas, a yawning misty channel into the highlands. It had been where Clark's last carved message had pointed.

As they glided, the denizens of the swamp noted their passage. A snow-white egret skimmed over the water, a hand span above the surface. Frogs leaped from boggy hummocks with loud splashes, and *hoatzin* birds, looking like some ugly cross between a turkey and a pterodactyl, screeched at them as they circled over their nests atop the palms that grew from the island hummocks. The only inhabitants that seemed pleased with their presence were the clouds of mosquitoes, buzzing with joy at the floating smorgasbord.

"Damned bugs," Manny griped, slapping his neck. "I've had it with flying insects making a meal out of me."

To make matters even worse, Okamoto began to whistle again, tunelessly and without the vaguest sense of rhythm.

Nate sighed. It would be a long trip.

After an hour, the little muddy islands vanished around them. In the swamp's center, the water was deep enough to drown away most of the tiny bits of land and jungle. Only an occasional hummock, mostly bare of trees, dotted the smooth expanse of the swamp's heart.

Here the sun, scorching and bright, shone incessantly down on them.

"It's like a steam bath," Carrera said from the raft's port side.

Nate had to agree. The air was thick with moisture, almost too heavy to breathe. Their speed across the swamp slowed as exhaustion set in. Canteens were passed around and around the raft. Even Tor-tor lounged in the middle of the bamboo planking, his mouth open, panting.

The only consolation was being temporarily free of the jungle's snug embrace. Here the horizons opened up, and there was a giddy sense of escape. Nate glanced frequently back the way they had come, expecting to see a tribesman on the bank back there, shaking a fist. But there remained no sign of the Ban-ali. The trackers of the ghost tribe remained hidden. Hopefully the group was leaving them behind and getting a few days head start on their pursuers.

Nate was tapped on the shoulder. "I'll take a shift," Kouwe said, emptying his pipe's bowl of tobacco ash into the water.

"I'm okay," Nate said.

Kouwe reached and took the paddle. "I'm not an invalid yet."

Nate didn't argue any further and slid to the raft's stern. As he lounged, he watched their old campsite get smaller and smaller. He reached back for the canteen and caught movement to the right of their raft. One of the bare hummocks, rocky and black, was sinking, submerging so slowly that not a ripple was created.

What the hell?

Off to the left another was sinking. Nate climbed to his feet. As he began to comment on this unusual phenomenon, one of the rocky islands opened a large glassy eye and stared back at him. Instantly Nate knew what he was seeing.

"Oh, crap!"

With his attention focused, he now recognized the armored scales and craggy countenance of a crocodilian head. It was a caiman! A pair of giants. Each head had to be four feet wide from eye to eye. If its head was that big . . .

"What's wrong?" Private Carrera asked.

Nate pointed to where the second of the two caimans was just slipping under the surface.

"What is it?" the Ranger asked, eyes wide, as confused as Nate had been a moment before.

"Caimans," Nate said, his voice hoarse with shock. "Giant ones!"

By now, his entire raft had stopped paddling. The others stared at him.

Nate raised his voice, yelling so all three rafts could hear him. He waved his arms in the air. "Spread out! We're about to be attacked!"

"From what?" Captain Waxman called from his raft, about fifty yards away. "What did you see?"

As answer, something huge slid between Nate's boat and its neighbor, nudging both rafts and spinning them ever so slightly. Through the swamp's murk, the twin lines of tail ridges were readily evident as the beast slid sinuously past.

Nate was familiar with this behavior. It was called *bumping*. The kings of the caimans, the great blacks, were not carrion eaters. They liked to kill their own food. It was why drifting motionless could often protect someone from the predators. Often they would bump something that they considered a meal, testing to see if it would move.

They had just been *bumped*.

Distantly, the third raft suddenly bobbed and turned. The second caiman was also testing these strange intruders.

Nate yelled again, revising his initial plan. "Don't move! No one paddle! You'll attract them to attack!"

Waxman reinforced his order. "Do as he says! Weapon up. Grenades hot!"

Manny now crouched beside Nate, his voice hushed with awe. "It had to be at least a hundred feet long, over three times larger than any known caiman."

Carrera had her M-16 rifle in hand and was quickly fitting on her grenade launcher. "No wonder Gerald Clark circled around the swamp."

Okamoto finished prepping his rifle, kissed the crucifix around his neck, then nodded to Professor Kouwe. "I pray you have another one of your magical powders up your sleeve."

The shaman shook his head, eyes wide, unblinking. "I pray you're all good shots."

Okamoto glanced at Nate.

Nate explained, "With their armored body plating, the only sure kill shot is the eye."

"No, there's also through the upper palate," Manny added, pointing a finger toward the roof of his mouth. "But to take that shot, you'd have to be damn close."

"Starboard side!" Carrera barked, kneeling with her rifle on her shoulder.

A rippling line disturbed the flat waters, ominous and long.

"Don't take a shot unless you're sure," Nate hissed, dropping beside her. "You could provoke it. Only shoot if you've got a kill shot."

With everyone dead quiet, Waxman heard Nate's warning. "Listen to Dr. Rand. Shoot if you have a chance—but make it count!"

Rifles bristled around the periphery of each raft. Nate grabbed up his shotgun with one hand. They all waited, baking in the heat, sweat dripping into eyes, mouths drying. Around and around, the caimans circled, leaving no sign of their passage but ripples. Occasionally a raft would be bumped, tested.

"How long can they hold their breath?" Carrera asked.

"Hours," Nate said.

"Why aren't they attacking?" Okamoto asked.

Manny answered this question. "They can't figure out what we are, if we're edible."

The Asian Ranger looked sick. "Let's hope they don't find out."

The waiting stretched. The air seemed to grow thicker around them.

"What if we shot a grenade far from here?" Carrera offered. "As a distraction, something to draw them off."

"I'm not sure it would help. It might just rile them up, get them snapping at anything that moves, like us."

Zane spoke from the farthest raft, but his words easily reached Nate's boat. "I say we strap some explosives to that jaguar and push it overboard. When one of the crocodiles goes for the cat, we trigger the bomb."

Nate shuddered at this idea. Manny looked sick. But other eyes were glancing their way with contemplative expressions.

"Even if you succeeded in doing that, you'd only kill one of them," Nate said. "The other, clearly its mate, would go into a rampage and attack the rafts. Our best bet is to hope the pair lose interest in us and drift away, then we can paddle out of here."

Waxman turned to Corporal Yamir, the demolition expert. "In case the crocodiles don't get bored, let's be prepared to entertain them. Prime up a pair of the napalm bombs."

The corporal nodded and turned to his pack.

Once again, the waiting game began. Time stretched.

Nate felt the raft tremble under his knees as one of the pair rubbed the underside of the logs with its thick tail. "Hang on!"

Suddenly the raft bucked under them. The stern was tossed high in the air. The group clung like spiders to the bamboo. Loose packs rolled into the lake with distinct splashes. The raft crashed back to the water, jarring them all.

"Is everyone okay?" Nate yelled.

Murmurs of assent rose.

"I lost my rifle," Okamoto said, his eyes angry.

"Better your gun than you," Kouwe said dolefully.

Nate raised his voice. "They're getting bolder!"

Okamoto reached out to one of their floating packs. "My gear."

Nate saw what he was doing. "Corporal! Stop!"

Okamoto immediately froze. "Shit . . ." He already had the strap of his rucksack in hand, half pulled out of the water.

"Leave it," Nate said. "Get away from the edge."

The corporal released his pack with a slight splash and yanked his arm back.

But he moved too slowly.

The monster lunged up out of the depths, jaws open, water sluicing from its scales. It shot ten feet out of the swamp, a tower of armor plating and teeth as long as a man's forearm. The Ranger was pulled off his feet and shoved high into the air, screaming in shock and terror. The huge jaws clamped shut with an audible crunch of bones. Okamoto's scream changed in pitch to pain and disbelief. His body was shaken like a rag doll, legs flailing. Then the creature's bulk dropped back into the depths.

"Fire!" Waxman called.

Nate had been too stunned to move. Carrera blazed with her M-16. Bullets peppered the underside of the giant, prehistoric caiman, but its yellowed belly scales were as hard as Kevlar. Even at almost point-blank range, it looked like little harm was done. Its weak points, the eyes, were hidden on the far side of its bulk.

Nate swung up his own shotgun, stretched his arm over Manny's head, and fired. A load of pellet sprayed through the empty air as the beast dropped out of range. A wasted, panicked shot.

The caiman was gone. Okamoto was gone.

Everyone was frozen in shock.

Nate's raft bobbed in the wake of the creature's passing. He stared out at the spot where the Ranger had vanished, Okamoto with his damn whistling. A red stain bubbled up from below.

Blood on the water . . . now the monsters know there's food here.

Kelly crouched with her brother in the center of their raft. Captain Waxman and Corporal Warczak knelt with their weapons ready. Yamir was finalizing his prep on two black bombs, each the size of a flat dinner plate with an electronic timer/receiver atop it. The demolitions expert leaned back. "Done," he said with a nod to his captain.

"Retrieve your weapon," Waxman said. "Be ready."

Yamir picked up his M-16 rifle and took up watch on his side of the raft.

A splintering crash sounded behind them. Kelly swung around in time to see the third raft in their flotilla knocked high into the air, the same as Nate's raft had done a moment before. But this time, its occupants were not as lucky. Anna Fong, her grip broken, went flying, catapulted through the air by the sudden attack. The anthropologist struck the water at the same time the raft crashed back down. Zane and Olin had managed to cling to the raft, as had Sergeant Kostos and Corporal Graves.

Anna popped to the surface, coughing and choking on water. She was only yards from the raft.

"Don't move, Anna!" Nate called. "Tuck your arms and legs together and float."

She clearly tried to obey, but her pack, waterlogged, dragged her underwater unless she kicked to keep herself afloat. Her eyes were white with panic; both the fear of drowning and the fear of what lurked in the waters shone bright in her eyes.

Movement drew her attention back to the assaulted raft. Sergeant Kostos was leaning out with one of the long bamboo poles that they had used to propel themselves away from shore.

"Grab on!" Kostos called to her.

Anna reached to the bamboo, fingers scrabbling for a moment, then clinging.

"I'm gonna pull you toward the raft."

"No!" she moaned.

Nate again called. "Anna, it should be okay as long as you don't make any sudden moves. Kostos, pull her very slowly toward you. Try not to raise a ripple."

Kelly trembled. Frank put his arm around her.

Ever so slowly, the sergeant drew Anna back to the raft.

"Good, good . . ." Nate mumbled in a tense mantra.

Then, behind Anna, an armored snout appeared, just the nose, its eyes hidden underwater still.

"No one shoot!" Nate called. "Don't rile it!"

Guns pointed, but there was no kill shot anyway.

Kostos had stopped pulling on the bamboo with the appearance of the caiman. No one moved.

A moan flowed from the woman in the water.

Ever so slowly the snout inched forward, rising slightly as its massive jaws yawned open.

Kostos was forced to slowly draw Anna toward him, keeping her just a couple of feet ahead of the approaching monster.

"Careful!" Nate called.

It was like some macabre slow-motion chase . . . and they were losing.

The snout of the creature was now less than a foot from the woman, the jaws gaping open behind her head. There was no way Anna could be pulled aboard without the creature attacking.

Someone else came to this same realization.

Corporal Graves ran across their raft and leaped over Anna's head like an Olympic long jumper.

"Graves!" Kostos yelled.

The corporal landed atop the creature's open snout, driving its jaws closed and shoving it underwater.

"Pull her aboard!" Graves hollered as he was sucked under by the caiman.

Kostos yanked Anna back to the raft and Olin helped haul her on board.

A moment later, the beast reared up out of the water, Graves still clinging to the top of its wide head. The caiman thrashed, trying to dislodge its strange rider. Its jaws reared open, and a bellow of rage escaped from it.

"Fuck you!" Graves said. "This is for my brother!" Clinging fast with his legs, he yanked something from his field jacket and tossed it down the beast's gullet.

A grenade.

The massive jaws snapped at the Ranger, but he was out of reach.

"Everybody down!" Waxman bellowed.

Graves leaped from his perch aiming for the raft, a shout on his lips. "Chew on that, you bastard!"

Behind him, the explosion ripped through the silent swamp. The head of the caiman blew apart, shredded by shrapnel.

Graves flew through the air, a roar of triumph flowing from his lips.

Then up from the depths shot the other caiman. Jaws wide, it lunged at the flying corporal, snatching him out of midair, like a dog catching a tossed ball, then crashed away, taking its prey with it. It had all happened in seconds.

The bulk of the slain caiman slowly rose to the surface of the lake, belly up, exposing the gray and yellow scaling of its underside.

The slack body of the huge creature was nudged from below. Ripples slowly circled it as the large beast was examined by the survivor.

"Maybe it'll leave," Frank said. "Maybe the other's death will spook it away."

Kelly knew this wouldn't happen. These creatures had to be hundreds and hundreds of years old. Mates for life, the only pair of its kind sharing this ecosystem.

The ripples faded. The lake grew quiet again.

Everyone kept eyes fixed on the waters around them, holding their breath or wheezing tensely. Minutes stretched. The sun baked everyone.

"Where did it go?" Zane whispered, hovering beside his ashen colleague. Anna, soaked and terrified, just trembled.

"Maybe it did leave," Frank mumbled.

The trio of rafts, rudderless, slowly drifted alongside the bulk of the dead monster. Nate's boat was on the far side of the body. Kelly met his eye. He nodded, trying to convey calm assurance, but even the experienced jungle man looked scared. Behind him, the jaguar crouched beside its master, hackles raised.

Frank shifted his legs slightly. "It must have fled. Maybe—"

Kelly sensed it a moment before it struck: a sudden welling of the water under their raft. "Hang on!"

"What—"

The raft exploded under them—not just bumped up, but driven skyward. Shattering up from the center of the raft jammed the massive armored snout of the angered caiman.

Kelly flew, tumbling through the air. She caught glimpses of the others falling amid the rain of bamboo and packs. "Frank!" Her brother splashed on the far side of the monster.

Then she hit the water—hard, on her stomach. The wind was knocked out of her. She spluttered up, remembering Nate's warning to remain as still as possible. She glanced up in time to see a chunk of the raft's log dropping through the air toward her face.

Dodging, she missed a fatal blow, but the edge of the flying log clipped the side of her head. She collapsed backward, driven underwater, darkness swallowing her away.

From the far side of the dead caiman's bulk, Nate watched Kelly get hit by debris and go under—dead or unconscious, he didn't know. All around the ruined raft, people, packs, and bits of debris floated. "Float as still as possible!" Nate called out, frantically searching for what had happened to Kelly.

The caiman had vanished underwater again.

"Kelly!" Frank called.

His sister bobbed to the surface on the far side of the debris field. She was facedown in the water, limp.

Nate hesitated. *Was she dead?* Then he saw one arm move, flailing weakly. *Alive!* But for how long? As dazed as she was by the blow, she risked drowning.

"Damn it!" He searched for some plan, some way to rescue her. Just beyond her body was one of the small hummocks of land with a single large mangrove tree sprouting up from it. Its thick trunk sprang from a tangle of exposed buttress roots, then fanned out into a branched canopy hanging over the waters. If Kelly could reach there . . .

A shout arose from the waters, drawing back his attention. The caiman's head appeared, rising like a submarine amid the debris. A large eye studied its surroundings. Shots were fired toward it, but it remained low in the water, blocked by the debris and the people. Then it sank quickly away.

Frank finally spotted his sister. "Oh, God . . . Kelly!" He turned, ready to swim to her aid.

"Frank! Don't move!" Nate called. "I'll get to her!" He dropped his shotgun to the bamboo planking.

"What are you doing?" Manny asked.

As answer, Nate leaped across the gap between the raft and the dead caiman. He landed on its exposed belly, landing in a half crouch, then ran down the length of the beast's slippery bulk, trying to get as close to Kelly as possible.

A scream rose on his right. He watched Corporal Yamir, struggling— then suddenly Yamir was yanked under the water, large bubbles trailing down into the depths. The caiman was picking off the survivors in the water.

Time was running out.

Nate ran and leaped from the belly of the floating caiman, flinging his body with all the strength in his legs. Flying out, he dove smoothly for Kelly, reaching her in a heartbeat. He rolled her face out of the water. She struggled weakly against him.

"Kelly! It's Nate! Lie still!"

Something must have registered, for her struggling slowed.

Nate kicked strongly toward the nearby hummock. He scrabbled through the debris. His hand hit something: a black dinner plate decorated with blinking red lights. One of the dead corporal's bombs.

Instinctively, Nate grabbed it up in his free hand and continued to kick.

"Behind you!" Sergeant Kostos called from across the water.

Nate glanced back.

A rippling wake aimed in his direction, then the tip of the snout broke the surface, then more of the bull's black-scaled head. Nate found himself staring eye-to-eye with the beast. He sensed the intelligence behind that gaze. No dumb brute. Playing dead wouldn't work here.

He turned and kicked and paddled with the napalm bomb toward the swamp island. His feet hit muddy ground.

With a strength born of fear and panic, he scooped Kelly under his arm and hauled them through the shallows, climbing the banks.

"It's right on top of you!"

Nate didn't bother to turn. He ran toward the tangle of mangrove roots, shoved Kelly between them, then dove in after her. There was a cramped natural cavity behind the main buttress roots.

Kelly groggily awoke, coughing out gouts of water and staring around in panic. Nate fell atop her in the small space.

"What . . . ?"

Then, over his shoulder, she must have spotted their pursuer. Her eyes grew large. "Oh, shit!"

Nate rolled around and saw the monster hurling itself up out of the lake, scrabbling up the short bank. It struck like a locomotive hitting a car on the tracks. The whole tree shook. Nate was sure it would crash atop them. But the tree held. The caiman stared at Nate between the roots, mouth gaping open, teeth glinting with menace. It paused, glaring at him, then backpedaled and slid into the waters.

Kelly turned to him. "You saved me."

He glanced to her, their noses almost touching in the cramped root prison. "Or almost got you killed. It's all perspective, really." Nate pushed to his knees. He grabbed one of the roots to haul himself to his feet. "And we're not out of the woods yet."

Nate studied the waters, watching for any telltale ripple. It seemed quiet. But he knew the caiman was still out there, watching. Taking a deep breath, he squeezed back out between the roots.

"Where are you going?"

"There are still others in the water . . . including your brother." Nate shoved the napalm bomb under his shirt and began to climb the mangrove, a plan slowly forming. Once high enough, he picked a good branch, clambered atop it, and slowly crawled down its length to where it hung over the water. As the branch thinned, it began to bend under his weight. He moved more cautiously.

At last, he could risk going no farther. He glanced down and around his perch. This would have to do.

He called to the other raft while pulling out the bomb. "Does anyone know how to arm one of these explosives?"

Sergeant Kostos answered, "Type in the time delay manually! Then hit the red button!"

Waxman yelled from where he floated in the water. Nate had to respect how calm the captain's voice was as he added a warning. "It's got an explosive radius of a couple hundred meters. Blow it wrong and you'll kill us all!"

Nate nodded, staring at the bomb. A simple sealed keyboard glowed atop it, not unlike a calculator. Nate prayed it hadn't been damaged by the dunking or abuse. He set the timer for fifteen seconds. That should be long enough.

Next, Nate cradled the bomb to his chest and snapped free his work knife. Clenching his teeth, he dug the blade into the meat of his thumb and sliced a deep gash. He needed the wound to bleed freely.

Once done, he used a secondary branch as support and climbed to his feet on the swaying perch. He pulled the bomb out with his bloodied hand and made sure he had a good grip. Stretching out over the water, Nate extended his arm, bomb in hand. Blood dripped over the weapon's surface and down to the waters below, plopping in thick drops and sending out ripples.

He held steady, his thumb on the trigger button. "C'mon, damn you." In Australia, he had once visited a live animal park and had seen a thirty-foot saltwater crocodile trained to leap after a freshly decapitated chicken on a pole.

Nate's plan wasn't much different. Only he was the chicken.

He slightly shook his arm, scattering more drops. "Where are you?" he hissed. His arm was getting tired.

Down below, he watched a small pool of his own blood forming on the surface of the water. A caiman could smell blood in the water from miles away. "C'mon!"

Squinting, he risked a peek toward the others still afloat in the debris field. With no way of knowing where the caiman was, neither of the other two rafts dared paddle to their mates' rescue.

Distracted, Nate almost missed the flash of something large heaving through the shallows toward him.

"Nate!" Kelly called.

He saw it.

The caiman lunged out of the water, blasting straight out of the lake and springing toward him, jaws wide open, roaring.

Nate hit the bomb's trigger, then dropped the blood-slick device down the open mouth. He realized at the same time that he had vastly underestimated how *high* a giant swamp caiman could leap.

Nate crouched on his branch, then leaped straight up, propelled by both his legs and the spring in the branch. Crashing through leaves, Nate grabbed a limb overhead. He yanked his feet out of the way just as the monster's jaws snapped shut under the seat of his pants. He felt its huffed breath on his back. Denied its prey, it fell back to the water, shooting spray almost as high as its leap.

Staring down, Nate saw the branch he had been perched on. It was gone, a stump, cleaved clean through by those mighty jaws. If he had still been standing there . . .

Nate saw the caiman again glide from the shallows into the deeper waters, but now it remained floating on the surface, revealing its length. A male, 120 feet if it was an inch.

Hanging from the branch, Nate caught a frustrated glower directed up at him. It slowly turned toward where the others were floating, giving up on him for the moment and going after easier prey.

Before it could complete its turn, Nate saw the beast suddenly shudder. He had forgotten to count the seconds.

Suddenly the belly of the beast swelled immensely. It opened its maw to scream but all that came out were jets of flame. The caiman had become a veritable flaming dragon. It rolled on its side and sank into the murkier depths, then a huge *whoosh* exploded upward in a column of water, flames, and caiman.

Nate clung to his perch with his arms and legs. Down below in the roots, Kelly yelled in shock.

The blast ended as quickly as it blew. In the aftermath, bits and pieces of flaming flesh showered harmlessly around the swamp. Insulated by the armored bulk of the great giant, the worst of the bomb's effect had been contained.

A shout of triumph arose from the others.

Nate climbed down the tree and retrieved Kelly. "Are you okay?" he asked her.

She nodded, fingering a gash at her hairline. "Head hurts a little, but I'll be fine." She coughed hoarsely. "I must've swallowed a gallon of swamp water."

He helped her down to the water's edge. While Kostos's raft went to collect the swimmers and packs, Nate's own raft, manned by his friends and Ranger Carrera, glided over to the pair to keep them from having to swim.

Carrera helped pull Kelly aboard. Manny grabbed Nate's wrist and hauled him up onto the bamboo planks. "That was some pretty fast thinking, doc," Manny said with a grin.

"Necessity is the mother of invention," Nate said, matching his expression with a tired smile. "But I'll be damned glad to be on dry land again."

"Could there be more of them out there?" Kelly asked as the group paddled toward the other raft.

"I doubt it," Manny said with a strange trace of regret. "Even with an ecosystem this large, I can't imagine there's enough food to support more than two of these gigantic predators. Still, I'd keep a watch out for any offspring. Even baby giants could be trouble."

Carrera kept watch with her rifle as the others paddled. "Do you think that the Ban-ali sent these after us, like the locusts and piranhas?"

Kouwe answered, "No, but I would not put it past them to have nurtured this pair as some de facto gatekeepers to their lands, permanently stationed guards against any who dared to enter their territory."

Gatekeepers? Nate stared at the far shore. The broken highlands were now clear in the afternoon brightness. Waterfalls were splashes of silver flowing down cliffs the color of spilled blood. The jungled summits and valleys were verdant.

If the professor was right about the caiman being gatekeepers, then ahead of them stretched the lands of the Ban-ali, the heart of their deadly territory.

He stared at the other raft, counting heads. *Waxman, Kostos, Warczak, and Carrera.* Only four Rangers remained of the twelve sent out here—and they hadn't even crossed into the true heart of the Ban-ali lands. "We'll never make it," he mumbled as he paddled.

Carrera heard him. "Don't worry. We'll dig in until reinforcements can be flown here. It can't take more than a day."

Nate frowned. *They had lost three men today, elite military professionals.* A day was not insignificant. As he stared at the growing heights of the far shore, Nate was suddenly less sure he wanted to reach dry land, especially *that* dry land. But they had no choice. A plague was spreading through the States, and their small party was as close to an answer to the puzzle as anyone. There was no turning back.

Besides, his father had taken this route, run this biological gauntlet. Nate could not retreat now. Despite the deaths, the dangers, and the risks, he had to find out what had happened to his father. Plague or not, he could only go forward.

Waxman called as they neared the far shore. "Stay alert! Once we pull up, move quickly away from the swamp. We'll set up a base camp a short distance into the forest."

Nate saw the way the captain kept scanning the swamps. Waxman was clearly worried about other caiman predators. But Nate kept his gaze focused on the jungles ahead. In his blood, he knew that was where the true danger lay—the Ban-ali.

Across the water, Nate heard the captain fall upon Olin Pasternak. "And you, get that uplink running as soon as possible. We have a three-hour window before the satellites are out of range for the night."

"I'll do my best," Olin assured him.

Waxman nodded. Nate caught the look in the captain's eyes: full of grief and worry. Despite his booming confident voice, the leader of the Rangers was as nervous as Nate. And this realization was oddly reassuring. Nervous men kept a keen eye on their surroundings, and Nate suspected that their survival would depend on this.

The pair of rafts reached the shallows and soon were bumping into solid ground. The Rangers offloaded first, rifles ready. They fanned out and checked the immediate forest. Soon, calls of "All clear!" rang out from the dark jungles fringing the swamp.

Nate glanced up as he waited for the okay to disembark from the rafts. Around him, the soft roar of countless waterfalls echoed. To either side, towering cliffs framed the narrow defile ahead, choked with jungle. Down the center of the canyon a wide stream flowed, emptying sluggishly into the swamp.

Warczak shouted from near the forest's edge. "Found it!" The corporal leaned out of the shadowy fringe and waved to his captain. "Another of Clark's markers."

Waxman motioned with his rifle. "Everybody on land!"

Nate did not wait. He hurried with the others toward Warczak. A few steps into the forest, a large Spanish cedar had been pegged with a strip of cloth. And under it, another carved marking. Each member stared at it with a growing sense of dread. An arrow pointed up the defile. The meaning was clear.

"Skull and crossbones," Zane muttered.
Death lay ahead.

3:40 P.M.

"Now that was quite entertaining," Louis said to his lieutenant, lowering his binoculars. "When that caiman exploded . . ." He shook his head. "Resourceful."

Earlier that morning, radioed by his mole, Louis had learned of the Rangers' plan to camp near the far shore until reinforcements could be flown in. He imagined the loss of three more men would cement Captain Waxman's plan. The group was now down to four Rangers. No threat.

Louis's team could take the other at any time—and Louis didn't want those odds changed.

He turned to Jacques. "We'll let them rest until midnight, then rouse the little sleepyheads and get them running forward. Who knows what other dangers they'll prepare us for?" Louis pointed to the swamp.

"Yes, sir. I'll have my team suited up and ready by nightfall. We're draining several lanterns now to collect enough kerosene."

"Good." Louis turned his back on the swamp. "Once the others are on the run, we'll follow behind you in the canoes."

"Yes, sir, but . . ." Jacques bit his lower lip and stared out at the swamp.

Louis patted his lieutenant on the shoulder. "Fear not. If there had been any other beasties lurking in the swamp, they would've attacked the Rangers. You should be safe." But Louis could understand his lieutenant's concern. Louis would not be the one using scuba gear to cross the swamp on motorized sleds, with nothing between him and the denizens of the swamp except a wet suit. Even with the night-vision lamps, it would be a dark and murky crossing.

But Jacques nodded. He would do as ordered.

Louis crossed back into the jungle, heading to the camp. Like his lieutenant, many others were on edge, the tension thick. They all had seen the remains of the Ranger back in the woods. The soldier looked like he had been eaten alive, down to the bone, eyes gone. A scattering of locusts had still crawled around the site, but most of the swarm had dispersed. Alerted by his mole, Louis had carefully kept burners of *tok-tok* powder smoldering as they crossed through the forest this morning, just in case. Luckily Tshui had been able to harvest enough dried liana vines to produce the protective powder.

Despite the threats, Louis's plan was proceeding smoothly. He was not so vain as to think his group moved unseen, but so far the Ban-ali were concentrating all their resources on the foremost group, the Rangers.

Still, Louis could not count on this particular advantage lasting much longer, especially once they entered the heart of the secretive tribe's territory. And he was not alone in these thoughts. Earlier, three mercenaries from his party had attempted to sneak off and flee, abandoning their obligations, fearful of what lay ahead. The cowards had been caught, of course, and Tshui had made an example of them.

Louis reached their temporary jungle campsite. He found his mistress, Tshui, kneeling by his tent. Across the way, strung spread-eagle between various trees, were the AWOL trio. Louis averted his eyes. There was surely artistry to Tshui's work, but Louis had only so strong a stomach.

She glanced up at his approach. She was cleaning her tools in a bowl of water.

Louis grinned at her. She stood, all legs and sinewy muscle. He took her under his arm and guided her toward their tent.

As Tshui ducked past the flap, she growled deep in her chest and, impatient, tugged his hand to draw him into the dark heat of the tent.

For the moment, it seemed rest would have to wait.

THIRTEEN

Shadows

Lauren knocked on Dr. Alvisio's office door. Earlier this morning, the epidemiologist had requested, rather urgently, a moment with her. But this was the first chance she'd had to break away and meet with him.

Instead, she had spent the entire morning and afternoon in video conference with Dr. Xavier Reynolds and his team at Large Scale Biological Labs in Vacaville, California. The prion protein they had discovered could be the first clue to solving this disease, a contagion that had claimed over sixty lives so far with another several hundred sick. Lauren had arranged for her former student's data to be cross-referenced and double-checked by fourteen other labs. As she waited for confirmation, she had time to meet with the epidemiologist.

The door opened. The young Stanford doctor looked as if he hadn't slept in weeks. A bit of dark stubble shadowed his cheeks, and his eyes were bloodshot. "Dr. O'Brien. Thank you for coming." He ushered her into the room.

Lauren had never been in his office, so she was surprised to see a whole array of computer equipment lining one entire wall. Otherwise, the room was rather Spartan: a cluttered desk, an overflowing bookcase, a few chairs. The only personal touch was a lone Stanford Cardinals banner hanging on the far wall. But Lauren's eye was drawn back to the computer bank. The monitors were full of graphs and flowing numbers.

"What was so urgent, Hank?" she asked him.

He waved her to the computers. "I need you to see this." His voice was grim.

She nodded and took the seat he offered before one of the monitors.

"Do you remember when I told you about the possible signature spike of basophils early in the disease process? How this clinical finding might be a way to detect and specify cases more quickly?"

She nodded, but since hearing his theory, she had already begun to doubt it. Jessie's basophils had spiked, but the child was recovering very well. There had even been talk of letting her out of the hospital ward as soon as tomorrow. This rise in basophils could be something that occurs with many different fevers and is not specific to this disease.

She opened her mouth to say just that, but Dr. Alvisio interrupted, turning to his computer keyboard. He typed rapidly. "It took me a full twenty-four hours to gather data from around the entire country, specifically searching for fever cases in children and the elderly with characteristic basophil spikes. I wanted to run a model for the disease using this new criteria."

On the monitor, a map of the United States appeared in yellow with each state mapped out in black lines. Small pinpoints of red dotted the map, most clustered in Florida and other southern states. "Here is the old data. Each area of red indicates current documented cases of the contagion."

Lauren slipped on her reading glasses and leaned closer.

"But using the basophil spike as the marker for designating cases, here is a truer picture of the disease's present status in the United States." The epidemiologist hit a keystroke. The map bloomed brighter with red dots. Florida was almost a solid red, as were Georgia and Alabama. Other states, empty before, now were speckled with red spots.

Hank turned to her. "As you can see, the number of cases skyrockets. Many of these patients are in unquarantined wards due to the fact that the trio of signs designated by the CDC have not shown up yet. They're exposing others."

Despite her doubts, Lauren felt a sick churn in her belly. Even if Dr. Alvisio was wrong about the basophils, he had made a good point. Early detection was critical. Until then, all feverish children or elderly should be quarantined immediately, even if they weren't in hot zones like Florida and Georgia. "I see what you're saying," she said. "We should contact the CDC and have them establish nationwide quarantine policies."

Hank nodded. "But that's not all." He turned back to his computer and typed. "Based on this new basophil data, I ran an extrapolation model. Here is what the disease picture will look like in two weeks." He pressed the ENTER key.

The entire southern half of the country went red.

Lauren sat back in shock.

"And in another month." Hank struck the ENTER key a second time.

The red mottling spread to consume almost the entire lower forty-eight states.

Hank glanced at her. "We have to do something to stop this. Every day is critical."

Lauren stared at the bloodstained screen, her mouth dry, her eyes wide. Her only consolation was that Dr. Alvisio's basis for this model was probably overly grim. She doubted the basophil spike was truly an early marker for the disease. Still, the warning here was important. Every day *was* critical.

Her pager vibrated on her hip, reminding her that the war against this disease had to be fought with every resource. She glanced down to her pager's screen. It was Marshall. He had followed his numeric code with a 911. Something urgent.

"Can I use your phone?" she asked.

"Of course."

She stood and crossed to his desk. Hank returned to his computers and statistical models. She dialed the number. The phone was answered in half a ring.

"Lauren . . ."

"What is it, Marshall?"

His words were rushed, full of fear. "It's Jessie. I'm at the hospital."

Lauren clutched the phone tighter. "What is it? What's wrong?"

"Her temperature is up again." His voice cracked. "Higher than it's ever been. And three other children have been admitted. Fevers, all of them."

"Wh . . . what are you saying?" she stammered, but she knew the answer to her own question.

Her husband remained silent.

"I'll be right there," she finally said, dropping the phone and scrabbling to replace it in its cradle.

Hank turned to her, noticing her reaction. "Dr. O'Brien?"

Lauren could not speak. *Jessie . . . the basophil spike . . . the other children.* Dear God, the disease was here!

Lauren stared glassily at the monitor with the map of the United States mottled entirely in red. The epidemiologist's theory was not a mistake. It wasn't overly pessimistic.

"Is everything all right?" Hank asked softly.

Lauren slowly shook her head, eyes fixed on the screen.

One month.

5:23 P.M.

AMAZON JUNGLE

Kelly sat hunched with her brother, both flanking Olin Pasternak. The Russian computer expert was screwing down the cover piece to reassemble the satellite communication system. He had been working on it all afternoon, trying to raise the States.

"This had better work," he mumbled. "I've torn it down to the motherboard and built it back up. If this doesn't work, I don't know what else to try."

Frank nodded. "Fire it up."

Olin checked the connections one final time, adjusted the satellite dish, then returned his attention to the laptop computer. He switched on the solar power, and after a short wait, the operating system booted up and the screen hummed to life.

"We've got a connection to the HERMES satellite!" Olin said, and sighed with relief.

A cheer went up around Kelly. The entire camp, except for the pair of Rangers on guard by the swamp, was gathered around Olin and his communication equipment.

"Can you get an uplink established?" Waxman asked.

"Keep your fingers crossed," Olin said. He began tapping at the keyboard.

Kelly found herself holding her breath. They needed to reach someone Stateside. Reinforcements were certainly needed here. But more important to her, Kelly couldn't stand not knowing Jessie's status. She had to find a way to get back to her.

"Here we go." Olin struck a final sequence of keys. The familiar connection countdown began.

Richard Zane mumbled behind her. "Please, please work . . ."

His prayer was in all their hearts.

The countdown blipped to zero. The computer screen froze for an interminably long second, then a picture of Kelly's mother and father appeared. The pair looked shocked and relieved.

"Thank God!" her father said. "We've been trying to reach you for the past hour."

Olin moved aside for Frank. "Computer problems," her brother said, "among many others."

Kelly leaned in. She could not wait a moment longer. "How's Jessie?"

Her mother's face answered the question. Her eyes fidgeted, and she paused before speaking. "She's . . . she's doing fine, dear."

The image on the screen fritzed as if the computer had become a lie detector. Static and snow ate away the picture. Her mother's next words became garbled. "Lead on a cure . . . prion disease . . . sending data as we speak . . ."

Her father spoke, but the interference grew worse. They seemed unaware that their message was corrupted. ". . . helicopter on its way . . . Brazilian army . . ."

Frank hissed to Olin, "Can you fix the reception?"

He leaned in and tapped quickly. "I don't know. I don't understand. We've just received a file. Maybe that's interfering with our downstream feed."

But for each key the man tapped, the signal deteriorated.

Static whined and hissed with occasional words coming through. "Frank . . . losing you . . . can you . . . tomorrow morning . . . GPS locked . . ." Then the entire feed collapsed. The screen gave one final frazzled burst, then froze up.

"Damn it!" Olin swore.

"Get it back up," Waxman said behind them.

Olin bent over his equipment and shook his head. "I don't know if I can. I've troubleshot the motherboard and rebooted all the software."

"What's wrong then?" Kelly asked.

"I can't say for sure. It's almost like a computer virus has corrupted the entire satellite communication array."

"Well, keep trying," Waxman said. "You've got another half hour before the satellite is out of range."

Frank stood, facing everyone. "Even if we can't link up, from what we did hear, it sounds like the Brazilian helicopter may be on its way here. Maybe as soon as tomorrow morning."

Beside him, Olin stared at the frozen screen. "Oh, God."

All eyes turned to the Russian communications expert. He tapped the screen, pointing to a set of numbers in the upper right-hand corner. "Our GPS signal . . ."

"What's the matter?" Waxman asked.

Olin glanced over to them. "It's wrong. Whatever glitched the satellite system must've corrupted the feed to the GPS satellites, too. It sent a wrong signal back to the States." He stared back at the screen. "It places us about thirty miles south of our current position."

Kelly felt the blood rush from her head. "They won't know where we are."

"I've got to get this up and running," Olin said. "At least long enough to correct the signal." He rebooted the computer and set to work.

For the next half hour, Olin worked furiously with his equipment. Oaths and curses, both in English and Russian, flowed from the man. As he labored, everyone found busy work to occupy the time. No one bothered to try resting. Kelly helped Anna prepare some rice, the last of their supplies. As they worked, they kept looking over to Olin, silently praying.

But for all the man's efforts and their prayers, nothing was gained.

After a time, Frank crossed and placed a hand on Olin's shoulder. He raised his other arm, exposing his wristwatch. "It's too late. The communication satellites are out of range."

Olin sagged over his array, defeated.

"We'll try again in the morning," Frank said, his encouragement forced. "You should rest. Start fresh tomorrow."

Nate, Kouwe, and Manny returned from a fishing expedition by the swamp. Their catch was bountiful, strung on a line between them. They dropped their load beside the fire. "I'll clean," Kouwe said, settling easily to the ground.

Manny sighed. "No argument here."

Nate wiped his hands and stared at Olin and his computer. He crossed toward the man. "There was something I was wondering about while fishing. What about that other file?"

"What are you talking about?" Olin asked blearily.

"You mentioned something about a file being downloaded during the feed."

Olin scrunched his face, then nodded with understanding. "*Da*. Here it is. A data file."

Kelly and Manny hurried over. Kelly now remembered her mother had mentioned sending something just before the system crashed.

Olin brought up the file.

Kelly leaned closer. On the screen appeared a 3-D model of a molecule spinning above pages of data. Intrigued, she settled nearer. Her eyes scanned through the report. "My mother's work," she mumbled, glad to occupy her mind on something other than her own worries. But the topic was troublesome nonetheless.

"What is it?" Nate asked.

"A possible lead on the cause of the disease," Kelly added.

Manny answered, peering over her shoulder. "A prion."

"A what?"

Manny quickly explained to Nate, but Kelly's attention remained focused on the report. "Interesting," Kelly mumbled.

"What?" Manny asked.

"It says here that this prion seems to cause genetic damage." She quickly read the next report.

Manny read over her shoulder. He whistled appreciatively.

"What?" Nate asked.

Kelly spoke excitedly. "This could be the answer! Here's a paper from researchers at the University of Chicago, published in *Nature* back in September of 2000. They hypothesized through the study of yeast that prions may hold the key to genetic mutations, even play a role in evolution."

"Really? How?"

"One of the major mysteries of evolution has been how survival skills that require multiple genetic changes could happen so spontaneously. Such changes are termed *macroevolution,* like the adaptation of certain algae to toxic environments or the rapid development of antibiotic resistance in bacteria. But how such a series of simultaneous mutations could be generated was not understood. But this article offers a possible answer. *Prions.*" Kelly pointed to the computer screen. "Here the researchers at the University of Chicago have shown that a yeast's prions can flip an *all-or-nothing* switch in the genetic code, causing massive mutations to develop in unison, to spark an evolutionary jump start, so to speak. Do you know what this suggests?"

Kelly saw realization dawn in Manny's eyes.

"The piranha creatures, the locusts . . ." the biologist mumbled.

"Mutations all of them. Maybe even Gerald Clark's arm!" Kelly said. "A mutation triggered by prions."

"But what does this have to do with the disease?" Nate asked.

Kelly frowned. "I don't know. This discovery is a good start, but we're a long way from a complete answer."

Manny pointed to the screen. "But what about here in the article where it hypothesizes . . ."

Kelly nodded. The two began to discuss the article, speaking rapidly, sharing ideas.

Beside them, Nate had stopped listening. He had scrolled back to the spinning model of the prion protein.

After a time, he interrupted. "Does anyone else see the similarity?"

"What do you mean?" Kelly asked.

Nate pointed to the screen. "See those two spiraling loops at either end?"

"The double alpha helixes?" Kelly said.

"Right . . . and here the corkscrewing middle section," Nate said, tracing the screen with his finger.

"So?" Kelly asked.

Nate turned and reached to the ground beside him. He picked up a stick and drew in the dirt, speaking as he worked. "The middle corkscrew . . . spreading out in double loops at either end." When he was done, he glanced up.

Stunned, Kelly stared at what Nate had drawn in the dirt.

Manny gasped, "The Ban-ali symbol!"

Kelly stared between the two pictures: one, a high-tech computer map; the other, a crude scrawl in the soft dirt. But there was no disputing the similarity. *The corkscrew, the double helixes . . .* It seemed beyond coincidence, even down to the clockwise spin of the molecular spiral.

Kelly turned to Nate and Manny. "Jesus Christ."

The Ban-ali symbol was a stylized model of the same prion.

11:32 P.M.

Jacques still had an unnerving terror of dark waters, born from the piranha attack that had left him disfigured when he was only a boy. Despite these deep fears, he glided through the swamp with nothing but a wet suit between him and the toothy predators of this marsh. He had no choice. He had to obey the doctor. The price of disobedience was worse than any terrors that might lurk in these waters.

Jacques clung to his motorized attack board as the silent fans dragged his body toward the far shore of the swamp. He was outfitted in an LAR V Draeger UBA, gear used by Navy SEALs for clandestine shallow-water operations. The closed-circuit system, strapped to his chest, rather than his back, produced no telltale bubble signature, making his approach unde-tectable. The final piece of his gear was a night-vision mask, giving him adequate visibility in the murky waters.

Still, the dark waters remained tight around him. His visibility was only about ten yards. He would periodically use a small mirrored device to peek above the water's surface and maintain his bearing.

His two teammates on this mission trailed behind him, also gliding with tiny motorized sleds held at arms' length.

Jacques checked one last time with his tiny periscope. The two bam-boo rafts that the Rangers had used to cross the swamp were directly ahead. Thirty yards away.

In the woods, he spotted the camp's fire, blazing bright. Shadowy fig-ures, even at this late hour, moved around the site. Satisfied, he motioned to his two men to continue on ahead, one to each raft. Jacques would drift behind them, on guard with his scope.

The trio moved slowly forward. The rafts were tethered to the shore and floating in waters less than four feet deep. They would all have to be even more careful from here.

With determined caution, the group converged on the rafts. Jacques watched above and below the surface. His men waited in position, hover-ing in the shadows of their respective rafts. He studied the woods. He sus-pected that hidden in the dark jungle were guards, Rangers on patrol. He watched for a full five minutes, then signaled his men.

From under the rafts, the men produced small squeeze bottles full of kerosene. They sprayed the underside of the bamboo planks. Once each bottle emptied, the men gave Jacques a thumbs-up signal.

As his men worked, Jacques continued to watch the woods. So far, there was no sign that anyone had noticed their handiwork. He waited a full minute more, then gave the final signal, a slashing motion across his neck.

Each man lifted a hand above the water and ignited a butane lighter. They lifted the tiny flames to the kerosene-soaked bamboo. Flames imme-diately leaped and spread over the rafts.

Without waiting, the two men grabbed up their sleds and sped toward Jacques. He turned and thumbed his own motor to high and led his men off in a swooping curve out into the swamp, then back around, aiming for a spot on the shore a half-kilometer from the enemy's camp.

Jacques watched behind him. Men appeared out of the wood, outlined by the burning rafts, weapons pointing. Even underwater, he heard muffled shouts and sounds of alarm.

It had all gone perfectly. The doctor knew the other camp, after the locust attack, would be spooked by fires in the night. They would not likely remain near such a burning pyre.

Still, they were to take no unnecessary chances. Jacques led his men back toward the shallows, and the group slowly rose from the lake, spitting out regulator mouthpieces and kicking off fins. The second part of his mission was to ensure the others did indeed flee.

Slogging out of the water, he breathed a sigh of relief, glad to leave the dark swamp behind. He fingered the unmangled half of his nose, as if making sure it was still there.

Jacques slipped out a pair of night-vision binoculars. He fitted them in place and stared back toward the camp. Behind him, his men whispered, energized from the adventure and the successful completion of their task. Jacques ignored them.

Outlined in the monochrome green of his night scope, a pair of men—Rangers, to judge by the way they carried their weapons—slipped away from the fiery rafts and called back into the forest. The group was pulling back. In the woods, new lights blinked on. *Flashlights.* Activity bustled around the campfire. Slowly, the lights began to shift away from the fire, like a line of fireflies. The parade marched toward the deeper ravine, up the chasm between the flat-topped highlands.

Jacques smiled. The doctor's plan had worked.

Still spying through his scope, he reached for his radio. He pushed the transmitter and brought the radio to his lips. "Mission successful. Rabbits are running."

"Roger that." It was the doctor. "Canoes heading out now. Rendezvous at their old camp in two hours. Over and out."

Jacques replaced the radio.

Once again, the hunt was on.

He turned to his other men to report the good news—but there was no one behind him. He instantly crouched and hissed their names. "Manuel! Roberto!"

No answer.

The night remained dark around him, the woods even darker. He slipped his night-vision diving mask back over his face. The woods shone brighter, but the dense vegetation made visibility poor. He backed away, his bare feet striking water.

Jacques stopped, frozen between the terrors of what lay behind him and in front of him.

Through his night-vision mask, he spotted movement. For the barest flicker of a heartbeat, it looked like the shadows had formed the figure of a man, staring back at him, no more than ten yards away. Jacques blinked, and the figure was gone. But now all the jungle shadows flowed and slid like living things toward him.

He stumbled backward into the waters, one hand scrambling to shove in his regulator mouthpiece.

One of the shadows broke out of the jungle fringe, outlined against the muddy bank. *Huge, monstrous . . .*

Jacques screamed, but his regulator was in the way. Nothing more than a wet gurgle sounded. More of the dark shadows flowed out of the woods toward him. An old Maroon tribal prayer rose to his lips. He scrambled backward.

Behind his fear of dark waters and piranhas was a more basic terror: *of being eaten alive.*

He dove backward, twisting around to get away.

But the shadows were faster.

11:51 P.M.

With a flashlight duct-taped to his shotgun, Nate followed near the rear of the group. The only ones behind him were Private Carrera and Corporal Kostos. Everyone had lights, spearing the darkness in all directions. Despite the night, they moved quickly, trying to put as much distance as possible between them and whoever had set the rafts on fire.

The plan, according to Captain Waxman, was to seek a more defensible position. With the swamp on one side of them, the jungle on the other, it was not a secure spot to wait for whatever attack the fires would draw down upon them. And none of their group was delusional enough to think another attack wouldn't come.

Always planning one step ahead, the Rangers had a fallback position already picked out. Corporal Warczak had reported spotting caves in the cliffs a short way up the chasm. That was their goal.

Shelter and a defensible position.

Nate followed the others. Carrera marched at his side. In her arms was a strange shovel-nosed weapon. It looked like a Dustbuster vacuum attached to a rifle stock. She held it out toward the black jungle.

"What is that?" he asked.

She kept her attention on the jungle. "With all we lost in the swamp, we're short on M-16s." She hefted the strange weapon. "It's called a Bailey. Prototype weapon for jungle warfare." She thumbed a switch and a targeting laser pierced the darkness. She glanced over her shoulder to her superior. "Demonstration?"

Staff Sergeant Kostos, armed with his own M-16, grunted. "Testing weapon fire!" he barked forward to alert the others.

Carrera lifted her weapon, pivoting it for a target. She centered the red laser on the bole of a sapling about twenty yards away. "Shine your flashlight here."

Nate nodded and swung his flashlight up. Other eyes turned their way.

Carrera steadied her weapon and squeezed the trigger. There was no blast, only a high-pitched whistle. Nate caught a flash of silver, followed by a ringing crack. The sapling toppled backward, its trunk sliced cleanly through. Beyond it, a thick-boled silk cotton tree shook with the impact of something slamming into its trunk. Nate's flashlight focused on the distant tree. A bit of silver was embedded deep in the trunk.

Carrera nodded toward her target. "Three-inch razor disks, like Japanese throwing stars. Perfect for jungle combat. Set to automatic fire, it can mow down all the loose vegetation around you."

"And anything else in its path," Kostos added, waving the group onward.

Nate eyed the weapon with respect.

The group continued up the jungle-choked ravine, led by Corporal Warczak and Captain Waxman. They were roughly paralleling the small stream that drained down the chasm, but they kept a respectable distance from the water, just in case. After a half hour of trekking, Warczak led them off to the south, heading for the red cliffs.

So far, there appeared to be no evidence of pursuit, but Nate's ears remained alert for any warning, his eyes raking the shadowy jungle. At last the canopy began to thin enough to see stars and the bright glow of the moon. Ahead the world ended at a wall of red rock, aproned by loose shale and crumbled boulders.

At the top of the sloped escarpment, the cliff face was pocked with multiple caves and shadowed cracks.

"Hang back," Captain Waxman hissed, keeping them all hidden in the thicker underbrush that fringed the lower cliffs. He signaled for Warczak to forge ahead.

The corporal flicked off his flashlight, slipped on a pair of night-vision goggles, and ducked into the shadows with his weapon, vanishing almost instantly.

Nate crouched. Flanking him, the two Rangers took firm stances, watching their rear. Nate kept his shotgun ready. Most of the others were also armed. Olin, Zane, Frank, even Kelly had pistols, while Manny bore a Beretta in one hand and his whip in the other. Tor-tor had his own built-in weapons: claws and fangs. Only Professor Kouwe and Anna Fong remained unarmed.

The professor crept backward to Nate's side. "I don't like this," Kouwe said.

"The caves?"

"No . . . the situation."

"What do you mean?"

Kouwe glanced back down toward the swamp. Distantly the two rafts still burned brightly. "I smelled kerosene from those flames."

"So? It could be copal oil. That stuff smells like kerosene and that's abundant around here."

Kouwe rubbed his chin. "I don't know. The fire that drew the locusts was artfully crafted into the Ban-ali symbol. This was sloppy."

"But we were on guard. The Indians had to move fast. It was probably the best they could manage."

Kouwe glanced to Nate. "It wasn't Indians."

"Then who else?"

"Whoever's been tracking us all along." Kouwe leaned in and whispered in an urgent hiss. "Whoever set the flaming locust symbol crept upon our camp in broad daylight. They left no trace of their passage into or out of the area. Not a single broken twig. They were damned skilled. I doubt I could've done it."

Nate began to get the gist of Kouwe's concerns. "And the ones who have been dogging our trail were sloppy."

Kouwe nodded toward the swamp. "Like those fires."

Nate remembered the reflected flash high in the treetops as they hiked through the forest yesterday afternoon. "What are you suggesting?"

Kouwe spoke between clenched teeth. "We have more than one threat here. Whatever lies ahead—a new regenerative compound, a cure for this plague—it would be worth billions. Others would pay dearly for the knowledge hidden here."

Nate frowned. "And you think this other party set those fires? Why?"

"To drive us forward in a panic, like it did. They didn't want to risk us being reinforced with additional soldiers. They're probably using us as a human shield against the natural predatory traps set by the Ban-ali. We're just so much cannon fodder. They'll waste our lives until we are either spent on this trail or reach the Ban-ali. Then they'll sweep in and steal the prize."

Nate eyed the professor. "Why not mention this before we set off?"

Kouwe stared hard at Nate, and the answer to his question dawned in his own mind. "A traitor," Nate whispered. "Someone working with the trackers."

"I find it much too convenient that our satellite feed went on the fritz just as we drew close to these Ban-ali lands. Plus it then sends off a false GPS signal."

Nate nodded. "Sending our own backup on a wild-goose chase."

"Exactly."

"Who could it be?" Nate eyed the others crouched in the underbrush.

Kouwe shrugged. "Anyone. Highest on the list would be the Russian. It's his system. It would be easy for him to feign a breakdown. But then again both Zane and Ms. Fong have been hovering around the array whenever Olin has stepped away. And the O'Briens have a background tied to the CIA, who have been known to play many sides against one another to achieve their ends. Then, finally, we can't rule out any of the Rangers."

"You're kidding."

"Enough money can sway almost anyone, Nate. And Army Rangers are trained extensively in communications."

Nate swung back around. "That leaves only Manny as someone we can trust."

"Does it?" Kouwe's expression was pained.

"You can't be serious? Manny? He's a friend to both of us."

"He also works for the Brazilian government. And don't doubt that the Brazilian government would want this discovery solely for itself. Such a medical discovery would be an economic boon."

Nate felt a sick sense of dread. *Could the professor be right? Was there no one they could trust?*

Before he could question Kouwe's assessment further, a scream split the night. Something huge came flying through the air. People scattered out of the way. Nate backpedaled with Kouwe in tow.

The large object landed in the middle of the crouched group. Flashlights swung toward the crumpled figure in their midst.

Anna cried out.

Transfixed in the spears of light, Corporal Warczak lay on his back, covered in blood and gore. One arm scrabbled up as if he were drowning in the spreading pool of his own blood. He tried to scream again, but all that came out was a croaking noise.

Nate stared, frozen. He could not tear his eyes from the sight of the ruined corporal.

From the waist down, Warczak's body was gone. He had been bitten in half.

"Weapons ready!" Waxman shouted, breaking through the horrified trance.

Nate dropped to a knee, swinging his shotgun out to the darkness. Kelly and Kouwe dove to aid the downed corporal, but Nate knew it was a futile gesture. The man was already dead.

He pointed his weapon. Throughout the jungle, dark shadows flowed and shifted, jiggled by the play of the group's flashlights. But Nate knew it wasn't all illusion. These shadows were all flowing *toward* the trapped group.

One of the Rangers shot a flare into the sky. The whistling trail arced high and exploded into a magnesium brightness that cast the jungle in silver and black. The sudden brightness gave those who crept up on them reason to pause.

Nate found himself staring into the eyes of a monster, caught in the shine of the flare. It crouched in the lee of a boulder on the cliff's escarpment, a massive creature, the size of a bull, but sleek and smooth. A cat. It studied him with eyes as black and cold as chunks of obsidian. Others lay nestled in the jungle and boulders around them. A pack of the creatures, at least twenty.

"Jaguars," Manny mumbled in shock over his shoulder. "Black jaguars."

Nate recognized the physique similar to Tor-tor's, but these creatures were three times as large, half a ton each. Prehistoric in size.

"They're all around us," Carrera whispered.

In her words, Nate heard the echo of his father's last radioed message: *Can't last much longer . . . oh, God, they're all around us!* Had this been his fate?

For another breath, neither group moved. Nate held his breath, hoping the nighttime prowlers would be intimidated by the flare's brightness and retreat. As if this thought were shared by one of the Rangers, a second flare jetted into the sky and burst with brightness, floating down on a tiny parachute.

"Hold steady," Waxman hissed.

The impasse stretched. The pack was not leaving.

"Sergeant," Waxman said, "on my mark, lay a path of grenades up toward the cliffs. Everyone else, keep weapons ready. Haul ass for the centermost cave on my signal."

Nate's eyes flicked to the yawning cavern in the cliff face. If they could make it there, the group could be attacked from only one direction. It was defensible. Their only hope.

"Carrera, use the Bailey to cover our—"

The sharp crack of a pistol cut off the captain's order. Off to the side, Zane stumbled backward from the recoil of his smoking gun.

One of the cats spat and leaped in rage. Other jaguars responded, growling low and bounding toward the group.

"Now!" Waxman yelled.

Kostos dropped to one knee, aimed his M-16 toward the cliffs, and fired. Carrera spun with her new weapon, blasting from her hip, laying down a swath of fire across their rear. A flashing arc of flying silver disks flew out, shredding the jungle.

One of the jaguars was caught in midleap, its exposed belly sliced open. It howled and collapsed to the jungle, writhing.

Its cries were cut off as Kostos's grenade barrage began booming, echoing off the cliffs, deafening. Rock dust and dirt flumed up.

Shots were fired all around. Frank guarded his sister and the professor as they knelt beside the slack form of Corporal Warczak. Manny was on one knee beside Tor-tor, whose eyes were wide, hackles raised. Zane and Olin stood with Anna Fong, firing blindly into the dark.

Nate kept his shotgun raised and centered on the giant fellow he had first seen, crouched by the boulder off to the left. Despite the noises and the chatter of rattling rock debris, the creature had remained stone still.

Other shadowy figures fled from the bombarded slope. Others lay unmoving, dead, shredded.

"Go!" Waxman barked sharply, his command cutting through the explosions. "Make for the cave!"

The group lurched through the fringe of brush and jungle toward the open rocky landscape at the foot of the towering cliffs. Nate kept his shotgun pointed at the cat, finger tensed on the shotgun's trigger. *If it even flicks its tail* . . .

Waxman waved them on, Kostos in the lead. "Get up there before they regroup!" The captain dropped beside Carrera. Behind them, the pack converged along their trail. Several limped or sniffed at a dead mate, but they kept a wary distance now.

Nate sidled past the silent cat off to the left. Only its eyes followed their passage. Nate suspected this was the leader of the pack. Behind that cold gaze, Nate could almost see the thing weighing these strangers, judging them.

Carrera had switched her weapon off automatic, conserving her ammunition. She fired at a lone cat getting too near. Her aim was off. The silver disk shaved the jaguar's ear and whizzed off into the jungle. The wounded cat dropped to its belly, glowering with pain and anger.

"Keep moving!" Waxman yelled.

By now, the cave was in direct sight. The group's tense pace collapsed into a panicked rout. Kostos led the way. He raised a flare pistol and fired it into the opening. A bright trace flashed out of the pistol's muzzle and exploded with light inside the cavern.

The deep cave was illuminated all the way to its rocky end.

"All clear!" Kostos hollered. "Move it!"

Olin, Zane, and Anna were the first to race inside. The sergeant stood at the entrance, M-16 in hand, waving his arm. "Move, move, move . . ."

Frank pushed Kelly ahead of him. Professor Kouwe ran beside him.

As the flares died out overhead, Nate took up a position on the other side of the entrance, shotgun ready.

Manny and Tor-tor followed with Waxman and Carrera on their heels.

They were going to make it, Nate realized.

Then a jaguar leaped from the deepening shadows, landing atop a boulder right beside the last two Rangers. Carrera dropped and aimed her weapon, but before she could fire, a paw struck out and raked into the chest of the team's captain.

Waxman was yanked off his feet, sailing into the air, claws sunk deep into his field jacket and chest. He bellowed, bringing up his own weapon. He fired over his head, striking the cat in the shoulder. The beast toppled backward, dragging the hooked captain with it. His body flew over the boulder, limbs kicking.

Carrera lunged up and ran around the boulder, going to the aid of her captain. Out of sight, Nate heard the characteristic whir of her weapon. Then suddenly she was backing into sight again. On her trail were a pair of jaguars. They were bleeding, embedded bits of silver decorated their flesh. Carrera was obviously struggling with the cartridge to her weapon, out of ammo disks.

Nate leaped away from the cave wall and ran toward her. As he reached her side, he shoved his shotgun to arms' length, the muzzle only a foot away from the snarling face of one of the jaguars. He pulled the trigger, and the beast flew back, howling.

Carrera unholstered her 9mm pistol. She fired and fired at the other jaguar, unloading the clip. It fell back, then collapsed.

They stumbled up the slope.

Around the other side of the boulder, the captain fell into sight, crawling, one arm gone. His face was a bloody ruin.

"I . . . I thought he was dead," Carrera said with shock, stepping in his direction.

The captain crawled half a step, then a paw shot out and dug into the meat of his thigh. He was pulled back toward the hidden shadows. He screamed, fingers digging at the loose shale, finding no purchase.

A shot cracked. The captain's head flew back, then forward, striking the rock hard. Dead. Nate glanced behind him and saw Kostos crouched with his M-16 in hand, eyes fixed to its sniper scope. The sergeant slowly lowered his weapon, his expression pained and ripe with hard guilt.

"Everyone, get inside!" he yelled.

The party had remained clustered near the entrance.

Nate and Carrera hurried toward the cavern mouth.

Frank and Kostos flanked the threshold, weapons ready. The men were limned against the glare of the dying flare inside the passage. Frank waved to them. "Hurry!"

From Nate's position several yards down the escarpment, he spotted a deeper shadow shift along the base of the rocky cliff. To the left of the cave opening. "Watch out!"

It was the largest of the jaguars, the one Nate had first spotted.

It sprang past the mouth of the cave. Frank was bowled over, flying high into the air and landing on his back. Kostos was slammed into the wall. Then the cat was gone, racing back into the shadows below.

Kelly screamed. "Frank!"

Nate ran with Carrera. Kostos picked himself off the ground, wheezing and holding his chest, dazed.

"Help me!" Kelly yelled.

Frank lay writhing in the shale. Kelly's brother hadn't just been knocked off his feet. Both his legs were gone from the knees down. Blood spurted and jetted across the stones. In those few seconds, the giant jaguar had sheared off the limbs, as cleanly as a guillotine.

Kouwe fell to Frank's other side. Olin helped drag the moaning man into the cave. Kelly followed, yanking tourniquets from her pack. Plastic vials of morphine tumbled to the floor. Nate retrieved them.

Near the entrance, a shot was fired. Light burst outside. Another flare. Nate held out the vials of morphine, feeling useless, stunned.

Kouwe took them. "Go watch our back." He nodded to the entrance.

Olin and Kelly worked on the stricken man. Tears flowed down Kelly's cheeks, but her face was tight with determination and concentration. She refused to lose her brother.

Nate turned with his shotgun and joined Kostos and Carrera at the cave's opening. The new flare showed that the jungle still moved with shadows. The bouldered slope offered additional cover for the cats.

Manny joined them, pistol in one hand. Tor-tor sniffed at Frank's blood on the rock and growled.

"I count at least another fifteen," Carrera said, face half covered with night-vision goggles. "They're not leaving."

Kostos swore. "If they rush us, we couldn't hope to stop them all. We're down to one grenade launcher, two M-16s, and a handful of pistols."

"And my shotgun," Nate added.

Carrera spoke, "I've fitted a new cartridge into the Bailey. But it's my last."

Manny crouched with his pistol. "There's some old debris blown in the back of the cave—branches, leaves, whatnot. We could light a fire at the entrance."

"Do it," Kostos said.

As Manny turned, a long, low growl rumbled up the slope. Everyone froze. Illuminated by the flare, a large shape revealed itself on the rocky slope. Weapons were raised.

Nate recognized the shadow as the largest cat.

"A female," Manny mumbled.

It remained in plain sight, studying them, challenging them. Behind it, the jungle churned with sleek bodies, muscled and clawed.

"What do we do?" Carrera asked.

"The bitch is trying to psych us out," Kostos grumbled, lowering his eye to the sight on his rifle.

"Don't fire," Nate hissed. "If you shoot now, you'll have the whole pack on us."

"Nate's right," Manny said. "Their blood lust is up. Anything could set them off. At least wait until we have a fire going here."

The cat seemed to hear him and let out a piercing yowl. In a surge of pure muscle, she leaped toward them, charging at an astounding speed, a precision machine.

The Rangers fired, but the she-beast was too fast, gliding with preternatural swiftness. Bullets chewed at the rock, sparking, missing, as if she were a true phantom. A single razored disk whizzed from the Bailey and zinged off a boulder to skitter harmlessly down the slope.

Nate dropped to one knee, shotgun pointed. "Here, kitty-kitty," he hissed under his breath. *Once she was close enough . . .*

Carrera repositioned her weapon, but before she could fire another shot, she was bumped aside. Tor-tor lunged past her, leaping from his master's side to the slope beyond.

"Tor-tor!" Manny called.

The smaller jaguar bounded a few yards down the slope and stopped, digging in, blocking the path of the larger cat. With a sharp snarl, he crouched low, rear haunches raised and bunched to spring, tail flicking with menace. He bared his long yellow claws and sharp fangs.

The giant black jaguar rushed at him, prepared to bowl him over, but at the last moment, she pulled up and stopped in front of Tor-tor, matching his stance, snarling. The two cats hissed and challenged each other.

Kostos lifted his weapon. "You're dead, bitch."

Manny motioned him not to shoot. "Wait!"

The two cats slowly padded around each other, circling, only a yard apart. At one point, the giant female's back was toward them. Nate could tell both Rangers had to restrain themselves not to fire.

"What are they doing?" Carrera asked.

Manny answered, "She can't understand why one of her own species, even a small one like Tor-tor, is protecting us. It has her perplexed."

By now, the two had stopped snarling. They cautiously approached one another, now almost nose to nose. Sharing some silent communication, the circling continued. Raised hackles settled back to sleek fur. A soft chuffing sounded as the larger cat took in the scent of this strange little jaguar.

Eventually they both stopped their dance, once again back to their original positions. Tor-tor crouched between the cave and the giant cat.

With a final grunt, the large jaguar leaned forward and rubbed her jowl against the side of Tor-tor's cheek, some understanding reached, a truce. With a blur of black fur, the giant cat spun and slipped back down the slope.

Slowly Tor-tor straightened from his crouch. His eyes glowed golden. With a feline casualness, he licked a patch of ruffled fur back into perfect place and turned to them. He padded back to the entrance as if he'd just come back from a stroll.

Carrera lowered her weapon and shifted her night-vision goggles. "They're pulling back," she said, amazed.

Manny hugged his pet. "You stupid bastard," he mumbled.

"What just happened?" Kostos asked.

"Tor-tor's close to being sexually mature," Manny said. "A juvenile male. The female, though huge, appears proportionally to be about the same age. And with all the blood in the air, tensions were high, including sexual tension. From their actions, Tor-tor's challenge was construed as both a threat and a sexual display."

Kostos scowled. "So you're saying he was making a play for her ass."

"And she accepted," Manny said, patting his jaguar's side proudly. "Since Tor-tor came out and met her challenge, she probably believes him to be our pack leader. An acceptable mate."

"What now?" Carrera asked. "They've pulled back, but haven't left. As a matter of fact, they seem to be massing down the chasm a bit, blocking any retreat back to the swamp lake."

Manny shook his head. "I don't know what they're doing. But Tor-tor has bought us some time. I say we use it. Get that fire lit and keep our guard up."

Nate watched the bulk of the pack flow down into the jungle chasm. What *were* they doing?

"We've got company," Carrera said, voice tense again. She pointed in the opposite direction, deeper up the canyon.

Nate turned his attention. In that direction, he saw nothing but the dark jungle and the broken landscape of rock at the foot of the cliff. "What did you—"

Then movement caught his eye.

A short way up the chasm, a dark figure stepped more fully out of the jungle fringe and onto the exposed shale. It was a human figure. A man. He was as much a shadow as the cats, black from head to toe. He lifted an arm, then turned and began to walk up the canyon, keeping in plain sight. They watched him, stunned.

"It must be one of the Ban-ali," Nate said.

The figure stopped, turned their way, and seemed to be waiting.

"I think he wants us to follow him," Manny said.

"And the jaguars aren't leaving us much choice," Carrera said. "They've settled into the jungle below us."

The distant figure simply stood.

"What do we do?" Carrera asked.

Nate answered, "We follow him. It's why we came. To find the Ban-ali. Perhaps this was their last test, the jaguar pack."

"Or it could be another trap," Kostos said.

"I don't see we have much choice," Carrera said. "I have a feeling we go or the pack will finish us off."

Nate glanced over his shoulder to the deeper depths of the cave. Ten yards back, Kelly, Kouwe and the others were still gathered around Frank, now stripped to his boxers. The man seemed to be sedated. Anna stood, holding an IV bag at shoulder height. Kelly had one of her brother's stumped limbs already wrapped in a bandage and was tying off a vessel in the other. Kouwe knelt beside her, ready with the bandages for this other limb. Around them, empty syringe wrappers and small plastic drug bottles littered the cave floor.

"I'll see if Frank can be moved."

"We leave no one behind," Kostos said.

Nate nodded, glad to hear it. He crossed to the others. "How's Frank doing?" he asked Kouwe.

"He's lost a lot of blood. Once he's stable, Kelly wants to transfuse him."

Nate sighed. "We may have to move him."

"What?" Kelly asked, tying off a suture. "He can't be moved!" Panic, exhaustion, and disbelief hardened her words.

Nate crouched as Kelly and Kouwe began bandaging the second stump. Frank moaned softly as his leg was jarred.

As they worked, Nate explained what had happened at the cave's entrance. "We've been contacted by the Ban-ali. Perhaps invited to continue on to their village. I suspect the invitation is a one-time offer."

Kouwe nodded. "We must've passed some last challenge, survived some gauntlet," the professor said, parroting Nate's early assessment. "Now we've earned the right to move onward by proving ourselves worthy."

"But Frank . . . ?" Kelly said.

"I can rig up a stretcher out of bamboo and palm fronds," Kouwe said softly, touching Kelly's hand. "Knowing these tribesmen, if we don't move him, he'll be killed. We'll all be killed."

Nate watched the woman's face tighten with fear. Her eyes glazed. *First her daughter, now her brother.*

Nate sank down beside her and put his arm around her. "I'll make sure he gets where we're going safely. Once there, Olin can get the radio up and running." Nate glanced to the Russian.

Olin nodded his head vigorously. "I know I can at least get the GPS working properly to send out a decent signal."

"And once that's done, help will arrive. They'll airlift your brother out. He'll make it. We all will."

Kelly leaned into him, softening against him. "Do you promise?" she said, her voice soft with tears.

He tightened his embrace. "Of course I do." But as Nate stared at the pale face of her brother, with blood slowly seeping through the man's new bandages, he prayed it was a promise he could keep.

Kelly shifted in his hold, and her voice was stronger when she spoke. "Then let's go."

He helped her to her feet.

They quickly began arranging for their departure. Kostos and Manny crossed to the jungle and gathered material to construct the makeshift stretcher, while Kelly and Kouwe stabilized Frank as well as they could. Soon they were ready to head out again into the night.

Nate met Carrera at the cave entrance.

"Our visitor's still out there," she said.

In the distance, the lone shadowy figure stood.

Kostos raised his voice, returning to make sure everything was in order. "Keep together! Keep alert!"

Nate and Carrera separated. The group filed out between them with the sergeant in the lead. Near the end of the line, Manny and Olin carried the stretcher, the patient lashed to the bamboo for extra security. The men in the party would take turns hauling Frank.

As the stretcher passed, Kelly followed last. Then Nate and Carrera moved in step behind her.

Just past the entrance, the toe to Nate's boot knocked an object from the shale, something dusty and discarded. Nate bent to pick it up and inspected it.

They couldn't leave this behind.

He knocked off the dirt and stepped forward. He slipped in front of Manny, wiped the last bit of dust from the brim of Frank's Red Sox cap, and placed it back on the stricken man's head.

As Nate turned to return to his place in line, he found Kelly's eyes on his, tears glistening. She offered him a shadow of a sad smile. He nodded, accepting her silent gratitude.

Nate took his position beside Carrera. He studied the dark jungle and the solitary figure in the distance.

Where did the path lead from here?

FOURTEEN

Habitation

Louis floated in his canoe, awaiting news from his trackers. Dawn was still hours away. Stars shone in the clear sky, but the moon had set, casting the swamp into deep shadows. Through night-vision scopes, Louis watched for any sign of his men.

Nothing.

He grimaced. As he waited in the canoe, he felt his plan crumbling around him. *What was going on out there?* His ruse to get the Ranger team fleeing had been successful. But what now?

At midnight, Louis's team had crossed the swamp in their canoes, hauled overland from the river. As the group neared the far shore, flares had blossomed into the sky further up the chasm, near the southern cliffs. Shots were fired, echoing down to the swamp.

Using binoculars, Louis had watched a shadowy firefight. The Ranger team was again clearly under attack. But from his vantage, Louis could not see who or what was attacking them. His attempts to contact Jacques's recon team had failed. His lieutenant had gone mysteriously silent.

Needing information, Louis had sent a small team ashore, his best trackers, outfitted with night-vision and infrared equipment, to investigate what was happening. He and the others remained a safe distance offshore in the canoes and waited.

Two hours had passed, and so far, there was no word, not even a radio message from the trackers. Sharing his canoe were three men and his mistress. They all watched the far shore with binoculars.

Tshui was the first to spot a man slip from the jungle. She pointed, making a small sound of warning.

Louis swung his glasses. It was the leader of the tracking team. He waved for them to cross to shore. "At last," Louis mumbled, lowering his scopes.

The convoy of canoes swept to the boggy banks. Louis was one of the first on shore. He silently signaled his men to set up a defensive perimeter, then crossed to the lead tracker.

The dark-haired man, a German mercenary named Brail, nodded in greeting. He was short, no taller than five feet, painted in camouflage and clad in black clothes.

"What did you find?" Louis asked him.

The man spoke with a thick German accent. "Jaguars, a pack of fifteen or so."

Louis nodded, not surprised. Across the swamp, they had heard the strange growls and cries.

"But these were no ordinary jaguars," Brail continued. "More like monsters. Three times normal size. There's a body I can show you."

"Go on," Louis said, waving this away for now. "What happened to the others?"

Brail continued his report, describing how the trackers had been forced to move with care so as not to be spotted. The rest of his four-man team were positioned in trees up the chasm. "The pack is leaving, heading deeper into the canyon. They appear to be herding the remaining members of the enemy team ahead of them."

Brail held out an open palm. "After the cats left the area, we found these on a mauled corpse." The tracker held two silver bars affixed to a scrap of khaki. They were captain's bars. The leader of the Rangers.

"Why aren't the jaguars attacking the rest?" Louis asked.

Brail touched his night-vision scope. "I spotted someone, an Indian from the look of him, leading them from farther up the canyon."

"One of the Ban-ali?"

The man shrugged.

Who else could it be? Louis wondered. He pondered this newest information. Louis could not let the others get too far ahead, especially if the Rangers had made successful contact with the strange tribe. With the prize so close, Louis dared not lose them now.

But the surviving jaguars could prove a difficulty. They stood between his team and the others. The pack would have to be eliminated as quietly as possible without spooking his true prey.

Louis studied the dark forest. The time of slinking in the others' shadows was nearing an end. Once he knew where the village was located and evaluated its defenses, he could take his plan to its final stage.

"Where are the cats now?" Louis asked. "Are they all heading up the canyon?"

Brail grunted sourly. "For the moment. If there's any change, my scouts will radio back to us. Luckily, with the infrared scopes, the bastards are easy to spot. Large and hot."

Louis nodded, satisfied. "What about any other hostiles?"

"We swept the area, *Herr Doktor*. No heat signatures."

Good. Then at least for the moment, the Rangers were still keeping attention diverted away from Louis's team. But this close to the Ban-ali lands, Louis knew such an advantage would not last long. He and his team would have to move quickly from here. But first, for his plan to proceed, the path ahead had to be cleared of the jaguar pack.

He turned and found Tshui standing at his shoulder, as silent and deadly as any jungle cat. He reached and ran a finger tenderly along her cheekbone. She leaned into his touch. His mistress of poisons and potions.

"Tshui, *ma chérie*, it seems once again we must call upon your talents."

5:44 A.M.

Nate's shoulders ached from carrying the stretcher. They had been marching for over two hours. Off to the east, the sky was already glowing a soft rose with the promise of dawn.

"How much farther?" Manny huffed from the head of the stretcher. He voiced the question on all their minds.

"I don't know, but there's no going back from here," Nate said, winded.

"Not unless you want to be someone's morning snack," Private Carrera reminded them, maintaining a vigil on their back trail.

All night long, the jaguar pack had dogged their trail, sticking mostly to the jungles that fringed the cliffs. An occasional bolder individual would stalk the loose shale, a silhouette against the black rock.

Their presence kept Tor-tor on edge. The jaguar would hiss under his breath and pace around and around the stretcher, on guard. His eyes flashed an angry gold.

For them all, the only safe path from here was forward, following the lone figure. The tribesman maintained a quarter-mile lead on them, keeping a pace they could follow.

But exhaustion was quickly setting in. After so many days with so little sleep, everyone was bone tired. The entire team moved at a snail's pace, feet dragging, stumbling often. Still, as hard as the night journey was on all their nerves, one member of their party suffered the most.

Kelly never left her brother's side: constantly checking Frank's vital signs and adjusting his bloody bandages as they walked. Her face remained ashen in the starlight, her eyes scared and exhausted. When she wasn't acting as his doctor, she simply held Frank's hand, just a sister at these moments, clearly trying to will him her own strength.

The only blessing was that the morphine and sedatives were keeping the wounded man in a doped drowse, though he would occasionally moan. Each time this happened, Kelly would tense and her face would twist as if the pain were her own, which Nate suspected was partly true. She clearly suffered as much as her twin brother.

"Attention!" Kostos called from up front. "We're changing direction."

Nate peered ahead. All night they had been trudging along the hard-packed soil where the jungle met the rocky escarpment of the cliffs. He now watched their guide cross the escarpment toward one of the many shattered cracks in the cliff face. It ran from top to bottom, as wide as a two-car garage.

The tribesman stepped to the entrance, turned back to stare at them, then, without a signal or any other sign of welcome, he strode into the chasm.

"I'll check it out first," Kostos said.

The Ranger trotted ahead as they slowed their pace. He had a flashlight secured under his M-16. The light remained steady and fixed on his target. He dashed to the side of the crack's entrance, took a breath, then twisted to shine his light down it. He remained fixed in this position for several seconds, then waved them over with one arm, maintaining his post. "It's a side chute! A steep one."

The group converged upon the Ranger.

Nate squinted up its length. The crack extended the full height of the cliff, open at the top to let starlight shine down it. The way was quite steep, but there appeared to be crude steps climbing the chute.

Professor Kouwe pointed. "It looks like there might be another canyon or valley beyond this one."

Anna Fong stood beside him. "Or perhaps it's a switchback of this same canyon, a shortcut to the upper level."

In the distance, the lone tribesman climbed the stone steps, seemingly unconcerned whether they followed or not. But his nonchalance was not shared by all. Behind them, the jaguar pack drew closer, growling and whining.

"I say we need to make a decision," Carrera said.

Kostos frowned at the tall walls that framed the crude staircase. "It could be a trap, an ambush."

Zane took a step toward the chute. "We're already in a trap, Sergeant. I for one prefer to take my chances with the unknown than with what lies behind us."

No one argued. The memory of the deaths of Warczak and Waxman remained fresh and bloody.

Kostos moved on ahead of Zane. "Let's go. Keep alert."

The chute was wide enough that Manny and Nate could walk side by side, the stretcher between them. This made mounting the steep stairs a bit easier. Still, the climb was daunting.

Olin moved down to them. "Do either of you need to be relieved?"

Manny grimaced. "I can last a little longer."

Nate nodded, agreeing.

So they began the long climb. As they progressed, Nate and Manny were soon lagging behind the others. Kelly kept near them, her face worried. Carrera maintained the rear guard.

Nate's knees ached, his thighs burned, and his shoulders knotted with exhaustion. But he kept on. "It can't be much farther," he said aloud, more to himself then anyone else.

"I hope not," Kelly said.

"He's strong," Manny said, nodding to Frank.

"Strong will only get you so far," she answered.

"He'll pull through this," Nate assured her. "He's got his lucky Red Sox cap, doesn't he?"

Kelly sighed. "He loves that old thing. Did you know he was a short-stop for a farm club? Triple A division." Her voice lowered to a strained whisper. "My father was so proud. We all were. There was even talk of Frank going into the majors. Then he got in a skiing accident, screwed up his knee. It ended his career."

Manny grunted in surprise. "And that's his *lucky* hat?"

Kelly brushed the cap's brim, a trace of a smile on her lips. "For three seasons, he played a game he loved with all his heart. Even after the acci-dent, he was never bitter. He felt himself the luckiest man in the world."

Nate stared down at the cap, envying Frank his moment in the sun. Had life ever been that simple for him? Maybe the man's cap was indeed lucky. And right now, they needed all the luck they could get.

Carrera interrupted their reminiscing. "The jaguars . . . they've stopped following us."

Nate glanced down the stairs. One of the giant cats stood at the entrance. It was the female leader of the pack. She paced back and forth below. Tor-tor stared down at her, eyes flashing. The female stared at the smaller cat for a moment—then, in a shadowy blur, she fled back into the jungle.

"The lower valley must be the pack's territory," Manny said. "Another line of defense."

"But what are they protecting?" Carrera asked.

A call sounded from up ahead. It was Sergeant Kostos. He had stopped ten steps from the end of the chasm and waved them to join him.

As the group gathered, the eastern skies brightened with dawn. Beyond the stepped chute, a valley opened, thick with dense vegetation and towering trees. Somewhere a stream babbled brightly, and in the dis-tance, a waterfall grumbled.

"The Ban-ali lands," Professor Kouwe said.

Olin approached Manny and Nate. He reached for the stretcher. "We'll take over from here."

Nate was surprised to see Richard Zane at the Russian's side. But Nate didn't complain. They passed the stretcher to the new bearers. Relieved of the weight, Nate felt a hundred pounds lighter. His arms felt like they wanted to float up.

He and Manny climbed up to Kostos.

"The Indian disappeared," the sergeant grumbled.

Nate saw that the tribesman had indeed vanished. "Even so, we know where we have to go."

"We should wait until the sun's fully up," Kostos said.

Manny frowned. "The Ban-ali have been tracking us since we first set out into the jungles . . . night and day. Whether the sun is up or not, we won't see a single soul unless they want us to."

"Besides," Nate said, "we have a man down. The sooner we reach a village or whatever, the better Frank's chances. I say we forge on."

Kostos sighed, then nodded. "Okay, but keep together."

The sergeant straightened and led the way from there.

With each step, the new day grew brighter. Sunrise in the Amazon was often sudden. Overhead, the stars were swallowed in the spreading rosy glow of dawn. The cloudless sky promised a hot day to come.

The group paused at the top of the chasm. A thin trail led down into the jungle. But where did it go? In the valley below, there was no sign of habitation. No wood smoke rising, no voices echoing.

Before moving forward, Kostos stood with binoculars, studying the valley. "Damn it," he mumbled.

"What's wrong?" Zane asked.

"This canyon is just a switchback of the one we were in." He pointed to the right. "But it appears this canyon is cut off from the one below it by steep cliffs."

Nate lifted his own binoculars and followed where the sergeant pointed. Through the jungle, he could just make out where a small stream flowed down the canyon's center. He followed its course until it vanished over a steep drop, down into the lower canyon, the one they had been marching through all night, the domain of the giant jaguars.

"We're boxed in here," Kostos said.

Nate swung his binoculars in the opposite direction. He spotted another waterfall. This one tumbled down into this canyon from a massive cliff on the far side. In fact, the entire valley was closed in by rock walls on three sides, and the steep cliff on the fourth.

It's a totally isolated chunk of jungle, Nate realized.

The sergeant continued, "I don't like this. The only way up here is this chute."

As Nate lowered his glasses, the edge of the sun crested the eastern skies, bathing the jungle ahead in sunlight, creating a green glow. A flock of blue-and-gold macaws took wing from a rookery near the misty cliffs and sailed past overhead. The spray from the two waterfalls at either end of the valley made the air almost sparkle in the first rays of the sun.

"Like a bit of Eden," Professor Kouwe said in a hushed voice.

With the touch of light, the jungle awoke with birdsong and the twitter of monkeys. Butterflies as big as dinner plates fluttered at the fringe. Something furry and quick darted back into the jungle. Isolated or not, life had found its way into this verdant valley.

But what else had made its home here?

"What are we going to do?" Anna asked.

Everyone remained silent for several seconds.

Nate finally spoke. "I don't think we have much choice but to proceed."

Kostos scowled, then nodded. "Let's see where this leads. But stay alert."

The group cautiously descended the short slope to the jungle's edge. Kostos led once again, Nate at his side with his shotgun. They marched in a tight bunch down the path. As soon as they entered under the bower of the shadowed forest, the scents of orchids and flowering vines filled the air, so thick they could almost taste it.

Still, as sweet as the air was, the constant tension continued. What secrets lay out here? What dangers? Every shadow was suspect.

It took Nate fifteen minutes of hiking before he noticed something strange about the forest around them. Exhaustion must have dulled his senses. His feet slowed. His mouth dropped open.

Manny bumped into him. "What's the matter?"

His brow furrowed, Nate crossed a few steps off the path.

"What are you doing, Rand?" Kostos asked.

"These trees . . ." Nate's sense of wonder overwhelmed him, cutting through his unease.

The others stopped and stared. "What about them?" Manny asked.

Nate turned in a slow circle. "As a botanist, I recognize most of the plants around here." He pointed and named names. "Silk cotton, laurels, figs, mahogany, rosewood, palms of every variety. The usual trees you'd see in a rain forest. But . . ." Nate's voice died away.

"But what?" Kostos asked.

Nate stepped to a thin-boled tree. It stretched a hundred feet into the air and burst into a dense mass of fronds. Giant serrated cones hung from its underside. "Do you know what this is?"

"It looks like a palm," the sergeant said. "So what?"

"It's not!" Nate slapped the trunk with his palm. "It's a goddamn cycadeoid."

"A what?"

"A species of tree thought long extinct, dating back to the Cretaceous period. I've only seen examples of it in the fossil record."

"Are you sure?" Anna Fong asked.

Nate nodded. "I did my thesis on paleobotany." He crossed to another plant, a fernlike bush that towered twice his height. Each frond was as tall as he was and as wide as his stretched arms. He shook one of the titanic leaves. "And this is a goddamn giant club moss. It's supposed to have gone extinct during the Carboniferous period. And that's not all. They're all around us. Glossopterids, lycopods, podocarp conifers . . ." He pointed out the strange plants. "And that's just the things I can classify."

Nate pointed his shotgun to a tree with a coiled and spiraled trunk. "I have no idea what that thing is." He faced the others, shedding his exhaustion like a second skin, and lifted his arms. "We're in a goddamn living fossil museum."

"How's that possible?" Zane asked.

Kouwe answered, "This place is isolated, a pocket in time. Anything could have sheltered here for eons."

"And geologically this region dates back to the Paleozoic era," Nate added, excited. "The Amazon basin was once a freshwater inland sea before changes in tectonics opened the sea to the greater ocean and drained it away. What we have here is a little peek at that ancient past. It's amazing!"

Kelly spoke up from beside the stretcher. "Amazing or not, I need to get Frank somewhere safe."

Her words drew Nate back to the present, back to their situation. He nodded, embarrassed at his distraction in the face of their predicament.

Kostos cleared his throat. "Let's push on."

The group followed his lead.

Fascinated by the forest, Nate hung back. His eyes studied the foliage around him, no longer peering at the shadows, but fixed on the jungle itself. As a trained botanist, he gaped in disbelief at the riotous flora: stalked horsetails the size of organ pipes, ferns that dwarfed modern-day palms, massive primitive conifers with cones the size of VW bugs. The mix of the ancient and the new was simply astounding, a merged ecosystem unlike any seen before.

Professor Kouwe walked beside him now. "What do you think about all this?"

Nate shook his head. "I don't know. Other prehistoric groves have been discovered in the past. In China, a forest of dawn redwoods was discovered in the eighties. In Africa, a grotto of rare ferns. And most recently, in Australia, an entire stand of prehistoric trees, long thought extinct, was found in a remote rain forest." Nate glanced to Kouwe for emphasis. "So considering how little of the Amazon has been explored, it's actually more surprising that we've *not* found such a grove before."

"The jungle hides its secrets well," Kouwe said.

As they walked, the canopy overhead grew denser, the forest taller. The morning sunlight dwindled to a green glow. It was as if they were walking back into twilight.

Further conversation died as everyone watched the forest. By now, even nonbotanists could tell this jungle was unusual. The number of prehistoric plants began to outnumber the modern-day counterparts. Trees grew huge, ferns towered, strange twisted forms wound among the mix. They passed a spiky bromeliad as large as a small cottage. Massive flowers, as large as pumpkins, grew from vines and scented the air thickly.

It was a greenhouse of amazing proportion.

Kostos suddenly stopped ahead, freezing in place, eyes on the trail, weapon raised and ready. He then slowly motioned them to get down.

The group crouched. Nate shifted his shotgun. Only then did he notice what had startled the Ranger.

Nate stared off to the left, the right, even behind them. It was like one of those computerized pictures that appeared at first to be just a blur of random dots, but when stared at cross-eyed, from a certain angle, a 3-D image suddenly and startlingly appeared.

Nate suddenly and startlingly saw the jungle in a new light.

High in the trees, mounted among the thick branches, platforms had been built, with small dwellings atop them. The roofs of many were woven from the living leaves and branches, offering natural camouflage. These half-living structures blended perfectly with their host trees.

As Nate looked closer, what had appeared to be vines and stranglers crisscrossing between the trees and draping to the ground were in fact natural bridges and ladders. One of these ladders was only a few yards to Nate's right. Flowers grew along its length. It was alive, too.

As he stared around, it was hard to say where man-made structure ended and living began. Half artificial, half growing plant. The blend was so astounding, the camouflage so perfect.

Without them even knowing it, they had already entered the Ban-ali village.

Ahead, larger dwellings climbed even taller trees, multilevel with terraces and patios. But even these were well camouflaged with bark, vine, and leaf, making them difficult to discern.

As they stared, no one in their party moved. One question was on all their faces: *Where were the inhabitants of these treetop homes?*

Tor-tor growled a deep warning.

Then like the village itself, Nate suddenly saw them. They had been there all along, unmoving, silent, all around. Bits of living shadow. With their bodies painted black, they had melded into the darkness between the trees and under bushes.

One of the tribesmen stepped from his concealing gloom and onto the path. He seemed undaunted by the weapons in their hands.

Nate was certain it was their earlier guide. The one who had led them here. His black hair was braided with bits of leaf and flower in it, adding to the natural camouflage. As he stepped forth, his hands were empty of any weapons. In fact, the tribesman was naked, except for a simple loincloth. He stared at the group, his face hard and unreadable.

Then without a word, he turned and walked down the path.

"He must want us to follow him again," Professor Kouwe said, climbing to his feet. The others slowly stood.

In the woods, more tribesmen remained silent sentinels, bathed in shadows.

Kostos hesitated.

"If they had wanted to kill us," Professor Kouwe added, "we'd be dead already."

Kostos frowned, but the Ranger reluctantly continued on after the tribesman.

As they walked, Nate continued to study the village and its silent inhabitants. He caught occasional glimpses of smaller faces in windows, children and women. Nate glanced to the men half hidden in the forest. *Tribal warriors or scouts,* he guessed.

Their painted faces bore the familiar Amerindian bone structure, slightly Asiatic, a genetic tie to their ancestors who had first crossed the Bering Strait from Asia into Alaska some fifty thousand years ago and settled the Americas. But who were they? How did they get here? Where did their roots trace? Despite the danger and silent threat, Nate was dying to learn more about these people and their history—especially since it was tied to his own.

He stared around the forest. Had his father walked this same path? Considering this possibility, Nate found his lungs tightening, old emotions surfacing. He was so close to discovering the truth about his father.

As they continued, it soon became apparent that the team was being led toward a sunnier clearing in the distance.

The forest around the thin track opened to either side as they reached the clearing. A ring of giant cycads and primitive conifers circled the open glade. A shallow-banked stream meandered through the sunny space, sparkling and gurgling.

Their guide continued ahead, but the team stopped at the threshold, shocked.

In the center of the clearing, practically filling the entire space, stood a massive tree, a specimen Nate had never seen before. It had to tower at least thirty stories high, its white-barked trunk ten yards in diameter. Thick roots knobbed out of the dark soil like pale knees. A few even spanned the stream beside it before disappearing back into the loam.

Overhead, the tree's branches spread in distinct terraces, not unlike giant redwoods. But instead of needles, this specimen sported wide palmate green leaves, fluttering gently to reveal silver undersides and clusters of husked seed pods, similar to coconuts.

Nate stared, dumbstruck. He didn't even know where to begin classifying this specimen. Maybe a new species of primitive gymnospore, but he was far from sure. The nuts did look a bit like those found on a modern cat's claw plant, but this was a much more ancient specimen.

As he studied the giant, he realized one other thing about the tree. Even this towering hardwood bore signs of habitation. Small clusters of hutlike dwellings rested atop thicker branches or nestled against the trunk. *Constructed to mimic the tree's seed pods,* Nate realized, amazed.

Across the way, their tribal guide slipped between two gnarled roots and disappeared into shadow. Stepping to the side for a better look, Nate realized the shadow was in fact an arched opening into the tree's base, a doorway. Nate stared up at the clustered dwellings. There were no vine ladders here. So how did one reach the dwellings? Was there a tunnel winding through the trunk? Nate began to step forward to investigate.

But Manny grabbed his arm. "Look." The biologist pointed off to the side.

Nate glanced over. Distracted by the white-barked giant, he had failed to notice a squat log cabin across the clearing. It was boxy, but sturdily constructed of logs and a thatched roof. It seemed out of place here, the only structure built on the ground.

"Are those solar cells on its roof?" Manny asked.

Nate squinted and raised his binoculars. Atop the cabin, two small flat black panels glinted in the morning sunshine. They indeed appeared to be solar panels. Intrigued, Nate examined the cabin more thoroughly through his binoculars. The structure was windowless, its door just a flap of woven palm leaves.

Nate's attention caught on something beside the door, a familiar object, bright in the sunshine. It was a tall snakewood staff, polished from years of hard use, crowned by *hoko* feathers.

Nate felt the ground shift under his feet.

It was his father's walking stick.

Dropping his binoculars, Nate stumbled toward the cabin.

"Rand!" Kostos barked at him.

But he was beyond listening. His feet began to run. The others followed him, keeping the group together. Zane and Olin grunted as they struggled with the stretcher.

Nate hurried to the cabin and then skidded to a stop, his breath caught. His mouth grew dry as he stared at the walking stick. Initials were carved in the wood: *C.R.*

Carl Rand.

Tears rose in Nate's eyes. At the time of his father's disappearance, Nate had refused to fathom the man could be dead. He had needed to cling to hope, lest despair cripple him, leaving him unable to pursue the yearlong search. Even when his financial resources had run dry and he was forced to concede his father was gone, he hadn't cried. Over such a prolonged time, sorrow had devolved into a black depression, a pit that consumed his life these past four years.

But now, with a tangible bit of evidence that his father had been here, tears flowed freely down his cheeks.

Nate did not entertain the possibility that his father was still alive. Such miracles were relegated to novels. The structure here bore evidence of long disuse. Dead leaves, blown from the forest, lay windswept into a pile against the cabin's front, undisturbed by any footprints.

Nate stepped forward and pushed open the woven flap. It was dark inside. Grabbing the flashlight from his field jacket, Nate clicked it on. A tailless rat, a *paca,* skittered from a hiding place and dashed through a crack in the far wall. Dust lay thick, tracked with little paw prints, along with rodent droppings.

Nate shone his light around.

Inside, near the back wall, four hammocks lay strung from the raftered ceiling, empty and untouched. Closer still, a small wooden bench had been constructed. Atop it was spread a collection of lab equipment, including a laptop computer.

Like the wooden staff on the porch, Nate recognized the tiny microscope and specimen jars. They were his father's equipment. He stepped into the dark space and opened the laptop. It whirred to electronic life, startling Nate. He stumbled backward.

"The solar cells," Manny said from the doorway. "Still giving it juice."

Nate wiped spiderwebs from his hands. "My father was here," he mumbled, numb. "This is his equipment."

Kouwe spoke a few steps back. "The Indian is returning . . . with company."

Nate stared at the computer for a second more. Dust motes floated in the air, sparkling bright in the morning sunlight streaming through the open flap. The room was aromatic with wood oils and dried palm thatch. But underlying it was an odor of ashes and age. No one had been here for at least half a year.

What had happened to them?

Wiping his eyes, Nate turned to the doorway. Across the glade, he watched the black-painted tribesman march toward the cabin. At his side strode a smaller man, a tiny Indian. He could be no more than four feet tall. His burnished skin was unpainted, except for a prominent design in red on his belly and the familiar blue palm print centered just above the navel.

Stepping back into the sunlight, Nate joined the others.

The newcomer had pierced ears from which hung feathers, not unlike the typical decorations of the Yanomamo. But he also bore a headband with a prominent beetle decoration in the center. Its black carapace glistened brightly. It was one of the carnivorous locusts that had killed Corporal Jorgensen.

Professor Kouwe glanced over at Nate. His friend had noticed the odd bit of decoration, too. Here was further evidence that the attack truly had originated from this place.

Like a knife through his gut, Nate felt a surge of anger. Not only had this tribe been instrumental in the deaths of half their party, they had held the survivors of his father's expedition prisoner for four years. Fury and pain swelled through him.

Kouwe must have sensed Nate's emotion. "Remain quiet, Nate. Let us see how this plays out."

Their guide led the newcomer to them, then stepped aside, in clear deference to the smaller man.

The tiny Indian glanced at the group, studying each of them, eyes narrowing slightly at the sight of Tor-tor. Finally he pointed to the stretcher, then jabbed at Olin and Zane. "Bring the hurt man," the Indian said in stilted English, then waved an arm at everyone else. "Others stay here."

With these simple commands, the diminutive man turned and headed back to the huge white-barked tree again.

Stunned, no one moved. The shock of hearing spoken English cut through Nate's anger.

Olin and Zane remained standing, not budging.

The taller Indian guide waved an arm angrily, indicating they should follow his fellow tribesman.

"No one's going anywhere," Sergeant Kostos said. Private Carrera moved forward, too. Both had their weapons ready. "We're not splitting up the group."

The tribesman scowled. He pointed at the retreating tiny figure. "Healer," the man said, struggling with the words. "Good healer."

Again the spoken English gave them pause.

"They must have learned the language from your father's expedition," Anna Fong mumbled.

Or from my father himself, Nate thought.

Kouwe turned to Kelly. "I think we should obey. I don't think they mean Frank any harm. But just in case, I can go with the stretcher."

"I'm not leaving my brother's side," Kelly said, stepping closer to the stretcher.

Zane argued, too. "And I'm not going at all. I'm staying where the guns are."

"Don't worry," the professor said. "I'll take your place. It's my turn anyway."

Zane was only too happy to be unburdened of the stretcher. Once free, he quickly scooted into the shadow of Sergeant Kostos, who wore a perpetual scowl.

Kelly moved to Olin at the head of the stretcher. "I'll take the other end." The Russian started to object but was cut off. "You get the GPS working," she ordered. "You're the only one who can get the damned thing fixed."

He reluctantly nodded and let her take the bamboo poles of the stretcher. She struggled with the weight for a moment, then with a heave, got her legs under her.

Nate shifted forward, going to her aid. "I can take Frank," he offered. "You can follow."

"No," she said harshly, teeth clenched. She tossed her head back toward the cabin. "See if you can find out what happened here."

Before any other objections could be raised, Kelly lurched forward. Kouwe followed at his end of the stretcher.

The tribesman looked relieved at their cooperation and hurried ahead, leading them toward the giant tree.

From the dirt porch of the cabin, Nate glanced again at the clusters of dwellings nestled high up the white-barked tree, realizing it was a view his father must have seen. As Nate stood, he sought some connection to his dead father. He remained standing until Kelly and Kouwe disappeared into the tree tunnel.

As the other team members began unhooking packs, Nate returned his attention to the empty cabin. Through the doorway, the laptop's screen shone with a ghostly glow in the dark room. A lonely, empty light.

Nate sighed, wondering again what had happened to the others.

Struggling under the weight of her twin brother, Kelly entered the dark opening in the massive trunk of the tree. Her focus remained divided between Frank's weakening state and the strangeness before her.

By now, Frank's bandages were fully soaked with blood. Flies swarmed and crawled through the gore, an easy meal. He needed a transfusion as soon as possible. In her head, she ran through the additional care needed: a new IV line, fresh pressure bandages, more morphine and antibiotics. Frank had to survive until the rescue helicopter could get here.

Still, as much as horror and fear filled her heart, Kelly could not help but be amazed by what she found beyond the entrance to the tree. She had expected to find a cramped steep staircase. Instead, the path beyond the doorway was wide—a gentle, sweeping course winding and worming its way up toward the treetop dwellings. The walls were smooth and polished to a deep honey color. A smattering of blue handprints decorated the walls. Beyond the entrance, every ten yards down the passage, a thin window, not unlike a castle tower's arrow slit, broke through to the outside, bright with morning sunlight, illuminating the way.

Following their guide, Kelly and Kouwe worked up the winding path. The floor was smooth, but woody enough for good traction. And though the grade was mild, Kelly was soon wheezing with exertion. But adrenaline and fear kept her moving: fear for her brother, fear for them all.

"This tunnel seems almost natural," Kouwe mumbled behind her. "The smoothness of the walls, the perfection of the spiral. It's like this tunnel is some tubule or channel in the tree, not a hewn passage."

Kelly licked her lips but found no voice. Too tired, too scared. The professor's words drew her attention to the floor and walls. Now that he had mentioned it, the passage showed not a single ax or chisel mark. Only the windows were crude, clearly man-made, hacked through to the outside. The difference between the two was striking. Had the tribe stumbled upon this winding tubule within the tree and taken advantage of it? The dwellings they'd seen on the way here proved that the Ban-ali were skilled engineers, incorporating the artificial with the natural. Perhaps the same was true here.

The professor made one last observation: "The flies are gone."

Kelly glanced over her shoulder. The flock of flies nattering and crawling among her brother's bloody bandages had indeed vanished.

"The bugs flew off shortly after we entered the tree," Kouwe said. "It must be some repellent property of the wood's aromatic oils."

Kelly had also noticed the musky odor of the tree. It had struck her as vaguely familiar, similar to dried eucalyptus, medicinal and pleasant, but laced with a deeper loamy smell that hinted at something earthy and ripe.

Staring over her shoulder, Kelly saw how heavily soaked her brother's bandages were. He could not last much longer, not with the continuing blood loss. Something had to be done. As she walked, cold dread iced her veins. Despite her exhaustion, her pace increased.

As they climbed, openings appeared in the tunnel wall. Passing by them, Kelly noted that the passages led either into one of the hutlike dwellings or out onto branches as wide as driveways, with huts in the distance.

And still they were led onward and upward.

Despite her anxiety, Kelly was soon stumbling, dragging, gasping, eyes stinging with running sweat. She desperately wanted to rest, but she could not let Frank down.

Their guide noticed them drifting farther and farther behind him. He backed down and studied the situation. He moved to Kelly's side.

"I help." He struck a fist on his chest. "I strong." He nudged her aside and took her end of the stretcher.

She was too weak to object, too winded to mumble a thanks.

As Kelly stepped aside, the two men now continued upward, moving faster. Kelly kept pace beside the stretcher. Frank was so pale, his breathing shallow. Relieved of the burden, Kelly's full attention focused back on her brother. She pulled out her stethoscope and listened to his chest. His heartbeat thudded dully, his lungs crackled with rales. His body was rapidly giving out, heading into hypovolemic shock. The hemorrhaging had to be stopped.

Focused on her brother's condition, she failed to notice that they'd reached the tunnel's end. The spiraling passage terminated abruptly at an opening that looked identical to the archway at the base of the giant tree. But instead of leading back into the morning sunshine, this archway led into a cavernous structure with a saucer-shaped floor.

Kelly gaped at the interior, again lit by rough-hewn slits high up the curved walls. The space, spherical in shape, had to be thirty yards across, a titanic bubble in the wood, half protruding out of the main trunk.

"It's like a massive gall," Kouwe said, referring to the woody protuberances sometimes found on oaks or other trees, created by insects or other parasitic conditions.

Kelly appreciated the comparison. But it wasn't insects that inhabited this gall. Around the curved walls, woven hammocks hung from pegs, a dozen at least. In a few, naked tribesmen lay sprawled. Others of the Banali worked around them. The handful of prone men and women were showing various signs of illness: a bandaged foot, a splinted arm, a fevered brow. She watched a tribesman with a long gash across his chest wince as a thick pasty substance was applied to his wound by another of his tribe.

Kelly understood immediately what she was seeing.

A hospital ward.

The tiny-framed tribesman who had ordered them here stood a few paces away. His look was sour with impatience. He pointed to one of the hammocks and spoke rapidly in a foreign tongue.

Their guide answered with a nod and led them to the proper hammock.

Professor Kouwe mumbled as they walked. "If I'm not mistaken, that's a dialect of Yanomamo."

Kelly glanced over to him, hearing the shock in the professor's voice.

He explained the significance. "The Yanomamo language has no known counterparts. Their speech patterns and tonal structures are unique unto themselves. A true lingual isolate. It's one of the reasons the Yanomamo are considered one of the oldest Amazonian bloodlines." His eyes were wide upon the men and women in the woody chamber. "The Ban-ali must be an offshoot, a lost tribe of the Yanomamo."

Kelly merely nodded, too full of worry to appreciate the professor's observation. Her attention remained focused on her brother.

Overseen by the tiny Indian, the stretcher was lowered, and Frank was transferred onto the hammock. Kelly hovered nervously at his side. Jarred by the movement, Frank moaned slightly, eyes fluttering. His sedatives must be wearing off.

Kelly reached down to her med pack atop the abandoned stretcher. Before she could gather up her syringe and bottles of morphine, the tiny healer barked orders to his staff. Their guide and another tribesman began to loosen the bandages over Frank's stumps with small bone knives.

"Don't!" Kelly said, straightening.

She was ignored. They continued to work upon the soaked strips. Blood began to flow more thickly.

She moved to the hammock, grabbing the taller man's elbow. "No! You don't know what you're doing. Wait until I have the pressure wraps ready! An IV in place! He'll bleed to death!"

The stronger man broke out of her grasp and scowled at her.

Kouwe intervened. He pointed at Kelly. "She's our *healer*."

The tribesman seemed baffled by this statement and glanced to his own shaman.

The smaller Indian was crouched by the curved wall at the head of the hammock. He had a bowl in his hand, gathering a flow of thick sap from a trough gouged in the wall. "I am healer here," the small man said. "This is Ban-ali medicine. To stop the bleeding. Strong medicine from the *yagga*."

Kelly glanced to Kouwe.

He deciphered. "*Yagga* . . . it's similar to *yakka* . . . a Yanomamo word for mother."

Kouwe stared around at the chamber. "*Yagga* must be their name for this tree. A deity."

The Indian shaman straightened with his bowl, now half full of the reddish sap. Reaching up, he stoppered the thick flow by jamming a wooden peg into a hole at the top of the trough. "Strong medicines," he repeated, lifting the bowl and striding to the hammock. "The blood of the Yagga will stop the blood of the man." It sounded like a rote maxim, a translation of an old adage.

He motioned for the tribesman to cut away one of the two bandages.

Kelly opened her mouth again to object, but Kouwe interrupted her with a squeeze on her arm. "Gather your bandage material and LRS bag," he whispered to her. "Be ready, but for the moment, let's see what this medicine can do."

She bit back her protest, remembering the small Indian girl at the hospital of São Gabriel and how Western medicine had failed her. For the moment, she would yield to the Ban-ali, trusting not the strange little shaman, but rather Professor Kouwe himself. She dropped to her medical pack and burrowed into it, reaching with deft fingers for her wraps and saline bag.

As Kelly retrieved what she needed, her eyes flicked over to the nearby sap channel. *The blood of the Yagga.* The tapped vein could be seen as a dark ribbon in the honeyed wood, extending up from the top of the trough and arching across the roof. Kelly spotted other such veins, each dark vessel leading to one of the other hammocks.

With her bandages in hand, she stood as her brother's bloodied wrap was ripped away. Unprepared, still a sister, not a doctor, Kelly grew faint at the sight: the sharp shard of white bone, the rip of shredded muscle, the gelatinous bruise of ruined flesh. A thick flow of dark blood and clots washed from the raw wound and dribbled through the hammock's webbing.

Kelly suddenly found it difficult to breathe. Sounds grew muted and more acute at the same time. Her vision narrowed upon the limp figure in the bed. *It wasn't Frank,* her mind kept trying to convince her. But another part of her knew the truth. Her brother was doomed. Tears filled her eyes, and a moan rose in her throat, choking her.

Kouwe put his arm around her shoulders, reacting to her distress, pulling her to him.

"Oh, God . . . please . . ." Kelly sobbed.

Oblivious to her outburst, the Ban-ali shaman examined the amputated limb with a determined frown. Then he scooped up a handful of the thick red sap, the color of port wine, and slathered it over the stump.

The reaction was immediate—and violent. Frank's leg jerked up and away as if struck by an electric current. He cried out, even through his stupor, an animal sound.

Kelly stumbled toward him, out of the professor's arms. "Frank!"

The shaman glanced toward her. He mumbled something in his native language and backed away, allowing her to come forward.

She reached her brother, grabbing for his arm. But Frank's outburst had been as short as it was sudden. He relaxed back into the hammock. Kelly was sure he was dead. She leaned over him, sobbing openly.

But his lungs heaved up and down, in deep, shuddering breaths.

Alive.

She fell to her knees in relief. His limb, exposed, stood stark and raw before her. She eyed the wound, expecting the worst, ready with the bandages.

But they proved unnecessary.

Where the sap had touched the macerated flesh, it had formed a thick seal. Wide-eyed, she reached and touched the strange substance. It was no longer sticky, but leathery and tough, like some type of natural bandage. She glanced to the shaman with awe. The bleeding had stopped, sealed tight.

"The Yagga has found him worthy," the shaman said. "He will heal."

Stunned, Kelly stood as the shaman carried his bowl toward the other limb and began to repeat the miracle. "I can't believe it," she finally said, her voice as small as a mouse.

Kouwe took her under his arm again. "I know fifteen different plant species with hemostatic properties, but nothing of this caliber."

Frank's body jerked again as the second leg was treated.

Afterward, the shaman studied his handiwork for a few moments, then turned to them. "The Yagga will protect him from here," he said solemnly.

"Thank you," Kelly said.

The small tribesman glanced back to her brother. "He is now Ban-ali. One of the Chosen."

Kelly frowned.

The shaman continued, "He must now serve the Yagga in all ways, for all times." With these words, he turned away—but not before adding something in his native tongue, something spoken in a dire, threatening tone.

As he left, Kelly turned to Kouwe, her eyes questioning.

The professor shook his head. "I recognized only one word—*ban-yi*."

"What does that mean?"

Kouwe glanced over to Frank. "Slave."

FIFTEEN

Health Care

Lauren had never known such despair. Her granddaughter drifted in a cloud of pillows and sheets, such a tiny thing with lines and monitor wires running to machines and saline bags. Even through Lauren's contamination suit, she could hear the beep and hiss from the various pieces of equipment in the long narrow room. Little Jessie was no longer the only one confined here. Five other children had become sick over the past day.

And how many more in the coming days? Lauren recalled the epidemiologist's computer model and its stain of red spreading over the United States. She had heard cases were already being reported in Canada, too. Even two children in Germany, who had been vacationing in Florida.

Now she was realizing that Dr. Alvisio's grim model may have been too conservative in its predictions. Just this morning, Lauren had heard rumors about new cases in Brazil, cases now appearing in healthy adults. These patients were not presenting fevers, like the children, but were instead showing outbreaks of ravaging malignancies and cancers, like those seen in Gerald Clark's body. Lauren already had researchers checking into it.

But right now, she had other concerns.

She sat in a chair beside Jessie's bed. Her grandchild was watching some children's program piped into the video monitor in the room. But no smile ever moved her lips, no laugh. The girl watched it like an automaton, her eyes glassy, her hair plastered to her head from fevered sweat.

There was so little comfort Lauren could offer. The touch of the plastic containment suit was cold and impersonal. All she could do was maintain her post beside the girl, let her know she wasn't alone, let her see a familiar face. But she was not Jessie's mother. Every time the door to the ward swished open, Jessie would turn to see who it was, her eyes momentarily hopeful, then fading to disappointment. Just another nurse or a doctor. Never her mother.

Even Lauren found herself frequently glancing to the door, praying for Marshall to return with some word on Kelly and Frank. Down in the Amazon, the Brazilian evacuation helicopter had left from the Wauwai field base hours ago. Surely the rescuers would've reached the stranded team by now. Surely Kelly was already flying back here.

But so far, no word.

The waiting was growing interminable.

In the bed, Jessie scratched at the tape securing her catheter.

"Hon, leave it be," Lauren said, moving the girl's hand away.

Jessie sighed, sinking back into her pillows. "Where's Mommy?" she asked for the thousandth time that day. "I want Mommy."

"She's coming, hon. But South America is a long way away. Why don't you try to take a nap?"

Jessie frowned. "My mouth hurts."

Lauren reached to the table and lifted a cup with a straw toward the girl, juice with an analgesic in it. "Sip this. It'll make the ouchie go away." Already the girl's mouth had begun to erupt with fever blisters, raw ulcerations along the mucocutaneous margins of her lips. Their appearance was one of the distinct symptoms of the disease. There could now be no denying that Jessie had the plague.

The girl sipped at the cup, her face scrunching sourly, then sat back. "It tastes funny. It's not like Mommy makes."

"I know, honey, but it'll make you feel better."

"Tastes funny . . ." Jessie mumbled again, eyes drifting back to the video screen.

The two sat quietly. Somewhere down the row of beds, one of the children began to sob. In the background, the repetitious jingle of the dancing bear sounded tinny through her suit.

How many more? Lauren wondered. *How many more would grow sick? How many more would die?*

The sigh of a broken pressure seal sounded behind her. Lauren turned as the ward door swished open. A bulky figure in a quarantine suit bowed into the room, carrying his oxygen line. He turned, and through the plastic face shield, Lauren recognized her husband.

She was instantly on her feet. "Marshall . . ."

He waved her down and crossed to the wall to snap in his oxygen line to one of the air bibs. Once done, he strode to the girl's bedside.

"Grandpa!" Jessie said, smiling faintly. The girl's love for her grandfather, the only father figure in her life, was special. It was heartening to see her respond to him.

"How's my little pumpkin?" he said, bending over to tousle her hair.

"I'm watching Bobo the Bear."

"Are you? Is he funny?"

She nodded her head vigorously.

"I'll watch it with you. Scoot over."

This delighted Jessie. She shifted, making room for him to sit on the edge of the bed. He put an arm around her. She snuggled up against him, content to watch the screen.

Lauren met her husband's gaze.

He gave his head a tiny shake.

Lauren frowned. *What did that mean?* Anxious to find out, she switched to the suit's radios so they could speak in whispers without Jessie hearing.

"How's Jessie doing?" Marshall asked.

Lauren sat straighter, leaning closer. "Her temperature is down to ninety-nine, but her labs are continuing to slide. White blood cell levels have been dropping, while bilirubin levels are rising."

Marshall's eyes closed with pain. "Stage Two?"

Lauren found her voice cracking. With so many cases studied across the nation, the disease progression was becoming predictable. Stage II was classified when the disease progressed from its benign febrile state into an anemic stage with bleeding and nausea.

"By tomorrow," Lauren said. "Maybe the day after that at the latest."

They both knew what would happen from there. With good support, Stage II could stretch for three to four days, followed by a single day of Stage III. *Convulsions and brain hemorrhages.* There was no Stage IV.

Lauren stared at the little girl in the bed as she cuddled against her grandfather. *Less than a week.* That's all the time Jessie had left. "What of Kelly? Has she been picked up? Is she on her way back?"

Her suit radio remained silent. Lauren glanced back to Marshall.

He stared at her a moment more, then spoke. "There was no sign of them. The rescue helicopter searched the region where they were supposed to be according to their last GPS signal. But nothing was found."

Lauren felt like a brick had been dropped in her gut. "How could that be?"

"I don't know. We've been trying to raise them on the satellite link all day, but with no luck. Whatever problem they were having with their equipment yesterday must still be going on."

"Are they continuing the air search?"

He shook his head. "The helicopter had to turn back. Limited fuel."

"Marshall . . ." Her voice cracked.

He reached out to her and took her hand. "Once they've refueled, they're sending it back out for a night flight. To see if they can spot campfires from the air using infrared scopes. Then tomorrow, another three helicopters are joining the search, including our own Comanche." He squeezed her hand, tight. "We'll find them."

Lauren felt numb all over. *All her children . . . all of them . . .*

Jessie spoke up from the bed, pointing an arm that trailed an IV line toward the video. "Bobo's funny!"

1:05 P.M.

AMAZON JUNGLE

Nate climbed down the fifty-foot ladder from the treetop dwelling. The three-story structure rested in the branches of a nightcap oak, a species from the Cretaceous period. Earlier, just after Kelly and the professor had left with Frank, a pair of Ban-ali women had appeared and led the party to the edge of the glade, gesturing and indicating that the dwelling above had been assigned to their group.

Sergeant Kostos had resisted at first, until Private Carrera had made an astute observation. "Up there, it'll be more defensible. We're sitting targets on the ground. If those giant cats should come up during the night—"

Kostos had cut her off, needing no more convincing. "Right, right. Let's move our supplies up there, then set up a defensive perimeter."

Nate thought such caution was unnecessary. Since arriving, the Indians had remained curious about them but kept a wary distance, peering from the jungle edges and windows. No hostility was shown. Still, Nate had a hard time balancing these quiet people with the murderous savages who had wiped out half their team by unleashing all manner of beasts upon them. But then again, such duality was the way of many indigenous tribes: hostile and brutal by outside appearances, but once you were accepted, they were found to be a peaceful and open people.

Still, so many of their teammates had died horribly at the indirect hands of this tribe. A burning seed of anger smoldered in Nate's chest. And then there were Clark and maybe others of his father's group, held hostage for all these years. At the moment, Nate found it hard to achieve professional detachment. As an anthropologist, he could understand these strange people, but as a son, resentment and fury colored all he saw.

Still, they *were* helping Frank. Professor Kouwe had returned briefly from the white-barked tree to announce that the tribal shaman and Kelly were able to stabilize their teammate. It was a rare bit of good news. Kouwe had not stayed long, anxious to return to the giant tree. The professor's eyes had flicked toward Nate. Despite the tribe's cooperation at the moment, Kouwe was clearly worried. Nate had tried to inquire, but the professor had waved him off as he left. "Later" was all he had said.

Reaching the last rung of the vine ladder, Nate jumped off. Clustered around the base of the tree were the two Rangers and Manny. Tor-tor stood at his master's side. The other members of their dwindling group—Zane, Anna, and Olin—remained secure in their treetop loft, working on their communication equipment.

Manny nodded to Nate as he crossed toward them.

"I'll keep guard here," Kostos instructed Carrera. "You and Manny do a sweep of the immediate area. See what you can discover about the lay of the land."

The private nodded and turned away.

Manny followed at her side. "C'mon, Tor-tor."

Kostos noted Nate's arrival. "What are you doing down here, Rand?"

"Trying to make myself useful." He nodded to the cabin a hundred yards away. "While the sun's still up and the solar cells are still juicing, I'm going to see if I can discover any information in my father's computer records."

Kostos frowned at the cabin but nodded. Nate could read his eyes, weighing and calculating. Right now every bit of intel could be vital. "Be careful," the sergeant said.

Nate hiked his shotgun higher on his shoulder. "Always." He began the walk across the open glade.

In the distance, near the clearing's edge, a handful of children had gathered. Several pointed at him, gesturing to one another. A small group trailed behind Manny and Carrera, keeping a cautious distance from Tor-tor. The curiosity of youth. Among the trees, the timid tribe began to reawaken to their usual activities. Several women carried water from the stream that flowed through the glade and around the giant tree in the center. In the treetop abodes, people began to clamber. Small fires flared atop stone hearths on patios, readying for dinner. In one dwelling, an old woman sat cross-legged, playing a flute made out of a deer bone, a bright but haunting sound. Nearby, a pair of men, armed with hunting bows, wandered past, giving Nate the barest acknowledgment.

The casualness of their manner reminded Nate that, though these folks were isolated, they had lived with white men and women before. The survivors of his father's expedition.

He reached the cabin, seeing again his father's walking stick by the door. As he stared at it, the rest of the world and its mysteries dissolved away. For the moment, only one question remained in Nate's heart: *What truly happened to my father?*

With a final glance to his team's temporary treetop home, Nate ducked through the door flap of the cabin. The musty smell struck him again, like entering a lost tomb. Inside, he found the laptop still open on the workstation, just as he had left it. Its glow was a beacon in the dark.

As he neared the computer, Nate saw the screen saver playing across the monitor, a tiny set of pictures that slowly floated and bounced around the screen. Tears rose in his eyes. They were photos of his mother. Another ghost from his past. He stared at the smiling face. In one, she was kneeling beside a small Indian boy. In another, a capuchin monkey perched on her shoulder. In yet another, she was hugging a short youngster, a white boy dressed in typical Baniwa garb. It was Nate. He had been six years old. He smiled at the memory, his heart close to bursting. Though his father wasn't in any of the pictures, Nate sensed his presence, a ghost standing over his shoulder, watching with him. At this moment, Nate had never felt closer to his lost family.

After a long time, he reached for the mouse pad. The screen saver vanished, replaced with a typical computer screen. Small titled icons lined the screen. Nate read through the files. *Plant Classification, Tribal Customs, Cellular Statistics* . . . so much information. It would take days to sift through them all. But one file caught his eye. The icon was of a small book. Below it was the word *Journal*.

Nate clicked the icon. A file opened:

Amazonian Journal—Dr. Carl Rand

It was his father's diary. He noted the first date. *September 24.* The day the expedition had headed into the jungle. As Nate scrolled down, he saw that each day had a typed entry. Sometimes no more than a sentence or two, but something was noted. His father was meticulous. As he once quoted to Nate, "An unexamined life is not worth living."

Nate skimmed through the entries, searching for one specific date. He found it. December 16. The day his father's team had vanished.

December 16

The storms continued today, bogging us down in camp. But the day was not a total wash. An Arawak Indian, traveling down the river, shared our soggy camp and told us stories of a strange tribe . . . frightening stories.

The Ban-ali, he named them, which translates roughly to "Blood Jaguar." I've heard snatches in the past concerning this ghost tribe, but few Indians were willing to speak openly of them.

Our visitor was not so reluctant! He was quite talkative. Of course, this may have something to do with the new machete and tangle of shiny fishhooks we offered for the information. Eyeing the wealth, he insisted he knew where the Ban-ali tribe hunted.

Now while my first impulse was to scoff at such a claim, I listened. If there was even a slim chance such a lost tribe existed, how could we not investigate? What a boon it would be for our expedition. As we questioned him, the Indian sketched out a rough map. The Ban-ali appeared to be more than a three-day journey from our location.

So tomorrow, weather permitting, we'll strike out and see how truthful our friend has been. Surely it's a fool's errand . . . but who knows what this mighty jungle could be hiding at its heart?

All in all, a most interesting day.

Nate held his breath as he continued reading from there, hunched over the laptop, sweat dripping down his brow. Over the next several hours, he scanned through the file, reading day after day, year after year, opening other files, staring at diagrams and digital photos. Slowly he began piecing together what had happened to the others.

As he did so, he grew numb with the reading. The horror of the past merged with the present. Nate began to understand. The true danger for their team was only beginning.

5:55 P.M.

Manny called over to Private Carrera. "What's that guy doing over there?"

"Where?"

He pointed his arm toward one of the Ban-ali tribesmen who marched along the streambed, a long spear over his shoulder. Impaled upon the weapon were several haunches of raw meat.

"Making dinner?" the Ranger guessed with a shrug.

"But for whom?"

For the entire afternoon, he and Carrera had been making a slow circuit of the village, with Tor-tor at their side. The cat drew many glances, but also kept curious tribesmen at a distance. As they trekked, Carrera was jotting notes and sketching a map of the village and surrounding lands. *Recon,* Manny had been informed, *just in case the hostiles get hostile again.*

Right now, they were circling the giant, white-barked tree, crossing behind it, where the stream brushed the edges of the monstrous arching roots. It appeared as if the flow of water had washed away the topsoil, exposing even more of the roots' lengths. They were a veritable tangle, snaking into the stream, worming over it, burrowing beneath it.

The Indian who had drawn Manny's attention was ducking through the woody tangle, squirming and bending to make progress, clearly aiming for a section of the stream.

"Let's get a closer look," Manny said.

Carrera pocketed her small field notebook and grabbed up her weapon, the shovel-snouted Bailey. She eyed the massive tree with a frown, plainly not pleased with the idea of getting any closer to it. But she led the way, marching toward the tangle of roots and the gurgling stream.

Manny watched the Indian cross to a huge eddy pool, shrouded by thick roots and rootlets. The water's surface was glassy smooth, with only a slight swirl disturbing it.

The Indian noticed he was being observed and nodded in the universal greeting of hello, then went back to his work. Manny and Carrera watched from several yards away. Tor-tor settled to his haunches.

Crouching, the tribesman stretched his pole and the flanks of bloody meat over the still pool.

Manny squinted. "What is he—?"

Then several small bodies flung themselves out of the water toward the meat. They looked like little silvery eels, twitching up out of the water. The creatures grabbed bites from the meat with little jaws.

"The piranha creatures," Carrera said at Manny's side.

He nodded, recognizing the similarity. "Juveniles, though. They've not developed their hind legs yet. Still in the pollywog stage. All tail and teeth."

The Indian stood straighter and shook the meat from his spear. Each bloody chunk, as it plopped into the water, triggered a fierce roiling of the still pool, boiling its surface into a bloody froth. The tribesman observed his handiwork for a moment, then tromped back toward the pair who stared at him, stunned.

Again he nodded as he passed, eyeing the jaguar at Manny's side with a mix of awe and fear.

"I want to get a closer look," Manny said.

"Are you nuts, man?" Carrera waved him back. "We're out of here."

"No, I just want to check something out." He was already moving toward the nest of tangled roots.

Carrera grumbled behind him, but followed.

The path was narrow, so they proceeded in single file. Tor-tor trailed last, padding cautiously through the tangle, his tail twitching anxiously.

Manny approached the root-ringed pool.

"Don't get too close," Carrera warned.

"They didn't mind the Indian," Manny said. "I think it's safe."

Still, he slowed his steps and stopped a yard from the pool's edge, one hand resting on the hilt of his whip. In the shadow of the roots, the wide pool proved crystal clear—and deep, at least ten feet. He peered into its glassy depths.

Under the surface, schools of the creatures swam. There was no sign of the meat, but littering the bottom of the pool were bleached bones, nibbled spotless. "It's a damn hatchery," Manny said. "A fish hatchery."

From the branches spanning the pool overhead, droplets of sap would occasionally drip into the water, triggering the creatures to race up and investigate, searching for their next meal. Tricked to the surface, the beasts provided Manny with a better look at them. They varied in size from little minnows to larger monsters with leg buds starting to develop. Not one had fully developed legs.

"They're *all* juveniles," Manny observed. "I don't see any of the adults that attacked us."

"We must have killed them all with the poison," Carrera said.

"No wonder there wasn't a second attack. It must take time to rebuild their army."

"For the piranhas, maybe . . ." Carrera stood two yards back, her voice suddenly hushed and sick. ". . . but not everything."

Manny glanced back to her. She pointed her weapon toward the lower trunk of the tree, where the roots rode up into the main body. Up the trunk, the bark of the tree bubbled out into thick galls, each a yard across. There were hundreds of them. From holes in the bark, black insects scuttled. They crawled, fought, and mated atop the bark. A few flexed their wings with little blurring buzzes.

"The locusts," Manny said, edging back himself.

But the insects ignored them, busy with their communal activities.

Manny stared from the pool back to the insects. "The tree . . ." he mumbled.

"What?"

Manny stared as another droplet of sap drew a handful of the piranha creatures to the surface, glistening silver under the glassy waters. He shook his head. "I'm not sure, but it's almost like the tree is nurturing these creatures." His mind began racing along wild tracks. His eyes grew wide as he began to make disturbing connections.

Carrera must have seen his face pale. "What's wrong?"

"Oh, my God . . . we have to get out of here!"

6:30 P.M.

Inside the cabin, Nate sat hunched over the laptop computer, numb and exhausted. He had reread many of his father's journal notes, even cross-referencing to certain scientific files. The conclusions forming in his mind were as disturbing as they were miraculous. He scrolled down to the last entry and read the final lines.

We'll try tonight. May God watch over us all.

Behind Nate, the whispery sweep of the cabin's door flap announced someone's intrusion.

"Nate?" It was Professor Kouwe.

Glancing at his wristwatch, Nate realized how long he had been lost in

Nate saw the other platters of food. Even a few pails of a dark liquid, smelling of fermentation.

Professor Kouwe examined one pail's contents and turned to Nate in surprise. "It's cassiri!"

"What's that?" Kostos asked from the doorway as he closed the flap.

"Cassava beer," Nate explained. "An alcoholic staple of many native tribes."

"Beer?" the sergeant's eyes brightened. "Really?"

Kouwe scooped up a ladleful of the dark amber liquid and poured it into a mug. Nate saw bits of slimy cassava root floating in the pail. The professor passed the mug to the sergeant.

He sniffed it, nose curling in disgust, but he took a deep swig anyway. "Ugh!" He shook his head.

"It's an acquired taste," Nate said, scooping a mug for himself and sipping it. Manny did the same. "Women make it by chewing up cassava root and spitting it into a pail. The enzymes in their saliva aid in the fermentation process."

Kostos crossed to the pail and dumped the contents of his mug back into the pail. "I'll take a Budweiser any day."

Nate shrugged.

Around the room, the others sampled the fare for a bit, then began to settle to woven mats on the floor. Everyone looked exhausted. They all needed a decent night's sleep.

Nate set up the laptop on an overturned stone pot.

As he opened it and turned it on, Olin looked at it hungrily, his eyes red. "Maybe I can cannibalize some circuitry for the communication array." He shifted nearer.

But Nate held him off. "The computer is five years old. I doubt you'll find much to use, and right now its contents are more important than our own survival."

His words drew everyone's attention. He eyed them all. "I know what happened to the other expedition team. And if we don't want to end up like them, we should pay attention to its lessons."

Kouwe spoke up. "What happened?"

Nate took a deep breath, then began, nodding to the open journal file on the laptop. "It's all here. My father's expedition heard rumors of the

Ban-ali and met an Indian who said he could take the research team to their lands. My father could not resist the possibility of encountering a new tribe and took the team off course. Within two days, they were attacked by the same mutated species as we were."

Murmurs arose from the others. Manny raised his hand as if he were in class. "I found where they incubate those buggers. At least the locusts and piranhas." He described what he and Private Carrera had discovered. "I've got my own theories about the beasts."

Kouwe interrupted. "Before we get into theories and conjectures, let's first hear what we know for sure." The professor nodded to Nate. "Go on. What happened after the attack?"

Nate took another breath. The tale was not an easy one to tell. "Of the party, all were killed except Gerald Clark, my father, and two other researchers. They were captured by the Ban-ali trackers. My father was able to communicate with them and get them to spare their lives. From my father's notes, I guess the Ban-ali native tongue is close enough to Yanomamo."

Kouwe nodded. "It does bear a resemblance. And isolated as the tribe is, the presence of a white man who could speak the tongue of the Ban-ali would surely give them pause. I'm not surprised your father and the survivors were spared."

The little good it did, Nate thought sourly, then continued, "The remaining party were all badly injured, but once here, their wounds were healed. Miraculously, according to my father's notes: gashes sealed without scarring, broken bones mended in less than a week's time, even chronic ailments, like one team member's heart murmur, faded away. But the most amazing transformation was in Gerald Clark."

"His arm," Kelly said, sitting up straighter.

"Exactly. Within a few weeks here, his amputated stump began to split, bleed, and sprout a raw tumorous growth. One of the survivors was a medical doctor. He and my father examined the change. The growth was a mass of undifferentiated stem cells. They were sure it was some malignant growth. There was even talk of trying to surgically remove it, but they had no tools. Over the next weeks, slow changes became apparent. The mass slowly elongated, growing skin on the outside."

Kelly's eyes widened. "The arm was regenerating."

Nate nodded and turned. He scrolled down the computer journal to the day almost three years ago. He read aloud his father's words. " 'Today it became clear to Dr. Chandler and me that the tumor plaguing Clark is in fact a regeneration unlike any seen before. Talk of escape has been put on hold until we see how this ends. It's a miracle that is worth the risk. The Ban-ali continue to remain accommodating captors, allowing us free run of the valley, but banning us from leaving. And with the giant cats prowling the lower chasm, escape seems impossible for the moment anyway.' "

Nate straightened up and tapped open a new file. Crude sketches of an arm and upper torso appeared on the screen. "My father went on to document the transformation. How the undifferentiated stem cells slowly changed into bone, muscle, nerves, blood vessels, hair, and skin. It took eight months for the limb to fully grow back."

"What caused it?" Kelly asked.

"According to my father's notes, the sap of the Yagga tree."

Kelly gasped. "The Yagga . . ."

Kouwe's eyes widened. "No wonder the Ban-ali worship the tree."

"What's a Yagga?" Zane asked from a corner, showing the first sign of interest in their discussion.

Kouwe explained what he and Kelly had witnessed up in the healing ward of the giant prehistoric tree. "Frank's wounds almost immediately sealed."

"That's not all," Kelly said. She shifted closer to get a better look at the computer screen. "All afternoon, I've been monitoring his red blood cell levels with a hematocrit tube. The levels are climbing dramatically. It's as if something is massively stimulating his bone marrow to produce new red blood cells for all he lost . . . at a miraculous rate. I've never seen such a reaction."

Nate clicked open another file. "It's something in the sap. My father's group was able to distill the stuff and run it through a paper chromatograph. Similar to the way the sap of copal trees is rich in hydrocarbons, the Yagga's sap is rich in *proteins*."

Kelly stared at the results. "Proteins?"

Manny scooted next to her, looking over her shoulder. "Wasn't the disease vector a type of a protein?"

Kelly nodded. "A prion. One with strong mutagenic properties." She glanced over her shoulder to Manny. "You were mentioning something about the piranhas and the locusts. A theory."

Manny nodded. "They're tied to this Yagga tree, too. The locusts live in the bark of the tree. Like some type of wasp gall. And the piranhas—their hatchery is in a pond tucked among the roots. There was even sap dripping into it. I think it's the sap that mutates them during early development."

"My father suggested a similar conclusion in his notes," Nate said quietly. In fact, there were numerous files specifically on this matter. Nate had not been able to read through them all.

"And the giant cats and caimans?" Anna asked.

"Established mutations, I'd wager," Manny said. "The two species must've been altered generations ago into these oversized beasts. I imagine by now they're capable of breeding on their own, stable enough genetically to need no further support from the sap."

"Then why don't they leave the area?" Anna asked.

"Perhaps some biological imperative, a genetic territorial thing."

"It sounds like you're suggesting this tree manufactured these creatures purposefully? Consciously?" Zane scoffed.

Manny shrugged. "Who can say? Maybe it wasn't so much will or thought as just evolutionary pressure."

"Impossible." Zane shook his head.

"Not so. We've seen versions of this phenomenon already." Manny turned to Nate. "Like the ant tree."

Nate frowned, picturing the attack on Sergeant Kostos by stinging ants. He remembered how an ant tree's stems and branches were hollow, serving both to house the colony and feed it with a sugary sap. In turn, the ants savagely protected their home against the intrusion of plants and animals. He began to understand what Manny was driving at. There was a distinct similarity.

Manny went on, "What we have here is a symbiosis between plant life and animal, both evolved into a complex shared interrelationship. One serving the other."

Carrera spoke up from her post by a window. The sun was slowly setting behind her shoulder. "Who cares how the beasts came to be? Do we know how to avoid them if we have to fight our way out of the valley?"

Nate answered her question. "The creatures can be controlled."

"How?"

He waved to the laptop. "It took my father years to learn the Ban-ali secrets. It seems that the tribe has developed powders that can both attract and repel the creatures. We ourselves saw this demonstrated with the locusts, but they can do it with the piranhas, too. Through chemicals in the water, they can lure and trigger an aggressive response in the otherwise docile creatures. My father believed it's some type of hormonal compound that stimulates the piranhas' territoriality and makes them attack wildly."

Manny nodded. "Then it's lucky we wiped out a majority of the adult horde so quickly. I imagine it takes time for their hatchery to grow a new supply. Just one of the disadvantages of a biological defense system."

"Perhaps that's why the Ban-ali keep more than one type of creature," Carrera noted astutely. "Backup troops."

Manny frowned. "Of course. I should've thought of that."

Carrera faced Nate. "Then there are those cats and giant caimans to consider."

Nate nodded. "Gatekeepers, like we thought, set up to defend the perimeter. They patrol the entry points to the heart of the territory. But even the jaguars can be made docile by painting a black powder over one's body, allowing the Ban-ali to pass freely back and forth. I imagine the compound must act like caiman dung, a scent repellent to the giant cats."

Manny whistled. "So our guide's body paint wasn't all camouflage."

"Where do we get some of this repellent stuff?" Kostos asked. "Where does it come from?"

Kouwe spoke up. "The Yagga tree." He had not moved, only grown more pale with the telling of the tale.

Nate was surprised by the professor's quick answer. "They're derived from the Yagga's bark and leaf oils. But how did you guess?"

"Everything ties back to that prehistoric tree. I think Manny was quite correct that the specimen behaves like an ant tree. But he's wrong about who the *ants* are here."

"What do you mean?" Manny asked.

"The mutated beasts are just biological tools supplied by the tree for its true workers." Kouwe stared around him. "The Ban-ali."

A stunned silence spread over the group.

Kouwe continued, "The tribesmen here are the soldier ants in this relationship. The Ban-ali name the tree *Yagga,* their word for mother. One who gives birth . . . a caretaker. Countless generations ago, most likely during the first migration of people into South America, the tribe must have stumbled upon the tree's remarkable healing ability and became enthralled by it. Becoming *ban-yin*—slaves. Each serving the other in a complex web of defense and offense."

Nate felt sickened by this comparison. *Humans used like ants.*

"This grove is prehistoric," the professor finished. "It might trace its heritage back to Pangaea, when South America and Africa were joined. Its species may have been around when man first walked upright. Throughout the ages, there are hundreds of myths of such trees, from all corners of the world. *The maternal guardian.* Perhaps this encounter here was not the first."

This thought sank into the others. Nate didn't think even his father had extrapolated the history of the Yagga to this end. It was disturbing.

Sergeant Kostos shifted his M-16 to his other shoulder. "Enough history lessons. I thought we were supposed to be developing an alternate plan. A way to escape if we can't raise someone on the radio."

"The sergeant is right." Kouwe turned. "You never did tell us, Nate. What happened to your father and the others? How did Gerald Clark escape?"

Nate took a deep breath and turned back to the computer. He scrolled down to the last entry and read it aloud.

"April 18

We've gathered enough powders to chance an escape tonight. After what we've learned, we must attempt a break for civilization. We dare not wait any longer. We'll dust our bodies black and flee with the setting moon. Illia knows paths that will quickly get us past any trackers and out of these lands, but the trek back to civilization will be hard and not without threat. Still, we have no choice . . . not after the birth. We'll try tonight. May God watch over us all."

Nate straightened from the laptop, turning to the others. "They all attempted to flee, not just Gerald Clark."

Across the many faces, Nate saw the same expression. *Only Gerald Clark made it back to civilization.*

"So they all left," Kelly mumbled.

Nate nodded. "Even a Ban-ali woman, a skilled tracker named Illia. She had fallen in love and married Gerald Clark. He took her with him."

"What happened to them?" Anna said.

Nate shook his head. "That was the last entry. There is no more."

Kelly's expression saddened. "Then they didn't make it . . . only Gerald Clark."

"I could ask Dakii for more details," Kouwe said.

"Dakii?"

Kouwe pointed below. "The tribesman who guided us here. Between what I know of the Ban-ali language and his smattering of English, I might be able to find out what happened to the others, how they died."

Nate nodded, though he wasn't sure he wanted to know the details.

Manny spoke up. "But what made them flee *that* night? Why the hint at some urgency in that last note?"

Nate took a deep breath. "It's why I wanted everyone to hear this. My father came to some frightening conclusions about the Ban-ali. Something he needed to relay to the outside world."

"What?" Kouwe asked.

Nate wasn't sure where to begin. "It took years of living with the Ban-ali for my father to begin piecing facts together. He noticed that the isolated tribe showed some hints of remarkable advancements over their Indian counterparts in the greater Amazon. The invention of the pulley and wheel. A few of the homes even have crude elevators, using large boulders and counterweights. And other advancements that seemed strange considering the isolated nature of this tribe. He spent much of his time examining the way the Ban-ali think, the way they teach their children. He was fascinated by all this."

"So what happened?" Kelly asked.

"Gerald Clark fell in love with Illia. They married during the second year of the group's incarceration here. During the third, they conceived a baby. During the fourth year, Illia gave birth." He stared hard at the gathered faces. "The child was stillborn, rife with mutations." Nate recalled his father's words. " 'A genetic monster.' "

Kelly cringed.

Nate pointed to the laptop. "There are more details in the files. My father and the medical doctor of the group began to formulate a frightening conclusion. The tree hadn't just mutated the lower species. It had also been changing the Ban-ali over the years, subtly heightening their cognitive abilities, their reflexes, even their eyesight. While outwardly they appeared the same, the tree was improving the species. My father suspected that the Ban-ali were heading genetically away from mankind. One of the definitions that separates different species is an inability to breed together."

"The stillborn child . . ." Manny had paled.

Nate nodded. "My father came to believe that the Ban-ali were near to leaving Homo sapiens behind, becoming their own species."

"Dear God," Kelly gasped.

"It was why their need to escape became urgent. This corruption of mankind in the valley has to be stopped."

No one spoke for a full minute.

Anna's voice, full of horror, whispered, "What are we going to do?"

"We're going to get that damn GPS working," Kostos said harshly. "Then we're gonna bug out of this damn place."

"And in the meantime," Carrera added, "we should gather as much of that repellent powder as possible, just in case."

Kelly cleared her voice and stood up. "We're all forgetting one vital thing. The disease spreading across the Americas. How do we cure it? What did Gerald Clark bring out of this valley?" Kelly turned to Nate. "In your father's notes, is there any mention of a contagious disease here?"

"No, with the inherent healing properties of the Yagga tree, everyone remained incredibly healthy. The only suggestion is the taboo against one of the Chosen, the Ban-ali, leaving the tribe. A shadowed curse upon he who leaves and all he encounters. My father had dismissed this as a myth to frighten anyone from leaving."

Manny mumbled, "The curse upon he who leaves and all he encounters . . . that sounds like our contagion."

Kelly turned back to Nate. "But if true, where did the disease come from? What triggered Clark's body to suddenly become riddled with tumors? What made him contagious?"

"I wager it has something to do with the Yagga tree's healing sap," Zane said. "Maybe it keeps the disease in check here. When we leave, we need to make sure we collect a generous sample. That's clearly vital."

Kelly ignored Zane, her gaze unfocused. "We're missing something . . . something important," she said, low and quiet. Nate doubted anyone else heard her.

"I can see if Dakii will cooperate," Kouwe said. "See if he has any answers—both to the final fate of the others and about this mysterious disease."

"Good. Then we have a working plan for now," Sergeant Kostos said by the door. He pointed around the room and assigned missions for each of them. "Olin will work on the GPS. At daybreak, Kouwe and Anna, our Indian experts, will act as intel. Gather as much information as possible. Manny, Carrera, and I'll search out where the repellent powder is stored. Zane, Rand, and Kelly will watch over Frank, ready him for a quick evac if necessary. While at the tree, it will be up to you three to collect a sample of the healing sap."

Slowly everyone nodded. If nothing else, it would keep them busy, keep their minds off the biological horrors hidden in the pristine valley.

Kouwe pushed to his feet. "I might as well get started. I'll chat with Dakii while he's alone down below."

"I'll go with you," Nate said.

Kelly moved toward them. "And I'm going to check on Frank one last time before full night falls."

The trio left the common room and crossed the deck to the ladder. The sun was only a sharp glow to the west. Dusk had rolled like a dark cloud over the glade.

In silence, the three descended the ladder in the gloom, each in a cocoon of their own thoughts.

Nate was the first one down and helped Kouwe and Kelly off the ladder. Tor-tor wandered over and nuzzled Nate for attention. He scratched absently at the tender spot behind the jaguar's ear.

A few yards away, the tribesman named Dakii stood.

Kouwe crossed toward him.

Kelly stared up at the Yagga, its upper branches still bathed in sunlight. In her narrowed eyes, Nate saw a wary glint.

"If you'll wait a moment, I'll go with you," he said.

She shook her head. "I'm fine. I've got one of the Rangers' radios. You should get some rest."

"But—"

She glanced over at him, her face tired and sad. "I won't be long. I just need a few minutes alone with my brother."

He nodded. He had no doubt the Ban-ali would leave her unmolested, but he hated to see her alone with such raw grief. *First her daughter, now her brother . . .* so much pain shone in every plane of her face.

She reached to him, squeezed his hand. "Thanks for offering, though," she whispered, and set off across the fields.

Behind Nate, Kouwe already had his pipe lit and was talking with Dakii. Nate patted Tor-tor's side and walked over to join them.

Kouwe glanced back at him. "Do you have a picture of your father?"

"In my wallet."

"Can you show it to Dakii? After four years spent with your father, the tribesmen must be familiar with recorded images."

Nate shrugged and pulled out his leather billfold. He flipped to a photo of his father, standing in a Yanomamo village, surrounded by village children.

Kouwe showed it to Dakii.

The tribesman cocked his head back and forth, eyes wide. "Kerl," he said, tapping at the photo with a finger.

"Carl . . . right," Kouwe said. "What happened to him?" The professor repeated the question in Yanomamo.

Dakii did not understand. It took a few more back-and-forth exchanges to finally communicate the question. Dakii then bobbed his head vigorously, and a complicated exchange followed. Kouwe and Dakii spoke rapidly in a mix of dialects and phonetics that was too quick for Nate to follow.

During a lull, Kouwe turned to Nate. "The others were slain. Gerald escaped the trackers. His background as a Special Forces soldier must have helped him slip away."

"My father?"

Dakii must have understood the word. He leaned in closer to the photograph, then back up at Nate. "Son?" he said. "You son man?"

Nate nodded.

Dakii patted Nate on his arm, a broad smile on his face. "Good. Son of *wishwa.*"

Nate glanced to Kouwe, frowning.

"*Wishwa* is their word for shaman. Your father, with his modern wonders, must have been considered a shaman."

"What happened to him?"

Kouwe again spoke rapidly in the mix of pidgin English and a mishmash of Yanomamo. Nate was even beginning to unravel the linguistic knot.

"Kerl . . . ?" Dakii bobbed his head, grinning proudly. "Me brother *teshari-rin* bring Kerl back to shadow of Yagga. It good."

"Brought back?" Nate asked.

Kouwe continued to drag the story from the man. Dakii spoke rapidly. Nate didn't understand. But at last, Kouwe turned back to Nate. The professor's face was grim.

"What did he say?"

"As near as I can translate, your father was indeed brought back here—dead or alive, I couldn't say. But then, because of both his crime and his *wishwa* status, he was granted a rare honor among the tribe."

"What?"

"He was taken to the Yagga, his body fed to the root."

"Fed to the root?"

"I think he means like fertilizer."

Nate stumbled back a step. Though he knew his father was dead, the reality was too horrible to fathom. His father had attempted to stop the corruption of the Ban-ali by the prehistoric tree, risking his own life to do so, but in the end, he had been fed to the damn thing instead, nourishing it.

Past Kouwe's shoulder, Dakii continued to bob his head, grinning like a fool. "It good. Kerl with Yagga. *Nashi nar!*"

Nate was too numb to ask what the last word meant, but Kouwe translated anyway.

"*Nashi nar.* Forever."

8:08 P.M.

In the jungle darkness, Louis lay in wait, infrared goggles fixed to his head. The sun had just set and true night was quickly consuming the valley. He and his men had been in position for hours.

Not much longer.

But he would have to be patient. *Make haste slowly,* he had been taught. One last key was needed before the attack could commence. So he lay on his belly, covered by the fronds of a fern, face smeared in streaks of black.

It had been a long and busy day. This morning, an hour after sunrise, he had been contacted by his mole. *His spy was still alive! What good fortune!* The agent had informed him that the Ban-ali village did indeed lie in a secluded valley, only approachable through the side canyon in the cliffs ahead. What could be more perfect? All his targets trapped in one place.

The only obstacle had been the valley's damned jaguar pack.

But his darling Tshui had managed to handle that nasty problem. Covered by the early morning gloom, she had led a handpicked team of trackers, including the German commando, Brail, into the valley's heart and planted poisoned meat, freshly killed and dripping with blood. Tshui had tainted each piece with a terrible poison, both odorless and tasteless, that killed with only the slightest lick. The pack, its blood lust already up from the attack upon the Rangers, found these treats too hard to resist.

Throughout the early morning, the great beasts dropped into blissful slumbers from which they would never wake. A few of the cats had remained suspicious and had not eaten. But hunting with the infrared goggles, Tshui and the others had finished off these last stubborn cats, using air guns equipped with poisoned darts.

It had been a quiet kill. With the way clear, Louis had moved his men into a guard position near the mouth of the side chasm.

Only one last item was needed, but he would have to be patient.

Make haste slowly.

At last, he spotted movement in the chasm. Through his infrared goggles, the two figures appeared as a pair of blazing torches. They slipped down the crude steps, alone. This morning, Louis had posted guards at the chasm mouth, ready to silence any tribesman who came down to scout for them. But none of the Ban-ali had shown their heads. Most likely the tribe's attention had remained focused on the strangers in their village, confident that the jaguar pack would keep them protected or alert them of any further intruders.

Not this day, *mes amis*. Something more predatory than your little pack has come to your valley.

The figures continued to thread down the chasm. Louis lowered his infrared goggles for a moment. Though he knew the figures were there, the black camouflage was so perfect that Louis could not spot them with his unaided eye. He slipped the goggles back in place and smiled thinly. The figures again blazed forth.

Ah, the wonders of modern science . . .

In a matter of moments, the two figures reached the bottom of the chasm. They seemed to hesitate. Did they sense something was amiss? Were they wary of the jaguars? Louis held his breath. Slowly the pair set out down the escarpment, ready for the night's patrol.

At last.

A new blazing figure stepped forth from the jungle, into their path. A slender torch that burned brighter than the other two. Louis lowered his goggles. It was Tshui. Naked. Ebony hair flowed in a silky waterfall to her shapely buttocks. She sidled toward the pair of scouts, a jungle goddess awoken from a slumber.

The pair of painted tribesmen froze in surprise.

A cough sounded from the bushes nearby. One of the Indians slapped his neck, then slipped to the ground. There was enough poison in each dart to drop a half-ton jaguar. The man was dead before his head hit the rocky ground.

The remaining scout stared for a moment, then fled as quickly as a snake toward the chasm. But Louis's mistress was even faster, her blood hyped on stimulants, her reflexes sharper. Effortlessly, she danced back into his path, blocking him. He opened his mouth to scream a warning, but again Tshui was quicker. She shot out her arm and tossed a handful of powder into his face, into his eyes, into his open mouth.

Reflexively choking, his call was gargled, more a strangled wheeze. He fell to his knees as the drug hit his system.

Tshui remained expressionless. She knelt beside her prey as the man toppled to the ground. She then stared over his body toward Louis's hiding place, a ghost of a smile on her lips.

Louis stood. They now had the final piece of the puzzle, someone to inform them about the tribe's defenses. Everything was now in place for the assault tomorrow.

Kelly sat cross-legged beside her brother's low hammock.

Wrapped in a thick blanket, Frank sipped weakly through a reed straw poking from a cantaloupe-sized hollow nut.

Kelly recognized it as one of the fruits that grew in clusters along the branches of the Yagga. The nut's content was similar to coconut milk. She had tasted it first when one of the tribesmen in the healing ward had brought it over to her brother. It was sweet and creamy with sugars and fats, an energy boost her brother needed.

She waited as Frank finished the contents of his natural energy drink and passed it to her, his hand trembling slightly. Though awake, his eyes were still hazy with a morphine glaze.

"How are you feeling?" she asked.

"Like a million bucks," he said hoarsely. His eyes twitched to the stumps hidden under the blanket.

"How's the pain?"

His brow furrowed. "No pain," he said with half a laugh, strained joviality. "Though I swear I can feel my toes itching."

"Phantom sensations," she said with a nod. "You'll probably feel them for months."

"An itch I can never scratch . . . great."

She smiled up at Frank. The mix of relief, exhaustion, and fear in her own heart was mirrored in her brother's expression. But at least his color had much improved. As horrible as their situation was here, Kelly had to appreciate the healing sap of the Yagga. It had saved her brother's life. His recovery had been remarkable.

Frank suddenly yawned, a true jawbreaker.

"You need to sleep," she said, getting to her feet. "Miraculous healing or not, your body needs to recharge its batteries." She glanced around and tucked in her shirt.

Around the cavernous chamber, only a pair of tribesmen remained in the room. One of them was the head shaman, who glared at her with impatience. Kelly had wanted to spend the night at her brother's side, but the shaman had refused. He and his workers, the tribesman had explained in stilted English, would watch over their new brother. "Yagga protects him," the shaman had said, brooking no argument.

Kelly sighed. "I had better go before I get kicked out."

Frank yawned again and nodded. She had already explained to him about tomorrow's plan and would see him at first light. He reached out and squeezed her hand. "Love you, sis."

She bent and kissed his cheek. "Love you, too, Frank."

"I'll be fine . . . so will Jessie."

Straightening, she bit her lip to hold back a sudden sob. She couldn't let go of her feelings, not in front of Frank. She dared not, or she'd never stop crying. Over the past day, she had bottled her grief tightly. It was the O'Brien way. Irish fortitude in the face of adversity. Now was not the time to dissolve into tears.

She busied herself with checking his intravenous catheter, now plugged with a heparin lock. Though he no longer needed fluid support, she kept the catheter in place in case of emergencies.

Across the way, the shaman frowned at her.

Screw you, she thought silently and angrily, *I'll go when I'm good and ready.* She lifted the blanket from over her brother's legs and made one final check on his wounds. The sap seal on the stumps remained tenaciously intact. In fact, through the semitransparent seal, she saw a decent granulation bed had already formed over the raw wounds, like the healing tissue under a protective scab. The rate of granulation was simply amazing.

Tucking back the blankets, she saw that Frank's eyes were already closed. A slight snore sounded from his open mouth. She very gently leaned over and kissed his other cheek. Again she had to choke back a sob, but couldn't stop the tears. Straightening up, she wiped her eyes and surveyed the room one final time.

The shaman must have seen the wet glisten on her cheeks. His impatient frown softened in sympathy. He nodded to her, his eyes intent, repeating a silent promise that he would watch closely over her brother.

With no choice, she took a deep breath and headed toward the exit. The climb back down the tree seemed interminable. In the dark passage, she was alone with her thoughts. Worries magnified and multiplied. Her fears bounced between her daughter, her brother, and the world at large.

At last, she stumbled out of the tree's trunk and into the open glade. An evening breeze had kicked up, but it was warm. The moon was bright overhead, but already scudding clouds rolled across the spread of stars. Somewhere in the distance, thunder rumbled. They would get rain before the morning.

In the freshening breeze, she hurried across the wide clearing, heading toward their tree. At its base, she spotted someone standing guard with a flashlight—Private Carrera. The Ranger pegged her with the light, then waved. At her side, Tor-tor lay huddled. The jaguar glanced up at her approach, sniffed the air, then lowered his head back to his curled body.

"How's Frank?" Carrera asked.

Kelly did not feel like talking but could not dismiss the soldier's concern. "He seems to be doing well. Very well."

"That's good." She jabbed a thumb to the ladder. "You should try to get as much sleep as possible. We've a long day ahead of us."

Kelly nodded, though she doubted sleep would come easily. She mounted the ladder.

"There's a private room on the third level of the dwelling left empty for you. It's the one on the right."

Kelly barely heard her. "Good night," she muttered and continued her climb, lost in her own worries.

At the top of the ladder, she found the deck empty, as was the common room. Everyone must have already retired, exhausted by the number of days with so little sleep.

Craning back, she stared at the dark upper stories, then crossed to the longer of the two secondary ladders.

Third level, Private Carrera had said.

Great . . . just what I get for being the last one to claim a room.

The third story was a good deal higher than the other two. Built on its own level of branches, it was more a separate structure, a two-room guest house.

Her legs aching, she mounted the long ladder. The wind began to kick up a bit as she climbed, whispering the branches, swaying the ladder ever so slightly. The gusts smelled of rain. Overhead, the moon was swallowed by dark clouds. She hurried up as the storm swept toward the village.

From this height, she saw lightning fork across the sky in a dazzling burst. Thunder boomed and echoed like a bass drum. Suddenly, living in a giant tree did not seem like such a wise choice. Especially the uppermost level.

She hurried as the first raindrops began pelting through the leaves. Pulling herself up onto the tiny deck, she rolled to her feet. The wind and rain grew quickly. Storms in the Amazon were usually brief, but they often came swiftly and fiercely. This one was no exception. Standing half crouched, she faced the doors that led to the two rooms on this level.

Which room had Carrera told her was hers?

Lightning crackled overhead in small angry spears, while thunder rattled. Rain swept in a sudden torrent, and breezes became fierce gusts. Under her feet, the planking rolled like the deck of a ship at sea.

Beyond caring if she woke someone, Kelly dove toward the nearest opening, half falling through the flap, seeking immediate shelter.

The room was dark. Lightning burst, shining brightly through a smaller back door to the chamber. The lone hammock in the room was thankfully empty. She stumbled gratefully toward it.

As she crossed toward the hammock, her feet tripped over something in the dark. She fell to her knees with a sharp curse. Her fingers reached back and discovered a pack on the floor.

"Who's there?" a voice asked from beyond the back door. A silhouetted figure stepped into the frame of the doorway.

On her knees, Kelly felt a moment of sheer terror.

Thunder echoed, and a new flicker of lightning revealed the identity of the dark figure. "Nate?" she asked timidly, embarrassed. "It's Kelly."

He crossed quickly to her and helped her to her feet. "What are you doing here?"

She wiped the wet strands of hair from her face, now burning hotly. *What a fool he must think I am.* "I . . . I stumbled into the wrong room. Sorry."

"Are you okay?" Nate's hands still held her arms, his palms warm through her soaked shirt.

"I'm fine. Just feeling especially foolish."

"No reason to be. It's dark."

Lightning crackled, and she found his eyes on hers. They stared at each other in silence.

Finally, Nate spoke. "How's Frank?"

"Fine," she said in a hushed voice. Thunder boomed distantly, rolling over them, making the world seem much larger, them much smaller. Her voice was now a whisper. "I . . . I never said . . . I was sorry to hear about your father."

"Thanks."

His single word, softly spoken, echoed with old pain. She moved a step toward him, unwilled, a moth drawn to a flame, knowing she would be destroyed but having no choice. His sorrow touched something inside her. That hard and fast wall around her heart weakened. Tears again welled in her eyes. Her shoulders began to tremble.

"Hush," he said, though she hadn't said a word. He pulled her closer to him, arms wrapping around her shoulder.

The trembling became sobs. All the grief and terror she had held in her heart released in a blinding torrent. Her knees gave out, but Nate caught her in his grip and lowered her to the floor. He held her tight, his heart beating against hers.

They remained on the floor in the center of the room as the storm raged outside, swaying the trees, booming with the clash of Titans. At last, she glanced up toward Nate.

She reached up to him and pulled his lips to hers. She tasted the salt of his own tears, of hers. At first, it was just survival in the face of the intense sorrow, but as their lips opened, an unspoken hunger awoke. She felt his pulse quicken.

He pulled away for a moment, gasping. His eyes were bright, so very bright in the darkness.

"Kelly . . ."

"*Hush,*" she sighed, using his own word. She pulled him back to her.

Wrapped in each other's arms, they lowered themselves to the floor. Palms explored . . . fingers loosened and peeled away damp clothes . . . limbs entwined.

As the storm hammered, their passions grew white hot. Grief faded away, lost somewhere between pain and pleasure, age-old rhythms and silent cries. They found the room too small, falling out onto the back deck.

Lightning rode the clouds, thunder roaring. Rain lashed under the awning, sweeping across their bare skin.

Nate's mouth was hot on her breast, on her throat. She arched into him, eyes closed, lightning flaring red through her lids. His lips moved to hers, hungry, their breath shared. Under the storm, under him, she felt the exquisite tension build inside her, at first slowly, then ever more rapidly, swelling through and out of her as she cried into his lips.

He met her cry with his own, sounding like thunder in her ears.

For an untold time, they held that moment. Lost to the world, lost to the storm, but *not* lost to each other.

Root

UNA DE GATO, "CAT'S CLAW"

FAMILY: *Rubiaceae*

GENUS: *Uncaria*

SPECIES: *Tomentosa, Guianensis*

COMMON NAMES: *Cat's Claw, Una de Gato, Paraguayo, Garabato, Garbato Casha, Samento, Toroñ, Tambor Huasca, Aun Huasca, Una de Gavilan, Hawk's Claw*

PART USED: *Bark, Root, Leaves*

PROPERTIES/ACTIONS: *Antibacterial, Antioxidant, Antiinflammatory, Antitumorous, Antiviral, Cytostatic, Depurative, Diuretic, Hypotensive, Immunostimulant, Vermifuge, Antimutagenic*

SIXTEEN

Betrayal

Nate woke to find his arms around a naked woman. Her eyes were already open. "Good morning," he said.

Kelly inched closer to him. He could still smell the rain on her skin. She smiled. "It's been morning for some time."

He rose to one elbow, which wasn't easy in a hammock, and stared down into her face. "Why didn't you wake me?"

"I figured you could use at least one full hour of sleep." She rolled out of the hammock, setting it swinging, and artfully drew off the single blanket and wrapped it around her.

With one hand, he grasped for her.

She stepped out of reach. "We have a long day ahead of us."

With a groan, he rolled to his feet and pulled his boxers from the pile of hastily discarded clothes as Kelly gathered her things. Through the rear door to the room, he stared out at the jungle.

Last night, he and Kelly had talked into the wee hours of the morning, about fathers, brothers, daughters, lives, and losses. There were still more tears. Afterward they had made love again, slower, with less urgency, but with a deeper passion. Sated, they had collapsed into the hammock to catch a few hours of sleep before dawn.

Stepping onto the rear deck, Nate studied the forest. The morning skies were blue and clear, last night's storm long gone, the light sharp and bright. Raindrops still clung to every leaf and blade, glistening like jewels. But that wasn't all. "You should see this," he called back to the room.

Kelly, now dressed in her khakis with her shirt half buttoned, joined him. He glanced to her, stunned again by her beauty. Her eyes widened as she stared beyond the deck's edge. "How marvelous . . ."

She leaned into him, and he instinctively circled her with his arm.

Covering the upper limbs of the tree, drawn by the moisture, were hundreds of butterflies, perched on branches and leaves, fluttering through the bower. Each had wings about a handspan wide, brilliant blue and crystalline green.

"*Morpho* species," Nate said. "But I've never seen this color pattern."

Kelly watched one specimen waft by overhead through a beam of sunlight. It seemed to shine with its own luminescence. "It's like someone shattered a stained-glass window and showered the slivers over the treetops."

He tightened his arm around her, trying to capture this moment forever. They stood in silence and awe for several minutes. Then distant voices intruded, rising up from below.

"I suppose we should go down," Nate finally said. "We have a lot to accomplish."

Kelly nodded and sighed. Nate understood her reluctance. Here, isolated above everything else, it was possible to forget, at least for a while, the heartaches and hardships ahead of them. But they could not escape the world forever.

Slowly, they finished dressing. As they were about to leave, Nate crossed to the rear deck and unhooked the bamboo-and-palm-leaf awning so it fell back across the rear door, returning the room to the way he found it.

Kelly noticed what he did and moved nearer, examining the hinges along the top margin of the door. "Closed, it blocks the doorway . . . pushed open and stilted, it's a shade cover for the deck. Clever."

Nate nodded. Yesterday he had been surprised by the ingenuity, too. "I've never seen anything like it out here. It's like my father mentioned in his notes. An example of the tribe's advancement over other indigenous peoples. Subtle engineering improvements, like their crude tree elevators."

"I could use an elevator right now," Kelly noted, stretching a kink from her back. "It does make you wonder, though," she went on, "about the Yagga—about what it's doing to these people."

Nate grunted in agreement, then turned to reassemble his own pack. There was *much* to wonder about here. Once ready, Nate gave the room a final inspection, then crossed to the door where Kelly crouched.

As Kelly slung her pack to her shoulder, Nate leaned in and kissed her deeply. There was a moment of surprise . . . then she returned the kiss with a matching passion. Neither of them had spoken of where the two would go from here. Both knew much of their urgency last night had come from a pair of wounded hearts. But it was a start. Nate looked forward to seeing where it would lead. And if her kiss was a clue, so did Kelly.

They parted, and without another word, they headed to the ladder leading down to the common areas of the dwelling.

As Nate descended, cooking scents swelled around him. He reached the bottom rung and hopped off. After helping Kelly down, they both walked through the common area to the large front deck. Nate's stomach growled, and he suddenly remembered his hunger.

Around a stone hearth set into the deck, Anna and Kouwe were finishing the final preparations for breakfast. Nate spotted a loaf of cassava bread and a tall stone pitcher of cold water.

Anna swung around with a platter of honest-to-goodness bacon in her arms. She lifted her bounty. "From wild boar," she explained. "A pair of tribeswomen arrived with a feast at daybreak."

Nate's mouth watered. There was also more fruit, some type of egg, even what looked like a pie.

"No wonder your father stayed here for so long," Private Carrera mumbled around a mouthful of bacon and bread.

Even this reminder of his father failed to squelch Nate's appetite. He dug in along with the rest.

As he stuffed himself, Nate realized two of their party were missing. "Where are Zane and Olin?"

"Working on the radio," Kostos said. "Olin got the GPS up and running this morning."

Nate choked on a piece of bread. "He got it working!"

Kostos nodded, then shrugged. "He has it recalibrated, but who knows if anyone's receiving."

Nate let this information sink in. His eyes flicked to Kelly. If the signal was received with the revised coordinates, they could be rescued as soon as this evening. Nate recognized the glimmer of hope in Kelly's eyes, too.

"But without the main radio to confirm," Kostos continued, "we may just be spittin' in the wind. And until I get solid confirmation, we proceed with our backup plan. Your mission today—along with Kelly and Zane—will be to make sure Frank is ready for a quick evac if necessary."

"Plus to gather some of the tree's sap," Kelly said.

Kostos nodded, chewing hard. "While Olin works on the radio, the others of us will split up and see if we can't find out more from the Indians. Get intel on those damned repellent powders."

Nate didn't argue with the sergeant's plan. GPS or not, it was safest to proceed as cautiously and expeditiously as possible. The remainder of the meal was finished in silence.

Afterward, the party vacated the dwelling in the nightcap oak and climbed down to the glade, leaving Olin alone in the dwelling with his satellite equipment. Manny and the two Rangers headed in one direction, Anna and Kouwe in another. The plan was to rendezvous back at the tree at noon.

Nate and Kelly headed toward the Yagga with Richard Zane in tow. Nate hitched his shotgun higher. The sergeant had insisted every member of the party go armed with at least a pistol. Kelly had a 9mm holstered at her waist. Zane, ever suspicious, had his Beretta in hand, eyes darting all around.

In addition to the weapons, each of the three teams had been equipped with one of the Rangers' short-range Saber radios, to keep in contact with one another. "Every fifteen minutes, I want to hear an all-clear from each group," Kostos had said dourly. "No one stays silent."

Prepared as well as they could be, the group split up.

As Nate walked across the glade, he stared up at the giant prehistoric gymnospore. Its white bark glistened with dew, as did its leaves, flickering brightly. Among the tiered branches, the clusters of giant nut pods hung, miniature versions of the man-made huts. Nate was anxious to see more of the giant tree.

They reached the thick, knobbed roots, and Kelly guided them between the woody columns to the open cavity in the trunk. As Nate approached, he could appreciate why the natives called their tree Yagga, or Mother. The symbolism was not lost to him. The two main buttress roots were not unlike open legs, framing the tree's monstrous birth canal. It was from here that the Ban-ali had been born into the world.

"It's big enough to drive a truck through," Zane said, staring up at the arched opening.

Nate could not suppress a small shudder as he entered the shadowy heart of the tree. The musky scent of its oil was thick in the passage. All around the lowermost tunnel, small blue handprints decorated the wood wall, hundreds, some large, others small. Did they represent members of the tribe? Did his own father's palm mark this wall somewhere?

"This way," Kelly said, leading them toward the passage winding up the tree.

As Nate and Zane followed, the blue prints disappeared eventually.

Nate glanced along the plain walls, then back toward the entrance. Something was bothering him, but he couldn't exactly put his finger on it. Something didn't look right. Nate studied the flow channels in the wood, the tubules of xylem and phloem that moved water and nutrients up and down the trunk. The channels ran down in graceful, winding curves around the passage walls. But down below, where the passage bluntly ended, the flow channels were jagged, no longer curving smoothly. Before he could examine this further, the group had passed beyond the tunnel's curve.

"It's a long climb," Kelly said, pointing ahead. "The healing chamber is at the very top, near the crown of the tree."

Nate followed. The tunnel looked like some monstrous insect bore. In his study of botany, he was well familiar with insect damage to trees: mountain pine beetle, European elm bark beetle, raspberry crown borer. But this tunnel had not been cored out—he would stake his life on it. It had formed naturally, like the tubules found inside the stems and trunk of an ant tree, an evolutionary adaptation. But even this raised a new question. Surely this tree was centuries older than the first arrival of the Ban-ali to this region. So why did the tree grow these hollowed tubules in the first place?

He remembered Kelly's muttered words at the end of last night's group discussion. *We're missing something . . . something important.*

They started passing openings through the tree's trunk to the outside. Some led directly into huts, others led out onto branches with huts beyond. He counted as they climbed. There had to be at least twenty openings.

Behind him, Zane reported in on the Saber radio. All was well with the other teams.

At last, they reached the end of the passage, where it ballooned out into a cavernous space with slits cut high in the walls to allow in the sunlight. Still, the chamber was dim.

Kelly hurried over to her brother.

The small shaman stood across the room, checking on another patient. He glanced up at their approach. He was alone. "Good morning," he said in stiff English.

Nate nodded. It was strange knowing these words were most likely taught to the man by his own father. He knew from reading his father's notes that this shaman was also the Ban-ali's nominal leader. Their class structure here was not highly organized. Each person seemed to know his place and role. But here was the tribe's king, the one who communed closest with the Yagga.

Kelly knelt at Frank's side. He was sitting up and sucking the contents of one of the tree's nuts through a reed straw.

He set his liquid meal aside. "The breakfast of champions," he said with his usual good-natured smirk.

Nate saw he still wore his Red Sox cap—and nothing else. He had a small blanket over his lower half, hiding his stumped legs. But he was bare-chested, revealing plainly what was painted there.

A crimson serpent with a blue handprint in the center.

"I woke up with it," Frank said, noticing Nate's gaze. "They must have painted it on me during the night when I was drugged out."

The mark of the Ban-ali.

The shaman stepped to Nate's side. "You . . . son of *Wishwa* Kerl."

Nate turned and nodded. Apparently their guide, Dakii, had been telling tales. "Yes, Carl was my father."

The shaman king clapped him on the shoulder. "He good man."

Nate did not know how to respond to this. He found himself nodding while really wanting to rip into the shaman. *If he was such a good man, why did you murder him?* But from working and living with indigenous tribes throughout the region, he knew there would never be a satisfactory answer. Among the tribes, even a good man could be killed for breaking a taboo—one could even be honored by being turned into plant fertilizer.

Kelly finished her examination of Frank. "His wounds have entirely sealed. The rate of granulation is amazing."

Her expression must have been clear to the shaman. "Yagga heals him. Grow strong. Grow—" The shaman frowned, clearly struggling to remember a word. Finally, he bent down and slapped his own leg.

Kelly stared at the shaman, then at Nate. "Do you think it's possible? Could Frank's legs really grow back?"

"Gerald Clark's arm regenerated," Nate said. "So we know it's possible."

Kelly crouched. "If we could watch the transformation in a modern medical facility . . ."

Zane interrupted her, lowering his voice and keeping his back toward the shaman. "Remember, we have a mission here."

"What mission?" Frank asked.

Kelly quietly explained.

Frank brightened. "The GPS is working! Then there's hope."

Kelly nodded.

By now, the shaman had wandered off, losing interest in them.

"In the meantime," Zane hissed, "we're supposed to gather a sample of the sap."

"I know where it comes from," Kelly said, nodding toward a channel carved deep into the wall. Shielded by the two men, she picked up the empty nut drained by her brother and pulled out the straw. She crossed to the wall and removed a small wooden plug. A thick red sap began to flow into the channel. She bent the nut's opening into the flow and began collecting the sap. It was slow work.

"Let me," Zane said. "You look after your brother."

Kelly nodded and stepped to Nate. "The stretcher is still here," she said, pointing an arm to the makeshift travois. "When and if we get the signal, we'll have to move fast."

"We should—"

The first explosion shocked them all. Everyone froze as the blast echoed away. Nate stared at the open slits high up the curved walls. It was not thunder. Not from blue skies. Then more and more booms followed. Beyond the roar, sharper cries arose.

Screams.

"We're under attack!" Nate exclaimed.

He turned and found a pistol pointed at him.

"Don't move," Zane said, crouching by the wall, a tight and scared expression on his face. He held the nut, now overflowing with sap, cradled in one arm, and the 9mm Beretta in the other. "No one move."

"What are you—" Kelly began.

Nate interrupted, immediately understanding. "You!" He remembered Kouwe's suspicions: *other trackers on their trail, a spy among them.* "You goddamn bastard. You sold us out!"

Zane slowly stood. "Back away!" The pistol was held rock steady on them.

Beyond the tense room, explosions continued to boom. Grenades.

Nate pulled Kelly away from Zane's threatening gun.

Behind them, the shaman suddenly bolted toward the opening, frightened by the explosions, oblivious to the closer threat. A sound of alarm rose on his lips.

"Stop!" Zane screamed at the tribesman.

The shaman was too panicked to listen or to comprehend the stranger's tongue. He continued to run.

Zane twitched his gun and fired. In the enclosed space, the blast was deafening. But not so deafening as to drown out the cry of surprise from the shaman.

Nate glanced over his shoulder. The shaman fell on his side, clutching his belly, gasping. Blood flowed from around his fingers.

Red with anger, Nate turned on Zane. "You bastard. He couldn't understand you."

The gun again pointed at them. Zane slowly circled around, keeping his weapon aimed. He even kept a safe distance from Frank's hammock, not taking any chances. "You were always the gullible fool," the Tellux man said. "Just like your father. Neither of you understood anything about money and power."

"Who are you working for?" Nate spat.

Zane now had his back to the exit. The shaman had rolled into a moaning ball off to the side. Zane stopped and motioned with his pistol. "Toss your weapons out the window slits. One at a time."

Nate refused to budge, shaking with rage. Zane fired, blasting wood chips from between Nate's toes.

"Do as he says," Frank ordered from the hammock.

Scowling, Kelly obeyed. She freed her pistol from its holster and flung it out one of the windows.

Nate still hesitated.

Zane smiled coldly. "The next bullet goes through your girlfriend's heart."

"Nate . . ." Frank warned from the bed.

Teeth clenched, Nate edged to the wall, weighing his chances of firing at Zane. But the odds weren't good, not with Kelly's life at risk. He unslung his gun and heaved it through one of the slits.

Zane nodded, satisfied, and backed toward the exit. "You'll have to excuse me, but I have a rendezvous to make. I suggest you three remain here. It's the safest spot in the valley at the moment."

With those snide words, Zane slipped out of the chamber and disappeared down the throat of the tunnel.

8:12 A.M.

Deep in the jungle, Manny ran alongside Private Carrera. Tor-tor raced beside them, ears flattened to his skull. Explosions ripped through the morning, smoke wafted through the trees.

Kostos ran ahead of them, screaming into his radio. "Everyone back to home base! Rally at the dwelling!"

"Could they be our people?" Manny asked. "Responding to the GPS?"

Carrera glanced back at him and frowned. "Not this quick. We've been ambushed."

As if confirming this, a trio of men, dressed in camouflage gear and armed with AK-47s and grenade launchers, trotted into view.

Kostos hissed and waved them all down.

They dropped to their bellies.

An Indian ran at the group with a raised spear. He was nearly cut in half by automatic fire.

Tor-tor, spooked by the chattering gunfire, bolted forward.

"Tor-tor!" Manny hissed, rising to one knee, reaching for the cat.

The jaguar dashed into the open, across the path of the gunmen.

One of them barked something in Spanish and pointed. Another grinned and lifted his weapon, eyeing down the barrel.

Manny raised his pistol. But before he could fire, Kostos rose up ahead of him, the M-16 at his shoulder, and popped off three shots, three squeezes of the trigger. *Blam, blam, blam.*

The trio fell backward, heads exploding like melons.

Manny froze, stunned.

"C'mon. We need to get back to the tree." Kostos scowled at the jungle. "Why the hell aren't the others responding?"

8:22 A.M.

Kouwe kept Anna behind him as he hid behind a bushy fern. Dakii, the tribal guide, crouched beside him. The four mercenaries stood only six yards away, unaware of the eyes watching them. Though Kouwe had heard the sergeant's order to regroup at the nightcap oak, with the marauders so near, he dared not signal his acknowledgment. They were pinned down. The group of mercenaries stood between them and the home tree. There was no way to get past them unseen.

Behind him, Dakii crouched as still as a stone, but the tension emanating from him was fierce. While hidden, he had watched more than a dozen of his tribesmen—men, women, children—mowed down by this group.

Further in the wood, explosions continued to boom. They heard screams and the crash of dwellings from the treetops. The marauders were tearing through the village. The only hope for Kouwe's party was to flee to some sheltered corner of the jungled plateau, hope to be overlooked.

One of the soldiers barked into a radio in Spanish. "Tango Team in position. Killzone fourteen secure."

Kouwe felt something brush his knee. He glanced over. Dakii motioned for him to remain in place. Kouwe nodded.

Dakii rolled from his side, moving swiftly and silently. Not a single twig was disturbed. Dakii was *teshari-rin,* one of the tribe's ghost scouts. Even without his paint, the tribesman blended into the deeper shadows. He raced from shelter to shelter, a dark blur. Kouwe knew he was witnessing a demonstration of the Yagga's enhancement of its wards. Dakii circled around the band, then even Kouwe lost track of him.

Anna grabbed his hand and squeezed. *Have we just been abandoned?* she seemed to silently ask.

Kouwe wondered, too, until he spotted Dakii. The tribesman crouched across the way. He was in direct sight of Kouwe and Anna, but still hidden from the four guards.

Dakii rolled to his back in the loam, aiming the small bow he had found high into the air. Kouwe followed where his arrow pointed. Then back down to the mercenaries.

He understood and motioned for Anna to be ready with her own weapon. She nodded, staring up, then back down, understanding.

Kouwe signaled Dakii.

The tribesman pulled taut his bowstring and let fly an arrow. A tiny *twang* was heard, as was the louder rip of arrow through leaf. The mercenaries all turned in Dakii's direction, weapons raised.

Kouwe ignored them, his gaze focused above. High in the branches was the ruin of a dwelling, but left intact among the branches was one of the little ingenious inventions of the Ban-ali, one of their makeshift elevators. Dakii's arrow sliced the support rope that held aloft a cradled counterweight, a large chunk of granite.

The boulder came crashing down, straight at the group of mercenaries.

One was smashed under its weight, his face crushed as he glanced up a moment too late.

Kouwe and Anna were already on their feet. From such close range, they emptied their pistols at the remaining trio, striking chests, arms, and bellies. The group fell. Dakii rushed out, an obsidian dagger in his hand. He ran at the mercenaries and slit the throats of any who still moved. It was quick and bloody work.

With a hand, Kouwe steadied Anna, who had paled at the display. "We have to get back to the others."

From the height of the chasm, Louis had a wide view of the isolated valley. A pair of binoculars hung around his neck, forgotten. Across the jungle, smoke rose from countless fires and signal flares. In just over an hour, his team had encircled the village and were now closing slowly toward the center, toward his goal and prize.

Brail, who had been assigned as his new lieutenant after Jacques disappeared, spoke near his feet. The tracker knelt over a map, marking off small *X*'s as his units reported in. "The net's secure, *Herr Doktor*. Nothing left now but mopping up."

Louis could tell the man was anxious to bag his own limit here.

"And the Rangers? The Americans?"

"Herded toward the center, just as you ordered."

"Excellent." Louis nodded to his mistress at his side. Tshui was naked, armed only with a little blowgun. Between her breasts rested the shrunken head of Corporal DeMartini, hung around Tshui's neck by the man's own dog tags.

"Then it's time we joined the party." He lifted his twin pair of snub-nosed mini-Uzis. They felt powerful in his hands. "It's high time I made the acquaintance of Nathan Rand."

"You watch over your brother and the shaman," Nathan said, sensing time was running out. "I'm going after Zane."

"You don't have a weapon." Kelly knelt beside the shaman. With Nathan's help, the two had wrangled the tribesman into a hammock. Kelly had shot him full of morphine, quieting his pained thrashing. A belly wound was one of the most agonizing. With no better solution, she was now slathering the entry and exit wounds with Yagga sap. "What are you going to do if you catch him?"

Nate felt a fire in his own belly, just as agonizing as a bullet wound. "First he betrayed my father, now he betrayed us." His voice choked with anger. He wanted only one thing from the man. *Vengeance.*

Frank spoke from his hammock. "What are you going to do?"

Nathan shook his head. "I have to try."

He headed toward the exit. Distantly the explosions had died down, but gunfire spat sporadically. The fewer the shots, the more obvious it became that the village was being wiped out. Nate knew they would fare no better, not unless something was done. But what?

Stalking down the passage, at first cautiously, then faster and faster, around and around, Nate was reminded of the serpentine pattern of the Ban-ali symbol, winding in a spiral. Could this passage be what the symbol represented, or was it what Kelly had conjectured earlier, a crude representation of the twisted protein model, the mutagenic prion? If it represented the Yagga's tunnel, what did the helixes at each end of the spiral mean? Did one depict the healing ward? And if so, what did the other represent? And the blue handprint? Nate recalled the painted handprints decorating the entrance to the passage and shook his head. What did it all mean?

He ran around a corner and stumbled over a dead Indian lying in the tunnel. Nate fell to his hands, skidding on his knees. Once stopped, he rolled around and saw the bullet hole in the man's chest and a second in the back of his head.

Nate looked down and saw another body, just its legs, around the next curve. Another Indian.

Zane.

Nate scrambled to his feet, his blood on fire. The man was picking off the unarmed stragglers here, healers and aides to the shaman, brutally clearing a bloody path to the tunnel's end. *The fucking coward.*

Nate shoved down the tunnel, counting off the openings on his left. When he reached the last one, he ducked out of the passage and through a small, empty dwelling. He found himself on a branch at least five feet thick. Before continuing, he needed some idea of what was happening below. Smoke billowed and wafted through the open glade.

In the clearing around the tree, a few Indians retreated toward the Yagga.

By now, an ominous quiet had settled over the village.

Nate edged along the branch, but he couldn't get a good look across the glade toward the nightcap oak and his team's temporary homestead. The branch pointed the wrong way. He couldn't even spy the entrance to the Yagga. *Damn it.*

Pistol fire sounded from below. Zane! A scream erupted from the field on the tree's far side. The coward must be hiding down at the tunnel's end, killing any Indians who neared. Nate knew the bastard had enough ammo to hold them off for a while.

The Indians in direct sight below fled toward the cover of the thicker wood.

Nate stared across the glade. There was no sign of his friends.

As Nate sidled along the thick limb, his toe nudged a rope coiled atop the branch. He looked closer. Not rope, he realized, but one of the vine ladders.

"A fire escape," he mumbled. An idea flashed into his mind—a plan forming.

Before he lost his nerve, he shoved the piled vine over the edge.

The ladder unrolled with a whispery sound until it snapped to its full length, only three feet from the ground. It was a long climb, but if Zane was down there, perhaps Nate could sneak up on him.

With no more plan than that, Nate mounted the ladder and began a hurried climb earthward. He raced down the rungs. If his group and the remaining Indians could fall back here, they might have a more defensible position. But before that could happen, Zane had to be eliminated.

Nate reached the end of the ladder and hopped off.

Tall roots rose all around him, and it took Nate a moment to orient himself. The stream was behind and off to the left. That meant he was about at the four o'clock position from the tunnel entrance. He began to wind counterclockwise around the trunk.

Three o'clock . . . two o'clock . . .

Somewhere off in the forest, a spatter of automatic gunfire erupted. Another grenade exploded. Clearly the fighting had not entirely ceased in some parts of the village.

Using the cover of the noise, Nate crawled and edged his way around the tree's base. At last, he spotted one of the tall buttress roots that flanked the entrance. *One o'clock.*

Nate leaned against the trunk. Zane was beyond the obstruction . . . but how to proceed from here was the tricky part. Another pistol shot rang out from Zane's bunker. Nate frowned down at his empty hands.

What plan now, hero boy?

9:34 A.M.

Zane knelt on one knee, aiming out with his pistol. Tiring, he supported his weapon arm with his other. But he refused to let down his guard, not when victory was so close. He only had to hold out a little longer, then his role in this mission would be over.

One eye twitched to the nut full of the miraculous sap. It was a fortune worth billions. Though St. Savin Pharmaceuticals had made a sizable deposit in Zane's Swiss account to buy his cooperation, it was the promised bonus of a quarter percentage point of gross sales that had finally sold him on the betrayal. With the potential in the Yagga's sap, there was no limit to the wealth that could flow his way.

Zane licked his lips. His role here was almost at an end. Days ago, he had successfully slipped the computer virus into the team's communication equipment. Now all that remained was the final endgame.

Late last night, Favre had instructed Zane to obtain a sample of the sap and protect it with his life. "If those damn natives pull some jackass stunt," Louis had warned, "like setting fire to their precious tree to protect their secret, then you're our fail-safe."

Zane had, of course, agreed, but unknown to his murderous partner, Zane had his own backup plan in mind, too. Once secure here, Zane had poured a small sample of the sap from the nut, sealed it in a latex condom, tied it off, and swallowed it. An extra bit of insurance on his own part. Any betrayal and a competing pharmaceutical company, like Tellux, would find itself in possession of the miraculous substance instead of St. Savin.

Distant rifle shots sounded from the woods. He spotted flashes of muzzle fire. Favre's men were cinching the noose. It would not be long.

As if confirming this, a grenade exploded at the glade's fringe. A dwelling in one of the huge trees blew apart, casting leaf and branch high into the air. Zane smiled—then he heard a voice within the echo of the blast. It sounded close.

"Watch out! Grenade!"

Something hit the trunk of the tree just over his head and bounced into the flanking root. *Grenade!* his mind echoed.

With a cry of alarm, he dove away from the entrance and rolled deeper into the shaft, arms shielding his head. He waited several tense seconds, then several more. He panted, ragged from the near escape. The expected explosion never came. Cautiously uncovering his head, he clenched his teeth. Still no blast.

He sat up, crawled slowly back toward the entrance, and peeked around the corner, where he spotted the small coconut-shaped object resting in the dirt. It was just one of the immature nut pods from the damn tree! It must have fallen from an overhead branch.

"Goddamn it!" He felt foolish at his panic.

He straightened, raising his weapon, and stepped back to his guard position. *Getting too damn jumpy . . .*

A blur of motion.

Something solid struck his wrist. The pistol flew from his fingers as his wrist exploded with pain. He started to fall backward—then his arm was grabbed by someone stepping from the blind side of the entrance. He was yanked out of the entrance and thrown bodily forward.

His shoulder hit the dirt. He rolled and stared back around. What he saw was impossible. "Rand? How?"

Nathan Rand towered over him at the entrance to the tunnel, a long, thick section of branch in his hand, which he raised menacingly.

Zane crab-crawled backward.

"How?" Nate asked. "A little lesson from our Indian friends. The power of suggestion." Rand kicked the immature seed pod toward him. "Believe something strongly enough, and others will believe, too."

Zane scrambled to his feet.

Nate swung the branch like a bat, striking him on the shoulder and knocking him back down. "That was for the shaman you shot like a dog!" Nate lifted the branch again. "And this is for—"

Zane glanced over Nate's shoulder. "Kelly! Thank God!"

Nate turned half around.

Using the moment of distraction, Zane shot to his feet and darted away. He cleared the side root in three steps.

He heard the blistering protest behind him and smiled.

What a . . .

. . . fool! Tricked by his own damn ruse! No one stood at the tunnel entrance. Kelly was not there.

Nate watched Zane race around the thick buttress. "No, you don't, you bastard!" With club in hand, he gave chase.

Still ringing with anger, Nate flew around the tree and spotted Zane fleeing along the base of the trunk, toward a tangle of roots. The traitor could easily get lost among them and escape. Nate thought of going back for the abandoned pistol, but he didn't have the time. He dared not lose sight of the bastard.

Ahead, Zane ducked under an arched root and wriggled through agilely. He was one wiry son of a bitch. In this race, Zane's smaller frame and lighter build were advantageous.

Realizing they were matched now fist to fist, Nathan tossed aside his club and pursued Zane. They fought through the snarl, crawling, climbing, leaping, squirming their way through the tangled maze. Zane was making headway on him.

Then the roots opened. They both stumbled onto some path amid the mess. Zane ran, pounding down the trail. Nate swore and went after him.

Ahead, water glistened. As they raced along the snaking trail, Nate saw the path ended at a wide pool, blocking the way. A dead end.

Nate smiled. *End of the line, Zane!*

As they neared the pool, his quarry also realized he had run himself into a blind alley and slowed—but instead of a groan of defeat, Nate heard a snarl of glee.

Zane leaped to the side, diving for the ground.

Nate closed the distance.

Zane swung to face him, a gun in hand. A 9mm Beretta.

It took Nate a startled moment to fathom this miracle. Then he saw his own shotgun, hanging by its shoulder strap from a rootlet a few steps to his right. The pistol was Kelly's! One of the weapons Zane had made them toss out of the treetop.

Nate groaned. The gods were not smiling on him. He took a step toward his shotgun, but Zane clucked his tongue.

"Move another inch, and you get a third eye!"

9:46 A.M.

Kouwe herded Anna ahead of him. The crack of rifle fire was closing all around them. Dakii led the way, expressionless, in scout mode. He wound with calm assurance through his village forest, guiding them back toward the nightcap oak. They needed to rendezvous with the Rangers. Put together some semblance of a plan.

Kouwe had been able to contact Sergeant Kostos over the radio and inform him of their status. He had also learned that Olin, left up in the dwelling, had been able to report in, too. The Russian was keeping himself well hidden in the tree. But so far no word had come from Nate's party. He prayed they were okay.

At last, Kouwe spotted sunlight ahead. The central glade! His team had been circling around from the south, keeping within the jungle cover. According to the sergeant, the Rangers were angling down from the north side.

Dakii slowed and pointed from a half crouch.

Anna and Kouwe moved up with him. Through a break in the foliage, Kouwe spotted the small log cabin in the clearing. He was able to orient himself. He followed the tribesman's arm. The nightcap oak, their destination, lay only fifty yards ahead. But that was not what Dakii was pointing out. Beyond the giant oak, Kouwe spotted Tor-tor. The jaguar raced along the clearing's edge. Drawn by the motion, Kouwe was able to see figures moving through the deeper shadows.

The Ranger team and Manny! They had made it back!

Dakii led them onward, speeding deftly through the glade's fringe.

In a few minutes, the two parties reunited at the base of the tree. Sergeant Kostos clapped Kouwe on the shoulder. Anna and Manny hugged.

"Any word from Nate?" Kouwe asked.

The sergeant shook his head, then waved to the dwelling. "I've ordered Olin to pack up his GPS and join us."

"Why? I thought the plan was to rendezvous at the tree."

"This is close enough. As near as I can tell, we're boxed in. The tree is no protection."

Kouwe frowned but understood. The marauders were systematically destroying every dwelling. They'd be trapped up there. "What then?"

"We bug out of here. Find a way through their line as silently as possible. Once past them, we'll seek shelter, somewhere where they can't find us."

Manny edged closer to them, glancing at his watch. "The sergeant set one of his napalm bombs back in the woods, timed to explode in another fifteen minutes."

"A distraction," Sergeant Kostos said. He hiked his pack on his shoulder. "And we have more if we need them."

"It's why we can't wait for Nate," Manny said, reading his friend's eyes.

Kouwe gazed at the Yagga. The sound of gunfire was trickling away . . . as was their time. If they were going to have any chance, they would have to take it now. Kouwe reluctantly nodded, conceding.

Overhead, the vine ladder shuddered. He glanced up. Olin was climbing down, his radio pack in place.

Kostos waved his M-16. "Let's get ready to—"

The blast rocked them all to their knees. Kouwe swung around and watched the roof of the cabin sail high into the air. Bits of debris blew outward with tremendous force. A section of log shot by overhead, a flying battering ram, slicing into the jungle and crashing into its depths. Smoke billowed outward.

That was no grenade blast.

Through the smoke, a cadre of soldiers appeared, weapons raised and ready.

Kouwe noticed two things simultaneously. First, walking in the lead was a naked woman, hand in hand with a tall gentleman dressed all in white.

But the second thing Kouwe noted was of more immediate menace, something carried by one of the soldiers. The man dropped to a knee and lifted a long black tube on his shoulder.

Kouwe had seen enough Hollywood movies to recognize the weapon. "*Rocket launcher!*" Carrera screamed behind him. "Everyone down!"

The first blast had frozen both Nate and Zane in place. Nate kept focused on his adversary's weapon. From only a few yards away, the pistol was pointing square at his chest. He dared not move. He held his breath.

What was going on out there?

As the second blast sounded, Zane's eyes twitched in the direction of the explosion. Nate knew he wouldn't have another chance. He was dead unless he did something . . . even something stupid.

Nate lunged through the air, not toward Zane, but toward the dangling shotgun. His movement did not go unnoticed. Nate heard the sharp report of Zane's pistol and felt something sting his upper thigh, but he didn't stop.

His body struck the root, his arms scrambling for the shotgun. He didn't have time to unhook the strap. From where it hung, he just blindly swung the barrel in Zane's general direction and yanked the trigger. Recoil tore the weapon from his hand.

Nate ducked and swung around.

He saw Zane flying backward, his belly bloody, arms flung out. Zane landed in the small pond at the end of the blocked trail. He sputtered to the surface—the water was surprisingly deep, even near shore—and cried in alarm and pain.

Zane was now learning the lesson he had taught the unarmed Ban-ali shaman: a belly shot was one of the most agonizing.

Nate pushed up and unhooked his shotgun. He pointed it at the floundering man. He had not seen where the pistol had gone and was taking no chances this time.

Zane, his face a mask of torment, struggled toward the shore. Then his body suddenly jerked, his eyes widened in shock. His moaning turned to fresh screams. "Nate! Help me!"

Responding instinctively, Nate took a step forward.

Zane reached toward him, face pleading, terrified—then all around his body, the waters erupted in a fierce churning.

Nate caught several flashes of silver bodies. *Piranhas*. He backed away, realizing where he was: the birthing pool, the hatchery that Manny had described finding.

Zane thrashed, jerking and twitching, screeching. He began to sink into the froth. His eyes rolled with panic as he fought to keep his mouth above water. He failed. His head sank away. Only one arm remained above the pool—then even this disappeared under the roiling waters.

Nate turned from the pool and crossed down the path, feeling no pity for the man. He briefly checked the stinging burn in his thigh. He found a bullet hole in his pants and a trickle of blood. Just a graze, nothing more. He had been damned lucky.

He clenched the shotgun in his grip and marched down the trail, praying his luck would hold.

10:12 A.M.

Manny shifted under a pile of debris, shoving with his shoulders. Smoke choked him. The explosion of the rocket in the treetop still rang in his head. It hurt to move his jaw. He crawled free amid shouts and yells. All commands.

"Throw down your weapons!"

"Show us your hands!"

"Move now, or I'll shoot you dead where you lie!"

That was incentive enough. Manny groaned and spat out blood. He glanced up into chaos. He saw Anna Fong on her knees, hands on her head. She looked all but unscathed. Professor Kouwe knelt at her side, bearing a scalp gash that dripped blood down his cheek. Dakii was also there, wearing an expression of stunned disbelief.

Turning, Manny saw Tor-tor's spotted face peering out from under a bush. He motioned the jaguar to stay put. Near the same bush, he watched Private Carrera furtively shove her Bailey under a section of the roof thatch from one of the abodes above.

"You!" someone barked. "On your feet!"

Manny didn't know who the man was talking to until he felt the hot barrel of a gun on his temple. He froze.

"On your feet!" the man repeated. His words were heavily accented, German perhaps.

Manny clambered to his knees, then to his feet. He wobbled, but this seemed to satisfy the mercenary.

"Your weapon!" he barked.

Manny glanced around him as if searching for a missing shoe or sock. He saw his pistol lying there and nudged it with a toe. "There."

A second soldier appeared out of nowhere and confiscated it.

"Join the *anderen*!" the man said with a shove toward the others.

As he stumbled toward his kneeling friends, Manny saw Carrera and Kostos escorted by other guards. Their holsters were empty, packs gone. They were all forced to their knees, hands on their heads. The sergeant's left eye was swollen, his nose crooked and bloodied, broken. Kostos had clearly put up more fight than Manny.

Suddenly a distant section of deeper forest blew up into a ball of fire. The soft explosion echoed out to them, along with the smell of napalm.

So much for Kostos's planned "distraction." Too little, too late.

"Herr Brail, this one's not moving!" one of the mercenaries shouted behind them in a mix of German and Spanish.

Manny glanced back to the base of the nightcap oak. It was Olin. He lay in a crumpled heap. A spear of wood had pierced through his shoulder and blood flowed brightly across his light khaki shirt. Manny saw he was still breathing.

The one named Brail tore his gaze from the burning forest and wandered over to check on the Russian. "*Hundefleisch,*" the German said. *Dog meat.* He lifted his pistol and shot Olin in the back of the head.

Anna jumped at the noise, a sob escaping her.

From near the ruins of the log cabin, the two leaders of the attack force casually wandered toward them. The small Indian woman, though naked, moved casually, as if through a garden party, all curves and smooth legs. She wore a talisman resting between her breasts. Manny had first thought it was a leather satchel, but as she neared, he recognized it as a shrunken head. The hair atop the disgusting trinket was shaved.

The slender man at her side, dressed in white khakis and a rakish Panama hat, noticed his attention. He lifted the necklace for the others' view.

Manny spotted the dog tags.

"May I reintroduce you to Corporal DeMartini." He laughed lightly, as if he had made a joke, a party amusement, and dropped the defiled head of their former teammate back to the woman's chest.

Sergeant Kostos grumbled a threat, but the AK-47 pointed at the nape of his neck kept him on his knees.

Louis smiled at the line of kneeling prisoners. "It's good to see you all together again."

Manny recognized a distinctly French accent. *Who was this man?*

Professor Kouwe answered his silent question. "Louis Favre," the professor mumbled under his breath, his expression sickened.

The Frenchman's gaze swung to Kouwe. "That's *Doctor* Favre, *Professor* Kouwe. Please let's keep this courteous, and we can be done with this unpleasant matter as quickly as possible."

Kouwe simply glowered.

Manny knew the man's name. He was a biologist banned from Brazil for black-market profiteering and for crimes against the indigenous people. The professor, along with Nate's father, had shared an infamous past with this man.

"Now, we've counted heads here and seem to have come up a few short," Favre said. "Where are the last members of your little troupe?"

No one spoke.

"Come now. Let's keep this friendly, shall we? It's such a pleasant day." Favre marched up and down the row of prisoners. "You don't want this to turn ugly now, do you? It's a simple question."

Still no one moved. Everyone stared blankly forward.

Favre shook his head sadly. "Then ugly it is." He turned to the woman. "Tshui, *ma chérie*, take your pick." He brushed his hands primly as if done with the matter.

The naked woman stalked before them, and hesitated before Private Carrera, cocking her head, then suddenly sprang two places over to kneel before Anna. Her nose was only an inch from the anthropologist's.

Anna recoiled, but the gun behind her held her in place.

"My darling has an eye for beauty."

Moving as quickly as a striking snake, the Indian woman drew a long, slender bone knife from a sheath hidden in her long tresses. Manny had seen knife sheaths like this braided into the hair of warriors in only one Amerindian tribe: the Shuar, the headhunters of Equador.

The bleached-white knife pointed into the tender flesh under Anna's chin. The Asian woman trembled. Red blood dribbled down the white blade. Anna gasped.

Enough, Manny thought, reacting reflexively. His right hand dropped to his waist, settling atop the handle of the short bullwhip. *He* could also move quickly when he wanted, reflexes developed from years of taming a wild cat. With skilled fingers, he snapped out with the whip.

The tip of the leather struck the bone knife, sending it flying, and nicked a cut under the Shuar woman's eye.

Like a cat, she hissed and rolled away, wounded. A second knife appeared in her hand as if by magic. It seemed this cat had many claws.

"Leave Anna be!" Manny yelled. "I'll tell you where the others are!" Before he could say anything else, Manny was clubbed from behind, knocked to his face in the dirt and leaves. A foot kicked his whip away, then stomped on the offending hand, snapping a finger.

"Drag him up!" Favre barked, all traces of his genteel mannerisms falling away.

Manny was hauled up by his hair. He cradled his injured hand to his chest.

Favre stood by the Indian woman and wiped the blood from her cheek. Favre turned to Manny and licked the blood from his fingertip.

"Now was that necessary?" he asked, and reached a hand behind him. One of the gunmen placed a snub-nosed rifle in his palm. Some type of miniature Uzi, from the looks of it.

The fist in Manny's hair twisted hard.

"Release him, Brail," Favre said.

The hand let go of him. Unsupported, Manny almost sagged to his face again.

"Where are they?" Louis asked.

Manny bit past the pain. "In the tree . . . the last time we saw them . . . they've not responded to our radios."

Favre nodded. "So I heard." He reached his free hand and pulled out a matching radio. "Corporal DeMartini was gracious enough to lend me his Saber and supply me with the proper radio frequencies."

Manny frowned. "If you knew . . . why . . . ?" He glanced over to Anna.

A long sigh followed, exasperated and bored. "Just making sure no one was attempting some deceptive tactic. It seems I've lost contact with my own agent in your party. And that always arouses my suspicious nature."

"Agent?" Manny asked.

"Spy," Kouwe said from the end of the row of prisoners. "Richard Zane."

"Indeed." Favre turned toward the tree and raised the radio to this mouth. "Nate, if you can hear me, stay put. We'll be coming over to join you."

There was no answer.

Manny hoped somehow Nate had fled with Kelly. But in his heart, he knew Kelly would never leave her brother's side. All of them must still be hiding in the ancient tree.

As the Frenchman stared at the white-barked giant, his eyes narrowed. After a moment, he swung back and focused on Manny again. "That leaves me only to address the insult upon my lady here."

The stubby Uzi again was raised in his direction.

"Not very gentlemanly of you, Monsieur Azevedo."

Favre pulled the trigger. Shots rattled and sprayed out.

Manny winced, but not a bullet struck him.

A grunt sounded behind him. The guard at his back collapsed into view, his upper body riddled. He lay on the ground, gasping like a beached fish. Blood poured out from his mouth and nose.

Favre lowered his weapon. Manny stared up at the Frenchman. Favre cocked one eyebrow. "It's not you I blame. Brail should have minded you better. He should never have left that damn whip at your side. Sloppy, sloppy work." Louis shook his head. "Two lieutenants gone in the same number of days."

He turned away and waved his weapon. "Bring the prisoners." He strode toward the Yagga. "I'm done chasing after Carl's boy. Let's see if we can coax the shy fellow to come out and join us."

Nate hid in the shadow of the Yagga's buttress root. Smoke clouded the glade. He heard intermittent gunfire and muffled shouts from the direction of the nightcap oak. *What was going on?*

The only object within sight inside the glade was the cratered husk of his father's log cabin. A mingled sense of dread and despair settled over his body like a shroud. Then, like ghosts from a grave, figures appeared out of the smoke, shadowy and vague.

He slipped deeper into the root's shadow, leveling his shotgun in their direction. Slowly, with each step, the apparitions took form and substance. He recognized Manny and Kouwe in the lead, guarding Anna between them. Kostos and Carrera flanked them, a step behind. Even the tribesman, Dakii, marched with them.

Blood stained all of them and they walked with their hands behind their backs, stumbling, prodded from behind by shadowy figures. As they approached, the others grew clearer: men in a mix of military and jungle fatigues. They had weapons of every ilk pointed at his friends.

Nate aimed down the barrel of his shotgun. A useless weapon against these odds, these numbers. He needed another plan. But for now, he only had stealth and shadows.

His teammates were drawn to a stop by their guards.

A man dressed all in white lifted a small bullhorn to his lips. "Nathan Rand!" he bellowed, aiming for the Yagga's treetop. "Show yourself! Come out freely or your friends will pay for your absence. I will give you two minutes!"

His teammates and the Indian were forced to their knees.

Nate lowered himself further into hiding. Without a doubt, the man out there was the leader of these mercenaries, a Frenchman judging from his accent. The man glanced at his watch, then back up to the treetop, tapping a toe impatiently. He clearly thought Nate was still in the upper bowers, relying on the last bit of intelligence from his dead spy.

Nate wavered. Show himself or flee? Should he take his chances in the woods? Perhaps try to get around behind the soldiers? Nate mentally shook his head. He was no guerrilla warrior.

"Thirty seconds, Nathan!" the man roared through the bullhorn.

A tiny voice echoed down from above. "Nate's not up here! He left!"

It was Kelly!

The Frenchman lowered his bullhorn. "Lies," he muttered under his breath.

Kouwe spoke up from where he knelt. "Dr. Favre . . . a word with you, please."

Nate found his fingers tightening on his shotgun, instantly recognizing the name. He had heard tales from his father about the atrocities attributed to Louis Favre. He was the bogeyman of the Amazon, a devil whispered about among the tribes, a monster banished from the region by his own father. But now here again.

"What is it, Professor?" Favre asked with irritation.

"That was Kelly O'Brien. She's with her injured brother. If she says Nate's not up there, then he's not."

Favre frowned and checked his watch. "We'll see." He raised his bullhorn. "Ten seconds!" He then held out a palm, and a wicked weapon was handed to him: a curved machete as long as a scythe. Even in the smoky sunshine, it shone brightly—freshly sharpened.

Favre leaned and placed the curve of the blade under Anna Fong's neck, then lifted the bullhorn. "Time is running out, Nathan! I've been generous giving you an initial two minutes. From here on out, every minute will cost a friend's life. Come out now, and all will be spared! This I swear as a gentleman and a Frenchman." Favre counted the last seconds. "*Five . . . four . . .*"

Nathan struggled for some plan . . . anything. He knew Louis Favre's sworn word was worthless.

"*Three . . . two . . .*"

He had seconds to come up with an alternative to submission.

"*One . . .*"

He found none.

"*Zero!*"

Nathan rose out of his hiding place. He stepped out with his shotgun over his head. "You win!" he called back.

Favre straightened from his crouch over Anna, one eyebrow raised. "Oh, *mon petit homme,* how you startled me! What were you doing down here all along?"

Tears flowed down Anna's stricken face.

Nate threw his shotgun away. "You win," he said again. Soldiers trotted around to circle him.

Favre smiled. "So I always do." His lips turned from amused to feral.

Before anyone could react, Favre twisted from the hip and swung the machete with all the force of his arm and back.

Blood flumed upward.

His victim's head was shorn clean off at the neck.

"Manny!" Nate cried out, falling to his knees, then his hands.

His friend's body collapsed backward.

Anna screamed, swooning into Kouwe's side.

With his back to Nate, Favre faced the shock and dismay of the other prisoners. "Please, did any of you truly think I'd let Monsieur Azevedo strike my love without recourse? *Mon Dieu!* Where's your chivalry?"

Beyond the kneeling line, Nate saw the Indian woman touch a gash on her cheek.

Favre then turned back around to face Nate. His white outfit was now decorated with a crimson sash of Manny's blood. The monster tapped his wristwatch and waggled a finger at him. "And, Nathan, the count *did* reach zero. You *were* late. Fair is fair."

Nathan hung his head, sagging toward the ground. "Manny . . ."

Somewhere in the distance, a feline howl pierced the morning, echoing over the valley.

SEVENTEEN

Cure

Louis surveyed the final preparations in the valley. He carried his soiled field jacket over one arm, his shirtsleeves rolled up. The afternoon turned out to be a scorcher—but it would get hotter here, much hotter. He smiled grimly, satisfied, as he stared over the ruins of the village.

A Colombian soldier named Mask snapped to attention at his approach. The fellow, standing well over six feet, was as lethal as he was tall. A former bodyguard for the captain of a drug cartel, the swarthy man had taken a face full of acid protecting his boss. His skin was a boiled mass of scar tissue on one side. He had been fired afterward by his ungrateful ward, too ugly and too awful a reminder of how close death had come. Louis, on the other hand, respected the man's show of stalwart loyalty. He made an excellent replacement for Brail.

"Mask," Louis said, acknowledging the man, "how much longer until all the charges are set in the valley?"

"Half an hour," his new lieutenant answered sharply.

Louis nodded and glanced at his watch. Time was critical, but everything was on schedule. If that Russian hadn't gotten that damned GPS working and a signal transmitted, Louis would have had more time to enjoy his victory here.

Sighing, Louis surveyed the field before him. There were eighteen prisoners in all, on their knees, hog-tied with their hands behind their backs and secured to their crossed ankles behind them. A loop of rope ran from the bindings and encircled their necks. A strangler's wrap. Struggle against your knots and the noose tightened around your neck.

He watched a few of the prisoners already gasping as the ropes dug deep. The others sat sweating and bleeding under the hot sun.

Louis noticed Mask still standing at his side. "And the village has been scoured?" he asked. "There are no more of the Ban-ali?"

"None living, sir."

The village had numbered over a hundred. Now they were just one more lost tribe.

"How about the valley? Has it been thoroughly scouted?"

"Yes, sir. The only way onto or off this plateau is the chasm."

"Very good," Louis said. He had already known this from torturing the Ban-ali scout last night, but he had wanted to be sure. "Do one last sweep through all stations. I want to be out of here no later than five o'clock."

Mask nodded and turned smartly away. He strode swiftly toward the giant central tree.

Louis followed him with his eyes. At the tree, two small steel drums were being rolled out of the trunk's tunnel. After the valley had been secured, men with axes and awls had hiked up inside the tree, set deep taps into the trunk, and drained large quantities of the priceless sap. As the men pushed the drums into the field, Louis studied another team laboring around the base of the giant Yagga tree. His eyes narrowed.

Everything was running with a clockwork precision. Louis would have it no other way.

Satisfied, he strode over to the line of segregated prisoners, the survivors of the Ranger team, baking and burning under the sun. They sat slightly apart from the remaining members of the Ban-ali tribe.

Louis stared at his catch, slightly disappointed that they hadn't offered more of a challenge. The two Rangers glared back at him murderously. The small Asian anthropologist had calmed significantly, eyes closed, lips moving in prayer, resigned. Kouwe sat stoically. Louis stopped in front of the last prisoner in the lineup.

Nathan Rand's gaze was as hard as the Rangers', but there was a glint of something more. A vein of icy determination.

Louis had a hard time maintaining eye contact with the man, but he refused to look away. In Nathan's face, he saw a shadow of the man's father: the sandy hair, the planes of the cheek, the shape of his nose. But this was not *Carl* Rand. And to Louis's surprise, this disappointed him. The satisfaction he had expected to feel at having Carl's son kneeling at his feet was hollow.

In fact, he found himself somewhat respecting the young man. Throughout the journey here, Nathan had demonstrated both ingenuity and a stout heart, even dispatching Louis's spy. And finally, here at the end, he had proven his loyalty, with a willingness to sacrifice his own life for his team. Admirable qualities, even if they were directed at cross purposes to Louis's own.

But finally, it was those eyes, as hard as polished stone. He had clearly known inconsolable grief and somehow survived. Louis remembered his elderly friend from the bar back at his hotel in French Guiana, the survivor of the Devil's Island penal system. Louis pictured the old man sipping his neat bourbons. The chap had the same eyes. These were not *Carl* Rand's eyes, his father's eyes. Here was a different man.

"What are you going to do with us?" Nate said. It was not a plea, but a simple question.

Louis removed a handkerchief from his pocket and wiped his brow. "I swore as a gentleman that I wouldn't kill you or your friends. And I will honor my word."

Nate's eyes narrowed.

"I'll leave your deaths to the U.S. military," he said sadly, the emotion surprisingly unfeigned.

"What do you mean?" Nate asked suspiciously.

Louis shook his head and took two steps to reach Sergeant Kostos. "I think that question should be answered by your companion here."

"I don't know what you're talking about," Kostos said with a glower.

Louis bent down at the waist and stared into the sergeant's face. "Really . . . are you saying Captain Waxman didn't confide in his staff sergeant?"

Kostos glanced away.

"What is he talking about?" Nate asked, directing the question to the sergeant. "We're well past secrets now, Kostos. If you know something . . ."

The sergeant finally spoke, awkward with shame. "The napalm minibombs. We were under orders to find the source of the miraculous compound. Once a sample was secured, we were to destroy the source. Total annihilation."

Louis straightened, enjoying the shocked expressions on the others' faces. Even the female Ranger looked surprised. It seemed the military liked to keep its secrets to only a select few.

Raising an arm, Louis pointed back to the small group of men gathered around the giant tree. They were his own demolitions team. Against the white bark of the trunk, the Rangers' remaining nine minibombs appeared like flat black eyes peering toward them. "Thanks to the U.S. government, there's enough firepower here to wipe out even a giant monster of a tree like this one."

Kostos hung his head, as well he should.

"So you see," Louis said, "our two missions are not so different. Only who benefits—the U.S. military complex or a French pharmaceutical company. Which in turn raises the question, who would do the greater good with the knowledge?" He shrugged. "Who can say? But conversely, we might ask—who would do the greater harm?" Louis eyed the sergeant. "And I think we can all answer that one."

A distinct quiet settled over the group.

Nate finally spoke. "What about Kelly and Frank?"

Ah, the missing members of the group . . . Louis was not surprised it was Nate who brought up the question. "Don't worry about their health. They'll be coming with my party," Louis explained. "I've been in contact with my financiers. Monsieur O'Brien will prove an ideal guinea pig to investigate this regenerative process. The scientists at St. Savin are itching to get their hands and instruments on him."

"And Kelly?"

"Mademoiselle O'Brien will be coming along to make sure her brother cooperates."

Nathan paled.

During the discourse, Louis had noticed Nate's gaze flick toward the tree. He waved an arm back to the giant. "The timers are set for three hours from now. Eight o'clock, to be precise," Louis said. He knew everyone here had seen the force of a *single* napalm bomb. Multiplied by nine, he watched the hopelessness settle into their faces.

Louis continued, "We've also seeded other incendiary bombs through-out the canyon, including the chasm leading up here, which we'll explode as soon as we vacate the area. We couldn't risk the possibility that we missed an Indian hidden up here who might free you. And I'm afraid, tied up or not, there's no escape. This entire isolated valley will become one mighty firestorm—destroying all remnants of the miracle sap and acting as a bonfire in the night to attract any helicopters winging this way. A fiery diversion to cover our flight."

The utter defeat in their eyes shone dully.

Louis smiled. "As you can see, it's all well planned."

Behind him, Louis's lieutenant approached briskly and stopped at his shoulder. The Colombian ignored the prisoners as if they were mere sheep.

"Yes, Mask?"

"All is in order. We can evacuate at your word."

"You have it." Louis glanced again at the line of men and women. "I'm afraid duty calls. I must bid you all a fond *adieu*."

Turning away, Louis felt a twinge of satisfaction, knowing that it was ultimately the young man's father, Carl Rand, who had truly brought his proud son to his doom. *Following in his father's footsteps . . .*

He hoped the old man was watching from hell.

4:55 P.M.

Nate knelt with the others, beaten and crushed by the news. He watched dully as the camp organized for their departure.

Kouwe spoke at his shoulder. "Favre has placed all this faith in the Yagga's sap."

Nate turned his head, careful of the noose around his neck. "What does it matter now?"

"He expects it to cure the contagion, like it does physical wounds, but we've no proof it can."

Nate shrugged. "What do you want us to do?"

"Tell him," Kouwe said.

"And help him? Why?"

"It's not him I'm trying to help. It's all those out in the world dying of the disease. The cure to the contagion lies here. I feel it. And he's going to destroy it, wiping out any chance to stop the curse of the Ban-ali. We must try to warn him."

Nate frowned. In his mind, he saw Manny's murder . . . his friend's body falling to the dirt. He understood in his mind what Kouwe was suggesting, but he just couldn't get his heart to go along with it.

"He won't listen anyway," Nate said, seeking some compromise between heart and mind, some justification for remaining silent. "Favre's operating under a strict timetable. He has another six to eight hours at the most before a military response is mustered. All he can do is plunder what he can and run."

"We must make him listen," Kouwe insisted.

Raised voices echoed to them from the Yagga. Both men glanced toward the tunnel in the trunk. A pair of mercenaries strode out with a stretcher between them. Nate recognized their own makeshift travois and Frank tied on top. He was bound like a trussed pig, ready for the spit.

Next came Kelly, walking on her own, her hands tied behind her back. She shuffled beside Favre and his naked Indian mistress. They were all trailed by additional gunmen.

"You don't know what you're doing!" Kelly argued loudly. "We don't know if the sap can cure anything!"

Nate heard their own argument from a moment ago.

Louis shrugged. "St. Savin will have paid me long before it's ever discovered if you're right or not. They'll look at your brother's legs—or what's left of them—and shovel the contracted millions into my account."

"What about all those dying? The children, the elderly."

"What do I care? My grandparents are already dead. And I have no children."

Kelly blustered hotly, then her eyes fell on the group of her friends. Her face crinkled in confusion. She glanced ahead to the trail of thirty or so men marching out of the valley, then back at the group of prisoners.

"What's going on?" she asked.

"Oh, your friends . . . they'll be staying here."

Kelly stared at the ring of explosives set around the tree, then over to them, her eyes settling on Nate. "You . . . You can't just leave them here."

"I can," Louis said. "I certainly can."

She stumbled to a stop, her voice soft with tears. "At least, let me say good-bye."

Louis sighed with dramatic exasperation. "Fine. But make it quick." He took Kelly by the upper arm and guided her out of line, accompanied by his mistress and four armed guards.

Louis shoved her in front of them.

Nate's heart ached at seeing her. It would've been better if she had simply continued past them.

Tears rolled down her face. Kelly shuffled before each of them and said how sorry she was—as if all this were her fault. Nate barely listened, drinking up the sight of her with his eyes, knowing this would be the last time he ever saw her. She bent and placed her cheek against Professor Kouwe's, then moved to Nate at the end of the line.

She stared down at him, then dropped to her knees. "Nate . . ."

"Hush," he said with a sad smile, the word a secret reminder of their night together. "Hush."

Fresh tears flowed. "I heard about Manny," she said. "I'm so sorry."

Nate closed his eyes and bowed his head. "If you get a chance," he said under his breath, "kill that French bastard."

She leaned into him, sliding her cheek next to his. "I promise," she whispered at his ear, like a lover sharing a secret.

He turned his face and met her lips, not caring who saw. He kissed her one last time. She met his kiss, gasping between their joined lips.

Then she was torn away, yanked to her feet by Favre. He had a hand clenched around her arm. "It would seem you two have been sharing more than just a *professional* relationship," he said with a sneer.

Favre whipped Kelly around and kissed her hard on the mouth. She cried out in surprise and shock. Louis released her, throwing her back toward the Indian woman. Blood dripped from his lip.

Kelly had bitten him.

He wiped his chin. "Don't worry, Nathan. I'll take good care of your woman." He glanced back to Kelly and his mistress. "Tshui and I will make sure her stay with us is an enjoyable one. Won't we, Tshui?"

The Indian witch leaned closer to their prisoner and fingered a curl of Kelly's auburn hair, sniffing at it.

"See, Nathan. Tshui is already intrigued."

Nate struggled to lunge at the man, fighting his bonds. "You bastard," he hissed, choking as the strangle noose tightened.

"Calm yourself, my boy." Louis stepped back, putting an arm around Kelly. "She's in good hands."

Tears of frustration rolled down his face. His breath was a ragged gasp as the noose dug into the flesh of his neck. Still he struggled. He would die anyway. What did it matter if he strangled or burned?

Louis glanced down at him sadly, then dragged Kelly away. The man mumbled as he left, "A shame . . . such a nice boy, but so much tragedy in his life."

Nate began to see stars dancing at the edges of his blackening vision.

Kouwe hissed at Nate. "Stop struggling, Nate."

"Why?" he gasped.

"Where there is life, there is hope."

Nate sagged in his bonds, not so much finding significance in the professor's words as simple defeat. His breathing became incrementally easier. He stared after the retreating mercenary band, but his eyes stayed focused on Kelly. She glanced back one time, just before disappearing into the jungle fringe. Then she was gone.

The group remained silent, except for a mumbled prayer from Anna. Behind them, a few of the Indian prisoners had begun to sing a mournful melody, while others simply cried. They continued to sit, with no hope, baking under the sun as it trailed toward the western horizon. With each breath or sob, their deaths drew nearer.

"Why didn't he just shoot us?" Sergeant Kostos mumbled.

"It's not Favre's way," Professor Kouwe answered. "He wants us to appreciate our deaths. A slow torture. It excites the bastard."

Nate closed his eyes, defeated.

After an hour, a huge explosion shattered off to the south. Nate opened his eyes and watched a thick column of smoke and rock dust blast into the sky.

"They blew the chasm," Carrera said at the other end of the line.

Nate turned away. The explosion echoed for a few seconds, then died away. All of them now waited for one last explosion, the one that would take their lives and burn through the valley.

As silence again descended over them, Nate heard a distinctive cough from the forest's edge. A *jaguar's* cough.

Kouwe glanced over to Nate.

"Tor-tor?" Nate asked, experiencing a twinge of hope.

From the jungle's edge, a jaguar pushed into the open glade. But it was not the spotted face of their friend's pet.

The huge black jaguar slunk into the open, sniffing, lips pulled back in a silent and hungry snarl.

5:35 PM.

Kelly walked beside Frank's stretcher. The two bearers seemed tireless, marching through the jungles of the lower canyon like muscled robots. Kelly, with no burden except for her heavy heart, found her feet stumbling over every root and branch.

Favre had set a hard pace for the group. He wanted to reach the swamp lake and disappear into the forests south of it before the fiery explosion ripped through the upper canyon.

"After that, the military will be flocking there like flies on shit," Favre had warned. "We must be well gone."

Kelly had also eavesdropped on the chatter among the mercenary grunts, spoken in a patois of Portuguese and Spanish. Favre had radioed ahead and arranged for motor boats to meet them at a river only a day's march from here. Once there, they would quickly speed away.

But first they had to get to the rendezvous spot without getting caught—and that meant speed was essential. Favre would brook no laggers, including Kelly. The monster had confiscated Manny's bullwhip, snapping it periodically as he moved through the line, like a slavemaster overseeing his crew. Kelly already had a taste of its stinging touch, when she had fallen to her knees as the chasm had exploded behind them. She had been so wrung with hopelessness, she had not been able to move. Then fire had lit her shoulder. The whip had split her shirt and stung her skin. She knew better than to falter from that point on.

Frank spoke from his stretcher. "Kelly . . ."

She leaned down toward him.

"We'll get out of this," he said, slurring. Despite her brother's earlier protests, she had given him a jolt of Demerol before being transported from the Yagga's healing ward. She hadn't wanted him to suffer by their manhandling. "We'll make it."

Kelly nodded, wishing her arms were untied so she could hold her brother's hand. But under the blanket, even Frank's limbs were secured by ropes to the stretcher.

Frank continued with his bleary attempt at consoling her. "Nate . . . and the others . . . they'll find a way to break free . . . rescue . . ." His words drifted into a morphine haze.

Kelly glanced behind them. The sky was mostly blocked by the canopy overhead, but she could still spot the smudge of smoke from the explosion, closing off the upper valley from the lower. She hadn't told her brother about the incendiary devices set throughout the primitive forest. They could expect no help from their old teammates.

Kelly eyed Favre's back as he marched ahead.

Her only hope now was for *revenge*.

She intended to keep her promise to Nate.

She would kill Louis Favre . . . or die trying.

5:58 P.M.

Nate watched the giant black jaguar stalk into the open glade. It was alone. Nate recognized it as the leader of the pack, the sly female. She must have somehow survived Louis's mass poisoning and instinctively returned to the valley of her birth.

Sergeant Kostos groaned under his breath, "This day just gets better and better."

The great beast eyed the bound prisoners, ready-packed meals. Without the repellent black powder, even the Ban-ali were at risk. The black feline god, created by the Yagga to protect them, had just turned feral.

The beast crept toward them, low to the ground, tail flicking.

Then a flash of fire drew Nate's attention over the cat's muscled shoulder. Tor-tor loped out of the jungle in its shadow. Showing no sign of fear, Tor-tor raced past the larger cat and rushed at Nate and the others.

Nate was knocked on his side by the cat's show of exuberance. With his master dead, Tor-tor was clearly relieved to rejoin them, seeking consolation, reassurance.

Nate choked on his tightening noose. "Th . . . That's a good boy, Tor-tor."

The large black cat hung back, watching the strange display.

Tor-tor rolled against him, wanting a pet, something to let him know all was okay. Nate, tied up, couldn't comply—but an idea formed.

Nate rolled around, earning a further twist of his noose, and held the ropes out toward the jaguar. Tor-tor sniffed at his bindings. "Bite through them," Nate urged, shaking his bound wrists. "Then I'll pet you, you big furry lug."

Tor-tor licked Nate's hand, then nosed him in the shoulder.

Nate groaned with frustration. Nate glanced over his shoulder. The giant black cat padded over to him and nudged Tor-tor aside with a small growl.

Nate froze.

The monster sniffed at the hand that Tor-tor had licked, then gazed up at Nate with those penetrating black eyes. He was sure it could smell the abject fear in the man curled at its feet.

Nate remembered how it had torn Frank's limbs off in a single swooping attack.

The jaguar lowered its head to Nate's arms and legs. A rumble sounded through it. Nate felt a fierce tug and was lifted off the ground, strangling in the noose. For a momentary flash, Nate wondered if he would be strangled before being eaten. He prayed for the former.

Instead, Nate found himself dropped back to the ground. He cringed a moment, then realized his arms were loose. Taking advantage of the opportunity, Nate rolled away with a kick and a twist. He sat up, glancing to the severed ropes dangling from his wrists. The cat had freed him.

Nate yanked at the constricting noose.

The large black jaguar watched him. Tor-tor brushed the giant cat's flank, a clear display of affection, and crossed to Nate.

After working free the noose, Nate tossed it aside. His ankles were still bound, but before he could free his legs, he had a friend to thank.

Tor-tor shoved into him, bowing his furry head into Nate's chest.

He scratched that special spot behind both ears, earning a rumbled purr of satisfaction. "That's a good boy . . . you did good."

A small sad whine flowed from the cat.

Nate pulled Tor-tor's head up and stared into those golden eyes. "I loved Manny, too," Nate whispered.

Tor-tor nuzzled his face, snuffling.

Nate endured it, making small soothing sounds to the cat. Eventually Tor-tor backed a step away. Nate was able to free his ankles.

Beyond Tor-tor, the giant black jaguar sat on its haunches. Tor-tor must have run into the female after Manny's death. He must have directed her here. Manny had been proven right a couple nights back. Some bond must have developed between the two young cats. Perhaps the ties had grown even deeper by their shared grief: Tor-tor for his master, the female for her pack.

Nate stood and freed Kouwe. Together they unbound the others. Nate found himself untying the ropes from Dakii's limbs. Here was the Indian scout who had been principally responsible for sending the piranhas and locusts upon their party. But Nate could no longer touch his old anger. The Indian had only been protecting his people—and as it turned out, rightly so. Nate helped Dakii up, staring at the smoky ruins of the village. Who were the true monsters of the jungle?

Dakii hugged Nate tightly.

"Don't thank me yet," Nate said. Around the glade, the other Indians were being untied, but Nate focused on the booby-trapped tree with its nine napalm bombs chained around its trunk.

Sergeant Kostos passed by, rubbing his chafed wrists. "I'm going to see about disarming the charges. Carrera's off to see if she can find the weapon she hid."

Nate nodded. Nearby, the freed Ban-ali gathered around the two jaguars. Both cats were now lounging in the shade, seemingly oblivious to the audience. But Nate noticed the larger female watching everything through slitted eyes. The cat was not letting its guard down.

Anna and Kouwe stepped over to join him. "We're free, but what now?" the professor asked.

Nate shook his head.

Anna crossed her arms.

"What's wrong?" Nate asked, noticing her deeply furrowed brow.

"Richard Zane. If we ever get out of this mess, I'm quitting Tellux."

Nate smiled despite their situation. "I'll be right behind you with my own letter of resignation."

After a bit, Sergeant Kostos strode back to them, wearing his usual scowl. "The bombs are all hardwired and booby-trapped. I can't stop the detonation sequence or remove the devices."

"There's nothing you can do?" Kouwe asked.

The Ranger shook his head. "I have to give that French bastard's team some credit. They did a great job, damn them."

"How much time?" Anna asked.

"Just under two hours. The digital timers are set to blow at eight o'clock."

Nate frowned at the tree. "Then we'll either have to find another way out of this valley or seek some type of shelter."

"Forget shelter," Kostos said. "We need to be as fucking far from here as possible when those babies blow. Even without the additional incendiaries placed by Favre's men, those nine napalmers are enough to fry this entire plateau."

Nate took him at his word. "Where's Dakii? Maybe he knows another way out of here."

Kouwe pointed to the entrance to the Yagga. "He went to check on the status of his shaman."

Nate nodded, remembering the poor man who had been shot in the gut by Zane. "Let's go see if Dakii knows anything helpful."

Kouwe and Anna followed him.

Sergeant Kostos waved them on. "I'll keep examining the bombs. See if I can come up with anything."

Once inside the tree's entrance, Nate again was struck by the scent, musky and sweet. They followed the blue handprints up the tunnel.

Kouwe marched at Nate's side. "I know escape is foremost on everyone's mind, but what about the contagious disease?"

"If there's a way out," Nate said, "we'll collect as many plant specimens as time allows. That's all we can do. We'll have to hope we stumble on the correct one."

Kouwe looked pensive, not satisfied with Nate's answer, but had no other rebuttal. A cure discovered here would do the world no good if they themselves didn't survive.

As they continued to wend their way up the tree, the sound of footfalls echoed down to them. Nate glanced to Kouwe. Someone was coming.

Dakii suddenly appeared around the corner, winded and wide-eyed. He was startled to find them in front of him. He spoke rapidly in his own tongue. Even Kouwe couldn't entirely follow it.

"Slow down," Nate said.

Dakii grabbed Nate's arm. "Son of *wishwa,* you come." He tugged Nate toward the upper tunnel.

"Is your shaman okay?"

Dakii bobbed his head. "He live. But sick . . . very big sick."

"Take us to him," Nate said.

The Indian was clearly relieved. They hurried up at a half trot. In a short time, the group entered the healing ward at the top.

Nate spotted the shaman in one of the hammocks. He was alive but did not look well. His skin was yellowish and shone with fever sweat. *Very big sick, indeed.*

As they approached, the prone man sat up, though clearly it pained him immensely to do so. The shaman waved to Dakii, ordering him across the room on an errand, then stared at Nate. He was glassy-eyed but lucid.

Nate noticed the ropes lying on the floor under the hammock. Even gravely injured, the man had been bound by Favre.

The shaman pointed at Nate. "You *wishwa* . . . like father."

Nate opened his mouth to say no. He was certainly no shaman. But Kouwe interrupted. "Tell him yes," the professor urged.

Nate slowly nodded, obeying Kouwe's instinct.

The response clearly relieved the suffering man. "Good," the shaman said.

Dakii returned, burdened with a leather satchel and a pair of footlong lengths of reed. He held the gear out to his leader, but the shaman was too weak. He directed Dakii from his hammock.

Obeying, Dakii lifted the pouch.

"A dried jaguar scrotum," Kouwe said, pointing to the pouch.

"All the rage in Paris," Nate grumbled.

Dakii fingered open the pouch. Inside was a crimson powder. The shaman spoke from the bed, instructing.

Kouwe translated, though Nate caught a word here and there. "He describes the powder as *ali ne Yagga*."

Nate understood. "Blood of the Mother."

Kouwe glanced at Nate as Dakii tamped some of the powder into the tips of the two straws. "You know what's about to happen, don't you?"

Nate could certainly guess. "It's like the Yanomamo drug *epena*." Over the years, he had worked with various Yanomamo tribes and been invited to participate in *epena* ceremonies. *Epena,* translated as "semen of the sun," was a hallucinogenic drug Yanomamo shamans used to enter the spirit world. It was strong stuff, fabled to bring the *hekura,* or little men of the forest, to teach medicine to a shaman. When Nate had tried the stuff, all he had ever experienced was a severe headache followed by swirls of color. Furthermore, he was not particularly fond of the drug's delivery system. It was snuffed up the nose.

Dakii handed one of the loaded straws to Nate and one to the shaman. The Ban-ali leader waved Nate to kneel beside the hammock.

Nate obeyed.

Kouwe cautioned him, "The shaman knows he's about to die. What he is offering is more than a casual ritual. I think he's passing the mantle of his responsibility to you, for the tribe, for the village, for the tree."

"I can't take that on," Nate said, glancing back at Kouwe.

"You must. Once you're shaman, the tribe's secrets will be open to you. Do you understand what that means?"

Nate took a deep breath and nodded. "The cure."

"Exactly."

Nate stepped to the hammock and knelt.

The shaman showed Nate what to do, but it was similar to the Yanomamos' ritual. The small man positioned the drug-loaded end of his reed straw to his own nose. Then motioned for Nate to bring his lips to the other end. Nate's job was to blow the drug up the other's nose. He, in turn, positioned his own straw to his left nostril. The shaman brought the other end to his mouth. Through the straws, the two men would simultaneously blow the drug into each other's sinuses.

The shaman lifted an arm. They both took a deep breath.

Here we go . . .

The Indian brought his arm down.

Nate exhaled sharply through the reed, while bracing for the jolt to his own sinuses. Before he even finished blowing on his end of the straw, the drug hit him.

Nate fell backward. A burning flame seared into his skull, followed by a blinding explosion of pain. It felt as if someone had blown the back of his head off. He gasped as the room spun. The sense of vertigo overwhelmed him. A pit opened in his mind, and he was falling. He tumbled, spinning away into a darkness that was somehow bright at the same time.

Distantly he heard his name called, but he couldn't find his mouth to speak.

Suddenly his falling body shattered through something solid in this otherworld. The darkness fragmented around him like broken glass. Midnight shards fell away and disappeared. What was left was a shadow shaped into a stylized tree. It appeared to be rising from a dark hill.

Nate hovered before it. As he stared, details emerged. The tree developed three-dimensional conformations, tiny midnight leaves, tiered branches, clustered nut pods.

The Yagga.

Then, from beyond the hill's edge, small figures marched into view, all in a line, heading up the slope to the tree.

The *hekura*, Nate guessed dreamily.

But like the tree, the figures grew in detail as Nate floated nearby, and he realized he was mistaken. Instead of little men, the line was a mix of animals of every ilk—monkeys, sloths, rats, crocodiles, jaguars, and some Nate couldn't identify. Interspersed among these darkly silhouetted animals were men and women, but Nate knew these weren't the *hekura*. The entire party marched up to the tree—and into it. The shadowy figures merged with the black form of the tree.

Where had they gone? Was he supposed to follow?

Then, from the other side of the tree, the figures reemerged. But they had transformed. They were no longer in shadow, but glowing with a brilliant radiance. The shining troupe spread to circle the tree. Man and beast. Protecting the Mother.

As Nate hovered, he sensed the passage of time accelerate. He watched the men and women occasionally wander back to the tree as their radiance dimmed. They would eat the fruit of the tree and shine anew, refreshed to take their place again in the circle of Yagga's children. The ritual repeated over and over again.

Like a worn record, the image began to fade, repeating still, but growing dimmer and dimmer—until there was only darkness again.

"Nate?" a voice called to him.

Who? Nate sought the speaker. But all he found was darkness.

"Nate, can you hear me?"

Yes, but where are you?

"Squeeze my hand if you can hear me."

Nate drew toward the voice, seeking it out of the darkness.

"Good, Nate. Now open your eyes."

He struggled to obey.

"Don't fight it . . . just open your eyes."

Again the darkness shattered, and Nate was blinded by brilliance and light. He gasped, sucking in huge gulps of air. His head throbbed with pain. Through tears, he saw the face of his friend leaning over him, cradling his head.

"Nate?"

He coughed and nodded.

"How do you feel?"

"How do you think I feel?" Nate wobbled up from the floor.

"What did you experience?" Kouwe asked. "You were mumbling."

"And drooling," Anna added, kneeling beside him.

Nate wiped his mouth. "Hypersalivation . . . an alkaloid hallucinogen."

"What did you see?" Kouwe asked.

Nate shook his head. A mistake. The headache flared worse. "How long have I been out?"

"About ten minutes," the professor said.

"Ten minutes?" *It had felt like hours, if not days.*

"What happened?"

"I think I was just shown the cure to the disease," Nate said.

Kouwe's eyes widened. "What?"

Nate explained what he saw. "From the dream, it's clear that the nuts of this tree are vital to the health of the humans in the tribe. The animals don't need it, but people do."

Kouwe nodded, his eyes narrowed as he digested what was said. "So it's the nut pods." The professor pondered a bit longer, then spoke slowly. "From your father's research, we know the tree's sap is full of mutating proteins—prions with the ability to enhance each species it encounters, making them better protectors of the tree. But such a boon must come with a high cost. The tree doesn't want its children to abandon it, so it built a fail-safe into its enhancements. Animals are probably given some instinct to remain in the area, something to do with territoriality, something that can be manipulated as needed, like the powders used with the locusts and piranhas. But humans, with our intellect, need firmer bonds to bind us to the tree. The humans must eat from the fruit on a regular basis to keep the mutating prions in check. The milk of the nut must contain some form of an *antiprion*, something that suppresses the virulent form of the disease."

Anna looked sick. "So the Ban-ali have not stayed here out of obligation, but enslavement."

Kouwe rubbed his temples. "*Ban-yi*. Slave. The term was not an exaggeration. Once exposed to the prions, you can't leave or you'll die. Without the fruit, the prion reverts to its virulent form and attacks the immune system, triggering deadly fevers or riotous cancers."

"Jekyll and Hyde," Nate mumbled.

Kouwe and Anna glanced to him.

Nate explained, "It's like what Kelly reported about the nature of prions. In one form, they're benign, but they can also bend into a new shape and become virulent, like mad cow disease."

Kouwe nodded. "The nut milk must keep the prion suppressed in the beneficial form . . . but once you stop using the milk, it attacks, killing the host and spreading to everyone the host encounters. This again would serve the tree's end. Clearly the tree wants to keep its privacy. If someone flees, anyone the escapee encounters would sicken and die, leaving a trail of death."

"With no one left to tell the tale," Nate said.

"Exactly."

Nate felt well enough to try to stand. Kouwe helped him up. "But the bigger question is why I dreamed up the answer in the first place. Was it just my own subconscious working out the problem, unfettered by the hallucinogenic drug? Or did the shaman communicate it to me somehow . . . some form of drug-induced telepathy?"

Kouwe's face tightened. "No," he said firmly and pointed to the hammock. "It wasn't the shaman."

The Indian lay in his hammock, staring up at the ceiling. Blood dripped from both his nostrils. He was not breathing. Dakii knelt beside his leader, head bowed.

"He died immediately. A massive stroke from the look of it." Kouwe glanced to Nate. "Whatever you experienced didn't come from the shaman."

Nate found it hard to think. His brain felt two sizes too big for his skull. "Then it must have been my subconscious," he said. "When I first saw the pods, I remember thinking that the nuts looked like the fruiting bodies of *Uncaria tomentosa*. Better known as cat's claw. Indians use it against viruses, bacteria, and sometimes tumors. But I didn't make the correlation until now. Maybe the drug helped my subconscious make the intuitive leap."

"You could be right," Kouwe said.

Nate heard the hesitation in the professor's voice. "What else could it be?"

Kouwe frowned. "I talked with Dakii while you were drugged out. The *ali ne Yagga* powder comes from the root of this tree. Desiccated and powdered root fiber."

"So?"

"So maybe what you dreamed wasn't your subconscious. Maybe it was some type of prerecorded message from the tree itself. An instruction manual, so to speak: *Consume the fruit of the tree and you will stay healthy.* A simple message."

"You can't be serious."

"Considering the setup in this valley—mutated species, regenerating limbs, humans enslaved in service to a plant—I wouldn't put anything beyond this tree's abilities."

Nate shook his head.

Anna frowned. "The professor may have a point. I can't even imagine how this tree is able to produce prions specific to the DNA of so many different species. That alone is miraculous. How did it learn? Where did the tree even get genetic material to learn from?"

Kouwe waved an arm around the room. "This tree traces its roots back to the Paleozoic era, when the land was just plants. Its ancestors must have been around as land animals first evolved, and rather than competing, it incorporated these new species into its own life cycle, like the Amazon's ant tree does today."

The professor continued with his theories, but Nate found himself tuning him out. He was drawn back to Anna's last question. *Where did the tree even get genetic material to learn from?* It was a good question, and it nagged at Nate. How *had* the Yagga learned to produce its wide variety of species-specific prions?

Nate remembered his dream: the line of animals and people disappearing inside the tree. Where had they gone? Was it more than just symbolic? Did they go *somewhere*? Nate found his eyes on Dakii, kneeling by the hammock. Maybe it was another intuitive leap, or a residual effect of the drug, but Nate began to get a suspicion where that *somewhere* might be.

Ali ne rah. Blood of the Yagga. From the root of the tree.

Nate's gaze narrowed on Dakii. He recalled the Indian's description of his father's fate, spoken with gladness. *He's gone to feed the root.*

Nate found his feet stepping toward the tribesman.

Kouwe stopped his discourse. "Nate . . . ?"

"There's one piece of the puzzle we're still missing." Nate nodded to Dakii. "And I know who has it."

He crossed to the kneeling tribesman. Dakii glanced up, tears running down his face. The loss of the leader had struck the man hard. He hauled to his feet as Nate stopped before him.

"*Wishwa,*" he said, bowing his head, acknowledging the passing of power.

"I'm sorry for your loss," Nate said, "but we must speak." Kouwe came over and assisted with the translations, but Nate was now becoming

"Is there another way out of the valley?" Nate asked again.

Dakii pointed to where the tunnel ended at a slightly concave wall covered with the blue prints. "Through the root. We go through the root."

"Yes, I want to see the root, too, but what about the way out?"

Dakii stared at him. "Through the root," he repeated.

Nate nodded, finally understanding. Their two missions had just become one. "Show us."

Dakii crossed to the wall, glancing over the prints, then he reached out to one near the innermost wall. He placed his palm over it and pushed with arm and shoulder. The entire wall pivoted on a central axis, opening a new section of passage, winding deeper underground.

Nate glanced up, recalling that the flow channels here hadn't exactly matched. A secret door. The answer was before him this entire time. Even the palm prints on the walls—they were like the one on the Ban-ali symbol, guarding the double helix that represented the root.

Anna slipped a flashlight from her field jacket. Nate patted his own jacket, but came up empty. He must have lost his. Anna passed him hers, indicating he should go first.

Nate moved to the door. Wafting out was the musk of the tree, humid and thicker, dank like the breath from an open grave. Nate readied himself and pushed through the opening.

EIGHTEEN

The Last Hour

As Louis's band took a rest break, he checked his watch. It was an hour before the explosion would turn the upper valley into a whirling firestorm. He focused his attention on the swamp lake ahead. The setting sun had turned the water a tarnished silver.

They were making good time. Skirting to the south of the swamp, where the jungle was thickest and the river channels many, they would easily slip away through the dense forest. He had no doubt of that.

He sighed contentedly, but with a trace of disappointment. Everything was downhill from here. He always felt this way after a successful mission. Some form of postcoital depression, he imagined. He would return to French Guiana a much richer man, but money didn't buy the excitement of the last couple of days.

"*C'est la vie*," he said. *There will always be other missions.*

A small ruckus drew his attention back around.

He saw Kelly being shoved to her knees by two men. A third was on the ground a couple of yards away, rolling, cursing, clutching between his legs.

Louis strode over to them, but Mask was already there.

The scarred lieutenant pulled the moaning guard to his feet.

"What happened?" Louis asked.

Mask thumbed at the man. "Pedro reached a hand down her shirt, and she kneed him in the groin."

Louis smiled, impressed. One hand settled to the bullwhip trophy at his waist.

He sauntered over to Kelly, now on her knees. One of her two captors had his fist tight in her hair, pulling her head back to expose her long neck. She snarled as the two men taunted her with the vilest innuendoes.

"Let her up," Louis said.

The men knew better than to disobey. Kelly was yanked to her feet.

Louis took off his hat. "I apologize for the rudeness here. It won't happen again, I assure you."

Other men gathered.

Kelly fumed. "Next time I'll kick the asshole's balls into his belly."

"Indeed." Louis waved off his men. "But punishment is my department." He tapped the bullwhip on his side. Earlier he had struck the woman as a lesson. Now it was time for another.

He turned and struck out with the whip, splitting the twilight with a loud *crack*.

Pedro screamed, covering his left eye. Blood spurted through his fingers.

Louis faced the others. "No one will harm the prisoners. Is that understood?"

There was a general sound of agreement and many nods.

Louis replaced his whip. "Someone see to Pedro's eye."

He turned back around and saw Tshui standing near Kelly, one palm raised to the woman's cheek.

As he watched, he noticed that Tshui had wrapped her fingers around a curl of fiery auburn hair.

Ah, Louis thought, *the red hair. A unique trophy for Tshui's collection.*

7:05 P.M.

In the flashlight's glow, Nate noticed that the passage beyond the hand-printed door was similar to the main tunnel, but the woody surfaces were of a coarser grain. As he walked, the musk of the tree flowed thick and fetid.

With Dakii at his side, he led Anna and Kouwe down the tunnel. It narrowed rapidly, twisting tighter and tighter, causing the group to crowd together.

"We must be in the tree's taproot," Nate mumbled.

"Heading underground," Kouwe said.

Nate nodded. Within a few more twisting yards, the tunnel exited the woody root, and stone appeared underfoot, interspersed with patches of loam. The tunnel headed steeply downward. They now ran parallel to the branching root system.

Dakii pointed ahead and continued.

Nate hesitated. Strange lichens grew on the walls, glowing softly. The musk was almost overpowering, now rich with a more fecund odor. Dakii pushed on.

Nate glanced to Kouwe, who shrugged. It was encouragement enough.

As they continued forward, the root branch that ran overhead split and divided, heading out into other passageways. From the ceiling, drapes of root hairs hung, vibrating ever so gently, rhythmically swaying as if a wind blew softly through the passage. But there was no wind.

The top of Nate's head brushed against the ceiling as the tunnel lowered. The tiny root fibrils tangled into his hair, clinging, pulling. Nate wrenched away with a gasp.

He shone his flashlight overhead, wary.

"What is it?" Kouwe asked.

"The root grabbed at me."

Kouwe lifted a palm to the root branch. The smaller hairs wrapped around his fingers in a clinging embrace. With a look of disgust, Kouwe tugged his hand away.

Nate had seen other Amazonian plants demonstrate a response to stimulation: leaves curling if touched, puff pods exploding if brushed, flowers closing if disturbed. But this felt somehow more malignant.

Nate fanned his flashlight across the path. By now, Dakii was waiting several yards down the passage. Nate urged the others to catch up. Once abreast of Dakii, Nate studied the splitting roots that now turned riotous, dividing and cross-splitting in all directions. Small blind cubbyholes dotted the many passages, each choked and clogged with a tangle of roots and waving hairs. The little cubbies reminded Nate of nitrogen bulbs, seen among root balls of many plants, that served as storage fertilizing sites.

Dakii stood before one such alcove. Nate shone his light into the space. Something was tangled deep inside the mass of twining branches and churning root fibrils. Nate bent closer. A few wiggling hairs curled out toward him, questing, waving like small antennae.

He kept back.

Deep in the root pack, wrapped and entwined like a fly in a spider's webbing, was a large fruit bat. Nate straightened in disgust.

Kouwe leaned in and grimaced. "Is it feeding on the bat?"

Anna spoke behind them. "I don't think so. Come see this."

They both turned to her. She knelt by an even larger cubby, but one similarly entangled. She pointed into its depths.

Nate flashed his light inside. Entombed within was a large brown cat.

"A puma," Kouwe said at his shoulder.

"Watch," Anna said.

They stared, not knowing what to expect. Then suddenly the large cat moved, breathed. Its lungs expanded and collapsed in a sigh. But the movement did not look natural, more mechanical.

Anna glanced back at them. "It's alive."

"I don't understand," Nate said.

Anna held out her hand. "Can I see the flashlight?"

Nate passed it to her. The anthropologist quickly surveyed several of the other alcoves, moving through the neighboring, branching passages. The variety of animals was impressive: ocelot, toucan, marmoset, tamarin, anteater, even snakes and lizards, and oddly enough one jungle trout. And each one of them seemed to be breathing or showing some signs of life, including the fish, its small gill flaps twitching.

"They're each unique," Anna said, eyes bright as she stared down the maze of passages. "And all alive. Like some form of suspended animation."

"What are you getting at?"

Anna turned to them. "We're standing in a biological storehouse. A library of genetic code. I wager this is the source of its prion production."

Nate turned in a slow circle, staring at the maze of passages. The implication was too overwhelming to contemplate. The tree was storing these animals down here, learning from them so it could produce prions to alter and bind the species to it. It was a living, breathing genetics lab.

Kouwe gripped Nate's shoulder. "Your father."

Nate glanced to him in confusion. "What about my—?" Then it hit him like a hammer to the forehead. He gasped. His father had been fed to the root. *Not as fertilizer,* Nate realized, swinging around, aghast, *but to be a part of this malignant laboratory!*

"With his white skin and strange manners, your father was unique," Kouwe said in a low voice. "The Ban-ali or the Yagga would not want to lose his genetic heritage."

Nate turned to Dakii. He could barely speak, too choked with emotion. "My . . . my father. Do you know where he is?"

Dakii nodded and lifted both arms. "He with root."

"Yes, but where?" Nate pointed to the closest cubby, one with an enshrouded black sloth. "Which one?"

Dakii frowned and glanced around the maze of passages.

Nate held his breath. There had to be hundreds of passages, countless alcoves. He didn't have time to search them all, not with the clock running. But how could Nate leave, knowing his father was down here somewhere?

Dakii suddenly strode purposefully down one passage and waved for them to follow.

They hurried, winding deeper and deeper into the subterranean maze. Nate found it increasingly difficult to breathe, not because of the sickening musk, but because of his own mounting anxiety. All along this journey, he had held no real hope his father was still alive. But now . . . he teetered between hope and despair, almost panicked with trepidation. *What would he find?*

Dakii paused at an intersection, then stepped to the left passage. But after two strides, he shook his head and returned to follow the trail to the right.

A scream built up inside Nate's chest.

Dakii continued down this new passage, mumbling under his breath. Finally, he stopped beside a large cubby and pointed. "Father."

Nate grabbed the flashlight back from Anna. He dropped to his knees, shining his light inside, oblivious to the questing root hairs that wrapped around his wrist.

Within the mass of roots lay a shadowy figure. Nate moved his light over its form. Curled in a fetal position on the soft loamy floor was a gaunt naked frame, a pale man. His face was covered by a thick beard, his hair tangled with roots. Nate focused on the face hidden beneath the beard. He was not entirely sure it was his father.

As he stared, the man inhaled sharply, mechanically, and exhaled, wafting root hairs from his lips. Still alive!

Nate turned. "I have to get him out of there."

"Is it your father?" Anna asked.

"I . . . I'm not sure." Nate pointed to the bone knife tucked in Kouwe's belt. The professor passed it over to him.

Nate stood and hacked into the root mass.

Dakii cried out, reaching to stop him, but Kouwe blocked the tribesman. "Dakii, no! Leave Nate be."

Nate fought through the outer cords of woody roots. It was like the husk surrounding some nut. Beneath this layer was a mass of finer webbings and draperies of rootlets and thready hairs.

Once through, Nate saw the roots penetrated the man's body, growing into it as if it were soil. It must be how the Yagga sustained its specimens, feeding them, supporting organ systems, delivering nutrients.

Nate hesitated. Would he harm the man, kill him, if he hacked the root's attachments? If this was indeed some type of suspended animation, would its interruption trigger a massive systems failure?

Shaking his head, Nate slashed through the roots. He would take his chances. Left alone, the man would surely die a fiery death.

Once the body was free of the root hairs, Nate tossed the knife aside, grabbed the man by the shoulders, and hauled him into the passage. The last clinging roots broke away, releasing their prey.

In the tunnel, Nate collapsed beside the man. The naked figure choked and gasped. Many of the tiny rootlets and hairs squiggled from his body, dropping away like leeches. Blood flowed from some spots where larger rootlets had penetrated. Suddenly the man seized, contracting, back arching, head thrown back.

Nate cradled the man in his arms, not knowing what to do. The thrashings continued for a full minute. Kouwe helped to restrain the man and prevent further injury.

The figure jerked into a final convulsion, then collapsed with a mighty gasp.

Nate exhaled with relief when the man's chest continued to rise and fall. Then the eyes fluttered open and stared up at him. Nate knew those eyes. They were his *own* eyes.

"Nate?" the figure asked in a dry husky voice.

Nate fell atop the figure. "Dad!"

"Am . . . am I dreaming?" his father asked coarsely.

Nate was too choked to speak. He helped his father, who was light as a pillow, all skin and bones, to sit. The tree had been sustaining him, but just barely.

Kouwe bent down to help. "Carl, how are you feeling?"

Nate's father squinted at the professor, then a look of recognition spread across his face. "Kouwe? My God, what's going on?"

"It's a long story, old friend." He helped Nate get his father on his feet. Too frail to move on his own, Carl Rand clung to Nate and Kouwe. "Right now, though, we have to get you out of this damn place."

Nate stared at his father, tears streaming down his face. "Dad . . ."

"I know, son," he said hoarsely and coughed.

There was no time for a proper reunion now, but Nate wasn't going to let another moment go by without saying the words he had regretted withholding the day his father left for this expedition. "I love you, Dad."

The arm around his shoulder tightened, a small squeeze of affection and love. A familiar gesture. Family.

"We should fetch the others," Anna said. "And head out of here."

"Nate, why don't you stay with your father here?" Kouwe suggested. "Rest. We can collect you both on the way out."

Dakii shook his head. "No. We not come back this way." He waved his arm. "Other way to go."

Nate frowned. "We should stay together anyway."

"And I can handle myself," Carl argued hoarsely. He glanced back to the cubbyhole. "Besides, I've been resting here long enough."

Kouwe nodded.

With the matter settled, they began to climb toward the surface. Kouwe gave a thumbnail sketch of their situation. Nate's father only listened, leaning more and more heavily upon them as they walked. The only words his father spoke during the discourse were at the mention of Louis Favre and what he had done. "The goddamn bastard."

Nate smiled, hearing a bit of the old fire in his father's voice.

When they reached the surface, it was obvious the two Rangers had been busy. They had all the Ban-ali gathered. Each bore packs full of nuts and weapons.

Nate and his father remained in the entrance, while Kouwe explained about the addition to their team and what they had found below. "Dakii says there's an escape route through the root's tunnel."

"Then we'd best hurry," Sergeant Kostos said. "We have less than thirty minutes, and we want to be as far away from here as possible."

Carrera joined them, her weapon on her shoulder. "All set at our end. We have a couple dozen of those nut pods and four canteens of the sap."

"Then let's haul ass," Kostos said.

7:32 P.M.,

As they wound through the root tunnels, Kouwe stayed with Dakii, periodically glancing back at the trail of Indians and Americans. Watching Sergeant Kostos help Nate with his father, Kouwe wished he had had time to rig up a stretcher, but right now every minute was critical.

Though Sergeant Kostos believed the subterranean tunnels would shield them from the worst of the napalm's fiery blast, he clearly feared the maze's integrity. "The rock here is riddled and weakened by the roots. The explosions could bring the roof down atop our heads or trap us here. We need to be well clear of these tunnels before those bombs go off."

So they hurried. Not only for their own sake, but for the world. Inside their packs, they carried the fate of thousands, if not millions—the nut pods of the Yagga, the suppressant for the virulent human prion. The cure to the plague.

They could not be trapped down here.

Glancing over a shoulder, Kouwe again checked the party. The dark tunnels, the softly glowing lichens, the dreadful cubbies with their captured specimens . . . all made Kouwe nervous. This deep in the system, both walls and ceilings ran wild with roots, zigzagging everywhere, crossing, dividing, fusing. Everywhere were the mounds of ubiquitous root hairs, waving and probing toward any passerby. It made the walls look furry, like a living thing, constantly moving and bristling.

Behind Kouwe, the others looked equally wary, even the Indians. The line of men and women ran out of sight around a curve in the twisting passage. Back at the end, pulling up the rear, was Private Carrera. She kept a watch behind them—where Tor-tor and the giant black jaguar followed. It had taken some coaxing to encourage the two cats inside, but Nate had finally been successful in luring Tor-tor. "I'm not going to leave Manny's cat here to die," Nate had argued. "I owe it to my friend to save him."

Once Tor-tor entered, the large female jaguar had followed.

Carrera remained alert, her weapon ready, in case the wild cat decided it needed a snack while traveling.

Dakii paused at the intersection of trails. Sergeant Kostos grumbled, but they dared not force a faster pace. It would be easy to get lost down here. They depended on Dakii's memory.

The tribesman selected a path and led the others. The tunnel descended steeply. Kouwe stared at the low roof. They must be a hundred yards underground . . . and going deeper still. But oddly, instead of the air growing more dank, it seemed to freshen.

After a few minutes, the tunnel leveled out and made a sharp turn, emptying into a huge cavern. The tunnel opening was halfway up one wall of the chamber. A thin trail continued along the nearest wall, a stony lip high above the bowled floor. Dakii stepped out onto the trail.

Kouwe followed, gaping at the room. The chamber had to be a half mile across. Through the center of the chamber, a massive root stalk, as thick around as a giant redwood, penetrated from the roof and continued down through the floor like a great column.

"It's the Yagga's taproot again," Nate said, coming up beside them. "We must have circled back to it."

From the main root, thousands of branches spread like tree limbs in all directions, toward other passages.

"There must be miles and miles of tunnels," Kouwe said. He studied the taproot. The giant tree above must be but a tiny fraction of the plant's true mass. "Can you imagine the number of species encased down here? Suspended in time?"

"The tree must have been collecting its specimens for centuries," Nate's father mumbled beside his son.

"Maybe even longer," Kouwe warned. "Maybe as far back as when these lands first formed."

"Back to the Paleozoic," Nate murmured. "If so, what might be out there in that vast biological storehouse?"

"And what might still be living?" Anna added.

Kouwe cringed. It was both a wondrous and frightening thought. He waved Dakii onward. The sight was too terrible to stare at any longer, and time was running down for both them and the world.

They wound along the lip as it circled the chamber. Dakii led them to another opening, back into the tunnel maze again. Though they left the chamber behind, Kouwe's mind dwelled on the mystery there. His feet slowed, and he found himself marching near Nate and Carl. Sergeant Kostos was on the other side.

"When I studied anthropology," Kouwe said, "I read many myths of trees. The maternal guardian. A caretaker, a storehouse of all wisdom. It makes me wonder about the Yagga. Has man crossed its path before?"

"What do you mean?" Nate asked.

"Surely this tree wasn't the only one of its kind. There must have been others in the past. Maybe these myths are some collective memory of earlier human encounters with this species."

He recognized the doubt in Nate's eyes and continued, "Take, for example, the Tree of Knowledge from the Garden of Eden. A tree whose fruit has all the knowledge in the world, but whose consumption curses those who eat of it. You could draw a parallel to the Yagga. Even when I saw Carl trussed up among the roots, it reminded me of another Biblical tale. Back in the thirteenth century, a monk who had starved himself seeking visions from God told a tale of seeing Seth, the son of Adam, returning to Eden. There, the young man saw the Tree of Knowledge, now turned white. It clutched Cain in its roots, some penetrating into his brother's flesh."

Nate frowned.

"The parallels here seem particularly apt," Kouwe finished.

Noticeably quiet for several yards, Nate was clearly digesting his words. Finally he spoke. "You could be on to something. The tunnel through the Yagga's trunk is not manmade, but a natural construct. The tunnels had to have formed as the tree grew. But why would the tree do so unless its ancestors had encountered man before and had evolved these features in kind?"

"Like an ant tree has adapted for its six-legged soldiers," Kouwe added.

Nate's father roused. "And the evolution of the Ban-ali here, their genetic enhancements," Carl rasped. "Have such improvements of the species happened before? Could the tree have played a critical role in human evolution? Is that why we remember it in our myths?"

Kouwe's brow crinkled. He had not extrapolated that far. He stared behind the others to where the giant cat stalked. If the Yagga were capable of enhancing the jaguar's intelligence, could it have done the same to us in the distant past? Could humans owe their own intellect to an ancestor of this tree? A chilling thought.

A silence fell over the others.

In his head, Kouwe reviewed the history of this valley. The Yagga must have grown here, collecting specimens in its hollow root system for centuries: luring them in with its musk, offering shelter, then capturing them and storing them in its cubbies. Eventually man entered the valley—a wandering clan of Yanomamo—and discovered the tree's tunnels and the wonders of its healing sap. Lured in, they were captured as surely as any other species and slowly changed into the Ban-ali, the Yagga's human servants. Since that time, the Ban-ali must have brought other species to the tree—feeding the root to further expand its biological database.

And left unchecked, where would it have led? A new species of man, as Carl had feared after the stillborn birth of Gerald Clark's baby? Or maybe something worse—a hybrid like the piranhas and locusts?

Kouwe squinted at the twisting passages, suddenly glad it was all going to burn.

Dakii called from up ahead. The tribesman pointed to a side tunnel. From the passage, a slight glow shone. A dull roar echoed back to them.

"The way out," Kouwe said.

Nate hurried as best he could with his father.

Sergeant Kostos growled constantly under his breath on the other side, counting off the minutes until the bombs blew.

It would be a close call.

The group sped toward the sheen of moonlight flowing from ahead. The roaring grew in volume, soon thundering. Around a corner, the end of the tunnel appeared, and the source of the noise grew clear.

A waterfall tumbled past the entrance, the rush of water aglow with moonlight and star shine.

"The tunnel must open into the cliff face that leads to the lower valley," Kouwe said.

They followed Dakii to the tunnel's damp exit. The rushing water rumbled past the threshold. The tribesman pointed down. *Steps.* In the narrow space between the waterfall and the cliff, a steep, wet staircase had been carved into the stone, winding back and forth in narrow switchbacks, down to the lower valley.

"Everyone head down!" the sergeant yelled. "Move quickly, but when I holler, everyone drop and hold on tight."

Dakii remained with Sergeant Kostos to guide his own people.

Kouwe helped Nate with his father. They scrambled as well as they could down the stairs, balancing between haste and caution. They hurried as the others followed.

Nate saw Kostos wave Carrera down the stairs, then followed.

Behind them emerged the two cats. The jaguars hurried out of the opening and onto the stair, clearly glad to be free of the confining tunnels. Nate wished he had their claws.

"One minute," Kouwe said, hobbling under Carl's weight.

They hurried. The bottom was still a good four stories down. A deadly fall.

Then a sharp call broke through the water's rush. "Now! Down! Down!"

Nate helped his father to the steps, then dropped himself. He glanced up and saw the entire group flattened to the stone. He lowered his face and prayed.

The explosion, when it came, was as if hell had come to earth. The noise was minimal—no worse than the dramatic end of a Fourth of July fireworks show—but the effect was anything but insignificant.

Over the top of the cliff's edge, a wall of flame shot half a mile out, and flumed three times that distance into the sky. Currents of rising air buffeted them, swirling eddies of fire moving with them. If it wasn't for the waterfall's insulation, they would've been fried on the stairs. But the waterfall was a mixed blessing. Its flow, shaken by the blast, cast vast amounts of water over them. But everyone held tight.

Soon bits of flaming debris began to tumble over the edge and down the fall. Luckily the swift current cast most of the large pieces of trunk and branch beyond their perch. But it was still terrifying to see entire trees, cracked and blown into the stream, tumble past, on fire.

As the heat welled up and away from them, Kostos yelled down. "Keep moving, but watch for falling debris."

Nate crouched up. Everyone began to climb to their feet, dazed.

They had made it!

As the others started down, he reached for his father. "C'mon, Dad. Let's get out of here."

With his father's hand held in his own, Nate felt the ground vibrate, a tremoring rumble. He instinctively knew this was bad. *Oh, shit . . .*

He dove atop his father, a scream on his lips. "Down! Everyone back down!"

The second explosion deafened them. Nate screamed from the pain. It blew with such force that he was sure the cliff would fall atop them.

From the mouth of the tunnel above, a jet of fire belched out, blasting into the fall of water. Scalding steam rolled down over them.

Nate craned upward and watched a second belch of fire blow from the tunnel, then a third. Smaller flames shot out of tinier crevices in the cliff face all around, like a hundred flickering fiery tongues. All of them an eerie blue.

All the while, the ground continued to shake and rumble.

Nate kept his father pinned under him.

Rocks and dirt shattered outward. Entire uprooted trees shot like flaming missiles through the sky to crash down into the lower valley.

Then this too died down.

No one moved as smaller rocks tumbled past. Again the waterfall protected them, deflecting most of the debris, or reducing their speed to bruising rather than deadly velocities.

After several minutes, Nate raised his head enough to view the damage.

He spotted Kouwe a step above his father. The professor looked dazed and sickened. He stared back at Nate, face pale with shock. "Anna . . . when you yelled . . . I was too slow . . . the explosion . . . I couldn't catch her in time." His eyes flicked to the long tumble below. "She fell."

Nate closed his eyes. "Oh, God."

He heard mournful cries flow up around them. Anna had not been alone in falling to her death. Nate pushed to his knees. His father coughed and rolled onto his side, looking ashen.

After a time, the group crawled down the stairs, beaten, bloody, and in shock.

They gathered at the foot of the falls, bathed in cool spray. Three Ban-ali tribesmen had also met their deaths on the stair.

"What was that second explosion?" Sergeant Kostos asked.

Nate remembered the strange blue flame. He asked for one of the canteens with the Yagga sap. He poured out a grape-sized drop and used Carrera's lighter to ignite it. A tall blue flame flared up from the dollop of sap. "Like copal," Nate said. "Combustible. The entire tree went up like a roman candle. Roots and all, I imagine, from the way the ground shook."

A deep mournful silence spread over the smaller camp.

Finally Carrera spoke. "What now?"

Nate answered, his voice fierce. "We make that bastard pay. For Manny, for Olin, for Anna, for all the Ban-ali tribespeople."

"They have guns," Sergeant Kostos said. "We have one Bailey. They outnumber us more than two to one."

"To hell with that." Nate kept his voice cold. "We have a card that trumps all that."

"What's that?" Kostos asked.

"They think we're dead."

NINETEEN

Midnight Raid

Kelly's eyes still stung with tears. With her hands bound behind her back, she couldn't even wipe them away. She was secured to a stake under a lean-to of woven palm leaves that deflected the gentle rain that now fell. The clouds had rolled in as full night had set, which had suited her kidnappers just fine. "The darker the better," Favre had exulted. They made good time and were now enveloped in thick jungle cover well south of the swamp.

But despite the darkness and the distance, the northern skies glowed a fiery red, as if the sun were trying to rise from that direction. The explosions that had lit up the night had been spectacular, shooting a fireball high into the sky, followed by a scattering of flaming debris.

The sight had burned all hope from her. The others were dead.

Favre had set a hard pace after that, sure that the government's helicopters would be winging to the fires posthaste. But so far the skies had remained clear. There was no whump-whumping of military air vehicles. Favre kept a constant watch on the skies. *Nothing.*

Maybe Olin's signal had never made it out. Or maybe the helicopters were still en route.

Either way, Favre was taking no chances. No lights, just night-vision glasses. Kelly, of course, was not given a pair. Her shins were bruised and thorn-scraped from falls and missteps in the dark. Her stumblings had amused the guards. Without her hands to break her fall, each trip bloodied her knees. Her legs ached. Mosquitoes and gnats were attracted to the wounds, crawling and buzzing around her. She couldn't even swat them away.

The rain was a relief. As was the short break—a full hour. Kelly stared over at the glowing northern skies, praying her friends hadn't suffered.

Closer at hand, the mercenary band celebrated its victory. Flasks of alcohol passed from hand to hand. Toasts were made, and boasts declared amid jovial whispers of how their money would be spent—much of it involving whores. Favre circulated through the group, allowing his men this celebration but making sure it didn't get out of hand. They were still miles from the rendezvous point where the motorboats were waiting.

So for the moment, Kelly had a bit of relative privacy. Frank was under another makeshift lean-to in the middle of the camp. Her only company here was the single guard: Favre's disfigured lieutenant, the man named Mask. He stood talking with another mercenary, sharing a flask.

A figure approached through the drizzle. It was Favre's Indian woman, Tshui. She seemed oblivious of the rain, still naked, but at least she no longer wore the head of Corporal DeMartini around her neck.

Probably didn't want to get the foul thing wet, Kelly thought sourly.

Mask's companion slid away at the approach of the woman. She had that effect on most of the mercenaries. They were clearly frightened of her. Even Mask took a few steps from the lean-to and sheltered under a neighboring palm.

The Indian woman bent out of the rain and knelt beside Kelly. She carried a rucksack in one hand. She settled it to the dirt and began to rummage silently through it, finally pulling out a tiny clay pot and freeing the lid.

Filling the container was a thick waxy unguent. The witch-woman scooped a dab on a finger, then reached to Kelly.

She flinched away.

The Indian woman grabbed her ankle. Her grip was iron. She slathered the material on Kelly's abraded knees. Instantly the sting and burn faded. Kelly stopped fighting and allowed the woman to treat her.

"Thank you," Kelly said, though she was not sure the treatment was solely for her comfort as much as to make sure she could continue to march. Either way, it felt good.

The Indian woman reached again to her pack and removed a rolled length of woven linen. She carefully spread it open on the soggy ground. Meticulously lined in tiny pouches of cloth were stainless steel tools and others made of yellowed bone. Tshui removed a long sickle-shaped knife, one of a set of five similar tools. She leaned toward Kelly with the knife.

Kelly again flinched, but the woman grabbed the hair at the nape of her neck and held her still, pulling her head back. The Indian was damn strong.

"What are you doing?"

Tshui never spoke. She brought the knife's curved edge to Kelly's forehead, at the edge of her scalp. Then returned the tool to its place and took another of the curved knives and positioned it at the crown of her scalp.

With horror, the realization hit Kelly. *She's measuring me!* Tshui was determining which tools would be best to scrape the skin off her skull. The Indian woman continued her measuring, fingering different sharp instruments and testing them against chin, cheek, and nose.

She began to line up the proper instruments on the ground beside her knee. The row of tools grew: long knives, sharp picks, corkscrewing pieces of bone.

A noise, a throat being cleared, drew both women's attention outside the lean-to.

Kelly's head was released. Free, Kelly twisted around, kicking, trying to get as far away as possible from the witch. Her feet sent the line of cruel instruments scattering in the dirt.

Favre stood outside the door. "I see Tshui has been entertaining you, Mademoiselle O'Brien."

He entered the lean-to. "I've been trying to gather some information on the CIA from your brother. Information to assist us in escaping now and planning future missions. A valuable commodity that I don't think St. Savin will mind me gleaning from their patient. But I can't have Frank coming to harm. That my benefactors wouldn't appreciate. They're paying well for the delivery of a *healthy* little guinea pig."

Favre knelt next to her. "But you, my dear, are a different story. I'm afraid I'm going to have to give your brother a little demonstration of Tshui's handiwork. And don't be shy. Let Frank hear your screams—please don't hold back. When Tshui comes over afterward and hands him your ear, I'm sure he'll be more cooperative with his answers." He stood. "But you'll have to excuse me. I don't care to watch myself."

Favre made a half bow and departed into the rainy night.

Kelly's blood iced with terror. She didn't have much time. In her fingers, Kelly clutched a tiny knife. She had grabbed it a moment ago from among the tools she had scattered. Kelly now worked to cut through the ropes behind her back.

Nearby, Tshui picked through her pack and gathered bandage material—to wrap the stump of Kelly's amputated ear. Without a doubt, they would torture her until they had drained every bit of information from her brother. Afterward, she would be tossed aside as unnecessary baggage.

Kelly would not let that happen. A quick death would be better than a tortured one. And if she could believe Favre, no harm would come to Frank—at least not until after he was delivered safely to the scientists at St. Savin.

Kelly sliced savagely at her bonds, covering her motions with jerky thrashings and moans that were only half faked.

Tshui turned back to her, a hooked knife in hand.

The ropes still held Kelly.

The witch leaned over her and grabbed her hair again, yanking her head back. She lifted her knife.

Kelly struggled with her own blade, tears flowing.

A chilling wail split the night, high and feline, full of fury.

Tshui froze with the knife poised at Kelly's ear. The witch cocked her head and glanced to the dark forest.

Kelly could not pass up this opportunity. She bunched her shoulders and ripped free the last fibers of the rope that bound her.

As Tshui turned back to her, Kelly swung around with her knife and planted it into the witch woman's shoulder. Tshui screamed and fell back in surprise.

Adrenaline racing, Kelly burst to her feet and leaped toward the forest. She ran with all the speed in her legs but slammed into a figure who stepped around a tree.

Arms grabbed her. She stared up into the leering and twisted face of

Mask. She had forgotten in her panic about the guard. She struggled but had no weapon. He yanked her around, lifting her off her feet, an arm around her throat. She was carried, kicking, back into the open.

Tshui knelt in the dirt, wrapping her wounded shoulder with the bandages meant for Kelly's ear. The glower the woman shot at Kelly burned with intensity.

Kelly stopped kicking.

Then the oddest thing happened—Mask jerked and let her go. Kelly dropped to her knees in the dirt at the sudden release. She turned as the muscled guard fell face forward to the ground.

Something glittered at the back of his skull, embedded deep into it.

A shiny silver disk.

Kelly instantly recognized it. She stared off into the woods as screams began to erupt from all around the camp. She saw men drop where they stood or tumble where they sat. Feathered arrows protruded from necks and chests. Several of the bodies convulsed. *Poisoned.*

Kelly stared again at the limp form of Favre's former lieutenant . . . and the silver disk.

Hope surged.

Dear God, the others must still be alive!

Kelly turned and found Tshui gone, likely fleeing toward the center of camp, toward Favre, toward where her brother was still held prisoner. By now, the camp was in chaos. Shots began to ring out, orders were yelled, but so far not a single attacker appeared.

It was as if they were being attacked by ghosts.

Men continued to drop.

Kelly grabbed the pistol from Mask's dead body. She could not gamble that the others would reach her brother in time. She darted toward the roiling center of camp.

Nate saw Kelly lunge with a gun in hand. *Going after her brother,* he knew with certainty. They could wait no longer. He signaled to Private Carrera. A sharp whistle blew and an ululating wail arose from the score of Indian throats all around the camp. It was a chilling sound.

Nate was already on his feet.

They had painted themselves all in black.

As a group, they lunged into the jungle camp, armed only with arrows, blowguns, and bone knives. Those who knew how to use modern weapons confiscated them from the dead.

Kostos opened fire with an AK-47 on the left. Off to the right, Carrera switched her Bailey to automatic fire and laid down a swath of death. She emptied her weapon, tossed it aside, then grabbed up a discarded M-16, probably one originally taken from the Rangers.

Nate grabbed up a pistol from dead fingers and ran headlong into the main camp. The mercenaries were still in disarray, only now beginning to fall back into a defensive line. Nate raced through the wet shadows, meaning to get behind their lines before they tightened.

As Nate ran, he was spotted by one frightened man, hiding under a bush, clearly unarmed. The man dropped to his knees at the sight of Nate's gun, hands on his head, in a clearly submissive posture.

Nate ran right past him. He had only one goal in mind: to find Kelly and her brother before they came to harm.

On the other side of camp, Kouwe ran with Dakii, flanked by other Indians. He paused to collect a machete from a dead body and toss it to the tribesman. Kouwe confiscated the rifle for himself.

They hurried forward. The line of fighting had fallen toward the camp's center.

But Kouwe suddenly slowed, an instinctual warning tingling through him. He twisted around and spotted an Indian woman slinking from behind a bush. Her skin was dabbed in black like theirs.

Kouwe, having been raised among the tribes of the Amazon, was not so easily fooled. Though she might paint herself to look like them, her Shuar features were distinctive to the educated eye.

He lifted his rifle and pointed it at the woman. "Don't move, witch!" Favre's woman had been trying to slip past their lines and escape into the woods. Kouwe would not let that happen. He remembered the fate of Corporal DeMartini.

The woman froze, turning slowly in his direction. Dakii held back, but Kouwe waved him forward. There was fighting still to be done.

Dakii took off with his men.

Kouwe was now alone with the woman, surrounded by the dead. He stepped toward her with caution. He knew he should shoot her where she stood—the witch was surely as deadly as she was beautiful. But Kouwe balked.

"On your knees," he ordered in Spanish instead. "Hands high!"

She obeyed, lowering herself with subtle grace, slow and fluid like a snake. She stared up at him from under heavily lidded eyes. Smoldering, seductive . . .

When she attacked, Kouwe was a moment too slow in reacting. He pulled the trigger, but the gun just clicked. The magazine was empty.

The woman leaped at him, knives in both hands, poisoned for sure.

Kelly stared at the two mini-Uzis held by Favre. One was pointed at her brother's head, one at her chest. "Drop the pistol, mademoiselle. Or you both die now!"

Frank mouthed to her. "Run, Kelly."

Favre crouched under the lean-to, using her brother's body as a shield.

She had no choice. She would not leave her brother with the madman. She lowered her pistol and tossed it aside.

Favre quickly crossed to her. He dropped one of the Uzis and pressed the other against Kelly's back. "We're going to get out of here," he hissed at her. He snatched up a pack. "I've got a backup supply of tree sap, prepared for just such an emergency."

He shouldered the pack, then grabbed Kelly by the back of her shirt.

A shout barked behind them. *"Let her go!"*

They both turned. Favre twisted around behind her.

Nate stood, bare-chested, in his boxers, painted all in black.

"Gone native, have we, Monsieur Rand?"

Nate pointed a pistol at them. "You can't escape. Drop your weapon and you'll live."

Kelly stared at Nate. His eyes were hard.

Gunfire sounded all around them. Shouts and screams echoed.

"You'll let me live?" Favre scoffed. "What? In prison? I don't like that proposition. I like freedom better."

The single gunshot, at close range, startled her—more the *crack* than the pain. She saw Nate fly backward, hit in the hip, his weapon spinning away. Then she felt herself fall to the ground, to her knees, pain registering more as shock. She stared at her stomach. Blood soaked her shirt, welling through the smoking hole.

Favre had shot her through her belly, striking Nate.

The pure brutality of the act horrified her more than being shot, more than the blood.

Kelly looked at Nate. Their eyes met for a brief instant. Neither had the strength to speak. Then she was falling—slumping toward the ground as darkness stole the world away.

Kouwe butted the first knife away with his rifle, but the witch was fast. He fell backward under her weight as she leaped on him.

He hit the ground hard, slamming his head, but managing to catch her other wrist. The second knife jabbed at his face. He tried to throw her off, but she clung to him, legs wrapped around him like a passionate lover.

Her free hand scratched gouges in his cheek, going for his eyes. He twisted his face to the side. The knife lowered toward his throat as she leaned her shoulder into its plunge. She was strong, young.

But Kouwe knew the Shuar. He knew about their secret arsenal of weapons: braided in the hair, hidden in loincloths, worn as decoration. He also knew women warriors of the tribe carried an extra sheath as a defense against rape—a common attack between the Shuar tribes during their wars.

Kouwe used his free hand to snatch between her legs as she straddled him. His fingers reached and found the tiny knobbed hilt hidden there, warm from her body heat. He pulled the blade free of its secret leather scabbard.

A scream rose from her lips as she realized this most private theft. Teeth were bared.

She tried to roll away, but Kouwe still had her wrist in his grasp. As she spun, he followed, holding her tight and using her strength to pull himself to his feet.

They crouched at arms' length, Kouwe keeping an iron grip on her wrist.

She met his eyes. He saw the fear. "Mercy," she whispered. "Please."

Kouwe imagined the number of victims who had pleaded with her—but he was no monster. "I'll grant you mercy."

She relaxed ever so slightly.

Using this moment, he yanked her to him and plunged the knife to its hilt between her breasts.

She gasped in pain and surprise.

"The mercy of a quick death," he hissed at her.

The poison struck her immediately. She shuddered and stiffened as if an electric shock had passed through her from head to toe. He pushed her away as a strangled scream flowed from her lips. She was dead before she hit the ground.

Kouwe turned away, tossing aside the poisoned blade. "And that's more than you deserve."

The gunfire had already died around the camp to sporadic shots, and Louis needed to be gone with his treasure before his defenses completely fell.

Gathering up the second Uzi from the ground, he watched Nate struggle to his elbows, a fierce grimace on his face.

Louis saluted him and swung around—then froze in midstep.

Standing a few yards away was a sight that made no sense. A pale, frail figure leaned against a tree. "Louis . . ."

He stumbled back in fright. *A ghost . . .*

"Dad, get back!" Nate called in a pained voice.

Louis collected himself with a shudder of surprise. Of course it wasn't a ghost. *Carl Rand! Alive! What miracle was this? And what luck?*

He pointed an Uzi at the wraith.

The weak figure lifted an arm and pointed to the left.

Louis's gaze flicked to the side.

Hiding under a bush, a jaguar crouched, spotted and golden, muscles bunched. It leaped at him.

He swung his weapon up, firing, chewing up dirt and leaves as he slashed toward the flying cat.

Then he was struck from the other side, blindsided, sacked, carried several yards, and slammed into the ground, facefirst. With the wind knocked out of him, he snorted and choked dirt. A large weight pinned him.

Who . . . what . . . ? He twisted his neck around.

A black feline face snarled down at him. Claws dug into his back, spears of agony.

Oh, God!

The first jaguar stepped into view, padding with menace. Louis struggled to bring his Uzi around, lifting his arm. Before he could fire, his limb exploded with agony. Teeth clamped to bone and ripped backward, tearing off his arm at the shoulder with a crunch of bone.

Louis screamed.

"Bon appétit," Nate mumbled to the two cats.

He ignored the rest of the attack. He had once watched a documentary of killer whales playing with a seal pup before eating it: tossing it through the air, catching it, ripping it, and tossing it again. Savage and heartless. Pure nature. The same happened here. The two cats showed a pure feline pleasure in killing Louis Favre, not just feeding, but enacting revenge upon the man.

Nate turned his attention to more pressing concerns. He dragged himself toward Kelly, crawling with his hands, pushing with his one good leg. His hip flared with agony. His vision blurred. But he had to reach her.

Kelly lay crumpled on the ground, blood pooling.

At last, he fell beside her. "Kelly . . ."

She shifted at the sound of his voice.

He moved closer, cradling against her.

"We did it . . . right?" Her voice was a whisper. "The cure?"

"We'll get it to the world . . . to Jessie."

His father stumbled over to them and knelt beside the pair. "Help's coming. Hang on . . . both of you."

Nate was surprised to see Private Carrera standing behind his father. "Sergeant Kostos found the mercenary camp's radio," she said. "The helicopters are a half hour out."

Nate nodded, holding Kelly to him. Her eyes had closed. His own vision darkened as he held her. Somewhere in the distance, he heard Frank call. "Kelly! Is Kelly all right?"

TWENTY

Eight Months Later

Nate knocked on the door to the O'Brien residence. Frank was due back from the hospital today. Nate carried a present under his arm. A new Boston Red Sox cap, signed by the entire team. He waited on the stoop, staring across the manicured lawn.

Dark clouds stacked the southern skies, promising a storm to come.

Nate knocked again. He had visited Frank last week at the Instar Institute. His new legs were pale and weak, but he had been up on crutches, managing pretty well. "Physical therapy's a bitch," Frank had complained. "Plus I'm a goddamn pincushion to these white-smocked vampires."

Nate had smiled. Over the past months, the researchers and doctors had been carefully monitoring the regeneration. Frank's mother, Lauren, had said that so far the exact mechanism for her son's prion-induced regeneration remained a mystery. What *was* known was that while the prions triggered a fatal hemorrhagic fever in children and the elderly—those individuals with immature or compromised immune systems—the opposite was seen in healthy adults. Here, the prions seemed capable of temporarily altering the human immune system, allowing for the proliferative growth necessary for regeneration and rapid healing.

This miraculous effect was observed in Frank, but not without danger to the man. He had to be maintained on a diluted mix of nut milk to keep the process from running rampant and triggering the devastating cancers that had struck Agent Clark. And now that the regeneration was complete, Frank was under a more concentrated treatment with the milk to rid his body of the prions and return his immune system back to normal. Still, despite Frank's status as guinea pig, much about the prions and their method of action remained a mystery.

"We're a long way from an answer and even longer from replicating the tree's abilities," Lauren had said sadly. "If the tree's history dates back to the Paleozoic era, then it's had a hundred million years' head start on us. One day we might understand, but not today. As much as we might vaunt our scientific skills, we're just children playing in one of the most advanced biological experiments."

"Children who came damn close to burning down their own house this time," Nate had added.

Luckily, the nut pods had indeed proved to be the cure to the contagion. The "antiprion" compound in the fruit, a type of alkaloid, was found to be easy to replicate and manufacture. The cure was quickly dispatched via a multinational effort throughout the Americas and the world. It was discovered that a month's treatment with the alkaloid *totally* eradicated the disease from the body, leaving no trace of the infectious prion. This simple fact, unknown to the Ban-ali, had left them enslaved for generations. But luckily, the manufactured nut milk was the immediate cure the world had needed. The plague was all but over.

Contrarily, the prion itself had proved beyond current scientific capability to cultivate or duplicate. All samples of the prion-rich sap were considered a Level 4 biohazard and confined to a few select labs. Out in the field, the original source of the sap, the Ban-ali valley, was found to be a blasted ruin. All that was left of the great Yagga were ashes and entombed skeletons.

And that's just fine with me, Nate thought as he waited on the stoop and stared at the setting March sun and the brewing storm.

Back in South America, Kouwe and Dakii were still helping the remaining dozen Ban-ali tribesmen acclimate to their new lives. They were the richest Indians in the Amazon. Nate's father had successfully sued St. Savin Pharmaceuticals for the destruction of the tribe's homelands and the slaughter of its people. It seemed Louis Favre had left a clear paper trail back to the French drug company. Though appeals would surely drag on for several more years, the company was all but bankrupt. In addition, its entire executive board faced criminal charges.

Meanwhile, his father remained in South America, helping resettle the Ban-ali tribe. Nate would be rejoining his father in a few more weeks, but he was not the only one heading south. In addition, geneticists were flocking to study the tribe, to investigate the alterations to their DNA, both to understand how it had been achieved and perhaps to discover a way to reverse the species-altering effects of the Yagga. Nate imagined that if any answers ever came, they would be generations away.

His father was also assisted by the two Rangers, Kostos and Carrera, newly promoted and decorated. The pair of soldiers had also overseen the recovery of the bodies. Difficult and heartbreaking work.

Nate sighed. So many lives lost . . . but so many others saved by the cure their blood had bought. Still, the price was too high.

The sound of approaching footsteps drew Nate's attention back around. The door opened.

Nate found his smile. "What took you so long? I've been waiting here like five minutes."

Kelly frowned at him, holding a palm to her lower back. "You try lugging this belly around."

Nate placed a palm on his fiancée's bulging stomach. She was due in another couple of weeks with their child. The pregnancy had been discovered while Kelly recuperated from the gunshot wound. It seemed Kelly had been infected with the prions during her examination of Gerald Clark's body back in Manaus. Over the two-week Amazon journey—unbeknownst to her—the prions had healed Kelly's postparturient infertility, regenerating what had been damaged. It was a timely discovery. If the prions had been left unchecked for even a couple more weeks, the ravaging cancers would have started, but as with her brother, the nut milk was administered in time, and the prions were eradicated before they could do harm.

As a result of this joyous gift, Nate and Kelly had been blessed. During their treetop lovemaking on the eve of Louis's attack, Nate and Kelly had unwittingly conceived a baby—a brother for Jessie.

They had already chosen a name: *Manny*.

Nate leaned over and kissed his fiancée.

Distant thunder rolled from the skies.

"The others are waiting," she mumbled between his lips.

"Let 'em wait," he whispered, lingering.

Thick raindrops began to fall, tapping at the pavement and rooftop. Thunder rumbled again, and the sprinkle blew into a downpour.

"But shouldn't we—"

Nate pulled her closer, bringing her lips back to his. "Hush."

Epilogue

Deep in the Amazon rain forest, nature takes its own course, unseen and undisturbed.

The spotted jaguar nudges its litter of cubs, mewling and whining in the den. His black-coated mate has been gone a long time. He sniffs the air. A whiff of musk. He paces anxiously.

From the jungle shadows, a silhouette breaks free and pads over to him. He huffs his greeting to his larger mate. They busily rub and brush against each other. He smells the bad scent on her. *Flames, burning, screaming.* It triggers warnings along his spine, bristling his nape. He growls.

His mate crosses to the far side of the glade and digs deep into the soft loam. She drops a knobby seed into the pit, then kicks dirt back over it with her hind legs.

Once done, she crosses to the litter of cubs—some black, some spotted. She sniffs at them. The cubs cry for milk, rolling over one another.

She rubs her mate again and turns her back on the freshly dug hole, the planted seed already forgotten. It is no longer her concern. It is time to move on. She gathers her litter and her mate, and the group heads deeper into the trackless depths of the forest.

Behind, freshly turned soil dries in the afternoon sun.

Unseen and undisturbed.

Forgotten.